T0367414

"THE LOST CODEX OF PALENQUE"

A sequel to
"THE FIELDS ARE BARE!"

S.J.Parsons

Order this book online at www.trafford.com
or email orders@trafford.com

Most Trafford titles are also available at major online book retailers.

Printed in the United States of America.

ISBN: 978-1-4669-0820-8 (sc)

Library of Congress Control Number: 2011962838

Trafford rev. 12/16/2011

 www.trafford.com

North America & international
toll-free: 1 888 232 4444 (USA & Canada)
phone: 250 383 6864 ♦ fax: 812 355 4082

PROLOGUE

It was early morning when Arnie came out his front door wearing only his cotton pajama bottoms. He slowly stepped to about the middle of the long porch and sat the steaming cup of coffee on the large wooden handrail. Briskly rubbing his arms and chest, he still enjoyed the shock of the cool morning air. Even though it was almost mid-summer, the air was only about seventy degrees. He ruffled his hair, thought, 'I guess I'm lucky to have any hair at all—being close to seventy years old!' He decided to tighten his bottom's drawstring before his pajamas pants fell off his skinny ass.

He got his cup, sipped and then looked to the top of the ridge at the far end of the narrow valley. The sunshine had just reached the tops of the tall trees on the ridge. With the sun rising to his back, behind the house, behind the Eastern ridge—it would be a while before sunshine reached down into Arnie's Hidden Valley. Before it reached the crops—the young, but healthy plants for this year's food supply.

In this silent time, if Arnie tried, he could hear the brook that flowed along the right side of the valley. At these times, it sounded relaxing. Now, listening, he closed his eyes and recalled his memories— memories from a long, long time ago—of when he and Ellen, just married youths, had frolicked in the stream while nude. And played with their new puppy. She had named him Duke. But these memories always ended the same—the scene of years later when he realized Ellen had died in their car crash. Shaking his head, he opened his eyes and wiped them with his bare hand. Another sip of coffee, he turned from the brook, and looked to the opposite side of the fields, the valley.

He concentrated on the barn as he thought about the couple now living in the barn's loft they had repaired. It was Tom Stapleton and Alex, no one here ever referred to her by her 'real' name, Alexandra Hawkins.

Tom, ex-military—numerous combat missions—still a member on 'call' for a secret Delta Force unit. Mid fifties, big, hard, and mean—very mean when he loses his temper. Or drinks too much alcohol! An expert in all forms of combat and weapons. Owner of a special Dodge van: armored, special systems and lockers full of weapons. Elected by the others as the 'Chief of Defence.' With Arnie, at Tom's insistence, as 'Commander in Chief.' Never married, Tom felt he was 'too dangerous' for a family life.

Alexandra 'Alex' Hawkins; Petite, short black hair, black eyes, a young lady in her early thirties and in excellent physical condition, a computer genius, and a fanatical collector of gold—a habit she gained through her father. Alex had been on her own—in and out of private schools—since her Mother's suicide when Alex was in her early teens. Hard working, independently successful, owns an expensive home on Lake Lanier. And is extremely private with her inner emotions. She has a 'sharp-tongue', which earned her the nickname of 'Brainy-Bitch'—BB for short—in her working world.

Arnie, Tom and Alex had been Buyers for separate food supply companies but were teamed together the year of the collapse—the collapse of the entire food system for the USA. This was about three years ago. During their travels that year, it was Alex who had discovered 'something was wrong'. And through her computer work, she 'nailed' the two Company Managers that were bleeding the food companies just prior to the collapse.

Alex had joined with Arnie and Tom in their fight and flight for survival, and she had been introduced into the world of combat and weapons.

Alex and Tom had, reluctantly at first, agreed to try and make a go of it as a couple.

Over the pleasant 'shock', Arnie had enough. With his cup, he went inside. Returning to the porch with a shirt on and a fresh cup of hot coffee, he looked toward the re-worked corncrib. It was now where the youngest couple lived. This was Mike Harder and 'Tiger'. Her real name, so she had told the others—she had no other proof— was Margarita Calienta.

Mike Harder in his mid forties was third generation farmer from South-Central Georgia. Big—but not as big as Tom—Mike had served missions with Tom. Mike was also an expert in combat and weapons.

He and his two brothers have a 'strong-hole' in South Georgia. They had joined Arnie, Tom and Alex in the rescue of Jim from the CIA. Mike and Alex, during that period of time, had a 'running affair', nothing mentally serious, just raw sex. While at Hidden Valley with his brothers, Mike had 'captured' Tiger. This led to Mike's decision to stay there instead of returning south with his brothers.

Margarita 'Tiger' Calienta, young—about twenty—a Maya 'runaway', had been survived in and around Hidden Valley during Arnie's absence.

Shortly after the Harder brothers, Jim and Nat arrived, Mike caught her one night while she was stealing food. Mike's brothers nicknamed her 'Tiger' because of Mike's difficulties in catching her. The two, Mike and Tiger had instantly become a couple.

Tiger was short—similar to Alex's height—but stockier, healthy, dark skinned, strong, well endowed with her large bosom. She was from the southern mountainous state of Chiapas in Mexico. She had fled the mortal conflict between 'Condor' and the Federal troops in and around her home village of Amatenango. She knew some English, and she had one very special ability—the ability to disappear and reappear when she wanted to!

Arnie shifted his position as he looked through the front windows of the living/dinning area inside. The sound of Nat and Jim moving about inside had caught his attention. And Arnie thought of these two. Dr. Natashia Karsky; Russian scientist of agriculture and the foremost expert of Maya hieroglyphics. A collaborator with Dr. Jim Shirley on the study of long term storage of food.

Just before the collapse, Nat had slipped out of Russia and joined Jim in Atlanta. Via computer link-up Jim had asked her to marry him. Tall, slim, well tanned from her years of rugged field research, Nat, as she became known to the other members, was in her mid fifties. She had brought with her computer disks concerning her life-long work. A computer 'wiz', and an expert at faking identifications, and other documents, she is also an expert at slipping in and out of different countries.

She had, just prior to leaving Russia, broken the secret of long—term storage without the use of modern machines.

Dr. James 'Jim' Shirley was Arnie and Ellen's life long friend. He had talked the two into going to the University of Georgia. A couple of years older, they—Jim and Arnie—had served in the Army together in Korea

Jim had suddenly retired from his long career as Professor of Agriculture at the U. of G. when Arnic informed him of the situation just prior to the collapse of the food system. A fellow collaborator in the study of long-term storage—and Jim had worked with Nat on field trips to ruins at different places in the Americas. As Arnie looked at the couple inside he briefly thought of himself. Arnold 'Arnie' Douglas. Since losing his childhood sweetheart, Ellen, he had no interest in establishing a close relationship. And they never had children. His entire working career had been in the food business. His entire spare time had been spent in developing Hidden Valley. Until, years ago when he and Jim, and later Dr.Karsky, got interested in the long-term storage of basic foods. Storage without freezing, canning or artificial preservatives. The 'ancient-ones' seemed to know how—but not 'modern-man'! Why not? But Dr.K's research had finally solved the problem! He had planned on retiring the year of the collapse—the collapse took care of that! These seven people came to be known and referred to as HVG for 'Hidden Valley Group'. Members that now stayed at Arnie's Hidden Valley, a isolated mountain valley in the Northeastern section of Georgia. Opening the door, Arnie started inside as he said, "Good morning, folks!" Opening the door, Arnie started inside, he said, "Good morning, folks!"

CHAPTER 1

During the nearly three years since the collapse of the food system, the monetary freeze, and with the military control being imposed on just about everything, the country had more or less stabilized into small groups of traders. These had worked out their own methods and contacts. For the HVG, Arnie, because of him knowing the people of the area and because this was how he first got into the food supply business, was leader of their efforts—their contacts, their trades.

The restoration of the oil refinement and distribution of fuels, and finally, the re-establishment of the electrical generation stations operations had been a major improvement. The night the centrally supplied electricity was turned back on, the members of HVG had a celebration. Their own supply of fuel for their generator was almost depleted.

They had been only generating enough for the freezers and for the computers.

The Federal Government, through FBI investigations, had voided all recent foreign holdings of lands, lands bought just prior to the collapse. And returned ownership to the previous USA natural citizens. Freezing all foreign bank holdings, the Government tried to stabilize the monetary system. It still wasn't actually being trusted—trading seemed more positive and safer.

The Government was still trying to re-establish some sort of basic food supply system. Secretary of Agriculture, Bill Stillwell had returned to D.C. to head up this effort. He had escaped the chaos of the inner cities during the early days by fleeing to his house in the Bahamas.

He and Jim Shirley had made contact—not directly, but via computers.

Through Jim, the HVG was persuaded to provide a major input. They, in return, encouraged legalizing the importation and planting of the 'illegal' winged-bean. The law against these wonderful plants was over-ridden at Secretary Stillwell's insistence. Nat quickly contacted her friends in South Africa for a supply of seeds. At long last, it was legal to import these!

After a while, after getting their ideas together Alex typed out and forwarded via computers to Stillwell an extensive, detailed plan. It was based on returning to the original farming/consumer concept similar to before World War II. But of course with modern equipment and facilities. The basic idea was for the farmers to raise the variety of food needed for their families. But much more than needed just for their family.

The dealers would be independent individuals or small companies— no more 'mega-companies'. The dealers to buy the 'excess' from the farmers and either distribute this to the retailers or the processors. Processing to be centralized and specialized, still modern. But encourage the return of local wholesalers. And no more Commodities Markets dealing in billons of tons 'sometime' in the future! Only real food, in real time—farmer to consumer basically. But of course, still use modern systems, computers, communication and transportation.

Bill Stillwell was surprised at Alex's detailed report—her historical references—and he nodded at the end of her closing summary—'the food system had advanced itself right into a corner, no way out! Being controlled by one system, one computer, and one bastard that threw a 'glich' in it and the system crashed like a fat cow being hit in the head with an axe.

Bill was also surprised at Alex's prompt response—especially after his and her face to face conflict during the kidnapping of Jim Shirley affair'. He laughed to himself as he remembered her—so small— standing toe to toe to him—so large—and her bringing him to his knees, so to speak!

Sometime during the early days of this depressing period, by listen-ing to the radio and through contacts with other 'Ham' radio operators, (Mikes's brothers had setup and left an old fashion hand generated 'Ham' radio and left a list of call signs) Tom decided that he, Mike and Alex should make a run into Atlanta to recover Alex's and Arnie's cars. These had been left at the company parking lot. And go to and check on Alex's home at Lake Lanier.

Alex? Mike? Because Tom knew if there was any serious 'problems', he didn't know anyone better than Mike. And Alex? She was his 'seasoned' tailgunner. She had shown her real toughness during their run back to Hidden Valley from North Dakota. Besides, she could decide what to do at her place. Tom did know that Mike had recovered her cache of gold just before chaos hit. Now, the gold was again hidden at Hidden Valley.

Tom had quietly steered Mike and Alex to where his van and Mike's pickup was parked. He explained his plans to go to Atlanta and Gainesville. They nodded in agreement, but as he looked toward his van, Alex suddenly said, "Let's take Mike's pickup! Mike, round up some tools—a hacksaw, an axe or a hatchet—maybe a chainsaw, a few pipe wrenches, some small diameter Rope." Tom asked,"What's that about?" "If it's still there, I want my hot tub! And—and—my bed." "Hot tub? Up here? Where? Arnie's house is full to the brim now!" "This was your idea! We'll sit the damn thing outside! Things aren't always going to be like they are now! We'll just have to fix up our own place—if necessary! OK?" Alex snapped back.

Tom knew better than to argue, he went and got a good selection of weapons from his van, And he checked to be sure he had his 'Delta Force' identification card—he felt sure this would get them through any military checkpoints.

"You got good identification—proof that you have a house in that swanky subdivision, B.B.?"

"Why? **11**

"You'll probably need it when we start ripping out plumbing in a fancy house like yours!"

"Got it!" as she patted her hip pocket.

They had no problems at the checkpoints, Tom's card worked. And no problems getting Alex's sports coupe and Arnie's station wagon. Tom led the way in Arnie's wagon, clearing the checkpoints again with his 'magic-card'. At the security entrance to the housing complex on Lake Lanier, Alex had to prove property ownership, which she did.

At her house, from the outside, things appeared to be in fair order, only a couple of small windows broke and the set of double glass sliding doors between the fenced-in back yard and the master bathroom had been forced open. But inside it was a different matter—everything in disarray, all food and Alex's prized collection of champagne was gone, all her clothes were gone or destroyed beyond use! The hot tub and her basic bed had been spared. No bed cloths or pillows left. As she looked about, Mike and Tom discussed the approach to removing the tub. By lifting the two doors from their lower tracks, these were set aside. Then sawing out a section of the fence, Mike was able to back his truck close to the tub. As the two men disconnected the tub's plumbing, Alex took the hatchet and went out on her dock to her thirty foot sailboat. It was still tied up, all the working ropes were missing and all the hatches had been broken open.

Tom and Mike heard the loud unusual noise out at the boat, they went there. Alex was inside, hacking at a blank fiberglass bulkhead. "What are you doing?" Tom shouted down the passageway. "Something I forgot!" She ripped out an area about one foot square then reached into the hollow cavity, felt about, then jerked out a canvas bag. She turned to the two staring down through the companionway, said,

"Gold! Traveling change! I had it built in!"

Mike and Tom shook their heads, went back to the job at the house.

When Alex returned, she said, in almost a whisper, to Mike, "Sorry I didn't get to keep that promise to teach you about sailing—maybe someday." He just nodded in understanding.

The three made a strange entourage as they returned to Hidden Valley. Mike's pickup loaded with the tub, mattress and springs, Arnie's wagon and Alex's coupe loaded with computer files and anything else worth bringing back.

They unloaded the tub at a flat and level spot close to the old barn, put the springs and mattress on top of it and covered the pile with plastic. Alex stepped back, looked at this, put her arm around Tom's waist, said,

"Tom, you once told me you never owned your own place—there's the beginning—a hot tub, a king size bed, and the old barn. All we've got to do is get it all together!"

Tom didn't reply, he pulled Alex tight, and kissed her sweaty forehead.

The first winter, all seven members spent crowded into Arnie's house. Early the following spring Mike, and Tiger, Tom and Alex began work on rebuilding the old corncrib and the upstairs loft of the barn. The men found and traded for enough metal roofing to cover the two buildings. With warm weather coming, the two couples moved in—Tom and Alex into the loft, Mike and Tiger into the crib. Mike and Tiger had located an old fashion steel bed, with springs and mattress. Alex's king size was finally inside. The hot tub was left outside. Tiger showed Alex how to use the old iron wash kettle and heat water with an open fire. Occasionally the two young women would have a frolicking good time in Alex's hot tub. The others thought the 'show' beat any TV they had ever seen! Jim, Nat and Tiger had quickly gotten use to the fact that Alex's body was naturally 'hairless'—Tom, Mike and Arnie had learned this in their previous escapades.

Early on, the three women had discussed birth control—'normal' supplies' were not available because of the country's unsettled and abnormal situation. All three agreed this wasn't the time for newborns.

Again it was Tiger who showed Alex and Nat a solution—she knew of a wild plant—and she had found it in the surrounding woods—if steeped into a 'tea' and one cup drank monthly at the 'proper time' in relation to their 'periods, they would not become pregnant. An old Maya trick, the three started this routine without letting the men know it.

With the two couples moved into their own places, and the four staying busy on the re-building, the daily routine had progressed into Alex and Tiger helping Tom and Mike until about a hour before sunset. The two women would then join Nat and prepare a 'community' supper. With swapping tales and interests afterward on the huge upstairs porch of Arnie's place. Or if too cold, indoors around the fireplace. The porch faced West toward the usual beautiful sunset over the ridge.

One day about mid-morning on a bright beautiful June morning, Jim and Arnie came from the 'main-house' and left in Arnie's station wagon. The four younger people, at work on their places, stopped and watched.

"Strange!" Tom said loud enough for the other three to hear, he added, "Wonder where those two are going?"

The others just shrugged, went back to work.

That evening, after the meal, Arnie returned inside, then came back out with a Maya style hammock. Without an explanation, he went down into the edge of the woods between the house and the barn. Selecting a clear ground area, the 'right' two trees, he strung up the hammock. After trying it out, he returned up on the porch. The others didn't ask, they just waited. Arnie let them wait. Not able to stand it, Alex asked,

"OK! Old Man! What's up? You moving out? Or—going camping?"

"Camping", as he glanced toward Nat and Jim who stood close to each other at one end of the porch. He added, "Tomorrow is a holiday—a special day—don't plan on working tomorrow, everybody!" Again he hesitated.

"Are we missing something?" Alex asked.

"I think so", he replied, "Tomorrow the Preacher Man is coming—we're having the first ever wedding in Hidden Valley! Jim and Nat are getting married —tomorrow—mid-day!"

The five faced Jim and Nat and applauded. Then joining them, they all hugged, shook hands, and kissed one another.

The three women immediately began to chatter about what needed to be done—to wear—what to fix for the reception. Arnie motioned for Mike to follow him. They went to the cellar and returned with several bottles of Arnie's prize home made wine. The celebration had begun. Arnie informed the others that he and Jim had invited about twelve guests to come &or the occasion. He added, "Jim has contacted Bill Stillwell, invited him and his wife. Bill said he wouldn't miss it for the world—especially the opportunity to meet the Bride! And Bill promised, "No FBI! No CIA!" They all laughed—knowing how USA Agents had chased the famous Dr.K all around the world!

Arnie asked of Tom, "Please don't let me forget—one of us needs to pickup the Stillwells at the Blairsville airport. Bring his pilot—crew-if they can leave their plane, that is." Alex asked, "Secretary Stillwell is bringing his wife! Shucks! I thought I might have a chance to put the move on that Big Dude!" Tom roughly grabbed her elbow, said, take you to the barn now!"

"No! No! Not now! There's too much to talk about here, now!"

The others laughed—they knew of Alex's 'problem'! And Tom's promise to keep 'it' under control!

The three ladies gathered at the cooking end of the porch, they talked intensely as they cleaned up the supper situation. Finished, they stayed in this area for a while—still talking. The four were at the opposite end. Suddenly, the women came, led by Alex, she asked to Arnie,

"Could we", she nodded to Nat and Tiger, "take over the house. You guys—with Jim's—whatever he'll need for the glorious occasion tomorrow-well—more or less—move over to our place", she nodded toward Tom and Mike, "or Mike's place—for tonight. You all know, the Bridegroom isn't suppose to see the Bride, on the day of the wedding, before the wedding ceremony!"

Arnie looked to the other men, they all shrugged with no open objections. the ladies, as they twittered, twisted about like 'sugared-up' thirteen year olds planning a, slumber party, ran inside. They rushed to the master bedroom—still chattering like mocking birds.

Arnie said to the others,

"Ok, let's gather up Jim's gear—and move out!"

"I'm not sure about the wedding, but tomorrow night, all Old Jim Boy will need is a riding crop—and his cowboy boots!" Mike interjected. The others laughed, Jim blushed, said, "Hey guys! I'm just an old man!" "Old? Like longevity! The best kind! No rush at all!" Tom remarked.

It was revealed in "The Fields Are Bare" that Alex's problem was nymphomania. They laughed again.

"Besides, with Tiger and Alex's help, you are probably in for a big surprise tomorrow night!" Mike added. They laughed, went and got Jim's stuff—and moved to Mike's place.

With the men finally gone—the three women had been completely motionless and silent as; Jim's clothes and etc. were gotten from the master bedroom— they immediately began over. After explanations, encouragement and coaxing, Nat finally agreed to Tiger's and Alex's 'plan'. Tiger quickly rushed out, over to her place, through the guys, and returned with several brown paper bags. As she had left the men, Mike said, "See, Jim? The Maya Herb Doctor is going to work her magic spell! I'm telling you, be ready for surprises!"

"What can they possible do?" Jim asked.

"Are you questioning someone who can disappear in front of your eyes!" Tom remarked. The guys laughed.

The first thing, the three ladies did was to strip naked—this was going to get complicated, and very wet. Alex and Tiger told Nat to take a light shower and to shampoo with regular shampoo. After this, Alex trimmed her hair—the few extra long sprigs, nothing drastic—Nat's hair was already rather short. Alex backed off, checked the trim, nodded in satisfaction, then said, "Ok, Tiger, powder her—all over!" With a large soft powder-puff, Tiger covered Nat—then rubbed this in, and the excess off. Looking about in Ellen's closet, the two found a package of ladies razors. "Just what we need!" Alex exclaimed.

Being European, especially Russian, Nat had never completely developed the habit of body shaving and only occasionally did she shave her legs— and just her legs. Alex began, and shaved Nat from her fingernails— her head—down to her toenails. To 'do' Nat's pubic hair—her complete crotch—it took some extra encouragement. Alex said,

"Look, Nat, if you don't, or Jim doesn't like it—but I guarantee you he'll be pleasantly surprised—it will grow back! At least yours is not like mine! Always hairless!"

This opened the subject, Nat asked,

"Alex, has your entire body always been—well—you know?"

"Yes, the doctors—and in the beginning I saw several—said it had something to do with my small size, an anatomical condition. As a teen, it really bugged me! But the doctors finally convinced me that I wasn't the only woman to have this 'unusual problem'. I first accepted myself, takes all kinds, I guess."

"And, is it complete?" Nat asked.

Alex raised one arm straight up,

"Complete! See my armpit? Slick as a whistle, and never touched by a razor!"

Finishing Nat's crotch, Alex asked, "Tiger, as a matter of fact, if we have to dress tight, and thin, tomorrow, as thick and coarse as your bush is, it might should at least be trimmed."

Tiger didn't object. With only scissors, Alex cut it short—not a complete shave—just a close trim.

The two briskly brushed Nat with towels, then she took another light shower and shampoo. Tiger washed out the tub and began to run a tub of hot water—as hot as she could stand with her hands. While this ran—Nat didn't towel dry—the other two got Aloe prongs from one of Tiger's bags. By cutting these into small sections and squeezing these, Tiger and Alex completely coated—including Nat's **wet** hair—her with a liberal coat of Aloe. The two rubbed, very hard, and very completely—toenails, face—especially around her eyes and mouth—crotch, buttocks—ever thing! Nat said she had never felt so completely slick—all over! She was amazed at the sensation!

With the tub to the proper level and the proper temperature—hot—Tiger added a large double hand full of honeysuckle blossoms, a small hand full of crushed ground-nettles and the 'used' Aloe prongs.

"Ok, Nat, it's ready! Get in!"

Nat, still coated with Aloe—but it was now dry—eased in, "Hot! Hot!"

"You'll get use to it! It has to be hot, to open your pores!" Tiger laughingly responded. Nat did adjust, and soon was completely submerged except for her face. As she relaxed, Tiger rinsed her hair and rubbed her face—a facial and scalp massage. Alex worked on her fingers, toes and torso.

As Nat soaked and completely relaxed, Alex went to the kitchen and returned with a bottle of wine and three glasses. The three sipped and waited—Tiger had advised, "Don't wait until the water cools off too much, get out while it is at least warm." And Tiger covered the bed with towels. Returning to Nat, she said "When you get out, don't dry with a towel—it has to be a slow drying—laying down—while we rub you dry."

Nat couldn't imagine—she was already so soothed, slick, smooth, and hairless! Relaxed but tingling all over, much more and she was just going to fade out!

After the brisk rubdown—Nat was now dry—she fell immediately into a deep sleep. Tiger got a sheet and gentle covered her. Tiger silently motioned to Alex to follow her to the tub. It had been left as Nat had used it. Easing the door shut, Tiger said, "No need to let this go to waste." With fresh glasses of wine, and adding more hot water, the two slid into the tub and began to soak. After a spell, Tiger remarked, "Senor Jim is going to be surprised."

"Surprised? He's going to think he just received a present of a thirteen year old virgin."

The two snickered.

Early the morning of the wedding, Tiger and Alex rushed about prep paring food, gathering flowers from the woods fields and decorating the house. Mike made a quick run to the local 'moonshiner'—Mike had located him early on—traded a hunting knife for a couple of gallons of 'white-lightning'. This was to reduce the drain on Arnie's supply of homemade wine. Tom tied some orange ribbons down next to the paved highway, the entrance was difficult to notice. Then he headed to the airport to pickup the Stillwells. Arnie helped Jim get ready—dressed—and as tradition required, kept Jim from seeing Natashia before the wedding.

Nat had selected Tiger as Maid-of-Honor because of Nat's life long work concerning the Maya. Nat felt privileged for such a 'happening'. Alex agreed, she thought this was a fitting arrangement. Arnie was Best-man, and he insisted that Jim give Ellen's rings to Nat. Nat's dress was of lace, it hugged her body completely, the hem down to about half way between her knees and her ankles. It was split on one side, up to almost the mid-point of her thigh. The upper portion a fitted brocaded front, open back—deeply cut to the cleft of her buttocks. Tiny spaghetti straps held this in place—one across the hollow of her lovely back, one across inline with her breasts, and two crossing over her shoulders to the outside edges of her breasts. The thin veil came down in front to about her nipples—it was topped with a diamond studded head band. She wore a single hair comb—it too was diamond studded—in the rear of her fluffed short hair, And medium height strap pumps.

Everything was a light peach color that blended beautifully with her tanned, smooth skin. The high split in the skirt accented her long legs. For accessories, Nat wore diamond bracelets on both wrists, single diamond ear studs and a hanging diamond necklace—it dangled into the cleavage of her firm breasts. All her cosmetics were in matching peach colors; eye shadowing, brows, lips and nails. She did not wear any rings. Her long slim fingers were left empty to emphasize the acceptance of the wedding rings. It would be a double ring ceremony.

There were a few things Dr.K made sure she brought out of Russia—her jewelry was one of these!

In the rush prior to the ceremony, Alex had decided to wear her 'regular'—her reliable white slip dress with tiny straps—the one custom made to accommodate her abnormally large and prominent nipples. With shiny white panty hose and white very high-spiked heels. And her 'regular' accessory set of gold nuggets; two 'pinky' rings, two middle finger rings, two tiny bracelets of gold nuggets, a close clasped chain necklace ringed with nuggets and a set of single nugget ear studs. For make-up, it would all be her custom mixed gold lipstick, eye shadowing, and nail polish. But her eyebrows would be expanded jet black to match her black hair pageboy cut, smoothed down. Being coarse, it was like a skullcap. Alex knew this routine very well. She would wait and be the last to get dressed.

During the fun and partying the night before, the three had over—looked the fact that there may be a 'problem'—finding something to dress Tiger with. After finishing the morning domestic preparations, and deciding it was time to dress, Alex quickly laid out her apparel. Then she started on Tiger. As she went through Ellen's wardrobe, Nat realized the problem—she got involved. The three narrowed the possibilities down to a white slip style dress. It had spaghetti straps and a back zipper. Alex and Nat helped 'stuff' Tiger into a pair of flat white pantyhose, then proceeded skinning Tiger with the dress It was obvious that Ellen had been much slimmer and taller. It was the zipping up that was the snag. No way! With Tiger's abundant bosom, the zipper couldn't be closed for the last three or four inches. And with the skirt length being longer than needed and no side splits, Tiger's legs were hobbled—she couldn't walk! As she stood as stiff as a manikin, Alex and Nat backed off and thought, wondered.

"We're running out of time!" Alex screamed as she looked for 'some-thing' to solve the situation. She found a long, narrow white silk scarf, as Nat got Ellen's sewing box. Draping the scarf around Tiger's neck, Alex pulled the ends over her shoulders to the rear, pulling it across the open zipper she said, "If we pin it here, it'll hide the 'problem'!"

Nat quickly got from her jewelry case, a set of matching pearl accessories. A single studded pearl was used as the pin—it worked.

Finding a seam-ripper, Nat got on her knees and said, "Alex, you pull on that side, I'll pull on this one—we'll split it up to about half way of her thigh—at least as high as needed so she can walk!" Alex got down and they began. And opened the seam to about half way up. Nat, using a pair of tweezers, removed the tiny cut threads. Standing, Alex said, "Ok, walk!" Tiger could, but still at only a half shuffle! "Ok! That'll have to do—but—" "But what?"

"It just doesn't look right! Too much white! "It is the white pantyhose! Hold still, Tiger! I'm going to skin you!"

Alex began, it wasn't easy, but finally she got them down to her feet, said, "Ok, step out." Placing a hand on Alex's shoulder, Tiger was able to release her feet.

"There! That's much better! Honey, with your beautiful skin color, it should show—well—at least as much as is legal!" "Shoes! Find shoes!" Alex snapped. The only plain white pumps were going to be tight—very tight! Tiger couldn't possibly sit—Alex and Nat struggled as they stuffed Tiger's feet in with a shoehorn—they finally got the shoes on. They stood, Tiger gave an expression of pain, Alex said, "Take a few steps, the shoes will get better—or—", she hesitated, didn't say it outloud, but thought, 'your feet will get numb!'

Nat quickly added single pearl ear studs, two single strand pearl bracelets and a long loop pearl necklace—this hung into Tiger's vast cleavage. One matching pearl ring completed this.

Nat did Tiger's face, with pink eye shadow, pink lips, and with Alex's black eye brow marker she extended Tiger's heavy brows. The two pulled Tiger's long, straight, coarse, shiny, jet black hair back—it came down to her waist. "Hold it, Alex, while I find a white satin ribbon!" Pulling it tight, then with a large bow, they were finished with the young beautiful Maya lady. The contrast of her skin—especially the high split in the skirt and her enormous over flowing breasts—with the brilliant white of the dress and the scarf was very outstanding!

Alex touched Tiger's cheek and said,"Smile! Show those pearly white teeth!" She did, Alex slapped her on the rump, added, "Great! Knock em' dead! Kid!" And Tiger smiled—a really big beautiful grin.

Alex helped Nat get dressed, and then quickly threw her outfit on. Tiger couldn't help much she was dressed skin tight, so tight she could hardly move.

"Flowers! We're forgetting the flowers!" Alex snapped. Quickly stepping to the end of the hall where it ended at the living /room, Alex saw that the furniture had been pushed to one side, and someone had brought in and setup about twenty folding chairs. An aisle was left between the chairs. The Preacher's podium was close to the far wall—the wall between the room and the front porch. Tom was standing at the front door, she caught his attention, motioned for him to come to her. "Tom, please get me the tray of flowers from the 'frig'."

Back with Nat and Tiger, Alex pinned these on—She and Tiger had gathered these yesterday, these were mountain laurel blossoms, pink fading to deep purple. Alex pinned one to Nat's left hip, and gave her the larger—three blossoms—hand bouquet. She pinned one to Tiger's left top—between her breast and arm—the waist of her dress was entirely too tight to pin. Then Alex pinned one to her own dess to the left shoulder strap. They were now ready.

The wedding processional music started. The three shifted about—Nat got first in line in the hall, Tiger followed by about two paces, Alex trailed about three steps back. Nat slowly lowered her veil, Tiger stepped closer, straightened the sides and then stepped back. Nat started the slow, odd skip-step march. Alex, looking at Tiger's tight dress and shoes, wondered if this strange step, hesitate, step wasn't developed just for such trying conditions.

As Nat entered the living area, she quickly saw the path—and the Preacher, Arnie and Jim at the far end of the room. She proceeded, Tiger and Alex followed. The entire group of guests turned—and gasped or sighed at the three beautiful ladies. Alex spotted Mr. and Mrs. Stillwell, they were seated on the left, near the rear. When Alex knew Bill Stillwell was staring directly at her face, she flashed an extra large smile and slightly nodded to him. He nodded back in recognition. Not that she had any doubts, but she was pleased to think he hadn't forgotten her.

The vows went very well—when the Preacher got to the ring part, Nat gently handed Tiger—who stood to Nat's left—the hand bouquet. As he finished with, "You may kiss the bride", Nat turned to Tiger. She raised Nat's veil and the two smiled proudly into each other's eyes.

With the kiss completed, and as she and Jim still faced each other, Nat slightly stepped back, caught both of his hands with her hands. She began, in Old Russian, with the vows of her homeland—Old Russia. Jim had a broad grin, but was briefly surprised. She finished, hesitated, continued to hold his hands. Jim knew what she expected. He repeated the Old vows, in Old Russian. Finished, they boldly kissed each other on both cheeks, then very hard on the lips. The guests had been totally silent. Bill Stillwell bent close to his wife's ear, whispered, "The Agents had been correct—Old Jim Boy learned Russian just to impress the lovely Dr.K" "I think he just did that, perfectly" Mrs. Stillwell whispered back and added "That was gorgeous." Bill nodded in agreement. Stillwell remembered that he had seen many photos of Dr.K but this was the first time he had ever seen her in person. She was even more beautiful than expected—even more sumptuous than rumored! He quickly thought, 'I know the 'others', but who in the world is the young, healthy, black-eyed Maya?'

That, he had to find out!

It was obvious the ceremony was over, Arnie calmly steered the four 'stars' into a line beside the podium toward the front door. Then he motioned for the guests to rise and come forward. As they shifted about, several of the men quickly and smoothly gathered up, folded, and stacked the chairs out of the way. The guests formed into a line to congratulate the Bride, Bridegroom, Tiger and Alex, Arnie decided to mingle with the guests. None of the men missed this opportunity to kiss the three lovely ladies.

Some of the guests drifted onto the porch, some even down to the yard, a few ladies went to the kitchen and prepared to serve the food and drinks. It was clear that these locals knew their way around weddings at home! And Mike and Tom fell right in.

After the formal reception line duties, Nat whispered 'something' to Tiger and Alex. Alex shook her head in disagreement. Nat guided Tiger thru the people as they headed for the rear bedroom. Stillwell saw the opportunity, stepped in front of Nat, gently took her hand, asked "Natashia, aren't you going to tell me about your lovely young Maid of Honor? Maya?" Nat and Tiger wavered, then Nat responded, "Secretary Bill Stillwell, this is my close friend, Margarita 'Tiger' Calienta, an assistant archaeologist I have worked with in Southern Mexico on several occasions. And, yes, Maya. Tzental Maya to be exact. Her family's home is in Chiapas. You do know where that is—don't you?" Stumped, he hesitated. She added, "If you will excuse us, we'll change into something more comfortable. You care to join us?" Stumped again, he apologized, but added, "I would like to hear more—maybe later?" "Sure, maybe later." He stepped aside, Nat and Tiger went on in and closed the door. The two laughed. Well, Tiger as much as she could without splitting the dress!

"An archaeologist's assistant?" Tiger questioned. "Well, I wasn't going to give him the knowledge that you were a 'wayward kid lost in the woods'! See Tiger? You can be who ever, what ever you want to be with total strangers!" "I never thought of that." "Sure, I'm an old hand at it—sure comes to good use at times—especially when slipping in and out of tight situations!"

They undressed each other—it was just about as difficult to get the skin tight satin dress off of Tiger as it had to put it on. Re-dressed, Nat stood in front of the full length mirror, pulled Tiger close, said, "See, you in your traditional wrap-around tie-top, full, dark red skirt, your pull-over, loose, scooped neck blouse with puffed short sleeves and your leather strap sandals—and—me in my tan, all cotton safari pants and shirt and my high top boots—w1ith my pants in the boots, we would be right at home as a team at any 'dig' in South America! Oh! Wait!" Nat quickly got her low crown, wide brimmed cotton hat—the one with a leather chin strap. She sat the hat tight, with a slight cock, to one side, then pulled the 'glyph' carved Bezal nut strap retainer tight.

"Now! Let's go. What was that Alex said?" "Knock em' dead!"

Nat didn't mention that her pants were of a stretch material and were skin tight. Her shirt was also tight, and unbuttoned down below the level of her nipples—she didn't wear a bra either. And the tan boots were of a 'kid' leather and very tight. And with medium heels. The outfit was rather flamboyant and sexy.

As they entered the front, the guests—especially the Stillwells— again stopped, stared and sighed or awed. Nat whispered to Tiger, "See? They came to see a real Archaeologist and her Assistant—no need to disappoint them!" Alex began to clap—even she was surprised! The others joined in, Nat and Tiger bowed.

About five P.M., the group began to splinter—some of the guests had already left—Mike was engrossed with a few of the local men about the best method of hunting deer in the mountains. Being a 'lowlander', Mike took this opportunity. Arnie and Jim were discussing 'trade-deals' with some of their older friends. Mrs. Stillwell had gotten involved with several of the older local women about 'something'. Bill caught up with Tom and Alex when they were alone. "Alex, I really appreciated your concise report, and you folks' prompt response—I'll probably be in touch again. If any of you—you, Tom or the others, want a job in the 'Ag' Department—", Bill hesitated. Tom was at Alex's side, one arm over her shoulders. Alex responded, started, "Mr. Stillwell—I'd rather be—", Tom slipped his hand—the one across her shoulders—over her mouth, he guessed what she was going to say wouldn't be NICE! She thought out the rest, 'I'd rather be shoveling horse crap than working for the Federal Government!'

Tom quickly finished it for her, "Thanks, Bill, we'll keep that in mind!"
Alex had opened her teeth and bit down on the fleshy inside of one finger.
Tom exclaimed, "Honey, I think you're needed in the kitchen!" Alex felt
her face flush—she wasn't sure if it was Mike's 'spiked' punch—or just an
instant 'piss-off'! She thought she was getting the 'little—lady-bug-out'
treatment! Tom jerked his hand loose, Alex gritted a smile, said, "Excuse
me, Mr. Secretary, I need to go piss!" She turned, and stomped off—well,
as hard as 110 pounds in high spike heels can stomp.

Tom and Bill ambled inside, lightly chatted some, Bill got another
glass of Mike's punch, Tom, another can of grape soda. Stillwell saw his
opportunity—Nat and Tiger were free. He quickly excused himself from
Tom, went directly to Nat. Nat had a feeling this might get serious—after
greetings, she casually guided Stillwell out and down to the front yard as
she held Tiger's hand. After some small talk, Stillwell felt comfortable with
Tiger hearing anything he had to say.

"Dr. K—sorry—you have no idea how many times that reference
has come up 'inside' the various Departments—" Natashia just smiled,
waited.

"Nat—I want to apologize for that fiasco about three years ago—
before the collapse. Truly I, and my Department had nothing to do with
it. That crap was all CIA! If anything, I helped as much as possible to find
Jim—" She interrupted, "So I heard, no apology necessary. If any-thing,
I think it—the problem—made Jim decide to this!", she waved an arm
around, then pointed at her 'new' rings. "Really? Great! That makes me
feel relieved—it had been bothering me! Thanks! Ok, change of subject—
have you got any new projects in mind? Off the record of course." He
hesitated, tried to 'read' her reaction. Nat was blank. Tiger stared at his
eyes. He started again, "That ceremony—in Moscow—where you and your
African group were so highly decorated—about three years ago—would
you possibly, please, give me a hint of what it was all about?" This time
he would wait her. Suddenly, totally unexpected by him, she said, "Sure,
why not! The project was completed before the ceremony! Corn! It was all
about corn!" Now she would wait. Bill remembered, 'Corn—the Agents
conclusions were correct—all they could uncover was corn—present corn
and very, very old corn! "Corn?" He replied, then continued, "Really?
Just corn??" "Really, just corn", she repeated. hand?" "Better still, I'll kiss
you—Russian style!"

At first Stillwell chuckled, Nat and Tiger joined in, and then the
three had a good laugh. Nat remarked, in a slightly more serious tone,

"Speaking of new projects, Mr. Secretary, if the CIA or any of the other USA Agencies want to know what I'm doing, tell them to contact me—you know how—and I'll see that they get a job on my next project—you know, trench-digger! Or maybe even head water boy!" then she laughed loudly. Stillwell caught it, joined her, said, "That's the best news—great line! Best I've heard in years! You can be sure—I promise—I'll get that in the D.C. rumor mill! Tomorrow! It's time those 'secret-agent' bastards were the blunt of a joke! Dr. K, you really are something! May I kiss your hand?" "Better still, I'll kiss you, Russian style." She kissed each cheek, then hard on his lips. He gasped as she drew back, and Bill said, "Nobody up there will believe this! Those bastards have chased you for years! And today, you kissed me! Not once—but what? Three times! Wait until I rub this day in their faces! I've heard all sorts of tales about how you slipped between their fingers—and now—here we are like old classmates!"

Nat glanced about, and at the ground—they stood in the open, the ground was smooth packed clay—no loose rocks, no dry leaves. She tilted to Tiger's ear and whispered something. Nat released Tiger's hand, took one step to the side, and asked Stillwell, "Do they think I'm slippery? Do you think I'm elusive?" "Well, I guess so, from all the remarks I've heard—why?" "Tiger, please say goodbye to Mr. Stillwell." He was puzzled at this sudden change in direction. Tiger extended her right hand, gave his a,:short, light shake, said, "Goodbye, Mr. Stillwell, nice meeting you", she stared into his eyes, then released his hand. "Goodbye, Tig—" he didn't finish—Tiger had disappeared! He quickly looked around, she wasn't in sight! "What the hell! Where did she go?" Nat just smiled, wavered as he stepped about, looked around. "Now that is slippery!" she exclaimed, added, "How would the Agents like to deal with her?"

"That's impossible!" He turned back, faced Nat. "You looking for me Mr. Bill?" Tiger said as she tapped the rear of his shoulder. He twisted around, "Well I'll be damned! How did you do that?" Tiger placed a vertical index finger across her lips, whispered, "Tzental secret", and she disappeared again! While Bill thought he was staring directly at her!

Stillwell again looked about, walked around, then returned to Nat, shook hands with her, remarked, "It's been a real treat—really—but I think I better head for the airport before I get really spooked. Please say goodbye to beautiful little Tiger—where ever she is." He smiled, dropped the hand shake with Nat. "Why don't you say goodbye yourself?" Tiger asked—she was standing beside him. He quickly grabbed her and lifted her up, snapped, "Gotcha!" and he kissed her full on her lips then added,

"Goodbye!" As soon as he lowered her, he headed for the house. Tom, who was up on the porch was still laughing as Stillwell approached. He said, "See you got the old Tzental treatment! Don't worry, you're not going crazy!" Stillwell didn't react, he just asked Tom if he would carry them back to the airport. But Bill did glance down at Nat and Tiger—they were hugging and laughing. He thought,'Ok, ok, the great Dr. K gets the last laugh—again!'

As Bill located his wife, his coat, she her purse and jacket, Tom found Alex in the kitchen. She had changed to jeans, low heels and an older loose 'outdoors' shirt. With the sleeves rolled to above her elbows, she was washing dishes in the sink. Tom stepped close to her back, placed a hand on each hip. She leaned back against him, twisted her head around, tilted it back and rolled her eyes upward. "I thought you might want to go with—" She didn't wait for him to finish, said "Go? I'd go anywhere now to get away from this sink!" She slung the water from her hands, wiped them with a cloth then followed him out of the kitchen.

After saying their goodbyes—Nat had joined Jim—the Stillwells headed out, they followed Tom and Alex. Jim and Nat waved from the porch and Alex as the four got into Tom's van. Mrs. Stillwell were in the rear, the two men up front. At first, Alex sat next to Mrs. Stillwell on the side bunk, but after a little chitchat, Alex apologized, said, "I'm about pooped, I think I'll lay down". She felt slightly dizzy-headed, probably too much of Mike's punch, Alex thought. She did notice that Bill was on Tom's phone talking to the crew telling them to warm up, they were on the way.

Alex slid to the rear cross bunk, pushed the pillows to the driver's side and lay down. She closed her eyes.

The bright flames were everywhere—outside all the windows—for as far as she could see! The van was at 'warp-speed', speeding along the endless four lane highway in North Dakota. She was tangled in the tall, ripe wheat! The brilliant, high, whipping flames were getting closer and closer! She couldn't get loose! She screamed, Daddy! Daddy! He answered but it was from a far away distance, Alex! Alex! Suddenly something poked her, she slapped at it very hard, twisted over, grabbed for her AK-47 but she couldn't get a hold of it. Daddy! Daddy! She screamed! Over and over!

"Alex! Alex! It's Mrs. Stillwell!"

Alex snapped upright, brushed her eyes and wiped the cold sweat from her forehead. She shook the cobwebs from her confused mind then she noticed Mrs.Stillwell as she rubbed her hand.

"Oh, sorry—"

"I guess you were having a night—having a dream. We're almost to the airport. I thought I had better wake you. Are you Ok?"

"Yes—just a bad dream".

But Alex knew better—she had it fairly often—ever since the real thing over three years ago.

Slipping around next to Mrs. Stillwell, Alex said as to herself, "We don't have anything to drink—I'm not talking about soda-pop—do we? Of course not! We're in Captain Tom the Terrible's van! He never keeps anything stronger than one year old grape soda in here!" Mrs. Stillwell gave her a puzzled expression. "Tom, doesn't drink alcoholic drinks! Didn't you know?" Mrs. S just shook her head, "Mrs. Stillwell, please excuse me—I'm just—", Alex let it drop.

At the boarding steps—Mrs. S went on up and inside—Bill hesitated, asked, "You two want to come aboard?" "Nope, guess we'd better get back!" Tom replied over the scream of the engines. Alex stepped up a couple of steps, "Mr. Stillwell—Bill—if you've got a couple of those small bottles of whiskey, like the Commercial People offer, I'd take that!" Bill bounded up, disappeared inside, returned with an unopened quart of Jack Daniels. As he passed it down to Alex, he remarked, "To you, little lady, personally—from me to you! I know big Cap. Tom-the-Terrible doesn't drink the stuff!"

Bill slowly stuck one index fingertip to Alex's nose, said, "Just remember, if there's ever anything you need—anything—just ask! Maybe someday you and I will be real friends! Ok?" "Ok! Maybe someday!" Alex responded as she stepped back from the steps. She and Tom waved then left.

On the way back to Hidden Valley, as Alex took another swig of J.D., Tom suddenly asked, "I wonder how he knew about Cap. Tom—the-Terrible?" Alex didn't try to reply, but she tilted her face toward the side window, remembered Secretary Stillwell's key words—'anything you need-just ask!' She prided herself on storing away key words! And promises!

It was almost midnight, Alex was on their new small balcony across the front of their loft, she glanced toward the main house. She thought; everything is cleaned up—back in place—everyone is gone except the 'Newlyweds', the last light went off about an hour ago. Alex felt good how well everything had gone. Sweeping her view to the right, she saw the glowing bed of coals where Arnie had his hammock, he was rolled in a light blanket as he slept in the hammock. Alex shifted the light wood chair slightly, sat down and propped her feet on the rail—it was made from a small sapling. She only had on her long sleeve 'work' shirt—nothing else. After taking another swallow of Jack Daniel—she had a large glass, the bottle was inside—she looked to her left. The light at Mike and Tiger's had been off for some time—it was still off. She leaned her head far back, studied the stars—the sky was clear—and no moon yet.

Tom softly came out, looked at her, returned inside and brought out another chair. Placing it at the opposite end, he sat down and placed his feet on the rail also. He only had on a pair of loose underdrawers. He didn't say anything. As Alex, he looked at the 'zillion' of stars. "Tom, I don't feel right", she gently spoke. Tom knew she didn't like the word 'scared'—but he wondered—and he remembered the time in North Dakota when she had said, "I'm scared—" and he had responded with the thought, 'The day Alexandra Hawkins gets scared, it is the day the world as we know it ends!' And it had. Tom waited, he knew something else would follow.

"I think I'm going honkers", she started. He waited. "I've had that nightmare again—It seems to be more frequently." He knew what she was talking about—the one with the flames, the tangled wheat, the one of calling her father. Tom had previously given this—her dream—a lot of thought—he knew it was hopeless to follow the path of her concern about her father—she hadn't heard from him in years. "Alex, I think it may be caused by you not having enough required mental activities. Your brain, your mind just over works and regenerates that scene." They both went silent for minutes, then Alex responded, "You may be right—no wheeling and dealing—no contract responsibilities—-no gold trading—very little computer work, serious work anyway", she hesitated, continued, "No more thrill of the challenge. Please don't take that wrong—I love you deeply—You keep me satisfied. I wouldn't trade you for a thousand Friday night 'pick-ups, but—", she let it drop. Tom understood, he let it drop. No doubt, her Friday night 'habit' had been drastically changed.

She started again, "The raising our own food—the planting—waiting-hoping the small plants will grow—the harvesting—storing—I know all that is very important—necessary—but—", she stopped, took another drink of J.D. "But it just isn't you, is it, Alex?" "It just isn't me—right", she waited, then added, "And I miss my gold activities. I don't think you fully understand that process—my full feelings for it. It's like high stakes poker, high roller dice—it's an inner thrill. I know, I know, it's an addiction. But remember, I've been hooked for years—and years! I keep having this sinking feeling—with no growth to my gold stock."

They waited, unaware of the passing of time. "So, what's the answer?" Tom asked. She waited, emptied the glass, stood and stepped close to Tom, said, "That's the biggest problem of all—I don't know! And you know how much I hate to NOT KNOW The answer to anything! I'm turning in before I can't resist the urge to get sloppy drunk! Come on, Stud! And bang out what little brains I have left!" Tom didn't like the implications, but he didn't mind the required treatment either!

But, Tom knew, deep down, Alex had to find something—and find it soon—to keep her mind busy, interested. But what? When?

CHAPTER 2

For the days following the wedding, none of the 'five' went to the main house where the 'honey-moon' couple was. Except Tiger did occasionally quietly slip in and out of the kitchen for food supplies. During this time, Tiger did all their cooking on her 'three-rock' outdoor grill. The 'five' had immediately gotten back to the work in the fields. After three days of isolation, about mid-morning, Jim and Nat joined the 'five' in the outdoor work. The honeymoon was over. That evening, the three women resumed the habit of cooking the evening meal on the porch of the main house. After supper, Arnie took down his hammock from the trees and 'moved' back into the guest bedroom. His camping out was over.

Tom noticed that Alex worked as hard as ever—maybe even harder. He wondered if her 'problem' was over, maybe the daily hard physical activities had taken care of her anxiety. As the fieldwork became < pit, she met Arnie. He was waiting beside a sack of shelled corn,> less and less necessary, Alex took a different turn—she began to cut-short the normal after supper conversation session, she would excuse herself and head for her place—to her computer. Daily, she would work on the computer until about midnight, Tom knew this wasn't inane exercises and he didn't question. Over her shoulder observations indicated it was complicated, seemed to be system or systems design. But at least Alex was busy, very busy, and seemed the happiest he had seen in a long time.

In early September, the fieldwork picked up as the crops matured—the work was now from sunrise until after dark. One day, mid-afternoon, as Alex came up the ladder from down inside the massive underground storage headed for the storage jugs below. Alex hesitated, Arnie wiped the sweat from his face. She said, "Old Man, looks as if you could use a break— and a drink of cold mountain water." She came on out, took his hand and as leading him toward the main house, said, "I've got something I want your opinion about."

As they slowly walked, Alex explained that she had been working on a plan, a design of systems, intercoupling control systems, for a company—a small buying, distribution, selling company. No processing. A company just for the Southeast, not the entire Nation. A company a hand full of people could run—no 'Mega-buck operation. And later if things panned out Ok, a series of these small companies could be set-up to handle the rest of the country—and exchange commodities. Annie seemed to listen, with only an occasional 'un-hu.'

At the water faucet, Alex stopped talking, got a glass of water and handed it to Arnie. After he drank, she asked, "Well? What do you think?" "Sounds like you got it all figured out. Except for one thing." He got another glass of water, handed it to Alex. She held it, asked, "What's that?" "People. Who is going to run what? Bear with me a few minutes. Systems operators, we don't have. Computer 'hacks' you probably could find—but—and this is a big but—they would need good supervision. Particularly if they had no experience in the food world. I'll put it bluntly, Alex there's no doubt you're a genius at systems—design, anything from the ground up—but, and again this is another big but—face the facts, you expect too much, you expect others to work as hard as you do, you expect others to be as totally dedicated to what ever task is at hand as you. And you're not a 'people's person'—you're a 'loner', sure, you can bullshit a farmer out of his overalls—but that's not like working people! Now, how about field personal? You know I wanted to retire the year of the collapse. And Tom? I think he's perfectly happy right here with you—us—he feels at home, probably for the first time in his entire life. Scratch Tom. And you know how important good Field Buyers are!" He stopped talking, just nodded directly into Alex's face.

She replied to the last statement first, "Sure, there's no substitute for personal contact with the farmers—someone that can sit on the edge of their porches and pet their dogs—like you. Or kick the tires, drive their new tractors, talk old 'war stories'—like Tom. Or a cute ass and nice nipples—like nine." She wavered, then, "With the demise of the Big Three—the companies we had worked for—there has to be other Buyers—good Buyers—out there somewhere. Give me a chance, I think we could work that out. Ok?"

Finished at the house, they both slowly headed back to the fields and the storage pit. As they walked, Alex thought about the other question; experienced computer operators—with knowledge of the food business—and most of all, a 'peoples person, an experienced supervisor. Alex started, more as to herself than as directly to Arnie, "A people's Super—like John King was—tying things together, smoothing out relationships between people. Maybe I should regret putting John in the 'slammer', but the S.O.B. shouldn't have gotten greedy, became a common crook." She went silent, then, "I'll work on that—you really think I couldn't handle that?" Arnie simply replied, "No, you could not." She slapped his back, snapped, "That's what I like about you, Old Man! Straight to the heart of the matter!" They chuckled together—and went back to moving the goods into storage.

That evening as the three women got together the items for supper, Nat abruptly said to Alex, "You must have not looked at your E-mail lately, in the three or so days." "No, I've been busy on something else. Why?"

"I got an 'E' from Secretary Stillwell—says he's been trying to contact you for the last three days. With no response from you, I guess he tried me. There's a hard copy by my computer if you're interested." Alex sat down the pan of venison steaks by the grill and went to Nat's computer.

The message was simple; 'been trying to e-mail you for three days, please contact me. The following is a list of phone numbers feel free to call collect. And a list of 'E' addresses if you prefer that. All list the times when I'll be available. I would greatly appreciate your response. Bill Stillwell.' She folded it up and stuck it in her hip pocket.

That night, Tom noticed that Alex didn't go back to work on her computer as she had been doing. Instead she searched about and located the bottle of Jack Daniel, went on the balcony, sat down and propped her feet up on the rail. He joined her—he didn't ask. It was just after ten, she took another heavy tug at the bottle, sat it down, then went in to her computer. She sent a brief message. 'Secretary Stillwell, what do you want? Alex. Then she returned outside and sat down. And had another drink.

Later she returned to the computer—there was a reply; 'Alex, I want to meet with you. Face to face. ASAP. Please reply now. I'll wait. Bill.' She typed the outgoing message. 'Ok. When? How? Alex.' She waited, the response was prompt. 'Tomorrow, I'll send the plane at sunrise. Be at the Blairsville airport by eight A.M. Ok? Bill.' She returned, 'Ok. Alex.'

Shutting down, she began to pack a small soft travel bag—the first thing she stuffed in were copies of her recent computer work. Tom came in, watched as she threw in odds and ends of clothes and 'make-up' stuff. He asked, "Going some where, Alex?" "Yes, D.C. I'll be back—whenever. Ok?" "Sure, whatever." He went back to the porch. Finished, she came out, leaned on the rail, then turned to Tom, "Tom, please, just go with the flow—I'm not sure where it's going—but—maybe at least somewhere!" Tom stood, stepped to her and then they embraced and kissed.

It was just before seven when Alex in her sports coupe roared up the incline and left Hidden Valley. At the airport, she stood beside her car, her travel bag in one hand, her strap purse on the other shoulder. The Gulfstream jet landed exactly at eight. She locked the door, slipped the car keys in her purse and shut the door. As the jet taxied back to the hanger apron and turned around, Alex briskly walked out. The forward door opened and the steps were extended. The attendant rushed down to meet her, said, "Good Morning, Miss Hawkins!" She pulled her shoulders back, raised her chin, replied, "Good morning—" she glanced at his identific- ation badge, "Bruce. Did you have a pleasant flight down?" "Very nice. My I take your bag?" "Sure, why not!" Alex was the only passenger—her 'private' jet!

After the plane punched thru the scattered cloud cover and leveled Off, Bruce asked, "Miss Hawkins—", she interrupted, "Please call me Alex", he continued, "Alex, would you care for a bite? A cup of coffee? Or whatever?" Thanks, I'll take black coffee with a shot of rum—and maybe a bun or muffin if possible, please." "No problem, I can even fix bacon and eggs!" "No thanks, just coffee, rum and a roll is plenty."

Back at Hidden Valley, Arnie noticed Tom hadn't said a word to any- one. And no one had asked. Of course they all knew that Alex had left— but—. He moved close to Tom, said, "Let's take a walk, Tom." As soon as they were out of ear-shot of the others, Arnie asked, "Tom, did Alex explain what she was—has—been working on?" "No, not really, something to do with systems design I would guess. No details. And nothing about what she was leaving to do." "I'm not sure even she knows—", then Arnie related his conversation with Alex yesterday. And about the 'E'mail Nat bad received from Stillwell. "So, that's why D.C." Tom remarked. "She's headed for D.C.?" "Yes, that's all she said—D.C." "Don't worry, Tom. Alex will take care of herself." Tom smiled, replied, "I never doubted that!" They chuckled together, and returned to their work.

As Bruce opened the door and extended the steps, there was a cold, brisk wind. A long black limousine pulled close to the steps. Alex wondered if her short black business suit was enough clothes. But at least she had worn panty hose. Reacting to the cold, she flipped up the collar to her long sleeve jacket. Bruce followed her down with her bag. The chauffeur opened the rear door of the limo, said, "Welcome to D.C., Miss Hawkins!" "Thanks" she replied. As the driver pulled away, headed out, he adjusted his rearview mirror to see her face then asked, "Ever been to D.C. before, Miss Hawkins?" "Alex call me Alex. Yes, as a matter of fact, I went to Georgetown U. for a while!" She didn't mention that she had been to a lot of Universities for a 'while'—or that she had been kicked out of a lot of schools after 'a while'! Usually for 'hacking' into the school's 'protected' systems—or for screwing the wrong people!

As the limo stopped at the end of a paved walkway which led into an end door of the large building, a young man briskly walked to the vehicle and quickly opened the door. "Welcome to the Department of Agriculture! Miss Hawkins!" Alex instantly thought—'Who are these turkeys trying to impress? And, everyone in the food world knows I detest that name! Alex! Damnit, Alex!' But she let it slide. She just nodded, looked at his plastic badge—'Wayne'. She got out, turned back toward the open door, said, "Get the bag, Wayne!" She headed for the building's door. As she followed the guide along the long, empty hall, up the elevator, along another long, empty hall with no windows, she had an inner vision. She was dressed in a loose, long black skirt almost down to her ankles, a loose, floppy long sleeve black blouse and she had a plastic badge, It showed, 'Spinster A. Hawkins'. Alex shook her head to clear the cobwebs.

Wayne stopped at the door, the gold leafed printing displayed 'Secretary of Agriculture' 'William F. Stillwell' He opened the door, stepped aside and allowed Alex to enter. There were four secretaries at individual desks. The one closest to the inner office stood, came forward, extended her right hand and said as they shook, "Welcome, Miss Hawkins." She didn't wait for any reply. She turned, opened the door to Stillwell's 'private' office, and waved Alex in. Alex just nodded to her.

Bill Stillwell was standing, and quickly stepped to Alex with his right hand extended, boldly said, "Alex! I'm so glad you could make it!" As she took his hand, she thought,'At least Mr. Secretary didn't screw-up!' "Bill, nice to see you again!" He motioned her toward a deep leather chair facing the front center of his huge desk. His receptionist left, she left the door open. Alex declined the chair, "I've been sitting." Bill went to his big chair and sat down. She waited. "I'll get someone to show you our facilities—our equipment—and point out some of our capabilities. Then we'll grab lunch and discus a few things!" Alex didn't falter, "No." "No?" "No, Mr. Stillwell,

I didn't come here to get the 'grand-tour', or to get some sort of beat-around-the-bush conversation. Exactly what is it you want? Exactly what do you want from me?" Stillwell realized—and remembered Oklahoma! Alex is a no bullshit person! To the point! He stood, stepped around his desk, went and closed the door. Turning back to Alex—she faced him—he started. "I've seriously considered your—your people's report—let's call it a proposal. I've also reviewed many more—mostly crap, but—at least I went over those too." He walked to the window, and while looking out, he continued.

"What your report showed may come to pass—by itself—over time. It seems to be an account of how the agriculture business did develop—years ago. But, as in the past, it may take years and years!" He turned, faced Alex, stepped to the edge of his desk, placed his big hands on the top, leaned toward Alex, added, "Alex, what I need—what the country needs, is your ideas, your plans spelled out in concrete terms! Item 1, so & so; item 2, so & so; etc! etc! I understand the general concept. So does some of my people but we need detailed, specific steps! Specific systems! Damnit! We need you! And your peoples help!" He hesitated took a deep breath—and waited. Alex waited, silently. "Alex, money is no problem! Personnel—or—or our facility is no problem!" She didn't respond, she waited. She guessed there was more, something Stillwell had not said yet.

He straightened up, turned back and faced the window, started,"I—we are afraid the wrong elements will beat us to a solution and gain control while everyone is in this unstable condition. I—we—have already seen signs of hoarding, price inflation, 'black-marketing'—and all in the wrong hands! The military has their hands full—they can't—hell! They don't know how to handle the situation! Or maybe they don't care—or worst they may become part of the wrong elements!" Turning back to face Alex, he softly said, "Under the hodgepodge, half-assed arrangements the country is now in, I—we—think there may be another crisis. The cities are barely surviving now." Now he would wait—it was Alex's turn to bet. "Bill, I think you finally got to the core of this discussion. You say money is no problem?" She didn't wait, added, "You have the personnel? Available? The facilities available?" He nodded.

"Well", as she extended her right hand, "Let's see what we can work out!" As they shook, she said, "Please introduce me to your best Supervisor—say under fifty years old." "Alex, you know I can't make any determinations based on age—that's against the law!" "But I can! We just will not mention it to anyone! Will we?" He nodded, they released the shake. She added for clarification, "A supervisor you would personally hire if you wanted to start a business which employed about ten of your best 'present' operators. Good reliable experienced operators—real computer 'Freaks'—with no personal problems." Alex knew she was sitting up Bill. She gave him a big smile, pulled her jacket off, threw it on the back of a chair, pulled her shoulders back, added, "Bill, let's work together on this,ok?" As he stared at her proud, prominent nipples through her thin white blouse. He mumbled, "Sounds—sounds great—really great—", he didn't finish.

She reached over—she was even closer—and depressed the button on the intercom—she pointed to it. Bill batted his eyes, then said, "Louise, please get Jerry White to come in here." "Yes sir—is that all?" He looked at Alex, she nodded. Bill stepped to a side cabinet, slid it open, "This may take a minute or two—you care for something to drink?" "Sure, I'll take a cup of coffee with a shot of rum. By the way, I've really enjoyed that bottle of Jack Daniel you gave me!" "Oh, really? How long did it last?" "I still have a little left!" "No kidding! Around your bunch, I would have thought it had a life span of about two hours!" They chuckled together. Alex thought, maybe they could be friends after all! As they sipped coffee—his without rum—he looked at Alex closely, and thought, 'what ever she says, what ever she does to Jerry White, the poor guy doesn't stand a chance!'

Alex broke his stare with, "When Mr. Jerry White gets here, Bill, please just tell him to show me around. The old standard tour scene. I want to feel him out without any influence from you. Ok?" "Sure, Alex, how ever you want to handlle it."

After casual greetings—Bill introduced her as 'a prominent senator's daughter—Alex left with Mr. White. He was mid-forty, appeared to be in good physical condition, about five-ten, well dressed. As they slowly walked along the aisle between the many work cubicles, he gave a 'standard spiel. Alex watched him, his eyes, his hands, his manners, his manner of walk and his tone of voice. He seemed good solid material. Casually, Alex slipped him a few very technical questions. His answers were crisp, prompt, and best of all, correct. As they approached the end of the long room,

Alex purposely went all the way to the wall—there was an empty area there probably out of hearing distance of the closest workers.

At the end wall, Alex turned and backed up to the wall, she waited. White was not staring at her nipples—he was looking directly into her eyes. That cinched her opinion of Jerry White. "You aren't a senator's daughter, are you? Who are you really?" "Just call me Alex. No, I'm not a senator's daughter. And I'm not some dip-shit agent from the FBI or the CIA checking up on Mr. Jerry White either. I'm the person that got FBI warrants issued for two crooks—the FBI didn't even know them, or know they were wanted. I'm the one who, with a close friend, communicated via Satcom III with a very prominent Russian Scientist just so my friend could ask her if she would marry him." White slowly raised an index finger toward her face, said, "Dr.K'! That one, I've heard about!" Alex held a vertical finger in front of her lips, whispered, "Not so loud. The 'Feds' may be listening."

Alex slowly slipped her arm in the crook of his elbow, they headed back. She gently said, "Now, introduce me to your very best operator—a real cracker-jack on anybody's computer." He did, and at Alex's request, he introduced her to five more of the 'best'. Back close to Bill's office, she asked, "Don't mention our conversation—any of it—to anyone, please?" "Sure, as far as I'm concerned, it was only small talk anyway. But could you please explain—" Alex pursed her lips, threw him a fingertip kiss, almost whispered, "Later, I promise."

Back in Stillwell's inner office, Bill asked, "Well, was the senator's little girl impressed?" "Oh, yes sir! I think she was very impressed!" Jerry White snapped. Then he bade them goodbye and left. Bill glanced at his watch, Alex said, "Now, let's get that lunch you mentioned. But, please, make it a quiet place, I've got a proposition you can't refuse!"

Bill led Alex to a rear booth in the small restaurant, it was quiet, there wasn't anyone within several tables or booths. She ordered a Caesar's salad and a martini. Bill ordered onion smothered steak, a small toss salad and a martini. After eating and ordering coffee, he asked, "Ok, Alex, what's your proposition?" She started with, "You want concrete, firm plans? I'm proposing a small company, about fifteen or twenty employees. This company buys, handles the transportation, sells to the processors, the retailers, nothing unusual, nothing gigantic. They handle all food supplies for—say—the South East. But they also, via computers, see that the food supply flows in an orderly manner. All above board."

"And each transaction pays their bills—each profit transacting pays their taxes. Isn't that one problem you failed to mention? Under the present situation—free-lance vendors, under-the-table buying and selling, hardly anyone pays taxes!"

"The systems are interconnected by the company, from farmer to the retailers or the processors. Get the retailers back on their feet. The company has their own Buyers—no free-lance operators. All transactions are accountable."

"And I'm talking about a proven company—all the start-up kinks worked out. No stumbling in the dark, no fragmented, half-assed or temps, and failures! And everything documented so that any other similar company—to cover other areas of the country—could start off running—and profitable from day one. And your Department could organize these additional companies, even help select the people—or at least encourage good, down to earth, honest people! No hoods, no crooks, no black-market bastards! What would you say to that?" Alex stopped and waited.

"Great! But I don't recognize which company you're talking about." "Mine! Well, ours! The group at Hidden Valley!" He cocked his head, "Did not know about that! Really?" "Yes, with your help. Here's the proposition part. For one year, you assign Jerry White to a 'special project', let him pick five of his best people—operators—five to begin with—this is part of the sorting out the kinks—I think five will be enough—but if he needs more, give him additional people. But please let Jerry pick them!'

"I'll finish designing the systems—a lot I already have, the basic control, and the interconnecting systems—and I'll direct the installation, the proper use, the proper interface. We, my group, will hire the Field Personnel—the Buyers. And, we, our group, will be advisors—work out any kinks that might develop." She hesitated, took a sip of coffee.

"Who pays Jerry and his people? That's a good bit of change!" "You do—you keep them right where they are—on the Fed payroll for just the first year. After that, after we work out the kinks, after we make operating capital, we put them on our payroll. I know, you know, how many millions of Fed dollars are pissed away on much less important, useless crap! Just call it development cost! Call it Project 'X'! Whatever!"

She went quiet, felt around in her purse, pulled out several printouts. "Here, look at these. These are flow charts for the interconnecting systems. And these", she pasted the papers over, and pointed, "are itemized lists of necessary pieces of information needed." He looked, remarked, "This is a bit too technical for me—I'm just not sure—"

"Ok! Ok! we'll play 'make-a-deal'! You set it up for me to spent—say at least four hours with Jerry. After that you can de-brief—isn't that what you Government people call it, de-brief him privately. I'll not influence him then. If he rejects it—if he says it's all bullshit, I'll catch a taxi to the bus station and ride Greyhound back to Georgia!" She didn't mention that between the HVG people, they actually had enough cash to do the whole project WITHOUT the Fed's money! But she felt The Feds should pay for something! Besides, this was probably her best opportunity to 'get' an experienced supervisor and operators!

They finished their coffee, and stared at each other a lot—it was like a high stakes two-handed poker game. Finally, Stillwell broke,

"Ok, deal! Let's go back to the office. When do you want Jerry?" "What's today? We don't exactly keep track of days at Hidden Valley", she chuckled. "Thursday, why?" "Damn! I have to be back home before Friday night! Back to Tom!" "Tom?" he questioned. "Private joke—but I do HAVE to be back! Ok?" "Ok, lets try to do it tonight, is that Ok?" "Sure, the sooner, the better! You want to sit in?" "No, I've got something I really need to do tonight. Political 'stuff' but necessary anyway."

As they got out of the limo, Bill told the driver, "Don't leave, wait here until Miss—Alex—just Alex, returns with Jerry White!" They approached his Receptionist, Bill stopped, tilted over said, "Louise, get Alex a hotel room—no—a suite at the Empire. All charges to be billed to us. And get Jerry White in here pronto!"

In his office, he told Alex, "I'll schedule your flight back. You plan on being picked up at the hotel at eight A.M. Ok?" "Sure thing, Boss!" as she threw him a broad smile. He returned with a grin.

When Jerry White came in it was close to quitting time. Bill said, "Close the door" and he started immediately, "Jerry, do you have import-ant—very important plans for tonight?" Jerry could read the message,

"No Sir, nothing that couldn't be skipped if I call my wife, by cell phone," "Good, call her on your way. I want you to join Alex, at the Empire Hotel, directly from here. Stay and listen—and listen very carefully to what she tells you. If you need to, take notes, I'm sure she'll understand. Right? Alex?" "The more notes, the better" she replied.

"The limo is waiting downstairs. Jerry, have him bring you back here whenever, if you need to pick up your car. I don't want to chance you two getting separated this afternoon or tonight. Got it?" "Yes, Sir. No pro-blem." "Alex, feel free to use room service if you two need anything—food, drinks, anything. And it's all on the Fed's tab!" "That's my kind of talk! Thanks!" "Jerry, Alex will explain—and when you two have finished, call me at home immediately. Regardless of when it is. Alex, I'll let you know then—Ok?" "Ok." "You two get out of here! Before the cattle stampede for the gate!" Alex reached around and got her travel bag, Jerry just auto-matically took it from her, and they left. They did miss the stampede.

As the limo got caught in heavy, slow traffic, Jerry slipped to the far side—away from Alex. Using his cell phone, he dialed his wife at home. His explanation went well until he got to the part concerning when he would get home. It wasn't going well at all. Alex noticed, slid close to him, motioned that he give her the phone. But he ignored her. Abruptly, she reached and took it from him.

"Mrs.White, you don't know me. My name is Alexandra Hawkins— but please call me Alex. I represent a group that has proposed a very serious, and important project to the Agi Department. I regret inconveniencing your husband, but, I flew up this morning and I have to be back in Georgia tomorrow. Secretary Stillwell assigned your husband the responsibility of reviewing the technical details of our proposal. The Department's decision depends on your husband either accepting—or rejecting our operation— our proposal. These details are extremely complicated—I don't even know how long it will take your husband to develop a clear understanding. But it has to be tonight, there just will not be another opportunity."

Alex listened, replied, "No, we're not working at the office, we're now headed for—", Alex covered the phone, asked Jerry, "Where?" She had missed the details back at the office. "The Empire Hotel. But we will not know the room number until after you check in." "Pardon me, Mrs. White—seems we are headed for the Empire Hotel—where ever that is!" Alex again listened, then, "To be honest, I've just about run my little tail off today. I wanted a more relaxing situation than that huge, empty, cold tomb they call an office!" She slightly laughed, replied, "Yes, I think I'm safe to call it little! I'm one hundred and ten pounds soaking wet! And just barely over five feet tall. Black,coarse, straight hair, 'page-boy' cut and black eyes—a dash of Cherokee from my rascal kin's past." Jerry heard his wife laugh over the phone. Then Alex, "No, I've never been married. You haven't asked, but I'll tell you anyway, I'm thirty-six". And as usual, she had added years to her age. Alex thought it made her 'seem' more mature. She continued to Mrs. White, "No kids either, but I can insure you there is no chance of hanky-panky, I'm seriously involved with the biggest, meanest, son-of-a-bitch you can ever image!"

After Mrs. White's remarks, Alex answered, "No, never has harmed me— well—in a meanway. Alex laughed, added, "No, he's not jealous— we're still our own free selves—He just can't drink!" Then, "If Tom—" "Yes, Tom, his military 'handle' was Cap. Tom the Terrible", they both laughed, "If Tom drinks too much hard likker, he'll kick the crap out of anyone that gets in his way! Anyone! I'm very fast on my feet!" More questions, "Oh, he's just a big pussy cat with me, I just have to encourage him to not drink—only a little wine, or champagne at special, quiet, at home, occasions—you know what I mean?"

Alex wavered, the questions seemed to be over, Alex carried it on, "Mrs. White, we plan to buckle down, work for a couple of hours, then have a bite to eat catered up. Would you care to join us? Your husband can call you back the room number—we'll not know that until I check in. Mr. Stillwell's gal made all the arrangements. Then, we'll finish up—regardless of how long it takes." Alex waited as Mrs. White responded. "I understand, yes, it could be quiet late. Sorry you can't come over—if things go in the right direction, your husband will probably wind-up in a very important position—in a very important project—one that could effect the entire Nation. And there's a possibility of tremendous financial advantages to your husband." Alex didn't wait, she quickly concluded with, "Mrs. White, I've enjoyed talking to you. If things are approved, you and I are bound to become very close friends. Oh! Bye the way, is it ok if your husband drinks? Say champagne with his snack? He doesn't turn into a horror-creature, does he?" Alex laughed at Mrs. White's reply, said, "Thanks! Goodbye!" Alex just smiled at Jerry as she returned his phone and slid back to the other side of the seat.

As the chauffeur held the door of the limo open, Alex exited, and when Jerry White slid out with Alex's bag, he said to the driver, "Joe, don't bother to wait—I'll catch a taxi." The big driver smiled with a broad grin, replied, "Thank you Mr. White!"

Entering suite 518, Alex glanced around at the interior. There was a sizable living room with sofas, stuffed chairs, a side bar, small end tables, cabinets and a four place dinning table with chairs directly in front of full height glass panels. The curtains were pulled open, the view faced the Potomac River to the West. A small kitchenette was to the left. Through an open door to the right, she saw the bed beyond which was another open door to the large bathroom. Everything was beautifully color coordinated in pale blues and light rose reds. She headed for the bedroom, motioned to Jerry to follow her.

The bedroom was with rich wooden chairs, and dressers with a large mirror—European Villa style, and a huge king sized Sleigh bed. A full height glass panel was in the West wall. Alex indicated to put her bag on the dresser top as she removed her suit jacket and roughly tossed it toward a chair. She missed. Stepping to the chair, she jerked her skirt up, almost to her crotch, sat down and began unbuckling one of her shoe's strap. Jerry turned toward her after placing the bag down, asked, "What you were saying to my wife—'important position, financial advantages was that just loose comments, or what? And this, your important proposal project. I recall you saying that could effect the entire nation. Miss Hawkins—or whoever you really are—" "Alex! Please call me Alex! Don't call me Miss Hawkins! Ok! And I don't make loose comments! Especially about money! You got that?" "Ok, Alex! I feel it is obvious this is more—much more than a simple analysis of some sort of systems design. I don't appreciate being kept in the dark!"

Alex got one shoe off, stopped then replied, "Sorry, it wasn't intentional. Things are—were—moving so fast, I really haven't had the opportunity to fully—even if that's possible yet—explain." She leaned back in the chair, added, "Let's start over. Did you—I'm almost sure you did—it was E-mailed to 'Still' several months ago?" She waited. "The one about going back to the old days, independent operators? No Mega-buck centralized companies? And about the farmers raising a variety of crops? That one?" "Yes. Do you recall the details? All the details? Now?" "Of course not. I've read a lot of suggestions recently—some were bullshit, some were entirely too far out. I do recall, that yours' was highlighted as the pick-of-the-litter. But nothing has happened since then. ""Well, it's happening now! There's a copy of that original in the very bottom of my bag. There are also other papers in there." She crossed her foot with the shoe still on it over her knee, added, "Get those out, re-read the original report, refresh your memory—please." She started on the shoe's buckle.

He unzipped the bag and began to fumble his hand through her clothes, her hose, her panties and her make-up accessories. He wasn't making much headway. Alex stopped on the difficult buckle, hobbled over—one shoe on, one shoe off—snatched up the bag, turned to the bed and dumped the entire contents out. Then she pulled the many papers out, handed these to Jerry, remarked, "Pick it out, should be on the bottom." She hobbled back to the chair, added, "I'm going to catch a quick shower, I feel like the South end of a North bound mule! Stick close, if you got any questions, just shout it out as I shower!" It didn't require any answer.

Alex finally got the last shoe off, threw it over her shoulder, snapped, "You bastards were killing my feet!" She stood, unbuttoned her blouse, dropped it to the floor. As she headed for the bath room, she wiggled her skirt down, stepped out of it as she walked. It lay where it fell. She only had on her pantyhose as she started the hot water to running in the shower.

"Ah! Hot running water!" She stripped down the tight hose, threw these back in the bedroom—she didn't want these to get wet.

Jerry had started to read, but he hesitated as he watched Alex—completely nude—and most shocking, completely hairless on her body—as she unwrapped a bar of soap, ripped open a packet of shampoo and got a wash cloth. And as she stepped into the cloud of steam. Reading again, Alex staring talking. He stepped close enough to hear her. She started with the lunch she had with Stillwell. Jerry had a question—a point in her report. He interrupted her account, asked the question. Without hesitation, she elaborated until he understood. Then she resumed her tale of today. Another question, same reaction. Alex hardly missed a word—either her story or her answer to his question. While shampooing, and washing the rest of herself, all at the same time.

He suddenly realized that the visual scene was secondary—even thru the clear but steamed up glass doors of the shower. They continued to communicate. Alex turned off the water, hardly missing a word she slide open the shower door, asked—just the interjection of a few words—"hand me a towel, please." And she continued whatever she was saying. Drying her body first, she folded and dropped the towel on top of her head, stepped out and went to the side of the bed. Roughly spreading the pile of clothes, she picked up an oversized, long tail cotton teeshirt. After removing the towel, she slipped this over her head and pulled the tail down. The old faded printing on the back read, "What is it you don't understand about the word no?" As Jerry noticed this, he thought, 'really represents little Alex!' She stepped around the huge bed, faced the mirror over the dresser, roughly dried her hair, and smoothed it down and in place with her fingers. Then she threw the wet towel toward the bath doorway—she missed.

Jerry finished with the original report. He lowered the hand with the papers. This was when Alex finished with the part about keeping Jerry White and 'his' operators on the Government payroll for one year. He was impressed, asked, "And Stillwell agreed to that?" "Yes, but of course only if he buys the whole project. And that depends on your assessment of the details—the feasibility of the systems, the logic of the project." She remembered saying to Stillwell, 'I'll not influence Mr. White's opinion DURING his de-briefing—she had not promised to NOT influence Mr. White before the de-briefing!' Inwardly, Alex felt she had just rounded second base!

She reached and took the papers from his hand, said, "Let's find some place to spread these out." She headed for the dining table in the living

room. Quickly removing the decorative items—she sat these on the floor
to one side, shoved the chairs back—Jerry saw the plan. He moved the
chairs to one side of the room as she began to look at, and spread the many
flow charts—in order—on the table. Shifting a few, then she straightened
up, stepped back, snapped, "There! It all starts there", she pointed, "goes
that way, then down a line, then again that way!" She swept the directions
with a stiff index finger. "You smoke it over! I'm about to dry out here! I'll
order something cold to drink—champagne

Ok with you?" Jerry had started on the analysis, he just mumbled,
"Sure—"

The phone closest was on an end table at the closest sofa. Alex sat
down, propped her bare feet on the coffee table, glanced at the phone
number index, dialed room service. "This is Alex in suite 518. Please send
up a bottle of cold champagne—California champagne, no specific brand
or blend—just say in the thirty to forty dollar range. And two glasses."
There was some sort of reply, Alex countered, "Believe me, Honey, Alex is
enough name—I don't have a last name! Ok?" She hung up not waiting
for a reply.

Springing to her feet, she moved to the dining table, shifted her
position until she could see Jerry's eyes. He was intensely studying the
various documents. Gently, she said, "If you got questions, just ask."
He just nodded. 'Great concentration', she thought—'good!' She turned
away, eased to the huge glass wall, spread her feet, stretched her arms high
overhead and placed her open palms against the glass. The sun was low,
just about to set. The scene, far below and far away, was glorious. She held
this position until there was a tap-tap on the front door.

"I'll get it." She swiftly bounded to the door, checked through the
'peek-hole'—it was room service. "A man after my heart!" As she swung
open the door and motioned the young man in with the pushcart. He
pushed it in, then hesitated. He wanted some sort of indication as to where
she wanted it placed, he had seen all sorts of requests! She quickly under
stood, motioned to the opening at the kitchenette, closest to the dining
table yet out of the way. She added a handsome tip to the bill, then signed
it, 'Alex'.

He smiled, stared at her outfit. She stepped between his eyes and the
backlighting of the setting sun through the glass wall. She slowly shifted
her feet wider and wider apart then suddenly she twisted away from
him, back toward the cart. Feet still far apart, she bent forward a deep,
full—with stiff knees—bend and reached to the bottom shelf of the cart.

There really was not anything down there. Alex just felt it was a 'fun' thing to do—and the full view of her naked bottom would give the kid something to tell his buddies! Jerry ignored them both. Straighten up, she walked back to the waiter, smiled and gently raised his dropped jaw, and then whispered, "Run along, cutie before you choke on your tongue." He reluctantly left.

Alex could see from the direction of Jerry's stare that he was less than half finished. "Take a break—have a glass of champagne," as she stepped to the cart and began to 'pop' the cork. She added, "And take that stupid tie and jacket off!" He straightened up, stretched his back and arms, stepped toward the bedroom. Removing his jacket, then his tie, he folded these and placed them on the end of another sofa. After pouring the drinks, she sipped hers, turned to face the Western view—and waited as the sun sank below the horizon. The city lights began to come on below and spread out like thousands of fireflies coming to life. "It is a fantastic view, isn't it?" Jerry had joined her, was standing at her side, "Yes, yes indeed!" The two watched as they slowly sipped the delicious, cooling drinks.

Finished with his drink, Jerry turned to the cart and as he sat his glass down, he calmly asked, "Alex, you wrote all those?" he pointed to the dining table. She nodded, took her last sip. "How is it you know so much about the food industry? You've listed items, people with years of experience still don't know. So far, I don't think you've missed anything pertinent. How? It just doesn't seem possible", he waited, but she didn't respond. He added, "Especially if someone saw you—", he let it trail off. She abruptly realized, 'Jerry White doesn't know me from Adam's ant. I've explained the project, but he knows nothing about who 'we' are! Where 'we' came from! He probably wonders, 'what makes me think—out of the clear blue sky—that I know all the answers—the right answers!

She slowly turned, refilled her glass, motioned to his—he indicated a decline—she said, "Let's sit on the sofa—I need to fill you in—some background explanations. I think it will help clear up some of your reservations." As they stepped to the huge, soft sofa, she added, as she glanced up to the ceiling, "Sorry, Mrs. White—this may take even longer than I expected!" Lowering her stare into his eyes, she asked, "Is this going to be Ok with you? It isn't simple—or short. Maybe you had just as soon skip it?" "No, I agree, details, background may help a lot. Don't be concerned about time—I think you cleared that 'problem' up with my wife rather nicely!" They both chuckled and sat down. He kicked off his shoes, they both propped their feet on the coffee table. Alex took a sip, tilted her head far back on the loft cushion, stared up at the ceiling, calmly started, "Well, let's see? Where shall I begin?"

She started with Arnie and his new bride, Ellen, graduating from the University of Georgia, went through them starting with a pickup truck, buying and selling local foods. And the facts that Arnie was the historian of the HVG, he was the one with almost fifty years of involvement—first hand—fields to dining table knowledge. Arnie knowing the old systems, habits and seeing, over the years, the changes that drastically effected how food was raised, distributed—even consumed. She covered a lot, ended with, "It really is Arnie's proposal, his project! Even thou he is retired! Willing or unwilling, Arnie created the project—I just documented it all." She, on purpose at this point, had skipped the fact that 'The' Dr. Jim Shirley was Arnie's and Ellen's best friend, from childhood.

After getting another glass full—again Jerry refused—she covered Tom's background, making a strong point that Tom saw things from a different view. He saw it as a job—but a job worth doing well. It wasn't a life long addiction, passion, a dedication as Arnie did. And that Tom had about fifteen years of experience—but only experience in the modern world—the 'mega-company world'. He could influence their ideas—Arnie and her ideas from an 'outsiders' point of view—respect. She more or less, didn't explain any of Tom's military past—and present involvement.

When she started on her own background, she started when she began to attend private—usually very highly respected—all girls schools. This was when she was fifteen. Covering the school years, she highlighted that she only studied—seriously studied—courses in math, computer science, and at college level, the theory of logics, and interconnecting commun-ications—never any serious efforts on inane (Alex's opinion) subjects. And the fact that she would 'jump' schools if things didn't go her way.

She did admit that her 'tendency' to be 'impatience' was 'probably' developed then. She only hinted that money was never a problem. And she had been employed in the food business for about ten years—her only employment was with a major 'Mega-company—one of the Big Three. She felt 'needed' in the food game. Nothing else even caught her attention.

On purpose, she skipped any comments concerning her 'addition' to gold. But a 9 to 5 hacker's job? No way! She couldn't stand to be that tied down, especially to a desk! She didn't work because she had to, she worked—and worked very hard—because she loved it. "So, you can see, I'm just the technician who just happens to know how to put Arnie's old-ways into modern world technology. Of course, with Tom's help to smooth things out and blend things together in a workable fashion. And you can see that my few years are only a drop in the bucket—but combined, we three represent about seventy-five years of actual real world experience!"

Alex hinted at the 'last season'—the year of the collapse, and unintentionally, she let it slip out that she had met Secretary Stillwell that season in Oklahoma. Jerry caught this very tiny detail, suddenly he jumped to his feet, turned to her, slapped his hands together, almost shouted, "Little Alex! Now I remember! That's been bugging me! You're the one that got in Old Still's face and threatened to expose the silo problems! Man He fumed for weeks! Isn't that right? It really was you, wasn't it?" Alex pulled her feet from the coffee table, stood, took a bow, smiled widely, said, "I'm guilty ! It was the one and only Alex! Brainy Bitch! B.B. for short!"

Jerry laughed, turned and went to the cart, got the bottle and his glass, returned to Alex. He filled their glasses, added, "And now, Stillwell is practically on his knees begging for your help! And you're going to take him to the cleaners to start your own business! Strange things never fail to happen!" They laughed together again.

Alex shuffled around the low table, clicked their glasses together, sipped, put her arm around Jerry's waist, looked deep into his eyes, said, "Jerry, I'm not finished—you're about to hear the strangest part of this tale!" He pulled back, sat his glass down, and remarked, "Alex", he pointed a stiff index finger at her face, "Hold that—I've got to piss!" "That's not a bad idea!" She joined his remark.

After taking turns in the bathroom, they returned to the bigger room. Jerry poured the last of the bottle, said, "Ok, Alex, let me hold it! You're just a bag of surprises!" "You remember, earlier today? At the end of that 'main prison', I mentioned that a friend of mine and I 'hacked' into Satcom III? So he could ask for a Russian Scientist's hand in marriage?" "Yes, sure—so?" "The friend is Professor Dr. Jim Shirley, recently of the U.of Ga!" "Dr. Shirley! I know of Dr. Shirley—he has handled so many of the Departments 'special projects', at one time, I thought he was a 'regular' on our payroll! It was really Dr. Shirley?" "Yes! Hold on! And the Russian Scientist was—none other than—the elusive Dr. K! Of course, you said you heard her name in connection with the Satcom III thing." "Yes, but all I heard was that she was 'someway' connected." Alex quickly clicked her glass to his, added, "And they both live with us at Hidden Valley! And! And! They are HVG members! As our 'Special Advisors!'" He backed up, stuck his empty hand straight up, shouted., Alex! You aren't kidding me, are you? Dr. Shirley AND Dr. Natashia Karsky! Unbelievable!" "Her name is now "Nat' Shirley!

Didn't 'Still' mention that he and his wife came to their wedding back in June?" "Not exactly—there were some rumors about him getting to meet Dr.K, getting to kiss her even, and something about her offering the CIA and FBI guys jobs—but I don't pay much attention to D.C. rumors, this city is full of rumors—but very seldom the truth!" "You will not tell anyone, will you? We would be ass-deep in Secret Agent men and damn News Reporters! Please! Promise!" "Ok! Ok! I promise! Unreal! No damn wonder you're such a cocky little bitch! You hold all the aces! Remind me to never play cards with you!" Alex took another bow, said, "Guilty! That's me!"

She looked at the empty bottle—their empty glasses—and the spread of papers still on the dining table, she thought, 'What the hell', she asked, "You about ready to eat a bite? I'm going to order another bottle anyway—may as well get diner started. What do you say?" "Sounds great— maybe it'll get me back down to earth!" "And back to your analysis?" "Right, Boss Lady—and back to work!"

She sat down next to the phone, asked, "What'll you have?" "T-bone, medium rare, a side order of sauteed mushrooms, a small toss salad—ranch, low fat. Rolls, margarine—no butter. That'll do it." He had began to survey the documents again.

"This is Alex, suite 518, please send up another bottle of champagne—just the bottle, we've got the rest. And Hon' rustle up some grub—", she relayed Jerry's wishes, added, "and a steamed lobster—large. And a side order of steamed asparagus with sauce, a bowl of melted butter—real butter, you know—that stuff made from cow's milk?" She hesitated, continued, "And two large cocktails, raw oyster cocktails with plenty of hot sauce—Tabasco sauce! Send the bottled on. Ok? Got that?"

Standing again, she remarked in a low tone, "I think I'll get dressed for supper." Without looking up, Jerry said, "Why? I was just getting use to being around a beautiful young lady with a cute little ass." "It is cute, isn't it?" Alex snickered, waited, he didn't comment. She added, "Because we're not eating watermelon!" That caught his attention. He twisted his head around, looked at her as she headed for the bedroom door. "Watermelon?" he questioned. About half way to the door, she stopped, turned back, put her hands on her hips and told an old farmer's joke.

"There was once two farmers sitting on low benches at a low table. They were eating a watermelon. The flies were very bad—all over the melon. One farmer stood, said, "I'm going to get Mable to come and eat watermelon with us!" "Why?" the other farmer asked. "Because when she sits down, and spreads her knees, the flies go away!" At first Jerry's expression didn't change, then he bent his head to the table in deep laughter. Between laughs, he managed to get out, "Alex! Where did you hear such?" "When you're a Buyer, you've got to know a lot of 'farmer jokes'!" She went on to the bedroom.

Alex stripped off the old tee shirt, added a liberal coating of Lady Power Roll-on to her armpits, went to the bathroom and wiper her face with a damp cloth. Back at the bed, she surveyed her clothes—not much choice—she picked up her black suit skirt and wiggled it on. Getting a thin white crop-top from the pile, she first tried this on in front of the mirror. Her nipples were so clearly displayed in a prominent manner. She thought, 'No way! Mr. White will never get finished!' Jerking this off and throwing it back to the pile, she got her suit jacket, shook the wrinkles out, and put it on. She buttoned only one button—the one in line with her nipples. She thought this was acceptable for 'working' conditions. She made-up her eyes, lips and hand brushed her short,cropped hair. Still looking in the mirror, she felt thankful for her coarse, easily controlled hair. Unconsciously, she unbutton the jacket—let it hang loose by her sides. She was staring at her flat, tight stomach—she gently rubbed it. Suddenly, she realized what she was doing. She was imaging what it would look like if she was pregnant! She whispered, "Have you lost your frigging mind, Miss Hawkins?" Quickly she re-buttoned the jacket, found her medium heel, comfortable shoes, slipped these on. No panties, no pantyhose this time—she didn't care to get THAT dressed! After locating her small pump bottle of body perfume spray, she gave a shot to each side of her neck, then she pulled her skirt up and gave her crotch a liberal pump or two. Telling the old farmer's joke reminded her that there may be some truth to the old joke!

She returned to the living room, Jerry was still at work, and the bottle of champagne hadn't arrived. Dialing room service, she asked, 'Why?' "Sorry, Alex, The food went so quickly—it is all on the way up, now." She hung up, mentioned this to Jerry. Alex quickly got a pen, asked, "If you agree to this sequence", she waved a finger at the papers, "I want to number these as pages. I had generated these in a rather random fashion. Agreed?" He looked at the overall arrangement again, replied, "Agreed." "Jerry, why don't you freshen up, I'll handle the diner." He headed for the rear. Alex numbered the papers, stacked these in order and placed them on one of the small end tables. Placing an empty ash tray on top of the stack, she leaned back and smiled.

'Tap-tap' at the door, she briskly stepped over, opened it. There was the same young man from earlier—and two other young guys. Assistants, she guessed. The previous waiter looked disappointed at her dress outfit. Obviously, he had expected her to be in her 'bare-bottom' tee shirt. Alex didn't feel as if she should disappoint him and his buddies. She stuck her thumbs into the waistband of her skirt, pulled it up very high. Turning her back to them as they came in, she dropped the pen, and slowly did a deep waist bend, with stiff knees—she felt the cooler breeze from the open door to the hall on her bare bottom. She also heard them gasp.Not too loudly, but just enough gasp for her to hear. Straighten up, she pointed to the dining table. Stepping aside, she pulled her hem up almost to her crotch and sat down on the sofa. She propped her heels on the coffee table.

As the three guys setout the meal, she slowly spread her feet—wider and wider—until she was sure the view was excellent! Her jacket being buttoned was tight in the seated position—slowly, she unbuttoned it. The waiters were in mid-motion, froze stiff, staring at her actions. The jacket sprung open to her sides, her large, stiff nipples jumped out when released from the pressure of the light coat. Now Alex was concerned that they may drop the food! Sure that they had seen her beautiful nipples, she slowly re-button her jacket. The three resumed their motions and were almost finished when Jerry retuned. The head waiter, placed and lit a single candle in the center of the dining table, a pleasant arrangement. The waiters probably thought this was a romantic occasion. Again, Alex added a 30% gratuity and signed the bill, 'Alex'. The head waiter opened one of the bottles of champagne and)helped Alex with her chair, then poured their drinks. The two assistants waited at the door. The head waiter, still at the dining table, asked, "Miss Alex, do you want me to stay and serve?" She glanced at the setup, replied, "No thanks, I think everything is in perfect order, We'll manage. Thank you!" "No, Miss Alex, thank you!" The guy smiled broadly, bowed, then the three left.

Lifting their glasses, they touched these together and held it, "Here's to you, Alex! I don't think I've ever met anyone so briefly that was so interesting. Lots of luck on your project!" They held the glasses together, Alex countered with, "Here's to you, Mr. Jerry White, I wish you the most of luck in any future endeavors!"

They sipped, then Alex reached over with one hand's fingers, slightly stroked Jerry's chin, "Mr. White, I do believe you shaved." "Just a bit,

I found a new razor in the bath—compliments of the hotel—thought I might be getting slightly bristled there", he rubbed his chin, "And I borrowed a dash of your body perfume—hope you don't mind." "Not at all, another nice touch, thank you." And he had replaced his tie and suit coat. As Alex stared into his eyes, she thought, 'I wonder if he sprayed his crotch?'

'Miss Hawkins! You must NOT think such evil things!' It was from somewhere in her past—sometime during her years at some suppressing all girls school, some old maid who had probably never been 'laid' in her entire life! Alex slightly shook the cobwebs from her mind. Jerry questioned, "Something wrong, Alex?" She realized her stare into his eyes had changed to a blank stare—that she really wasn't seeing anything!

Abruptly, there was just a flicker of a thought—'she was looking but she didn't see—or was it she could NOT see? She tried, very hard to make it a complete thought—it should tie with something—connect to something, something from deep—very deep—inside her mind, but she couldn't complete it. But she did recall Tiger saying, 'they can look, but they can NOT see!'

Jerry reached over and gently rubbed her cheek, she jerked her head aside, batted her eyes. She was not smiling. "Alex? Are you Ok?" "I guess—please excuse me", she pushed back, stood and stepped to the glass wall and looked across the city lights below. She knew 'it' had to mean something—but what? Where? Jerry joined her, placed an arm around her small shoulders, gently remarked, "Alex, the food is getting cold—you want to postpone it? I can call room service—" She turned, placed a flat hand against his chest, replied, "No, silly, I'm Ok—let's eat, I'm famished!" She was now smiling.

The meal proceeded with no additional problems, and with the heavy pre-warmed plates, it didn't get 'too' cold. The food was delicious. Alex enjoyed her lobster in a very slow sucking fashion—dipping chunks into the melted butter, sucking the butter from the pieces, and after slowly chewing, sucking the juices from her finger tips, and wiping her lips with the tip of her tongue. And the raw oyster cocktail—she would tilt her head back, and with the small dainty fork—drop an oyster into her open mouth and swallow it whole. The asparagus spears she would lift by the root end with her delicate fingers and insert the tip between her pursed lips and suck the sauce off, slowly insert it farther and suck again repeatedly until the entire spear was in her mouth—and throat. And with a final push with one finger tip between her juicy lips, it was gone. Jerry watched her—most of all, her mouth, her lips, as she sucked down the last spear. Unable to resist it, he said, "Alex, you really know how to—enjoy your food." That wasn't exactly what he wanted to say, but—. "You know the old saying—practice makes perfect!" Alex quipped as she pushed away the last empty dish. Jerry asked, in an effort to change what was on his mind, "Just out of curiosity, how did Dr. K slip out of Russia and into the USA?" Alex stopped in mid-motion, "You aren't a secret agent man are you? Plying me with wine and food, so I'll spill the beans on a fellow comrade, are you?" He looked disappointed at such a reply. Alex laughed, "Jerry! I'm just kidding! I don't actually know, but from some of her tales, and Jim's tales, that lady could slip an elephant into a Piper Cub and no one would ever notice it! One thing I do know, she's an expert at making passports and forging documents! I think she could replicate the proper papers to get you on the space shuttle!" "As if I would want to get on the space shuttle!" he laughed.

As she served coffee after the meal, Jerry gently expressed his desire—'if the project is a 'go' or if it is rejected, regardless, he wanted to join their group.' Leaning forward and paying close attention, Alex waited until he was completely finished. Then, "Jerry, you don't have any idea of what the HVG members did today—or what they are doing right now." He just slightly shook his head. "Today, all six of them picked beans, pulled and shelled corn, cut and put up cabbage. And stored food in our massive underground storage pit. Hard, physical work! Then they had a 'community' supper, cooked on an outdoor grill on Arnie's front porch. After which, they sat around for a couple of hours and discussed things." "Things?" he was very attentive. "Yes, things—things from the heaven's star patterns to microbiology, to what funny looking little pictures 'say'! Yes, 'say', as with words. Things such as when the first snow will fall—or—when the next deer would need to be killed, or was the trout population in 'our' stream on the increase or the decline. Things, thousands of different things." She stopped and sipped her coffee. "The way you say it, it doesn't sound half bad—not bad at all." "And now, they're all asleep—as happy as full pigs in a warm mud puddle!" She waited, then changed to a much more serious tone, added, "All happy—except me. I'm sorry, I don't mean right now, I'm the happiest I've been in a long, long, time."

She stood, carried her cup, and moved to face the glass wall, she continued, "I regret to say, this is my world. Here, today is what I enjoy. You don't have any idea but I've got enough money—real money—to not have to work another day—even one hour—for the rest of my life—even if I live to be a hundred and ten. But—right now, I want this project to be a success. It's just the challenge, just seeing if I can make it a success!" She turned back, faced him and said, "Can you understand that?" He saw the few tears as they slowly drained from her black eyes. He stood, and with his napkin, softly wiped her eyes and cheeks, and in just above a whisper, "Yes, I think I can understand." He lightly kissed her on one cheek then backed off.

"Alex, I'll clear off the table if you'll pour us another round of champagne. Fair deal?" She smiled, replied, "Fair deal! Besides you've got to finish your analysis of my silly project!" "There's nothing silly about it. It will probably be the best thing to happen to this country since Henry Ford's 'silly' little Model T!"

He started stacking the dishes, she opened the second bottle of champagne and poured drinks. As she topped the second glass, she thought, 'Alex, baby, you're sliding into home plate—all you've got to do is be damn sure and touch the bag!'

Jerry was again deeply studying the charts, the interconnection of the different systems. After about thirty minutes—up until then he had not noticed Alex at all—the clatter of dishes caught his attention. He sat back, looked into the kitchenette. Alex was in front of the small sink, she was washing dishes! And she had removed her jacket and hung it on the handle of the compact refrigerator. She was nude from her waist up. "Alex! WHAT are you doing?" He almost shouted at her. "What?" Then she realized she didn't have to wash dishes—it had been the results of the habit back at 'home'. She stepped back, looked seriously at the sink—the dishes. Wiping her hands, she got her jacket and slipped it back on—she didn't bother to button it up, "Sorry, just nervous habit, I guess." Jerry went back to work, she poured herself another drink, went to the bedroom and exchanged her 'too' tight jacket for her old baggy tee shirt. And she pulled off the heels, but she kept on the skirt.

Another hour or so, then Jerry slid his chair back, brushed his hair, and stretched his arms. Rising, he looked toward Alex, asked, "Any more coffee?" Without saying anything, she got up from the sofa, patted her bare feet through the thick carpet and got the coffee pitcher. "Yes, I'll 'nuke' you a cup!" Handing him the cup of heated coffee, she asked, "Well? Where do we stand?" He sipped and then replied, "The only thing I would recommend is to combine some of the paths. Some of the inputs and outputs. With our advanced hardware, this would be a snap to process." "If combined, could Joe Blow use a eight hundred dollar PC bought across the counter at the local discount outlet?" "No" was his reply. "Then I'll say we leave it like it is. We—anyone—could buy cheap, across the counter hardware. Buy one unit, start, and as the cash flow was predictable, buy another unit. And as the workload increased, buy another cheap set-up. Got the picture?" "Yes, sounds very logical, very basic business. Alex, you see, you look through different eyes We've got 'Mega-buck stuff', so we—I—think in 'Mega-buck' terms." Alex started again, "What I see, is the Department furnishing the game plan, even the operational programs. Spelling out exactly what the next group will need, even hardware wise. Hell—maybe even furnishing it—giving it to the next group." She continued, "Have you ever heard how Mexico, Thailand, other so-called 'third world' countries operate? Get their people in business? Businesses the people need? The Government gives the hardware—Ok, so some of it is old, or 'hand-down'—to whoever has the potential to make it work for their people." "No, I guess that's another strike against us—the Department—our Government?" "Damned straight!" "Alex, are you proposing that all this," he waved a hand toward the documents, "with operational programs, be GIVEN to the next groups? Lady, you're talking stuff that's worth a fortune! Do you think Micro-Soft gives their programs away?" "I intend for our profits to come from a small, a reasonable percentage of difference between the buying price and the selling price—not from selling what the groups—the next groups, the next 'cell' needs to get started! Besides, that was the exchange proposed with 'Still', he gets the operational details, a proven system, I—we—get you people and the use of the Department's hardware for one year. After that, we're on our own. A deal is a deal, understand?" "Ok, no shirt off my back." They both waited, he drank coffee, she sipped champagne. Then Jerry went to the phone and dialed Stillwell's home number. It was about eleven thirty. As it rang, Alex asked, "Do you want me to leave the suite?" "Hell no! You and I don't have any secrets—well—concerning this subject anyway!" Alex smiled, "About this subject, you may be correct!"

It didn't take long—Jerry explained to Stillwell, "It's all very well planned, very feasible, interconnected correctly. I don't recommend any changes—none what so ever." He listened, then, "Yes sir, we've discussed that. We agreed to start by Alex furnishing the detail operational programs—to me. I'll use Yevona, she can load—get set-up as the programs are transferred up via computers. She can do that part-time, work off her present Department project. I just don't reassign her any new Department projects. We, Yevona really, can feed back to Alex the results of 'dummy' examples, problematical exercises to check out the programs, their relationships. In the mean time, HVG will get their Field Buyers in place. We feed schedules down, info, etc to HVG. And as the action starts, all inputs will come directly to us. D.C., Yevona. Then when the work load increases, I can reassign another of our operators—and another." Jerry listened, then, "Yes sir, we have—we, Alex and I, can foresee a max. of ten. "He waited, "Yes sir. You want to talk to Alex directly? Ok, I'll tell her." Stillwell talked, he listened, "No sir, that has not been discussed. I'm of the opinion HVG is planning to pick up the tab for their Field Buyers and use private sub-contracts for all the transportation needs. Of course, that cost will be added into their selling price."

Again Jerry went silent, then, "Really? You would agree to that? Ok, I'll tell her. I'm sure it would be appreciated." He waited, "Got it, ten operators max, one year only!" he listened, "No problem, sir. It has been very interesting indeed! Mr. Stillwell, Alex is one 'crackerjack' little gal. Shame, the Department couldn't get her!" He waited, then laughed, said, "Goodnight, sir!" He hung up, sighed, went for a glass of champagne, Alex joined him.

As they clicked glasses, he said, "Alex, you're in business! I guess you caught most of that—the details, but the part you didn't get—the part about the Field Buyers, Stillwell said he would—he did agree—for you—HVG—to bill the Buyer's expenses, their wages, their traveling expenses, through me, really directly to Yevona. She will process with your programs but, get this! The Department will actually PAY THEIR EXPENSES! From the Department's 'developmental expense account!" Alex put one flat hand against her chest, leaned back, gasped, then she jumped to her tip-toes and kissed Jerry hard, on his lips. Exclaiming, "I can't believe it!" She kissed him again. And again.

Alex relaxed, asked, "What was that last laugh, just after, 'shame the Department couldn't get her'?" Jerry backed up, answered, "Stillwell said, 'The Brainy Bitch would have my job and your job before the year was out!" Alex laughed, and playfully punched Jerry in his stomach. He playfully doubled forward.

The two walked back and forth some with their arms around each other's waist, Jerry said, "Well, are you going to call someone in Hidden Valley tonight? Now?" She waited, thought then replied, "Nope! Those tired folks are getting much needed rest! They've got a day of hard work ahead! It can wait until I get back and catch them all together after supper time! But it will be tommorow! And we can celebrate—besides it'll be

Friday night!" "Friday night? Stillwell mentioned, earlier to day that you had to be back by Friday night—You even mentioned that to my wife, but yet I haven't heard you say why you had to be back by Friday night. So?" Alex stepped away, turned her back to him, stepped to the glass wall—to her own reflection—after a while, she said, "Well—we are partners now—besides, you're bound to find out sooner or later—", she wavered. Then, in a low tone, "I'm a Friday night nympho." Jerry opened his eyes wide, shook his head, asked, "I didn't hear you—or maybe I don't believe what I thought I heard. You're a—what?" "It's a very old, old habit." She turned, faced him, "I'm a nympho on Friday nights! Did you hear that?" "Yes—I'm." He went silent. He really didn't know what to say!

She walked briskly to the kitchenette, poured herself another drink, said, "Well, Mr. White, thanks a heap, thanks very much for your help. You take all those papers—I've got it on disk. My 'E' mail address, phone numbers are at the top—and—", this time she let it drop. He put his coat on, gathered up the documents then headed for the door. At the door, and holding it open, he turned toward her, nodded, said, "We'll stay in touch. Don't forget your 8 A.M. pick up. Have a nice flight back. Goodnight." He left and closed the door behind himself. Alex leaned her face to her cupped palms and softly sobbed, "Damn—damn—"

CHAPTER 3

The next few months were a flurry of activities at Hidden Valley. Alex had quickly convinced the others to be working partners. Nat and Jim, with occasional interjections by Arnie, were busy finishing up their manuscripts—these were basically translations, from Russian to English, of Dr.K's years of research concerning the effects, and results, of long term storage of food. These included her conclusions that had culminated with the 'African Project'—the one for which she and her assistants were highly recognized in Moscow. This was just prior to the collapse of the food system in the USA.

Their basic plan was to distribute these—thru Jim's contacts—to the colleges and universities to be used as teaching material. At Alex's suggestion, they were also writing a more concise version. Less technical, to be distributed to farmers. By 'private' conversations with Secretary Stillwell, Alex had convinced him to handle this distribution thru his county agents. And she persuaded him to do the printing of these manuscripts. As usual, she had 'leaned' on Stillwell rather hard. But by now, he didn't expect any less from her.

The HVG's personal farming activities were finally finished for this season. Mike and Tom had quickly cut and stacked enough wood for this winter's needs. They had also located—and traded for—two small cast iron pop-belly stoves for the 'barn' and the 'crib'.

Alex had worked late nights writing detail operational programs, she forward these to Jerry in D.C. via computers. Set-up for the 'project' had progressed well—and rapidly.

By Arnie supplying a list of ex-buyers from his 'little black book', the two of them narrowed the search down to four potential HVG Field

Buyers. But at the last moment, Alex had the feeling that Tom felt 'left-out', would 'miss his freedom' of being a Buyer—on the road again. Suddenly, before final deals, she reduced the number of needed Buyers to three—and convinced Tom that he could handle 're-calls', unusual cases, and most importantly, he could be a 'point-man' for contacting the retail stores. She impressed the fact that she wanted HVG's name and all contact numbers and 'E' addresses in their face! Tom seemed very pleased with the prospects of his 'new' duties—and of being on the road again!

At a group meeting in Atlanta—Arnie, Alex, Tom and the three prospective new buyers—Alex explained the details. Similarly, all three of the new men agreed to join up, with something like, "little Alex, you got a deal!"

After giving the details of the new employees to Jerry over the phone, Alex asked, "Jerry, I promised I would personally stake these four guys— she 'failed' to mention that Tom was the fourth man—$1000 each, 'front-money' so they wouldn't need to dip into their own money while waiting for payments, salaries, to be processed, but—", she hesitated. Jerry got the message, said, "Alex, file that through 'expenses', your account. Hell, we spend more than that each month on toilet supplies!" She chuckled, replied, "Jerry, you're a real doll! Thanks!"

In Alex's spare time, she had persuaded Mike and Tiger to be in charge of all transportation details—selection of companies, or even private truckers—personal contacts—explanation of HVG's intentions—even scheduling. But of course by the D.C. programs and direct computer Link ups to D.C. Mike and Tiger both became enthused with the prospects Of 'getting-out', back to work for Mike, a very new experience for young Tiger. They were also placed on the D.C. payroll—in a roundabout fashion through the HVG programs—this was similar to Tom's situation and the three new Buyers.

During this period, Alex flew, via commercial flight to D.C. She spent a couple of days with Jerry and Yevona. Just before leaving, she 'borrowed' seven new lap top computers—these were top-of-the-line units. And like Jerry said, "this is just another drop in the bucket for Big Government!" With a previous meeting of Stillwell, Jerry and Alex, it had been agreed that the beginning of Alex's 'year' wouldn't start until the first Field Expense report from her Buyers were received at D.C. Then she had one year—and only one year! After that, she—the HVG—was on their own. This start of the year began on November 15. The entire system was off and running!

By mid January, the HVG felt secure—every aspect was showing to be efficient and reliable. And firm contracts—mainly out of Florida—were pouring in. Firm sales—with firm cash flow—were out stripping supply. And turn-around times on all the information and payments were even faster than Alex had expected. Jim and Nat had finished the manuscripts and the Ag Department had covered the expenses of printing the many, many copies. Distribution to the schools and the farmers was planned for early spring.

Word about HVG's efforts—and success—was beginning to spread across the country. The Ag Department had even produced a TV Special concentrated on their success. And Stillwell had induced Alex, Arnie and Tom to be the TV 'stars'!

Alex was back in D.C. in a private meeting with Stillwell when he told her that he didn't want to wait out her one year deal—he would stick to the original agreement to cover their expenses, all that, but he could already see that her project was the way to go. Their HVG had tied up the entire Southeast into one neat and effective package And it was all above board just as she had promised. He planned to start action immediately to promote other groups—cells—for the entire country. But, but, of course this depended on her agreement. She still, more or less, owned the programs being as she was an independent, private 'writer'. She asked for one week to think it over.

Alex didn't return immediately to Hidden Valley. Privately, she asked Jerry to join her for supper—and a very confidential meeting—she didn't want any witnesses, as a matter of fact, she didn't want anyone to know that the two of them were meeting together. She impressed this on Jerry. And she hadn't told anyone else that she was staying over in D.C.

Leaving the office, she declined the limo, went down and out and caught a taxi on the street. On the way to the Hotel Empire, she asked the driver to stop at a Chinese 'take-out'. At the hotel, she got a suite, it just happened to be 518 again. Entering 518, she smiled at the fact that everything was the same. Quickly setting the bag of food on the dining table, she turned back toward the door, the bellhop waited, holding her travel bag. Alex said, "Just put that on the dresser, the one with the large mirror, next to the bed" He did, she tipped him then he left.

Alex quickly dialed Jerry's number at his office and told him where she was. She went to the bedroom and removed her full length fur coat.

She had 'recovered' it from storage when on her way to Hartsfield in Atlanta.

She removed the black wool suit jacket and the long, full, black wool skirt. This was a new suit she had bought on her way through Atlanta this morning. She had been reminded in September how cold it could be in D.C. this time of year—she didn't intend on being caught under-dressed again. Removing the long sleeve black lacy blouse, with a high ruffled collar, she was down to her mid calf length black slip and black pantyhose—with a slight pattern—and black high heel pumps. This felt more comfortable, she opened her bag, felt around and pulled out a loose, long sleeve white blouse—it was plain—especially compared to the one she had just removed. She slipped the white one on, left it unbuttoned up the front.

Calling room service, she asked that they send up a jug—1.5 liter jug—of Sangria wine, no glasses or cart, just the wine. She had decided to use some of the fancy glasses in the bar/cabinet. This arrived soon, she made it quick by accepting it at the door—and she left the door unlocked.

Alex poured herself a glass of the wine and looked out the glass wall. She wasn't sure—something unusual for her—which way this was going to go. She had no documents, no hi-tech schemes—just one simple decision to make. She smiled, thought, ok, maybe two decisions!'

In about thirty minutes, there was a tap-tap on the door, she didn't bother to turn, she said, "Come in, it's unlocked!" As Jerry closed and locked the door behind him, he stood, waited and stared at Alex. She was beautiful he thought—regardless of what she wore. Standing in front of the window, with the low sun beyond, she was extremely attractive. She turned, said, "Get a glass from the cabinet there—a jug of wine is here on the counter." He got a drink, stepped next to her side, slipped his free hand around her waist. They sipped, he slid his hand lower, down to her buttock—nothing rough, just a gentle pressure. She didn't flinch. Suddenly, he realized it was Friday night! The first Friday Alex had been In D.C. since he knew her! He tilted over, and softly kissed her neck. Still no reaction—or resistance either.

"I'm out of wine", she broke the silence, twisted away and poured herself another glass full, added, "I've got Chinese take-outs—I didn't want us disturbed by room service—well—no more than necessary anyway! You ready for a snack? I haven't eaten today." He took the hint, replied "Sure." He turned and began to unload the bag. They ate, more or less, walk-about—a little of this, a little of that. Almost finished, and with a full glass of wine, she stepped to about the center of the room, and began to fill him in on her 'private' meeting this morning with Stillwell.

"And he admitted you own the programs? But, I'm not surprised, you really do, you know." "Jerry, you said, back in September—our first meeting here", she waved a hand around, continued, "that the programs were worth a lot of money. What are you calling, 'a lot of money?" He stepped closer, faced her, "Alex, are you serious about selling? You made a high and mighty speech about giving them away." He waited, then she shrugged her small shoulders, "Well—they are working—" "Yes, working flawless, a real god-sent," he interjected. "Just for example, nothing concrete-yet—what if the Department bought them? It wouldn't be like hustling the poor people for their needs to set-up a new group—would it?" "No, it wouldn't be! Alex, you've been thinking too small! In this city," he waved toward the glass wall, added, "Money changes hands, Departments pay for 'things'—don't forget, I have access to all the bills, all the checks, Hell, in this city, millions are paid just so someone will leave—disappear-or keep their mouth shut. Paying you for something so needed, would be peanuts. And—and—Stillwell would not dare to proceed without a signed, witnessed, and notarized receipt—a contract—with you. Especially you! He knows you would sue him—rake his ass over the coals in a heart beat! Alex! You've got him by the balls! He wants to push this 'group'—cell'— business! He wants to be the hero of the hour! Hell, yes, make him a deal!" They were silent as she headed for the wine jug.

Back facing the glass wall, they waited and watched as the sun set. "Beautiful," she calmly remarked, "Why can't things be as simple as that?" She turned, faced Jerry, added, "I have no idea what kind of money, how much we're talking about." Jerry placed one hand under her chin, stared into her eyes, said, "Two million. Oh, he'll huff and puff, maybe even shout—then he'll counter with one and a half. Don't snap at it, stand your ground for a while, then bat those beautiful black eyes, get humble and take the damn one and a half—and laugh all the way to the bank!" "No", she said. "No? Are you crazy! Three months ago, you were willing to give it all away!" "I meant about going to the bank. I don't think

I've told you YET, but I only deal in gold—real gold preferred. But I will accept gold certificates—if by a very reputable dealer. Or certified checks directly to my dealer." "Gold? Damn, Alex, you never fail to amaze me! Is there no end to your surprises?" "Jerry, you're only heard the beginning of Alex—and Miss Hawkins." He was shocked that she used the name she so obviously hated so much—Miss Hawkins!

He turned away, added, "You asked, that's my suggestion—but—please keep my name out of it! Or I'll be a street sweeper! Soon! No wonder you were so secretive about this little ta-de-ta! I need a drink, and I don't mean wine!" He headed for the phone.

As room service delivered the cart with the pitcher of cold martini mix and glasses, Jerry stayed in the bedroom out of sight. Alex noticed it was the same young man she had first received room service from back in September. She slightly fingered his name tag, asked, "Timmy, I see. Are you going to be working all night?" "Yes, Miss Alex! Great to see you back! How long are you going to be here—in 518?" "I'm not sure, exactly, probably through Monday night at least." She added the tip, signed the bill and she smiled broadly at him, said, "We'll probably be seeing a lot of each other. You scheduled to work this weekend?" "Yes, Mam, all weekend—even all the nights next week!" As he left, he thought, 'Man! Some chick, that Alex!' He couldn't wait to see his buddies!

Jerry came out, and as he poured drinks, Alex called Stillwell's home number. After greetings, Alex said, "Still, if you're available Monday morning, I'm ready to discuss the details of what you proposed earlier today." She listened, "Ok, nine A.M. Your office! Thanks, see you then. Good-by." She hung up, turned to Jerry, stuck both her thumbs up, snapped, "Now! This is fun! Let's celebrate!"

She downed the 'martini, she removed her blouse, threw it toward a chair—she missed it. Pulling her black slip straps over her shoulders, she pulled it down to below her hips, then wiggling, it fell to the floor. She stepped out of it, said, as she headed for the pitcher, "How the hell did we every get ram-roded into wearing clothes? A real pain in the neck!" In only her high heels, and black pantyhose, she twisted over to the room's temperature control switch and turne d it to the highest setting possible.

Facing Jerry across the room, she leaned one hand against the wall, cocked her hips to one side, snapped, "Let's get some heat in here! You like it hot? Really hot? Sticky hot? Hot enough for two people to stick together. Hot enough for my crotch to drip?" He removed his coat, then his tie, placed these on one end of the sofa. Stepping closer, he lifted her chin with one set of his fingers, said, "Are you giving me the come-on?

"It's Friday night—it's time to let Evil Little Miss Hawkins out of her cage!" "So, it's Miss Hawkins with the problem?" She snapped straight, strutted around him, quipped, as she headed for the drink cart, "Take it anyway you want to!"

He followed her, said, "Alex—I don't want Miss Hawkins—I want you, Alex, I want to love you, I want to work shoulder to shoulder with Alex—forever! I want to keep you." "Keep! Wrong word!" she turned, faced him, snapped, "No one keeps us!", she pointed an index finger to her chest, continued, "Alex—and Miss Hawkins—can take care of our selves! We have been doing it since—", she hesitated, and she didn't say 'since our mother sat in a tub of hot water and slit her wrists'—instead she continued with, "since we were fifteen years old! So don't talk to us about KEEP! OK!" He didn't respond.

She walked across the room and back several times, then abuptly stopped mid-ways, and in a much softer tone—almost normal—said directly to Jerry, "You want to—or not? It isn't difficult—it's just like those computers we play with. Seems complicated but really, just a little click here, a click there, a little flash here, and there—a bunch of little things that add up—hopefully to a conclusion—or a climax—or a—He headed for his coat and tie. As he picked these up, he said, "No, Alex, this is not uhat I want—I want something—a relationship-that means something—a real meaningful relationship!" "A meaningful relationship! Everyday thousands starve while rich countries watch—one country kills half of another country—now, those are meaningful relationships!"

She stomped pass him, snapped, "I'm taking a long hot bubble bath—you do what you want to!" He left 518.

Uhile she ran hot water in the tub, she got her cell phone from her purse, dialed the number at Arnie's—she guessed Tom and the others would still be there. She slipped her shoes off and pulled the pantyhose down. Opening a package of bubble bath solution and squeezing it along the water, she waited for the connection. Nat answered, they talked some, then Alex asked, "Is Tom still there?" "Yes, you want to speak to him?" "Yes, please." Alex climbed in the tub and sat down while Tom came to pbo)ne. "Tom, Honey, I'm—yes, I'm still in D.C.Look, I've got a glich here"—"no, nothing serious, but I've got to stay over—until Monday night for sure. I'll call then if it takes longer"—"Ok, love you! Bye!"

Alex broke the connection, speed dialed Jerry White's home phone. She had slid deep in the hot bubble bath, soon, Mrs.White answered. They greeted one another, then Alex said, "Lilly, Honey, I've got a small problem." "What, Alex, anything I can do?" "Yes, that's why I'm calling you. I came up with a minimum of clothes—but something is requiring me to stay over until next week, I need to buy some extra clothes!"

Jerry came in his front door just in time to hear his wife say, 'Why sure, Alex honey, then you're interested mainly in a business suit "or two?"—"Sure, I know exactly the best places." Lilly glanced at Jerry, he was waiting, listening, she continued, "Alex, how about I get Jerry to drive us around? Ok?"—"Would it be Ok if we pick you up, say at ten?"—"And you are at the Empire?" "Great, we'll see you tomorrow morning at ten! Bye!"

Lilly hung up, turned to Jerry, said,"It was that sweet little Alex, she wants me to help her shop for new clothes! Isn't that just lovely!" He nodded and headed for their bar.

The water in Alex's tub was cooling off, she jumped out, grabbed a huge towel and as she roughly dried off, she ran to the hotel phone. She dialed room service,"Hon, this is Alex in 518"—"Yes, the martinis were just right! But I guess I'm just not a Martini lady! You recall that champagne I got back in September?"—"Yes, it was in the thirty dollar range. Please sent me up two bottles. Hey! Make that three—looks like I'm stuck here for the weekend!"

She continued, "Hon, I need a tiny favor. I sort of made a mess in the kitchen"—she lied, "No! Not maid service! If you could, please let that cute Timmy bring up the champagne, and stay over to help me out, I'd be more than happy to pay for his service"—"How long? Let's just say for the balance of his night. I'm not sure how long this will take—you got what I mean?" She gave a slight chuckle into the phone, added, "You're a real sweety, I would appreciate that!"

Hanging up, she quickly checked to be sure the door was unlocked, ran back to the bedroom, finished drying, found a spaghetti strap, short, thin, 'Baby-doll' gown and slipped it on. She rubbed her hair in place then made-up her face. Being as she already had on red fingernail polish she put on bright red lipstick. She exaggerated it a lot, and as she added much longer than usual eyebrow make-up—black—she hesitated as she looked into the mirror, and said calmly, "Miss Hawkins, I think you would have made a very successful whore—if you had just needed the money!" Alex laughed.

Locating her black, strap, high spike heels, she struggled and got these on. Moving to face the full length mirror in the bath, she slowly looked at her reflection as she turned around. Facing the mirror, she slipped both hands up under the gown and with her thumbs and index fingers she began to twist and pull her nipples—she continued for several minutes. With a final hard snap, she said, "There, you beautiful suckers, it's Friday night! It's time you two perform!" With no pantyhose, no panties, her nipples proud and erect and clearly visible through the thin material, Miss Hawkins was ready. "Thank you so much, Alex, it has been a long time since you let me play—", the different tone of voice died away.

She stared at the mirror until she heard the tap-tap on the front door. "Come on in, Tim!" She headed for the bed. Hearing him enter, she called out, "Bring the cart back here—and lock the door, please!" "Yes mam" Tim answered in reply. As he entered the bedroom, he saw that she was lying spread out on the huge bed. She remarked, "Tim, Honey, for tonight, please call me Miss Hawkins—but for tonight only."

The early morning sun through the glass strip near the head of the bed woke Alex. With a start, she sat upright, quickly jumped up, grabbed her watch from the top of the dresser—it was only seven-thirty. She realized she had plenty of time before the Whites were to pick her up.

Sighing, she lay back down on her back. Glancing at the naked young man still sleeping next to her—he was face down—she thought, 'Not bad! Not bad at all!'

Alex was in the lobby, she wore her long black skirt, a thin white blouse, black pantyhose and her comfortable black pumps. And her full length black Russian mink fur coat with a matching 'Cossack's' cap. It too was black Russian mink. Nat had loaned it to her. Too warmly dressed to wait much longer inside, she stepped thru the double front doors and went outside. The doorman asked, "Taxi, Miss?" "No thanks, someone is to pick me up."

Alex guessed the temperature outside to be in the high twenties or the low thirties—light snow flurries were blowing about, it was solid gray, the trees in sight were bare. Decided that she had cooled off enough, she started to the doors. But a black Mercedes pulled under the canopy—she recognized it as Jerry's. The doorman opened the front passanger's door, but the lady declined to get out. Jerry got out, stood, and called over the top, "Alex! You ready?" She waved, nodded and stepped to the rear door. The doorman opened it and helped her get in.

Pulling out into the street traffic, the blonde in the front twisted around, said, "Well! Alex! We finally meet! I'm Lilly! So nice to see you!" She stuck her right hand over to Alex. Alex took it, said "Nice to meet you, Lilly, we've talked and talked, but never met. It's really nice for you to help me out today! I can't believe I've got caught in such a situation!" "One never knows, does one?" Lilly remarked then she proceeded to explain where they were headed.

Alex sized up Mrs. Lilly White; she looked to be about forty, about five eight or nine, about the correct weigh for her height, a very attractive face—it was made-up to perfection—and 'just right' curly blonde hair. About all Alex could see of her dress, she too had on a fur coat—it was slipped back off her shoulders—when she twisted around, Alex saw her ruffled front, thin, white blouse. And Lilly's rather large bosom. Overall, so far, Alex guessed her to be a very beautiful lady. No wonder Jerry didn't seem 'too' anxious! For the first time ever, Alex viewed another woman as a competitor! This thought had never crossed her mind before!

Mrs. White was still elaborating on the shopping possibilities when they approached the huge mall. As soon as the three got together inside— Jerry had dropped the ladies out close to the door, went and parked—Lilly asked, "Exactly what did you have in mind? You mentioned a business suit. Anything else?" "I guess, maybe a new leather travel bag—If I buy clothes, I'll need another bag—or two. You know, one thing leads to another—or two!" Alex lightly laughed. As they slowly strolled, Lilly placed her arm over Alex's shoulders, "Yes, Honey, I know!", she laughed, glanced to Jerry. "And I'm thinking about a new brief case—I'm about tired of stuffing papers in my old travel bag!"

"Alex, I'll ask, being as I have no idea of your preferneces—I—are you talking expensive items? Or bargain prices? I know that sounds so personal, but—" "Not too expensive, I'd say about medium—no need to waste time looking for bargains." "Ok, I've got the picture! Let's head this way!" And she headed off.

The first store specialized in ladies business suits, with a broad range of styles. Alex was out of the habit. She had forgotten there would be so much available in one store. It went slowly—she decided on a penstrip outfit—but with a skirt—she didn't—never had—appreciated the 'men's' style pants suits so pushed by the fashion world. But with her small size, that was some what of a problem. After several attempts, Alex whispered to Lilly, "Maybe I should try the little girls department." Lilly whispered back, "I should be so lucky."

While fitting, Lilly remarked, "Black really is your color—I think your Indian heritage—your hair is very attractive—it must be a dream to fix!" "Yes, I can't image any other—I'm lazy when it comes to dressing up," Alex chuckled then added, "If I had my way, we'd all go around in the buff—except in this damn cold weather! Maybe we could just wear our fur coats!" "Alex! My, how you talk!" Lilly wavered, looked blankly, then added, "I was trying to image such! Might be a scream!" They laughed together.

Alex finally bought a snug fitting black—with light gray tiny strips— skirt and matching jacket—suit style, with lapels and the 'standard' suit pockets.

With the activities and the heat inside the mall, the two resorted to carrying their fur coats dripped across one arm. While strolling, Lilly slipped closer to Alex and placed her 'free' arm around Alex's small shoulders. In almost a whisper, she asked as she looked at Alex's breasts, "Alex, can't help noticing you are not wearing a bra. With your small size— no pun intended—what size do you wear?" "Bra size? I have not a clue!

I don't even own bra!" "None?" "Nope, None at all—what would I do with one?"

Alex chuckled, grabbed Lilly around her waist, pulled her tightly, said, "I notice your bra is very attractive"—it was clearly visible through Lilly's thin white blouse—Alex added, "If I may ask, what size is it?" Lilly pulled on Alex's shoulder, tilted close to her ear, whispered, "34-'C'—a 'D' if I want real comfort." "That's a lot of—I can't image" Alex remarked. "Yes, they are." The two laughed.

Being how Lilly had started this conversation, and not to be out done, Alex asked, "Lilly, what do you think of my nipples?" "Cute, precious, tantalizing, very impressive—they must be a lot of fun—" "Yes, they are." They laughed again.

At another store Alex bought a black skirt and a black rather plain blouse—just 'spares'. "What next?" Lilly asked as she automatically took the bags from Alex and handed these to Jerry. She added, "Travel bags? Briefcase? Shoes? Boots?" "Boots!" Alex snapped, "Let's leave the bags until last." She glanced to Jerry and smiled. He nodded in appreciation. Alex nor Jerry showed any indication of their 'misunderstanding' yesterday. "I want a pair of tall, tight, zip-up the side black boots—kid glove leather! I have a friend—she looks great in her boots!" She was thinking of Nat's 'safari' outfit. "As a matter of fact, let's go to a store where they may have a pair of black, tight, stretch pants to go with the boots—I want the boots to fit over the bottom of the pants. And a black, tight safari jacket—it must have epaulets" "Epaulets?", Lilly questioned. "Yes, Shoulder straps—the little straps on the top of both shoulders—epaulets!" "That sounds—well— exciting! And maybe a whip?" Lilly asked. "Yes! You're right! Must have a black whip!" The two laughed, Jerry didn't, he thought it all sounded weird—and Alex didn't need more weird!

But the two made it a theme effort, finding the pants first, Alex kept these on—she packed away her heavy wool skirt. Then the jacket— just large enough to be very tight over her white blouse—was added.

Alex had proposed that she take off the blouse and leave the upper buttons open. But Lilly had raised her eyebrows, said, "Alex, we may lose our 'bag-man' if you do that—keep the blouse on." But Alex did leave the upper buttons open—the white blouse contrasted beautifully with the new black outfit.

Lilly knew exactly where to go for the boots. When they got to selecting the boots—Lilly had really gotten enthused in fixing Alex's outfit—the store clerk was very impressed by the outfit and got the idea—high heels, black, soft leather and to be worn over the skin tight pants. After finding and fitting, Alex decided to continue to wear the outfit. With her black fur coat on, but pulled far back and the black Cossack's fur cap, it wasn't 'too' shocking for the public.

Leaving the boot store, Lilly whispered, "I know where a shop is that specializes in leather goods—briefcases, jackets, vests, hats—and, yes, even whips. Are you ready to go 'all the way'?" "Why not." Alex pushed her coat even farther back, strutted a couple of quick twisting steps ahead of them, swung around and made a couple of swinging motions with her right hand above her head, shouted, "Crack! Crack!" "Alex! You are too much!" Lilly exclaimed loudly. Then she stepped forward and grabbed Alex in a bearhug. They laughed, Jerry said, "I'm getting a buggy!"

In the leather shop, the two first got a clerk to one side and described 'the whip'. Alex impressed, "Not too long, smallish in size"— to match her stature—"and it has to be black—see my outfit? Ok? That's one. And there is to be another one—" "Another one? Two whips?" Lilly interrupted. "Yes, I've got this friend, she is where I got this wild idea, She has a tan 'safari' outfit—she's as tall as you are—and she's a real—" Alex let it drop. No need to say too much about Dr. K. Back to the clerk, who had gotten interested in the tale, "The second one has to be a medium tan and longer than the black one! Do you think that is possible?" "Yes, I think so, but it will take sometime hunting! Are you two ladies in an extreme hurry?" Alex glanced to Lilly, who replied, "No, no hurry at all! Besides, Little Alex here wants a couple of leather travel bags!" "Feel free to look! The bags are over there." He pointed, then headed for the rear.

Jerry had returned with a buggy and taken a seat outside the store. He settled in to watch the foot traffic in the huge mall.

While they looked at bags, Lilly suggested a large rigid case. "No, got to be smaller—even if it takes more than one." Lilly looked a question. "I've got a small sports coupe, not much room." Lilly shifted to the smaller sized selection, but still rigid. "No, soft—the kind you can push flat—well, nearly flat." "Why?" "In case you need to use it for a pillow!" "A pillow? Who would want to do that?" "I have—I've used my travel bag as a pillow, lying on the ground, with my AK-47 as my bed fellow." "My! Alex, so exciting!" "Not really—having my face three inches from bulletproof glass and watching bullets splatter on the other side—Now that's exciting! Or throwing hand grenades! That's exciting!"

"Alex, what kind of life have you lived?" "A kind that is seldom boring!" Lilly hugged her, said, "To look at you, one would size you up as a little rich, pampered, snooty kid—can't judge one by looks, can one?" Alex didn't reply, she just waited for Lilly to release her.

Finished, as they headed for the door, Alex stopped, said, "Let's surprise Jerry. Here, hold my coat and shoulder purse." The clerk waited with the cases and bags. Alex pulled her Cossack's cap tight, got the black whip from the bag, coiled it properly, stepped out the door, glanced around to be sure there were no people in the way. She drew back and 'cracked' the whip—fairly close to Jerry. He fell back as far as possible on the bench and shouted, "What the hell!" Alex, Lilly and the clerk laughed. "I don't think that's so damn funny!" he snapped. Alex recoiled the whip, held it in the ready position, quipped, "Watch your language Hombre! There are ladies present!" Jerry covered his face and shook his head. The other three laughed again.

They settled down, the clerk helped Jerry arrange the cases and bags on the buggy. As Alex put her coat back on, the clerk stepped to her, shook her hand, said, "Little lady, you've made my day—maybe even my week! Thanks so much! Who are you?" She had paid with cash—"Alex-that's all, just Alex!" "Well, Alex, you are something else!" "Thanks".

"In case you two haven't noticed, this buggy is full. Are you two ready for a bite to eat?" Jerry asked. Lilly and Alex looked at each other, nodded, Alex said, "Sure, thanks for reminding me, I haven't eaten a thing today!"

On the ride back into the center of the city, Lilly tilted to Jerry, whispered something. He replied, "An AK-47? That's a Russian designed automatic rifle. Why?" "Alex said she slept with one." 'I wouldn't doubt if Alex slept with a rattlesnake!' he thought.

They were quiet, then Lilly turned around to face Alex, said, "I've got an idea! When we get to the Empire, you just drop off your things, and you can change outfits, then go with us to our place! I'll invite a few friends over." Turning to Jerry, she added, "And Alex can tell some of her amazing stories!" Jerry just nodded, Alex said, "Sure—why not? But change clothes?" Alex had her coat thrown open and pulled off her shoulders. She rubbed her thighs and torso, "I kind of like this outfit! It makes me feel—not bigger—feel—like more macho!" "No, Alex, it's that you feel more intimidating!" Jerry responded. "Oh, Jer—don't be such an old stodgy! Alex will be the hit! And she can bring her whip and demonstrate 'cracking! No one's going to believe me!" Alex leaned forward, touched Lilly's arm and said "How about me bringing my AK-47?" "Oh, NO! Now that may be really intimidating!" Lilly laughed as she grabbed Alex's hand.

Pulling in front of the Empire, Alex said "Jerry, let them park your car. You two come up, I want to show Lilly my place." Then to Lilly, "If I have to spend much more time in D.C., I think I'll lease 518! I think I could get a price cut! At five hundred a day, any cut would be nice!" Lilly raised her eyebrows then remarked, "I'd like to see that!" As the bellhop unloaded Alex's items, he glanced at her, recognized her and said, 'Miss Alex, love your outfit!" She spread her coat wide, turned around, remarked, "It is smart, isn't it?" "You planning a trip?" Lilly was listening. Alex answered, "Yes—the Amazon, soon!" and she gave a big, smile to the bellhop. Lilly put her fingers to her lips and repressed a laugh.

Arriving at the door of 518, Alex didn't hand the key to the bellhop, instead she unlocked the door herself as she said to Lilly, "Let me check it out—I left a mess this morning—and there may be one or two rapists still in the bed!" Lilly laughed as they entered, the place was perfect. Alex stuck her head into the bedroom, said, "No such luck, they're all gone!" The ladies dropped their coats on the closest sofa, Alex removed the cap and brushed her hair straight. The bellhop unloaded the things in the bedroom and Alex tipped him. As Lilly looked about, made compliments about the suite, she said, "Alex, are you always so much fun?" Alex shrugged, but Jerry answered, "No! You don't want to be involved with little Alex when she is working!" Alex smiled and nodded at Lilly, then as she headed for the bedroom, she said, "Jerry, I think there's some champagne in the frig, please pour us a round—I'm going to brush my teeth and touch-up my face. Lilly, if you need the bathroom, it's back this way—just make yourself at home!"

While Alex was out of the living room, Lilly looked at the dining table, it had a beautiful table cloth and an attractive arrangement of fresh flowers as a centerpiece. She said, "So, this is where you two worked until midnight in September?" "Yes, Alex wiped that table clean and covered it with documents—and documents." "Are you sure it wasn't her cute little ass that she spread on the table?" "I'm definitely sure!" He stepped to Lilly and lightly kissed her on the cheek, added, "Don't worry, Alex lives in her own world—and I'm not part of it!"

Alex was still in the rear when Lilly noticed that her drink was still on the kitchen counter. Stepping close to the bed room doorway, she asked, "Alex, honey, you want me to bring your glass?" "That would be nice—I kind of got caught up here—maybe you could help." With the two glasses, Lilly went in the bedroom, she stopped and stared.

Alex had changed blouses, her face was finished, and she was painting her nails. Alex had decided, as Lilly had said earlier, 'to go all the way'. She had done her standard gold theme; gold eye liner, gold lips, gold nails and her gold nugget jewelry. Her brows were exaggerated in length with jet black.

Lilly wasn't sure which was the most shocking—Alex's gold face trim, or her gold jewelry, or her very unusual 'blouse'! The top was sleeveless, the material was more like pantyhose than cloth—so stretchy it didn't compress anything, in particularly Alex's prominent nipples. It was white—more or less, so much showed through it—and about as transparent as clear plastic film. And as tight as a coat of paint! There was a stand up collar—it too was the stretchy material.

"Lil, honey, would you please put my choker necklace on me—I think my nails may still be wet." This broke Lilly's spellbound attitude—she sat both glasses down on the dresser close to the dazzling gold necklace. It was about one inch wide—rows and rows of tiny gold nuggets— with a full width gold clasp. Standing behind Alex, Lilly began to fit the necklace around the collar of her 'blouse'—or was it a tee shirt? Or a tank top with a fancy collar? Or a 'special' pantyhose?

Finished with the difficult clasp, Lilly lightly stroked the back of Alex's top, and asked, "Where did you find this—this top?" "From the ballet crowd, it's called a body stocking. The dancers use these when they want to appear nude—it makes them legal! And there are many different styles available. Lilly, you should check it out—you would be a real 'knock-out with your gorgeous breasts!" "Maybe I will, maybe I will—" "Ask at any high level dance studio they can put in touch with a supplier."

Stepping to Alex's side, Lilly got her glass, sipped then asked, "Alex, where in the world did all this beautiful jewelry come from?" "The nuggets, from my dad over the years. I had those mounted, converted to what you see." "He was in the gold business?" Alex chuckled, "You might say that— I'll explain tonight." Alex blew on her nails, gingerly lifted her glass—she drank it completely in one effort. Twisting in front of the mirror, she asked, "Well! Do you think that's impressive enough?" "Honey, if that doesn't impress them, they're blind!" The two laughed. "Lets get another drink—I think my nails may be dry by then."

As they entered the living room, Jerry stared at Alex's bosom then he shook his head and slowly covered his eyes with one hand. "Oh, Jer, you've seen nipples before! Don't put on so!", Lilly joked. "It wasn't her nipples—it was all that gold!" He laughingly replied. By now, Alex was wearing her rings, ear studs and left bracelet in addition to the C.) wide choker necklace. "Right, sure, gold." Alex remarked as she pulled Lilly toward the kitchen. They both chuckled.

Just prior to leaving 518, Lilly watched closely as Alex wiggled into her safari jacket, buttoned only the lower buttons, then unbuttoned her left epaulet. Tightly coiling her whip, she then slipped it up her left arm and on to her shoulder. The handle hung straight down in the front, between her left arm and her left breast. Then she re-buttoned the epaulet over the whip. It held the whip tightly in place. "Bet you didn't know what these small straps on the top of these shirts or jackets were for, did you?" Lilly just shook her head.

Alex put her purse close up under her right arm, pulled the strap over her head—this held the purse tightly up into her armpit. After slipping on her fur coat, Alex picked up the cap, asked Lilly, "Cap?" "By all means, it just goes naturally with your coat. Where did you happen to get the coat and cap?" "My dad had the coat made when he was in Russia years ago. A friend of mine recently loaned me the cap. It's just a miracle that they're both of exactly the same breed of mink!" "They both look lovely—especially together." Alex chuckled. "What?", Lilly questioned. "Oh, I just remembered about the coat. I asked my dad how he got the size so correct. He said that the Russian seamstress used a ten year old gi±l as a model! That lets me know where I stand—an old middle aged woman in the body of a little girl." She didn't smile. "Oh, Alex, you're as cute as—" Alex interrupted, "I know! Anything that can be considered cute has been used as an euphuism for me! I'm sorry Lilly, I didn't mean to snap at you—but—", she let it drop.

On the way to the White's home—it was definitely out of the city—Lilly called on her cell phone and invited the guests for tonight.

The White's place was a rather large, two story house with a connecting hall to a cottage style two car garage. The main house was faced with flagstone on the first story—the second story and the attic walls were shiplap boards painted white. All the roofs were steep. The buildings were set well back on a large, slight knoll—there were many old oak trees about.

The front of the house faced the river across the way. The place was by no means new or cheap. As Jerry eased to the garage, Alex asked, "This is very attractive. It looks like family property. Is it?" "Yes, my mother's and father's. I inherited it." Jerry replied. "Any brothers or sisters?" "No, an only child thing. You?" "Only me," Alex cut it short.

As they hung coats—Alex put her purse and cap on the upper shelf— Lilly said to Jerry, "Jer, hon, would you—" she didn't have to finish. "Sure, I'll take care of everything!" He went off, Lilly said, "Jerry is such a darling—he loves to direct the kitchen help—explain exactly what he wants—and when. And he loves to fix-up the bar—drinks, all that! Come on, I'll give you a personal tour of the old homestead!" It took a while.

They ended back at the huge den that had a lot of glass that looked out to a large patio in the rear of the house. The patio was surrounded by a hedge. Being winter, the outdoor furniture was pushed close to the stone barbeque pit and grill. As they looked out to the patio, Lilly said, "Jerry loves to cook outdoors—in better weather. Maybe we can do it soon. Alex, you'll just have to come back when the weather warms up." They went silent for a while then Lilly remarked, "I'm sorry, would you care for a drink? Wine? Whatever? Jerry has about everything!" "Sure, say Sangria—I rather favor that." "No problem, just make your self at home! Be back in a jif!"

Back with the drinks, Lilly lit the gas logs in the two opposing old fireplaces then she returned to Alex who still looked outside. Outdoor automatic lights came on—the entire patio area was flooded with bright light.

"Alex, you mentioned, back in September, that you—well—were having a relationship with—Tom? It was Tom, wasn't it? I don't want to appear—"

Alex quelled Lilly's apprehension, "No problem—yes, Tom and I have been together since the collapse." Alex took a sip, decided she might as well elaborate, "We live in the loft of an old barn—on a place, a valley farm owned by a very close friend. Tom just this winter put in a wood stove—an old cast iron pop-belly one he traded for. My hot tub is still outside. I guess it'll have to stay there—no room inside—well, not yet anyway." Lilly was floored! Something didn't fit! Alex just spent close to a thousand dollars today! And pays five hundred a day for a suite! All without batting an eye!

Alex looked directly at Lilly's face—her mouth hung open, her eyes as far open as possible. Alex didn't want her to faint. She smiled, said, "Don't worry, Lilly, we're not poor. We just love it like that—back to nature, hard physical work, cutting wood, crawling under a pile of quilts, snuggling together just to keep warm!", and Alex laughed. Lilly's expression changed back to a pleasant one, she sighed, "You scared me, Alex! Was that a joke? Your description?" "No joke. And there are five others that live there—in the valley together. We all eat a community supper each evening together. And discuss all sorts of subjects."

"A sort of commune?" Lilly asked. "No, no 'hanky-panky' like the wild sixties—strictly monogamous relationships—loving relationships. Hey, don't worry, I own—free and clear—a large home on a very expensive piece of property, at a lake, with my own private dock. And my own thirty-foot sailboat—fiberglass, very nice! I just didn't enjoy living by myself—no real close friends. The ones where we live now—well—we've saved each others asses! We would die for each other! One can't ask for more than that, could one?"

Lilly looked back toward the patio, "No, guess not—I just never would have guessed you were so—complicated." Alex laughed, placed her arm around Lilly's back, "That about sums up little Alex! Complicated, yes! That fits me!"

"And your family?" "Let's get our glasses refilled and check on Jerry, he may need some help", Alex avoided Lilly's question as she headed for the other part of the house. Lilly followed and she quickly decided THAT question was a definite 'NO-NO'! And to be sure and steer any of the guests away from it!

Jerry didn't need help. With full wine glasses, they made a brief trip through the kitchen—the two maids were bring everything together to Lilly's satisfaction. She led Alex on to the formal living room, turned on the proper lights and straighted up a few things.

Moving to the front door and looking through the glass, Lilly called out, "Here they come! Let's meet them out on the walk! Quick, slip on your coat and cap! I want a great first impression!" And it was—the two couples appeared to be stunned at Alex's appearance—and with Alex! Back inside, Lilly graciously took everyone's coat—and the men's hats, then led the group to the den.

Jerry came in with a tray of drinks—he knew exactly what the guests liked—he had casual greetings then disappeared again, but soon returned. Lilly had skipped formal introductions until now. She went through the lengthy procedure—one by one with Alex. And she was careful to avoid using Alex's last name. Jerry had cautioned her about that, Alex and only Alex!

The couples were in their mid fifties, all appeared to be in good physical condition, the men were dressed in three piece suits and wore ties. The ladies wore rather modest evening gowns and beautiful jewelry. Their make-up and hair styles were according to the latest fashion.

Lilly opened the conversation, "As I told you on the phone this afternoon, I thought you would enjoy meeting Alex. Only today, she was telling me about sleeping in the woods on the ground, snuggled up to her own AK-47!" The AK-47 caught everyone's close attention. Alex decided to start with just after her first encounter with Secretary Stillwell. Not using real names, especially the CIA, she covered Jim's rescue and continued through their struggles—she was sure the shoot-outs, the bullet proof glass, and her throwing grenades were included in their efforts to get from North Dakota back to Georgia. The others, even Jerry who had never heard these tales, was awed. When she came to where they arrived at Hidden Valley, she suggested another round of drinks and then she would gladly answer any specific questions. She sensed they had questions, but had been polite enough to not interrupt. Jerry quickly added another suggestion. The buffet was ready, why didn't they get food, eat lap style, while Alex answered any questions. Alex, and the others agreed.

During the serving at the buffet, there was a flurry of conversation among the others as they exchanged questions and eliminated duplications. Their talking to each other even created additional questions. During this time, Jerry caught Alex alone, he said, "You avoided Dr. K's identity very smoothly." "Of course, I don't know who these people are, or their connections. I hope you do the same." He nodded, "Of course."

As the others ate—Alex only nibbled at the delicious food—she answered questions. When the others were almost finished eating, Alex sat her plate aside, left the den. She soon returned with a tea glass full of red wine, she said, "Jerry, your wine glasses are beautiful—but just too damn small!" The others laughed. She resumed her answers. The eating over, one of the maids gathered up the dishes as the other maid offered strong coffee. The questions concerning a particular subject seemed over.

One of the guest ladies asked, "Alex, your whip—do you really know how to use it?" "Yes. If you folks will stand at the glass doors, I'll go outside and demonstrate—I'll trim Jerry's hedge for him!" With Lilly close, Alex slipped off the ring on her right hand and put it on Lilly's finger. The others quickly made their way to where they could see the patio. Alex went out, removed the whip, flipped it a few times to be sure it was properly uncoiled, then in a swift slashing overhead swing, the whip's tip clipped twigs from the top of the hedge. Several times, in a continuous motion—clip—clip—clip. Then swinging to the center of the patio—the open area—she cracked it—a very loud report, like a gunshot, again and again—over and over without stopping between cracks! In one swift, continuous movement, she twisted around and cracked it directly at the glass doors—just a few inches from the glass, she knew it could actually break the glass! The people inside flinched back from the glass! And made loud sounds.

Alex stopped, slowly coiled the whip and replaced it to her shoulder—just right. She was warmed up by now—the others thought she had finished. But she stepped close to the glass, facing the glass, she saw that the others were still watching. In one flashing smooth motion, she twisted her back to them, jerked the whip—it snapped the epaulet loose, the whip uncoiled too fast to be seen and continuing the swing, she clipped the hedge again! And again! One of the men said to Jerry, "Man! You wouldn't want to piss her off!" Jerry just nodded—he had seen still another side of 'Little Alex'—one that would not be wise to cross! Now she was finished, she came back inside.

The group applauded her as Lilly replaced her ring. Someone asked, "Where in the world did you learn that?" "Guatemala—I spent one summer down there with my dad, while he was looking for gold!" She lay the whip aside, got her 'tea' glass. "Learned from whom?" "The Cholti Indians—now there's a bunch of real men!" Alex smiled, left it hanging. But, gold? Guatemala? Cholti Indians? There was a flurry of questions! She more or less replied to these with brief answers.

"Did you have other interesting summer vacations?" "A few—learning to ride horses in Argentina—skiing in Switzerland—mountain climbing in Colorado—sailing in the 'Med'—Oh! And probably the most fun, bicycling Italy! Skin diving in the Polynesian Islands. And some I can't seem to remember—must not have been much fun!"

"Alex, your father"—Lilly stood, prepared to interrupt, bluntly if nessessary—"was he a professional miner? Or a professional dealer? Or just on vacation?" Alex didn't show much resentment—Lilly waited. But Alex's facial expression did become more serious. "No, he was a professional bum!" "Excuse me—you said—a bum?" "Yes, in the beginning, about when I was born, a real bum. But he knew the power of concentration—gold, and only gold—the only thing he was interested in. He made deals, found a little—here—there, then being a hopeless bum became his cover. Buy here, sell there, good luck, find Indians with a bag, a pouch here—there—buy below market, sell, buy more. Gradually his stake grew. Later, when I was a teen, he deposited in a gold account. When I became eighteen, we had a deal—he put gold in, I took it out! And I began to trade on the 'Boards'—the markets—national and international. Then I also began to put gold into the account. When I turned twenty one, I decided I could trade and hold a job—so—I got a job. A Buyer for one of the Big Three food companies." She hesitated, added, "And that brings us—more or less—up to date!"

She left the room with her empty glass. Soon she returned with a bottle of champagne and a cork remover and said, "Sorry Je, but I found your cache. Anyone care for a swallow?" She removed the cork and drank directly from the bottle, sat down, spread her knees wide and held the bottle out to the others. No 'takers', she took another gulp.

Alex was tired, it had been an exhausting 'event'. She decided to bring it to a quick conclusion. Sitting the bottle aside, she stood, faced the guests, then slowly unbuttoned her jacket and removed it. The guests gasped at the sight of her body stocking—at her nipples. Alex twisted to one side, tossed the jacket at a chair—she missed—she turned back and faced the guests again. She cocked her hips to one side, placed her finger tips to her hip bones, pulled her shoulders far back, and said, "You people want to hear about when I got kicked out of Georgetown U. for banging the History Professor?" No one said a word—they stirred, shifted about then began to say their good-bys. Lilly was the gracious hostess and saw the four to the door. Jerry accommodated her. Alex sat back down and had another drink from the bottle.

Returning to Alex, Lilly sat next to her, took the bottle from her hand, took a deep slug, patted Alex's knee and remarked, "Kid, I would have given a hundred bucks for that! Those two 'biddies' will talk about it for weeks! Hell! Maybe months! Did you really—do—the History Professor?" "Yelp, sure did! Right on the top of his desk!" Alex got the bottle back, added, "See? I told you we'd become close friends! Now, if one of you will speed dial me a taxi, I'll get out of your hair! I'm about bushed!" "Don't be silly! Jer can run you back to the hotel!" Lilly went to find Jerry, Alex finished off the bottle of champagne.

On the way to the hotel, Jerry asked, "What are you doing tomorrow? Maybe we, just you and I, could get together?" "Don't think so, I'm going to sleep in, get some rest before that meeting with Stillwell. I think I'll need it."

As Alex slipped out the right car door at the hotel, she turned back toward Jerry, held the door open with her right hand, leaned in, said, "Tell Lilly if she wants a great 'lay', I made connections with a young stud that works here!" Jerry tilted toward her face said, "Alex, you really are a bitch!" "I wanted you to know Miss Hawkins doesn't do without on Friday nights."

Sunday, as she had told Jerry, Alex slept late, got lightly dressed, went down and had a salad for lunch. And walked about the lobby for a while— nothing interesting—she went to the gift shop. Here, she bought a few items for her new briefcase; pencils, pens, pads, letter opener, a small stapler, paper clips and a small pencil sharpener. Most of which she already had back home in her old shabby case.

Back in 518, she arranged the expensive case, removed her present notes and documents from her travel bag and put these in the new case. And she located her official 'Department of Agriculture' identification badge, put this in a noticeable place on the dresser—she didn't want to forget this tomorrow morning. And she laid her 'false' eyeglasses next to this. The glasses were plain heavy black rims, with plain glass—Alex only used these to make her appear older and more businesslike. Then she located and laid out her plain black business watch. And then her new pen stripped suit, plain skin toned hoses and her medium plain black pumps.

Finished with the 'work items', she transferred her other clothes and articles to the new leather bags. Folding up the older cloth travel bag, she stuffed it into the trash container in the bath—Alex was to regret this later! The packing complete, she stepped back, looked at the new expensive leather bags, and thought in admiration, smart, impressive, cosmopolitan, suave, chick. Later, she was to regret this thought!

Glancing to the glass strip in the bedroom wall, she realized it was getting close to sunset. Quickly she completed her 'fiddling' with her stuff. She rushed to the glass wall in the living room and watched the beautiful sunset beyond the river, beyond the city below.

Restless, she checked the 'frig'—only about one or two glasses of wine left. She slipped on her heels, got her purse and headed down. Wasting sometime it the lobby, Alex then went to the restaurant, had a club sandwich and hot tea. Then she cruised the bar—still nothing interesting—had a couple of martinis in a quiet side booth and later returned to her suite.

Quickly stripping naked, she located and put on her old, loose sleeping tee shirt. Taking a note pad and a pencil to the dining table, she pushed the cloth and decorations to the far side then sat down.

Thinking about each situation, she listed all the possibilities that might happen during her meeting with Stillwell. With these in a two column fashion—Stillwell's actions, reactions, comments on the left—hers on the right, she revised these until she became satisfied. For a two million dollar deal, she didn't intent to slip up. Taking the pad in hand, she paced the floor as she memorized the list—she acted out several of the 'key' parts.

Feeling pleased with her effort, she laid the pad on the edge of the table, stepped to the TV, clicked it on, shifted to the weather channel—the one with a constant display of the current time. After getting her watch, she checked it with the TV—it was still correct. Watching the weather report for a few minutes, she saw no problems with the predicted weather—still low thirties, no ice, no snow. Alex switched off the TV.

Getting the wine jug and a glass, she went and took a long soaking, hot bubble bath. And she finished off the wine.

The taxi stopped at the end door of the 'Ag' building in time for Alex to arrive before the other workers—but when the early morning clean-up crew would be inside. Before getting out of the cab, she slipped on her glasses, got her brief case then she smartly stepped out and briskly walked toward the door. The young marine on duty snapped to attention, glanced at her badge clipped to her jacket pocket—he pulled the door open. Alex didn't smile at him, with a serious expression she only slightly nodded.

Upstairs at the main office door, she looked inside and saw a cleanup man there. She rushed in, walked directly to the coffee counter, asked, "Coffee ready yet?" "Yes, Mam!" the crewman snapped. She got a cup, swiftly went straight to Yevona's work station. Setting her case on the floor, she flipped on the computer, quickly 'booted' it up, clicked in several commands. The CRT displayed a complicated master flow chart. It was one of Alex's. Entering 'alt', then changing the font size to four, shifting to the upper right corner of the document, she typed in a capital 'R'. She moved back one space, shifted the font size to twelve, and typed in a zero. The screen showed the very small capital 'R', encircled by the larger zero. Alex activated the print cycle. When a hard copy was produced, she took it and looking at it, she thought, 'perfect!'

She backed out of the system, and switched off the computer. She carefully folded the page to fit in her jacket's pocket. With her briefcase, she left, then rode the elevator down one floor. She went into the 'public' women's restroom, and waited until 8:55, until she knew everyone was upstairs in place.

Retracing her steps, Alex walked in, said. "Good morning, Louise! I've got a nine with 'Still'" "Good morning, Alex, Let me see if he's ready for you!" Louise stuck her head in the inner office, turned back, said, "Come on in, he's waiting for you." "Thank you." As she walked past, Louise thought, 'Is this a different Alex? No make-up, no lipstick, no glittery jewelry, skin colored hose, plain pumps, a business suit, a new briefcase and glasses! Some differences!'

After brief pleasant greetings—Alex thought Stillwell seemed happier than usual—she used only a very sly, tight smile, and no joking or cute remarks—they got down to business. Stillwell slipped her a list, said, "These are the programs—according to Jerry—in question." He asked her to either agree or disagree with the list. Alex didn't need her copy—she knew it by memory. Running an index finger down it, she saw that one program was missing—a very important one, the one that commanded the interconnection of the other programs. She didn't say anything, but she wondered. This list had to have been produced BEFORE Friday! BEFORE her decision to sell! Was Jerry covering her ass? Or covering his own ? She knew, and she knew that Jerry knew, the other programs were worthless without this one—the 'missing' one! Was Jerry holding an ace in the hole for when he shifted from the 'Fed's' payroll to the HVG payroll? Or just in case if things went 'sour' between HVG and the 'Fed's'? Either way—or whatever—it was an advantage for her!

Alex finished her review of the list, looked into Stillwell's eyes, calmly said "Looks ok to me. And we're talking about me retaining ownership, and you—your department buying reproduction and use rights?" "Yes— even sales rights—but, of course, not exclusive sales rights"

"Sounds ok", she waited—and she intended to wait until he asked! After a spell of silence, he casually rose, stepped and faced the window, and asked, "Have you thought about what you want for this?" "You're asking, 'what is the price? In US dollars?" He didn't face her. But answered, "Yes, in US dollars." She didn't hesitate, "Two million, US dollars—BUT— in gold! Either real gold, or certified checks deposited with 'Bosh & Bosh, New York, New York!" He spun around, but waited—he didn't want to lose it—his composure—not yet!

He stared at her, then raised his head far back, snapped, "Ha! No way!" Alex waited, but only briefly, then she slowly stood, reached down and lifted her briefcase, straightened up, turned toward the door. "Alex! Alex! Hold on! Let's talk a deal here!" She stopped, turned back. She wasn't smiling, she glanced at her business watch, gently said, "I've still got time to catch the noon flight to Hartsfield." She let it drop off. Raising her eyes toward his, she calmly added, "Ok, deal" "One point five", he sternly offered. "One point seven five" She countered. He leaned both his big fist to his desk top, snapped, "F—k you!" "Your place? Or my place? Or here and now?" "I believe you would!" he quipped. She stepped to the edge of his desk, placed her free fist on it, tilted her face close to his face, replied "Mr. Stillwell, for a quarter of a million dollars, I would screw the entire Corp of Engineers!"

Stillwell pulled up, she pulled up, they stared. He started, "Missy, we could claim we wrote those", he pointed at the list, added, "You have no proof that you wrote those first! That you are the original author!" From her pocket, she calmly pulled out the 'doctored' copy—the one from Yevona's computer earlier, said, "See that small capital R? With the circle AROUND IT? You can walk down the street, to the Office of Patents and Registrations and ask them who owns First Rights! All these", she pointed at the list, "are copyrighted by me!" She bluffed, thinking he wouldn't check!

Suddenly he stepped around his desk, past her, jerked the door open, and shouted. "Louise! Get one of those 'prick' lawyers from upstairs—and—get Jerry White in here—both! Now!" He returned to Alex, stuck out his right hand. She hesitated, asked, "One point seven five?" "One point seven five." She took his hand, and as they shook, she said, "Deal!" He repeated, "Deal!"

Alex relaxed, asked, "Bill, why don't you pour us a stiff drink?" He did, they downed these. He poured another round. As they sipped, he said, "Alex, do you always drive a hard bargain?" "I didn't get 'well-off' playing 'penny-poker'!" Then she smiled for the first time this morning.

Soon Louise, the lawyer and Jerry White came in. Louise automatically uncovered the typewriter, switched it on, set the margins. Stillwell more or less sat back as Alex, the lawyer, and Jerry worked out the details of the contract. Bill gave 'it' to the lawyer who said, "This list is what we are buying?" The lawyer passed it to Jerry, who nodded, then passed it to Alex, she nodded. The two slightly smiled at each other—they both knew if there was any 'problems' down the road—if anyone ever got 's—, either one of them—Jerry or Alex—could jerk the rug out from under the Department—and Stillwell—and sue. And have a 99.9% chance of winning! Alex passed the list to Louise. She had already started typing on the contract.

Alex stood, stepped to the side cabinet, poured herself another shot of Jack Daniel as she thought, 'Alex, you just hit a home run with the bases loaded!'

When Louise got to Terms of Payment, Alex removed from her purse a business card, said, "This is my gold dealer in New York." Flipping it over, she wrote, 'To the account of Alex and William Hawkins—account number 762837', as she said, "They'll accept certified checks, deposit those to this account, it will show up on my monthly statement. I want payments to be—one hundred and ninety-four certified checks of nine thousand dollars each, and one check of four thousand dollars—I believe that makes a total of one point seven-five million dollars. You folks want to check my addition?" She smiled at Jerry. Both the lawyer and Jerry quickly got out their small calculators and confirmed the total as correct.

Alex gave the card to the lawyer, he passed it to Louise, asked, "You got all that?" "Yes sir!" Then she turned toward Stillwell, slightly waved the small card at him and asked—as a joke—"Sir? Will there be any sales tax on this?" All five broke out in laughter. Stillwell stepped to Louise, patted her shoulder, said, "The way Alex is having those checks made, the IRS will not even get ANY taxes!"

They all knew that checks under ten thousand dollars were not reported to the IRS! Bill straighten up, said to Alex, "You are a smart kid, aren't you?" She stuck two thumbs up and smiled.

Alex whispered to Jerry, "Sorry about the extra printing work." "No problem, the computer will not even notice it."

It took until almost three—they had all worked through lunchtime. After signing, witnessing and notarizing, Louise moved back to her desk in the outer office. Alex and the three men said their good-byes. Jerry and the lawyer left. Alex said to Stillwell, "Friends?" "Friends—Alex, if you ever need anything—anything at all—just contact me!" "Promise?" "Promise!"

As Alex approached Louis, she stopped, asked, "Dear, would you speed-dial me a Taxi—ask that he come to the end door. I'll wait inside—the driver can just honk." Before Alex turned to leave, Louise smiled, winked, and stuck both thumbs up. Alex returned the sign with her one free thumb.

Waiting just inside the glass doors of the 'Ag' building, Alex took out her cellphone and dialed Jerry's number upstairs. He answered, she said, "Jerry, are you where you can talk freely?" A phase then "Yes." "Jerry, in what fashion would you—and Lilly—like to receive one hundred thousand? After I get confirmation of course." She waited, then he replied, "Your deal with Bosh & Bosh sounded attractive—say an account transfer?" He paused, then, "I'll let you know the proper numbers later. Ok?" "Ok, catch you later!"

As Alex put her phone back in her purse, she looked to the outside, it was gray and it had started to snow—snow rather hard. 'So much for weather forecasters!' she thought.

CHAPTER 4

It was Tuesday, February the fifth, the sky was completely gray and with light snow flurries—the ground was covered with snow. It had been about two weeks since Alex returned to Hidden Valley. During this period of time, she had received confirmation from the gold dealer in New York. And Jerry and Lilly's new account numbers at Bosh & Bosh. Alex had, via, computer, transferred the one hundred thousand dollars she had promised Jerry from her account to their account.

But she still had not said anything to anyone at Hidden Valley—not even Tom—about her 'deal' with Stillwell. When she had received the statement from Bosh & Bosh, she had folded it to fit in her hip pocket of her jeans. And she had carried it around since then.

At mid-afternoon—their 'regular' time—Alex met Tiger at the wood pile. The routine was to meet, then help each other carry in firewood for their pop-belly stoves. As the two lifted the pieces of old metal roofing that covered the wood—to keep the snow off the wood—Alex noticed that Tiger had tears in her eyes. "Tig—What's wrong?" "Oh, Alex! It's the beginning—February the fifth—of fiesta back at home! I'm so sad that I'm not there." "After all these years away?" "It's even worst—I'm beginning to not remember—I can't recall some of the happy times! I'm scared that I'll forget everything!" She began to sob. Alex hugged her, brushed the snow from her hair, said, "Come on kid! Let's get the wood in, then we'll find something to cheer you up!"

Doing Tiger's first, they finished up at Alex's loft upstairs.

Alex searched around, found her bottle of Jack Daniels, poured two cups about half full, handed one to Tiger, said, "Sip on that while I check my E-mail, it has been a few days, then we'll go to Arnie's, see if we can get the others to party a bit!"

After boot-up, Alex clicked to 'incoming '—there was a new listing from last night. It was from Jerry White.

'Alex, got a confirmation on the transfer a while back. Sat on it until last night, wanted to surprise Lilly—it was our twentieth wedding anniversary. Told her I had saved it *over* years and decided we should try gold. She says 'hi'. I say thanks—thanks a lot!

Love, J&L

She quickly removed it from her mailbox and shut down. Turning to Tiger, she casually remarked, "Nothing important. Cheers! Down the hatch!" as she finished off her drink.

The men were gathered about Arnie's fireplace, mumbling about something. Alex pulled Nat and Tiger into the kitchen—she explained to Nat what Tiger had told her when out at the woodpile. She added suggestions concerning fixing something Mexican style for supper. They all got busy, with Tiger directing the other two. With coarse ground corn meal, they started by making tortillas. Nat and Alex tried their hand at fixing these but they were not nearly as proficient as Tiger. With Tiger doing the patting, Alex and Nat pan cooked, they soon had a stack. While still hot, they converted fourteen to Quesodillas. Tiger quickly started a huge pot of rich, thick bean soup while Nat and Alex spread the cheese and folded the Quesos. Alex fixed a meat hash filling for tacos.

Tiger got seven ears of corn—these still had the husks—ran outside, lit the grill and started the corn to roasting. She ran back in, removed seven dried chili peppers from the string hanging by the window, put these in a pot of shallow water. Later, after these were pliable, she split and scrapped out the webs. Back to the grill, she quickly roasted these. Returning inside, she covered these with grated white cheese then heated the peppers in the oven—just enough to melt the cheese. This finished the Quesopimientas.

Nat made 'her' special sauce; chopped greens, a small amount of chopped onions and garlic—sauted this in butter until completely tender. She added cream cheese and seasoned with thyme, rosemary, soy sauce, mustard and 'Tabasco' sauce. Over a very low flame, this was slowly reduced to a thick, creamy sauce. Without a specific 'name', this delicious sauce was called 'Stuff' by the HVG members.

"La maize! La maize!" Tiger screamed as she ran out to the grill. Grabbing the ears of corn from the grill—the husks were almost flaming— she quickly stripped the husks off. Placing the ears back over the open flame, she waited as the kernels 'blackened'. Shutting off the flame, she gingerly gather up the corn in her skirt and returned inside.

Finished with the food preparation, they sat it out on the dining table. Alex said, "Come on guys! It's Mexican tonight! Tiger, Nat and I want to have a Mexican party tonight!" She went into the rear of the house, returned with a portable cassette player—she had it loaded with Franco's version of "Toda la Viva!" Placing it on a side table, she turned the volume up very loud! Back to the bedroom, Alex jerked off her flannel shirt, located one of Tiger's pullover, scooped neck short sleeve blouse—she put this on. Finding one of Arnie's old black felt hats, she pulled it tightly on her head—it came down to her ears, almost over her ears! She kept on her tight jeans—the monthly activities statement from Bosh & Bosh was still in her hip pocket. Returning to the living room, she stopped, stuck her hands up and shouted, "Ole! Ole! Let's party!" The men noticed her, but went back to getting their food. Alex shrugged.

After eating—he finished before the others—Mike left the house. Returning soon, he had a jug of 'shine', he said, "People, if we're going to party, I'll fix some real drinks—except for Tom!" Eating, drinking, dancing to Franco—Mike and Tiger danced fast Mexican style, the others not so fast. By ten or eleven, they were about 'tuckered-out'.

The three ladies flopped down on the sofa—Tiger at one end, Nat in the center, Alex at the other end. Jim wandered to the rear and came back with a book. He sat close to Tiger. Opening the book to where he had a marker, he began to study the photos with a hand held magnifying glass. The photos were of the so-called 'Paris' codex and the 'Dresden' codex. Tiger leaned closer, looked with intensity at the photos, said, "I've heard of those things—you call it—codex?" "Yes, codex—books." Nat turned to Tiger, asked, "Where did you hear of the codex?" "From my Grand mama." Jim quit studying and looked at Tiger—then to Nat, who exchanged the glance. "When?" he asked. "Oh, since I can first remember—a very little girl. The Old Ones used to sit us around them, tell us stories about seeing the codex—one at least." "Do you recall the stories?" Nat asked. "I'm not sure—maybe—"

Alex had ignored them, but then Nat said to Tiger, very seriously, "Tiger, it could be very important. Please try to remember. I know of the codex you were probably told tales about. Franz Blom chased it for most of his adult life. It is called, "The Lost Codex of Palenque", and it is priceless! Worth more than a lot, a very lot, of gold!" On the words, 'priceless' and 'gold', Alex turned, asked, "What are you talking about, Nat?"

The other three men pulled their chairs closer. They knew they were in for another interesting tale by the eminent Dr.K! And it was a tale about 'something' priceless! Worth a lot of gold! Nat waited until they got settled, then she began.

"There are—or maybe were, I haven't heard any mention in years—tales, stories, maybe just rumors. These were about the priest, or someone, escaping from Palenque—the temple—with one codex containing the history of the Maya from their beginning. Or of their coming—maybe." "Escape? Were they at war? Or captured?" Alex asked. "Not a fighting war—this was after the fighting of the actual Spanish Conquest—it was during the early days of the Spanish settlement—call it the Conquest of the Maya Religion."

"There was one Spanish Priest—Diego de Landa—he was the first bishop of Yucatan, his church, his center of operations was at Izamal during the mid-fifteen hundreds. Seems Landa got this idea, if he could destroy all the codices, they, the Maya, would be easier to convert to Christianity. In the beginning, he thought the codices were their 'bibles', their religious records, or commands. Or ritual procedures."

"Similar to Hitler in the nineteen thirties?" Alex asked.

"Somewhat, but there was a big, big, difference! In Hitler's case, he had all the writings by the Jews, rounded up. These were burned at Berlin. But, he, his people, was only able to destroy what was in Germany! Other copies, naturally, were scattered in other parts of the world. The Germans didn't really destroy, completely destroy, the writings by the Jews. And by no means, destroy ALL the copies of ALL the writings." Nat hesitated, said, "Mike, I could use another drink, please?" He nodded, asked the others if they wanted something to drink—most did. Tom went and helped Mike fix and get drinks. Nat waited. The others waited.

With everyone settled back down, she resumed her explanation. "In the case of Landa and the Maya codices—all, completely every 'written' word was still in 'Mayaland'— their world. Not any had every been'exported', nothing was 'outside' the Maya world. There were not any copies of any of the existing codices! When a certain codex was burned—and that's what Landa had done, he had the codices rounded up and burned! It was gone, completely—totally—destroyed! Forever lost! Most historians, historians of any history, agree this was the greatest crime ever committed! Even greater than the most disastrous of all wars! Wars don't necessarily destroy all one's history, their records! Sure, it kills people, destroys buildings, things—but these can be replaced. Knowledge, histories, can not be replaced!" she stopped. She wiped her eyes, threw down the last of her drink.

"Ok, we've got the picture. Are there any codices left? Any at all?" Mike asked. Nat straightened her shoulders, regained her composure, replied "Yes. Four parts—not the complete codex—just parts of four.

These are referred to as the 'Paris' codex, the Dresden codex, the Madrid codex, and the Grolier codex—named for the cities where they are now. And then there just may be—'The Lost Cordex of Palenque'—if there is any truth to the tales about it." "I understand why it could be so valuable!" Alex remarked, then added, "Wouldn't that be the find of the century!"

Nat turned to Tiger, repeated, "Like I said, it is terrible important you remember all you can about the old-tales." Tiger looked at the others—they seemed to be waiting for her to do 'something'—say 'something'! "Oh—", she slumped almost off the front of the sofa, leaned her head far back and closed her eyes. She began. "They—the Old Ones—at the temple—had to move it—keep from bad white men—men with hair on their faces—burning—moved—to river—found out—moved again—higher—there for a long, long time—bad men looking—moved higher—long time—Chamula—I remember, I liked Chamula—I liked the runners, the flags, fiesta—another white man—yes! Franz Blom! I remember his name—funny name—close—returned to—to river—closer to home—river, water, some thing about water—over the river—Oh!"

Tiger opened her eyes, said, "If I could just talk to Granny, just get her to remember—repeat the old story, I might understand! As a little girl, I didn't care to understand! It was a beautiful story, lots of action, chasing, hiding—That's all I can remember!"

Alex stood, stepped around Nat's feet, patted Tiger on her shoulder, said, "I thought it was great! Don't worry!" Then Alex turned to the others, added, "We'll just have to go and talk to Granny!" The others would not have been more shocked if she had thrown ice water in their faces!

Tom jumped up, shouted at Alex, "Have you lost your frigging mind! The season has just really started! Those guys in Florida are really cracking! And that is just the beginning! And, most of all, I haven't even scratched the surface on contacting the retailers—who the hell are we going to sell to? Alex, I—we—know you. When you suggest doing something—anything—you mean yesterday!" He stomped toward the kitchen.

"Tom's right!" Mike set-in, "I've got over twenty appointments in Florida with truckers! Some of that stuff is ready to roll—now! And there's much more already contracted for! I think you should forget any new Wild Goose chase!" He went to the kitchen to be damn sure Tom didn't locate that jug of 'shine'!

Alex looked at Arnie, he shrugged, remarked, "Forget it! I'm too old for chasing Wild Geese!" She turned to Nat and then to Jim. They both shook their heads, Nat answered Alex's stare, "Alex, you know we're deep, very deep, in getting these publications out. With me not being able to go to D.C.—the CIA would catch me as soon as I stepped in the 'Ag' building—Jim and I will have endless communications back and forth. Sorry."

Mike and Tom returned, Tom had a large bottle of grape soda. Alex took a slow sweep of the others, softly began, "All of you know how hard I've worked for HVG, since before June. You all know I wouldn't run out if I had even the slightest idea of any problems. But I don't. Everything is in place—everything has checked out—flawlessly. Tom, Mike, I agree, you both have very important jobs to do—jobs that have to be done. And I can't do these for you! And neither one of you need, much less want, me to get in your way! Those 'super-computers' in D.C. will do everything else!"

Alex stepped to the sofa, indicated for Nat to slip over. Then she sat down next to Tiger, and slipped her arm around Tiger's neck. Looking at Tom and Mike, she said, "Who do you two think you're talking to? A couple of junior high virgins? None of you", she made a sweeping motion with her hand toward the others, continued, "None of you can think—even the least—that Tiger and I can't handle a simple trip south to see her family! Besides, I've finished my part—I need a vacation!" Then she smiled, Tiger smiled. No one replied, Alex waited, still no arguments, no rebuttals. Alex pulled Tiger's head close to her face and kissed her on the cheek, and whispered, "Got em."

The others realized what she had said was true, they shifted about, seemed to relax and face the facts that they had 'made a mountain out of a mole hill'. Alex decided that now—right now—was as good a time as any. She stood, moved to the center of the group. They watched her as she stuck one set of fingers in her hip pocket and said, "Folks, I've got some more news. Please pass this around and closely review it—it is for real!" She handed the Bosh & Bosh statement to Nat first. Alex then went to the kitchen and poured a glass of 'shine'—she knew where Mike kept it.

Still in the kitchen, Alex glanced briefly into the living room. Tiger had moved to Mike's knee. Alex concluded he would be the last to get the statement—and he would explain it to Tiger. She waited in the kitchen and sipped the drink. It took about fifteen minutes. Tiger screamed, then ran into the kitchen with the statement clutched in her hand. She waved and waved it in Alex's face as she screamed "Alex! Alex! Alex! Over a million dollars! Over a million dollars! How! How! How?"

Gently, Alex placed one hand over Tiger's mouth, calmly said. "Easy, I sold one computer disc—you know, those small, flat, round, plastic things I stick in the front of my computer?" Tiger's eyes were extremely large. Alex decided she better uncover her mouth or her eyes were going to jump out! Tiger gasped then shouted, "We go on vacation? We go to Amatenango? To see my family?" "Yes, Tiger, we go to Ama—where—ever—the hell-that-is!" They hugged and kissed—and kissed!

Returning to the living room with their arms still around each other's waist, Tom said, "No wonder you want to go on a vacation! One point seven-five million! How? Where?" Abruptly Mike snapped toward Tom, "Man! That kind of money—I wouldn't give a damn where or how my lady got it!" They all laughed. It was almost midnight, but no one was about to leave!

For the next thirty or so minutes, Alex explained. But at no time did she mention Jerry White's name. Finally, Alex's and Tiger's 'Mexican' party had taken off!

Later, about two A.M., Tom and Alex were under their thick pile of quilts—it was dark except for tiny flickers of light from the fire in the old pop-belly stove. In almost a whisper, Alex asked, "Tom, you still awake?" "Yes, Alex." "There's something I want to do before Tiger and I leave." "Yes, Alex." "Will you help me?" "Yes, Alex." "I want us to dig that—my gold—out of that crack up there in the cliff and deposit it—well, we'll weight out enough, say about one hundred thousand dollars worth, leave that buried up there—just for emergencies. Deposit the balance in the local bank. I'll electronically transfer that to Bosh & Bosh."

"They—I've been in touch with them—showed me some past activities charts—now, gold is the best game in town. I've decided to play gold again.

I want to do this before we leave."

Alex was silent while she estimated how much may still be buried up the mountain. She knew she had brought $184,000 from Bismarck when they had started their run for Georgia. And Mike had gone to her house at Lake Lanier and got what she estimated to be half a million dollars worth of gold. Minus about twenty thousand—ten thousand here and there, and the ten thousand she had recently deposited in HVG's new operating account. And minus the hundred thousand she would leave buried, there should be somewhere between point six and point five-five million to deposit. And then to transfer to B&B.

"Tom, you want to know about how much it is? To be deposited?" 'No, Alex." "No!" "No! I want you to stop thinking about money!

Gold!" "And what?" "Roll your little ass on top of me." She punched him in his ribs—then rolled on top of him.

Early on in their intimate relationship, Alex had convinced—and shown—Tom that despite her diminutive size, she could be treated just as rough and 'play' back just as rough—as any 'full-grown woman'. Alex's words. She actually enjoyed 'rough sex'.

After a terrific session of heated passion, Tom was still lying flat on his back, Alex still on top of him, he calmly asked "That one hundred thousand, that 'out-flow', the last activity listed on your B&B statement, what was that for?" "Security." "Security?" he questioned. "I thought you wanted me to stop thinking about money?" "Yes, Alex."

CHAPTER 5

Alex jerked upright, the quilts fell from her naked body, "Oh!" She pulled one back up and wrapped it tight around her neck. "Well! Well! Sleeping Beauty has awaken!" Tom laughed as he turned toward her—away from his view outside. Seeing and smelling the coffee Alex tilted her head back and sniffed, "Is there any more of that?" Tom stepped to the old stove, topped up his cup from the old metal coffee pot steaming on the top of the stove, said, "Here, take this", as he handed the cup to Alex, "I'm about coffee'ed out here!"

With Mike's and Tiger's help, the four began to retrieve Alex's gold from the cliff. After the second difficult climb up to the water-box, Alex hesitated, backed her butt to the edge of the concrete container, gasped and said to Tiger, "I've got to catch my breath—" Tiger backed up and sat next to Alex. Tom and Mike had already turned right, and were making their way along the narrow tedious path toward the small cave under the overhanging ledge—the cave where the gold was hidden. "Tig, we'll take this vacation—this trip—first class! Fly down to the closest swanky 'tourist-trap', party a bit, rent a car and drive on to your hometown! Expenses are no problem! Only the very best!" But, unexpected by Alex, Tiger dropped her head, more or less muttered, "Like all the other rich-gringas—" She had just as soon stuck Alex in her eye with a sharp stick! Alex snapped her face toward Tiger, narrowed her eyes, and opened her mouth—but she didn't speak. Alex suddenly realized Tiger's opinion-—probably the same as millions of others from Tiger's background. Rich Gringa! Alex had always, all her life, despised that expression! That image!

Alex slowly smiled, gently reached over, and lifted Tigers face toward her own, calmly responded, "No—Tiger—we will not go as rich-gringas', rich American Assholes, we'll go how ever you want. Hell, we'll hitch-hike if you want to!" They smiled at each other. Tiger said, "Do you understand? Really understand?" Alex hugged her, replied, "Yes, I really understand!" And Alex thought of the days before she was 'well-off'.

Tom and Mike returned from the side path, they stopped next to the women. "You two aren't back-slacking, are you? There's more left!" Mike asked. Alex just pushed around them, Tiger followed. The men headed on down with the plastic bags of gold.

"That's enough—it's about all we can carry this trip", Tiger remarked. Alex was still on her knees, the upper part of her torso inside the small opening—the crack in the cliff, under the ledge overhead. Looking with her small penlight, Alex replied, "There's only two left—I'll get those!" She forced the flashlight into the breast pocket of her one-piece, zip-up, insulated jump suit. Getting the two bags—one in each hand—she shuffled backward with her knees and toes. She felt as if her back muscles were going to cramp—she had to straighten up! With her head finally out of the crack, she raised—but too swiftly, and too high! Striking her head against the ledge above, her reflexes jerked in response to the blow, she stepped back, hard with her right foot. The edge of the path gave way! Her right foot slipped into open air! And her left knee buckled! She was falling! Falling off the cliff!

Tiger yelled, "Alex! Alex!" Swinging her arms madly, Alex tried to get back to the path—or something! The bag in her right hand struck the rocks overhead—it burst! She struck the edge of the rocky path with the bag in her left hand, it too burst! Gold coins rained down the cliff! Continuing to fall, she grabbed at everything—her feet were in open space! With a sharp blow, her left hand hit a small sapling, she was able to grab it, this swung her closer, she latched on with her other hand. The little tree was only about two inches in diameter. But it held.

She kicked and scratched with her toes, but, at first, she was unable to get a toe-hold! Tightening her grip, she looked up—it was about eight feet up to where she had fallen from! She quickly glanced down, she saw some of the coins still tinkling down the hillside far below.

Alex knew that she should be able to pull up, give a quick jerk and get her waist over, above, the small tree. She tried, and got her chin almost over, but she saw the tree bend more—and the ice around its base crack—and a little of the earth around the roots fall away. Easing back down, letting her arms straighten out again, she decided to not try that again. Instead, she slowly worked both her hands closer to the roots in an effort to reduce the bending of the tree. Besides, her heavy clothes and snow boots were working against her.

"Alex! Alex!" Tiger was down on her knees above, "Are you ok?"

"I guess, if hanging in open space very high above the valley below is ok, then I guess I'm ok!" Tiger stood and yelled for help, she yelled down toward the houses far below. "Hang on, Alex, I see Mike coming up!"

Alex leaned her head forward, tried to relax her neck and back. Slowly and cautiously she began to search with her toes for anything to get her toes on. With her right toe, she felt a slight protrusion. She began to kick away the frozen cover, and soon was able to hook her boot's toe on it—just enough to help relieve the strain on her hands and arms. Without help from her legs, Alex knew she couldn't last long.

Fairly stable, she had a 'strange' thought. Headlines—'Young millionairess Falls to Her Death While Watching Her Gold Slip Below Her' Hearing Tiger's screams for help, Tom and Mike stopped, looked back up. Seeing Alex hanging by her hands below the ledge, they dropped the bags. Mike snapped, "I'm faster—you get rope!" he ran uphill, Tom ran toward the barn!

When Tom arrived back to the others, he saw that Tiger had moved back out of the way. Mike was on his knees, talking calmly to Alex. He was encouraging her to maintain her stable position. "Don't struggle, you'll lose strength." Feeding one end of the rope to Mike, Tom controlled the rest of it and prepared himself to be the 'anchor-man'. Tying a bowline knot close to the end of the rope, Mike lowered the rope, said, "Alex, stick one arm through the loop, pull it as close to your armpit as possible—grab the rope above the knot with that hand. Got that?" "Yes." she answered. "Hold your weight with that hand—the one on the rope! Then thread the other arm through the loop and again grab the rope above the knot with that hand! Got that?" "Yes!" another reply. "Spread your elbows! For once, it is your elbows—Not your knees! Let your armpits take your weight—Not your hands! Ok?" "Right."

Doing exactly as Mike ordered, she began to feel more secure. "You may get some swinging, we're going to pull you up—just spread your feet, let your toes stabilize the swing—BUT DO NOT release your grip with your bands! Got that?"

Slowly she was drawn up by Mike, with Tom, who had a turn around his waist, taking up the slack.

As she made it over the edge, she rolled onto her back, one side next to the cliff above. She looked into Mike's eyes—he was still on his knees—and said, "I can't believe that wise-crack about NOT spreading my knees!" All four of them laughed!

Back at the bottom of the cliff, where the mountain leveled off, Alex stopped, turned and looked up as she said, "Well, folks", she pointed back up, "There is our emergency funds! Up there!" and she laughed.

The four quickly changed clothes, then 'played Wells Fargo' and transferred the gold to the bank. The other three waited in Tom's van as Alex took care of the banking business. Mike and Tom discussed their plans to leave and get on the road. Again. It had been a few years. Tiger just listened. "Ok! Hit it! I've got everything settled!" Alex shouted as she jumped in the van.

On the way back to Hidden Valley, Alex and Tiger got far back in the rear and discussed their travel plans. "I think Senor Arnie's station wagon would be best. More room, besides, no one would want to steal it! Your beautiful sports coupe would have a life expectancy of about twenty-four hours where we may go!" Tiger said to Alex. "Ok, ok! I'll ask Arnie if we can swap vehicles!" Alex conceded. "And just head west?" Alex asked. "SI, I'll explain on the way!" They were already pulling into Hidden Valley.

'As the three women prepared supper, Alex explained to Nat that Tiger needed some 'official' identification—Passport, birth certificate, "You know, the poor child", she patted Tiger's healthy rump, "doesn't have a thing to prove who she is! There could be problems at the border, especially getting BACK in the USA! Those Border People are regular bull-heads! "Nat laughed, "I know! How do I know!" Nat laughed, then said, 'We'll make her a Morley. Birth certificate—a few back-up documents—the granddaughter of the great Sylvanus G. Morley! And Tiger is presently an Assistant Archaeologist to—to—I'll think of someone! A 'new'—being as she has never had one!—USA passport. I have many blanks still left! And you're driving?" "Yes and just between us ladies, I'm planning on asking Arnie for his station wagon!" "Ok. I'll need the details—for Mexican insurance! No need to waste money on that crap!" The three continued to prepare the meal.

During the supper, Tom, then Mike, announced that they were leaving first thing in the morning. Tom toward Ashville, N.C. to get together with the major chain grocery stores. Mike to Florida and meet with some trucking firms. Alex waited until they finished, then she said, "Well! It looks like February the seventh is the day for people to leave! Tiger and I have decided to leave tomorrow also! That is, if Nat", she looked at her, continued "can finish some 'necessary' documents—and", she turned, faced Arnie, "If Arnie and I can workout a deal to swap vehicles!" All of this was a surprise—the others knew the two younger women had been talking about it—a vacation, according to Alex, visit home according to Tiger—but no one realized they were talking about NOW! And the news concerning a vehicle swap was completely new!

Arnie raised his eyebrows, but Alex quickly explained their reasons. He listened closely, and after she finished, he sipped his coffee, shrugged his shoulders, answered, "I don't see why not—if you two gals trust my old 'Betsy'—besides, Jim's Bronco will still be here." Alex leaned to him, patted a kiss on his cheek and said "Don't worry, we'll get the old gal back in one piece!" Little did she know.

Soon afterwards, Nat asked Arnie for the information in order to prepare the 'false' insurance papers for the Mexican Officials.

The two younger men broke away soon after the meal, left to pack for their trips. Alex and Tiger stuck around while Nat produced the papers—and they helped with the photos for Tiger's 'new' passport. Nat had a variety of notarizing machines and numerous government stamps and passport blanks—especially USA ones! And Nat made several documents Alex had not thought of, especially 'official' papers for her pistol! And an 'official' badge for Tiger—similar to Alex's 'Ag' Department badge. And with 'special' modifications to both badges.

Shortly after midnight, they were finished. Alex and Tiger agreed to leave soon after Tom and Mike got off. Walking through the dark, as the two got close to their places, where the paths split, Tiger hugged Alex and said, "Thanks so much! It will be wonderful to get home again! I can't wait!"

Going around 'downtown' Atlanta on I-285, Alex split off on I-85, headed for Montgomery Alabama. After they were out of the heavy traffic, Alex asked, "You said you wanted to enter Mexico at El Paso-Ciudad Juarez, any particular reasons for there? Other crossings are closer." "Alex, you said that you had never heard of Barranca del Cobre—or—Copper Canyon—you're in for a surprise! We have to go to Chihuahua and the best highway from the north, headed south, is Mex Forty-five from El Paso. The road between Chihuahua and Ojinaga is very bad, very slow!"

"So you are going to surprise me! The way we're heading west takes us by New Orleans—you're in for a surprise!" "What?" "No! No! You'll have to wait! We should be there tomorrow!" They laughed.

After a spell of silence, Tiger asked, "Have you ever been to Mexico before?" "A few times, several 'spring-breaks' at Cancun when I was in college—a few week-end 'quickies' again at Cancun after I was working. Didn't see much, mostly the ceilings of bedrooms or—", she thought, added, "You don't see a lot with your ass hiked up and your face buried in the mattress do you?" They laughed. Alex continued, "Oh! I spent one summer in Merida Yucatan—but—I was just a teen then. That summer I really enjoyed! Except for one 'bad' incident." She dropped it. 'What?' Tiger insisted. "Not much, I just picked up the wrong bastard. He thought I was a punching bag—but—it came out ok anyway." "Sorry I asked." "Don't be, kid, we've got no reasons to hold back between us!" Alex laughed, Tiger joined her.

Alex drove straight through—she took I-65 at Montgomery, south to Mobile, then I-10 west—and made the way as far 'downtown' New Orleans as she could go. It was just after sunrise. The streets were a mess;

paper, ribbons, cans, bottles, even pieces of clothing were everywhere. Hundreds of street cleaners were busy. Easing forward, she approached a street barricade.

"Hey! Turn right or left!" the big cop barked. Thrusting her head out the open window, Alex asked "Mister dear policeman, can you'en tell little ole me where a couple of poor gals can get a cheap room for a couple of nights?" The Policeman stepped to Alex's window, looked in, asked, "You two hookers?" "Lord, no! I is just a farm girl from Gerogee! She" Alex shook her head in Tiger's direction, "is, as you can see, is just a poor Mexican child" At the word 'child' Tiger twisted slightly to her right, pushed her left shoulder forward in an effort to hide her 'poor child's' thirty-four 'Dees', Alex continued "I'm carrying her west to see her dear Granny!"

The cop straightened up, pushed his cap back, then leaned down again, "Turn right, go two blocks—on your right—house number eight-zero-four. A lady rents beds just to young ladies. You can probably make a deal with her now that the crowd had began to thin out!" "Thanks a heap!" as she eased the car toward the side street.

An old lady, she was rather large, was sitting in a rocking chair on the front portion of the huge wrap-around porch. After greetings and the enquiry, she led them to a side door. Placing a finger vertically to her lips, she said, "Not too loud, most are asleep—or fixing to be."

The huge room was filled with single bunk beds, very closely spaced— most had young women, in various positions, fast asleep. A few milled about in various forms of dress. Or undress. "The bath's that way, storage lockers in the hall. You gals got pad locks?" She pointed, then motioned that they go back outside. She said, "Ten dollars per night—a night is noon till noon, each, cash upfront, you're responsible for your own things. Ten dollars extra for puking anywhere except inside a toilet. No drinking on the property. No fighting either! Towels, sheets, one light blanket, once a day clean-up, we furnish. No guys! No girl-girl stuff! If you want to exercise your tongues and your vulvas, go elsewhere!" She seemed to be finished.

"Ok, we'll take it," Alex snapped as she reached in her jean's pocket and 'fished-out' what she thought was about forty or maybe fifty dollars.

Alex stuck out forty dollars, the lady said, "No, only pay for each night up front," she smiled, added, "You'd be surprised how many don't show up for the next night!" Alex smiled, gave her only twenty dollars. The lady said, "Forget about any charges for this morning, being as there are empties anyway", she looked closely at Alex's eyes, added, "Been driving all night—catch a nap now—you'll need the rest for tonight!" "Thanks." Alex responded.

At the empty bunks—they had located two that were side by side— Tiger showed Alex how to knock any loose dirt from their shoes and roll these up in their jeans. Then use that as her pillow. Security for whatever you may have in the pockets of the jeans was provided in this fashion. "If you've got a purse—and it should be a soft one—roll that in the jeans also," Tiger said as they 'crashed-out'. As Alex fell asleep, her last thought was 'I think I'll learn a lot from Tiger—a lot about her world, the 'real' world!

Alex jerked upright on the hard, small bunk. The noise—talking, occasional squeals, and bumps on her bunk-had startled her awake. Quickly glancing at her outdoors/sports watch—she had left her business watch and her gold nugget dress watch hidden in 'Betsy'—she saw it was five P.M. As she cased the situation, she deducted that most of the young women, the gals, were using a 'buddy system'. With their gear piled on their bunks, in various fashions of disarray, one would stay there while the other one would do the bath scene. When the first gal returned—usually naked and wet and drying with a towel—the other would strip, then head for the showers. Alex imaged that the showers were very wet—particularly the floors— and carrying clothes in there was a definite no-no.

The hectic, frantic scene in this room—gals either naked, wet, maybe drying with a towel, naked and getting dressed, getting naked and heading for the showers, or a few already dressed—was one of chaos! It all reminded her of the younger years, as a teen, when she was in private, girls schools. But the schools had not been nearly as crowded. The girls not nearly as tall, not nearly as big 'up-there', and not nearly as bushy 'down-there'! Alex didn't see another smooth crotch, as she thought about her own naturally hairless body.

Bending over to Tiger's bunk, she gently shook Tiger, said, "Tiger, Tiger, its time to get up." Slowly rolling her face toward Alex, and barely opening her eyes, she asked, "What?" "It's time to rise and shine! These gals are getting ready to do something! And we want to follow them to whatever it is!" Knowing Tiger was slow to wake, Alex jumped up. She had slept in her long sleeve, long tail 'driving' shirt. She threw on her jeans and shoes then ran out to the car. Jumping and running seemed to be the only version of motion here!

Returning to their bunks with the two beautiful, expensive leather cases she had recently bought in D.C., Alex threw her bags on her bunk, and Tiger's on her bunk. The gals within sight of the gorgeous, stiff cases, stopped in mid motion and stared at the cases. Alex swept the room with her sight, she saw that the only other type of bags were either; well worn, soft, nylon hand travel bags or backpacks also well broken-in, and these far out numbered the hand bags. The gals remained motionless and continued to stare. "They were a gift! I couldn't refuse them!" Alex practically shouted. While pulling out something to wear for tonight, Alex realized the cases were definitely 'out-of-place' for the style of traveling that she and Tiger were doing—and were going to do!

"Tiger, you hang close here while I shower, then you can shower after I come back! Ok?" That was ok with Tiger, she still wasn't fully awake. Alex stripped, and glanced around at the others. They had again stopped in mid motion as they stared at her body—mainly her crotch and her prominent nipples! Alex just shrugged her shoulders as she looked back at the gals close to her. She ran from the large, full, room. Soon she returned, naked, wet and drying with a towel. She now knew why this was the procedure! The shower room was deep in water, the spray and steam made it impossible to dry anything. The many dry towels were on shelves in the hallway.

As she dried and Tiger stripped, a tall—almost six feet tall—blonde smartly stepped close to Alex. The naked, beautiful, well-endowed 'up-there' blonde said, directly to Alex, "You are the cutest thing I think I have ever seen!" The blonde's eyes continuously swept up and down Alex's body—most of all, from her crotch to her nipples! Alex got the implication, she leaned her head against Tiger's shoulder and gave the blue-eyed blonde a tiny sly smile, almost whispered, "I'm her's." Tiger got the idea, put her arm around Alex's backside and gently patted Alex's small bare rump, said, "Yes, she's mine," as she stared the tall blonde in the eyes. "Hey, can't blame me for checking." She turned to leave, stopped, twisted back, added, "Still the cutest I've seen!" And she stared at Alex's crotch and nipples again.

Alex had just a flash of a thought, 'I bet I could charge these bitches for just looking at my nipples and crotch. Maybe I could pick up a few bucks?

After dressing and fixing their faces with wild patterns and locking their stuff in the station wagon, they followed the crowd. Tiger was dressed in black pantyhose, black spandex short-shorts and a white—very thin—silky crop-top. Alex wore her white 'custom' slip-dress with a pair of black tiny tong panties—these could be seen through the dress. They both wore medium height comfortable heels and carried their shoulder strap purses. They were ready for whatever was ahead.

Everyone was headed in the same direction. The crowd got larger, thicker, and slower. As the crowd came to a slow shuffling motion, Alex saw steel barricades that lined both sides of the street ahead. "Where are we!" she shouted above the loud music to a man next to her. "Rue Bourbon—Bourbon Street!" "So?" "The route of the parade!" "Great! When?" "About a hour or so—" "Great!"

Looking about, Alex spotted a sign hanging between the false 'palm trees', it showed, Patio La Fitte. Still holding Tiger's hand tightly, Alex pulled, said, "Tiger! Let's squeeze this way!" The Patio lounge was a group of many small tables on the sidewalk at an intersection with a smaller side street—this was Alter Street, the sign overhead showed. After a brief wait, they grabbed two empty chairs—a couple had moved on. Many people slipped between the tables—coming and going with large paper cups of beer.

Alex leaned across the small table, said, "Tiger, we can at least drink expensive, can't we?" Tiger tilted closer, "Yes, Alex, if that's what you want!" "Aw, come on, Tig, I just can't hold much beer! I want something with some 'pow' to it!" "Ok! Ok! Order us some 'pow juice'!" They laughed as Alex stuck up her hands and waved for a waiter.

A waiter finally came, Alex ordered two Tequila 'Slammers'. Just as the waiter started to slam the special glasses on the tabletop, Alex yelled to Tiger, "Throw it down! All in one big gulp!" They did, Alex ordered two more. Still in slight shock, Tiger got it out, "Wow! Never had that before! That's a real blast!" A few more Slammers, then Alex switched them to something to sip slowly—champagne, by the bottle.

As the parade started, Alex paid with a Platinum credit card, and taking the bottle of champagne, they began a slow struggle to get close to the street barricade.

Being tiny—and very determined—Alex wormed her way forward and pulled Tiger close behind her. When within one row of the barricades, Alex looked to each side until she spotted two tall men against the rail and not far away. Moving laterally, and saying, "Excuse us", and pointing at the two men, adding "Husbands" they were able to get directly behind the two she had 'selected'. Tapping both on their shoulders, Alex asked, "Would you two tall handsome dudes let a couple of short hot-assed gals slip in front of you? So we could see at least something!" Alex stood on her tiptoes, stretched up, said to the man directly in front of her, "And you can play with my cute little ass!"

The four shuffled about, Tiger and Alex pushed tight against the rail, the two men tight against their butts. Alex bent close to Tiger's ear, asked "Tig—are we going to get laid tonight?" "Not me, not really laid—maybe a few feels here, a few there—that's not real sex, is it?" "Guess not, say a 'helping hand'—or two!" Alex grabbed the rail and shoved her ass backward. It felt his nob, which was already 'at attention'.

The parade moved by; the many tremendous floats, the torchbearers, flag bearers, dancing musicians, marching bands. The people on the floats threw trinkets and strings of beads—the beads seemed to be the most prized of all. Both sides of the street were lined with packed crowds, all the overhead balconies were full—some guys up there occasionally flashed the crowds below with their bare butts. And gals pulled up their blouses to above their bare bosoms. Overall it was a wild and loud scene.

"Wow! What a show!" Tiger shouted into Alex's ear. "Yes! Well, Kid, what do you think of your surprise?" "So, this was the surprise? I think it is just fantastic! Fantastic!"

The guy tight against Alex's backside had settled into a steady hunching motion. Alex guessed what ever 'it' was, it wasn't a pair of rolled up socks!

Alex's hem slowly began to rise. Tilting her head back and slightly twisting it around, she said, "Sport! I don't want this dress screwed up! If you'll just hang in there, I'll give you a 'helping hand'!" Her dress fell back down. She slipped one hand behind her back.

Tiger looked at Alex, saw her manipulations, thought, 'Why not? A feel here, a feel there'. She copied Alex's activities.

Feeling the spasm, Alex gave a couple of hard, quick rubs. The guy dropped his face to her bare neck, said something—it wasn't words, it was more like, "Oh, aw, oh, aw." She squeezed hard, then pushed 'it' away, pulled her butt hard forward—she still didn't want her dress messed up. He moved his mouth close to her ear, said "Thanks!" "You are welcome."

Alex laughed, leaned to Tiger and said "I'm heading for Patio La Fitte! You?" "I'll be on as soon—shortly! Get us a table! I'd like another Slammer!" Tiger laughed.

Tiger arrived soon, sat down as she laughed, "What a scene!" After a round of Slammers, Alex shook her head trying to clear it, said, "Tig—I think I better eat something!" Tiger went to the waiter, they talked, she returned, said, "Come on, he told me how to get to where there was reasonably priced, good food."

They went through the narrow side street, turned left on to an 'off-parade' street and continued on until they came to a huge building up on the bluff along the river. It wasn't crowded. First, a trip to the public restroom, then one slow pass through as they surveyed the many open-air vendors—there were all sorts of food available. Turning around, Tiger said "I think that place", she pointed "had the best looking food, and at great prices!" Back to there, Tiger remarked, "Let's share—I'll get Creole and rice, and you—" "The grilled shrimp caught my attention, I'll get an order of that. And some bread and butter!"

After eating, Tiger asked, "Do you feel better?" "Sure—just too much booze too fast! The last thing I want to do is pay Mrs. Whoever ten dollars for throwing up on her floor!" They both chuckled. Then unexpected by Alex, Tiger asked "Alex, do you feel ok? About this?" She slightly waved a hand to indicate 'everything'. Alex didn't fully understand, she didn't reply.

Tiger seemed to understand, she even realized Alex was confused. She added, "The 'cheap' approach? Not rich Gringa? And—and—it is Friday night!" They both knew, clearly, that implication. The 'cheap approach', Alex understood what Tiger meant, and she knew the answer. "Yes, I'm enjoying our 'cheap' method—I think it's fun—really!"

But Alex was slow to realize her answer to the other part—the 'Friday night' part. She slowly tilted her head back, and stared at the ceiling far above. She couldn't exactly put it into words to Tiger—to a very close friend. After a few minutes, Alex realized that she had not 'heard' anything from Miss Hawkins since she and Tiger had left on this trip. Strange—and it was Friday night!

Slowly Alex smiled. She lowered her head then she stared into Tiger's large, beautiful, black eyes, got up, went around the table and sat on the bench next to Tiger. Slowly, she hugged Tiger, and sobbed, "Tiger, I don't give a damn if it is Friday night or not! To hell with **Miss Hawkins!"** The last part Tiger didn't understand being as she had never heard Alex use that expression—but she felt it was not necessary to ask. She hugged Alex back, and gently wiped Alex's tears away.

It was after 2 A.M. as they left the huge building, Alex asked, "What now?" "My ears are still ringing, my rump is still numb from all the pinches, pats, and slaps! As far as I'm concerned, we can head for the house." She waited, then asked, "Alex, do you have any idea where it **is?"** Alex grabbed her around her waist, pulled and replied

"Of course NOT!" They laughed and wandered on, holding each other tightly.

The next day was almost an exact repeat, sleep till about five, then jump up—a lot of nude bodies, some wet, some drying, some dry, some getting dressed—and the owner came through and collected her ten dollars. As Alex stepped out of the shower, out of the cloud of steam, she realized the tall blonde was also coming out. "Hi", the blonde said. "Hi", Alex replied. As they got towels, the blonde asked, "How'd it go last night?" Alex responded with casual remarks, then, "You?" "So, so. I think this may be my last year—it seems to be the same old thing, over and over.

Guess I'm just burned out on Mardi Gras!" As they entered the huge sleeping room, the blonde said, "Let's start over. I know this nice quiet restaurant around the corner. They have absolutely the best fried shrimp you can image! Let's—the four of us—get an early bite to eat—just chit-chat a while—then, whatever. You know if you eat before the parade thing, you will not piss away so much money on drinks!" "Yes, I found that out last night! I almost got dumb-faced before I remembered to eat!"

Approaching Tiger, the blonde waved her friend over. With Alex and the blonde continuing to dry, and Tiger and the 'friend' undressing for their trips to the showers, they had very casual introductions.

The tall blonde's name was Gail—T.G, short for 'Tall Gail'. The friend's name was Gloria—S.G., for 'Short Gloria"—even though she wasn't THAT short, she was two or three inches taller than Alex and Tiger. Gloria had brown hair medium length, and medium built—attractive— but not what anyone would call beautiful. Both of the new friends were from California. They all agreed that TG's suggestion about eating at the quiet restaurant 'around the corner' was a good idea. 'Dutch' of course. And a casual discussion might be interesting.

On their way out, when Alex and Tiger locked their gear in the station wagon, Alex saw that the gals from California noticed the older, plain vehicle and the tag from Georgia. As the four walked toward the restaurant, Alex decided she would mimic the other couple's actions. This was without any discussion with Tiger. They walked with their arms around each other's waists, Alex slipped her arm around Tiger's waist, and Tiger responded with the same. After being seated, when ordering, TG ordered for the both of them—Alex let Tiger order their meal All four were having fried shrimp and beers. Alex noticed that TG kept one hand on top of one of SG's hands. Without being too noticeable, Alex placed one of Tiger's over one of her hands.

The conversation—carried by TG, then by Tiger as she got the idea—started with the usual; where you from, what do you do, how long you staying, some family or some similar background information. The two from California were very much alike; from Northern Cal., both in their last year of college—but TG, who was doing all the talking, didn't mention which college or university, both from 'normal' medium income families. And they both had 'always' been girl-girl but only 'came-out' since starting college. They had 'been-together' since then. With the

Cal. gals' explanations and descriptions finished, Alex was anxious about Tiger's response. She kicked Tiger's foot under the table, and gave her a slight nod.

Tiger started "My real name"—only Tiger had been used up until now—"is Margarita Morley. The nickname, Tiger, I guess, started years ago because of my work in the jungles—I'm an Assistant Archaeologist! My last field project was with Dr. Michael Smith—that's with a 'I', not an 'Y'—of Rollins University."

TG interrupted with, "Morley? Why does that sound familiar?" "I'm not sure, my Grandfather was Syvanus G. Morley—the 'G' is for Griswold—he did a lot of work with—and wrote books about—the Maya. My Grandmother was full blooded Maya. That's where this came from", Tiger flipped her straight black hair, continued, "And these!" she slightly lifted her huge breasts. TG and SG chuckled. Alex leaned toward the two, whispered, "I just love to nuzzle those—oh, it makes me cream in my panties to just think about them." She winked at TG.

Abruptly TG said, "Sylvanus—yes! Old Sylvanus! Wrote 'The Ancient Maya'! I knew I'd heard that name—Morley—before!" "How do you know this?" Tiger fired back. We go to Sanford! That book was published by the Sanford University Press! I've been working, since being at Sanford, with the Press! I've run across that name several times! The unusual name, Sylvanus, that's hard to forget!"

"So! You're following in the 'old Man's' steps! That's just great!" TG exclaimed. Alex patted Tiger's hand, the one on top of her hand, and smiled at Tiger. The 'poor child' had performed magnificently. And from then on, Tiger was the hit of the evening! Alex relaxed and enjoyed it all. She thought, 'Tiger may even become a bigger bull-shit artist than I am!'

Their food arrived, and as TG had said, it really was great! Alex admitted it was the best fried shrimp she had ever had. Finished and settled back with coffee, TG asked, "And little Alex, how about you?" "Not much to talk about, I came from an average, middle income, stable family in Atlanta, specialized in computer work, got a job—that fell through—then I met Tiger—love at first—well—whatever." She knew she had lied, and most of all, she had skipped what TG really wanted to hear—her 'hairless situation'.

Alex waited. She wanted to see where it went from here. "Alex, I think you're short changing us!" TG started, added, "What about the expensive leather travel cases? A gift? And—and—your beautiful 'unusual' body?" Alex responded, "A boss lady thought she could 'buy' me—she couldn't. I kept the cases. My hairless body?" Alex brought it directly to the point, "A rare anatomical case—but the doctors assured me I'm not the only case—not having any hair at all on my body." She cut her eyes down, pursed her lips as if her feelings had been hurt.

"I'm so sorry Alex, really I am. I shouldn't have been so blunt. Please forgive me", TG remarked. Slowly Alex lifted her eyes, and meekly replied, "I do—I shouldn't be so sensitive. No one knows how many times I feel like a little Hairless Mexican Chihuahua among a bunch of Saint Bernards!" Alex just couldn't resist it! TG looked as if she would 'slime' under the table!

Following hours of the parade, crushing crowds, loud music, drinking, street dancing—mostly with each other or other girl-girl 'buddies', the four stumbled and staggered their way back to the 'big-house'. Stepping up on the porch TG said "Well! We're flying out in the morning! And you two?" Tiger answered that, "We're driving on out west—then down into Mexico to visit some of my family—some I haven't seen for years. Guess this is good-by." At the door, they kissed each other good-by then eased in, found their bunks and 'crashed-out'.

Alex snapped upright, quipped, "What! What the hell is going on!" The strange gal who had shook Alex's shoulder stepped toward her feet, out of arm's reach, and said, "Didn't mean to frighten you, but it's almost noon. Unless you want to pay for another night, you'd better hop-to! And—I'm the last person here, except you two," she waved an arm in a horizontal motion. Alex rubbed her eyes, looked around at the many bunks. Empty! No jumping and running naked girls—no one else! "Sorry I barked at you. Thanks for waking me." Alex extended her right hand, added, "I'm Alex!" As they shook, the young lady said "I'm Betty, and I'm out of here! Got a bus to catch! Bye!"

CHAPTER-6

Alex roughly pushed the cover down she saw her 'hot-pants' and 'crop-top', purse and shoes piled under the pillow. After standing and stretching, she jerked the cover off Tiger, slapped her bare rump, yelled "Tiger! Tiger! The house is on fire!" Tiger slowly rolled her face toward Alex, mumbled, "Really?" "No, not really, but we got to get out of here, or it'll cost another twenty bucks! Rise and shine!" As Alex jerked on her shorts, she thought, 'I can't believe what I just said! Twenty dollars! I've spent ten times that on a single meal!' With her top on and the car keys, she ran out, saw the 'old lady' on the porch, said, "Sorry, we'll be out of here in a 'jiff', only got to get traveling clothes on!" Digging out jeans and loose shirts from the awkward stiff leather cases in the rear of the station wagon, she said, "I'm going to get rid of you! Really I am!" Alex looked in all directions—no one! Everybody gone!

Leaving the big, old house, the two said good-by to the Owner and Alex got the mailing address and phone number. As they got in the car, she called back, "We plan on coming again! Thanks! Bye!"

It was almost 2P.M. before they cleared New Orleans and began to really roll west on I-10.

It turned dark before Alex worked their way around Houston, then continued west on I-10. Leaving the city's traffic behind, and the freeway being almost straight and level, she suddenly realized she was bushed—little sleep, little food nourishment, jumping, pushing and yelling had all taken a toll. Not to mention the groping, pinching, patting, slapping and hunching her body had received! The on-coming lights were huge blurs, and she began to see double and have difficulty maintaining a constant speed. Saying 'toward' Tiger—she was inclined against the side, fast asleep—"I can't believe how sleeping I am! It's only", she glanced at her watch, "Damn! Only eight-thirty! And we're in the middle of no-where!" During one of her slow spells—only the semi-trucks roaring past kept her awake—suddenly Alex saw something small at the edge of the highway. It was someone, somebody thumbing for a ride. She slowed and stopped at the who-ever. Leaving the engine running and the headlights on, she reached under the seat and got her double-stack 40 caliber Da-Wo automatic pistol, the one that Tom insisted she carry. She opened the door, stood up and slipped the gun into the top of her pants. Then she pulled the tail of her loose shirt over it.

The young man—Alex guessed to be about thirty—stooped to get his backpack and his soft travel bag, both appeared well worn. He loudly said, "Thanks for stopping!" "Not yet", Alex came back, "Leave the bags for a second!" He released the articles, stood stiff and still. "Can you drive?" "Yes", he answered. "Got a valid license?" "Yes—you want to see it?" "Yes, and step to the headlight!" As he opened his wallet and held it to the light, Alex saw it was a California one, and it was still in date.

"You feel like driving?" she asked, added, "I'm about out on my feet! I've got to get some sleep!" The man pointed toward the 'sleeping Tiger', asked, "Can't your—partner drive?" "No, no night experience!" she failed to mention that she had very little experience at all! "You aren't sleepy, are you?" "No, not at all. I'll gladly drive—if you want me to." "Yes, I want you to. Get your stuff." as she walked around to the passenger's side rear door and opened it.

As he approached the door, she said, "Got anything in those that is easily broken?" "No, just clothes, tent, soft stuff." "The back is full. Lay your bags on the floor, in front of the seat." She pointed. He then stepped away. "Just a minute", and Alex opened Tiger's door—Tiger almost fell out, but Alex caught her head, said, "Help me get her to the back seat! She sleeps like a log!" Half asleep, and with Alex's and the guy's help, Tiger was moved, and laid down on the seat. "You drive, I'll crawl on top of your bags. Is that Ok? And I'll catch some shut-eye!" "Yes, no problem! By the way, my name is Jay!" "If you get to El Paso, stop! That's as far as we're going. Ok?" "Ok", he ignored the fact that Alex didn't introducing herself. Or the other person. But he did notice the bulge at Alex's stomach! Wouldn't want to mess with this little gal—who ever she is!

As she crawled in, squeezed between Tiger and the back of the front seat, she asked, "Where the hell are we anyway?" "About half way between Houston and San Antonio where route seventy-seven crosses I ten, near Schulenburg." "Would you please shut the door and drive west?" "Yes, no problem!" He also decided this little gal didn't waste words! Before Jay got up to speed, Alex was asleep.

Alex's mind was still in deep fog as something kept poking her in her side and her stomach. She thought she heard, "Miss! Miss! Miss Hawkins!" With her left hand, she grabbed 'it', twisted 'it' very hard, while she groped for her pistol. It was still in place, in the front of her jean waistband. She jerked her shirttail up, snatched out the gun. But as she tried to raise upright, something on her side held her down. She twisted harder, pointed the barrel up and toward the voice. She yelled,

"Don't call me Miss Hawkins! Ever again!" "Hey! You're hurting my wrist!" He raised slightly in his seat, turned his head sideways, looked over into the 'business-end' of the forty caliber barrel. "Hey! Point that thing somewhere else! I'm just trying to wake you! Ok? "Jay retorted.

Alex lowered her hand, and gun, to her chest, and released her grip on his wrist. Awake, she realized where she was—mainly she was under Tiger's arm and leg! Tiger hung off the seat, half covering Alex in the floor. Glancing back again, and not seeing the gun, Jay said, "I called you Miss—and only Miss—because I don't know your name! I've driven over five hundred miles! I've got to have a break! I'm about to nod out here! Ok?" With her left arm pushed above her head, Alex twisted her nose close to her armpit—and sniffed—she almost gagged from the foul odor.

She asked, "Where are we?" as she forced Tiger off. She glanced at her watch, it showed five fifteen, 'Almost sunrise', she guessed. Jay replied, "Just west of the get-off to Balmorhea, to our left—south. It is about twenty miles to where I twenty from the north-east joins with I ten," he waited. She thought, then, "At the first motel, whatever, that has a restaurant, gasoline pumps, and a damn shower—I've got to bath! Stop, we'll take a break, eat, rest a spell, sleep if we need," she hesitated, then continued, "And it is all on me! Ok?" She said as she climbed over into the passenger's front seat.

Jay glanced at Alex several quick times as she removed the pistol from her jeans and slid it under her seat. "Do you always travel with that thing?" "Yes, always!" she didn't explain any more than that.

Far ahead on their left, the two made out the sign; it was faded, rusted around the edges, on tall wooden poles. It displayed; 'Water, Oil, Gas, Food'. Alex guessed that was in the order of importance. Soon, they saw the arrangement; one long, low building, a canopy next to large glass panes at the end nearest the highway—three cars close together at this end, four cars scattered along its length and a pile of maybe twenty cars off from the far end heaped together in the scrubby countryside.

"You want to stop there?" Jay asked. "Hell yes! It looks—well—at least alive!" It was beginning to be sunrise. And there wasn't a tree in sight—with the flat terrain that was a very long ways! Parking at the cafe and getting out—Tiger had finally woke up—Alex asked Jay, "What first? For you, eat? Sleep? Bath?" "I'd just as soon sleep first!" "Ok. I'll handle this." While the other two stepped about outside and tried to shake out the kinks, Alex found someone to inquire about rooms. It was the waitress—the only waitress.

Returning to Tiger and Jay, she snapped, "Got a deal!" she threw Jay a key—it had a large wooden fob attached. "Your's. Our's is next door, drive about half way, we'll walk!" She motioned for Tiger to follow her. As they approached the station wagon and the room doors, Jay was going in with his gear. He glanced back, said, "The car keys are in the switch." "Hey! Aren't you afraid someone will steal it?" Alex laughed. He looked about, replied, "Who?" There were no others in sight as far as they could as see. He added, "Besides, who would want it?" The three chuckled, Tiger grabbed Alex's hand, jerked it, said, "See? I told you so!"

It was shortly before one P.M., Alex and Tiger had bathed, and bathed, repacked their things, relaxed and were now strolling along the front of the long building just enjoying the warm, sunshine. Hesitating in front of Jay's door, Alex thought she heard a sound inside. She lightly tapped on the door, Jay immediately opened it—he was dressed and looked refreshed. "Good! We put off eating until you were up and ready. Let's get a bite and bug-out of here! This place," she waved a hand around, "is so lonely, I bet the rattlesnakes use binoculars to look for a mate!"

With Jay's smaller travel bag in one corner of the rear seat, Alex lay back and stretched out. Jay was driving, Tiger up front. "Man! That was the most food I ever seen for only a few bucks! Thanks, Tiger for introducing me to Navajo tacos!" Alex sat up and watched as the traffic from 1-20 blended into I-10. Not far on, she tapped Jay on his shoulder, said, "Pull over, stop—I've got a deal for you!" As he did, she explained that Tiger was a 'beginner-driver'. And she wanted Tiger to get some more driving experience while they were in open, flat land. She also wanted him to keep an eye on her as she drove. He agreed, the two swapped places, Alex added, "Let's say, Tiger drives to just before Fabens—east of Fabens. Ok?" The two up front nodded as Tiger pulled off.

Up to speed and looking stable, Alex lay back down again. After staring at the overhead for a while, she asked, "Jay, where are you from?" "San Diego." "What do you do? For a living I mean?" "Well, just between jobs now—anything I can pick-up. I had started my own Brokerage when—" Alex interrupted, "When the collapse knocked the blocks from under it!" "Right! Overnight it turned into like trying to sell ice cream to—to—those rattlesnakes you mentioned!" They laughed, she responded, "I was a major food buyer! You can image how it hit me!" Alex didn't elaborate.

"And you, Tiger?" he asked. "Me? I'm an Archaeologist!

Except for problems getting something to eat, the collapse didn't bother my line of work. You know, the stuff that's been buried for centuries doesn't know crap about the national economy!" They laughed again. "Jay, you married? Got family? Responsibilities?" Alex asked. "Nope" was his only reply. "Are you gay?" Alex decided it was simpler to ask than to waste time trying to figure it out! "Nope" again. Alex slid down, went silent as she thought. 'Jay loose—no strings attached—and he probably isn't planning beyond the next ride—maybe he could go with us? Naw! Come the first Friday night, I'd be screwing him like a mink in heat that just drank a soft drink laced with 'Spanish-fly'! Besides, what's that old sailor's saying? Never ship three on a boat! Bad luck—major bad luck! Anyway, me and young Margarita Morley are getting along just fine!

With the steady hum of the car and no conversation, Alex's thoughts drifted deeper. 'That last night in New Orleans, surprisingly, had been pleasant. And with no serious sexual overtones—just a hug here, a gentle pat there, a sweet kiss now and then, and holding hands, or holding each other around the waist or hips. And with no grabbing, rough stuff, struggling to size up some guy's ego—and the seemingly constant 'I want, I want from the 'Master Members of Society'! Alex rolled to her side, crossed her arms over her face, thought 'Maybe I'll back off the sex game—with guys at least—maybe I'll just check into a nunnery, become a nun—I understand there are a lot of convents in Mexico—donate all that worthless money to a church, check in—', Alex drifted into sleep.

"Alex! Alex!" Jay had learned to not shake her, he called as Tiger stopped on the shoulder of the highway. "Alex! We're close to Fabens!

/Wake up!" She snapped upright, wiped her eyes, glanced at her watch, it was about five P.M. She replied, "Ok! I'm awake!" She realized they were stopped, said, "I'll take over from here!" Moving to the driver's seat, Alex indicated for Tiger to slip over, and for Jay to get in the rear.

They passed through Fabens and just before getting into the heavier traffic of El Paso, Alex said, "Jay, this is where we part company. Thanks for the help! Any particular place you want to be dropped off at?" "Yes, there's one of those 'Super Truck Stops just a head. I'll probably have a better chance for a ride there. Maybe even a lift directly—and all the way—to San Diego. I really appreciate the ride, it's been fun. And, Alex, thanks for picking up the tabs!" He expected her to just pull over at the truck stop and let him out, but instead she entered the busy, large parking area, worked to the restaurant parking spots.

Easing to a stop, Alex said, "Let's have a snack—it may be a while until another opportunity! Jay, leave your bags in the car, and, please order for us," she indicated herself and Tiger. "I'll have a ham and cheese on rye, black coffee," she pointed to Tiger, who replied, "I'll have the same." "We got a little something we've got to do! We'll come in ASAP—I've got the tab. Please sit as close to the entrance as possible, so we will not have trouble spotting you. Ok?" "Ok—but—", she didn't wait, snapped, "Run! Run! We're rather in a hurry!"

As the two stepped through the entrance to the cafe, Jay saw them—he guessed it was them! He fell back, gasped—they wore matching business outfits; black dress suits—skirts and long sleeve jackets, plain man style white blouses, tan hose and medium heeled pumps, also black. They wore matching black strap purses and they both had identification badges clipped to their breast pockets. Alex held an expensive looking leather travel case, Tiger held a very nice briefcase. But the most outstanding different feature was the black, heavy rim glasses that Alex wore. As they sat, Jay was still in shock over their different appearances. Tiger's long black hair was twisted into a bun on top of her head. They both had on a minimum of make-up.

The food arrived and as they began to eat, Jay leaned forward and read their badges, "The Department of Agriculture, Miss Alexandra Hawkins, Special Agent." "Special Agent?" he asked. "Not so loud, please, you'll start half of the guys in here running for the door!" Alex almost whispered. Looking at Tiger's, he read, "The Department of Interior, Miss Margarita Calienta Morley, Archaeologist, Special Projects Director." He slid back, took another bite, said, "And I thought you two were just a couple of 'twits' hooking your way across country. No kidding, who are you two anyway?" "That's an entirely too complicated question—we don't have time to even begin to explain. Next trip, maybe." Alex and Tiger laughed, he looked rejected. Tiger reached and took his hand, pleated, "Oh, don't feel so bad, maybe just a little—like where are we headed?" "Ok, I'll bite, where?" "About two thousand miles due south to Amatenango and Palenque." He looked puzzled. The other two chuckled. He let it drop, regardless, he didn't think he would get the truth, he finished the meal without any more questions.

As Alex eased away from the Mexican Customs station, she suddenly laughed, grabbed Tiger's knee, shook it, and said "Tig Baby! We are the Greatest! Together we may be the best B.S. artist since P.T.Barnum!" "P.T. who?" "Forget it—old joke! Did you see those guys when I showed them the permit for my pistol!" "Yes! And when you pulled it out of your purse, I thought they were going to vamos! Pronto! Run all the way to Mexico City!" "And when you showed them the document proving Ole Sylvanus was your Grandfather! I thought their eyes were going to pop out. And when we showed them with the laptop computer, how we could communicate with our bosses! Mine, Nat at Hidden Valley! And yours, Jerry White at his home! They flipped out! Gave up!" "And your 'official letter of introduction from Dr. Smith, the 'Project Leader' at Palenque! They swallowed it all! Hook, line and sinker!"

They entered the busy section of downtown Ciudad Juarez, Alex asked, "What now?" "It is too late to head on south. We'd better find a room here, spend the night and get an early start tomorrow morning." Alex cast her a questioning look, it was just after six, and it wasn't even dark yet. Tiger responded, "One only drives at night if absolutely necessary! Or one is a professional bus driver!" "Oh," was Alex's only comment—she had learned to pay attention to Tiger's knowledge of the 'real' world. "Maybe a motel?" Alex added. "No, something—a hotel—in the heart of town is better, things will be within easy walking distances. The cities, the towns, down here, start and end suddenly. City—bang! Nothing at all!" Alex eased on, the traffic along the broad street was moving at a crawling pace.

Approaching the junction with Avenue Lopez Mateos, Tiger said, "Go left here, follow route forty five. Tomorrow, we'll take that route south on to Chihuahua." The traffic continued to creep forward. "Alex! Look at the people—look where they are all walking!" Alex looked toward the sidewalks, replied, "Yes, so, they are all going in the same direction as we are. So what?" "That means we are going in the RIGHT direction! "Looking as far ahead as possible, Tiger saw the flow of people on their left, turned left. And the ones on their right crossed the avenue and blended in with the others headed left. "See—up there," she pointed, "Everyone is going left at that side street. Turn left there! Follow the people!" Alex didn't question. But as she came to the 'crossing' crowd, she stopped. It was a solid mass of people—all kinds of people! "Why did you stop?" Tiger asked. Alex pointed out the windshield, "To keep from killing anyone!" Tiger laughed, replied, "Go ahead! And turn left! You couldn't possible hit those people!" Alex eased forward, the people jumped around, parted, without stopping their scurry toward 'something'.

Around the corner, now on the smaller side street, Alex again followed the people—both sidewalks, and most of the street was now packed crowds. And they were still making better time than she was! Ahead, she saw that the street appeared to be blocked by a huge, open shed! "It's the market!" Tiger screamed! "We've found the Central Market! El Mercado!" She was like a kid that had seen Santa for the first time!

"Park at the first place barely big enough—just leave enough room for a car—a single car—to get by!" It had been almost five years since Tiger had been to a real Mexican Central Market!

Alex had to turn one way or the other. There didn't seem to be any indication of one being any better than the other, she turned left. And just after, she saw a car backing out. She waited then slipped old 'Betsy' in the parking space. Looking out the rear, she estimated that one car— Ok, one very small car—could 'maybe' get by!

Tiger forced out through the partially opened door—it was that tight—she stood and screamed, "Home! I'm finally home!" As Alex stood outside, she saw that Tiger had tears on her cheeks.

Turning to Alex, Tiger wiper her eyes as she smiled, then she glanced down at her manner of dress. She shook her head at Alex, motioned that they go to the rear of the station wagon. There, she pointed at Alex's business suit dress, shook her head, said, "No way! We have to change clothes!" "Where? How?" Alex snapped. "Here! Now! Open the tailgate!" "Have you lost your mind? We're standing in the street! Almost being rubbed by the cars slipping by!" "No one will even notice us! Believe me, Alex! No one!"

With the rear hatch up, they quickly got their jeans, the loose traveling shirts and their low-quarter tennis shoes. They pulled off the dress jackets and heels. At first, they tried to slip the jeans on over the pantyhose and under the skirts—it didn't work. They rapidly unzipped the skirts, slipped these off. Alex looked around as she slipped her feet into the legs of her jeans. True, no one even looked at them. It was as if they were invisible! Feeling better about the situation, they unbuttoned their nice 'uniform' blouses, removed these and put on the loose shirts. Again, no one paid them any attention.

With their shoes on, and only their wallets—Alex had the car keys— which they stuffed deep into their front pockets, they headed in under the huge market. Tiger had previously warned Alex "never, ever, carry anything in your hip pockets! There are people who, with razor blades, can slit a hip pocket open and be gone with 'whatever' and you'll never know it! Until you feel for 'whatever', or take your pants off!"

The subject of getting a room—somewhere—wasn't mentioned for the next three or so hours!

After a hour of *aimlessly wandering*—pushing really—through the crowd, picking up, looking at many items, Tiger asking questions, asking prices, Alex realized that Tiger had returned to her 'rapid-fire' Spanish—all the words hooked together—endlessly! Sentence to sentence, endlessly! Alex thought, 'and teaching for nearly two years, I thought she had learned to pause between words! All that hard work went down the drain in about fifteen minutes!

They came to a pile of 'somethings'. These were beautiful cloth objects. The vendor-lady handed Alex one from under the table. It was stuffed with old newspaper—the thing was soft, even cuddly soft—the material was brightly decorated with woven patterns. There were two sling straps and a zipper lengthwise. The vendor unzipped it, indicated you put things in the bag. It was about two feet long, and being stuffed, it was almost a foot in diameter—it had flat circular ends. Closing the zipper, Alex slipped both straps over one of her shoulders—it was comfortable! Tiger took it from her shoulder, spread the straps, said "Stick one arm in each strap", as she held it to Alex's back. It was now a backpack, in a horizontal fashion. "And if you have to—", Tiger got another one from the huge pile and holding it horizontal to Alex's chest, she hooked both straps over her head, "Another pack! A chest pack!" Tiger picked up two more, and slipped both straps of one over one of Alex's shoulders. She did the same with the other bag, over Alex's other shoulder. Then she placed one in each of Alex's hands! "Now! You're ready for traveling! With six bags!" The three women laughed at Alex's six bags, all over her!

Alex screamed, "Yes! Yes! I've got to have these!" Tiger quickly put her hand over Alex's mouth, said, "Si, you'll drive the price out of sight!" Then she added, "Slowly shake your head, slowly return the bags to the pile—and I'll try making a deal, Tiger almost whispered. Alex did, but instead of letting Tiger play 'let's make a deal', she pulled her head close, said into her ear, "Tiger, ask if she would trade six of her bags for my two leather cases." Tiger did, turned to Alex, "She said no." Alex didn't like the word no, she pulled on Tiger, and said "follow me!"

Among Alex's many good attributes, one was an excellent sense of direction—physical direction—in the simplest fashion possible. There are seldom straight paths in Mexican markets—too easy to move too fast, definitely not good for business. Alex led them back to the station wagon. As soon as she opened the rear hatch, she grabbed up one of the leather cases, and she said to Tiger, "Dump that one! I'll do this one! If that lady ever sees these, I guarantee we can make a deal!" Little Alex knew she could haggle with the best!

In about thirty minutes, they returned to 'Betsy' with eight of the 'Mitla bags—Alex had finally learned the name, and she had learned these bags were made—even the cloth was woven in a small town just outside of the city of Oaxaca. How these bags got this far north, no one seemed to know! Completing the 'trade-deal', the vendor lady had shown Alex a much smaller version. Alex got two of the smaller ones—but, she had to pay cash—the deal had already been 'closed'! Money wise, Alex knew she had lost—lost a lot! But she was so disgusted with the stiff leather cases, and so pleased and delighted, with the Mitla bags, it was ok.

At the tailgate, the two began to re-pack. They decided on using four bags, two for their individual 'work' clothes, two for their 'dress' clothes. And one each of the smaller bags for make-up and panties. While doing this, Alex asked, "it's nearly ten, and I don't notice that the crowd has dropped off any—do these people do this all night?" "Some times, just depends." As people squeezed pass, Tiger began to ask, then she filled Alex in, "This is the eve before Ash Wednesday! Tomorrow is a holiday! A celebration! Alex! Can we stay, through tomorrow?" And Tiger added quickly, "And tonight there's a celebration also! With fireworks and all! It should be great!"

Suddenly, she hesitated, then meekly said "That is, if we can find a room." "What? I didn't hear you!" "There may be a room problem!" "You mean like—a problem with the room we don't have!" Tiger just hung her head, and slowly nodded. "I'm teasing! Hell, if we have to, we can spend the night in the wagon! Right here! One thing for sure, we sure as hell will not starve!" She pointed around to the piles and crates of fresh fruits and vegetables.

Finished with the packing, and more room being available inside, Alex gave the pile a couple of hardy shoves, cleared the rear edge of the floor. She turned, backed up and hooked her butt on the edge of the floor and put her heels on the bumper. She propped her elbows on her knees and propped her chin on her fists. Tiger matched Alex's position. Soon, Tiger said, "There's another way to get a room." "Really? How?" "We don't look, we ask—we ask everyone that passes us!" "Hey, not a bad idea—besides, my 'doggies' are tired!"

"How does that go, in Spanish? Donda esta su casa para un, ah, noche?" "No, no silly! You just asked, where is your home or, ah, night'!

It is, 'Donda es un cuarto para esta noche?'—Where is one room for this night?" Tiger corrected Alex as she laughed. They started, got a lot of nos. But, finally, one man with his family—wife and three little daughters, they looked three, four, and five—,said, "Si, just up the street, upstairs! If you two don't mind that each of you sleep with one of my daughters!" "Bath? Con banos?" Alex quickly asked. "Si, if you wait your turn!" "Deal!" Alex stuck out her right hand. As they shook, Alex asked, "Oh, price? Cuanto para un noche?" "Free—we're glad to help two young pretty Senoritas in distress!" They all laughed, even the three small muchaches! The nice man said "You should just leave your car—your wagon", the girls thought that was funny, "where it is, there's no other place close by." Alex checked her pocket to be sure she had the keys then she quickly locked up. They followed the family.

The three-story apartment building was on the side street, and one block in the direction they had come this afternoon. The family's apartment was to the left of the top of the narrow stairs—it was a corner unit on the top floor, the third floor. The place consisted of a large living/dining/kitchen, two bedrooms separated by the bath. As the three darling girls jumped, ran, and explained everything—especially their room—in 'rapid-fire', Alex commented to Tiger, "It's lovely! The girls' room all in pink, three individual single beds and three dressers just alike with no signs of partiality at all! How sweet!"

La Senora asked Tiger if they wanted anything to eat—the family.

Had 'snacked-about' at the market. "No gracias, we ate too at the market."

Then El Senor explained; they were going back out, soon, as he got out-door blankets from the closet, to watch the fireworks, from the roof! He didn't have to ask if Alex and Tiger would join them, Tiger jumped up and down as she explained to Alex! Senor got three blankets out!

The beautiful and very continuous display of fireworks lasted until the wee-hours of the morning. Returning to the apartment, Senor carried the largest girl, Tiger the middle girl, and Alex, the three year old. The girls were asleep.

As the dim light from the city outside drifted through the window,

Alex pulled the three year old child close and cuddled her tightly. She cautiously brushed the little girl's long, black hair from over her precious face. "Mas benito muchacha" Alex whispered as she closed her own eyes.

Alex fell back through her mind's time; the wild college years, when Miss Hawkins ran rampant, studying only what she wanted, her problems, changing from school to school without a second thought. And money not being of much concern—that seemed to be in an endless supply.

Her memory slipped farther back—back to the period of time—to the 'awful' years, between when she found her mother dead and when she first entered 'higher' education. The time when she was forced by circumstances to mature. The time when the evil Miss Hawkins ruthlessly became dominate with her insatiable, insidious desires for sex. And the suppressions by the matrons upon Miss Hawkins. And the years of being forced to attend church by the demanding matrons.

Her mind churned forward all the transfers, from one private all girls' school to another similar awful school. Never transferred by a human being—always transferred by letter, even telephone calls. No one to help with the confusing impact of starting over again. And with each transfer, Miss Hawkins increased her control over Alex.

Her mind recalled the period before her mother's death, the very beginning of being forced into maturity. She could remember only little, her father occasionally dropping-in, and never staying for long at the time—him bringing presents—him acting as if nothing was 'wrong', and she could remember her sexual attraction to him and their intimate, but brief encounters. But, always he would leave—he always left, over and over again, no explanations, no reasons, he just would suddenly be gone. She never knew her father. 'He' was just a stranger passing through her young years.

Her mind could travel back to the first time he was 'just gone', but, beyond that, the years before that—she must have been five or six years old, her youngest years—she couldn't remember a single thing. She could only guess—or hope—she must, at least she hoped, have had a 'normal' childhood. Happy, a real family, a father and mother, games, playing with other kids, pets—but she could only recall nothing! It was as if she had never existed then! Trying as hard as possible, NOTHING!

Alex squeezed her eyelids tighter—nothing—she softly sobbed as her tears forced their way out. She pulled the little girl closer.

"Come on! Let's run! I'll race you to your wagon!" the middle girl yelled as she struck out and quickly got a head start! Tiger, then Alex and the oldest sister caught up, Tiger grabbed 'runner's' hand, the other two linked-up as they crossed the street to the station wagon. A quick glimpse—everything inside appeared to be exactly as they had left it. They ate breakfast. This was snack-about on fresh fruit and fresh hot rolls. They had not brought the 'Babina'—the baby sister—the two older ones had said she was too young! Alex thought, 'Amazing! What difference being one or two years older makes!'

They returned to the apartment with a basket full of fresh fruit and hot tortillas. They had forgotten to carry a basket, Alex bought one, saying, "We'll need one anyway, we'll buy it now!" They were greeted by the parents who were in the process of getting dressed for mid-morning church services. As La Senora quickly began to dress the two older sisters, she—through Tiger—insisted that Tiger, and in particular Alex, join them.

"Go to church?" Alex pulled Tiger to one side, whispered, "I haven't been to church since the time I entered college!" "Well? What's the problem? What difference does that make?" "Besides, we—I—don't have anything proper to wear! Skin-tight short tail cocktail dresses will not exactly work!" Alex argued. "Alex, you're just trying to excuse yourself out of this! You know, I know, we can wear our business suits, out 'Official Uniforms! And I'm sure the Senora has extra shawls, all women down here always has extra shawls! Quit acting like a 'bad little boy' trying to skip Sunday school!" Alex didn't concede, she just quit objecting.

After services—Alex had relied on her years of 'learning' to carry her through—as the seven of them walked back along the eight or so blocks, Senor asked, "What are you Senoritas going to do next?" Alex felt this was a proper opening, "It's about two hundred miles to Chihuahua, I think if we leave soon, we can make it before dark—do you think that's possible?" "Yes, should be no problem. The highway, most of it, is level and reasonable straight. Closer to Chihuahua, it does begin to climb, but still no major twisting curves, switch-backs, that sort of difficulties."

The two older girls swung Alex's hands as the family continued to stroll. Tiger was carrying the youngest one on her hip when she said, "Alex, I thought we may stay here until tomorrow. That is", she turned toward the parents, asked, "If it is ok with you lovely people?" They both replied it would be perfectly acceptable. Then El Senor added, "My family—my Mother, brothers, sisters, and of course all the kids—has a traditional diner on this night, out at the old hacienda—the home place—we would love to have you two as guests. I think you both would make a grand impression—especially on my brothers! Please stay and join us!"

"Oh, Alex! Doesn't that sound like fun? Please—", Tiger pleaded, then waited. "Sure! We would be happy to join your family for diner!" "It will be rather late—we usually go out to Mother's about nine at night. Is that ok?" "Sure, we're regular 'night-owls' anyway!" Alex quickly replied.

For the balance of the day, everyone changed into casual clothes, the parents stayed in the apartment with the 'little-one', Alex, Tiger and the two 'older girls' went to the market—they wandered, shopped didn't buy much, Alex only bought a few things for the girls as they snacked about. Alex was amazed at the great variety of articles being offered for sale. Almost anything, everything one could think of was there—from live animals to custom blended on the spot facial make-up supplies—even lipstick! This was done by a couple of beautiful young ladies. On the way back to the apartment, they picked up their dress clothes Mitla bags and their smaller 'make-up' Mitla bags.

When it was time to get dressed for the evening, Alex and Tiger consulted La Senora about what they should wear—they were not sure. The Lady's basic reply was; as fancy, as sexy, as pretty as possible—beautiful young ladies should definitely 'show-off' on these occasions. And, several of the brothers are not married—they would appreciate you two! Alex and Tiger were thrilled at the opportunity! And the two did just that; skin tight 'cocktail' slip-dresses—black for Alex, white for Tiger—spike heels, and Alex 'decorated' the two of them with lots of fancy jewelry—Alex, her 'nugget' set, Tiger in pearls! And the three muchachas helped! The three little girls thought Alex and Tiger were 'Real Showgirls! Even Actresses! Or Real Dancers! The two didn't spoil their young imaginations! La Senora and El Senor were also very favorable impressed!

With the traffic much less than the day before, El Senor brought his sedan around and all the 'ladies' packed in. "Get comfortable, it is almost a hour drive out to the hacienda", he advised.

The place was a Colonial Period hacienda, a long narrow driveway with lights led up to the front of the large, spread out ranch style home. There were numerous outbuildings, including a couple of huge barns. From what Alex saw, she asked, "This was a working ranch at one time—right?" "Si—up until the land reform of ninety twenty four, then it gradually couldn't be operated profitably. My Father sold off most of the open land, then he became a merchant." Alex, and in particular, Tiger, knew he had 'slightly stretched' the truth. In the land reform act, the majority of the land was taken from the hacienda owners and given to the 'residents' of the places—that just didn't work in the long run! Most descendants didn't like to talk about the real—the true—details of this disastrous period of time.

They were met at the heavy front door by a butler who led them to the formal living room. The two little sisters, leading the 'baby', immediately disappeared into another portion of the huge house—they knew the routine very well—the kids under thirteen would be fed and entertained 'somewhere else'—not in the formal dinning room with the adults.

Some members of the family were already here. The introductions were formal, one on one, to every body—to the Mother first. Alex and Tiger were introduced as USA Government Employees. The two didn't bother with specifics. And, as La Senora had said, all the ladies were extremely well dressed and bedecked with jewelry. And the men were handsomely suited—very stately, with gracious manners. Two of the younger—Alex guessed to be in their mid to late thirties—brothers were without 'dates'—guests. Things were looking-up for a very enjoyable evening. These two immediately 'accepted' Alex and Tiger as their guests—their dates. The two—Alex and Tiger—didn't object to this at all.

The meal was fancy, elegant—three main courses—all the proper condiments, and unfailing glasses of superior wine, the food was delicious, and expertly prepared and served. It was relaxed, drawn out, never rushed, the conversation—most spoke perfect English—was pleasant and relaxed, without probing questions. Alex and Tiger just 'went with the flow' and enjoyed the scene—the company. Overall, the meal was stupendous!

At the end of the meal—this was when the Mother stood from her chair at the end of the long table and indicated—they all moved to the formal living room. It was almost 2A.M., the two brothers offered to carry Alex and Tiger back to the city—but—to Tiger's surprise Alex declined their offer, said she thought they—she and Tiger—should help with the three little girls. After getting the girls, the seven of them returned to town.

Back at the apartment, Alex and Tiger expressed their gratitude to their host and hostess. And, as the night before, Alex and Tiger slept with two of the girls. And Alex slept peaceably. And all the 'girls' slept late that morning.

Getting up about mid-morning—El Senor had already gone to work, the two had learned he was the Manager for one of the several 'Family' stores—the girls and women casually stirred about, and slowly got dressed. Alex and Tiger in their 'traveling' jeans, loose shirts and tennis shoes. Shortly after noon, the two said their 'good-byes', and left, headed south for Chihuahua.

As Alex pulled away from the market, Tiger remarked, not as to Alex, but more to her self, "That—last night—was the side of my country, I never expected to see—", she didn't elaborate. Alex turned and saw the few tears in Tiger's eyes. She gently patted Tiger's knee, softly responded, "Tig—you're still growing up—you'll probably see more that you thought you would never see—", she also dropped that subject.

CHAPTER 7

Clearing the traffic of Juarez, Alex began to slow and pull to the shoulder of the highway. "What?" Tiger asked. "The traffic isn't bad, the road looks ok, it's your turn to drive!" "No, I've—this is a two lane road, I." Alex interrupted "Tiger! Don't act like a 'bad little boy' trying to skip driving duties! Get out, and let's swap places!" They both chuckled at the touche' touch.

As Tiger drove and after a period of silence, Alex had a 'conversation'—not so much with Tiger, she was in deep concentration—but with herself. "Is that what's missing from my life?" She didn't expect any answers, and she didn't get any. "Family? Running, jumping, dancing little kids? A real, loving, caring family life? Someone who will always be there? Someone who will never leave? Never leave me again? Walk the kids—and me—to church every Sunday or whenever? Am I headed down my same old path? Lonely—to spend the rest of my life alone? And no one else at the end?"

Suddenly, Alex leaned forward. Tiger was in a rather tight 'pass—not pass'-situation. Alex snapped back to reality as she gave instructions about the driving. After Tiger worked her way out of the close condition, Alex slid back, said, again as to herself, "I need a drink."

Alex even let Tiger drive thru Anumada and Moctezuma—both were straight thru affairs, no turns, or necessary intersections. As they began to see the mountains ahead, Alex told her to pull off at the intersection with route 120. Alex took over driving and when near the edge of the city—it was about five p.m.—she asked, "You said the surprise was at—or—in? Chihuahua? We are near the outskirts, what next?" "We stop and ask for instructions to the railroad, the trains—the place where the vehicles are loaded!" "Train? Load vehicles?"

Alex turned her right hand toward Tiger, her fingers up, made a flipping motion, "Come on Tig—give me more!" "They load cars—whatever—on flat rail cars—we ride across Copper Canyon." "Load this car on a train? Just to cross a crack in the ground? To look down into a single canyon?" Alex laughed. "Not exactly. We ride along the canyon—up to the Continental Divide—then down into the canyon—and out to the Sea of Cortes—the Golfo de California." Alex got serious as she realized they were a hell of a ways from the Pacific coast! "What! Exactly how long is this—this—train ride?" "Over four hundred miles long," Tiger calmly replied.

Alex quickly estimated the difficulties—up mountains, down into 'something', all the way to the coast—she asked, "And, more or less, how long is this adventure going to take?" "More or less, twenty hours," Again she was calm, cool, with her reply. Then she added, "We can either ride in a passenger rail car—or—ride in 'Betsy'—or—or—ride out on the flatcar." "Oh, really? And what, where, do we eat—drink—piss for twenty hours?" "We should buy some supplies." "Should! Should! Tiger! That is an understatement—try! Ha! Make that, be damn sure we buy supplies! Especially—and I ain't talking soft drinks here—buy something 'hard' for me to drink!" "Ok! Ok! Or we could, like I did on one trip—but of course, I was younger, wilder, and with a guy friend—jump from flatcar to flatcar, make our way forward, jump to the last passenger car, make our way to the diner car. There will be a nice diner—" Alex didn't comment, she just shook her head.

After a brief silence while Alex conjured up wild and bad thoughts, she asked, "What happens if you fall off?" "If the fall doesn't kill you, another train will come along in about twenty-four hours—but— of course, they wouldn't stop—bandits, Indians, that sort of stuff." "Bandits! Indians! You aren't using that to represent Mexicans, are you?" "No. This is Indian country!""Real Indians?" "Yes, real Tarahumara Indians—but I guess, the drug smugglers are really more of a threat, especially during the 'off season', like now." Alex looked serious, and waited as she began to watch for a Pemex station. "Don't worry, Alex! It'll be great fun! It is a fantastic scene! Just fantastic!" as she tickled Alex in her ribs.

As Alex 'negotiated' gasoline, she was quickly learning it was not as simple as in the USA, Tiger asked directions to the 'loading yard' of The Chihuahua Al Pacifico Railroad. Back in the car, Tiger began to explain the way to go, she closed with, "And the man said, have plenty of cash, it's a cash only deal!" "I've got about three hundred in US cash—but very little, only some change I picked up at the market, in Mexican pasos. You think that will work?" Tiger just shrugged.

Several turns later, they approached a large paved parking lot, or staging area. It was level—almost like a mound that had been leveled off—one side, the side next to the rail yard was straight and had a low concrete curb. Next to this, and with the tops of the flatcars level with the top of the curb, were ten or twelve flat-bed railcars. Several vehicles—mainly large expensive RV's and large pickups with camper bodies—were in a straight line. Outside along the passenger's side stood the people from the vehicles.

A huge diesel powered forklift, with long forks and huge pneumatic tires, and all-wheel steering, was busy as it lifted, backed up, lumbered with a vehicle on its forks to a railcar and shifted for the correct position, then lowered the vehicle onto the flat car. A crew of four men on the flat car chained the vehicles down as fast as these were loaded. A Railroad Agent walked among the owners and processed the necessary papers, and collected the fare.

Alex signed the forms—there were several—and paid the fare, she had not a clue what it had cost, she had given the Agent two one hundred bills, he had given her back a hand full of 'funny-money'—pasos—and the Agent gave her a carbon copy of the forms. Looking at 'Betsy', out 'there', chained on a flat car to 'somewhere', Alex realized, and snapped to Tiger, "What the hell do we do now?" Without a reply, or hesitation, Tiger ran after the Railroad Agent.

With 'Betsy' 'out-there', and Tiger tagging along beside the Agent, Alex felt deserted—alone—as she stood' there with only the clothes she wore, her wallet in one hand, and in her other hand a fist full of papers and strange money.

But soon Tiger ran back, rapidly said "We've got options. We can return to out there", she pointed to beyond the loading track—out into the rail yard—"Find our car, climb on and ride in—or—with it. At THREE A.M.! Or—or—we can take those forms." she pointed to the copies Alex held, "To the passenger's terminal, down there," she pointed far beyond the switch yard, "At FOUR A.M., and show that", again she pointed to the forms, "to the Conductor and ride in the passenger cars!"

Alex looked at 'Betsy'—so far, Betsy was the smallest, and oldest vehicle on the train—then she swept the horizon with her view, saw a simple, direct paved street across the wide rail yard, and across that way was a sign, 'Hotel', next to that, another sign, 'Bar', and next to that a sign that indicated a grocery store. Alex pointed that way, said, "I'm for sticking with Betsy, but first, we go that way", she pointed. "Tig, remind me to buy a flashlight, we're going to need it!" Tiger smiled as she nodded to Alex, Alex smiled back. They walked off, arm in arm.

It was 2:45 A.M., they didn't need the new flashlight long, only as they stumbled and tripped, with their arms loaded—they had bought food, drinks and tequila—over the several sets of tracks next to the business district. Most all the loaded RV's and even several of the camper/pickups had their interior lights on. And several were playing loud music. Moving along the flat cars, they spotted 'Betsy'—the huge Winnibago loaded behind Betsy was brightly lit. Alex hesitated, called very loud, "Ahoy! Ahoy!" Immediately a middle-aged man swung open the door of the RV, called back, "Ahoy!" He looked down at Alex and Tiger, said, "Welcome! You look like the two gals that belong to—to—that!" He pointed at their small, old station wagon—that's what 'Betsy' looked like in the presence of the Winnibago.

"Yes, that's us! May we come aboard?" Alex asked. "Of course! Hold on a 'sec'—we've got a step ladder." They sat their load on the edge of the flat car near the station wagon, returned to the light from the open door of the RV, and waited. As the big, jolly man lowered the ladder, he said, "Hold on! I'll come down, help you ladies up!"

As Alex stepped from the ladder to the flat car, she turned and headed in the direction of 'Betsy'. Woah! Little Lady! Come Inside! Let's have instructions—and a bite of breakfast! Twenty hours is going to be a long haul—we just as well be like family!" "You sure it's ok?" she asked. "Heck, two more ain't nothing! Especially two as pretty as you two!" She faced Tiger and smiled, Tiger met her with a broad grin and winked

The Rvers were three couples from Dallas, four of them had made this trek before. They all appeared to be in their mid—fifties. After introductions—first names only—and after the delicious breakfast, as they were having another cup of coffee, the train, the RV, suddenly gave a jerk, The train was 'taking up the slack', trying to get started. Alex and Tiger both jumped up and said, "Our things! Our stuff is still on the edge of the flat car!" Running out into the much dimmer night-light, Alex fumbled with the keys as Tiger slid their supplies away from the edge and toward the tailgate. Someone in the RV switched on a set of out-door flood lights—it was bright as day. Alex waved 'thanks' as she finally got the car open and they began to load their supplies.

One of the men stepped close, glanced inside the still open tailgate, asked, "You two ok?" "Yes." Still looking inside 'Betsy' he added, "Traveling light, aren't you?" "I guess so—just an impromptu vacation—kind of a 'lark' some people would say." Alex answered—but she didn't explain anymore than that. At least for now.

"Might as well come back in the RV, as soon as you like; it's still hours till daylight! No need to—", he let it drop. "Thanks, we'd be glad to! Thanks a heap!" Alex replied. He started to leave. Tiger whispered To Alex, "See? I told you things would work out Ok." As the man went toward the RV, he suddenly stopped, turned back, called out. "If you two plan on riding outside at all, you'd better get out jackets, sweaters, warm clothes! We'll probably go through snow as we go over the mountains!" "Snow? Is he kidding?" Alex asked Tiger. "No, not at all!" she replied. They got out two light weight—but insulated—jackets. And two pairs of socks. "Snow?" "Really!" again Tiger answered. Alex dug out two tee shirts. Then two pairs of flannel jogging pants. And two scrafs. "No kidding? snow?" "Yes! ALex! Snow!" Alex looked in the new supplies, got the bottle of tequila.

It was still dark, they returned to the inside of the RV, piled their clothes to one side, and as another round of coffee was poured, Alex asked if it was Ok for her to 'lace' her coffee with tequila. "Yes, but tequila? Ug! Little lady, you ain't got much taste in drink'g! I've got plenty,and I do mean plenty! Of good old Jack Daniels!" Alex sat her bottle of tequila to one side and winked at Tiger'.

As the owner added a shot of JD to everyone's cups, his wife continued to elaborate on THE TRIP. "Up the Sierra Madre Mountains, across the Continental Divide—even along on top of the Divide for a ways, back down the Eastern slope again—but for only a short time to the village of San Juanito, back across the Divide again to the Pacific side, down—but not much down—to the village of Creel—,"

She took a short break, poured more coffee, then started again, "At Creel, a few passengers usually get off for a few days lay-over.

We did on our first trip—before we got in RV'ing. Then, after the RV, we learned how much more fun it was to ride the flat cars! With our own 'private passenger car'—our RV!" She continued, and explained that after Creel, one was really AT the canyon—at first along the top edge. And the great depth and width was absolutely fantastic!

As her husband got a well worn map of Mexico out of a cabinet and passed it to her, he said, "Hon, hold it a minute"—he had heard the tale many times, but he still appreciated his wife's version—"I've got to take a piss"—he looked to Alex and Tiger, added, "If you two need to use the 'john', just make your selves at home!"

One of the women poured more coffee, one of the men added more JD, the other lady checked outside the door to see if sunrise had began yet. She said back to the others, "Not long! A glow has started in the East!" She came back and joined the others.

With everyone settled down again, the owner's wife resumed her story. "Pass Creel, only about twenty miles, the train stops for almost a half hour. The place is named the 'El Divisadero'. The inside passengers-the ones up-front, can get out—we usually just stay on the flat car. That place is the last of being 'up' on the rim, not far on it is as if the train turns left, and dives—DIVES! Down into the canyon! Fantastic! A lot of 'first-timers' are actually frightened! That leg—the diving—is a lot of switchbacks! One after the other! At one place I know, you can look down and see the front section of this train on two different levels of the track! Unreal!"

The others—even her husband—were spell bound! Even Tiger, at the lady's exciting account of what Tiger had seen before! "Of course, once the down starts, that's when we leave the snow behind!" Alex asked, "And there's really snow when we climb to the Continental Divide?"

"Sure, honey, as soon as light gets up, you'll see that we are already into—up to—snow level! There's snow outside now!" Alex leaned to a window, peered out, but it was still too dark.

When the 'story-teller' realized the others were getting anxious about sunrise, she cut her tale short, "Down, down, it gets hot—palm trees, fruit trees, crops ripe. At the bottom, the tracks follow the Rio Fuerte on to about San Blas, and then on to Los Mochis. End of trip." Everyone thanked her, then quickly they all got on heavier clothes for 'outside'—it was coming daylight.

Standing at the front door, before any of the others went out, the owner gave a very clear warning. He was serious and very stern, "Under no conditions—none what so ever—do any of you—no one—stick anything—hands, arms, and especially legs, out beyond the edge of the flat car! Understand? Any questions?" He waited then Alex asked. "Why? What's the problem?" "Tunnels—bridges—cliffs—and even trees! The passenger cars in front, fairly well keep it clean—knocked back—broke off—but only to the size and shape of the outside of the passenger cars!" He waited again. "There are tunnels? Bridges?" "That's right, Little Lady—eighty six tunnels and thirty-seven bridges—one is the highest above the water below in all of the Americas!" he added, "And there aren't any lights inside the tunnels!"

As they filed out the passenger's front door, he stopped Alex and Tiger, said to the both of them, "The others know this—so I'm telling you two. There's a rope strung between cleats on the driver's side—that's where most of the spectacular views will be—hang on to the rope when you're along that side of the RV, Of course, you can hold on to

A the rearview mirrors also! Got it?" "Yes, thanks, that's nice to know!" Alex responded. She had already envisioned clawing holes in the metal siding of the RV!

Outside, Alex screamed to Tiger, "There really is snow! Look at the patches in the shade!" Everyone had to speak loudly because of the rumbling of the train. The scene, the scenery, was much, much more awesome than either the 'story-teller' or Tiger had conveyed to Alex! Passing through the colonial town of Cuauhtemoc, the route really began to climb, at the village of La Junta, they were on the top of the Divide. On one side, it fell off to the East—the other, to the West!

The eight of them staggered, grabbed things, grabbed each other as they got their 'sea-legs' against the jostling of the train's movement. Uphill, it wasn't moving very fast. Alex guessed the speed to be only about ten or occasionally fifteen miles per hour. "It's cold", Alex shouted to the owner, she added, "Why is it so cozy inside?" "Thermostatically controlled propane heater!" he replied.

A pattern of activity soon developed; dash out the door with a foam cup of hot coffee or hot chocolate. "Only foam or cheap plastic containers allowed outside, in case you have to 'pitch' it, to grab on!" the owner's wife had announced early on—stay until you've had enough of the amazing scene—or got cold, stagger, bump, grab and make your way back inside. Then snack—the Texas women had set out muffins, cookies, hot tortillas, hot sauna, sliced cheese and sliced ham. One lady said to Alex and Tiger, "Eat up! You both look as if you could use some meat on your bones!" By comparison, true, Tiger, and Alex in particular, were the smallest on-board.

Standing close to the driver's outside mirror of the RV, Tiger held on to the mirror's brace with one hand—she faced forward. Alex had turned around and faced Tiger with the intention of asking her a question. Swiftly Tiger grabbed her around the shoulders, pulled Alex tight. "What are y—" The darkness was complete! And abruptly! The sound was as if someone, somehow, had slammed it all into Alex's ears at once! Alex jerked, more from fright than anything! Tiger squeezed her tighter, screamed, "Tunnel! Don't move! Hang on to me!" As suddenly as it had started, it was over! They were out of the tunnel. Alex quickly learned to watch out for tunnels! And she remembered the owner's warning—there would be eighty-five more! In several cases, a few tunnels were in rapid succession—one right after the other! Some more were like the first one, short and quickly over. Others were rather long, some even curved.

Alex and Tiger learned if they made their way along the driver's side—using the 'safety-line'—to the rear of the RV, they could sit on the rear bumper, spread their feet for balance, and be out of the wind. Best of all, they faced the rising sun most of the time, The generator's motor must have been just inside the skin here, there was a warm area to the rear metal panels.

As the train slowed for the stop at Creel, Tiger looked forward around the RV, and sensed a longer than usual stop—she had seen a larger than normal crowd at the terminal up ahead. The train's schedule didn't seemed fixed, the Conductor controlled it accordingly to the situation, not his watch. Suddenly, Tiger yelled, "Alex! You got your money?" "Sure! Why?" "Come on! Let's run! Forward!" Tiger shouted as she started to run! "We'll be back! I guess!" Alex shouted back to the owner as she tried to catch up with Tiger. They broad jumped, from one flat car to the next, dashed around the other vehicles and people—the 'riders'. Alex screamed, "Tiger! Where are we going?" "Sightseeing! Into the passenger cars! And the diner! Hurry!"

Jumping to the rear of the 'last' passenger car, and almost falling through the door, then inside, Alex gasped, flopped down on a seat, said, "Tig—I'm out of breath—wait—" "No! You'll miss seeing the Indians! Come on!" as she jerked Alex to her feet. They ran, pushed, shoved their way forward—through the cars, through the vestibules. Suddenly, at one of the vestibules, Tiger stopped, leaned out as far as possible, and jerked Alex to her side, screamed, "See? There are the Tarahunara Indians!" Alex pushed tight against the handrail, bend forward, snapped "Those small people? They're the Big Bad Indians? And—and—what is that?" she pointed to a group of small skinny men that stood slightly aside from the other Indians. "Those are the 'runners', the competitors, must be either the beginning, or the end of a race!" "But—they only have on baggy diapers! And strap sandals! And it is snowing! And what are they doing—kicking around 'something'? A ball! Damn! I never—"

Tiger laughed, hugged Alex, and started to explain as it continued to snow lightly. "They run foot races—never short ones—for miles and miles, even hundreds of miles! No regulated stops—rest periods—run day and night, stopping only when an individual runner wants to!" Alex had continued to stare at the runners who were constantly kicking about the 'somethings', she asked Tiger, "And those things—white, and about the size of a softball?" "Wooden balls, hand carved to a specific size—they kick those along the trail as they race! Have to start with it on the ground, can't touch it with anything except their feet, and they have to finish the race with their ball—and it still on the ground." "Sounds serious!" Alex remarked. "It is, very serious. Each village that sponsors a runner bets a certain amount of corn. If one village increases the amount of the bet, the others have to match that, or withdraw their runner." "Like poker!" "Yes, like poker, and also like poker, the winner takes all! There are no second or third place prizes!" "Wow! Now that is serious!"

The train gave a jerk, Tiger headed for the door, "Come on Alex, let's go to the diner!" As they went forward in the diner, the headwaiter led them to two chairs next to the window on the left side. Tiger whispered to Alex, "We're in luck—this side is where the fantastic views will be." "You mean we're not to the fantastic part yet?" "Oh, no! Not yet! But just out of Creel—south—the fantastic begins!"

"You want to eat? Say breakfast?" Tiger asked. "Well, I've snacked—but—'what-da-hell', let's eat! You order for both of us!" Tiger ordered, and ordered—the waiter brought food, and brought food. As they stuffed, Alex thought 'the kid didn't want to travel like a rich Gringa, but she sure doesn't mind eating like one!'

Tiger continued her tale about the 'Tara' runners; "—locked away from any women—fed only specially prepared corn and 'corn' water—the winner get his pick of the women after the race—or, if a 'poor' showing, a 'screw-up', he can become an 'outcast'." She finished with a story about the one occasion when the Olympic Games were in Mexico—the best of the 'Tara' runners were entered in the marathon—all the 'Taras' out ran all the other competitors by hours! But they were later disqualified." "Disqualified? For what?" Alex asked. "For betting! Betting among themselves!" They laughed, Alex asked, "Have they ever entered again?" "No, said they wouldn't bother if they couldn't bet!" They laughed again!

While eating, the two enjoyed the beautiful scenes outside the windows; the canyon sides had gotten closer together—these became much steeper, more like cliffs—with more rocky outcroppings and less trees. The scenes, across and down into the deep canyon, were indeed fantastic now! And the train now followed the very edge of the rim of the canyon—in some places, only feet from the edge! The train's path began to wind as it followed the canyon, it was no longer nearly as straight.

Suddenly, Tiger shouted "I see it! I see it!" She jumped up and waved frantically to the waiter—and called him. From reaction, Alex also stood and waved. "What?" Alex asked Tiger. "El Divisadero! We have to get out here!" Alex quickly settled with the waiter and followed Tiger.

Leaving through the rear door, she went to the side of the vestibule—the canyon side—"We aren't going to run, hop and skip back to the vehicles?" Alex asked as she squeezed next to Tiger. "No, we'll get off here!" "We can actually get off?" "The train has a thirty minute wait here—for sightseeing, taking pictures, shopping, whatever! We'll get off, spend some time, not long—we have to move fast because we'll have to run to the flat car and climb up!" As Alex glanced at her watch, she thought, 'Nothing like experience—And for a gal barely twenty, Tiger seems to have experience!'

They ran across the huge apron, dodged the vendors, went directly to the pipe handrail. Where they stood, it pavement overhung the wall of the canyon under their feet. Spreading her arms out straight to each side, Tiger shouted, "There! Alex! Is the most fantastic view of all from the top of the entire canyon!" Alex was dumbfounded at the scene! And it was—as she had heard so many times—fantastic! Just Fantastic! In silence, the two stood and stared. Twisting in both directions, Alex saw that the canyon—the magnificent views—extended farther than she could see! Alex looked down—it was deep! So deep, the river appeared as a silver thread. "You know, it is deeper than 'your' Grand Canyon", Tiger commented when she noticed Alex's stare at the bottom far below. "And, back toward Creel, it is wider than the Grand Canyon", she added. Alex just shook her head in wonder, then asked, "Is it longer, also?" "Yes, it is." Alex grabbed and hugged Tiger, shouted, "Oh! Tiger! I can't imagine a bigger surprise! Thank you so much! This is indeed a surprise! I never expected any thing so beautiful! So—so—shockingly wonderful! I'll never forget this moment!" Alex pulled the two of them tightly together and kissed Tiger hard on her lips.

'Ding-ding', it was Alex's watch—she had set it for fifteen minutes from when the train had stopped rolling. "Time's up, Tiger—maybe we should, as it's said, 'make a run for it'!"

As the Texans on 'their' flat car saw Alex and Tiger running toward them, they whooped, yelled and called out! One of the men got the ladder and helped the two aboard. The RV owner's wife hugged them, said, "I didn't think we'd ever see you two again! We thought you two were skipping-out, maybe even running from the Law!" They all laughed, Alex responded, "Nope! Just checking out the passenger cars!" One of the other Texas ladies added, "That's some way to just see the inside of the passenger cars! I thought you two were 'death-wishers', or something else not normal!" More laughter.

Alex stepped to 'Betsy', unlocked the doors, opened the driver's side rear door, and backing up to the end of the seat, she fell backward, shouted, "Man! What a morning!" Someone shouted back, "Alex! We're just coming to the good part!" She raised, twisted her head toward the 'Texas' group called back, "You're kidding, aren't you?" "Nope—this has been just the 'fluff' part—the first half! The next half is the ass-puckering section!" As she fell back in on her back, she shouted, "Jezz! How much fun can one have!" The others laughed.

The train jerked, and began to roll. Tiger joined Alex, opened the driver's door and fell in on her back. The others returned to inside the Winnibago. A brief silence, then Tiger softly said, "Get ready, Alex, for the thrill of a lifetime." Alex didn't respond to Tiger, she slowly got out and left. Soon, she returned with two large plastic 'glasses' full of ice cubes, and her bottle of tequila, and said, "Let the fun and thrills begin! And my ass can pucker all it wants to!" Tiger smiled at Alex as she took one of the glasses and waited while Alex poured it half full of straight tequila. Alex poured her own drink, then they touched the rims together, Tiger remarked, "You'll never know how much I appreciate this trip." "No problem, Kid, let's just enjoy!"

The canyon walls became closer together and the cliffs along it became even steeper. Alex was standing between the open door and the door's opening—she had her backside braced against the framing around the door opening. With her right hand, she held onto the top of the door's window frame. She sipped the tequila from the plastic container—there wasn't much left and only a few ice cubes. Alex glanced toward the RV—all six of the Texans were sitting on the front bumper. Each man had one arm around his mate's shoulders. The other hand gripped a rope that they had rigged across the front. They looked—they stared unblinkingly—slightly to the left of dead ahead. And they all looked serious—not a smile on anyone.

"What the—", Alex turned and looked in the same direction—slightly left of center, forward—"Wholly crap!" She snapped, she clamped tighter to the window frame, her entire body went rigid—drum tight! The forward cars, as these swung left slowly were gradually disappearing from her view—the cars were smoothly dropping out of sight—dropping over the rim of the canyon! Her mind instantly popped-up all sorts of images; Wreck! We've been derailed! Hi-jacked! But there's no dust, no loose steam, no flames—maybe the entire train is free-falling in the open air, headed to crash in one tremendous pile at the very bottom of the canyon! The flat car with the vehicles directly in front of Alex began the slow swing to the left, then the slow dive down. She tightened every part of her body even tighter—especially her ass!

As their car went over the edge, the Texas lady who had not been on this trip before screamed! Great idea, Alex's brain signaled, she opened her mouth very wide, but nothing would come out! She just gasped! Once their car was pointed down—the angle was steep, but it was about the same as the cars in front of them. The forward cars were now clearly visible as they descended. The railroad bed was cut into the side of the canyon wall! The engine and the first few cars below were going around a switchback, now headed in the opposite direction. Below there, another switchback headed the tracks back in the original direction—and another switchback even lower!

Feeling 'better'? Or'safer'? Now that Alex could see where the train was headed, and seeing the cars up front were all in good condition, she somewhat relaxed. She felt something wet on her left thigh. Looking down she saw her left hand, she had crushed the plastic container into a tight ball around the few remaining ice cubes! The melted ice continued to drip on her thigh. "Whew! I thought I'd pissed in my pants!" she said out loud as she slung the ball of plastic over the side. She thought 'that was the reason for no glass containers outside!

For hours, the train switch backed its way downward and southwest. Alex's first sight of debris—the scattered remnants of rail cars along the bottom of the canyon far below sent shivers up and down her spine. The canyon gradually became more confined as they went deeper into it. The railroad tactics changed—bridges! And bridges—back and forth across the canyon—each bridge lower than the previous one. Crossing one bridge, Alex was able to count ten bridges in easy view! All this time still headed down and west. The vegetation slowly changed, it became tropical! The air became much warmer.

Realizing there was little possibility of the air becoming cold again, Alex said to Tiger, "I'm going to change clothes—change to something a lots cooler! You?" "Sure, why not!" While Alex opened the tailgate, she glanced at the Texans who were still seated on the bumper, they seemed to be interested in the fantastic scenes—she decided to not bother them. Tiger asked, "Where? When?" "Here! Now!" was Alex's simple reply. They picked out and laid in order what they would put on. The stripping order was; scarves, jackets, shoes and the heavy socks, jeans, pantyhose, shirts, then tee shirts last—keep the panties. As Alex and Tiger stripped, in unison, down to the pantyhose, they turned, backed their butts to the edge of the floor and started the struggle with the hoses. Alex cast a quick look up—the Texans were still looking away. Hose off, then the loose shirts, and as they pulled off the tee shirts, they were down to panties only. The applause began.

Alex and Tiger turned, faced the RV, all of the Texans were clapping, and smiling. The men added, "Take it off! Take it off!" as they laughed. Alex and Tiger smiled at each other, nodded, faced the others, gave them a slight bow. The two slowly wiggled their panties to the floor of the flat car, more applause, even 'cat-calls and whistles. Even a few "Poco Chihuahua" for Alex's 'hairlessness'. Show just started—Alex and Tiger slowly got dressed—taking each piece, showing it to 'their' audience then slowly wiggling into it. The two wound up dressed in short-shorts, crop tops and strap sandals. They both got out their larger shoulder strap purses—they had to, these outfits didn't have pockets!

Alex shut the tailgate, got the tequila then they joined the Texans. To the man that had warned about the 'puckering situation, Alex gave a Hi-five, he returned it, she said, "You were right! That's about the tightest 'pucker' I've had in years!" They fixed another round of drinks—Alex and Tiger had tequila on the rocks.

The 'Story-teller', the owners wife, caught Alex and Tiger off to one side—they were all back inside now—and she gently asked, "Not that it is any of my business, not that it matters—are you gals 'Pros'?" Alex and Tiger smiled at each other, then Alex thought, 'what the hell, these people have been so nice—'. She slowly opened her purse as she said "As a matter of fact, we are", she removed her official identification badge—'Department of Agriculture, Miss Alexandra Hawkins, Special Agent'— and handed it to the Texas lady. Tiger saw the game plan, she removed her, Archaeologist badge—'Department of Interior, Miss Margarita Calienta Morley, Special Projects Director', she also handed it to the older lady. The Texan stared then slowly shook her head. She turned toward the front where the others were, called out, "Hey! Everyone! Look here! We've got two very special young ladies here!"

All close around and the badges passed to each other, one of the men asked, "This—Special Agent, Alex, that's for real?" "Licensed to kill real! Got my own semi-automatic pistol with me!" She slipped out the 40 caliber, double-stack, removed the clip, slipped the breech back just far enough to check the barrel to be sure it was empty. Keeping the clip, she handed him her favorite gun. All the Texans were very impressed! The owner started, "Sorry, I, we, thought you two—" Alex interrupted, "A couple of poor gals 'hooking' our way across country! We've heard that before!" She and the others laughed. She added, "And that's exactly what we want people to think—so—please, keep it under wrap, Ok?" "No problem—

none what so ever!", the Texans agreed. "I take it you two are on assignment?" One man asked. "Yes, and all we can say is, we're going to talk to someone." "I take it a telephone call will not work?" As Alex slapped the clip back in her pistol and stuffed it to the bottom of her purse, she narrowed her black eyes, stared into his eyes, gave the man a tiny sly-smile, replied, "No, that wouldn't work." He didn't ask any more questions, but he thought, 'I wouldn't want to be in that poor bastard's shoes!'

Someone asked Tiger, "And you—you're an archaeologist! Are you on this same assignment?" "Yes, I'm the interpreter—the person only speaks Tzental." Not knowing anything else to ask that they couldn't get answers to, their attention returned to the travel scenes outside, they went back outside.

The train was finally to the bottom of the canyon. It now followed the Rio Fuerta for hours. Tiger pointed out several different groups of women as they washed their clothes in the edge of the river—these scenes were very close to where the train passed.

It started to approach darkness—sunset—Tiger and Alex got busy straightening out their things in the rear of the station wagon—the Texans had told them it would be about midnight when the vehicles were unloaded and the railroad yard would be very dark, almost no lights at all.

To view the sunset, everyone gathered along the passenger's side of the RV and watched the brilliant display of nature. There was still about five more hours of traveling left.

In the darkness, village lights could be seen—some at great distances away. As the train stopped at San Blas, they knew they were only a hour or so out of Los Mochis—the end of this journey.

When the train slowed as it approached the yards at Los Mochis, the owner of the RV filled Alex in on the unloading procedure. Then they all said good-byes and thanks to each other. Alex And Tiger moved into 'Betsy' and got ready to be unloaded.

While the two of them waited—their seat belts tight, the engine warming up, the transmission in neutral, the interior light on, Alex remarked, "I've been f—ked a lot, but I can say, this is the first time I have ever waited to get forked!" They laughed—until the bright headlights of the mammoth forklift rushed to their side and jostled them up in the air! When the forklift sat them down and backed away, Alex drove forward. "What—where—do—" she terminated that question, answered herself, "I know! Follow the crowd!" Tiger laughed, said, "You catch on quickly, Alex!"

For a few miles, there was no problem—all the vehicles were headed in one direction—toward the city lights. Realizing they were downtown and the traffic she had been following had now scattered in different routes, Alex began to cruise as the two of them looked for a cheap hotel. Spotting a likely one, she slowed and looked for a parking place—the closest was about a half block from the hotel.

As Alex jockeyed into the tight spot—it was directly in front of an all-night bar—Tiger asked, "Is there anything from in here that we need for tonight? Anything you want?" Alex finally got parked, replied, "Just maybe that half bottle of tequila—I might want a slug to help me sleep!" Tiger reached over into the back and got the bottle. There was not a bag for it. "Anything else?" "Nope! Got money, got my gun," she patted her purse, added, "Got my ass! Now, if that hotel just has a room!"

After being sure she had the car keys in her purse, Alex checked the doors and the tailgate to see that these were locked. Still wearing their short-shorts, crop-tops, strap sandals and their shoulder strap purses and Alex holding the half full bottle of tequila, they looked as if they were 'in business'. Heading toward the hotel, two of the several guys leaned against the front of the bar quickly fell in behind them. Nearly half way to the hotel the guys got closer. "Do you think those two could be trouble?" Alex asked. Tiger suddenly stopped, whipped around, and in rapid-fire Spanish said 'something' to the men. Without saying a word, the two immediately turned and headed back toward the bar. Going on toward the hotel, Alex asked, "What did you say to them?" "I just asked if they had one hundred dollars, US, each!" then she added, "With our strap sandals, they probably thought we were a couple of amateurs that just walked out of the jungle!" Alex took Tiger's elbow, remarked, "Oh, Tig, you say the cutest things!"

In luck, they were able to get a room—the clerk had first asked if they wanted it for the night, or by the hour—but a room with only one double bed. And the bath was 'down the hall'—no problem with that, they would use the toilet first. But the price was cheap. Very cheap, Tiger had argued the price down. As they climbed the stairs, Alex led, the room was on the third floor. Alex suddenly stopped, and chuckled. "What?" Tiger asked. "Kid, if I keep hanging out with you—haggling about a buck here, a buck there—I might forget how much money I really have!" Tiger laughed, and poked Alex in her butt, said, "Gettyup, rich Gringa!" Alex jumped and they both laughed.

The room left a lot to be desired; one dim light bulb hung from the center of the high ceiling, a small table and two straight back wooden chairs, and 'the' bed—a double bed? Not quiet, more like a single bed with only a few inches in width added. They quickly stripped, but Alex kept on her watch. After nearly three years of not wearing a watch, she was again back in the habit. In the bed, with the sheet pulled up, they both laid on their right sides, Alex said, "If I count to three, on 'three', roll over!" Tiger barely chuckled. Suddenly Alex realized she was 'bushed—very tired, and not normal for her, she was very sleepy. Softly Tiger asked, "What time is it?" Alex thought 'Who cares!', but she looked at her watch, replied, "It's two a.m." "What day does your watch show?" Alex again looked, replied, "Saturday, February, the sixteenth." She thought she would save Tiger the next question. But Tiger waited, and Alex anticipated something— anxiously, she asked, "Tiger, what difference can that make? The time, whatever?" "Think Alex, it is past midnight, a Friday night—and I have not heard, or seen, any indications about sex from you—since—I can't remember when. Nothing at all, today or tonight." Alex grabbed Tiger's left shoulder, pulled her over—they were face to face—responded, "And I—", she wasn't sure how to say it, explain it, "And I—haven't heard a single thing from that bitch-you-know-who! Has she gone away? Gone at last?" Tiger hugged and pulled Alex very close, and very tight as Alex began to sob. Alex cried herself to sleep in Tiger's embrace. Later, Tiger drifted off.

CHAPTER 8

Rolling over to her back, Tiger swung her arm out, it hit only the mattress—something was wrong, different! She quickly propped up on her hands and looked around the small room. Alex was gone. Jumping up, she jerked on her shorts and top and noticed that Alex's clothes, shoes and purse were gone. She stepped closer to the small table and looked at the bottle of tequila—the level seemed to be the same as when Alex sat it down last night. A quick check of the bath—she used the toilet—but still no Alex.

Running down to the lobby—still no sign of Alex—she went directly to the skinny man behind the counter. "Have you seen a young lady, slightly older than me, short black hair, black eyes, dressed like me?" "Yes, she left about a hour ago." He replied. "Do you know where she went?" "Maybe she's working—on her back!" as he gave a s—t eating grin. Without thinking or hesitation, Tiger grabbed his tie and snatched him forward, hard into the counter, almost over the counter, said, "You slimy bastard! She is a—", 'fine lady' were the words intended, but the front door flying open interrupted her.

It was Alex—she had kicked the door open with her foot—she had the two large and the two small 'Mitla' bags, her purse, and a plastic bag which contained papers and booklets. Alex stopped, looked at the scene at the counter, but she didn't bother to ask, instead she shouted, "Tiger! We've got to hurry!" Stepping to Tiger, she added, "Here! Take these two, those are your bags! Come on upstairs, we've got to get dressed-up!"

Tiger relaxed her pull, but still holding his tie, she pushed very hard, this slammed the clerk into the rear wall. He choked and coughed as he struggled to loosen the tie.

Running up the stairs, Tiger asked, "What's up? Are we going some-where?" "Yes! I found a Travel Agency close bye! Made a deal! We're going to La Paz!" "That's on the Baja!""Yes! We'll be a couple of 'Baja Babes! The ferry leaves at ten! That's why we have to rush!" Inside the room, Alex dropped her stuff, said, "No time for showers! We can just wash our faces, do our teeth—" she lifted one arm, sniffed toward her armpit, continued, "And I can wash under there!" Over the pass years with and around Tiger, she had learned the Maya were not plagued with that problem.

Completing the bath business, they quickly picked out what they would wear; short skirts, dress blouses, medium comfortable heels and panties—it was too hot for pantyhose and modest jewelry. Then the two began to re-pack what they would carry with them on the ferry; cocktail dresses, spike heels, tongs, dress jewelry, nightgowns—and if these weren't 'needed', two old loose sleeping tee shirts. And their bathing suits— Alex held up Tiger's, said, "Really, Kid, this is—well—'homey' old fashioned!" As stuffed it in the bag, she added, "We'll just have to find you something 'modern'!" These articles were combined and packed into one of the larger bags, they also combined their make-up stuff and their identification articles—along with Alex's pistol—were packed into one of the small Mitla. This was stuffed inside the larger one. They finished with only one large Mitla to carry on the ferry. The rest would be locked away in Betsy.

Alex quickly drove—passing in tight situations, running red lights and stop signs, driving as fast as possible—through the traffic of Los Mochis and continued on to the port town of Topolobampo. This was where the dock for the ferry was. Parking the station Wagon in the 'protected' area— the sign indicated 24 hour guards—they boarded as deck passengers.

Leaving the shoreline behind, the huge ship style ferry was soon in the open sea. Then Alex told Tiger that she had gotten hotel reservations being as they were on a tight schedule. Alex added. "And it—the hotel room—was the cheapest thing the Agent had a listing for, The Hotel Arcos, downtown La Paz. See? I learning, aren't I? I'm beginning to see things your way!" Tiger tilted her head to Alex, hugged her, replied, "Oh, Alex, and I'm beginning to see things your way! If you want to spend money, go ahead!" Alex hugged her back, "Thanks, I needed that!" The two went to the bar, got a couple of fancy drinks and returned to stare over the rail at the beautiful deep blue Sea of Cortez.

After a while, Alex slipped her arm around Tiger's waist, softly said, "This is really a fantastic vacation. I can't remember when was the last time I have enjoyed so much. No computer writing, no hustling, no petty competition, just relaxing—go with the flow." Tiger put her arm around Alex's petite waist.

The ferry docked at La Paz about three, after catching a taxi, by four p.m., the two stood on the balcony of their room—it was on the second floor—in the Hotel Los Arcos. They stared at the bay offshore. The hotel was Spanish architecture, highlighted with archways, courtyards and fountains. As they had passed through downstairs, they had noticed the two swimming pools, a disco, and the restaurants—there were more than one. The hotel was ocean front, and within easy walking distance of shopping, markets and all types of small businesses.

Alex turned toward the room, reached back, caught Tiger's wrist, said, "Come on, Kid, it's time to shop for you a new bathing suit!" Shopping wasn't easy—there was so much! Small shops that specialized— one after the other—almost anything imaginable! And open-air restaurants, snack stands, and bars of all sorts. It had been about a hour of browsing, and after returning to the sidewalk following another round of fancy drinks on a deck that overhung the water, Alex asked, "How late do you think these shops will be open?" "As long as they can see a potential customer in sight!" "Great! I think we'll need all the time we can get! We've got to concentrate Swimwear! Swimwear!"

Holding up the two small pieces and lightly shaking these, Tiger remarked, "These weight, what? Probably less than two ounces? And for that price!" "It isn't how much it weighs! Or how much it costs! It is how much it shows!" Alex had encouraged Tiger to review only white Bikini 'tongs'. "White shows off your beautiful skin tone. Try it on!" She did, then returned and twisted about for Alex to see it. The 'suit' was two very small triangles—these barely covered Tiger's nipples—with spaghetti straps, and a tiny 'tong' bottom—mostly only the waist strap and the two short, vertical parts showed—the rest was 'hidden', buried in her crotch.

"Great! Just right! Beautiful!" Alex exclaimed, then she reached to Tiger's crotch, pinched a tuft of hair, added, "We may as well hunt a safety razor—this—", she gently pulled the hair, "has got to go!"

Tiger changed back to her skirt and blouse while Alex paid the clerk with a credit card. "You got a couple of those thin—see through—beach blouses—jumpers? In both our sizes, in white?" Alex asked the clerk. "Sure, no problem!" She quickly located these. "How about low crowned, wide brimmed fancy hats? White of course." "No, no hats. Hats, you can get next door." "Thanks", as she paid for the 'jumpers'.

After buying hats, and back on the sidewalk, Alex said "Beach towels! We've got to have beach towels!" "No! There's something down here that is better! It's a woven mat—sometimes woven from real reeds, tiny reeds, sometimes from plastic that looks like reeds. You can roll these into very small bundles—these hold no sand, and can't get wet!" "Ok, two reed mats it'll be!" They searched and shopped on. They found and bought two mats. With the mats, the other clothes, they needed a new straw beach bag, the kind with the large looped handles. And the new beach jumpers needed new strap sandals—with straps up nearly to their knees and high platform heels. And the outfits needed hew fancy sunglasses!

When they remembered the razors, Tiger asked, "Have you got plenty of suntan lotion?" "No, didn't need any in North Georgia—and what I had at my place at Lake Lanier was stolen!" At the drug store, after selecting lotion, razors, and a small can of shaving cream, Alex picked out a box of condoms. Showing these to Tiger, she whispered, "Just in case—besides— I've lost track of when I had my last cup of your 'special' tea." Tiger just nodded and smiled at Alex.

It was a little before eight when they got back to the hotel room. They quickly removed the tags from the new items, then they stripped, and Alex helped Tiger shave—they both decided to clean shave her entire crotch. They showered, primped and got dressed for a night on the town—or whatever. Downstairs, in the largest restaurant, they both ate grilled lobster, small salads and a common side dish of asparagus with sauce, with a bottle of California champagne.

About midnight in the disco—they had danced some with each other, then a couple of nice looking guys got interested, after dancing with them and while the men were away, Alex patted Tiger's hand and said, "I, we, are going to slip upstairs to our room. If you want in, tap three times, wait, tap three more times. I'll probably see you in—say—two, hours at the most. Ok?" "Ok, I'll be right here." Tiger smiled as she replied, then she added, more seriously, as she held Alex's hand hard to the table, "You aren't having problems, are you? Problems with 'her'?" "Hell no! Just good clean fun! I could just as well skip this!" "Ok! Have fun!" Tiger encouraged.

In less then a hour, Alex and her 'date' returned to the table, but before she could sit down, Tiger stood and motioned her head in the direction of the 'ladies' room. As they straightened their make-up using the huge mirror in the restroom, Tiger asked, "Well? How was it?" "Let me say, he isn't no Tom-the-Terrible! But Ok, I guess—" Another young lady—looked USA, California type, mid-twenties—stepped to almost between Alex and

Tiger, she said, "Please excuse me, couldn't help hearing, but you were talking about that 'dude' you left with?" "You noticed, did you?" "Yes, he has kind of caught my attention, just wondering—" Alex touched her arm with one set of her fingers, said, "Well, Honey, if you like 'lickin' better than 'the other', then he's your man. Sure knows exactly where the 'little lady in the boat' is!" The three laughed, Alex added, "If you want to, come back to our table and I'll introduce you to him." She nodded. Turning to Tiger, Alex remarked, "If you're ready, we'll take a hike, get some fresh air—try that place down the street, the one that overhangs the water—the one with a bandstand." "Suits me, I can see this disco thing is going no where!" Tiger replied.

The open-air dance bar was a wild scene! The music was live, loud and hetic! The people were mostly local young men and 'foreign' Baja Babes! Everyone danced with everyone! Alex and Tiger switched to tequila slammers, a much bigger 'production' here than in New Orleans! After a hour or so, as Alex was returned by a guy not much larger than she, she flopped down, Tiger too had just flopped down, Alex said, "Tig! I done shook my 'boddy' till I just can't shook it no mo!" "Time to turn in!" Tiger helped Alex to her feet, got their purses and settled the bar bill with Alex's credit card. Helping Alex sign the tab, they headed for the hotel.

In their room, Alex kicked off her spikes, fell face down on 'her' huge double bed—there were two beds, both huge! She mumbled, "Early-tomorrow—we go to a very quiet beach—soak up sun—relax—", she dozed off. Alex didn't wake up as Tiger 'skinned' her white slip-dress up and over her head. And Tiger folded the beautiful bed cover over Alex's naked body.

Alex fell someone shake her hip—and through her mind's fog, she made out, "Alex! Get up! If you want to go to the beach! Get up!" Alex pushed up with her arms and hands, replied. "Ok! Ok! I'm up!" "I've got your swim suit, your new beach jumper, your new sandals laid out! Get dressed!" Tiger encouraged. "I've got to piss and brush my teeth first!" Tiger helped her to the bathroom. Alex came out drying her face, asked, "I'm guessing you have found out where we're going?" "Yes, a little village, Las Cruces, about twenty miles North-East of here. The desk clerk said it was beautiful, quiet, and 'native'. And we could catch a taxi to there!" Alex held her head with both hands, muttered, "I need a drink." "No, no, you need to put some clothes on your little white ass!" And Tiger began to help her get dressed.

At the end of the unpaved road was a small village, all native with local style of construction. Beyond, was the beautiful, deep blue Sea of Cortez. Along the white sand beach were several palapas—thatched roofs on poles with no sides. And there was only a handful of people, all locals and mostly kids. After getting out with their beach bag, Tiger paid the driver and again emphasized the importance of him returning about two o'clock—no later than three, the ferry left La Paz at five—and carrying them back to the Hotel Los Arcos. He promised, and promised.

"Gorgeous! Beautiful! Mas bonito!" Alex exclaimed as she stood and looked about. Close by was one snack/beer/drink stand. The sides had not been opened yet, but the taxi man insured the two that it would open soon. And it would have food, very good food! Finding the perfect spot— at one end of a palapa they could put the beach bag and their other items in the shade and lay in the early morning sun, then move into the shade without actually re-locating. They put their gear under this palapa then removed their covers, hats and sandals. At Tiger's insistence, the two went for a quick dip then walked along the beach while they dripped dry. Returning to the palapa, they rolled out the new mats and lay down. Tiger applied a liberal coat of suntan lotion all over Alex. She only put some on her own shoulders, nose, and the tops of her feet.

After about an hour of lying in the sun, they repeated the first routine— except while strolling, kicking the sand and looking for seashells, Tiger broke the silence. "Do you think you and Tom will ever get married?" Alex stopped walking, she wavered, even thou she had expected this question from Tiger, or the others for a long time, she still wasn't sure how to answer it. "I'm not sure—maybe Tom is too set in his ways—or doesn't want the responsibility—or has seen too much horror in his military days. Every time 'something' brings it up, like Nat and Jim's wedding, Tom just sidesteps, wanders off—alone again." She took a break, then, "And me? Hell, I don't even know me at times—" She stopped, stared into Tiger's eyes. "And?" Tiger asked, she sensed Alex wanted to say more. "I'm not sure about Miss Hawkins! How she would take it—us getting married. There! I got that out! Ok?" Tiger didn't reply, she took Alex's hand, started them walking again.

Tiger turned them back toward the palapa and the snack stand, said, "I see the drink place is open, let's get a beer! Or, several beers!" She laughed as she started swinging Alex's hand hard. "Ok! Let's race!" Alex snapped and jerked loose, got a head start on Tiger. But, as expected, Tiger beat her to the stand. Alex was out of breath, Tiger got out, "Dos cervezas, por favor!" When Alex was about half finished with the first beer, she strolled to where their gear was, dug out a handful of paso bills, returned to Tiger. Taking Tiger's hand, she placed the money in it, said, "You pay for this, what ever we get here—today."

Another round, then they went to the palapa and moved the mats into the shade. It was about eleven, Alex knew about avoiding the noonday sun, from eleven until one thirty or two. And she knew it was especially critical for her—with her extra white skin pigment and her natural hairless body, that did makes a difference, she was very easy to sunburn. She didn't avoid the sun, she loved to sunbath but she just had to start slowly.

When the two had laid down, just relaxing, Alex asked, "Tig, what about you two, you and Mike? Have you two discussed anything serious about getting married?" "Oh, Mike wants to get married, he asks me all the time. He wants a house full of kids!" She stopped. "So? What's the problem? You're young, as healthy as a horse, why wait?" "I'm not sure" she stopped. Alex asked, "Sure of what? You do love him, don't you?" "Sure! That's not the problem" again she hesitated. "Tiger! You're stalling! Tell me! You know you can tell me anything!" "It's my skin. I am dark. I couldn't bear it if Mike had to suffer—because of other's remarks, their reactions. And you and I both know it—my brown skin color—would show up in our kids! And how would they suffer? I can't take the chance! No! Not yet! Alex, you're Lilly white, you can't know how I feel!" Alex quickly replied, "You're right! The person who says 'I know how you feel' is a liar!"

Alex waited, she didn't press, but suddenly she lifted to her right elbow, turned to face Tiger, said, "Why can't the two of you live down here? Mike loves Mexico! And, if things go right with HVG—and I believe it will, I'm sure it will—after this first year, he would—might would—have to come to the States only a few times a year. Tiger, I haven't fully explained the business arrangements to you. If HVG is successful, we're all going to have a decent living's income! Forever! And Mike sure as hell wouldn't have to be in the USA all the time and go to some C.S. job every day! And for damn sure, your kids' skins are at home down here!

And Mike's white ass? Let him suntan it!" Tiger jumped up, almost screamed, "I never thought of that! You're right, Alex, that would work!" She dropped to her knees and kissed Alex hard on her lips.

The wonderful odor from the grill at the snack place seemed to drift under the palapa and fall directly down on their faces. Like cats, they jumped up from a half-sleep and ran to the source. Leaning over the counter, they saw; very large shrimp—the diameter of broom handles-spot-tail sea bass—about one pounders—cactus fronds and chili peppers, all being cooked on an old homemade grill. The fire was a bed of coals from palm frond stalks. Occasionally, the man would rip off a strip of banana leaf and lay it on the coals. Using an old brush, he would wipe the hot food with his own seasoning sauce from another old pot on the end of the grill.

He turned to them, asked "Si?" A quick collaboration, the two requested a single order; one fish, ten shrimp, one cactus 'pad' and one chili—split and smeared with the melted white cheese—Mozzarella, they guessed. The cheese was warming at one end of the grill in an old beat-up pot. And 'enough' tortillas. The serving platter was a well-worn metal cookie sheet. He brushed on a thin coating of the seasoning, placed the fish in the center and spred the shrimp around it. And spread slices of lime among the shrimp. The cactus and the cheese coated chili were put on a separate plate. The tortillas were wrapped in heavy brown paper. After placing the food between Tiger and Alex, he put out Tabasco sauce, salt, red pepper and two old forks. Without asking, he handed each of them a cold beer. They saluted him with their beers, clicked the bottles together and began to eat.

Almost finished—it all was delicious—Alex tilted far back, stared up, remarked, "Jezz! I'm going to turn into a butter-ball, and die of fat!" Tiger snickered, "You can't die from just being fat, Silly!" "How about dying from too much cholesterol!" Tiger nodded, "Now that, could get you!"

Back under the palapa, they were getting their stuff in carrying order when they heard the taxi's horn. They waved, and rushed. From then until the ferry sailed exactly at five, it was a blur of scrambling. But they made it! After watching the coastline disappear and before dark, Alex dug out their copy of the AAA map of Mexico. As she carefully studied it—mentally calculating some distances. Tiger asked, "What?" She sensed Alex was up to 'something' other than just returning to Los Mochis and spending the night. The ferry was scheduled to make Topolobampo about eleven P.M.

"I'm so refreshed, I'm thinking about driving straight through to Mazatlan!" "You're crazy! That would take—until sunrise—or later!" "It's only just over two hundred and sixty or seventy miles!" Tiger didn't respond. "You said the over-night—the long-haul—buses ran through the night, I'll just follow them!" "You want a beer? Or a drink?" Tiger side stepped Alex's idea. "No, I'm finished for tonight!" Tiger left, headed for the bar inside.

It had been a tiring haul, but once Alex got the hang of hooking-up with and drafting the huge—and fast—buses, she made good time. And Tiger had slept on the back seat all the way. Daylight began as she closely followed the 'last' bus into the edge of Mazatlan. Near the heart of the city, and as she realized the bus was going to turn into the station, she turned right on to a side street headed west. She knew the Pacific Ocean was west, she drove until she could see the ocean. She stopped at the stop sign for the Olas Avenue, it crossed in front of her, it was broad, and sweeping to follow the beach line. Alex glanced at her watch—she had re-set it to Mountain Time as they had arrived at Los Mochis—it showed 7:10 A.M., Monday morning. February 18th.

MEXICO CITY CENTRAL DATA PROCESSING BUILDING (Hidden 'somewhere', in a 'safe' place) Holding his coffee cup, the man, in his late thirties, stepped close to the computer terminal. He glanced at his watch. It showed 8:10 Central Time, Monday, February 18th. 'Right on schedule', he thought, 'and the same old routine—over and over—nothing ever develops with an interesting twist.' He switched on, booted-up, and punched-up the last twenty-four hours of entries to the SUA files. SUA was the acronym for Suspicious and Unusual Activities.

For the S portion, the computer had arranged the entries in alphabetical order, using the first letter of the last name of the persons 'suspected' of 'something'.

The U portion was arranged alphabetically by the first letter of different categories—such as; A for air, B for blast, etc.—these entries were filed, under a given category, by the first letter of where the unusual happening occurred.

The man at the computer was Antonio—Tony—Valdes. His job was to isolate any entries he thought needed additional investigation, then inform the proper authorities via electronic hook-up, or whatever method available. He had tight guidelines for the immediately dangerous down to petty thieves and drug dealers. It was almost impossible to investigate all suspicious activities—or suspicious persons. Tony's main responsibility was to narrow the field—reduce the number of investigations to a workable level.

He sat down and began with the S files; the boring entries came from many sources; Border Customs Stations, airport flight records, private plane flight plans, or just suspicious flights within Mexico. Or just observations by anyone via 'proper' channels. All the various departments of the—any—government were expected to report anything that seemed out of the ordinary.

The computer stored all the details of any entry, summarized this to a brief statement for easy review. Tony worked down the S list; such entries as; Brown, Joe, male, Caucasian, USA passport, 24 years old, crossed border at Ciudad Juarez three times between 10 A.M. and 2 P.M., Feb, llth. Suspect drug trafficking.

'So what', Tony thought, 'That's the other guys, the USA Border officers problem!' He moved fast on down the list. Then he came to; Hawkins, Alexandra.

'Hawkins, Alexandra, female, Caucasian, USA passport, 32 years old, crossed border at Ciudad Juarez, 5:45 P.M. Feb, 12th. Acceptable weapon's permit issued by USA Government. Suspect foul play.'

Tony stopped and stared at this entry. He wondered, 'What is the problem, Geni? The young lady has a permit, from the USA Government!' He quickly punched-up for all the details on file.

'Hawkins, Alexandra, female, Caucasian, USA passport, 32 years old, crossed border at Ciudad Juarez, 5:45 P.M. Feb. 12th. Acceptable identification as Special Agent for the USA Department of Agriculture, weapons permit issued by same Department; one 40 caliber DaWo semi-auto pistol, ser.no.143056. two clips, loaded.' The computer also listed the general physical description of Hawkins, and, continued with, vehicle description and details available. Also 'facial photo reproduction available on request.' Then the screen displayed, 'Hawkins, Alexandra accompanied by Morley, Margarita Calienta, female, Maya, USA passport, 21 years old.'

Tony held the display, leaned back, thought, 'Now this seems interesting even if not particularly dangerous—two young ladies, proper credentials, and one nice gun!' While still on Hawkins, he punched-in for the vehicle's info and the facial photo repro. The additional data identified the vehicle—one so-so older station wagon—and one very attractive face! While he had all the info on Hawkins 'up', he requested hard-copies. This process started, he went and got another cup of coffee.

Returning to his station—the printing cycle was completed—he shifted his search directly to Morley, Margarita Calienta, and commanded up all the details available.

'Morley, Margarita Calienta, female, Maya, USA passport, 21 years old, crossed border at Ciudad Juarez, 5:45 P.M. Feb.12th. Acceptable identification as Archaeologist, Special Project Director, for USA Department of Interior.' As he looked at the face displayed, he thought, 'Definitely Maya, and also a real 'looker'!' He tilted back, sipped his coffee then requested hard-copies to be printed. While this went on, he leaned back again, and thought, 'Morley, a beautiful face, and her physical descriptions indicated a nice size, but—but—an Archaeologist? And a Project Director? At only twenty-one? And traveling with a Special Agent? A Special Agent with a semi-automatic 40 caliber pistol! And they drove down—into—Mexico in an old station wagon? Did they drive from D.C.? And both had listed their destinations as Mexico City—What's wrong with a direct flight from the USA to Mexico City?

The printer finished, he got the papers for Hawkins and Morley together, placed these in a file folder, wrote on the front, 'check 2/25 for additional info'—this would allow one week for more data to come in. He then put the folder in his file drawer. Back to the computer, he activated the 'notification' portion of the SUA program, and entered Hawkins and Morley to the 'Special Notice' list. Then he entered the departments he decided to notify; The Department of Agriculture, The Department of Interior, and Senora Gomez—because of the 'gun' situation, and the 'Special Agent' from the USA. 'They could decide what to do next', Tony thought. He was finished with Hawkins and Morley for the time being.

As he typed in Senora Gomez's name, he remembered her 'official' positions—yes, more than one! Senora Gomez, private secretary to El President—and Colonel Gomez, Head of Internal Security. Gomez, AKA, 'The Ferdelance', 'special' private bodyguard to El President. And he recalled Gomez's able assistant—and El President's chauffeur—Carlos! Gomez's personal protector and her own hit man, if necessary!

Tony returned to the basic S list, started again where he had left off—Hawkins, Alexandra. He smiled, thinking about his brief, interesting interlude to his normally dull daily routine. And he had an idea that he hadn't seen the last of Hawkins and Morley.

MAZATLAN

Alex waited, the traffic—most headed north—was heavy and it moved fast. She caught fleeting glances at the scene beyond the Oltas—the four lane avenue. The dark blue Pacific with a slight ruffle on its surface, a ground swell of only two or three feet, it rhythmically rolled between the offshore rocky mountainous islands. The many sea birds had started their early morning feeding frenzy. Beautiful! Beaches with clean sea water, sun and fun ahead! Again!

But suddenly, she felt very tired, exhausted after hours of hectic, straining, night driving. Tilting her forehead to her hands on the top of the steering wheel, she closed her eyes. 'Honk! Honk!' It was a car behind her. Startled, she took only a flashing glance at the traffic and plunged across it, swung left, headed south again. This brought Alex awake—to her 'emergency' strength.

Several blocks ahead, as the avenue swept right and started up a slight noll, she saw a white building—it was four stories tall, and near the roof, painted across the front, in big black, bold letters was; 'Hotel Oltas Altas'. It was on the mainland side, across the northbound traffic lane—the 'wrong' side—she would have to cross the heavy traffic again. Or whatever. Approaching the location of the hotel, she saw a wide place on her side—it looked like an unloading area for the over-look platform that had two sets of wide steps that led down to the beach below. All this was concrete, similar to the waist high wall that separated the wide sidewalk from the beach below.

Pulling over and parking in the unloading zone, she switched off, took the keys, glanced at Tiger—she was still asleep on the rear seat—got out, stretched, then studied the hotel. Alex didn't see any activity inside or outside. But it was the traffic that was going to be her first problem. She had seen 'it' before—she slowly walked to the centerline, raised both hands as high as possible, and dashed forward. No one hit her but they didn't miss her by much either!

Alex eased the front door half open, sticking her head in she called out, "Ola! Ola!" No one. She went inside. A combined reception area and a small bar—with a few stools, and behind the bar were shelves filled with whisky bottles and a small TV, there was a large cooler below, was just inside the main entrance door. To her left, down a couple of wide steps, was what was obviously a huge restaurant. Looking around the corner of the wall at these steps, she saw the stairs leading up. "Ola! Ola!" she called toward the rear of the dining area. No one. Turning back to the reception section—it was all neatly and tightly arranged—she stepped behind the bar, between the bar and the cooler. At the end where the bar closed to the sidewall, there was a stool.

She opened the cooler's lid. It was full of beer and soft drinks— only bottles of course. Canned drinks were very, very rare in Mexico! Taking out a very cold Corona Gold, she snapped off the cap with the opener on the front of the cooler. Turning her back to the stool, she hiked her tired little ass up on it, hooked her heels on one rung—she was still dressed in her 'traveling' dress outfit; short skirt, long sleeve blouse and medium heels—and took a large gulp of the cold beer. Leaning her head against the wall, she shut her eyes. She still clutched the car keys in one hand, the bottle of beer in the other.

She was about to nod-out when she heard, "Senorita, may I help you?" Slowly, she opened her eyes, took another swallow, answered, "I surely hope so." The man was in his late fifties, maybe early sixties, tall, trim, salt and pepper wavy hair, with black flashing eyes and a pleasant smile. Alex pulled her skirt even higher, took another drink and then started her description of what she wanted—"room, as high up as possible—" "Si." he replied. "With a balcony facing that way—", she pointed with the bottle toward the ocean. "Si, I have that." "And a private banos." "Of course. All our rooms have private baths." "And two single beds." "No. There is a room available on the top floor, but it has a double bed—a nice big double bed." Alex nodded, said "That's Ok."

She emptied the bottle, handed it to him and asked, "Could I please have another?" "Si", he got one, opened it and handed it to her. She took a long, slow draft, leaned back again and closed her eyes. "Senorita, you appear very tired, can I help?" "Yes", without opening her eyes, she again pointed across the street, "See the dull black station wagon?" "Si." "That's mine—I don't think I can get back to it." "We have a parking lot behind my hotel—fenced, secure, would you like for my man to move your car over here for you?" "I would love that!" she opened her eyes, looked into his, and smiled.

The man rang the announcement bell three times and soon a handsome young man appeared. He was dressed in white jeans—very tight jeans—a white long waiter's jacket, a 'ducky' little cap and white tennis, shoes. He smiled, first at the owner, then even wider at Alex—he cast a look at her bare legs, bare to almost her crotch. Alex slowly spread her legs—enough until she knew the two men were looking at her black panties squeezed between her white thighs. She waited, took a slow sip, slid slightly more forward on the stool as she still leaned against the wall. The older man broke the silence, he patted the younger man on the shoulder. It was introduction time: The owner was Senor Zazueta—'Senor Z, his friends called him—the young man was Juan. She countered with, "Alex! Just call me Alex, and don't use my 'other' name, please." While Senor 'Z' explained her situation, Alex tossed the car keys to Juan.

When Juan opened the front door, she added, "Oh! There should be another young lady. She's probably still asleep on the rear seat! Her name is Tiger. If she's not in the car—please find her and either tell her where I am—or bring her with you!" Juan had listened then he waved, responded, "Si, Senorita Alex!" Alex suddenly remembered, called out, "And Juan! Please bring my purse to me, it's on the front floor!" She turned to Senor 'Z', added, "So we can settle my bill." Juan left and dashed through the traffic.

Still on the 'owner's' stool, Alex thought, 'I'll reduce the guessing game about what he thinks we're doing.' Looking at Senor 'Z' eyes, she calmly stated, "So you don't have to guess, we're just a couple of hookers on vacation—working our way across country." He laughed, reacted with, "That, I don't believe! Hookers don't work when on the road. They may— more than likely will—get in trouble with the local Law—and the local hookers!" They both laughed, but Alex didn't change her 'story'.

Tiger came around the corner of the dining room sidewall and up the steps. She had both their purses in one hand and her shoes in the other. She looked down at her feet, said, mainly to Senor 'Z', "Sorry, I got my feet sandy!" "Tiger, this is Senor Zazueta—Senor 'Z'—Owner of the Hotel Oltas Altas!" Alex turned to him, "Senor 'Z', this is"—she decided to skip her real name, "we call her Tiger!" They shook, Alex asked Tiger, "I take it you've met Juan?" "Yes, he found me on the beach—I was wading in the surf."

Alex slipped from behind the bar, went to the front, pulled out a bar stood, said, "Tig—pull up a stool, I want to order some food—I'm famished, and I guess you are too!" But Alex waited to order—she thought she may as well give it directly to Juan, she felt sure he would be responsible for preparing the meal.

"Coffee?" Tiger asked Senor z, he pointed toward the opening to the dining room and replied, "Turn right, go through to the kitchen, there's a huge pot on the stove. Help yourself." She looked at Alex, waited. "No, not me! As soon as I eat, I'm hitting the sack for at least four hours! I don't want coffee to interfere with that!" As she waited for Juan, Alex asked Senor Z, "You got some of those huge shrimp? Up at La Paz, we had some that big!" she showed him with her hands. "Si, I have those!" "And, how about raw oysters?" "Si, those too!"

Alex watched as Tiger came up the steps from the dining room—she held a large cup of coffee in one hand, the fingers of her other hand were extended and placed on her hip bone, she had a large smile on her face, a twinkle in her black eyes, and an extra snappy twist to her rump. Juan followed directly behind her. As she met Alex's look, she winked.

Juan lightly tossed the keys to Alex, said, "Everything Tiger showed me is now in room 304 and your station wagon is out back locked up. Is there anything else I can help you two with?" He glanced back and forth between the two. Alex didn't hesitate, "Yes, we want some food! Start with two raw oyster cocktails—no cilantro! Plenty of Tabasco! Then—", she looked at Tiger, who just nodded. "Then two orders of shrimp fixed in whatever way your best fashion is! You and Senor Z can decide that— Ok?" "Ok, Senorita Alex!" "Oh, three beers for me—", Tiger spoke up, "Orange juice for me—please?" "That's for starters!" Alex exclaimed, they all chuckled. "And, Juan Honey, would it be too much trouble for you to bring that up? These tight clothes—and these damn shoes—are killing me!" "No problem—it may be about twenty or thirty minutes—Is that Ok?" "Sure! Tiger, let's hit those thirty-nine steps up!"

Alex used one of her credit cards and signed in as Alexandra Hawkins, destination, Chiapas, no particular town.

After entering 304, Alex noticed that all the Mitla bags and even the new beach bags were in the room. Out of habit, she quickly located her pistol and checked it—Ok. The two stripped except for their panties. Tiger washed her face and put on new make-up. Alex wondered 'has handsome Juan caught Tiger's attention?' Alex dug out her loose sleeping shirt and slipped it on. Tiger found her Maya pullover blouse. It was straight, loose tailed—the bottom barely came below her ample breasts, and the blouse hung direct off her nipples. The body of this was colorful—medium and puffy white sleeves red with a darker band around the bottom edge—the dress of Amatenangoians.

But, unlike at 'Home', Tiger didn't put on her colorful skirt! She didn't put on any skirt! But she did slip on a pair of spike-heels!

While she looked in the mirror, Alex stepped to behind her, looked into the mirror at Tiger's face and said, "Are those young Tiger's black eyes flashing I see before me?" Tiger just smiled even bigger, reached back and pushed Alex away from the view of the mirror. Alex chuckled, headed for the_balcony.

Moving the chair until it was just right, Alex sat down and propped her feet on the balcony rail. She knew better than to lay down—not before the food! Tiger came out and stood at the rail. Alex relaxed and enjoyed the beautiful scene, the wonderful weather, and her very pleasant feeling.

Hearing the tap tap on the door, Tiger turned and briskly stepped to the center of the room, she stopped, put most of her weight on her left foot, slightly moved her right foot away and cocked it outward. She placed her right fingers—spread apart—on the front of her hip. Her white nail polish really showed up against her dark skin. Spreading her left fingers, palm to her rear, she let her left arm hang straight down. Pulling her head well back, she sweetly said, "Please come in, Juan, the door is unlocked."

With the heavy tray balanced on one hand and his shoulder, Juan slowly opened the door. At the stunning sight of Tiger, he stopped, held the door knob and gasped. Motionless, he stared at her—naked from just below her beautiful bosom except for the tiny panties and the tall spike heels. "Come on in Sweety. Please come—", she almost whispered. It was difficult, but he regained his composure, turned loose the knob, shifted the tray to both hands, then asked, "Where would you love to have it—this set-up—Tiger?" He had visions of why her name was Tiger!

"Could you possibly do it, on the balcony? Close to Alex? The poor lady is really give out, too tired to get up."

During this 'performance' Alex had watched over her shoulder, and heard. She had thought 'Kid! Kid! You're over acting! His hands are full, just go to him and grab him in his crotch! Get to the point!' Alex placed a hand over her own mouth to keep from laughing—at her own ideas!

The ta-de-ta over, Juan left after setting the tray on a small table next to Alex—it was within her reach. Juan had pulled the other chair over, held it back and helped Tiger get seated. The food was delicious; the shrimp were fried but in a different sort of fashion—no batter, yet slightly crusty, seasoned delightfully and these were juicy inside. And the cocktails were very hot with Tabasco and not a hint of cilantro. And there was a basket with a cloth that covered rolled tortillas, these had been smeared with a garlic buttery, slightly cheese coating before being rolled tight while hot. Tiger's orange was obviously fresh squeezed. The beers were wrapped in a small towel and in another basket. All very nice indeed!

Finished eating, Alex leaned back and said, "I'm telling you, I'm turning to a butter-ball!" as she rubbed her stomach. "Like the lady from Texas said 'You could use some meat on those bones!" Tiger responded. "If you, **Miss** Smart-ass, will help this poor tired old lady to the bed, I'll crash!" They laughed as Tiger removed the tray and table. And crash she did—out like a light! Tiger had helped; she removed and folded the beautiful bed cover, put it aside, and pulled down the sheet before Alex fell face down on the bed—about the center of the large bed.

Before going to the balcony, Tiger gently pulled the sheet over Alex. Outside on the balcony, Tiger leaned forward and gripped the rail with both hands. She wasn't smiling as she stared north. North through the dim mist of the beach front spray. North—she could barely make out the tall high-rise hotels. And she fell into deep thought. Hotel Row—Playa Northa—The Golden Zone—The zone of the rich Gringas and Gringos. Shifting her view, she made a slow sweep of 'Old Town', downtown Mazatlan. She had intended to never see either of these places again, never, ever, be here again! She stopped the sweep when her eyes were again focused on the beach far to the North—Playa Northa.

At first, she didn't realize it, but as her arms began to tremble—inside first, then visibly—she noticed that her grip on the rail had gotten tighter, very tight. Jerking her hands loose, she wrapped her arms around her torso, just under her breasts. "Damnit" she muttered. She turned and stomped inside. Almost frantic, she searched through their gear until she found the half full bottle of tequila. Returning to the balcony, she sat down, propped her feet on the rail, removed the cap from the bottle, then, she threw the cap as far as she could toward the beach. A heavy gulp, then she leaned back, let the drink burn its way down. She closed her eyes—it had been over six years—but her memories—the hellish nightmare was still just as clear as if it happened yesterday—last night—she was skinny, very skinny, actually starving. She had only two things; an old loose, dirty, pullover dress and a short piece of rope that she tied around the dress. Nothing else—nothing at all.

Tiger started to stare—at Playa Northa—she took another drink. Continuing to stare, but she saw that night long ago—she had heard that there—up there, Playa Northa—there were rich people—she could beg for pennies up there—Everyone was rich—maybe she could beg enough pennies to buy some food to eat—she was so hungry. And she walked up there—and begged while the fat rich Gringas ignored her. While the fat rich women stuffed their big bellies with expensive food—and wasted enough to feed many poor people—like me.

Tiger shook her head, wiped the tears away, and had another slug of tequila. Still staring North, she recalled the real nightmare—how it began—she sat down on the beach sand and leaned back against the still warn, concrete retaining wall in front of the fancy high-rise hotel—it was the Hotel Riviera—in the Golden Zone. She still shivered—more from the lack of food than from the cool night air. And some fat rich Gringa had called the Poliza—she came with the big ugly cops—she pointed out 'the trash'—her, shinny, 'filty trash', skinny Margarita Calienta.

She was too weak to scream or struggle—the cops dragged her—mostly by her bare ass, her small breasts, her skinny arms and legs, and her matted hair. They roughly threw her in the rear of the large van—there were others—but she didn't care—she only wanted to die. Downtown—she guessed, she' didn't really know where—the cops separated the males from the females—the cops knew who the females were because the cops looked, grabbed, slapped, and poked fingers in the women to be sure—and the cops laughed among themselves. She, with the other females` were thrown into one huge holding cell—it was crowed, filthy, filled with all kinds; whores, 'butches' and puking drunks, even one old hag that thought she was a witch! And even starving little girls.

The next day—there was no trial, no hearing—they just took down the names of those who could and would tell them—she told them her name, she saw them write it down—then most of the females were loaded again into the huge van, trucked North-East on highway 40, toward Durango, and shoved out—along the edge of the highway—nothing in sight—no one anywhere—skinny, weak, fifteen year old Margarita Calienta headed North-East and never looked back.

Tiger stood, took another swallow, went inside and sat the bottle—there wasn't much left—on the dresser in front of the mirror. She stared at her image in the mirror then roughly she pulled the blouse over her head and dropped it to the floor. Slipping the panties down, she stepped out of those. She kept on the high spike heels as she continued to stare in the mirror. Lifting her breasts several times, she then raised her hands and arms above her head and slowly turned a couple of circles. And softly said, "Look at skinny, poor Margarita Calienta now, you rich bitches!"

Holding her pose, her hands still high, facing the mirror, she stared. From behind her, Alex said, "What are you doing?" This startled Tiger, she jerked her hands down and reached for her blouse and panties. Stepping to the bags, holding the blouse and panties, she casually replied, "I thought I'd get my swimsuit on—maybe go to the beach for a while." But Alex saw her wipe her eyes, and Alex saw the nearly empty tequila bottle—the one without a cap. And she saw that Tiger was not smiling.

Alex jumped up, stretched, smoothed down the tail of her tee shirt, ran out on the balcony. "Fantastic! It is just beautiful!" Alex shouted then she rushed back in, stopped and asked "Isn't it, Tiger?" Tiger didn't respond as she located her new bathing suit. Quickly looking at her watch—it was on the dresser "It's only three fifteen! You're right! Let's tug on our straps"—the tong suits Alex meant—"and hit the beach!" After the two had on the very skimpy suits, Alex glanced toward the city just outside, she quickly got both their 'traveling' jeans and loose shirts and their low tennis shoes—no socks—, said, "Here, slip these on—until we get down past the retaining wall at least—we wouldn't want to cause any wrecks on the 'old Oltas', would we?" Covered up, Alex got the beach bag, checked for the mats—she had really fallen for these—they beat the hell out of cloth towels—and for suntan lotion. She threw the room key and her wallet in, and as they passed the dresser, heading out, she hesitated, lifted the bottle, said, "Evaporation is really bad here, isn't it?" And she turned up the bottle and emptied it. Tiger didn't answer, and Alex didn't expect any reply. But Alex thought 'Something is wrong!'

Crossing Oltas Avenue in mid-afternoon wasn't very difficult, the traffic wasn't heavy. Down on the beach, they had the mats spread out,

Alex lay on her back as she rubbed suntan lotion on her arms and shoulders. Tiger was on her knees—at Alex's hip—as she rubbed lotion on Alex's feet and legs. Alex asked, "What's wrong? You don't seem your jolly self."

Tiger hesitated with the rubbing, but she didn't react to Alex's question. Alex asked again, about the same. Throwing the lotion tube down close to Alex's side, Tiger straighten her back, twisted toward Alex's face, snapped, "Don't you ever mind your own business?" And she slightly moved as if to get up.

In a flash, Alex raised at her waist, hooked her right elbow behind Tiger's neck, grasped her hands together and jerked Tiger down on top of her chest. Alex now was flat on her back, she tightened the headlock and pulled Tiger's face within inches of her own face, said, "Your business is my business. Your troubles are my troubles. Your problems are my problems." Twisting Tiger's head to the right, Alex pulled until her mouth was even with Tiger's ear. In almost a whisper, Alex said, "Can't you see? I've fallen in love with you—I would do anything possible for you. Don't shut me out, just tell me what is wrong." At first Tiger had resisted Alex's unexpected move, but, slowly she relaxed. Alex gradually felt Tiger's weight increase as she lay on top of her. Alex whispered, "Please, please, let me know—" Tiger pushed her face tight against Alex's neck, whispered back, "Yes, but not here, not now." Alex relaxed the pressure of the headlock, but she maintained the hold. Tiger slipped her right arm tight around Alex's waist and hugged her very tightly.

After a few minutes, Alex took the sides of Tiger's head in her hands, pulled Tiger's face to hers and asked, "You promise?" "Yes. I promise." Alex kissed her hard lips to lips. Tiger didn't resist, the two relaxed as they held the kiss for a very long time. And they both felt relieved, and stimulated—even sexually aroused.

Rolling off of Alex, they both were flat on their backs and both stared up at the blue, clear sky. They both were silent—soon Alex dozed off, but Tiger didn't. "This side is about 'done'", Alex broke the long silence, she added, "Would you please rub some lotion on my backside if I roll face down?" "Sure, of course." As Tiger began to rub Alex's naked, tight buttocks, Alex felt a tingeing sensation—almost a twitch inside—she hadn't felt this in a long, long time. She knew it came from anticipation— but anticipating what? Alex contracted her butt very tight to prevent any uncontrolled quivering. She finally reached behind, and gently moved Tiger's firm, strong hands up higher onto her back. Alex didn't think she could stand it any longer.

The air temperature was dropping, the sun's steep angle no longer did any good as far as getting a tan was concerned, they slipped their jeans, shirts, and shoes on, gathered up the other articles and headed for the steps up to the avenue. Traffic was heavy—they had to use the wave, hop, skip and dodge run method to cross the broad street. Running to the hotel, Alex commented, "Do you think some people get over to the beach side, and can't get back? Ever!" Tiger chuckled, and smiled.

When they entered the room, they saw that all the dishes and the tray from this morning had been removed—and the bed was made-up.

Stepping from the bathroom, Alex was still drying, she said, "What do you think about us staying in—watch the sunset, order up a snack—just girl talk?" Tiger headed for the shower, hesitated, replied, "Sure, sounds good." "See? Not only am I getting fat, I'm also getting lazy!" Tiger stepped to Alex, hugged her, "Little Alex? Lazy? That'll be the day! Hey! You're wet!" They laughed. While Tiger showered, Alex called down, ordered two Caesar salads—with low fat dressing, a 1.5 liter jug of white wine and two servings—she wasn't sure how—of yogurt, low fat. She continued with Juan, "Juan? We may be on the balcony watching the sun set—we'll leave the door unlocked, just come on in" "Yes, Miss Alex! Anything else?" "Yes! You can drop the Miss! It's just Alex! Ok?" "Ok, Just Alex!" She fell back on the bed and laughed into the phone. Juan also laughed. She added, "Joan Wilder! The Jewel Of The Nile! And—The Jewel! What was his name?" "Al Jerha! I've been waiting for ages for this to happen!" Juan laughed back.

"Juan, what do you think of Tiger?" "Man! She's the greatest! And so—so—" "Nice big tits! That's what you were looking for?" "Yes! And her" "Her ass is lovely?" "Yes!" "Juan? Are you married? Got kids? That kind of situation?" "No—Why?" "Just checking, we don't want to cause any problems! What time do you get off—stop working?" "Eleven, but sometimes, if something is needed, maybe later." "We are not planning to go out tonight. When you finish your duties to Senor Z, check around, see what we're doing—I think Tiger is interested in you—but-Juan, don't come-on to her when you bring up our food this evening. Ok? We—I—have got a little hitch to work out—oh, say, until well after sunset. Understand?" "Sure—wait until I'm off duty, then find Tiger—see where it goes from there!" "Right! And I promise I'll stay out of the way!" "Alex hung up, found her loose tee shirt, slipped it on and went out onto the balcony.

Watching sunsets—and sunrises—was almost a ritual with Alex. Almost the only 'leisure' activity when her mind would seem to shove all other thoughts off to one corner—and relax—and enjoy the scene. Juan had politely slipped in and out as he brought the food and wine. They had eaten before it was 'show-time'—Nature's 'show-time'. And it was spectacular! Just enough low clouds to reflect the last rays after the sun was actually below the horizon—this created a complete coverage of all the hues of red and yellow. And it had been fantastic as the sun slowly disappeared between the two islands not far off shore! Alex and Tiger continued to watch even after it was completely dark in the West. The sidewalk lights along the Oltas had come on, then the numerous 'night' businesses' lights joined these. Standing, Alex exclaimed. "Bravo!

Buenos Nochas, El Sol!" and threw the West a kiss from her finger tips. She gathered up the empty dishes, carried these inside to the tray and filled their glasses.

Returning to Tiger on the balcony, as she handed the glass to Tiger, Alex simply commented, "You promised." Tiger sipped the wine, then started, "I've never told anyone this—not even Mike—", then she told Alex everything she could remember about the 'last' time—over six years ago—when she was here—Mazatlan, Playa Northa, and 'Downtown', in jail. Everything to when she walked away from Matazlan and never looked back. Alex had pulled her chair close enough so that she could touch Tiger—hold hands, pat her knee or stroke her arm, as Tiger's tears flooded. Alex got the box of tissues from the bathroom. When Tiger seemed finished, Alex stood close and gently pulled Tiger's head against her hip, and stroked her long hair. And Alex just waited—waited as Tiger drowned her terrible memories.

Alex knelt beside Tiger's chair, pulled Tiger's face around, said, "Would you like to do something—something to try and re-write your memories?" Tiger's appearance—her eyes—questioned Alex's confusing statement. Alex added, "Sometimes, to over come a bad memory, it is possible to return to the source, change what happened, change the impressions, change 'it'—whatever—to a more pleasant story—with good luck, maybe come out with a happy memory. Would you want that? Would you want to try?" "But—but—how?" Tiger finally asked.

Alex stood, stroked Tiger's long hair again, replied, "Let's have some wine—hell, maybe a lot of wine! Let me get'loose', let my 'wild' imagination—my thoughts—loose! We'll kick it around, see where it lands! We'll come up with something!"

After a few more rounds, Alex unconsciously took to one of her old habits—pacing and sipping wine. Feeling too drained to join her, Tiger just watched—Alex was like a wild cat in a new cage. Abruptly, she stopped, jerked around—she spilled wine on her tee shirt—and snapped, "I've got it! We go there!" She pointed north toward the string of lights far up the shoreline. Tiger frowned. "No, not JUST go there! WE go in magnificent style! We'll be the Stars! We'll be the rich Gringas! We'll show them—we—you—are just as damn good—even better! And we visit every place up there! A brilliant entrance! And a snotty exit! And we make everyone—all the rich acting bitches and bastards notice us! Notice you!" Tiger just smiled and nodded.

"Come on, Kid, throw on some clothes, jeans, shirts, we've got work to do!" Alex glanced at her watch—it was almost ten. As Alex fumbled with the tray full of dishes, they ran down the stairs. At the bottom, Alex turned hard right, went straight back into the kitchen, fitting the tray in an empty spot, she threw a kiss at Juan, and winked at him. Returning through the nearly empty dinning room, Alex and Tiger—who had waited at the bottom of the stairs—located Senor Z. He was on his stool behind the bar, leaned back against the wall watching the small TV—the sound was not turned up—on the opposite end of a shelf. Alex rushed to the bar, opposite Senor Z, reached far over the bar, and took his hand. He turned, leaned toward her, extended his other hand—she grabbed it.

"Senor Z, I need help!" "Sounds like how we first met, Alex!" he responded. "No, no! I was bushed then! Now I'm all fired-up! Can you—

will you help? Please?" "Depends, is it legal?" "Yes!" She started, avoiding the 'why', just explained the 'what'! She wanted to rent, borrow, whatever, the biggest, longest, blackest, limousine in Mazatlan—or wherever! She didn't care about the details, or how much it cost—for all day and all night! And she wanted two escorts—the most handsome, best mannered, real gentlemen, great dancers with fitted tuxedos, black shoes so shinny one could comb their hair with the reflection from the shoes! She wanted flowers—for their evening gowns, she pointed to Tiger and herself. The gowns would be white, and boutonnieres for the men—and the tuxedo had to be black! As Alex talked, she motioned for him to pass her a beer, as she drank, he got a notebook and pencil—he could see little Alex was serious, and it was going to be complicated! She kept right on talking—And she wanted to know where she could buy beautiful evening gowns—gowns good enough for the most fancy places in town! And where the best beauty shop was—one where the social elite women of Mazatlan went! Suddenly Alex hesitated, turned to Tiger, asked, "Kid, would you please go to the kitchen and get me a cup of strong, black coffee?" Tiger left.

Quickly while Tiger was gone, she explained. "We want the Social Editor of the 'main' daily newspaper, with his—or—her—photographer for the entire night! To follow us to wherever we go! And if it cost money, that's Ok too! Money is no object!" Senor Z looked questionly at this 'request'. Alex snapped, "Don't ask, can you arrange this—without Tiger knowing before we are picked up tomorrow night by our limo?" He thought, then, "Yes, I know how I can work it out—you will have to pay their expenses." "No problem!" she replied.

Tiger returned with the coffee, Alex gulped at it, "Dam! That's hot!" then she began again to Senor Z—"And I want diner reservations for our party—including you-know-who—at the Hotel Riviera—say at nine—and I want their fanciest suite reserved, just for tomorrow night!" "Are you moving out?" he questioned. "Hell no! We'll just parade up, in, take some pictures, mess it up a little, maybe a bottle of champagne—and leave!" She laughed, and winked at Senor Z.

"Can you get all this? Will you make all the arrangements?" She again pulled on his hands. He thought, then, "Yes, I know exactly where, how these can be taken care of—one of my several son-in-laws is in the wedding business! He can handle it all! Complete! And he is used to instant notices! Last minute demands!" They leaned closer to each other, Alex kissed his cheek, said, "Senor Z, you're a real doll!" "But, Alex can you—", she guessed the rest, interrupted, she almost whispered, "It— everything—will not cost over two million, US dollars, will it?" He straightened up, smiled, replied, "By no means!" "Good! I didn't want to dig into my 'piggy-bank' account!" The three laughed. But Alex knew, if Senor Z wanted to—and he probably would—he could check her credit card limit—being as he already had that number—the platinum card she had used here had a one million dollar limit—US dollars.

"If I may ask, why are you doing this?" he asked the both of them. He had picked-up that it seemed to be something Alex was doing for Tiger. Alex reached over, took Tiger's hand, they looked into each other's eyes, Alex softly remarked, "Let's just say Mazatlan and Playa Northa owe little Margarita Calienta an apology." Senor Z thought, 'Who? But it sounded too deep to question.' He didn't ask any more about that subject.

First things first, Senor Z held up a stiff index finger, made a telephone call. Hanging up, he said, "One long, black limo, with a chauffeur, will pick up you two ladies at nine A.M. tomorrow morning. The driver will know which beauty parlor—with spa—to carry you to. Wherever you go, he waits for you—all day and all night!" Tiger and Alex yelled cheers and hugged each other.

Alex and Senor Z discussed the details for tomorrow's 'event' some more. Alex glanced at her watch—it was only a few minutes before eleven.

Juan stepped up from the dining room, said, "Senor Zezueta, everything is finished. Is there anything—", he glanced toward Alex, then Tiger, "—else I need to do?" The older man just shook his head, and then he looked to Alex, then Tiger. Alex grabbed Tiger's thigh, gave it a squeeze. Tiger stood, stepped to Juan at the end of the counter, and with direct eye contact, softly commented, "Juan—there is something you can do for me", she wavered, then added, "There seems to be a slight dribble to the toilet—Could you please-look at my little problem—The dribble?" Juan glanced at Senor Z, asked, "Is that Ok?" Z nodded, replied, "Sure, take care of whatever Senorita Tiger wants", as he smiled at the young man. Tiger led the way, Juan followed close behind as the two went upstairs. With her fists balled up, her thumbs stuck up, Alex said to Senor Z, "Yes! She needs it!" Senor Z leaned closer to Alex, asked, "Juan isn't going to have to pay, is he?" Tilting farther back on the bar stool, Alex laughed, then bending to the bar, she replied, "About my tale of us hooking our way across country—that was just a joke!"

Because of the complicated conversation, Senor Z asked, "Who are You two anyway?" "I can only say a little." She got serious, asked, "The truth?" "Yes, please—no more jokes—the truth!" "I'll simplify it—I'm a Special Agent of a 'special department of the USA government. I'm assigned to protect Tiger—she is an Archaeologist—and we're headed for a special project—I can't say what." "Special Agent?" "Yes, and I'm licensed to carry a weapon—even down here—I have it with me." Senor Z leaned back, raised his eyebrows. Alex added, "Of course, this doesn't need to leak out. Ok? Two gals on a lark, a vacation, is our cover. Ok?" "No problem, I understand!"

"And the millions of dollars—US—, is that a joke? Or the truth?" "The truth, I have a side-line job—getting rich! But! I'm not a rich-bitch Gringa! OK!" He felt he had touched a sore spot, he hesitated. Alex realized this, continued, "Besides, Tiger and I—independently— own a sizable share of a huge food distribution company—a new and fast growing company. There's a rather healthy income from that!" She stood, strolled to the front door, looked out then turned back.

"Do that again!" Senor Z exclaimed. She did. "It's your—the little— twisting walk!" "You mean my cute little ass, don't you?" "Well, yes, but I've seen you before, Alex, somewhere, somehow!" He waited, thought then, "You say you're into a new food company? Yes, that's it! You were on TV! With some high ranking government man—and a couple of guys, one older man, and one very big dude!" Alex laughed, responded, "Yes! That was I! And that show was played down here? I'm surprised!" "Yes, some documentary program thing—I watched it right here" He pointed to the small TV up on the shelf, added, "Since first seeing you, I've felt as if I had seen you before!"

Suddenly, Alex wanted sex, now. And it wasn't at Miss Hawkin's insistence—the feeling had started when she was down on the beach. She stepped around the counter, leaned over the drink cooler—with her backside toward him—and took out a cold beer. She then leaned over to the opener on the front of the cooler—again with her butt toward Senor Z. She felt sure he was watching her bottom in her skin-tight jeans. He was still on his stool, still leaned back against the wall, his feet on a rung of the stool, his knees stuck out. She took a gulp, stepped close, and placed her crotch directly—and firmly—to one of his knees, and asked, "How would you like to have some of my cute little ass?"

He smiled, replied, "Let me lock the front door and turn off some lights—there's a cot—for naps and whatever—in the back storage room. That Ok?" "Anywhere, anyway!" she snapped as she smiled into his eyes.

As he reached up and pulled on the dim overhead light in the small room, he said, "I'm not going to have to pay, am I?" "Yes! You are!" Alex quipped, then poked him in his ribs, pulled his head down to her face, and she whispered into his ear. "So, Little Alex likes—!

I guess that's cheap enough!" They both laughed.

CHAPTER-9

It was almost nine the next morning, the two were dressed in their matching tight, short, white cocktail dresses—these were slip style, with tiny spaghetti straps. And their highest heeled strap dress shoes—these were black. No hose—Alex knew how awkward these were at a spa, just 'tong' panties, black, so these would be barely noticeable through the thin dresses. They had already fixed their hair, they were finished except for jewelry. It had been decided; pearls for Tiger, and for Alex, her 'normal' nugget accessories.

As Alex fitted Tiger with pearls, she said "One's jewelry can become like a personal signature—like Barbara Bush's pearl necklace, or Jackie K's small diamond one, or Taylor's diamond 'rock' that she beat everyone in the face with!" Then the two quickly got Alex's nuggets on her. They both looked in the mirror, Alex jerked her purse strap on her shoulder, grabbed up their sunglasses, snapped, "Ok, Kid, bet's go knock em dead!"

Coming up out of the dining room, they rounded the bar, turned then stopped facing where Senor Z sat—he was on his stool reading the morning newspaper. Alex made a slight noise, he looked up. Startled, he dropped the paper, stood and said, "My God! You two are beautiful!" Alex's 'nuggets' caught his attention. He briskly stepped around and lifted one of her hands to look more closely at her rings and bracelet, then at her necklace. "Wait, just hold that pose!" He went toward the back. Soon he returned with Juan, said to him "Juan, I want you to meet the latest guests of Hotel Oltas Altas!" The young man was taken back, just stared with his mouth open. "Ah, come on, Juan, you can say more than that!" Alex quipped. He came forward, lifted Tiger's hand and slowly turned her around, commented, "Tiger, you are gorgeous!" She curtsied, replied, "Thank you!" Behind the two, the front door briskly opened, they turned around as the big man stepped to them. He wore a black uniform; long tailed jacket, 'riding' pants and high-top black boots—with a small driver's cap under his left arm. He clicked his heels, bowed and asked, "Senoritas Alex and Tiger?" Alex took one step forward, extended her right hand, flat, palm down, fingers slightly limp, said, "Senorita Alex!" It was obvious someone, probably Senor Z, had warned the chauffeur about not using her last name. He stepped to her, bowed again, gently lifted her hand and kissed it. Still holding her fingers, he snapped up straight, and waited. "And this", as Alex slowly moved her other limp hand in Tiger's direction, "is—." Senor Z and Juan—behind her—waited and listened very closely—they had only heard 'Tiger'. Alex continued, **"Is** Senorita Margarita Calienta Morley. For this day and this night, you're to address her as—Senorita Margarita Calienta! And you are to announce her each and every time she gets in or out of the limo! And at any other time or place you feel is appropriate! Understood?" He continued to stare into Alex's black—and serious—eyes, he answered, "It is clearly understood, Senorita Alex!" He dropped her hand, twisted to face Tiger, bowed, lifted her right hand and kissed it, and gave an example of his announcement, "Senorita Margarita Calienta! It is my pleasure!" Tiger smiled, and would have blushed if it had been possible—Maya can't blush. The big driver stepped back, exclaimed, "I am Maxillian Hernandz— please call me—Max!"

As Max gently lowered Tiger's hand, Senor Z stepped forward, said, "Forgive the intrusion, Max, this is a list of places, things, the ladies are interested in, it may help." Max took the list, glanced at it then put it in a pocket, said "Thank you, Senor Zazueta!" Reaching in another pocket, Max removed a calling card, presented it to Alex—rightly, he had quickly deduced that Alex was 'the boss-lady', and Margarita was to be 'presented'—to be toured among the social scene. "This is my Employer's card", Max said, then he turned the card over, added, "With special instructions to whomever you present it to, and, the explanation that both of you are only here for a brief period—that service is to be prompt, no waiting, and service is to be superb! And, all billing will be to", he turned the card back to the front, "to these numbers and this address! He hesitated then added, "You, Senorita Alex, are not to pay for any services! Do you understand, this is to prevent the possibility of double payment." "It is clearly understood!" Alex returned 'his' answer. As she took the card and dropped it in her small black purse, she said, "Thank you, Max, how nice! I think you and I are going to get along just fine!" She wavered, stared into his eyes, softly added, "Or—even much better than—fine."

Again, Alex hesitated, still looking in his eyes, she suddenly realized it was 'her move', she said, "May we go?" She then Tiger, slipped on their sunglasses, nodded to Senor Z and Juan as Max escorted them out. The big, long, black limo was parked directly in front of the door, at the curb, in a no-parking area—the traffic on the Oltas just had to 'make-do!

After helping Alex in the limo—Alex first being as she was the older of the two—and as Max took Tiger's elbow, in a strong but pleasant voice, he said, "Ah! Senorita Margarita Calienta! What a pleasure to have you aboard!" The few people in hearing range stopped and looked at beautiful 'little Margarita'—exactly as Alex wanted!

In less than two blocks, Alex saw a sign, 'Banco'. "Dear Max, please stop in front of that bank—we want to look around inside—see if they look worthy of holding a few million of our money!" Besides, there were more people around the bank!

Max repeated his performance—and again everyone stopped and looked at Tiger. Inside, Alex, with Tiger's arm hooked in her elbow, strutted to the Main Receptionist, asked "May we have a brief look about? Senorita Margarita Calienta", she nodded to Tiger, "is looking for a new bank!" "What sort of accounts is the Senorita interested in?" the clerk asked. "Checking mainly, say one million, US. To start with, but one never knows, does one?" Alex replied. Tiger just smiled. "Please, look around, if I can be of additional help, please return to me." The two slowly strolled to the far end of the huge room, slowly turned around, and slowly walked directly out the front door, to Max. Again he welcomed Tiger. Back in the limo, which Max headed North, Tiger whispered to Alex, "Did you see? Everyone dropped their teeth?" Alex just smiled, and nodded in return.

They hadn't gone far when Max twisted his head back, said, "Senorita Alex, we have someone following us. Do you want me to lose them?" "No, please don't—do you have any idea who it is?" "I think it is that nosey Social Editor for the newspaper, and his Photographer, they very often try to 'crash' private weddings!" "As a matter of fact, please be sure that they do follow us! After we get beautiful, we—you and I—may ask them to take some photographs!" Alex leaned back and thought, 'I think Senor Z has started our plans even sooner than I anticipated! Great!

She tilted forward again, said, "Max, inside here, in the limo, you can call me Alex, Ok? And Senorita Margarita, you can, if you want to, call her Tiger, Ok?" "Tiger?" but he didn't ask any more about the 'unusual' name. "Max? Where is our next stop? I understand you have the list, you know the places that we need to go to—", Alex asked.

"El Cid Mega Resort for the spa, the beauty salon, almost anything a lady can desire." "Tell us about it, please." "Over nine hundred acres, fourteen restaurants, private golf course, six swimming pools, seventeen tennis courts, a complete night club—and deep sea fishing is also available. And it is located about center of the so-called Golden Zone." "It sounds rich, alright", Alex responded.

"Max, while you wait, please spread the word that your client is Senorita Margarita Calienta", Alex said as they pulled up to the front of the El Cid. He just nodded. After helping them out under the canopy at the entrance, and 'announcing' Tiger, Max stepped to the Doorman, handed him one of the 'cards' and said something in rapid-fire Spanish. The Doorman motioned for Alex and Tiger to wait. Going inside, he soon returned with a bellhop, who now had the card. He stepped to Tiger, extended his right elbow, asked, "Please follow me, Senorita Margarita Calienta!" Alex took his other elbow then they set out. And it was a good thing they had a guide—the place was enormous!

Entering the main entrance to the spa/salon facility, the bellhop released them, passed the card to the Head Receptionist. She glanced at the special instructions, stood, smiled and asked that they follow her then she motioned in a certain direction. But Alex held up a 'halting' signal with one hand, said, "I am Senorita Margarita Calienta's personal bodyguard. Please inform your people—the ones that serve us— that we are not to be separated—out of sight of each other—under any conditions. Is that understood?" The beautiful, trim, middle-aged lady hesitated, glanced back and forth between Alex and Tiger. "This is most unusual—", the receptionist replied in perfect English. She looked toward the depths of the long interior, thought, then added, "Yes, I think our facilities are suited for that—If you two—", again she looked back and forth at Alex and Tiger, "don't mind using a large whirlpool, a hot-tub, together—as a soaking tub. Our regular tubs are in individual cubicles—these are NOT within sight of each other! Is the hot-tub acceptable?" "Perfectly!" Alex answered as Tiger nodded.

They were led into the depths of the huge, complicated compound. Then two assistants were assigned to each Alex and Tiger—their 'own' two young attractive female attendants. First thing, their jewelry was removed—this was locked in individual cases and put in a vault. Alex and Tiger were given claim-check tickets. They were able to keep their purses. Next, they were stripped—not much trouble for them, they hadn't wore much.

For the next three hours, they were; oiled, rubbed, patted, bathed, shampooed, plucked, caked, bathed more. And hot-waxed—Tiger's legs and armpits, of course, Alex didn't need this. The four assistants had a problem understanding Alex's 'unusual' condition, but they agreed it was cute. Because of Tiger's crotch being shaved when they were at La Paz, 'it' didn't need to be hot-waxed either.

Then they were soaked in the large (large enough for four friendly people.) whirl pool, the assistants turned it into a bubble bath—with the numerous jets activated, it was a fantastic bubble bath!

Extending one arm straight up—she was chin deep in bubbles—Alex snapped her fingers. All four of the attendants responded, she smartly said, "We would enjoy a bottle of your best champagne, and a light finger-snack as we linger in here in lavishness!" The closest one replied "Yes! Of course, Alex!" She ran off. The four had quickly understood Alex's demand about the 'name-thing'! They had been sternly instructed by Alex during introductions—"Alex! And only Alex! And only Senorita Margarita Calienta—her full name! And it is to be used complete, exact, and it is to be used in any reply or comment!"

While soaking, sipping and snacking, Alex explained to Tiger, "Tig, the nice mild manners of your race—the Maya—are beautiful and should be appreciated more—but—in this world—", she waved a bubbly hand around, "You should get used to—even accomplished at—directing others, demanding. One doesn't have to be rude—just be firm, stern, clear and expect—and get—the response you want." "But—that is so unusual for us, I—", Tiger wavered. "I know, but please try—it will take practice, but I think you'll enjoy it once you learn how. Please?" "Of course—I'll try—" Tiger didn't seem exactly positive.

"Ok, practice, ask one of your girls—the one you think is the cutest—to refill our glasses." Alex said as she pushed Tiger's thigh with her foot. Tiger looked at the two who stood next to her side of the hot-tub, she stuck up one arm, and snapped her fingers, then she pointed at the shorter of the two. The attendant immediately stooped down, asked, "Si? Senorita

Margarita Calienta?" "Please, our glasses are empty!" The young lady rushed, got the bottle and refilled the two's glasses. Tiger nodded to her, smiled and remarked, "Thank you so much!" Then softly to Alex, she said, "That does feel good."

As they sipped and continued to soak, Alex asked, "Why did you pick that one as the cutest?" **"I'm** not sure, her smile, her bigger breasts— I guess." "Of the four, I would like—", Alex wavered, then, "I would pick that one", she nodded toward the tallest of the four, "The one with the slim, long legs—she could wrap those—long—slim—beautiful legs around my neck and back anytime!" "Alex! What are you saying?" "I'm not sure, it just popped out!" They laughed and shoved each other with their feet.

"I think we better get out! Or we'll look like prunes!" Alex exclaimed, added, "You ask them to help us, Ok?" Tiger stuck up one arm, snapped, made a circle motion with her index finger. The four rushed forward, "We're finished here, please help us." There were showers off to one side. 'Their own' attendants assisted them to rinse off and dry. As Alex's two were drying her off, she thought, 'What a place—and lovely company—for a party!' After being 'dressed' in loose bathrobes, the assistants led them to the salon section—to the beauticians.

It was time for their hair; Alex's was to get only lightly fluffed, Tiger's was to receive much more. They divided her hair into three strands. One smaller one on each side, these were tightly braded. The large one down the back was fixed in a looser twisted arrangement. The hair dressers-there was two for each person—tied little ribbons on Tiger's 'tails'.

Alex didn't like the ribbons. She snapped for one of 'her' assistants, whispered something to her. The girl left, and soon returned with a clerk.

He was dressed in a black suit and he carried a fancy jewelry case. As the beauticians continued with Alex's hair, she selected what she wanted— it was three pearl clasps for Tiger's 'tails'. Pointing to Tiger and clearly saying her name, Alex instructed that the pearl clasps were to replace the 'cheap' ribbons. Alex signed the clerk's ticket and waved him away. He stepped to Tiger, and personally replaced the ribbons with the clasps. Alex could see that Tiger was surprised at her gifts. Tiger waved to Alex, who stuck her two thumbs up, and nodded back. And it was obvious that all the beauticians and the attendants were very impressed.

Their nails and their toenails were done while their hair was being fixed. Their faces were done last. Alex suggested 'wild' rather than 'mild' for Tiger—she wanted Tiger to be 'outstanding'—something no one was likely to forget! And 'it' was to go with a white evening gown—both of them would be wearing white! Alex thought, 'If we can't be virgins, maybe we can look like virgins!'

Somehow, Max must have known about when they would be finished, he was waiting in the lobby of the salon. As they approached, he said, "Ah Senorita Margarita Calienta! How beautiful!" As the two strutted from the salon, with their arms hooked in Max's elbows, he whispered to Alex, "Alex, you're as cute as—", she interrupted, "I know, I know! I've heard all the 'cutes' anyone can come up with!" As they walked on through the extensive compound, Alex asked Max, "Is it acceptable for you to have a drink with us?" "No, but I can wait in another place if you and Senorita Margarita Calienta", he 'announced Tiger again, "want a drink or two. What ever you prefer." Alex snapped, "I don't prefer that! Let's get out of this clip joint! And, you can stop at the first bar, dive, whatever, where all three of us can drink together, all we want to!" He tugged Alex's arm with his elbow, softly said, "Alex, you're my kind of gal." She tugged back, responded with, "And Max, big boy, you're my kind of guy—when this 'gig' is over, I might just— your brains out!" They smiled at each other, he added, "You got a deal, Little Alex."

As the three—still arm in arm—exited the main front entrance, flash bulbs went off. They stopped, Alex said, "Smile—and throw that 'cocked hip' thing you do, Tige. It's show time!" A few more photos, then the Editor rushed forward—Max released the two, and stepped to the door of the limo—"Which of you are Senorita Margarita Calienta?" Alex stepped to one side, and bowed a wave at Tiger. The Editor began to ask questions, to which she mostly replied, "No comment!" "Come on, Senorita, give me something! Please!" "Ok. I'm an archaeologist on my way to a project. I was here six yeas ago, we, Alex"—she waved toward Alex, "and I just swung by to see if anyone remembered ME!" "And Alex?" he looked at Alex, "She is—what? A good friend?" "Yes, and also my personal bodyguard!" "Bodyguard? She is very small!" Tiger leaned close, "But she packs a very mean gun."

The Editor backed off this subject, he asked, "And tonight?" Tiger waved one arm, "Tonight, we'll be back! Get ready Playa Northa, little Margarita has returned!" Tiger had gotten into this 'revenge' idea very well. The Editor didn't understand, but he didn't ask. Tiger and Alex didn't notice the TV cameraman off to the side of the crowd that had already gathered at the entrance because of the sight of the photographers.

After Max helped Tiger into the limo, he turned back to the crowd, and he spread his arms, announced, in a loud voice, "Senorita Margarita Calienta has left the building!" As he drove away, the three doubled up with laughter. Even Max had gotten in the mood!

Max drove South, out of the Golden Zone, he passed the bullfight ring, and when at the outskirts of the city, he turned left on a paved road, he slowed, turned left on a 'white' gravel drive way—almost like a beat out path through the large open field. This ended at a low spread out building with an old rusty metal roof—it looked as if it had been expanded one board at the time. Beyond this, there were several native style houses. Max parked close to the entrance of the bar/club, a small sign showed, 'Marie's Place'. The two cars that had followed them parked about thirty feet away.

Getting out in a hurry, Max didn't open the rear door, instead, he took long, strong strides back to the cars. Leaning in the first, then the next car, he then returned and helped Alex and Tiger out. Alex glanced toward the cars—the three men were outside, she didn't see any cameras. "I've got some good friends here I'd like for you two to meet." Max explained, "And we can sure as hell drink together!"

Inside, he introduced them to a robust Native woman—Marie, the owner, she was behind the bar wiping out glasses—and then to the three much younger women who 'hung-out' here. The Editor, his photographer, and the TV 'stringer' came in, took seats at a table off to one dark side. Alex saw that Max, Tiger and the other women were into a rapid-fire marathon. Alex asked the owner for a bottle of tequila, a bottle of ginger ale and three 'slammer' glasses. She quickly fixed Tiger one first, then Max, and one for herself. They had waited, Alex lifted her drink, they followed suite. She said, "Ok, on three, slam! One, two, three!" Bang! They downed that round. "Excuse me," the others had resumed the 'talk-a-thon, they didn't notice Alex as she got one more 'slammer' glass, gathered up the other three and with the two bottles, she went to the reporter's 'conference' table.

Kicking a fourth chair to the table, she asked "Looks like you guys could use a drink. Slammers, anyone?" They jumped at the opportunity. After the first round, Alex turned her chair around, pushed the back to the edge of the table, pulled up the hem of her tight cocktail dress to her crotch, she straddled the chair, then leaned forward toward the table, said, "Fellows, I know you have all wondered what this is about! I'm going to tell you a brief—and true—story about a poor starving little girl—and as

I know you know, then you can do what you want with it. And I'm going to tell you another tale—about a success story—a very successful story." She hesitated, looked at each one of them, one by one. She didn't smile. They waited, then she said, "You guys can stay and listen, or you can get the hell out!" One guy started mixing slammers, he said, "Little Lady, we're all ears! Fire away! On three, slam!" They did, then Alex started.

Alex told Tiger's story about her horrible time here six years ago. She closed with, "And you", she pointed a stiff index finger at the newspaper Editor's face, "Can check with your local jail-keeper!" Alex hadn't used any specific name for the story, she only used, "little girl". Alex stood, she didn't bother to pull her dress down, turned toward Tiger at the bar, shouted, "Tiger! Come over here!" "Tiger?" the Editor questioned. "Yes! She devours people when she loses her-temper!" Tiger rushed over, stopped, stared at Alex. "Please lean your knuckles to the center of the table—show these guys how undernourished you are!" Without questioning, she did. The three men were breathless at the sight of Tiger's beautiful, enormous breasts. While they stared, Alex snapped, "Men, this is that poor starving little girl! Margarita Calienta Morley!" Alex laughed, and slapped Tiger on her rump, said, "Ok, shows over!" Tiger returned to the others at the bar—they went back to talking again.

Alex fixed herself another slammer. The Editor asked, "You said there was another tale—" Alex slammed, threw down the drink, caught her breath, "Yes! Sure! It's shorter! A male member of our business group found her", she pointed toward Tiger, "They fell in love. Now, she is an equal partner in a very successful company—it promises a sizable income for the rest of her young life, without her even having to lift a finger! Besides that, she is an Archaeologist working for the US Government on Special Projects. And I'm a Special Agent for a department of the US Government assigned to Senorita Margarita Calienta as her personal bodyguard." She stopped, slipped her purse's strap off her shoulder, slowly laid the purse flat on the table—it was unzipped—slowly she moved her hand inside, then slipped out the 40 caliber DaWo pistol. The three men's eyes got as large as possible. She left it lying on the table, her right hand on the grip, her right index finger slowly slipped toward the trigger. But she stopped, held her pose, asked, "Any questions, Boys?" With their sights glued to the pistol, they all shook their heads.

In a flash, Alex jerked her purse and the gun—it was properly gripped, straightened her back and pointed the pistol at them, all in one swift, smooth motion. All three snapped back, almost fell over backwards. She laughed, then replaced the gun in her purse. Without another word, she picked up the bottle of tequila and headed for the bar. But the Editor quickly called out, "You used a different last name, Morley! What's that about?" She stopped, turned back, snapped, "That's her USA family name! Morley! She's a descendant of S.G.Morley! You know, the famous writer!" She went on to the bar.

The Editor leaned back, put his hands behind his head as he said, "Man! What a story! Wait until this hits the streets!" "Wait? Streets? This is going on the air—tonight! On the six P.M. news!" The TV stringer exclaimed as he stood, nodded, added "I've got to run! See you two where ever they are!" He started to leave, but the Editor stopped him with, "Hey! Aren't you going to check out these gals before putting anything on the air? Who knows, these two could be B.S. artist!" The stringer stepped back, leaned over the table and asked, "So?" "Listen, I've got connections with Central Data in Mexico City. I'll check them out ASAP, give you a call—Ok? Just a favor, to be sure we both put out the same story—the true story, Ok?" "Sure, but no later than five! Our drop-dead is at five—at five, we go with whatever!" The TV stringer left.

The other two men stood, started to leave, but the Editor went to Alex, asked, "Ok, Sweetheart, we believe you. What about tonight? Is there more to this 'revenge' show?" "Yes, today was just the warm up, tonight, be at the entrance to the Riviera! We start at nine P.M.!" "Thanks, Alex! I wouldn't miss it for the world! I guess you know there will be coverage of you two on the six P.M. local TV newscast! There will be a crowd at the Riviera if what you just told me JUST HAPPENS TO LEAK OUT!" "The more, the merrier! Help that leak get started!" "No problem, no one can keep a secret in this town!" He smiled, lifted her right fingers and kissed the back of her hand and then he left.

Alex slipped between Max and Tiger, said, "I hate to break up a party, you two, but it is almost three. And we've still got to buy dresses!" Around of goodbyes, and Alex paid the bill—she didn't want Marie to have to wait for a payment from 'somebody'—the three left.

At three fifteen, the Editor rushed off a 'E" mail to Central Data Center in Mexico City—it requested confirmation about Alex and Tiger's identity, and if any, their official titles or connection with the US Government, and to confirm the date of their entry into Mexico. He waited, and off and on, checked his incoming 'E' mail box. By three-thirty, it showed up;

'Hawkins, Alexandra, white female, USA citizen, Department of Agriculture, Special Agent—licensed to carry weapons, permit accepted by Mexican Officials, age 32'—and the rest of her physical description. And,'Photo copy, frontal view, available on request. Entered Mexico Feb. 12th, at Ciudad Juarez'

Morley, Margarita Calienta, Maya female, USA citizen, Department of Interior, Archaeologist, Special Projects, age 21'—and then the rest of her physical description. And, 'Photo copy, frontal view, available on request. Entered Mexico Feb. 12th, at Ciudad Juarez,'

He requested a display of the photo copy of Alex's frontal view. Almost immediately her face appeared. He printed a copy. Then he repeated this routine for Tiger. Holding up the two printouts, he leaned back, said, "Well, I'll be damned! Dead ringers! And I thought these gals may be B.S. artists!"

Then he called a 'friend' in the City Police Records Department and asked for a favor.

As soon as he got all he wanted, he called the TV stringer, gave him the news—and he mentioned that the two gals would be at the Hotel Riviera at nine tonight. Stringer came back, "I got one better than that! They are staying at the Hotel Oltas Altas! And 'old 'Z' is giving a private reception party tonight at eight! See you there before eight!"

When the three left Marie's native bar/club, Max turned East at the paved road, went to the junction with the major North-South highway, route 15. Heading South, Max followed Business 15 into the heart of Mazatlan—passed the Central Bus Station, the huge Mercado (Market), and continued south. Turning East, and approaching a warehouse section of 'Old Town', he made a phone call—he didn't say anything to Alex. Slowing at a huge brick building—it covered an entire block—he turned in through a set of heavy wood doors. Driving into the open courtyard, he swung right, close to a set of personnel steps at a single door. Alex saw to the left of the courtyard, many garages with several other limos—some were white, some black—and many trucks—different sizes and types. There were several men working among the vehicles. Some of the open front storage portals were filled with chairs, tables, and what appeared to be disassembled tents—all the articles were white.

As Max helped Tiger, then Alex, out, a man who looked to be in his mid-forties opened the door at the head of the step's platform. He was dressed immaculately in a gray pin-stripped three piece suit. Talking on a cell-phone, he casually waved for them to come up. A much younger man joined him—he held a note pad and was jotting down as the older man almost whispered to him. He too was finely dressed.

Max followed the two up, clicked his heels and bowed to the older man. Max quickly introduced Tiger, then Alex to the two gentlemen. Holding the phone to one side, the older one said. "I'm pleased to finally meet you both", he lightly chuckled, added "You seem like close friends, I've heard so much from my Father-in-Law Senor Zazueta since late last night! My name is Hernando Montejo—please call me 'Herny'!" He kissed the ladies' hands, motioned that they enter—he went back to talking on the phone.

Max returned to the limo. Quickly, Herny said "This is my Secretary, Tony, please excuse us, but we're in the middle of something here."

A female Manageress met them, bowed, introduced herself, motioned for Alex and Tiger to follow her. Herny just waved them on, and continued to whisper details to Tony. Deeper into the huge building they went; there were rows of doors on both sides of the narrow hall—the doors on the left were continuous sliding ones. The older lady slid some open as they walked on—it was all closets, filled with different groups of clothes—men's tuxedos, little boys' tuxedos, ladies gowns—on and on—shoes, hats, veils, gowns' 'trains'—on and on! The many doors on their right were to 'private' fitting rooms.

"We have several gowns already selected—Senor Z was kind enough to describe you two lovely ladies—he has a excellent eye for guessing sizes, and—well, he knows the ladies!" She chuckled, added, "You're both in white I see, Senor Z had also guessed you wanted white gowns—Is that right?" "Yes, for both of us", Alex replied. "Are you to be individually fitted? Or had you rather be together—help one another? Some ladies are particular about—well—undressing with friends." Tiger and Alex smiled at each other, Alex answered, "Together—we are very, very close!"

The lady smiled, nodded, as she led them into a larger dressing room. The walls were completely covered with mirrors, there were four young ladies—the 'fitters', Alex assumed. For the next hour, it was almost a frenzy! But, finally it came down to two gowns. As Alex and Tiger turned, twisted, bent, sat and got up, they finally hugged each other. Then Alex said to the Manageress, "A favor, please—I want Max's opinion! Would you please get him in here?" "That's highly unusual." Then she hesitated. "Do you want me to go get him?" Alex snapped. "No! No!" The lady then snapped her fingers to one of the younger ladies then pointed a finger toward the outer door. The 'fitter' ran.

Both gowns were white, both tightly fitted, the hems just above the knees, splits on both sides—these came up to about mid-thigh—and all the straps on Tiger's gown were tiny 'spaghetti' straps. They wore white spike heels, with tiny straps around their ankles.

Tiger's gown had a brocade, panel in the front—it started just above her crotch, very 'Veed' here, and gradually widened as it came upward to each side of her ample bosom. Under her breasts, the panel stiffened into support cups that barely covered her nipples' red areas. To the outside, two straps extended up and tied behind her neck. The back was cutout, very wide—straight down under each armpit, then in a gently curve as the cut-out crossed the top of her_buttocks. The rest of the gown was a soft, thin satin material.

At Alex's insistence, the cutout exposed the upper part of her buns cleavage—and the most important thing—as Alex insisted—it exposed Tiger's Maya spot. Technically, this is named 'A Mongolian Spot'. And Tiger's was perfectly placed—dead center of her cleavage, and it was purple-black, the size of a half-dollar coin.

At the small of Tiger's back, there was another tie-strap—and higher, inline with the bottom of her bust cups, there was another strap.

"That's beautiful! Alex exclaimed as she admired Tiger's lower back, particularly her 'Beauty Spot'. The Spanish attendants and the Manageress seemed—but they didn't say anything—rather putout at Alex's insistence that the spot be SO revealing! And that was exactly the reaction Alex wanted! And the reaction she wanted tonight!

During Tiger's early days at Hidden Valley, she was extremely shy about her 'mark', but the others convinced her it was attractive, and, besides, no other race carried a 'build-in' identification! Of course, this includes the Maya's 'home-race', The Mongolian Race.

With Alex's small bosom, the stiff 'push-up' cup approach just didn't work. 'They' decide on a tightly fitted body, satin, to under her bust line. In front, above here was a panel of stretchy, see-thru material. It was soft enough to not depress Alex's nipples, and open-laced enough to show the dark shade of her nipples. The front continued up, over her shoulders and around her neck, The extreme cut-out back was also of this material as was the stand up, ruffled collar. The see-thru portion of the back dipped down to cross over the upper part of her buns. But, of course, she didn't have a 'beauty spot', what little Cherokee blood she had just didn't warrant the 'spot'! Three small cloth covered buttons closed the back—the dress definitely required an assistant!

Max entered the room, led by the young 'fitter', the others stood back as Alex and Tiger turned and turned, and twisted. Finally they stopped. Facing Max, Alex asked, "Well? You think this is impressive enough?" "Yes! Indeed! You both are amazingly gorgeous! You two will set the Golden Zone on its—head!" Alex extended her right hand, they shook, she said, "Thanks! I wanted a man's opinion!" He left. Alex turned to the Manageress, remarked, "Ok! That's a wrap! Now, get us out of these! Please!"

Two assistants—with the two huge boxes—led Alex and Tiger toward the exit door. Herny and his Secretary caught up with them, he said, "You ladies finished already? Some take days!" "We don't have days! Thank you for everything!" Alex responded. "I'll see you two tonight! 'Poppy'—Senor Z—is having a reception for you two in the restaurant at eight!" He stopped and began on his phone again. As they got into the limo, Alex thought, 'That's nice to know! Now it's be ready by eight! Instead of nine! Wow! What a rush!'

As Max pulled up in front of the Hotel Oltas Altas, they saw the sign on the restaurant glass, "Closed tonight-Private Party".

It was exactly eight as Tiger stepped to the bottom step leading into the dining room. With all the pearls to accent her stunning dress, she was magnificent.

Stopping, she slowly cocked her right hip—the split revealed a lot of her gorgeous brown thigh. Smiling, she turned her face toward the center of the room. There were about twenty guests, mostly middle or older aged couples, everyone was dressed excellently for this occasion—The ladies wore a lot of jewelry. The dining room had been rearranged—only two tables, one at the center with a large punch bowl and crystal cups, another smaller table near the front glass. This had a silver bowl filled with ice packed around a bottle of champagne. There was only four wine glasses there.

Dressed in a medium gray pin-stripped suit, Senor Zazueta stepped to Tiger, lifted her right fingers and kissed her hand. Still holding her hand, he turned to the group, said, "Please allow me to present Senorita Margarita Calienta!" The guests patted-patted a pleasant applause. Everyone smiled and nodded toward Tiger. Senor Z slowly led Tiger to the side of Juan at the punch table. Juan was dressed in a brilliant white uniform—well starched and ironed. He didn't wear his usual cap, his hair was combed back in perfection. The two smiled at each other, and waited.

Senor Z returned to the bottom of the stairs, extended his hand upward as Alex slowly stepped to the last step. He kissed her hand then announced her, "Senorita Alex, Special Agent of the USA Government!" The group again applauded softly. Alex, escorted by Senor Z, was joined

with Tiger at the punch table. Juan served them—just the two of them—cups of punch. Tiger extended hers toward the guests, slowly moved it from side to side as she said, "To all our friends. Thank you for being kind enough to come tonight!" Alex clicked Tiger's cup, they sipped. The guests began to come forward to the table as Juan served them. The front curtains were pulled open, Alex looked out. The entire length was filled with faces and cameras—all as close as possible. Over the heads, she saw the top of the TV station's van. Searching among the faces, Alex recognized the TV stringer, the newspaper editor and his photographer. Moving to each, she pointed and 'mouthed', 'you', 'you', and 'you'. Then she pointed toward the front door. The door was locked. After locating Senor Z, she asked if he would go with her and let the three 'special' reports inside. The two left the dining room, he unlocked the door but held it tightly. Only opening it slightly, Alex peered through the crack, saw that the three had shoved their way to the door. Senor Z let them in, one at the time, then forced the door shut—and locked it.

With the five in the lobby/bar, Alex and Senor Z explained the plans— get ready to record and take photos, Max was to blow his horn when he arrived, Alex wanted coverage of their first meeting with the escorts, then the formal introductions in the dining room at the smaller 'champagne table. And their first toast to each other, then everyone was on their own.

Senor Z glanced at his watch, made his way to Tiger and guided her back to the lobby. The three newsmen got behind the bar and got their equipment ready—even the editor had a camera. Outside, the right lane- the one closest to the hotel—had been barricaded off by a squad of City Policemen. They were still outside, controlling the traffic and the crowd. So far, only the TV and official reporters' vehicles were inside the blocked off area directly in front of the hotel.

As Max approached from over the knoll to the South, two cops removed the barricade at that end and let him 'inside'. At exactly the pre-arranged time, Max blew the horn, got out and let the two gentlemen out. Max roughly pushed a path through the crowd, the escorts followed him.

The two professional escorts were indeed handsome. Alfonso Morales; six feet tall, slim, tight looking, white skin, and with slightly wavy, black hair—trimmed close and parted on one side. And Estrada Landivar; about two inches shorter, broader shoulders, slightly round face, coarse straight black hair pulled back to a small pony-tail. And his skin was darker, his eyes black, revealed a definite 'splash' of Indian blood somewhere in his history. They both wore black tuxedos and white carnation boutonnieres in their lapels. Alfonso held a clear plastic box that contained a black orchid wrist bouquet. The bouquet Estrada had was a white orchid.

The two smiled as they—side by side—followed Max. Alfonso waved slightly and nodded at several of the newsmen. Max held the door widely open, the two entered together. "Senor Estrada Landivar!" He nodded at the shorter, darker gentleman. Then, "Senor Alfonso Morales!" Max nodded at the other. Max went back outside, closed the door behind himself, took a guard's stance with his arms crossed, he stood as big as possible—that was very big! Several of the 'fans' had felt Max's wrath before—they didn't want to again. The crowd backed away a few feet.

The TV camera had started 'rolling' as soon as Senor Z unlocked the door and let Max and the two escorts in. The newspaper photographer snapped photos as the two gentlemen were introduced by Max. And both had taken 'shots' of Tiger's and Alex's expressions as they first saw the escorts.

Before the escorts could reach for the ladies' hands, Senor Z raised a finger, glanced at the photographers and said, "Excuse me, we want to take the next photos in the dining room." Taking Alex and Tiger in tow, he led them to the smaller champagne table, turned them to 'proper positions', returned to the escorts, took the boxes with the wrist bouquets. He nodded to the two escorts indicated that they follow him. At the table, he positioned them. Estrada facing Tiger and Alfonso facing Alex. Juan quickly fitted the flowers on the ladies wrists. Senor Z saw that the three newsmen were in position. Then, one couple at the time—and loud enough for the guests, and the TV camera to hear—he formally introduced the four. The bows, kissed hands, the ladies' curtsies were all recorded on film. Senor Z stepped back to the far end of the ceremony as Juan came and served the champagne—one glass at the time—and each couple, individually, with

Tiger and Estrada first, toasted their dates. As the cameras ran or recorded, Senor Z, Senor Montejo and Juan were visible in the backgound.

With Tiger and Alex at their elbows, the escorts slowly, gracefully, moved among the guests and personally introduced the ladies to 'old acquaintances'. The professional escorts knew everyone there!

And Tiger beamed with happiness!

When Alfonso started with Herny, he said, with a pleasant chuckle, "I'm sure you two have met." "Yes, we have", Alex replied as she took Herny's hand. She leaned forward, almost whispered, "What? No cell phone?" the three chuckled, then Al completed the formalities. Alex finished with, "Senor Montejo, we are so grateful, we couldn't have done this without you—and your gracious people." He leaned close, softly said, "Thanks, but it is I who am grateful—", he smiled into her black eyes, squeezed her small hand tighter, added, "You'll get the bill tomorrow." The three chuckled again.

Shortly before nine, Alex glanced out the front glass—there wasn't anyone there! And only Max's limo and the two cars of 'their' reporters were parked outside! She thought, 'The news has leaked out! Great! With Al in tow, she quickly went to the reporters, said "You guys stick with us! You three can work the 'inside' coverage!" They thanked her and began to get their gear ready for traveling!

As their limo approached the Hotel Riviera, the crowd was easily visible, including the TV van and the reporters' cars and the policed again with barricades trying to maintain a path for vehicles to get under the entrance canopy. As Max slowed, he slid open the sun-roof panel, leaned back and said, "Estrada, I think you and Senorita Margarita should stand and wave to her fans!" Estrada knew the routine, he pulled out the box mounted into the rear-facing seat, took Tiger's hand, the couple stood—and the crowd cheered as the handsome—and beautiful—couple waved back!

The two escorts had been informed 'up-front' 'that Senorita Margarita Calienta was to be the STAR! And everyone else was to support her 'role'!

The four in the rear had been arranged so that Tiger would be the first to exit the limo. As Max helped her out, she hesitated, cocked her hip, placed her hands 'just right' and Max loudly announced, "Senorita Margarita Calienta has arrived!" The crowd went wild, surged the police line, but it held them back. Flash bulbs were almost constant! As they entered the building, Max led, Tiger and Estrada—her arm hooked in his elbow—Alex and Al next. Alex cast a quick glance over her shoulder—she saw that the three 'special' reporters had fallen in close behind her, she gave them a quick smile and nodded to them.

The group—Tiger's party—didn't wait for the Concierge, Max led them all the way to the dining room doors. He held the door open, and bowed as 'his' party entered. Then he returned to the limo and moved it to the special parking zone just for limos. He checked his cell phone—he had slipped Alex a very small one for her purse so she could call ahead when she wanted the limo moved into position. It would be simple, the phones had direct dialing keys.

Estrada felt Tiger's hand on his arm tighten, and suddenly she placed her other hand on his forearm. Her grip gradually clamped more and more, and she slowed her steps. He sensed something wasn't pleasant to the beautiful young lady he was escorting into the dining room. Tiger continued to sweep her view from one side of the huge elegant room to the other side—he couldn't decide if she was looking for someone or something in particular or not. When the Maitre d' approached them, he would have sworn that Tiger flinched, and she squeezed his arm even tighter. And she stopped walking. Except for her head and her hands, she tighten and 'froze'in place.

The opulence, the lavishness, the people shocked young Tiger, she had never seen such a display. And when she abruptly realized she was among 'them'—a room full of 'them'—her entire mind and body wanted to rebel, run away from 'them'!

She jerked her head to the right, and stared out through the huge glass wall—the lights were bright around the magnificent swimming pool area—beyond there, she saw the concrete retaining wall. Suddenly, she was not in the lavish dining room any more—she was sitting on the warm sand, leaning back against the warm concrete wall. But she shivered any-way—she was so hungry—so skinny—she was fifteen-'filthy trash'—she shivered again.

Estrada felt her tight hands as they began to quiver—short jerking motions as she stared off to their right, out through the large glass wall.

Instantly-she wasn't at the wall, she briefly glimpsed the beautiful white, fluffy clouds stream about her. "Hold me, hold me tight." she gently, softly asked—to no one in particular—to anyone.

"Hold me, hold me tight", Estrada heard, he twisted to face her and wrapped his big arm around her shoulders, her back. He pulled her tight to his large chest, and said, "It is Ok, I have got you, I am holding you. Hold on."

The Maitre d' stepped back and waited.

Alex saw, and felt, something was wrong, she pulled Alfonso with her as she stepped close to Tiger's back. With her right arm, Alex hugged around Tiger's neck, and leaning to Tiger's ear, Alex whispered, "Hold on, Kid, It's Ok. We have got you. Hold on. Hold on."

Tiger knew—she had heard it long ago—seeing, going to the upper-world, the white clouds, without asking to, was the prelude to disappearing without control. Most never came back! But, she heard their soft voices—'hold on, hold on—'

Alex felt Tiger as she slightly shook her head, and broke the stare to the pool area. Alex straightened up, and stepped back with Al. Squeezing his elbow, Alex said, in just above a whisper, "She'll be Ok, stage fright, I think—", but Alex wasn't really sure—she didn't really know.

"Margarita, it's Ok—just follow me, I'll take care of you. Don't worry, it is Ok." Estrada had leaned down close to her ear and calmly, smoothly spoke encouraging, soothing words to the frightened young lady. He lightly patted her hand, the one on his forearm, then he lifted her chin, lifted her face toward his, and smiled into her eyes. She slowly relaxed her vise-like grips, and slowly smiled back. He pulled her closer, gave a light tug—she leaned her head against his shoulder. He felt her give a slight sigh. Turning back to being side by side, he calmly spoke to the Maitre d' who had patiently waited, "We are the party of Senorita Margarita Calienta!"

The Maitre d' led them on into the huge dining room and he helped with the seating. Then he directed the three reporters with their camera gear to another table that was close by. As Alfonso held her chair back, Alex hesitated, she took her time before being seated, she glanced around. The magnificent dining room—it was full, their tables were about center, most all the ladies present were whispering to each other or their partners. The men just stared at Tiger and Alex. No doubt, they were the youngest and most beautiful in sight! Alex couldn't resist—she held both her

hands high above her head, slowly turned a full circle as she smiled and nodded in the direction of the guests. Then she sat down. As the head waiter came and removed the reservation cards from the tables, Alex noticed that the cards showed "Senorita Margarita Calienta and party", everything was working out as planned.

After ordering, and the first round of champagne—the three toasted to Tiger—Alex shifted the centerpiece out of her way. She stretched her arms to Tiger, took her hands, and asked, "Tig, are you ok? Really ok with this? We can call it off, if—" "Don't be silly! Sure, I'm ok—I guess I was just slightly amazed at all this!" They squeezed hands, Alex broke it off, dropped the subject and moved the centerpiece back in place, said, "Great! Let's have another drink!"

The meal was light for the ladies; Alex had stuffed mushrooms and a few fried oysters and a small salad. Tiger, scampied shrimp on a bed of satue' vegetables and a small salad. The gentlemen had steaks and salads. And they all drank champagne with the meal.

The band was playing soft, slow dance music. With the dishes removed, the escorts asked for them to dance—there wasn't anyone else on the dance floor. They danced, tightly squeezed together with an occasional sexy move, the others in the room continued to stare at the four. Alex decided the dancing wasn't really 'going any where'. Near the end of the second dance, Alex nodded to Tiger to follow her toward the front of the band stand. They 'danced' in that direction. When close and centered in front of the band, Alex said to Tiger, "Disappear." "Oh, Alex, I'm not sure that's a good idea—this tight dress—these shoes—holding hands—" Tiger made excuses. "Turn her loose" Alex said to Estrada. 254////

Without questioning, he released Tiger. Alex and Al were facing them—and suddenly Tiger was gone! Disappeared! The people gasped—stunned! Some said out loud "Where did she go!" Or, "Never!" Or the men, "What the hell!" Alex's date froze, the band stopped playing. And Estrada frantically looked about, totally confused! Alex broke Al's grip, stepped back, turned toward the other guests, and slowly bowed! Straightening up, She waved one hand toward Estrada—he was still searching for Tiger—then she began to clap! The crowd joined in—but they were still amazed! Placing her palms to each side of her mouth, Alex loudly called out, "Tiger! Ok! That's enough! You can come back now!" Tiger, as suddenly as she had disappeared, was back at Estrada's side. She bowed to the guests, turned, and as if nothing had happened, she took Estrada's hands in the dance position—they started dancing. Alex joined Al and the four finished without music! The members of the band were still stunned the Editor snapped to the two photographers, "What the hell was that? Did you two get that with your cameras?" The TV stringer quipped back, "Hey! Writer-man!

You can NOT record what is NOT there! Hell, no we didn't get that! Besides, if I had been filming, no one would believe it. It would look as if there was a 'cut-away', or I just stopped while she walked out of view!" The newspaper photographer just shook his head. There must be some way!" the Editor said. "Yes! See it with your own eyes!" Stringer replied.

As they headed for the table, Alex hugged Tiger, said, "Tiger, you were great! These rich bitches will never forget little Margarita! Let's get out of here!" The two escorts smiled, nodded at the two ladies! They too were amazed—and would never forget these two 'strangers from somewhere'! And what was this 'Tiger' thing Alex had said?

At the table, the headwaiter pulled out a chair for Alex, but she roughly shoved it back to the edge of the table, she snapped, "Don't bother! Just get the check! We're going up to OUR SUITE!" She turned to the reporters, almost shouted, "Follow us, Boys! The location is changing!"

After she quickly signed the bill, she took Al's elbow, they left the dining room—the others followed. In the hall, instead of turning toward the front entrance, she turned toward the elevators. "Where now, little Alex?" Al asked. Slipping her fingers in her purse, she pulled out a Hotel Riviera room key, shook it at the others, said, "Private photo session in the fanciest suite in this joint!" The reports heard, they slapped each other on the backs or shoulders. At the elevator doors, she saw a young man from room service, she snapped her fingers, motioned for him to come to her. "We're in a hurry, Sweetie, get us a bottle of cold champagne—", she glanced at their party, added, "And seven glasses up to—", she showed the young man the room key, "as soon as possible! Got it?" "Yes Mam! Senorita Alex!"

As they rushed inside the suite, Alex quickly informed the others of her plans; a few shot sipping glasses with their arms hooked together, 'us' sitting on 'their' laps on the sofa—both couples. She stopped, opened the curtains, the view looked North, Alex continued, a few maybe on the balcony—with the lights of the other hotels in the background. She moved to the bedroom, they followed. Maybe pile up the pillows, sitting back and sipping? Whatever! The others agreed as the cart with the champagne and glasses was wheeled in. It didn't take long—finishing off the bottle, they headed out and down. And Alex called Max on 'her' new cell phone.

After getting in the limo, Alex jerked around to Max, said, "Hold it ! Until I say go!" The sunroof was still open, she stood on the box, waved to the crowd and shouted as loud as possible, "Free drinks inside! On the Hotel Riviera!" The crowd—it looked even larger than when they had arrived—turned, pushed pass the cops, the Doorman, and then rushed in! As she dropped down inside, Al caught her around her hips—her butt. She said, "Hit it, Max! To the next hotel North!" Her date pulled her down into his lap, laughed, "Alex! Are you always this much fun? This wild?" "I hope the hell so!" she snapped, twisted and kissed him hard on his lips. Estrada laughed, asked Tiger, "Is she really?" "Most of the time—except when she is working! Then she is a heartless bitch!" He started to ask something, "Margar—" Tiger interrupted, "It's Tiger! My name inside this limo is Tiger!" "That's what I was going to ask! Tiger? Why Tiger?" "Because I eat people when I'm angry!" They all laughed, even Max.

Looking in the rearview mirrors, Max said, "I don't think that crowd will make it! There's a lot of flashing blue lights back at the Riviera!" Alex slapped the dates' knees, remarked, "I'm sorry guys! But I just had to do that! Will it harm your reputations? As perfect escorts?" Al spoke up, "Alex, with all this publicity, I might try making movies!" Estrada added, "I haven't seen such spell-bound fans since I saw Liz and Burton get in a shouting match at the El Cid! Man! Could those two cuss!" "So much for Liz's proper English up-bring!" Alex commented.

As Max pulled under the canopy of Playa Mazatlan Hotel, Alex said, "Ok, gang, we'll have to take a slightly different approach. How sexy can you two guys dance?" "X-rated, Sweetheart!" Al replied. Estrada nodded in agreement. "Ok, we hit the bars, make these old bitches eyes pop-out!" Ok?" "Suits me fine!" Estrada answered, then he placed his hand on Tiger's knee, asked, "Is that ok with you?" "Sure! I've been to Mardi Gras! In New Orleans!" She moved his hand up to her crotch and leaned her ample bosom closer to his face.

At Al's and Estrada's advice—they knew where the bars in the different hotels were that 'normally' had the most 'rich-Gringas'—the four were able to move along rapidly. As soon as the four were satisfied that the other guests knew who Tiger and Alex were, and the others were impressed—either favorable or not, it didn't matter which—with the two couples' sensuous, sexy—almost illegal dancing, they moved to the next bar which had a dancing area with 'rich-Gringas'.

Even at the first place, several of Tiger's fans showed up and supported their 'exhibitions'. As the four changed locations, Alex let the crowds know where they were going next. Before long, the number of fans that followed them and new ones that joined the group reached a sizable number.

In each place, the two couples were able to 'shut-down' any others that were already dancing there. And when the two couples had the dance floor to themselves, this was when they really got 'down and dirty' with their moves! If Alex hadn't known better, she would have sworn that she had sex with Al several times! The Man could move! And apply pressure to all the right spots!

By one A.M., as the four climbed back in the limo, and after they had visited the last of the hotels, Alex asked, "Well, Kid, do you feel better? Do you think we may as well call 'it' finished?" Tiger slipped to Alex's side, put her arms around her, softly said, "Alex, you were right. Yes, I think I'll remember this night—instead of—I am ecstatic!" Tiger hugged tighter, Alex gently took Tiger's face in her hands and kissed her hard in the mouth—and held the kiss for a while. Their dates just raised their eyebrows at each other. They knew not to ask. Alex suddenly pulled apart, twisted toward Max, patted him on his shoulder and screamed "Max! Head for Marie's! I just had a brilliant idea!" "Right on!" Max exclaimed.

Alfonso thought, 'It's after one, just had a very hectic evening, and little Alex has an idea? And a brilliant one at that! Man! What a woman!' Estrada thought, 'I don't recognized Marie's—but what the hell!' The two men didn't dwell on this very long—Alex suddenly shifted about, removed her heels, and wiggled her pantyhose down as she said, "These bastards are too damn hot! My little—thing—can't breath!" The two escorts double over with laughter, Tiger just gently kissed Alex's forehead and patted her on the top of her head, then softly said, "Poor thing, she gets bent out of shape about the least little things, like her tiny suffocating—" The two men folded up in deep belly laughs!

Alex reached around, got her shoes, and tossed these to Al. With the pantyhose still in her hand, she let the window down, and as she threw these out, she quipped, "I wouldn't want Max's big ole limo, to end up smelling like a two-bit whore house!" They all laughed. Alex shifted to the seat opposite Al, pulled her dress hem up to her crotch, sat back and placed one bare foot to the outside of Al's thighs, and the other bare foot to his crotch. "Al, Honey, please put my shoes back on for me." Alex smiled as he couldn't decide to look at her shoe, or her open-air crotch.

As Max turned left on the paved road leading to Marie's, he watched the mirrors, and said, "We've still got tails, and we picked up some more when we passed the Riviera. And it is not just the three reporters either, it's a lots more! "Alex snapped, "Great! The more the merrier! I want everyone to know where Marie's place is!" Then she explained to Al and Estrada; their 'duties' were completed—from here on, it was 'free-lance' party-time, Alex's fashion! Ok? "If you two want, Max can call you a taxi. This might go on until sunrise!" Alex closed with. The escorts, without hesitation, agreed to stick with Alex—they would love to see 'Alex's fashion!'

Parked around Marie's were seven or eight older cars, at one end of the building were many bicycles. Under the shadows of the overhanging roof were several couples. As Max wheeled the long limousine as close as possible to the open front door, one of the 'local' women—one that had met Alex earlier today— recognized the car—and Max. She screamed, "They are here!" And she ran in, continuously screaming, "They are here!" "The music from the local group had been so loud it rattled the old metal roof, but it abruptly stopped. And everyone inside ran out and swarmed around the limo.

Max got out, and in a jovial attitude, pushed his way through the crowd. Opening the rear door, and 'handing' Tiger out—as she stood—Max shouted, "Permitame presenter La Senorita Tiger Calienta!" A guy in the group called out, "Por que Tiger?" Tiger yelled back, "Because I eat smart-ass guys like you!" The crowd laughed, screamed and squealed, jumped and waved. Tiger moved just enough for the other three to squeeze out. On seeing Alex, there was another round of screams, cat-calls, jumping and waving. Alex extended her hands as high as possible, yelled, "The drinks are on me! Alex!"

The crowd switched their attention, forced their way inside. Max led the party of four in as he hugged, patted and grabbed in fun and joined cheers with the locals. Four of the local 'regular ladies' quickly fell in step with the two handsome escorts. And they began 'small-talk'. Bumping through the crowd was a young guy not much larger than Alex, he roughly grabbed Alex around her waist, said, "Alex! I saw you on TV—the news!" "How did I look?" she asked as she slipped her arm around his neck. "Good! Good enough to eat!" She pulled her arm tight, brought his face close to hers, "Eat? I want a drink! And you, wise guy! You're talking about eating! How good are you at mixing 'slammers?" She relaxed her grip. "I'm the best 'Slammer' in all of Mexico!" "Great! Let's slam some!" They made their way to the bar together.

After a couple of slammers, Alex glanced around, looked for Alfonso and Estrada—it looked as if they were ok, there was a local 'lady of the evening' on each knee—and they all had drinks. She then spotted Max and Marie—they were together. Pulling the small guy, she forced her way through the others and joined Max. She interrupted whatever they were talking about, said, "Marie, Max, let's step out side—where I don't have to scream!" The band was back at 'mega-watts' blasting out some warp speed Mexican number! As they pushed on, Alex noticed that the people from the cars that had followed them were now inside—having a great time—and spending lots of money. These people hadn't heard Alex's "The drinks are on me!"

Once they got outside, Alex turned loose of 'small-guy', she put one arm around Max's waist and the other over Marie's shoulders. Hesitating until she had their attention, she asked, "Marie, how much would it cost me, for you to put a sign", she released Max, waved her arm toward the ridge line of the roof, added, "up there—high up, in bright lights! A sign showing"—she waited, then, "Marie's Margarita Calienta Cocktail Lounge and Restaurant"!" Marie countered, "But I don't have a restaurant—and we only cook a little at special times on a old outdoor grill", she motioned toward the rear of the building, added, "And cocktail lounge? No way could this place be called that!" "Ok! Ok! How about, 'Marie's Margarita Calienta Bar and Grill?" Marie was not a beginner at being in business, or people—she said, "Alex, you aren't just talking about a sign—are you?" "No, I'm talking about a business partnership—I furnish all the money, you fix up an acceptable bar, night club, cafe—indoor, or outdoor—fine restrooms"—Alex hesitated as she noticed 'small-guy' pissing against the wall—"Pave the road, pave a parking lot, put up lighted signs!" Alex hugged Marie, and continued, "You know what to do—I have the money—lots of money—it could work beautifully!"

Max had been paying close attention, he asked, "Ok, Alex, say if, just if—what kind of percentage do you want?" He waited. The 'small guy' joined them, but he didn't say a thing as he looked from one to the other. "First, I want Tiger's name in lights—damn bright lights—right there!" She pointed toward the roof again, "And we—I, mainly—will keep track of how much is invested. When up and successful, we have it appraised— legal, local realtors. That value will be the base—the starting point. And if, just if, the business is ever sold—even after I'm dead and gone—I, or my legal heirs, get the difference—only the difference—between the original 'base value' and the selling price! I'm not interested in a percentage of the 'take'—that hampers the operation, it would hamper Marie's desire to make it a success! Do you two understand?"

"In other words"—Max started, "You invest, and count on capital, long term property gains? Marie does the project, complete control, but of course with your request about publicity for Tiger, Marie keeps all the profits earned." He hesitated then added, "Who pays the taxes?" Alex screamed, "You Bandido! The damn taxes are operating expenses! The Business pays the taxes!" she poked him in his ribs and laughed! "Just trying! Just trying!" he laughed.

Alex said to both of them, "Besides, we've got the publicity! Everyone knows Margarita Calienta now!" Max pulled Marie off to one side, they talked. 'Small guy' stepped to Alex and slipped one arm around her waist, and slowly let it slide down to her butt—he began a slow rubbing motion. Alex, in deep thought, ignored him. When the other two returned to Alex, Marie opened, "Alex, let me introduce my son, Jose!" He was 'small-guy'! "He is a fine cook, just never had a proper place or customers. Alex hugged Jose, said, "You sly, cute little—I should have guessed something was up! The way your Mother let you grab-ass with me!" They all laughed, then back to business, Marie said, "Ok, it's a deal!!' She stuck out her right hand, the two shook.

As they walked toward the front door, Alex stepped close to Max, said, "Remind me to speak to Senor Z about the legal arrangements, communications, etc, etc." Max didn't know Alex well enough to realize she was also reeling him in as a potential business partner too! Back inside, Alex noticed that Tiger was still the 'Star' with a mixed group—'regulars', and 'new customers'—at the bar. They were all talking at once—in 'rapid-fire' Spanish!

Alex went to the table far in the corner where Alfonso and Estrada were. She leaned over, said "Well! I see you two narrowed the field to only two apiece!" There still was one woman on each knee. "How are you guys doing?" She asked seriously. "Ok, no problem, except I'm concerned about messing up this expensive suit! It belongs to Herny!" Al stated jokingly. "Simple!" Alex quipped, "Take the damn thing off before you start!" They laughed.

Alex asked, "No kidding, you two want to go with us—soon—I'm about bushed—I think Tiger is about loaded—or had you rather stay, call a taxi—or what?" The two shrugged, Estrada answered, "We had rather stay—if that's Ok with you?" "Sure! Hey! Take all four of them! More the merrier!" As she started to leave, she turned back and remarked, "Thanks guys! You both were grand!" Then she left.

Back to Max and Marie, she said, to Max, "If you can pry 'Bell Star' away from her fans, I'm about ready to go." Max headed for Tiger, Alex said to Marie, "I'll either contact you tomorrow, or have someone—a legal representative contact you—tomorrow. For tonight's bill, just add up whatever, I'll get it to you through Max someway!"

Max—with Tiger in tow—as the three slowly made their way to the limo, he asked, "Alex, have you made quick deals—expensive decisions—like this before?" "Max, Ole Boy, my last quick-deal took about thirty minutes—and netted me—personally, not our company—one point seven five million! US million!" He didn't mention quick-deals any more. And he never questioned Alex's ability concerning business again.

Juan had been the one appointed to wait up for Alex and Tiger. He had spent the last several hours cat-napping on the stool behind the bar. After letting the three in, he replaced Alex at Tiger's arm. Alex led the way up as Max and Juan practically carried Tiger up the thirty-nine steps. Entering their room, the guys laid Tiger on the bed, Alex looked at her, commented. "She's ok" Turning to Max, she asked, "Would you please wait outside? I'll just be a jif—I've got to get out of this dress!" As Max eased the door shut, Alex snapped to Juan, "Unbutton this damn thing! And help me skin it off! You can undress 'Sleeping Tiger' there after I-we—are gone!" She wasn't being modest to Max, she didn't want to lose the 'element of surprise'!

Naked, she splashed perfume in all the right places, pulled on short-shorts, a light crop-top and comfortable low tennis shoes. Jerking up her purse, she headed for the door. But she stopped, went back to one of the smaller Mitla bags and grabbed up a few condoms—she slipped two in her purse and threw two to Juan as she snapped, "Be sure to use those! Ok?" He just nodded as he began to untie Tiger's back straps.

Back at the limo, Alex got in the rear as she commented "I've never done 'it' in a limo! Do we have far to go?" Max smiled then remarked "No. Just over the knoll and South only a few blocks there is a small secluded parking spot, this is above a sandy cove. A really lovely little beach among the huge rocks!" "That does sound interesting—and—attractive indeed!" She didn't say, but she thought, 'And real handy for a moonlight 'quicky' with some of Max's wealthy clients—like me!'

As she quickly got ready, with the sunroof still open, she saw the nearly full moon overhead, and the moon's reflection on the open Pacific, and the sky was clear—not a cloud in sight.

When Max opened the rear door, Alex was completely naked, laid back on the huge seat, her feet toward the door he opened, her feet spread very wide—one foot on the floor, the other on the top of the seat back. And as she wanted, Max was very surprised! Alex had already decided 'it' would be a two part series; a quick, rough and hard first part inside the limo. Then later it would be a slow, long drawn out affair on the beach.

Like other men at the beginning of their first 'trick' with her, Max had a demur approach. She knew this was caused by him seeing her completely naked for the first time. Her miniature size, her small breasts, the absence of any hair anywhere on her body—these things created in their minds the image of a young child-girl. He, as others, started with caution, gently, even carefully. But she relieved his unnecessary concerns by whispering into his ear, "Max, I'm not really what you think you see—I'm not a child—you don't have to treat me as one—I can take 'whatever'—I really appreciate rough and tumble, hardy wild raw action—would you please?" And that was what she got!

They took a brief break, had a couple of drinks, then got ready for the second part; the slow, drawn out, tender, gentle session. Max, with the trunk open changed from his uniform and boots—he had only removed his coat for the 'quick' affair—to a pair of soft cotton tie-top pants and low tennis shoes—these were pull-ons. Then with a blanket from the trunk, they climbed down.

There was a path, it was steep, very narrow—as big as Max was he almost had to squeeze between the gigantic boulders that lined both sides of the path that twisted between these. It went down about thirty feet to the very secluded cove. Max was right about it being small—it was semi-circled for only about fifty feet total! With the brilliant moonlight, the shadows of the large boulders, the bright reflections on the open ocean and the white sand of the small beach, the entire scene was fantastic!

"Oh! Max! This is beautiful!" She ran from one end to the other and back to Max as he spread out the blanket. She ran to him, jumped up, caught him around his neck and locked her legs around his waist. And kissed him about his face, "Thank you so much! This is a wonderful surprise! Can we go swimming? Are there any dangerous currents? Is it deep?" Alex was like a kid for the first time here! "Do you know how to swim?" "Like a fish!" "This is open ocean, there are no currents—not ever much rise and fall with the tide! And, yes, it is deep—too deep to standup, except on the beach!" "Great!" she exclaimed as she jumped down and jerked off her top, shorts and shoes. She asked, "You coming?" "Wouldn't miss it for the world!" as he kicked off his shoes and pulled his pants down and stepped out of them.

As soon as Alex saw Max was out of his pants, she ran and grabbed his hands, jerked, "Let's run and dive in!" They did, then swam, and played in the clear water for a while. Running out of the water, she shook, and wiped at the water clinging to her small body and hair. She grabbed and hugged Max, he picked her up like a doll, stepped to the basket, calmly remarked, "There's another surprise in the basket." She leaned her head away, said, "Surprise me!"

There was a cold bottle of champagne, slices of rich cheese and a loft of baked bread—and two dry towels in the basket. After drying each other roughly—the water was rather cold—the two snacked and sipped, and lay on the blanket and enjoyed the fabulous scene.

"I feel so relaxed—so at ease with everything—Oh, Max—", he didn't let her finish, he started the second part of this affair. It seemed to last for hours and hours. Finished, and completely drained, she lay on top of Max—her arms on his arms, her legs on his legs, Alex slipped from total frenzy to total relaxation—she dozed off.

At this time Alex had no idea how important this quaint place would become to her family. And to Max's family.

CHAPTER 10

'Tap-tap-tap'—Lying flat on her back, Alex opened her eyes and looked at the ceiling high above. She couldn't recognize where she was—or how she got here—or when. It was as if her mind, her body was still too deeply relaxed to function. 'Tap-tap-tap'—It wouldn't go away and leave her alone! She jerked the sheet from over herself, leaving it over Tiger. Dressed only in her sleeping tee shirt—she didn't know, or remember how, or when she put this on—she jumped up, ran to the door. Opening it only a small distance, she shouted, "What!" It was Senor Z, he didn't verbally reply, he placed a newspaper flat over the opening and held it still. In a flash, Alex had read enough! Throwing the door wide open, she snatched the paper and continued to read as she slowly turned toward the bed. Motioning with a wave of one hand, the three—Senor Z, Juan, and Herny Montejo—followed her.

Suddenly, she jumped up and down several times, as she screamed, "We did it! We did it!" The others just waited. Grabbing the bed sheet, she slung it to the floor—Tiger had only her sleeping tee shirt on, it was bunched up under her armpits. Lying almost face down, Tiger's bare rump was exposed—Alex slapped it hard, then screamed, "The house is on fire! The house is on fire!" The three men looked back and forth to each other. Tiger twisted her head toward Alex, opened her eyes and asked, "It isn't really on fire, is it?" "No! Get up!"—Alex realized Tiger was naked from her armpits down, "Ops!" as she pulled down Tiger's shirt tail. "We did it! We did it! Not only a comment or two in the Social Column!

Not only the complete column—but two entire pages! Tiger! You are famous!

The Social hit of Mazatlan! Playa Northa!" Tiger bounded up, jerked the paper from Alex. Reading only the highlights, then she threw the paper to the bed and grabbed Alex in a bear hug. The two jumped up and down, and around as they screamed and yelled!

They separated, both grabbed their heads—dizzy, almost out of breath and 'out-of-gas'—they realized that last night, they had too much dancing, too much drinking, too much whatever else they did! "Oh, oh" Alex moaned as she staggered toward the men. Herny saw his opportunity, he asked, "Alex, you aren't leaving today, are you?" This was very important to him—his people almost had her bill ready! She stopped, blinked her eyes as she tried to focus them, replied, "No", she wasn't sure how much she wanted to reveal yet—"No—I've got to close a business deal! No idea how long it will take!"

All together, the men retorted, "Business deal!" Then everyone was silent. Senor Z looked to Juan and Herny, softly said, "I hope she's not going into hotels." Herny said, "I hope she's not going into the wedding game." Juan added, "I hope she doesn't know how to cook!" "Right! Juan! I can't even boil water without burning it!" Alex quipped, then chuckled. "Ok, Alex, what are you up to this time?" Senor Z asked.

"I'd rather not get into the details yet—want to close before—well—it leaks out." They waited. "Ok! Ok! It's sort of a silent partner arrangement with a local bar and grill!" she responded. Herny put two and two together very quickly—Max and Alex, Max and Marie, Alex and Marie! Herny slapped his hands to Z and Juan's shoulders, loudly said, "She is buying Marie's bar!" Alex, with a finger at her lips, "Quiet—really guys, keep this on the Q.T.—please? Pretty please?" They just nodded.

Herny went directly back to—Max and Alex. He took one step forward, pointed a stiff index finger at Alex's face, snapped, "you're after Max! Alex! Max has been with me from the beginning! No way am I going to lose Max!" Alex stepped to him, twisted to his side, put her arm around his waist, sweetly said, "Senor Montejo, I want to talk to you about that delicate subject. Let's—you and I—step out on the balcony and have a private"—she glanced at Z and Juan and Tiger, added, "conversation."

As Alex led him, she began to whisper into his ear. Tiger shouted, "Alex! You are bare assed! Put something on!" Alex twisted, cast Tiger a 'nasty' look for interrupting. But Alex didn't say anything, instead she looked around on the floor, found a pair of her tongs, jerked these on and jerked up very hard. Then she quipped, "There! Kid, is that better?"

The tongs, of course, had 'snapped' into her bottom—they were not even visible! Tiger fell back, flat on the bed, grabbed her head, moaned, "Coffee, food, coffee, food—" Alex resumed her 'private' conversation with Senor Montejo out on the balcony. Senor Z looked at Tiger, then at Alex, then he said to Juan, "Let's go—get some food, coffee up here—I sure as hell don't want these two gals to starve to death—not in the Hotel Oltas Altas!"

DOWN TOWN MAZATLAN
'The Mazatlan News' Office.

The Social Editor's phone range. Picking it up, Joe—the Editor—held it away from his ear as the Mayor of Mazatlan shouted into the other end of the connection. "What's this crap in your article? This—this-Margarita Calienta gal? And her so-called body guard? An Archaeologist on a special—secret—project—somewhere! You believed those two publicity hungry bitches? Do you know we had a riot at the Riviera? I had cops all over the place because of those two! And this Alex—a special agent for the USA Government! Have you lost your mind?" "No sir, it's all true—you know, the truth? I checked them out with Central Data in Mexico City— their credentials proved out everything in my article!" "And this baloney about her—Calienta—being arrested six years ago—thrown in the cell block, with, whatever—and given a ride out of town! That can't be true!" "Sorry, Sir, but City records confirmed it." There was silence from the Mayor, Joe added, "Off-hand, I'd say your guys screwed up! They listed the young girl's real name—Margarita Calienta!" Again, no reply. Joe continued, "And sir, the Morley part of her name? The real last name? Again according to Central Data—that's her USA family name." "She really is the grand-daughter of the famous Maya Researcher Sylvanus Griswold Morley?" the Mayor asked. Joe remarked, "Off-hand, I'd say your guys arrested the wrong little girl six years ago!" "And the elections for my Office are next month—I didn't need this, particularly NOW!" "Sorry, Sir, but it is all true and it was too good to pass up!" 'BANG', as the Mayor slammed the phone down. Joe leaned back and smiled.

CENTRAL DATA-MEXICO CITY

Antonio Valdes was performing his normal review of suspicious people or events. His phone rang, it was a young lady from the newspaper review section. Each day, newspapers from all over Mexico were reviewed, scanned, for information that might relate to suspects or unusual events on their 'special' list. "Senor Valdes, there is an article in this morning's Mazatlan News that you might want to see." "Please, just read it to me." "It's two pages—full— and it concerns Hawkins, Alexrandra—and Morley, Margarita Calienta, Sir—" "Hawkins and Morley! I'll be right down!"

As he read the Social News—Special Edition—he commented, "So, little Alex is now an 'assigned bodyguard'! And they—'were on their way to a special, secret Archaeological project—somewhere—not at liberty to say where—'. He read on, and close to the end, he said, "Ouch! Those two really stuck it to the City Cops! And the Hotel Riviera!" He thought, 'so Alex is using her 'Special Agent' status to help her friend, Margarita, to get back at whoever! So what! That's been done before—we'll just keep an eye on those two—nothing serious yet, anyway!'

Back at his deck, his phone rang, it was Colonel Gomez from El President's office. He rarely got calls from her, he snapped to, as she asked, "Tony, did you see The Mazatlan News this morning—the Social Special, about Hawkins and Morley?" "Yes, I did as a matter of fact!" He felt lucky to at least be up to Gomez's level on the present information. "What do you think?" "Seems innocent—Alex just using her position to help Margarita slap those locals in the face." "Ok, I agree on that part. But it's the 'on the way to something else'—and besides, Alex being a Special Agent, and being assigned to Margarita as a bodyguard? That part seems so unnecessary for what they wanted to accomplish in Mazatlan. They could just have well B.S.'ed their way through that. It all brings us back to—what are they really up to? Doesn't it? And it does confirm they're headed for something! But, what?" She waited. Tony wasn't sure about an answer, he stammered, "I'm not—yes, they're up to something—maybe—but—" Gomez interrupted, understood his position, she added, "Well! Looks like some of my people may as well find out, doesn't it?" "Yes, Colonel Gomez. With the possibility of losing them—I'd say your approach seems the way to go." "Thanks for your agreement", as if she actually needed that, Tony though—"We'll feed any additional data to your Department as it is gathered." Then she broke the connection.

Placing the phone down, Gomez reached to the silver case on the top of the President's desk, got a long, slim, black cigar and lit it with the silver lighter. Leaning back in the huge comfortable chair, she slightly pushed back from the huge magnificent desk, crossed her long slim legs and propped her heels on the top edge of the desk. As she took long, slow draws on the cigar, she slipped her free hand under her skirt and slightly adjusted her two 'special' garters—the ones that held two all fiberglass knives up between her thighs.

And she thought 'Who is the main Actress in this play? Is Alex really 'just' a bodyguard? And is Margarita really going to 'just' do something? But,if it is 'just' something, why all the bother? It's obvious from the photos, they are staying at the Hotel Oltas Altas—two nice chicks—two handsome agents—it shouldn't be too difficult—she reached for the phone. But there was 'something' in the far back of her mind, it kept nibbling at her thoughts—Hawkins? Alexandra Hawkins?

MAZATLAN HOTEL OLTAS ALTAS

As Alex and Herny slowly walked—arm in arm—toward the door, He asked, "Where are you going to be at—say—one fifteen?" "I'm not sure." She saw his apprehension, quickly she added "Really! I've got to get a Lawyer—now! I'll call you", she released his arm, stepped to her purse, pulled out the small cell phone, asked, "Let's see—you're number three on the 'speed-dial'?" "Yes—Hey! That's my phone!" "So, bill me!" He slapped her on her rump, said, "Alex, I'm out of here! Call, we'll get together!"

Tiger still lying on the bed, didn't move—she was almost asleep again. Juan arrived with a tray full of food—and lots of hot coffee. Tiger jumped up, looked at the food, kissed Juan on his cheek, said, "You're the greatest!" Then she whispered, "Was I good last night?" "The best!" he replied as he left. "Kid, it's nice to be the BEST!" Alex quipped as she grabbed a cup of coffee and a plate of breakfast then went to the balcony. Soon, Tiger joined her. About half finished, Tiger asked, "What's next?" "Not sure, close this deal, just go with the flow, I guess."—"You do remember, we have to be in Chiapas BEFORE March the fifth—don't you?" "Yes" was Alex's only reply, but she thought, 'And it's February the twentieth now—not much time—I've got to move in a hurry!' Alex mentally added the days—only today plus twelve days—not long! And this year just HAD to be a 'Leap Year'—we lost one day there!

When Alex stepped from the bathroom, she heard the loud noise as it came from the open doors to the balcony. Drying, she stepped closer, saw That Tiger had on short-shorts, and a crop-top and was barefooted.

And she was waving both hands at the crowd below. "Alex! They're waving! And taking pictures! And screaming for me!" Alex thought, but she didn't say, 'Kid, the way your beautiful tits are showing out the bottom of that short top, a concrete statue would wave!' But, Alex did say, "Great! You're a Star! That newspaper coverage showed that you put down the Hotel Riviera—and 'Down-town'!"

Alex began to search for clothes, she called out to Tiger, "Kid! After you wear out your arms and shoulders, take a shower, primp, slip on that white cocktail dress—go down and let your fans have some more!" "Really? You think I should?" "Sure! Do your hip-thing, let them get some great close-ups!"

Alex slipped on her loose 'driving' jeans, loose 'mans' shirt—she left the tail hanging out—and her low tennis shoes. Finding an older scarf and older sunglasses, she put these on. But her purse! That just wouldn't do! Picking up one of the smaller Mitla bags, she dumped the contents on the bed, and then dumped her purse into the bag. She located a note pad and a couple of pens and also put these in the Mitla.

Tiger looked around, to Alex, asked, "Where are you going? Dressed like that?"—"First, I'm going to find Z, try to locate a lawyer, slip out of here, and take care of business! Are you going to be Ok? Here, alone?" "Sure—I'll do what you suggested. Get dressed up—go to my fans! When do you think you'll be back?" "Not sure, just hang around—I'll be back!"

Coming down into the dining room, Alex saw it was full—and she noticed a couple of guys working the crowd, she had not seen these waiters before. Stepping to the bar/lobby area she saw Senor Z was at the cash register, he was taking money as fast as possible. There were people waiting for seating in the restaurant. And the crowd was still outside. Standing beside Senor Z, she asked, "Sorry to bother you, but I—", "You need a lawyer", he finished it for her. He pulled a slip of paper out of his coat pocket, added, "I called", as he handed her the note, "Made you an appointment-eleven—only time I could talk him into—call or whatever." He glanced at her manner of dress, smiled, said, "You better go out the back—these people may still recognize you!" when she came close to the storeroom in the rear, she remembered something—she got an old straw hat from there and pulled it down to her ears. It was ten o'clock. Outside the rear door, she called the lawyer and 'sweet-talked' Senor Martinze—the lawyer—into meeting her at Marie's for her eleven o'clock appointment. She explained this would actually save time because Marie would be necessary to discuss the business arrangements. Alex had no idea of how to contact Marie—other than go and look for her!

Luckily, Marie was at the bar. Walking inside, Marie stopped wiping the glass she held in her hands, asked, "May I help you?" "It's me, Alex!" Marie was amazed at Alex's 'different' appearance. After greetings, Alex called Max—on Herny's phone—and asked about his schedule-—he didn't have a client until nine tonight. "Max, could you please come to Marie's, I've got a lawyer that has promised to meet us there at Marie's, at eleven." "Sure, I'll be there—in fifteen minutes." Alex wasn't sure why, but she felt, or guessed, that Max and Marie were much closer than just casual acquaintances. And she felt Max could help Marie make reasonable decisions. In this deal, Alex never wanted anyone to accuse her of taking advantage of a local woman.

Marie went back to wiping glasses, Alex stepped to the open rear door, leaned back against the frame, and asked, "Marie, what's that large building—that huge thing over there?" Marie looked to Alex, she was pointing off to the left. "That's the bullring." Alex had forgotten about there being bull fights in Mexico! "When are the fights?" "Every Sunday afternoon. Maybe you and Tiger can get to go!" "I'm not sure—don't know how much longer we'll be around." Alex thought, then asked, "They actually kill the bull?" "There are more than one fight—usually four or five—Yes, they actually kill the bulls." "What do they do with four or five dead bulls?" "The bulls are butchered—out back. And the meat is given to the poor people—they come and get it."

"Do you get business from the crowd? The spectators?" "Oh, yes! Sunday afternoons are our busiest times!" "Sunday afternoons—how about Sunday nights?" "Not as good—mostly men dropping by for a beer or two after the fights are over—five or six.o'clock." "What if, just if, you had some sort of attraction—entertainment—to hold over your customers?" Marie quit, joined Alex at the doorway, looked toward the bullring, replied, "Maybe—just maybe—" They let it drop as they heard a car out front.

Max arrived, the three discussed various aspects of the deal. Alex took notes. When the lawyer came, the details were already worked out. They quickly described these to Martinza—he made notes. By quarter to one,

Martinez had all the information he needed, including that he was to check on the property ownership—it must legally belong to Marie! "And by tomorrow morning, we can plan on signing the contract?" Alex asked. "Not morning, say mid-afternoon", the lawyer replied. Marie and Alex agreed—the plan was for Alex to pickup Marie, go to the lawyer's office, sign and the deal would be final. The lawyer left, and Alex immediately called Senor Montejo. "Herny, Honey, do you have my bill ready?" She listened. "Herny, would it be possible for you to run out to Marie's?

Max and I still have somethings to discuss with her"—"Yes, Max is here, maybe you would like to sit in on our discussion—Alex knew this would get his attention! "Ok! Great! We'll be here!" As she closed the cell phone, she smiled at the two, said, "Yes! He's interested!"

Before Senor Montejo arrived, the three talked about 'The Sign'. Marie thought she knew some guys—'regular customers'—who could, and would, be glad to make and erect a large sign—with lights. "Soon? I'm not sure if you two know it or not, but Tiger and I have to leave soon. And I would really appreciate it if Tiger could see the sign before we leave." Marie said, "Excuse me", she went out the back door and rung a large bell. Returning to them, she said, "That'll get Jose here! I'll send him to get the two workmen now!" "Marie! You're my kind of lady!" Alex responded, added, "I see we're going to get along just fine!"

"Max, when your boss gets here,—", she explained what she planned. She closed by asking Max if he agreed. He did.

Jose ran in, Marie told him 'something' in rapid-fire Spanish, he ran off toward the houses.

It didn't take long for Herny to arrive. Stepping out of his new Mercedes, he held a paper—her bill—in his hand. Alex quickly scanned the itemized list—it was extensive—then nodded. Turning to Marie, she asked, "Marie, what was the 'damage', the expenses for my drinks on Alex gig?" Without hesitation, she replied, "Five hundred, US!" Turning back to Herny, Alex said, "Please add that to the list! It will save me the trouble of getting another transfer here! You can 'cut' Marie a check, send it out by Max—or whatever." Herny hesitated, she took the bill, and added on the five hundred, said, "You'll see how it works! Excuse me."

Alex went to the station wagon, dug out her laptop and returned. Holding up Herny's 'special' card they had used the day before, she asked, "This is the proper account for a direct electronic transfer?" "Yes", Herny replied. She clicked in the address of her gold dealer in NY,NY, a few more numbers, then looking at the total of the bill, clicked in that amount.

She received info—clicked some more. Shutting the computer, Alex said, "There! That's taken care of! On to the next business at hand!"

"What do you mean—'taken care of'?" Herny questioned. "Oh, Honey, check that account, say, in thirty minutes, at the most—if your money is not there, contact me, or Marie! Please! Don't get bent out of shape over a few thousand—here or there!" The three laughed, Herny just slyly grinned, and looked at his watch. Alex patted his knee, started, "Now this is what I see—"

Alex, Marie and Max had already agreed on the atmosphere of the new Marie's—it was to stay the same, a real local, 'native' bar and grill. The local customers were to be encouraged to continue as if nothing had changed. The bar was to be an 'exciting', unusual experience for the 'rich-bitches' from 'Hotel-row'—no funeral hall music—keep that the same, wild and loud! No running off the 'ladies of the evening', they stay. Clean up some, patch up some, build modern, clean restrooms, a new out door grill arrangement that served only 'native' food, 'native' style.

With Herny 'aboard', the discussion was how his limos, his drivers would inter-play with Marie's—the driver would 'casually' hint at, or about an 'unusual', 'real native experience'—hustle rich-bitches to Marie's to put it bluntly. The drivers would be encouraged—by Max—to 'expand' their images. Keep what they have, but emit more of a 'personal bodyguard'—a hero image to the rich ones. And being local, the drivers knew the difference between rowdy, jostling, good-ole-boy horseplay and real dangerous situations. In that case, get the clients out! Alex closed that part with, "Just think! Normal for the locals—but so exciting for the 'rich-bitches', they will be creaming in their girdles!"

Alex had one thing left—she wanted more of Max's time available to help with the bar and grill! Knowing that a bar/grill busiest times were Friday and Saturday nights—and with changes, maybe Sunday night here, she asked Herny to not assign driver duty to Max for those nights EXCEPT for runs to and from Marie's! And if this—the lost of the nights would reduce Max's income, then Marie's—the business—would pay the difference. That is, unless Max was making 'special' runs to and from Marie's! Then he—Herny—would pay. This was the closest arrangement that Alex could devise where no one lost—except maybe Herny would have less use of Max's time. And as the years passed, Max could work toward a retirement with Marie's—quit that driving, and kissing rich-bitches ass! Alex closed with, directly to Herny, "This proposal is better for you than me hiring Max at twice what he is now earning! Isn't it?" Herny didn't see he had a choice—he agreed with the 'plan'.

Not sure if he was pleased, or displeased, 'had' or 'brought-in' as a partner, Herny looked at his watch. It had been over a hour—he punched up on his lap-top computer to Alex's account, and as she had predicted, the money had been deposited. "You were right, Alex, it's there! Marie, I'll have Max drop off your five hundred!" As the three walked with Herny to his car, he asked, "Whose old station wagon is that?" "Actually, it belongs to a dear friend of mine", Alex answered, added, "I can't afford to own a car!" She laughed then slowly the other three joined her. Herny shook his head and drove away.

Jose came with two men, and everyone discussed 'The Sign'. After an agreement—and Alex impressed the urgency of the project—the two workmen promised to have it up and lit in two days. That would be the night of the 22th—a Friday night. Alex was pleased with this.

With her left turn signal on, and her left arm stuck straight out, Alex eased close to the Policeman standing at the double centerline. Waiting for him to stop the on-coming North bound traffic, Alex looked at the scene around the hotel. Things had changed since she had left this morning. There was a huge, heavy canvas banner that hung from the bottom of 'their' balcony. It simply showed—'Margarita Calienta'. The crowd in front of the glass of the restaurant was now mainly teen-aged girls and young women,-screaming fans as they caught sight of Tiger inside.

The Cop stopped the cars, waved Alex toward the narrow alley between the hotel and the adjacent building. When she sneaked in the rear door, she pulled the old straw hat down tighter—it came to her ears, almost to her eyebrows—she had given up on the scarf trying to hide her 'page-boy' hair cut. She still had on the old sunglasses. Coming to the kitchen area, the delicious aroma of the cooking was shocking—she realized she hadn't eaten since this morning. Hesitating at the opening, Juan glanced at her and just waved a spatula at her. She nodded in recognition, and saw that he had a 'new' assistant—he was busy 'preping' the meals. And the two new waiters were very busy.

Easing to where she could *see* the dining area, Alex waited. It was full of guests, and Tiger was 'playing' the gracious Hostess. Between leading people in and helping them get seated, she was delicately moving among the guests—a wine glass in one hand, and when she stopped and chatted, her hip cocked with the other hand placed on her hip bone, Attractive indeed, and with the high split in the side of dress, an abundance of brown skin showed. And Alex noticed the two handsome men—one appeared to be mid-forty, the other, mid-fifty. Both were dressed in fine sports clothes. And there were not any ladies with them. Alex quickly moved to the bottom of the stairs, glanced into the bar/lobby-it too was filled, and Senor Z was still 'shoveling' money in!

After taking a quick shower, she modestly primped and pulled on her white cocktail dress—then only put on her nugget earrings and simple nugget ring. And medium heels. She re-packed her purse and headed down. She wanted something to eat! And drink!

Stepping to the last step, Alex stopped, posed. Most of the guests turned and stared at her. A few waved lightly, she nodded in return. One young lady waved and shouted, "It is Alex! The Bodyguard!" 'Great! I've got a new nickname! No longer B.B., Alex thought. Smiling and nodding, she slipped to Tiger's **side and** softly asked, "Have **you eaten** today? Since this morning?" "No—I guess I just forgot." "Come on, let's go toward the rear, get a bite from the kitchen." Alex could see that getting a table was next to impossible!

Tiger followed, Alex boldly went in the cooking/prep area and gathered up a plate full of fried shrimp, a few tortillas and some cocktail sauce. The others there ignored her. Moving on toward the rear door, she stopped at the huge cooler and got a bottle of cold white wine—she opened it there, went on out the back door.

Sitting side by side on one of the rear steps as they ate—and drank from the bottle—Tiger asked, "So? How did it go today?" Alex felt this was out of politeness. Tiger was beaming about 'something else'! Alex made it brief; "Ok, we sign tomorrow. And you? What kind of day did you have?" Tiger hesitated. "Tig! Just tell me! Before you bust!"

"Ok! Ok! Senor Z has come up with speaking engagements for me! The local clubs! Breakfast, luncheons, ever diners! Me! Poor starving, skinny Margarita! Margarita—who never went to school after being thirteen!"

"I think you did really well, Kid! You can speak, read and write Spanish and English. And you can speak your native tongue—what? Tzental! And you can speak enough French to get along!" Alex suddenly hesitated as she realized something, then she asked, "How did you learn French?" Tiger looked off to the distance, wavered, then softly replied, "You will not tell Mike, please?" "Of course not—", then Alex waited.

"While walking away from here—Mazatlan—I and another little girl became separated from the others—a Frenchman—a French-Canadian—

from Quebec—middle aged gentleman picked us—me and Poco—Poco was all I ever knew—up and nursed us back to normal health. He was very caring—and 'well-off', money wise. For about a year, we—the three of us—stayed together—Poco and I gained weight, recovered our strength and our bodies grew up with the proper foods! Please, don't ever tell Mike—but-about all the three of us did was eat, sleep—and screw, that was our exercise! And he taught us that we didn't have to beg for pennies anymore! So—that's how, when I learned to understand and speak French—that year."

Tiger wiped her eyes, twisted to face Alex, Alex kissed her on the cheek, patted her knee, almost whispered, "Kid, most everyone has secrets in their past—don't worry, I'll never mention this to anyone. It isn't what is in the past, it is what is going on now—in the present that really matters. And your present looks really fantastic! Tell me more about your speaking engagements—These are for how long? How many days?" "Oh, I'm not sure—there are all sorts of clubs here! I guess for as long as we stay—", she let it drop off.

"Kid, I can be finished by Saturday morning—we really have to move on—but if—", she too let it drop. "Yes, I know—Ok! What ever I can get—that's Ok! Just Fine! Just to know I've done it!" Tiger was again enthused! "Great—is there anything I can do to help?" "Guess not—Z gave me a list to start calling—he is so busy! I thought I'd start this afternoon, tonight—unless you want to go out?" "No, really—I'm about bushed. We'll stay in tonight—you call, I'll rest—whatever!"

Putting the plate from her knees to the step—it only had the shrimp tails on it—Alex took another swig from the bottle, passed it to Tiger. Placing her arm around Tiger's neck, she pulled their heads together, said, "Tig, maybe you had rather stay here, in Mazatlan longer, I could go on—" Tiger interrupted, "No! We're going to find the Codex! Together!" Alex lightly kissed her on the cheek, remarked, "It's getting dark—Let's not miss the sunset!" They headed in—at the cooler Alex got two more bottles of wine—and they went up.

Inside their room, the two decided to stay 'dressed'. Tiger because of the possibilities of meeting her fans or exposing herself over the balcony. Alex because she was tired of the ugly, 'workman's' clothes she had worn all day—she wanted to feel feminine—feel sexy.

Neither of them knew about the two 'bugs'—the tiny radio transmitters—that had been placed in their room, one in the globe of the overhead light, one in the telephone.

As Tiger began calling, Alex searched around and located her personal corkscrew and opened one of the bottles, then she stepped out on the balcony. Shifting the chairs to face the coming sunset, she sat down, and sipped from the bottle.

"Hi!" the male's voice behind her said. "Hi", she didn't bother to look. "Hi! I'm Kyle! I guess we're neighbors!" "Guess so!" Alex still didn't look over her shoulder. She knew it was coming from the balcony next to where she sat. "You're Alex! Right?" "I know!" she cut it short. "And your friend is the famous Margarita! Right?" "Yes, I know!" "You two have really made the news! Maybe I could come over, let's get acquainted?" "No!" she snapped. The Agent turned, went inside to where his partner was listening with the earphones. Kyle said, "Cold fish! This might not be as easy as we thought!" The other Agent just nodded as he continued to adjust the volume of the tape being recorded.

The Agent didn't give up, he went back outside, said toward Alex, "Should be a gorgeous sunset! I love sunsets! Do you? Are you a fan of the beauty of sunsets? I've—we've, me and my buddy, have a bottle of champagne! Maybe you'd like to come over for a drink as we—you and I—watch the sunset together!" He waited. Alex slowly raised her right arm straight up, and slowly folded all her fingers except the middle one.

When the sunset got close, Alex went inside—Tiger was propped up in the bed, sweet talking to someone about a luncheon—Alex shook her foot and pointed toward the balcony. Tiger followed with the phone—it had a very long wire—and the list. With only a side, quick, glance, Alex saw that the two men—the same two she had noticed in the dining room—were now out on their balcony.

The two Agents began to comment about the sunset loud enough for Alex to hear. Tiger had stopped her telephoning. She waited in silence for the moment of the actual dip below the horizon. As the rim of the sun seemed to touch the ocean—the men were still talking—Alex stood placed both her fists on her hips, turned to the men, snapped, "Would you two shut up! I'm trying to hear the sizzle!" She sat back down and propped her feet on the railing. The Agents went silent. And one of them remembered the warning—' Alex is armed!' He decided he didn't want to push her too hard!

THE LOST CODEX OF PALENQUE

The sunset over—Tiger with three engagements for tomorrow and it getting too late to bother the locals any more—Tiger asked, "Alex, do you think this publicity—the news about me—may have reached Hidden Valley?" "Maybe", as Alex stood, took the hotel phone and the list from her, went inside, and returned. Handing Tiger Herny's cell phone, Alex said, "Use this one, we'll not have to pay for the call!" Tiger began to dial Hidden Valley. Luckily, Tom and Mike were still up at Arnie's. Tiger talked, talked, and talked. Alex could see that Tiger was all bubbly about her new found fame! When Tiger got all 'mushy' with Mike, Alex went inside and opened the second bottle of wine. As she returned to the balcony, Tiger handed her the phone, said, "It's Tom—"

"Sounds like you two are having a great vacation! And what's this talk about you doing a deal? You two haven't forgotten about your prime mission—the Codex—have you?" "Yes! It's been fun—and so different, Tom, I just never imaged! Deal? Just a little something I stumbled on—no big deal. And, no, we haven't forgotten about the Codex! The way I see it, if I can pull the Kid loose from her screaming fans, we'll head on South Saturday morning." "It's really like that? Who would have ever guessed—sly little Tiger, a Star!" "I wish you, and Mike in particular, could see her—she has really became a show-off! Guess I better get off this phone before it runs out of time. We'll contact you guys when—I'm not sure when—just later, or after more info about the Codex. Love you!" Alex held the phone away from her ear, asked, "Tiger? Any more?" Tiger, with tears in her eyes, just shook her head. "Tom, tell everyone I—we—love them—guess it's goodbye." She broke the connection, tossed the phone to the bed then she stared across the ocean.

The younger Agent asked his partner, "Well? You got anything?" The other one removed the headset, shook his head, replied, "Missed it—the 'bugs' didn't pick-up the cell phone when they were on the balcony." "I would guess—the gals were almost whispering and with that noise from the crowd—"

It was almost eleven when Alex stood, extended one hand to Tiger—she took it. "It time for beddy-bye, Kid, you'll need it for tomorrow!" They went inside, Alex slid the door shut—and locked it. Both naked, Tiger got her sleeping tee shirt, but Alex took it from her in a gentle fashion and softly said, "Please, not tonight" and she smiled. In bed, Tiger shifted, said, "I'm so thrilled—I can't get over it." Alex rolled over on Tiger's arm, hugged her, whispered, "Go to sleep, little tiger, you need your beauty rest."

"But, I could—I could—" Alex nuzzled Tiger's breast, placed a hand to her flat, firm stomach—and began a firm circular motion, whispered, "Try the word—climax." "Oh, Alex-yes—I could climax." Alex took Tiger's nipple into her mouth and began a slow flipping action with the tip of her tongue—she moved her hand—still with the firm motion— lower, and lower. Tiger spread her thighs and thrust her firm, jutting bulge upward. A few hard squeezes of the protruding mound, Alex shoved her hand between the taut, smooth thighs and began a slow, searching, prying action with her fingers. Opening Tiger, she soon found her rigid, 'love-button'. "Oh, Alex—Yes!" Tiger, with both arms tight around Alex's back, began a slow clawing with her finger nails And a slow grinding action of her hips. It didn't take long, Tiger was ready, in one mighty thrust of her pelvic, and squeezing Alex's mouth hard to her breast, "Yes! Yes! Oh Alex! Yes!" Tiger's entire body became stiff, completely rigid! Then she fell limp, fell into the depths of ecstasy, and she let her hand Alex slowly fall from Alex's back rolled away, they both were asleep almost instantly. Up early, Tiger was in a dither trying to decide what to wear. Alex knew exactly what she would wear—it was the same as yesterday, her disguise, the 'man's' outfit. Seeing Tiger not make much headway, Alex said, "Wear that expensive outfit you wore to the Riviera! Make it your 'signature! Shock 'em!" "Really?" "Yes, you sure as hell will not need it back at Hidden Valley! To pick beans in!" They both laughed as Tiger began to wiggle it up. "But, I need someone to tie the straps!" "That's what I'm here for!" As Alex tied the one around her neck, she leaned to Tiger's ear, nibbled it, asked, "Did you enjoy—that—last night?"

"Oh, yes! It was exactly what I needed! Sorry I didn't return the favor." Then Tiger twisted her face side ways—Alex lightly kissed her cheek, whispered, "Next time."

But Tiger had a point about the clothes situation—they really had to get some laundry done! Alex telephoned down, asked "Sorry to bother you, Senor Z, but, we just got to get some clothes cleaned!" She listened as he quickly gave instructions. Hanging up, then Alex hurriedly gathered up whatever she suspected was dirty. Stuffing these in the straw beach bag, she headed out. Hesitating at the door, she said, "Knock 'em dead, Kid!" Tiger smiled, waved her away.

Next door, the Agent jerked off the earphones, snapped, "Alex is on the move—better run—I'm guessing she'll move fast! I'll tail the Star-gal!" The other Agent slightly opened the door just in time to see Alex's head—her old hat—disappear as she went down the stairs, then he followed her.

After Alex pulled out into the heavy North bound traffic on the Oltas, she recalled, 'Three blocks North, turn right, four doors—Chinese laundry. A quick stop, dropping off the clothes, she then made two left turns to return to the broad avenue, a right, she was again headed North, toward Marie's.

Pulling up to Marie's, Alex saw that the 'sign-fabricators' were on the job. One large pole—an old used telephone pole with many spike scars—was already in place. The hand mixed—on the ground—concrete was around the bottom drying. There were the two men from yesterday, plus two more. They were in the process of hoisting the second pole into position. With three smaller poles tied together at the upper ends–a gin pole arrangement—a block and a rope, three pulled the pole upright while the fourth guided the base end toward the hole in the ground. Close by was an old beat-up pickup with a long rusty boat trailer hooked to the truck. On the trailer were several timbers—also used—were sheets of metal. These appeared to be from a previous sign.

In front, outside, Marie and Jose sat at a table with four chairs. Alex guessed they were outside just in case the workers dropped 'whatever' through the roof! Hopping out, Alex spread her arms, shouted, "Great! No new stuff! No shiny metal! Just great! It goes with the rest!" The four workers, their hands full, turned, nodded and smiled to Alex. Stepping to the table, Alex flipped a chair 'backwards', straddled it as she said, "The sign looks well on the way! What next?" The three kicked around a few ideas then settled on 'restrooms' next. They agreed on two individual units—both behind the rear wall–concrete—floors, concrete block walls, and all this tiled inside. The roofs would be wood framed, with metal roofing.

As they walked about there, Alex asked if workers could be gotten–now—to start—now. Marie hesitated, then "Tonight, I'm sure the right ones will be here tonight—I'm sure they're already at work somewhere else—now." "Ok, but that—concrete, tile, hard plumbing and wiring, that'll take a while, yes?" "Yes, I'm guessing two, maybe three weeks", Jose interjected."

"Ok—but in the mean time—during the three or so weeks, let's do something about the rest room problem!" Jose nor Marie replied—they appeared confused. Alex started to clarify, "Go ahead with the concrete ones like we just discussed, get that started by making a deal with the workers tonight!"

"And", she reached over, took a hold of Jose's arm, added, "We, Jose and I will go—now—and buy two small trailers—new ones! Have these delivered today, and hooked up—water, drains and hot-wired—today. Or we don't buy! Got the idea? These we set"—she pointed—"out of the way of the expected construction of the permanent rest rooms—"the trailers, here and here!" Jose and Marie smiled.

"Alex! Don't forget, we have to be at the Lawyer's office by mid afternoon!" Alex looked to Jose, asked, "You know where we can buy new trailers? Now!" "Sure!" "How far away is it?" "Only a few miles!" "Ok, let's go! Marie, we'll be back—and we—you and I—will not be late!" As the two briskly stepped to the wagon, Jose asked, "You got enough money—with you—to pay for two new trailers?" "Better! I've got plastic!" You drive!" In Alex's tenacious manner, the two roared away in a cloud of white disc! Marie tilted her face to her open palms, muttered, "Oh, Lord, what a woman."

About noon, they drove up, stopped, Alex and Jose hopped out. In sight were two heavy duty pickups—each was pulling a trailer, both were about twenty feet long. "Jose, you direct them, show then exactly where the trailers go!" Alex snapped. "But, where?" he questioned. "Exactly where YOU want them!" and Alex laughed. He smiled, ran toward the lead truck and waved at the driver. Alex headed for the open front door, she called back, "Marie! You want something to drink?" "Yes! A cold beer!"

Before she got to the door, Alex glanced up at the progress on the sign—the second main pole was up—the concrete around the bottom—and two stub-poles on the roof, more or less, over the main roof support poles inside, were mounted. The tops of all four were, more or less, even. The workers were now installing the horizontal members.

As Marie and Alex sipped the cold beers, an old Ford van pulled up close to where they sat. On the top were several old ladders, most were homemade, and painted on the side of the van—in fancy letters—was 'Johnny-The Sign Painter'. Johnny got out, he looked to be over sixty, and with him was a younger man. His helper, Alex guessed. There was no doubt they were painters—their coveralls had splotches of every color imaginable. The two glanced up at the sign framing going together over the roof. The older man removed his bib-cap, scratched his hair then walked to Marie and said, "I guess I'm early—needed to find out the situation anyway."

He and Marie shook hands, and Marie introduced everyone. The younger helper was, "Johnny, Junior', and he was Johnny's grandson. Alex thought their names were cute!

Alex went to her station wagon, returned with a notepad and pencil. And she waited while Marie explained, "Ask Alex for the details! This is her project!" Alex drew a sketch—with 'Marie's' on a forty-five degree angle, then 'Margarita Calienta'—much larger letters—level across the main body of the sign. At the other end, same angle as the other, 'Bar/ Grill'. "White background, big bold black letters! And there's to be flood lights at each end and along the top or the bottom—which ever!" Alex explained. Both Johnnys nodded in agreement, the older one said, "Ok, guess we'll come back—"

Alex quickly interrupted, "Excuse me, Johnny, if you two will please follow me, we have another job!" Alex led the three around to where the new trailers were. Seeing that the trailers were already blocked up off the tires and stable, she said to the older Johnny as she made hand motions,"Mujers, and under that, Women" she shifted her view and pointed to the other trailer, "Caballeros, and under that 'Men', all in big bold black letters!" The trailers were white. "And you can paint that now?" "Si, Senorita Alex, Now!" The older one spoke to the younger one. He went and moved the van closer. And they ignored the trailer workers who were busy digging ditches for the plumbing. They started to pencil off the letters. Finished with one letter, Johnny Junior asked, "That size? That is Ok?" "Si! Si!" Alex replied.

Being rather busy, Alex had not noticed the car that was parked at the junction of the white side road—Marie's road—and the paved East-West street. Or the Agent who waited in the car.

Alex glanced at her sports watch—it showed after one. Jose appeared to have accomplished his job. "Jose, there is a small Mitla bag in the :1" front seat. Please get it for me." Alex had been paying attention to the 'trailer man' hooking up the wires for electrical service to the two trailers—she decided he knew his job very well, and was good at it. Jose returned with the bag, she removed her wallet, said, "Throw the bag under your Mother's counter, near the cash register—Hey! Don't throw it too hard! My pistol is in it!" Jose's eyes opened very wide, she laughed, added, "Doesn't every little gal carry one?" "Not in Mexico!" he replied, as he went in the rear door. It was about center of the building—between the two new trailers. Jose returned to Alex and his Mother.

Alex wasn't sure who did or who didn't speak English—she didn't want to have to stumble through her Spanish, "Jose, ask the man doing the wiring if I could have a minute with him. You can translate, Ok?" "Sure!" With the worker, and Jose, Alex said "I would like to have flood lights under the eaves, one pointed that way, one that way"—she pointed, then, "today, before dark." "That's not part of the trailer deal—"he hesitated. Alex pulled out two twenties—US twenties, "For this—"she extended the bills toward him. He reached for these as he remarked, "Sure thing—but the lights, supplies, I don't have with me!"

"Jose, can you go and get the supplies?" "Of course!" As she pulled out a handful of bills, she added, "And be back here by two-thirty?" "Yes, it is not far!" "Great! You two decide what is needed, then run get it! Ok?" The two just nodded. She started to walk off, but twisted back, pointed a stiff finger at the man holding the two twenties, said, "Remember, you promised—flood lights before dark!" He smiled and nodded.

Just Marie and Alex together, Marie said, "Alex, where did you learn all this"—she waved a hand at the activity around them, added, "I thought you were just a—", she stopped. "A rich-bitch? Come inside, Marie, I'll try—just try—to explain as we have a cold drink!" Alex was not nearly concerned about something being dropped through the roof as she was about getting too much sun! Inside, in the cool shade, She 'walked' her chair backward until it was right to hang her legs on the top of the table. She began with the collapse of the USA food industry. She ended with, "So you see, after taking one hundred year old farm buildings, trading for material and food, gravity water, even chamber pots, little Alex, and Tiger 'ain't' some gals that just fell off the cabbage truck!" Marie stood, rubbed her ample rump and said "Well! I'd say! I never expected such! And Tiger—Margarita—was there all the time—at your Arnie's Hidden Valley! Let's have another beer!"

Hearing the station wagon slide to a stop, Alex glanced at her watch-two-fifteen. Jose briskly walked in, threw the keys and a hand full of change and bills, and receipts on the table. He got a cold drink, took a long gulp, pulled up a chair, leaned forward to Alex—he wasn't smiling as he said, "Alex, you've got a tail!" She jerked her legs down, bent forward, snapped, "What? How? Who?" "Not sure, but, I guess you and I being about the same size—even dressed alike—the bastard thought I was you. The prick followed me everywhere I went! And, now, he is parked up at the street!" "Not just a 'crazy' fan? I've tried to avoid that!"

"No, he looks maybe mid or late forty, slick looking 'dude'! You aren't banging some 'sport', are you? Maybe a jealous lover? Some 'psycho?'" "Hell no! I hate 'sports', think all they got to do is smile, wag their— and you'll come a-running!"

Alex stood, walked to the doorway, looked out—the dark colored car with someone was still there. She turned back, said, "Regardless, Marie, we'd better head for the Lawyer's office. Jose, get the lights—the material out of the wagon—and keep things going here until we get back. Remember, flood lights out back—to the rest rooms—by dark!" She turned, looked again at the dark car over on the paved street, said, "Jose, bring me my bag! The mother—that screws with little Alex just might get his—I blown off!" Jose shuttered as he stood, then headed for the bar while holding his crotch.

While she and Marie got in the wagon, Alex saw the dark car ease off—West, toward the beach. At the street, she turned left—East—and watched in her rearview mirror. The car made a tight one-eighty in the street and began to follow her—not too closely, but close enough. Alex asked Marie for directions, then she made a couple of unnecessary turns—the car still followed. Alex decided 'screw-it', I'll ignore him, proceed with what we need to do.

After greetings-the Lawyer was ready—Alex's first question concerned the title of the property. "No problem, that entire open area, has been in the Hernandez family for generations." Alex almost fell out of her chair—Hernandez! That was Max's last name! The Lawyer continued—"It was willed to Marie in nineteen-seventy-three by her Father, Maxillian Hernandez, The Elder. And there are no outstanding loans or mortgages against it. It is all free and clear. Shall we proceed?" "Sure, please do!" But Alex was still stunned—Max and Marie were brother and sister! No wonder he seemed so concerned!

The Lawyer covered the details, Alex and Marie agreed, then signed the contract as the secretary watched and then notarized the documents. Leaving the office, Alex hugged Marie, and asked, "Why didn't you— or Max—tell me that you were brother and sister?" "Half brother and sister—we had different Mothers." Marie chuckled, commented, "Tell you? I left that up to Maxie!" "Which of you are the older? As if that makes any difference!" Alex laughed. "Max is by three years—his Mother died in Max's birth." As they approached the wagon, the dark car was parked at one end of the block. "And, is"—Alex thought,'while on the subject of Max's situation', "Is Max married? Got kids?" "No, and no—none he admitts to anyway!" The two chuckled as Alex pulled from the curb. She noticed the car fall in behind them.

From here, Alex knew which way she wanted to go, she turned right, headed for Avenue Oltas. On a side street that junctioned with Oltas, Alex parked. Marie questioned with her facial expression. "There's another little business deal we—you and I—need to attend to, before I leave. Please go with me, you'll need to sign also. Let me get my lap-top, I'll need it—I think." Alex saw the car park at the far end of the block—it was on the same side of the street.

Walking to the corner with Avenue Oltas, she looked North, then South. Seeing the bank's sign, she turned left. It was the same bank she and Tiger had checked out only two days ago. Opening the door, walking in, Alex glanced at her style of clothes, and thought, 'This is going to be just as big a shock as our cocktail dresses were—but in a different direction!' At the prudish Receptionist's desk, Alex waited until the lady looked up—then she removed the old straw hat, and said, "We'd like to open a joint checking account." Marie was dressed in typical native loose wrap-around skirt, scope neck blouse and strap sandals. The lady almost gasped, she did stare briefly, "Well, I—." Alex interrupted her stammer with, "I'm Alex—Alex—you remember—two days ago? Senorita Margarita Calienta and I were in here? Just two days ago? You do remember Senorita Calienta, don't you?" The woman's jaw hung open. Slowly, Alex reached over the desk and lifted it, added, "Just point—if you've lost your voice!"

Alex propped the end of her computer on the edge of the desk and waited. The woman finally pointed, muttered, "Third desk back—ah— Miss Alex." Mistake number three! Alex leaned close to her face, softly said, "Don't ever-never again, call me Miss—And don't ever call me by my last name. The name is Alex, and that's all—Alex. Is that perfectly clear? If not, I'll scream it in one ear—maybe it will come out the other side." The woman didn't say a word, but she nodded a lot! And pointed. Marie smiled, she had heard about Alex's 'name-wrath' from Max, but this was the first time she had seen it!

Greetings, then being seated, Alex started by removing one of her business cards for HVG from a side pocket in her computer's case. Handing it toward the clerk, she said, "This shows all the necessary addresses, communication numbers you may need. Keep it, it'll save us the trouble of transmitting this information." But before the lady took the card, Marie reached over, nodded to both of them, and took the card. She hadn't seen this before. The card showed Alex's home address—Hidden Valley and the numbers for there. And her 'office address—actually Jerry White's D.C. address and numbers—The Department of Agriculture, Washington, D.C., etc.—and the computer and phone numbers there. And bold print, her name and—Alex, Executive Director, HVG, Inc.

'IF IT IS EATABLE, WE BUY AND SELL IT!'

Looking from the card to Alex's eyes, Marie said, in almost a whisper, "Alex, you haven't mentioned this—I had no idea—" Alex just patted Marie's knee, replied, "It's Ok, you'll get used to me after a while." She smiled, took the card and passed it on to the clerk as she said, "Please use the Washington address and numbers—all my HVG business transactions go through there, Ok?" The clerk just nodded as she stared at the complicated business card.

Finishing the bank's paper work—it was a joint checking account—Alex impressed on the clerk that she was leaving Mazatlan soon—this was to be Marie's business account. The clerk indicated the need for some sort of deposite to actually open the account. Alex asked for the bank's incoming electronic transfer number. The clerk turned a document toward Alex, and pointed at a ten digit number. Alex opened her computer, and as she hooked up to her gold broker in NYC,.N.Y., she casually said, "This is an opener—There will be more to follow—depends on Marie's needs, Ok?" "Sure, how much are you having transferred—now?" The clerk saw what Alex was doing—a direct electronic transfer. "Twenty thousand—US dollars." The clerk gulped and batted her eyes, muttered, "Twenty—thousand." "Is that ok? Enough? To open with?" The clerk nodded, and Alex thought,'This crowd needs lesions in voice control!' After this was completed, the clerk gave Marie some temporary checks, promised that the printed ones would be ready in one week. Alex insisted that the name, 'Marie's Margarita Calienta Bar/Grill',be printed on the checks.

Back on the sidewalk, Alex hooked her arm into Marie's elbow—"Now here's the deal—You write checks for what you need to bring the place up to what we discussed. I'll monitor the accounts balance via computers, I'll transfer money in as needed. If there is any sort of emergency, contact me—I'll leave you one of my cards And you—by mail is Ok—send me receipts—not for every nickel and dime item, just the big stuff—and I'll see if I can 'write-off' some of the expenses—for taxes."

They slowly walked on, then Alex added, "And, when the business has stabilized, when you think all the improvements are complete, then we'll talk about getting the business appraised by a couple of local Realtors, Ok?" "Sure thing, Alex, what ever you say. It all Sounds too good to be true."

Walking on, Marie shyly asked, "Your food business, how big is it? Is it as big as—a central maket, down here? Or is it like a neighborhood grocery store?" Alex tugged on Marie's arm, chuckled, then replied, "No, neither one! We don't actually get the food—we sell it before it is delivered. Then it is delivered to the new owners! Size? I can only relate to the money part of it. And to tell you the truth, I have no idea! Roughly guessing, by the end of this season—this year—I would guess one, maybe two billion dollars will be passed through our accounts. I don't personally handle that line of the business—Our staff in D.C. does that boring crap!" "Billions? That is more than a million?" "Yes, Marie, a lots more."

On a few steps, Marie remarked, "I thought you were a Special Agent—a bodyguard—for the US Government—for Tiger—" Alex interrupted, "I am! HVG, the food business, is just a sideline! Like Tiger, she is a vice-President of HVG—but to her, it is just a sideline also!" "Alex, is there anything else you do?" "Oh, Marie! I'll just bore you!" "So bore me, little Alex!" "Well—I have written and sold computer programs—", she let it drop off. "Sold? People can sell that?" "Yes, my last set of programs got me nearly two million—and—" She again let it die. "Two million! US dollars?" "Yes, something like that—but—"

"But what?" Marie stopped walking. Alex twisted, turned face to face, softly said, "Marie, can you keep a secret? Really, really keep one?" "Of course—you said—but—but what?" Alex cast glances in both directions—no one in sight—then she almost whispered, "Tiger and I—like the TV and the newspaper said—we really are on a 'special project'. And if—just if—it is successful, the rewards will be unlimited. PossibLy the greatest ever—for most anyone. Completely unlimited—a fortune."

They stared into each others eyes, Alex added, "Please, not a word of this—to anyone, OK?" Marie nodded, Alex twisted to her side, pulled her arm, said, "Marie, please close your mouth—flys may get in it!" Then Alex chuckled, the two went on toward the station wagon. "And—you would make a fortune from this—whatever?" Alex laughed, tugged again on Marie's elbow, and replied, "Could—but—you may not believe this! I have promised to give it away!"

Back at the station wagon, Alex repacked her computer in the rear, and felt around for an old hammer she had seen. She slipped the hammer under her shirt, and held it with her elbow, then 'closed the tailgate. Instead of driving forward, Alex quickly accelerated backward, The Agent in the car, thinking she was going to ram his car, dropped down, lay across the front seats, braced for the impact. But she stopped a few feet short, hopped out—she left her door open—rushed back and broke out both head lights with the hammer. Dashing back into the wagon, she sped forward. She didn't stop at the junction, but skidded right, headed North on Avenue Oltas.

Laughing, Alex said, "Sorry, Marie, but I just had to do something! That should slow him down for tonight at least!" Marie suppressed deep laughter with her hands. It was only about a hour until dark, and this late, it just might be difficult to get new headlights—especially in downtown Mazatlan!

As the Agent looked at the damage, he said, "That little bitch! I'll have to find lights, now!" Looking toward Oltas, he added, "I've lost her, damnit!"

Settled down, and almost to the bar, Marie asked, "What are you going to do tonight?" "I don't know—Tiger has a speaking engagement—just hang around the hotel I guess." "Why don't you come back out? You can help me pick the guys for the rest room project—we can talk about—well—whatever." "Sure"—Alex pulled at her old loose shirt, she added, "Maybe I can get dressed up." A brief silence then Alex added, "You think Jose could cook up something to eat?" "Well, yes, he's good at rounding up something—you two might have to run get—whatever—is that a problem?" "No problem with me—unless—I have to hold the cow's head while he cuts off a hind quarter!" "Alex! You're too much!"

CHAPTER 11

Alex made a quick check on the projects; the sign workers were finished except for installing the flood lights. Johnny and Johnny were just finishing the white background—they promised that they would paint the black lettering tomorrow. The trailer guys were finished and gone. Alex and Marie checked these—lights, water, drains AND the two flood lights too! And the signs on the rest room were unmistakable! As Alex flushed the toilet after she 'used' it, she said, "Look! No more squatting in the weeds! Or pissing on the walls!" They hugged, went in the rear door to the bar—it was an easy walk with good visibility. They got a cold beer apiece. Jose was inside, beaming with pride. Alex went to him, put her arm around his neck, gave a light peck on the cheek, said, "I knew you could do it!" Straightening up, she added,"Now, if you can come up", she pulled out a handful of bills, "with enough lobster for the three—or four—of us, you'll be at the top of my list for free blow-jobs'!" Jose looked at Alex's eyes, replied, "Aw—you wouldn't! Would You?" "As certain as the suns sets over the Pacific!"

Alex pulled off the old straw hat, put it on Jose's head. And she had a spark of an idea! "Please hand me another one, Marie—And, Hey! Start me a tab! Don't want no 'free-bees' here—Now that I'm a business partner! If either of you see me start that 'Drinks are on me—or the house' crap, just hold my mouth shut!" Alex sat down on a bar stool next to Jose—and she thought, she was silent as Marie told Jose about the bank thing, and about Alex's 'respect' for stranger's headlights! Alex really wasn't listening.

"I've got it! I've got it!" Alex yelled. "Oh no! Not again!" Marie shouted. "No! Not another deal! Well, not a business deal at least!" Alex lifted the hat from Jose's head, and replaced it, said, "You keep the hat! Wear it all the rest of tonight! Don't take it off! And—and— after you cook, and we eat, later we'll just have to see how things go—we, you and I, will slip into the men's restroom and we'll SWAP clothes! Then I'll wear the hat! I'll wear some of Tiger's native dress—loose-about like your Mother has on now! And flat sandals! Then you—but you'll look like ME—can drive off in my car! Go—well—where ever you want to! Lead 'Tail-man' on a wild goose chase! We'll just have fun with that bastard! And if I want to leave before you get back, hell, I'll call a cab! Isn't that great! Just Great!" Jose didn't smile, he calmly asked, "Alex, did you fall on your head when you were a little girl?"

But after more definitions, and more of his rebuttals like; "What if someone sees us go in the restroom together?" "Hell, they'll just think we were getting a 'quicky'!—could be possible", Alex responded. Jose finally gave in and agreed. "Tonight, you be sure to wear light colored clothes—shirt, pants—because Tiger's native colors are red and even darker red. The more contrast, the better!" Alex impressed on Jose.

"Got to run! We'll have fun—that is, if 'whoever' shows up!" She left and went directly to the Chinese laundry and then on to the hotel. Getting out, she grabbed the Mitla bag from the front seat, but, at the rear, as she tried to get up the laundry—it had been wrapped in thin, slick paper as individual packages for each different type of garment—and with the laptop, she had a problem. Giving up on trying to carry it all on one trip, she considered 'duck, fox, and grapes', this would work.

until the stairs—but she surely didn't want to climb up and down the thirty-nine steps THREE TIMES, or even two times!

"May I help you? Looks as if you got more than you can carry! "the voice behind her asked. She whipped around, it was the younger man from 'next door', the one who had been following her. "Yes, you can!" as she glanced beyond him—she didn't see a strange car, or one with the head lights missing. He noticed that she was looking for his car, he said, "I had a little problem with my car this afternoon—vandalism, I guess, someone broke out my headlights." "Really? Who would do such a naughty thing like that?" She wondered why he told her—maybe just to let her know that he knew. But it also confirm the 'who'—he was definitely the one that had been tailing her.

"You don't have your straw hat," he remarked. Alex felt to her head, snapped, "Damn! I must have left it at Marie's! I'll have to pick it up when I go back there tonight!" She wanted him to know that! Alex jerked up her lap-top by the loop handles, said, "If you would please get those slick packages of laundry, I think we can make it to the top!" It was a double arm load. She shut the tailgate and led him in—opening and closing the door as they moved through. And she lead him up the stairs. About a third of the way up, Agent-man made the first serious mistake, he said 'something' that started with, "Miss—blab, blab" The other words didn't register in Alex's brain. At the last landing, he committed the second mistake—a very grave one—he started his sentence with, "Miss Hawkins—blab, blab.

Because of her internal boiling rage, Alex had difficulties unlocking the door. But she didn't want to explode yet—she wanted things to be just right! Opening the door only enough for her to pass through, she quickly dumped her load, turned back. The man was between the edge of the partially opened door and the doorframe with both arms full, and his feet spread apart, just wide enough. Taking swift, long strides, Alex kicked him in his crotch—and caught the packages as he fell to his knees and slightly back, but not far enough back. With her foot, she slammed the door very hard to his face.

Quickly tossing the packages on the bed, she hooked the night chain, opened the door the limited distance and looked though the gap. He was on his knees, one hand holding his crotch, the other at his bleeding nose. She saw that it wasn't split—just a simple nosebleed—and his eyes flooded with tears.

Loud enough to be sure he heard through the throbbing inside his head, she said, "Ops! Just a reactive reflex to some prick calling me Miss! And especially Miss Hawkins! If there IS another time, the reflex gets worse—much worse!" She slammed the door, then doubled over with laughter!

The fun over, Alex thought, 'I may have spoiled things for tonight. Naw! If he is, was, the 'Tail',the Agent-man—he would be at Marie's tonight. Even if he had to go by wheelchair—on the Oltas! If he is not Agent-man, then he is just some poor slob who made a couple of mistakes!'

In case she missed Tiger tonight, or even tomorrow morning, Alex wanted to leave Tiger a coded message. The code was one Dr.K used in her world wide escapades. Basically, you substitute Maya numbers for the letters of Modern English with 26 letters and the Arabic numerals of 1 thru 9 plus the Maya 'number' of zero. Substituting the Maya numbers for the letter's position in the alphabet (the numbers are direct) you then write your message in Maya numbers. Because there are only three different symbols for all the Maya numbers, the message becomes a series of dots, short lines, and the Maya 'conch'—Dr.K used what it really represents, the zero. Pulling out a sheet of hotel stationary, Alex wrote a brief coded message.

Tearing off the small portion required, she slipped the edge of the note into the gap between the mirror and the mirror's frame leaving the message visible. Standing back, Alex read **it** to herself. 'Do not trust men next door.'

Alex quickly stripped, dropped 'the workman's' clothes on the floor and **kicked** these to one side. Unwrapping the fresh laundry, she began to hang and put-away the clean clothes. Suddenly she stopped, realized what she was doing. She thought, 'hanging out with Tiger **is** turning me into a domesticated woman!'

After a brief shower, she took Tiger's traditional wrap-around—one size fits all—skirt and one of Tiger's pull over blouses. These on, she he located her own strap sandals. And she removed her earrings and didn't put on any jewelry—not ever rings—or any lip stick or eye make-up. She wanted herself plain, as plain as Jose would be when he 'took' her place! She was ready to display herself to Agent-man next door!

Throwing the sliding door to the balcony open, she went out; loudly moved the two chairs about, leaned over the rail and shouted down to the few teen aged girls below, "Ola! Ola! Bueno nochas!!Bueno!"

"Are those fans of Margarita? Or your fans? "He asked from the adjacent balcony. Alex intended to act as if nothing had happened earlier. "Si!—Yes! Both I hope!" She turned toward him,he was looking at her. "You like my new outfit?" She turned around and around, held the full hem up and out so it would flare. "Very nice! But I thought it was uncouth for a Gringa—like you—to wear traditional Maya dress?" She wasn't sure if he was just asking a question or being a smart-ass. With restraint, she replied, "Not any more—it is getting so one can actually buy these in the States! Don't you think I'll be a 'hit' at Marie's tonight?""Maybe—so, you're going back—", he didn't finish. He realized he had let Alex know that he knew she had been at Marie's. "Got to run!" She headed for the door, but stopped, turned back, added. "I'm driving there, you know!" She left.

Turning onto the 'white' road, she stopped. By the light from her headlights, Alex admired the new sign—the entire width of the building and faced almost exactly South—any one headed North to the 'Golden Zone' had to notice it! Of course, it didn't have the letters painted yet, and it didn't have the flood lights yet—but she could imagine it for tomorrow night! There seemed to be more cars than she had seen so far—and a lot of the cars were newer than usual. Alex eased on to the building—the music was blasting away, a couple stood in the dark shadows to one side of the doorway. Alex thought, 'Don't want too much light here at the front, the 'action' in the shadows is to be part of the thrill, the excitement for the 'rich Gringas!'

Alex went through, greeted everyone close by, went behind the bar, kissed Marie on the cheek, got a cold beer and went out the back door— the area was brightly lit! No problem of stumbling— this was a vast improvement! Jose was busy; he had removed all the cooking hardware from the old grill, had a charcoal fire going. And he had close by an old metal tub with several live lobsters swimming about in the seawater. Great! As he prepared vegetables for sauteeing, Alex gave him a 'peck' on the cheek, commented, "It looks delicious! Do you need anything else?" "No, don't think so, there's a wrap of tortillas in a foam container in the 'Men's room—those two trailers are going to be handy for storing stuff!" He smiled and went back to chopping.

"Tomorrow, we, you and I, are going shopping for more cooking gear, and outdoor furniture, tables, chairs, umbrellas, etc! Etc! Jose, you're going to be a Master Chef! A great Host! We'll make you as famous as— well—as anyone!

Back inside, Alex circulated among the women she had come to recognize as 'regulars'. Teasing, patting, hugging, cheek kissing, and Alex practiced her Spanish—that was always good for laughs! Behind the bar and standing close to Marie as she mixed drinks, Alex realized—for the first time ever, she was actually paying close attention to how certain mixed drinks were made. She had always been a champagne and wine gal herself—just pop the cork, and drink!

Alex glanced toward the front door—more people were coming in—even some that appeared to be 'Gringos', looked upper-middle class, probably staying in 'Old Town'—Great! Their money was as good as anyone's! She thought, 'Is it the sign? Not even painted? Is it catching people's attention?'

Again at Jose's cooking—the veg's were finished, the lobsters were on the grill—it seemed about ready. "Anything I can do?" she asked. "Yes, get three plates—shelve under the bar—dip the sautee'. I have to watch these!" Returning with the plates and as she dipped, she asked, "What's the routine here?" "We fix Mama a plate, take it to her—she snacks when possible. Drag out a couple of chairs, you and I can eat here by the grill—I don't like to leave the fire this hot, it'll burn down soon."

"Got it!" as she stirred the small pot of butter—real butter—on the end of the grill. Then she got the tortillas—Alex had no modesty about going in the 'Men's' room—unwrapped the pile and laid about nine or ten on the end of the grill to warm. The first plate finished, she carried it to Marie then returned to the grill with two old wooden chairs. "Beer?" she asked. "Yes" She went and got two cold beers and came back just as he laid the golden browned lobsters on their plates. It was delicious—and they dipped the chunks directly into the hot pot of butter still on the grill. The atmosphere was delightful! And Jose was indeed a great cook!

The business potential was enormous! All that was needed were people that could afford it! People from 'Hotel Row' and 'Old Town'!

Finished eating, Jose took Alex's plate, scrapped all the lobster hulls onto one plate and walked out into the darkness. Returning with the plates empty, he only said, "Nite-cats." "Nite-cats! Margays! Oncillas! Here! This close to the city?" Alex snapped as she jumped up, and twisted toward the back door! She had heard about 'Nite-cats' from Nat's and Jim's tales of jungle life! "No, Silly! Not real 'Nite-cats'. Domesticated cats! House cats—maybe a few 'Alley cats'! From the houses over there!" he laughed. The two sat back, stared at the glow of the coals and sipped.

As they drained the bottles, Alex asked, "Can you relieve your Mother for a while? There's something I want to talk to her about." "Sure, I'm— we're finished here. The fire looks ok to leave." They went inside.

Guiding Marie outside, Alex began in a delicate, gentle fashion.

It was about the 'regulars', the women that 'worked' the men in a routine manner. She explained—without being prudish or high-bowded— that she was interested in the girl's welfare and just maybe, improving their concern about their own bodies for their own protection.

"And, a supply of free condoms, and throw-away dues bottles would be here—in 'their' trailer." Alex hesitated. Marie expressed her agreement— she seemed deeply interested now that someone had openly brought up the subject. Alex added, "And I think—know—you're the one to talk to the ladies, not me! Rightly, they would resent me interfering in their business! Ok?" "When?" Marie asked, even though she was getting used to Alex's 'now'. Sure enough, Alex replied, "Now" "The two had worked their way into the 'Ladies' trailer. Marie nodded, and left. Alex slid back, propped in one corner of the sofa/bed, and waited, as she thought, 'I'm not going to say a thing, unless they ask.' Soon the ladies began to drift in—they almost completely ignored Alex as they primped, sat down on the floor and leaned back and smoked, or just whatever. When one of the gals took a piss, standing fashion, Alex noticed that she didn't wear panties, or wipe—and that she had a very 'healthy' bush. Alex was quickly getting used to the fact that people— especially the men—very seldom closed a toilet door.

When Marie finished, Alex was very pleased, Marie had handled it like a mother explaining the facts of life to a thirteen year old daughter—a virgin daughter! The ladies—there were six—seemed interested and concerned, and even pleased that anyone would agree to help. One attractive young lady, Janie—Alex guessed her age to be sixteen, or even younger— asked Alex, not in an air of resentment, but of real interest, "Alex, how do you know about whoreing? How could, someone like you—rich— even imagine what it is like?" "Sweetie, during my school years"—Alex didn't want to say college or university, besides her obsession with sexually activities had started long before that—"I was always the busiest whore in whatever school I was in! I was just too stupid to ask for pay! I may look like an innocent little rich kid, but I guarantee you all, I have been—and still am—a wild—bitch!" They all laughed, she quickly added, "Hell! I got kicked out of more schools than you can shake a stick at for—the teachers!" They laughed again, and began to leave the trailer.

With just the two of them left in the trailer, Marie asked, "Are you still planning to go through with this clothes swapping thing with Jose tonight?" "Yes, if Agent-man shows up, why?" "It's your hair—if Jose puts on your skirt and blouse, that part will probably be Ok—but his hair is much shorter, around the sides and back." "And, if I wind up with the hat—Jose will not have anything to hide his short hair. I see what you mean." The two thought, then Marie said, "You need to be wearing a scarf now. Then give the scarf to Jose, tie it in the same fashion—He'll then have something to cover his short hair." "Yes! That would do it—but—", Alex knew she didn't have a scarf with her—here— tonight.

"Janie is wearing one now—around her neck, and it is dark red. You wait here, I'll go borrow it!" In only a few minutes, Marie returned with it, and helped Alex tie it over her head, and down over the sides—it hung low enough in the back. Looking in the mirror, Alex saw that the scarf hid her 'page-boy' cut perfectly. And it would do the same for Jose's short hair.

They walked arm in arm back toward the rear door, Alex asked, "How about the workers for the concrete rest rooms project?" Marie thought, 'Doesn't she ever stop working?' She came up with her own answer, 'No'. Inside, and a few outside, with Alex in tow, Marie began to talk with several of the men. Slowly, they had selected and got together four at a table off in one corner. Marie explained the project, asked Alex for clarification on some of the details. A couple of rounds of beers later, the four men agreed—they could start at sunrise tomorrow!

Marie and Alex were seated side by side, Alex started, to the four men, "Great! The drinks are"—she couldn't finish! Marie had placed a hand over her mouth! Looking into each other's eyes, Alex realized, slowly removed Marie's hand and then she finished her statement with, "Just great at Marie's!" Marie and Alex chuckled, the men thought it sounded stupid!

The workmen left the table, and Alex saw 'him'—Agent-man, the neighbor from the hotel—as he came in the front doorway. He cased the scene, hesitated when he spotted her and nodded in her direction. Going directly to the bar—he limped slightly—he got a beer from Jose, turned and looked again at Alex. Laying one hand on Marie's arm, Alex said, "Well! Well! It's show time!" "What?" "It's him! There at the bar! Next to Janie!" Alex waited until Marie saw the man, then she asked, "Can you relieve Jose? I—want us—Jose and I—to dance some—clearly show ourselves—our clothes, the hat and my scarf. Let this guy see us together!" "Sure—You really are going to do this?" "Wouldn't miss it for the world!"

A couple of wild dances; Jose removed and waved the old hat, and hunched a lot—Alex spun until the full skirt swung out and high enough to reveal her bare ass with only her tongs pulled up tight in her bottom and she showed off her scarf as much as possible! Then they headed for the rear door. As they passed close to Agent-man, Alex said to him, "Hi! Glad you could make it! Should be a lot of fun tonight!" He just nodded back as they went on.

Quickly the two went in the 'Men's' trailer, there wasn't anyone else inside, she flipped on the door lock. They began to swap clothes. When she got down to only her tongs, Jose patted her cheeks a couple of times and mentioned her obvious 'hairless' condition. Alex snapped, "La Naturale!" For some strange reason, she had recalled—and used—Tiger's very first words to her, years ago, when she had made a 'smart' remark about Tiger's huge breasts. Alex made sure Jose had the scarf tied and pulled in the same fashion. She pushed up her hair and pulled the hat down tightly over it. And she made sure Jose had the keys and a hand full of money.

Back inside the bar, they passed around close to the walls, in the shadows. At the front doorway, they hesitated as Alex grabbed Jose by his butt and kissed him hard in the mouth. Glancing toward the bar, she saw that Agent-man was watching. Quickly, she headed back into the shadows near the inside walls. Jose stepped briskly to the station wagon, but waited after starting the engine. He could see 'Him' as he approached the open doorway. "Yes! Agent-man had taken the bait!", Jose softly said as he slowly drove away. On the streets, Jose made sure he was being tailed, then he headed South on Route 15. Jose checked the fuel gage—there was plenty for what he planned—a trip to the roughest, toughest bar in all the State, at the small beach town of Caimanero. Jose checked the passenger's seat—as Alex had promised, her 'workman's' jeans and shirt were there.

All he had to do was be sure Agent-man followed him, but beat him there by enough time to change clothes, and little Alex would disappear! And Agent-man would be on his own—among the meanest bastards in all of the State! And he would hang in the shadows, have a few beers, and watch the fun! Or slip out and drive back—he wasn't sure which yet.

Back at Marie's Alex removed the hat, rubbed her hair back down and in general, mingled with the customers, paying special attention to the USA couples and the ones from Old Town—she even led two couples out the rear door and showed the ladies the inside of the 'Ladies' trailer. They were favorably impressed. After the 'local' men recognized her in Jose's clothes, she danced with a couple of them. Time passed.

And Jose walked in the front doorway. Alex ran to him, asked, Well? Where is Agent-man?" "Don't worry, he's about sixty miles away with two flat tires—and stuck at a very, very, very bad place!" Jose was wearing Janie's scarf tied around his neck as he told of their 'game' and his trip. Several of the 'regular Ladies' gathered around and listened. Janie smoothly reached and removed her scarf—she didn't want it to get lost in the clothes shuffle.

Finishing his rendition, he pulled Alex face to face, said, "What about that blow-job you promised?" The 'ladies' went silent and pressed closer. "Real? I did that?", she didn't want, or wait for an answer.

She raised her hands to about shoulder level, slightly flipped her fingers open and to the sides, glanced to the 'ladies', said, "A promise is a promise!

Come on, little guy, this will not take long!" The 'ladies' smiled, and Janie slapped Alex on her butt, exclaimed, "Way to go Alex!"

She took his hand and led him to the dark side of the trailers.

It was late, the customers drifted away, and there had been no sign of Agent-man. Alex said her goodnights, thanked Jose for the excellent meal and reminded him of their shopping trip, she drove away. Slipping in the rear door of the hotel—Senor Z had given her a key—she quietly made her way to their room. It was dimly lit, the small light in the bath was still on and the door there was almost pulled shut. Tiger was spread out on the huge bed, hard asleep. Not turning on more lights, Alex hung up Tiger's skirt and blouse, stripped, and kicked these clothes to one side. She stepped to the bed, and hesitated.

Tiger was lying on her side, her beautiful limbs spread as if she was making a broad-jump, her long hair scattered over her face, shoulders and back—even her large breasts. Slowly moving around the bed, Alex enjoyed the quiet, undisturbed scene—the lovely sight of the beautiful young Maya. Tiger gave a slight twitch occasionally. Alex was tired, beat, but only physically. Her mind was still excited by the thrill of pulling off the trick on the Agent-man—and, yes, her paying off her promise to Jose. She hadn't thought much about it at the time—but now, she realized she wanted something more—but what?

Staring at Tiger's round buttocks and the deep valley between the two tight mounds, Alex had brief flashes of her early days—her first real exposure to other girls—at private all-girls schools. She had not been shocked nearly as much as she was pleased, excited, and sank quickly into intimate involvements, usually with more than one favorite 'mate' at the time. And she usually wound up in trouble with the Matrons. But all this had been replaced with her desire for men when she was 'released' into the world of dual sexes—the man/woman scene.

Alex had quick thoughts of Tom—and other men from her past—she turned away from Tiger, stepped to the door to the balcony and slid it open. The rush of the cool night air was refreshing on her naked body, she roughly rubbed it—this felt pleasant. The scene outside, with the huge full moon above the hilly offshore islands, the reflections of the moon and the many streetlights along Oltas on the ever lapping water was still fantastically beautiful.

Leaning against one edge of the doorway, she unconsciously twisted and snapped her large nipples—another of her nervous habits—Alex felt confused. Confused about what she wanted, even needed—sexually. Amazed that her hectic 'other' businesses seemed so in-place, and her satisfactions with such frantic activities in recent months, but now, confused about her inner-self—the two seemed to have landed worlds apart.

And to make it more complicated, she knew it was her choice— she could go in whatever direction she wanted. This compounded her confusion, it was seldom, but she couldn't seem to decide; boy/girl, girl/ girl, or girl/boy/girl? Or—even the option of no sexual relationship at all—without 'she-knew-who', this could, just maybe, be possible!

Or? Her thoughts briefly snapped, or settle down, forget all else, and have a house full of kids! Not necessarily her own, but kids! She had doubts of her ability to bear children. This thought was not new. 'Alex! You are no longer a 'spring-chicken'! Time is rushing forward!' Her mind shouted!

Seeming to be hypnotized by the moon, she was not any closer to understanding herself. "Alex? Is that you?" Tiger had rolled over and propped up on her elbows. "No, Tiger—It is the one hundred and ten pound Rapist! And I've come to rape you!" Without her decision, her mind had suddenly, quickly relieved that problem—she wanted Tiger—very strongly. Alex ran and jumped on top of Tiger, they both squealed and laughed as Alex played 'grab-ass'!

And by the bright moonlight, the two made passionate, hard physical love. And Alex thought—only briefly—to hell with serious decisions. This is what I want—now!

With her lust, her urge, satisfied,' Alex thought of her 'game' with Agent-man. If she could just think of a way to rub it in!

It wasn't difficult, early the next morning, in nothing but her sleeping tee shirt, Alex went out on the balcony, banged the chairs about, and waited as she leaned on the handrail with her bare bottom stuck out. She heard 'Him' as he came out. Holding her position, she twisted her face toward him—he was staring at her bottom—she said, without even greetings, "Roads down here are bad on tires, aren't they?" He gritted his teeth and glared at her. She jerked upright, laughed and went inside, still laughing out loud!

Agent-man returned inside, he pointed a stiff index finger at his partner, snapped. "From now on, that little bitch is your assignment!" The partner doubled up with laughter! "You will not be laughing when you see that she is as slick as a live snake dipped in mineral oil!" "Ok! Ok! Following this—this Margarita gal around is as boring as watching the hogs sleep! Ok! I'll take on Alex—starting this morning!" He was still chuckled.

Driving along Oltas, toward Marie's, Alex watched the mirrors, and thought, 'Well. I guess 'Sport' threw in the towel! I've got a new 'tail'—a light tan sedan!'

At Marie's, she saw Johnny and Johnny on the roof as they painted the letters on the sign. Two of the construction sign workers were busy installing the floodlights. And the four new men had started digging ditches for the foundations of the new rest rooms. Jose walked to the wagon, she returned his clothes, and asked, "You, or your Mother don't own a vehicle, do you?" Sheepishly, he replied, "Couldn't ever seem to afford one," he let it drop off. "Come on, let's pick out one—something to haul stuff in, a service for the business—not new, mind you, but good enough to not be too much trouble." She lifted his chin, threw her arm around his neck, gave a tug, said, "Come on! Let's ask your Mother what she thinks—Besides, it is her business!" The two chuckled and went to locate Marie. Alex closed her explanation with, "And all the expenses for a vehicle—pay out of the business money—that's deductible."

Marie had no objection, she only smiled at the idea.

As they walked back to the wagon, Alex handed him the keys, said, "I need a jog—you slowly turn the car around, point it that way", she pointed north-east—away from the in-coming road and the street where the tan sedan was now parked. She added, "When you see me at that car"—she slightly nodded her head toward the tan sedan—"Come in a hurry and pick me up. Ok?" "Yes, but—" "No buts, ok?" "Sure."

She,started to jog directly toward the car. The Agent saw the station wagon move but it wasn't pointed his way. Confused as to where the wagon may go and to why she was running here, he started the engine, but waited. She jogged to the car and leaned her elbows on the open window sill, said, "Buenos dias, Senor! So, It's your turn in the barrel!"

"My name is Alex, I guess you've heard the 'problem' of calling me anything else!" She straightened up, stepped toward the front of his car, leaned down slightly and said, "Nice headlights!" He quickly shut off the motor—but—he left the keys in the switch, opened the door and jumped out. "Alex! Don't screw with my headlights!" He stepped to the front, as if he was protecting the lights. "My! My! You really know how to talk to a Lady!" She jumped to the open door, reached in, and snatched out the keys and held these over her head, and shouted, "Let's play Finders Keepers!" she made a slight motion with her hand—the one with the keys overhead. He leaped at her, his right hand going for the keys. She hopped back, grabbed his wrist with her 'free' hand and pulled—very hard as she stuck her foot in front of his feet. He headed down, both hands out front, preparing to fall face down. She made a wide swing with her 'key' hand and shouted, "There they go! Finders, Keepers!" She hopped over his feet and ran to the station wagon—Jose had been waiting for her. Jumping in, she yelled back at the Agent who was on his hands and knees, "We'll be back! Got to go rob a few banks!" She and Jose laughed as he roared off. Out of sight, Alex held the car keys in front of Jose's face—she had 'palmed' these instead of throwing them out in the bushy field.

As Jose headed for 'used car dealer's strip', the two discussed the possibilities—they finally agreed on a van, a window van, with all the seats, if possible. And if the price was right. This could be used to haul people, or things, or to store stuff out of the weather. Over an hour later, they had located an older full-sized van, a Dodge with all the side windows and the original seats—a slant-6, automatic transmission, even a radio that worked. Alex let Jose do the haggling, she hung back. Finally Jose was satisfied he had the lowest price he was going to get. Alex wrote the Dealer one of Marie's 'new' checks, insured him it 'was 'good'—he could call the bank if he wanted to! He did, replied, "No problem!"

Completed with the purchase, Alex told him to follow her back to the bar, she would leave the wagon there, and then they could get on with their shopping. Approaching the 'white' roadway to the bar, they saw that the tan sedan was where they had last seen it. But there wasn't any sign of the Agent. Pulling up close to the front with both vehicles, Alex rushed inside—she wanted something cold to drink.

Agent-man was seated at the bar, having a beer, He didn't say anything as she got a cold beer from the cooler, came around and sat down next to him. She raised her frosted bottle to him, he nodded, she gulped a slug then she waited, it was his move.

"Alex, I could 'cuff' you now—I've got the authority—" She interrupted, "Ok, then what? You going to haul me downtown? Here? In Mazatlan? In case you haven't heard, the last thing the Mayor of this 'Burg' wants is trouble with—or out—of me or Margarita! I think you would look really silly hauling my little ass around chained to your wrist—day and night!" He waited—he knew he couldn't make anything stick—then he conceded; "Ok, so what's next?"

She reached in her pocket, pulled out his keys and tossed these on the bar, and said calmly, "Look, I'm just trying to wrap-up some business here—and as you know Margarita is involved almost day and night with her speaking engagements." She took another swallow, he nodded. She added, "You stay out of the way—it makes me nervous for anyone to sneak around behind my back—and we'll see where it goes from there. Ok?" He didn't reply as he picked up his keys, but he did nod. "Ok! Got to run! Got shopping to do! Why don't you just hang around here—and spend MONEY!" Again he only nodded.

In the newest addition to Marie's Bar and Grill, she and Jose went here and there—Jose knew where the best deals were for what they wanted; a new propane gas grill for quickies-keep the old charcoal one, it had character, and was better suited for larger affairs, new pots, pans, a few fancy spatulas, large forks and knives—and what ever else looked handy. Then for the 'service'; new plastic tables, chairs (also plastic—these held up better in the outdoor scene), table cloths, eating utensils and plastic storage boxes. And supplies; disinfectants, deodorizers, boxes of paper towels and toilet tissue and plastic trash containers—large and small. When Alex got to ; boxes of condoms, female sanitary napkins, and particularly d.isposable dues bottles, Jose was shocked. "Hey! Its just part of the female world! Don't get the 'willies' now!" Alex quipped. But he did know where to buy these items wholesale. By mid-afternoon, the van was packed full. They headed back to the bar.

The tan sedan was gone, Alex asked Marie about the Agent. She only shrugged, then replied, "He hung around a while, had a few beers, looked at the different things going on here, paid his bill, then I asked him who he worked for, and why was he concerned about you." "So? What did he say?" "Not a lot—said he was 'with' the Department of Internal Security. Wanted to know your plans—asked me a few questions—which I did not know anything about, then he left." Alex nodded, Marie added, "He seemed like a rather nice gentleman." "That's more like it—If they want to know, just ask, and I'll tell them—what I want to!" Alex laughed and rejoined Jose at the van, they began to unload and set-up all the new items.

The two spent the rest of the afternoon on this, and they also moved the old cooking grill from the rear to the East end of the building—close to the rear corner. And at this end, they sat-up the new tables, chairs and umbrellas. "Alex, I can't believe it! You buy things that we've wanted for years like—like buying a handful of tortillas! Where does all your money come from?" She stopped in mid-motion, her arms full, replied, "Jose, we don't have time now for me to fully explain—it's very complicated. I'll just say I didn't steal it"—she hesitated, added, "Well, not with a gun anyway!" She walked on laughing.

They took a break, got beers, sat under an umbrella at one of the new tables, in the new chairs. Marie joined them, looked at all the new equipment and said, "I'm impressed! And in such a short time!" Jose and Alex smiled and sipped.

"Excuse me, there's something else I need to do before—", Alex headed for the station wagon. Returning to the table where Marie and Jose still sat, she had her laptop computer. Alex began, she contacted Yevona directly in D.C. After several transmissions back and forth, Alex shutdown her computer, leaned back and said, "Well! That's taken care of! The Staff in D.C. is up to date on your accounts. From now on, they will handle the details—I can contact them whenever I want to."

She took a sip, added, "Marie, being as I am not sure how much longer we will be in Mexico—how long our 'project' will take—or what might happen—I left D.C. an order. If your bank checking account falls below two thousand—US dollars—D.C. will automatically deposit ten thousand—US. Do you think that will work out? Being as you—or anyone—may not be able to contact me—or Tiger."

The three were serious, and silent for a brief time. Then Marie leaned to Alex, covered her small hand with hers, and, in almost a whisper, "Alex, you are headed for serious trouble, aren't you?" They were staring into each other's eyes, then, uncommonly, Alex cut her eyes away and stammered, "I—we—not sure—don't—", she got it together, "Hell, nothing we can't handle—one way or the other!" Then she laughed, and smiled to both of them. Marie returned to the question, "Of course that will be ok, I've never had so much money in such a short period of time—I don't know how to thank you!" Alex patted her hand, replied, "Easy! Make YOUR business a real success! Think BIG! Think lots of c ustomers! With lots of money!", then she glanced to Jose, added, "And make Jose the most loved Chef in all of Mazatlan!"

"Alex, after the new restrooms are completed, what do we do with the trailers?" Marie changed the subject. "I don't know—that's your concern. Use for storage, employees comfort, changing rooms, whatever. Turn into 'mini' whore houses for all I care!" The three chuckled. Jose asked,

"You don't have any problems with whores?" "None at all—especially the 'working gals'—best buy in town. It's the expensive 'Pros' I don't have much use for. It's ok, but, outrageously over priced! Hey! A blow-job is a blow-job! If it cost two dollars or two hundred dollars!" "There are men that pay two hundred?" "Sure! You've just got to have the right customers! And those are the ones we're after—people who'll pay twenty dollars for the meal you cooked for me last night! See? The service is the same—It's just a matter of WHO pays for it! If we're talking about sex or food!" Jose remarked, as if to himself, "I'm beginning to understand what you are after here."

Suddenly Alex excused her self again, and she went around to the rear where the workers were busy doing the final smoothing of the two small concrete slabs. She had learned that the Bossman spoke fairly good English. Getting him off to one side, they talked, and she pulled out her wallet and gave him some bills. After a trip to the 'Ladies' trailer, she returned to Jose and Marie.

"Jose, where is the closest place to get the two new propane tanks filled?" Alex asked as she looked over the new grill. "Not far, why?" "Run get both filled—and while you're out, pick up something handy to cook—for customers—for tonight." She glanced up at the sign—the painters were almost completed. And she saw the flood lights being checked—all of these came on. Jose and Marie watched her. "I feel a party coming on! Tonight!"

She got her cell phone, dialed up Max. The other two listened, "Max! Tonight! We're ready! Bring us some Rich-bitches!" They laughed, Jose ran, grabbed up the two tanks and ran to the van—and roared away! Marie got the idea—she went inside and called the liquor /beer /wine distributor and ordered a lot! For tonight! Not tomorrow, but NOW! Alex's 'fever-pitch' had finally caught on!

The sign workers gathered around Marie as they tallied the bill. Alex came in, caught one by his arm—he really wasn't doing anything—pulled him aside, said, "Sweetie, please come with me." He did, and when outside at the 'cafe' area, Alex pointed up to the sign, said, "That top light—there at this end, please run up the painter's ladder and turn that one—just the one—back toward where I will be standing—like the spot light is on me!" Without hesitation, he was up. Alex moved to just beyond the tents to a clear area in the field. The man sighted the light, guessed it to be on her. Coming back down, she thanked him, then said, "After tonight, do me, do Marie a favor and turn it back toward the sign. Please?" "Sure, Senorita Alex! I'll be glad to!" He waited and watched her for a while. She stepped out to the bushes in the field, bent over and looked closely. The center stem was fairly straight and easily broken. Picking a few, she stripped off the bushy part, then brought these to the end of the building and stored these for later use. Scratching his head—he didn't ask—the worker returned inside.

The deal settled with the sign workers, Marie wrote them a check, and they left. Alex went to Marie—Alex was sure there were more, but one additional item she wanted to discus with Marie—she started. "On the paving—the parking lot or the roadway to here—I'm leaving that entirely up to you. If you do, or don't do, if you think it is too expensive for what good it will do—all that's your decision. I'll go with whatever you decide! Ok?" "I understand, Jose and I—and Max, will talk about it after—" she dropped it. Realizing that today was the last day together, they hugged, and had a few tears.

"Got to run! I want to see if I can catch Tiger between engagements! She just has to see that sign! Love you all! See you tonight!" Alex dashed for the station wagon as she wiped her tears away.

Racing toward the street, Alex saw that the tan sedan was back. It was pointed east and had not started its move. She faked a left, but when within about fifty feet, she turned right across the corner of the field. Barely missing his rear bumper, she completed the swing onto the paved cross street. Not stopping for the stop sign, she drove through the light North bound traffic and—among several horns blowing—she forced her way into the heavier fast moving South bound string of vehicles. By the time she pulled into the alley at the hotel, Agent #2 was not in sight! Hey, little Alex had learned how to drive in downtown Atlanta!

Running in, through the dining area, Alex rushed to the cash register. "Senor Z, where is Tiger?" He just pointed up as he took money. She slowed down, took her time with the many stairs. In the room, after greetings— and hugs—Alex asked, "What is your schedule for tonight? Can you finish soon, at a reasonable time? Say nine or ten?" "Let me see—", Tiger curled one hands fingers under her chin, looked up at the ceiling. "I've got a surprise for you!" Alex thought she would encourage the decision! "Ok! I'll cut it short! I'll say we're leaving early, blab, blab!" Alex grabbed her in a bear hug, "You'll love the surprise!"

As Tiger got all dressed up, Alex watched, said, "You will not have to re-dress tonight—that outfit will knock em' dead at Marie's!" Alex had already began to pack for leaving early—four or five—in the morning. "I'll layout our loose traveling jeans, shirts, our low tennis shoes", and as she held up a 'silence' sign to Tiger, she added, "No need for us to be uncomfortable on our flight to Mexico City tomorrow morning!"

Alex stood in the open hall doorway as Tiger left the room and headed down. When Tiger got down to the next landing, Agent #1 came out of their room. "Hey, I thought I'd save you two some trouble—no need to strain your ears listening to that rinky-dink radio! She is knocking off early tonight—nine or so, coming back here. Then we're going together out to Marie's for a going away party. You two sure don't want to miss that!" He just glared at her, then continued toward the stairs. "Still pissed about those lousy tires, I guess!" She laughed as he disappeared down the steps.

It took only a brief time for Alex to locate the two planted radio transmitters—the 'bugs.' Quietly removing both, she tip-toed to the toilet. Holding both in one hand, her other on the flush handle of the toilet, she screamed at the 'bugs', "Oh Lord! It's a bug! It's a bug!" She flushed the toilet, made sure the sound was relayed and then she dropped both of the 'bugs' into the toilet bowl—these were sucked down, gone.

Across the hall, Agent #2 jerked off the headphones, threw these downs snapped, "Damn it! She found them!" And he thought, 'At least we know they are flying to Mexico City tomorrow morning!'

Alex immediately got on the phone, called the Social Editor of the Mazatlan News. With him on the other end of the connection, she said, "Joe, Alex here, you may want to be at Marie's tonight—say nine or earlier. We're having a going away party for Tiger—Margarita—", she listened, then said, "Great, be sure to bring your photographer. I don't seem to find that sweet TV guy's number—could you possible see that he is there also? And Joe, this time things will definitely have a different twist!"—"No, let it be a surprise! See you tonight! Bye!"

Before the sign, before the changes at Marie's, Alex had another surprise for Tiger. Alex had not shown anyone at Hidden Valley her new 'safari' outfit—the one she bought in D.C. And she hadn't bothered to describe her night at Jerry and Lilly White's home—the night she had demonstrated her ability to use a whip. But of course, Tiger knew of her skill with a whip, they had played with one many times at Hidden Valley. Alex had brought the outfit and her whip on this trip without Tiger knowing it. Alex's reason? She had thought, 'Hey! We're going to the jungles of Chiapas—wherever that is!'

She had already showered, and had been puttering about in the nude. But suddenly she realized—She was about to forget! Jumping around, she located her sleeping tee shirt, jerked it on, grabbed up the bottle of white wine she had been sipping on and dashed out on the balcony. It was time for the sunset! Agent #2 came out on his balcony, but he didn't say anything until after the sunset was completely over—he had learned that was a 'no-no' with Alex. He saw Alex break her stare at the horizon, he calmly leaned his hands to the rail facing her, and said, "Alex, let's cut the crap. All we want to know is why you're down here, what you are going to do, and if it is dangerous for anyone."

She waited, then stood, moved her chair to face him and placed her feet up on the lower rail directly across from him, and slowly slid her feet far apart. She felt now, he wouldn't hear, or at least remember, what she was about to say. She took her time, took another sip from the bottle, then, "That's all? You sure?" "Yes, promise, that's all." He replied as he stared at her bare crotch. "If I tell you, you promise to go away, not bother us any more?" "Sorry, I have to follow orders—We're not a 'free-lancer' like you." Another sip, "Sure—Let's see, that was 'why are we here', simple, to take a trip. Next was, what are we going to do? Right?" He nodded. "We are going to get something very old that has been lost for a very long time—that's all! Oh, third, 'is it dangerous to anyone? Yes, very dangerous for anyone, you included, that gets in our way!" She stood, stepped to the doorway then turned back, asked, "Did you catch the info about tonight's party at Marie's?" He nodded. "Don't miss it!" Then she went inside.

Alex called down to the desk phone, said, "Sorry to interrupt, Senor Z, but you may want to add up my tab—I need to get that settled tonight, say about eight-thirty?"—"Thanks, I'll be down by then. We're heading to Marie's then, hey! You may want to come along, it's a going away party for Tiger"—"No? Sorry, I wish you and Juan could be there."—"No way?"—"See you shortly."

Back at Hidden Valley:

Nat was at her computer as she opened the recent E-mail. One was unusual.

To. HVG, Hidden Valley
From: JW, HVG D.C.

That Southern A-T account is getting questions from the Big M.C. Seems the 'top brass' is interested in the activities of the A-T account. So far we have been successful in 'fielding' the questions.

Dr. K stepped to the living room, motioned to Arnie, as she said, "You may want to look at this E-mail. It's from Jerry White—something concerning Alex's and Tiger's activities down South of the border." As the two stared at the display on the screen, Arnie softly commented, "Top brass—must be the Feds. Big M.C., that's Mexico City." He hesitated then asked, as to himself, "Why would the Mexican Feds be asking questions about those two gals' activities?" Dr. K just shrugged her shoulders.

Another quick rinse off, and Alex dried her hair as she rubbed it down. Next, she put on her gold nail polish, then made up her face; extended her black eyebrows, gold shadow liners under and over her eyes, and bright gold lip stick. She put on her gold nugget ear pins. After pulling on the skin tight leather pants, she put on the high top tight boots and zipped these up. Pulling on the tight fitted leather jacket—she had decided she didn't need a blouse—she only buttoned the two lowest buttons. It widely spread at her small breasts, but it did cover the red around her stiff nipples. She then put on two gold nugget rings on her left handy and her gold nugget 'dress' watch on her left wrist She didn't put any jewelry on her right hand or wrist—she didn't want anything to interfere with her whip handling. Taking her gun, she removed the clip, snapped out all the rounds into her purse then checked the barrel to be sure it was empty. She replaced the clip, and stuffed the pistol deep into her larger dress purse with her other 'necessities'. Adjusting the strap for a tight fit up under her arm, that was finished.

With the whip, she gently shook it out on the floor, checked for any cracks or broken strands, recoiled it to fit tightly around her left shoulder then snapped the epaulet over it. It felt comfortable. She had not brought the fur coat or the fur cap on this trip.

Checking her watch against her sports watch, she noticed it was almost eight-thirty, she headed down. At the bottom step, she hesitated, gave everyone—the dining room was again full—a chance to get a good look at her in the 'hunting' attire! She thought the guests were even more impressed than with her expensive evening dress she wore only a few days before. There were 'ohs' and 'ahs', and as she expected, one young lady said outloud,"It's Alex! The Bodyguard!" The group stared as Alex took a slow bow, then smartly stepped on down and went to Senor Z at the cash register. At the first sight, the others in the lobby and at the bar were taken back! Even Senor Z was surprised!

Alex politely nodded at the people. "Alex! You never fail to amaze me! Senor Z said as he stopped counting money and stared at her 'different' outfit. He couldn't help it, taking Alex's elbow he led her to the kitchen, pushed her in far enough for the guys to see her—mainly so Juan could see her! "See! I told you guys to tighten up! Here's your new Master!" Then he and Alex laughed, the others applauded for her!

The two slowly walked back through the dining Senor Z set the pace, mainly so all the guests could get a good look at them—together, and arm in arm! Back at the cash register, Alex paid her bill with her credit c card, then she slipped her purse under the counter—she knew it would get in the way for what she planned next.

Stepping out the front door—the crowd of fans had gotten smaller, but there was still a good size group—the cry went up, "Alex! Alex! Alex!" Not wanting to disappoint anyone, Alex stepped sideways until she was about middle of the glass front to the dining room. She stepped to the edge of the curb, removed the whip—she didn't have enough room behind her for 'overhead' cracks or a 'drawing crack'—and made several 'vertical' cracks in front of herself. The cracks were very loud! The crowd—outside and inside applauded And cheered, "Alex! Alex!" Glancing through the glass, she saw that Juan and his 'new' crew were also watching. And Senor Z was with them.

As Alex recoiled her whip, she bowed to the people several times. She heard a single applause from above, looking up, she saw it was Agent #2, he was leaning over the rail of his balcony. She waved to him, he waved back. Alex, still on the sidewalk, mingled, shook hands, and most of all told everyone about the party tonight at Marie's. People from inside had joined in the fun.

Suddenly, a police car whipped up to the curb and abruptly stopped. The two cops jumped out, one asked, "Ok! Who shot the gun?" Everyone laughed, but the cops didn't think it was funny, the other cop, shouted, "So, you all think that's a joke—everybody knows it is against the law to fire a weapon in the City limits! Now, who shot the gun?" The crowd laughed again, but Alex stepped forward, and shook hands with both the Policemen as she explained it was the 'crack' of her whip! The cops acted as if they didn't believe her, then one person in the by-standers yelled, "Show them, Alex! Show them!" Many others chimed in, "Show them Alex! Show them Alex!"

She bowed to the crowd, removed her whip and demonstrated several vertical cracks—"CRACK! CRACK! CRACK!" She didn't, but she could have kept it up continuously for almost a half-hour! The cops then believed, they shook their heads, got in their car. The crowd applauded as they drove away. Alex again yelled, "Tonight! Marie's!"

A long black sedan pulled to the curb and stopped—it was a chauffeur with Tiger! The fans were in luck tonight! The two of them together for the first time in days—or nights! And the fans went wild as the driver helped Tiger out of the car. Screaming, cheering, applauding, the crowd was in a frenzy! Tiger waved, threw kisses, and jumped up and down!

Alex stepped to her, they hugged and kissed, the on-lookers went frantic! Tiger held Alex off with stiff arms, asked, "Alex! Where in the world did you get that wild outfit!" "D.C., one time when I was up there!" Then the two faced the fans, and as they held hands, Alex yelled—with a wave toward Tiger, "La Tiger! La Tiger!" The crowd picked it up, "La Tiger! La Tiger!" It was Tiger's turn, she waved to Alex, shouted, "La Tamer! La Tamer!" The people joined in, "La Tamer! La Tamer!"

Alex realized the driver was still standing beside the car. Turning close to him, she asked, "Can you please drive us to Marie's Bar and Grill?" "Sure, wouldn't miss it for the world!" "Hold it just a second! I've got to get my purse from inside!" She dashed in, ran back, then he helped both of them in the back.

Agent-man had been watching all this time from his balcony, as he saw the car begin to leave, he said, "Oh damn! She's gone again!" He rushed inside at the same time his partner entered from the hall door, he shouted, "Let's go! Let's go! They're on the move!" "What? I just followed the Maya gal here!" "Well, they're gone!" They rushed out, #1 snapped, "What was the tag number?" as they took two steps at the time. "Tag? All I saw was a large black sedan!" "Like there's only one large black sedan in Mazatlan! Damn!"

As Alex looked back, she saw the fans run for their vehicles—Great! It's going to be a grand time tonight! She noticed the sunroof overhead, she tilted forward, asked the driver, "Would you please open the sunroof?" He did, and when Alex judged that the sign was visible, she stood up—Yes! She pulled Tiger to her feet, and screamed as she pointed, "Look! Tiger! That is for you! Look!" Tiger was shocked, she had no idea of this project.

All of Alex's efforts—and expense—were for this exact moment! They hugged! They kissed—lips to lips, with passion. And both cried with joy.

As the driver worked his way between the other cars, Alex was impressed with the number of cars already here; the local TV van, what appeared to be the 'regular' newsmen cars, the 'local, normal, customers plus a lots more—newer, nicer cars, she judged these to be 'Old Town' Residents or 'rental' by tourist types. Parking as close to the front door as possible, they got out. !'Thanks! Come on in! There's going to be a party—and a special show tonight!" And she noticed the new decorations under the eaves and around the front doorway.

With Tiger's hand hooked in her elbow, Alex led her in as the crowds— outside and inside— cheered "La Tiger! La Tiger!" The happy two nodded and waved in return! There were brightly colored ribbons strung in the ceiling, and behind the bar, there was a huge, long banner; 'Welcome to Marie's Margarita Calienta Bar and Grill" Alex had no idea these wonderful new friends had gone to so much trouble—such effort, in such a brief time. Not only was Tiger surprised but so was Alex!

Marie came around from the rear of the bar, hugged and kissed the two. Taking Tiger's arm, she began to tour her about as she explained Alex's work. Alex headed off in a different direction. She went back outside to the new tables with the umbrellas. The beer distributor's large truck and their service van were still parked out back. These Employees had finished with setting up several beer kegs, tables, and boxes of heavy paper cups. These four handsome men—they all wore white pants and shirts, and their bright, highly decorated 'Beer' windbreakers; gold with black for Corona Gold, green with gold print for Tecata, silver with red print for Superior, and, black with white print for Montejo—were not about to leave! They knew a great party when they saw one! They hung around, ready to offer service, or more beer, or 'whatever'.

Jose was very busy as Alex stepped close and lightly kissed his cheek then asked, "How's it coming? ""Wonderful! The charcoal is right! I've got a large pot"—he pointed, it was one of the new pots—"of taco filler, and kilos of tortillas! And several cases of prepared hamburger patties and buns!" Alex saw that the large old grill was completely covered with slabs of ribs! She sniffed the gray smoke as it drifted about, said, "If people don't buy something to eat, it's because they ain't got nose!" Jose smiled as he began to turn over the ribs as Alex strolled away.

She approached a beer table, it had beers already drawn, and she smiled to the 'operator' as she spoke to him—he was one of Marie's 'regulars', he pointed to the money box—it had the price written on the front. She fished out something. It was more than enough, tossed it in the box and got a beer from the table. 'Efficient', she thought! Casually moving about among the guests at the new tables, she nodded, shook hands and answered questions about her Safari outfit that the women seemed very interested in.

When Alex saw Janie with a tray full of fancy mixed drinks, she realized two things! Janie had come out a 'new' door in the East end of the building! A door, cut and installed since she had left here this afternoon! And Janie, the youngest of the 'Ladies of the evening', was working as a cordial waitress!

Moving on, Alex came close to the van—Marie's van—again she was surprised! On both sides, in large, bold letters were painted; "Marie's Margarita Calienta Bar and Grill' This too had been done since she left this afternoon! Great idea! Great response! These two, or whoever, have caught on in a hurry! She guessed that the two Johnnys had painted it after they finished with the overhead sign. She returned to Jose's cooking area.

'If Jose is cooking and Marie is showing Tiger around, who is mixing drinks?' Alex's brain snapped. Through the new door, she looked to the mixing counter behind the bar. A large, older man, in a nice white dress shirt was mixing drinks very fast. Again, she recognized him as another of Marie's 'regulars'. Great! She thought, 'All they needed were the customers!' Sweeping the inside with her sight—it was full—'Well, they've got that now!'

Slowly making her way to the front doorway, Alex saw that the other five 'regular ladies' were also working as waitresses. Recognizing Joe—from the newspaper—and his photographer, and the TV Stringer, she went to them. There was not a chair available, she pulled Joe's knee from under the table and sat down on it. "Well! Did you guys think you'd ever see this?" she waved toward all the customers. "No! Never!" Leaning her face closer, she remarked, "I have this theory—a few thousand here, a few thousand there, and it will make a difference!" The three held a hand up, joined them and as Alex grabbed them, Joe said, "Way to go, Alex!"

"Is this the surprise?" Joe asked her. "Yes and no—This, the improvements, and mainly the huge sign overhead is a surprise—but not THE surprise!" She pointed toward the new East doorway, said, "That will take place out there—beyond the tables—out in the brightly lit spot!" "When?" the Stringer asked. She glanced among the guests then responded, "It depends on a couple of special people being here." She looked off again, continued, "I don't see them yet. But you three should work your way out, as close to the bright spot as possible,the best 'shots' will be there!"

Alex stood first, said, "When you see me with a couple of well-dressed strangers, you'll know the time is getting close." The three stood with their drinks, Joe asked, "What 's with the outfit? And what do I write it is for? Or—why?" She hesitated, they waited. "Joe, just say it is my 'jungle expedition' get-up!" "Jungle? Expedition? Details, Alex! Please! My readers would love the details! They are crazy about you two!" "Sorry, Joe—I really can't say more! You do remember we used the word, 'secret', don't you? Well, that is part of the expedition—'secret'! Ok?" She headed for the front doorway as they went toward the East doorway.

Stepping through the doorway, the crowd outside began to applaud and cheer, "La Alex! La Alex!" She bowed, waved, and recognized that most were the people—fans—from the sidewalk scene earlier. Someone called out, "Alex! Crack your whip!" She stopped, pointed a finger in the direction of the voice and yelled, "Later! Over there!" she pointed toward the East, to the umbrellas, "Later! At the spot light! Beyond the umbrellas!" Looking off into the distance, toward the paved street, Alex saw the flashlights of several Policemen as they directed traffic headed for Marie's.

Continuing to scan the crowd for the two Agents, a calm voice behind her said, "Later, what, Alex?" She whirled around, grabbed the man—it was Ageht #2—by one elbow, said, "I'm so glad you could make it!" Agent#1 was just behind, Alex reached around with her right hand extended, looked at #1 eyes, said, "And you too! Friends?" She stuck her hand closer. He reluctantly took her hand, and waited. She violently shook it, said, "Yes, Friends!" she implied they were friends now. "Please, you two—-, follow me, I'll get you ring-side seats!" Holding #2 hand, she led them through the crowd—it quickly parted for 'La Alex'—and on to the East end of the umbrellas, right at the edge of the brightly lit open area.

There were two 'regulars' at the table, Alex leaned over and whispered to them. The 'locals' stood and without seeming resentful, offered the chairs to the two Agents, "What will you two have to drink? I think I can rush it up." They told her, she located Janie and relayed their request and asked for special service to the two. Alex pointed them out. Stepping back to the Agents, she looked for the three newsmen, they were seated with a good view of the place in mind, she waved and they nodded in return.

Alex looked about and spotted the four workmen, the ones on the restroom project. They stood at the edge of the brightly lit spot, East of the last table. Beyond the four was the Ford four-door sedan of the Headman. The car was pointed 'out'—East, away from the building and the bright spot. She thought, 'Yes, they are in position and ready!' Everything was ready—except for the 'star', Tiger!

Hearing an unusually loud cheer out front, Alex guessed it must be Tiger! She excused herself from the Agents, quickly rounded the corner of the building. Yes, Tiger was just outside the front doorway—she was waving to her fans as they cheered, "La Tiger! La Tiger!" The fans parted as Alex went to Tiger's side, took her hand and Alex also began to wave. Out of the corner of her mouth, Alex said, "Tiger, I need to talk to you—now."

But they both saw the slowly approaching headlights. The huge black limo was being escorted, as the two cops—one at each front fender—asked the people to make a path for the limo. The car stopped, Max stepped out, and someone in the crowd recognized him and began to cheer, "El Maxie! El Maxie!" Max was pleasantly surprised, he hadn't heard that expression since he was a star on the local pro-baseball team! He removed his cap, bowed, and waved back. Alex thought, 'Fantastic!'

Helping his clients out—they were four 'beyond middle aged' ladies, expensively dress and with a lot of jewelry—Max led the ladies forward as he waved at the crowd. The crowd politely parted. Alex and Tiger stepped forward, greeted Max, and without hesitation shook the ladies' hands, without their offer, or 'proper' introductions! Then Alex and Tiger led the five around the end of the building to the umbrellas. Max promptly— he knew all the 'regulars'—asked four 'regulars' to offer their seats to the ladies. They did with pleasure—even held the chairs for the 'Rich Bitches from Hotel Row'. Alex and Tiger held back, then quietly slipped off to one side. With 'his' ladies seated, Max asked for their orders, relayed this to Janie with 'special instructions'; increase the prices in exchange for prompt service and to let Marie know the drinks were for 'Max's Ladies'.

Alex quickly told Tiger the plans—at least the part that involved Tiger. But Tiger objected, "I got on heels—that ground is too loose for heels!"

"Take your shoes off!" "And this dress—it is too tight around my knees!" Bending down, Alex ripped the two side splits about six inches higher, quipped, "Try that!" Tiger glanced around, she didn't see anyone looking directly at her—for an instant she was gone! Then right back, she nodded, agreed, "Ok, let's do it!" she threw the shoes up next to the buildings. "You go to the spotlight, Ad lib something, I've got to get some thing", Alex said, as she headed to where she had placed the sticks earlier. Tiger headed for the spotlight area.

CHAPTER 12

Slowly walking into the bright light, Tiger held up both hands and arms, spoke loudly, "Ladies and Gentlemen, La Alex is up to something! I very seldom know what she is up to next!" The guests laughed and clapped. She bowed, then, "And my feet are killing me!" she showed a bare foot. Again the crowd roared and applauded.

Alex ran to Tiger's side, joined her, and said to the people, "Ladies and Gentlemen! Perhaps you were at The Riviera three nights ago! Perhaps not!" Many of the guests whispered to each other. "Or perhaps you have heard about Margarita, Calienta 's unusual ability! Her ability to disappear! Disappear in front of your very eyes! For those of you who didn't see her perform at the Riviera, she will do it tonight! Here! Now! Well—soon!"

While the spectators screamed and yelled, and applauded, one Agent asked the other Agent, "What the hell is Alex talking about?" The other just shrugged. An 'Old-Town guest next to them said to them, "Oh, yes! It was on TV news! She just vanishes!" The two Agents shook their heads.

The crowd quieted down, Alex turned to Tiger, said loud enough for the guests to hear "Ok! Tiger! Disappear!" Tiger acted shy, she didn't do anything else as she stuck one thumb tip in her mouth. Again loudly, Alex said toward the crowd this time, "Well! Maybe poor La Poco Tiger needs encouragement! If you will, please help me count down—three, two, one, then shout, 'Good-by! Ok?" The crowd yelled back their confirmation.

Alex began, lifting and dropping her arms, "Three! Two! One!" The crowd shouted along with Alex; "GOOD-BY!" Tiger was gone! No where in sight! Vanished! In front of their eyes!

Agent #2 said, "What the hell was that! She IS gone!" The other Agent's mouth was open, but he wasn't saying anything. `There were ohs and ahs, and the people twisted about as they looked for her. Then they began to applaud. Alex raised her arms, indicated for silence. They did, then Alex teased, "Ok, show's over, you can all go home!" The people clapped, yelled, screamed! Loudly, Alex shouted, "Just kidding! Please don't leave! Please spend more money!" They laughed and cheered!

"Now, Ladies and Gentlemen, you have to help me find Baby Tiger! We'll count down again, three, two, one, then, 'Hello Tiger!' Ok?"

There was a lot of nodding and cheering. "Ok, let's go! Three! Two! One!" The people joined Alex, "Hello Tiger!" Tiger was again standing beside Alex! More ohs and ahs, then heavy applause! "What are we going to write in our report?""#2 asked. #1 replied, "Not a damn thing! Nothing at all!"

When the cheering died down, Alex turned to Tiger—she was still at her side—said, loud enough for the crowd to hear, "Come on, Tiger, let's get a drink!" Tiger disappeared again! The crowd, not expecting this, went wild! Alex waved for calmness, then she called out, "Guess she didn't want a drink!" The audience laughed and cheered. "Let me try something else! Tiger! Let's eat!" And Tiger again reappeared, took Alex's hand and led her from the spotlight. The crowd was frantic with joy! But, Alex jerked loose, and dashed back to the light, shouted, "After I get a drink, I'll be back! There is more to come!" The crowd carried on with the merriment! And everyone talked to each other! And ordered more drinks! No one was about to leave!

Walking out of the spotlight, Alex cast a quick glance at the four workmen, and the Ford car, they were still in place.

When Alex approached the two Agents, #2 stood, offered her a seat. She sat back, waved and indicated to Janie to bring her a drink—almost any drink would do. "Alex, how does she do that?" #2 asked. "This is the honest truth", she felt she had to clarify her answer, "I have no idea! We've been together for years—years—and I still don't know!" The two men looked questionably. "Honest! I'm not sure she even knows what she does! But she says it is an old family secret, and all the girls—only the girls—at—", Alex suddenly realized she had almost said Amatenango. She changed it to, "her village can do it!" "And which village may that be?" #1 quickly asked. Waving a stiff index finger in front of his face, Alex replied, "No, no, Agentman!" She laughed, leaned far back as Janie brought her a glass of white wine. Alex reached for her pocket, said. "Hold it, Janie, I've got some money—somewhere!" "I've got it!" #2 said.

Alex glanced around at the crowd, and she spotted the two handsome men in black tuxedos—it was Alfonso and Estrada! And they had 'dates'. She waved, they waved back. Alex felt certain their 'dates' were really 'clients'. 'Great! She thought, 'Just the kind of publicity and customers that Marie's needs! Soon a chauffeur came to the Professional Escorts—this meant there was another of Herny's limos here! Even Greater! The 'Plan' was working!

Tiger had gone through the crowd, shook and patted hands, some cheek kissing and on to Jose's large grill. "Jose, I'm starved! Could I have a plate of those delicious looking ribs and a few tortillas?" "Of course!" and he fixed it for her. By the beer table, she got one, and looked about. Quickly a man offered her his chair. She sat down and began to eat in earnest. She still didn't know what Alex was going to do next.

Agent #2 got another chair and pulled up next to Alex. It didn't take long for her to see what she wanted—under their sports jackets they both wore under their left armpits a holster with a pistol. Finishing her wine, Alex leaned closer, patted #2's knee, said, in a rather sweet voice, "You seem like a good sport, would you please help with my show—my demonstration of the whip. It is simple, you hold a bush's stem, and I cut it off with my whip. Please?" It sounded easy enough, he replied, "Sure, if you promise you will not hit me!" She laughed—but recalled that he couldn't promise to go away and not bother them—"Yes, I promise!"

The two stood, Alex said, "Just a sec—", she went to the beer table and got six empty paper cups, returned and taking his hand, led him to the edge of the bright light. She lay down the cups and picked one of the sticks she had placed there earlier. As they went toward the center of the bright area, she stepped to his left side and looked toward the four workmen. Seeing they were watching her, she patted the left side of her chest—close to her armpit and beside her breast. The four men at the edge of the light nodded in recognition. The Headman said to the other three, "Holsters under their left arms, that means they both are right-handed. Go for the right hands."

Close to the center, Alex tugged on his hand, said "I'll cut the stick three times—three! Just don't flinch, wave it about, or move your feet. And—not likely—if I just happen to hit you—your hand or arm— please grit your teeth and we'll cover it up someway. Don't bolt and run. You know, 'the show must go on' thing. Ok? Please?" He just nodded as she stared into his eyes with her big black eyes. He thought, 'How bad can a little whip lash be?'

She stopped, turned and guided him then toward the crowd, she began, "Ladies and Gentlemen! This handsome gentleman has so graciously agreed to help me!" The crowd cheered and clapped. She again positioned him—turned him to about a forty-five degree angle to the center of the guests, and she leveled the stick he held in his right hand, she muttered, "Yes, that's right, now just hold steady." Alex stepped back, her line square to the stick. The whip was still snapped under her epaulette. "Ready?" she asked. He had expected her to take the whip off her shoulder and flip it straight. She didn't, he hesitated. Again, louder this time, she called, "Ready?" He nodded. In one swift motion, at flashing speed, she grabbed the handle, jerked it loose—it uncoiled by itself—the back swing, and, 'Crack!' and about the end four inches of the bush scattered as dust! Again, Crack!, the next few inches, again dust! He had expected a wait, another 'get ready', but instead Alex instantly adjusted her aim—no time at all, no hesitation at all—it was for the soft area between the base of his thumb and his index finger. 'Crack!' He dropped to one knee! He felt as if he had been shot!

Dropping the whip, she rushed to him, being sure to block the crowd's view with her back. She was there just long enough before the four workmen arrived to see his hand—there was 'only' a nasty welt, the skin wasn't broken. Two of the big workmen knelt to their knees, their backs to the guests. One jerked a white cloth from under his shirt—the cloth had a large bloody splotch on it. Quickly wrapping the hand with the cloth, he grabbed around it—the—Agent's entire hand and squeezed very hard. "The Senor needs to be carried to a Doctor! There's a Doctor just up the road!" the Headman shouted toward the crowd. The other worker, the one on his knees, caught the Agent's left wrist. "Leave me alone—", Agentman started, but the workman whispered, "You come with us, or you'll need a cast on your hand after I crush half the bones in it. Understand?" The Agent started to struggle, the workman tighten his grip. The Agent dropped his other knee and lowered his head as the pain became unbearable! The other worker removed the pistol and slipped **it** under his shirt, stuck the barrel in the top of his pants.

The other Agent rushed up, shouted, "I'll handle this! Back off!" The two workers that were still standing stepped close, one on each side, their backs to the crowd and one caught the Agent's right hand and squeezed very hard. Quickly flipping his shirt open, the worker 'showed' him Alex's pistol, then the other worker jerked out the Agents gun and hid it inside his shirt. The Headman, in a low tone, said, "You both come with us—or-else. Understand?" as he squeezed the Agent's hand much harder.

The workers stood, lifted the 'injured' Agent, Alex stepped close to the Agents' faces, softly said, "Sorry, but Tiger and have a project to complete, and you two insisted on getting in our way. Adios, Agentmen." As the four workers 'helped' the two Agents to the Ford and drove away, Alex calmly returned to her whip's handle and picked it up.

"Ladies and Gentlemen! Sorry for the little accident! A few stitches should take care of it!" She hesitated, the crowd was quiet. She shouted, "Maybe I was not warmed up enough!" She briskly stepped to the beer cups, picked these up and in a rather random pattern, scattered these on the ground. A few light flips to be sure the whip was not twisted. Then in a lightning flash,Crack!Crack!Crack!Crack! Crack!Crack! And all six cups were reduced to only small chip. The crowd applauded and cheered! Seeing Tiger at the edge of the umbrellas and not eating any more, Alex called out loudly, "Would someone please put a cigarette in Tiger's mouth and run her in my direction!" The two of them had done this before, back at Hidden Valley. There were a lot of ohs and ahs—but no cheers! And no offers!

Getting a 'white'—this showed up better against her darker skin— cigarette from one of the local men, Tiger briskly walked out and stood half sideways so the crowd could see. She stuck the cigarette in the center of her lips. Tiger nodded, Alex nodded back. 'Crack!', the cigarette exploded as the tip of the whip whipped within inches of Tiger's face. The two turned and bowed, the crowd went wild! As Tiger waved, threw kisses and bowed, Alex calmly recoiled her whip and replaced it on her shoulder. Seeing Alex finished, Tiger raised her hands high above her head and shouted "Now I need a drink!" The crowd went even wilder! Even Max's wealthy Ladies from Hotel Row!

Leaving the spotlight, the two went directly to Max's clients and thanked the Ladies for coming. One remarked, "It has been the most entertaining—and the most real fun I've had in years!" "Would you please tell your friends? And everyone you meet at the Golden Zone?" Alex asked. "Oh! Of course! I think everyone should come to Marie's—It is so exciting!" Marie joined them, and Tiger quickly introduced her to the four Ladies. Shaking hands, Marie continuously said, "Please come back!"

One of the Ladies asked Tiger and Alex, "Will you two lovely Entertainers be here tomorrow night?" Suddenly Tiger snapped as she bent forward, "Sorry? You must have just gotten to town?" Tiger waited, Alex stayed out of it—she was anxious to see where it went. "Yes! We all did, came in this afternoon! Why, may I ask?" Tiger and Alex looked at each other, lightly chuckled, Tiger answered, "I am Margarita Calienta" "The name on that big sign over the roof?" the Lady asked. "The one and same!" Tiger proudly replied—she even beamed! "My goodness! We've been in Mexico for several days—and everywhere we went, we heard your name and about your story. I'm so pleased to meet you!" A different Lady this time, as she pointed at Alex, "And you—you—must be her personal bodyguard!" "That's me alright—just a poor, hard working bodyguard!" Alex winked at Marie.

The three excused themselves, and as they walked toward the 'Ladies' trailer, Marie popped Alex hard on her tight little butt, said, "Alex! You should be ashamed! Putting-on those Ladies like that! Poor? Haw!" "Sometimes I just can't help myself!" "Sometimes? Try all the time!" Tiger quipped. The three women hugged each other and laughed.

Show over and getting late, the crowd began to drift away. And Alex and Tiger began to say their good-byes. During this, the four workmen returned, the Headman personally gave Alex's pistol back to her. He asked, "What do we do with the other stuff?" "What happened to—you know-who?" She asked. "We carried them for a moonlight boat trip." "You didn't—". "No, we didn't—we carried them over to Dear (this is the correct spelling!) Island, and left them there. No way can they get back before you two leave." "Great! Now what is this 'stuff'—you were concerned about?" "Their clothes, their shoes and their guns!" "Jezz! You mean you left them naked?" "Yes, sure did!" "And?" "The first tour boat goes to Dear at nine tomorrow morning! They're in for a surprise!" "Yes! They! The Tourist! And the Agentmen!" Everyone that had heard this tale doubled over with laughter!

"Get a bag—here—put their stuff in it, I'll drop it off, outside their room!" After a long, tearful round of good-byes—with everyone—and with Alex's faced streaked with her gold eye make-up, she asked Jose to take them to the hotel. Her last words to him were "Don't forget, you own me one!"

In their room, Alex quickly wrote a note and stuffed it in the bag with the two agents' clothes. It showed; 'See you two in Mexico City. It should not be difficult for you to find us, stroll around among that 'over' twenty-five million until you spot us!' She placed the bag at their door.

After quick showers and drying, they slid under the sheet. They were both naked—Alex had packed away their sleeping tee shirts, on purpose. Alex rolled over, and again rolled over. Putting an arm across Alex's chest, Tiger asked, "What's wrong—you're not sleepy?" "No, I'm still too 'wired'—all the excitement I guess. Usually, I would just drink more, but it is not very long until we leave, until I have to drive. I guess I could hunt some strong coffee and stay awake—"

Tiger started with long, soft kisses around Alex's face, her mouth, her neck, she moved lower, hesitated for minutes at each of Alex's stiff nipples. Then moved lower, and lower. As her entire body reached spastic pitch, Alex muttered, "Tig--you've--got---a--tongue -like a--like a--oh, I like that! Yes, right there! Like a--like——" Tiger got tickled at Alex's speech problem! Tiger's torso shook as she tried to laugh. Forcing Alex's thighs apart--these were tightly clamped around her head—she raised her head, said, "Alex! Try the words, 'like an Iguana!" "A What!" "An Iguana! The large lizards down here! They have huge tongues!" "Ok, Iguana, dive back in!" Then Alex pulled hard with her two hands full of hair on the back of Tiger's head.

It didn't take long until the two were soundly asleep, snuggled in each other's arms.

And again, Alex had made it through a Friday night without a 'visit' from 'Miss Hawkins'.

By six A.M.—it was February 23th Saturday morning—they were on the open road beyond Mazatlan and headed South on Route 15. Alex, feeling refreshed, settled in for the over two hundred and seventy miles to Puerto Vallarta, their next destination. Tiger was tilted over, hard asleep. The morning's light had just began behind the mountains to the East. In this quiet time, Alex thought, as she glanced at 'Betsy's' odometer, 'I need to get the oil changed—we've come over three thousand miles. Maybe in Puerto Vallarta, lay over an extra day. And also get the tires checked. And really rest! And I am not—not—going to get involved in anything serious! Well, at least until we get to Tiger's village any way!'

The miles rolled by, passing through the city of Tepic, she had to pick up Route 200. Just past Jalisco, Alex pulled over. Tiger had been awake for a while now, "Ok, Tig, It's your turn to drive!" She did until they approached Bucerias. Getting close to Puerto Vallarta, Alex offered to take over, the two swapped positions and they continued on South.

BACK AT MAZATLAN

Wearing borrowed hotel uniforms and riding in a taxi back toward the Hotel Oltas Altas, Agent #1 asked, "How's the hand? The welt?" "That's ok. It is my dignity that hurts! You saw those old rich-bitches laugh!" "Do we tell home-office we've lost them?" "No, not yet anyway! We check all the out-going flights—anyway the ones that are left—we've already missed the most likely ones, the early flights. And if nothing, and if they really have checked out of the hotel—guess we have to let the Boss know." A long silence, then, "I can't believe we fell for such a simple trap." "Wait until we call Boss and say, Guess what? We've lost two simple-minded split-tails! That's when IT hits the fan!"

During their 'stay' on Dear Island, the two had agreed to 'not mention' the boat ride incident to anyone—ever!

BACK ON THE ROAD

It was mid afternoon and Alex knew she had just about had enough. She shifted her weight from one bun to the other—the other was numb. She gently patted the top of the dash, said, "Betsy, ole gal, you're good—but I don't see how Arnie's old bony ass stands your hard bench seats!" Tiger chuckled, she asked, "How do you know Arnie's ass is bony?" Alex told her a tale about the time when fighting their way to Hidden Valley when she and Arnie went swimming in the nude. That swim was in the Little Tennessee River. When Alex finished, Tiger remarked, "I hadn't heard that one before!"

Alex knew they were getting close to Vallarta—they had recently passed through Bucerias, and had passed the junction—on the left—with the side road to Valle de Banderas. "Tiger, watch for any sign of, or to, Costa Azul Resort. Should be on our right, maybe a turn off or whatever. I'm about ready to call it a day!"

Not much later, Tiger said, "Si! Ahead, two kilometers—a right junction!" At this side road there was a small native style village with a Pemex gas station and next to the gas station was a small shed type garage. As the station attendant pumped gas, Alex took Tiger's hand and headed to the garage. "I want to ask about getting the oil changed—in Betsy— and getting the air pressure in the tires checked, Would you interpret?" "Si!

Si! Senorita! La Tiger esta su interpreter para esto noches!" "Ok Senorita Smartass, rub it in!", and Alex jerked Tiger's arm.

It went about like this: Yes, he could, tomorrow, yes in the morning. How early? Seven! Promise? Si! I'll either bring it here at seven—you

sure at seven? Si at seven! Pronto seven! Or have someone from the hotel bring it! Si! Si! And the tires? Si, no problem, complete! Si! Si! And it all had been Alex to Tiger, Tiger to garage owner, owner to Tiger, Tiger to Alex, and reverse, and reverse! Headed west on the side road to find The Resort, Alex said, "Your people—use a lot of SI! Si! Don't they?" "Si! Si! Mas bonito mujer!" "You know what I mean!" "A lot of my people don't know the word, 'no'." Alex held up a hi-five, Tiger joined it, Alex snapped, "My kind of people! I know the word, I just don't like it!"

After only a short ride through dense jungle and as they approached the resort—it appeared expensive—Alex asked, "If you had rather not go this route—expensive—Maybe I could drive on into 'downtown', find a cheap room—" she let it drop. "Cheap?" Tiger pushed on Alex's shoulder, continued, "Haven't you heard? I'm a Star! I'm famous! I've got my name in lights!" "Oh, crap! I've created a monster!" Alex laughed. They were still laughing as they went into the lobby. The Reservation Clerk asked if he could help. And before Alex could reply, Tiger asked him, "Have you heard of Margarita Calienta?" "Ha! Who hasn't heard of her!" Turning to Alex, she simply said, "See?"

The clerk passed them a price list, it showed: Hotel Suite Adventure Packages, Villa Adventure Packages, Two bedroom Villa Adventure Package. Alex summed it up in a hurry, she asked, "What's the Villa like?" And we're not interested in Adventure, and for sure if it's wrapped in a Package! We've had enough Adventure—very recently! We want peace and rest—not in a damn package!" "Excusre her, she's the driver!"—Tiger couldn't resist it! Then she added, "And I'm Margarita Calienta!"

The clerk didn't change his expression, he dryly remarked, "Right, sure. I had three Margarita Calientas yesterday. Which accommodations do you—ladies—want—if any?" Alex saw Tiger's eyes flash as she tighten her jaw muscles and raised her right hand to above counter level. Quickly, Alex bumped her out of arm's reach—Tiger's arm and his tie! "We'll take a Villa! Please!" Alex snapped and tossed him a Platinum MasterCard.

As the bellhop carried their bags in, Alex walked close to him and talked 'Let's make a deal'. The young man, for the right price, agreed to drive the station wagon to the garage, wait for the oil to be changed and the tires to be checked, bring it back, find Alex—wherever she was—and give the keys directly to her. "At six-fifty-five AM?" "Si! Si!" "Ok!.Deal! Shake!" They did, and Alex gave him more than enough money for the garage work and the keys, and again impressed, "You watch that the oil is actually changed! Ok? It has over three thousand miles on it—it must be changed! Ok?" He waited until he was sure she was finished, then **"Si! Si!"** Then he left, headed back toward the lobby area—it was a ways off, in a much larger building.

Alex needed to walk, to work off her numbness. At first she slowly strolled around the pool area, among the many beautiful palms—these had protective retainers around their root systems. The Villas' were individual units about twenty feet square. Their unit had a bed area—a huge bed— along one side and a conversation area—sofa, huge stuffed chairs and a few small tables—along the other side. There was a small kitchenette with a small four place dining table close by and a nice fully equipped bath. And there were closets and dressers. The place had good cross ventilation from lots of windows and double sliding doors to a small porch which faced the beach—it was only about fifty feet away.And there were individual parking spots at each cottage. All the buildings in sight had steeply sloped thatched roofs—tropical style. The entire complex was surrounded by dense jungle—palms with thick underbrush. Sheds and outbuildings for their 'Adventure' equipment were shoved back into. the jungle. She saw bikes, ocean-going kayaks, and even horses. After seeing the equipment, she looked more closely at the jungle along both sides of the open resort area. There were a couple of paths, maybe wide enough for two horses to get through. 'Through' seemed to fit: the path was surrounded—both sides and even overhead—by jungle too dense to see into. Her mind ran amok as she stared into the 'tunnel' of jungle—she imagined a scene: her on a huge run-away horse who was spooked by spiders dropping from above, gigantic snakes leaping from the sides, and Iguana standing stone-fast in front, and being chased by 'Nite-cats' with a 'sleeping problems'. Alex shook her head, clearing away her not uncommon imagination's wild side then she headed for the beach—the wide open beach.

Stepping onto the white, powder soft sand of the beach, Alex's low tennis shoes immediately filled with sand. She and Tiger were both still wearing their jeans, loose over sized men's shirts and their low top shoes. Quickly removing the shoes, she tied the strings together & slung these over one shoulder. Turning northwest, she saw Tiger farther along the beach. Beginning a slow, easy jog, she soon caught up with Tiger. She had also taken off her shoes. "Kid! Let's roll up our pants and wade in the water!" Tiger stopped, turned around, replied, "Oh, it's you." Without saying more, she began to roll up her pant's legs.

In the calm surf, and only about ankle deep, the two waded on—there wasn't any other signs of man's construction—only jungle—as they got a ways from the Resort.

Without saying, they turned around, headed back. "Do you think that prick—that slimy old clerk—was telling the truth? About someone else saying they were Margarita Calienta?" Tiger asked as she looked down. "Wouldn't doubt it—at one time—a long time ago—there were at least six Marilyn Monroes! And even more Liz Taylors! Hell! Southern California at any one time, has at least two dozen Jesus Christs! People say they are popular there because they think they are in Israel! I think it's because of all the beautiful 'chicks' there!" "Really?" "Look, Tig, you know who you are! Don't let some smart-ass get under your skin!"

Alex jerked up Tiger's rear shirt tail, jammed her hand deep inside Tiger's jeans and pinched her butt, said, "I'll race you back!" From the pinch, Tiger already had a head start—and being faster, she beat Alex to the Resort area.

Stopping to catch her breath, Alex saw something farther on—at the surf's edge. Walking on, it was a dock, with a couple of offshore power boats for fishing. And pulled up on the beach, close to the palm trees were several Hobbie Cats—fourteen and sixteen footers. Set back in among the palms, was an equipment building. A portion of the front was still propped up. "Hobbie Cats!" Alex screamed. "What kind of cats?" "The small sail boats! Those are Hobbie Cats! Let's check it out!"

Running to the building—there was a young man inside on a stool, leaded back against the wall. He was looking at a 'girlie magazine', and was holding it sideways—by one edge of the pages. He was seriously looking at the 'center-fold'. "Hey!" Alex surprised him!

He quickly placed it down, face down on the countertop. It was still opened to the 'center-fold'. He appeared to be about mid twenty, wore cut-off jeans and an old 'Captain's' cap. And he looked Maya, almost the same skin tone as Tiger and big black eyes and straight glossy black hair.

Alex decided she would 'break-the-ice' in a smashing manner! She picked up the magazine, in the same fashion that he had held it. She looked at the 'center-fold', then turned it toward Tiger, said, "That's a lot of meat! Tiger, would you look at the 'split' on this gal!" The three chuckled.

Alex turned the 'center-fold' back to her self, added, "Nice tits—but I don't think they are as pretty as yours!" The young man quickly got interested, he hopped off the stool, leaned his hands to the counter and tilted forward—toward Tiger's chest—her bosom. And he waited. Alex glanced at his actions, his position, him waiting. 'No need to disappoint the fellow', she thought, then said to Tiger, "Tig—show him yours before he faints from holding his breath too long!"

And for the first time since the incidence at the front desk, Tiger broke into a broad grin, and slowly began to unbutton her loose, floppy shirt. The man stared at Tiger's bosom, Alex stared at his face—his eyes got bigger and bigger, but he didn't bat, and his mouth slowly opened—more and more! Completely unbuttoned, Tiger slowly pulled it open, and even slightly slid it off the back of her shoulders. His face got closer and closed, and suddenly, Tiger twisted her shoulders several times—her enormous mounds jiggled. He snapped back, covered his face with both hands, and muttered, "You're right, Little One! Now that's a set of beautiful jugs!" As he sighed, Alex and Tiger laughed as she re-buttoned her shirt.

As she placed the magazine to one side, Alex asked the smiling, very healthy appearing young man, "Are the Hobbies for rent?" "Si!" "What's the deal?" "Little gal, you got the money, I'll let you have it any way you want you want it!" "I bet!" Tiger quipped. He just smiled larger at both of them.

"We're staying in—" Alex pulled out the key, "Villa number nine, and we've got tomorrow morning free—say four hours or less. Is that possible? Say a sixteen footer?" He realized she was serious, not just a 'come-on', "Sure—you know anything about sailing? It is rather complicated! Even dangerous if one doesn't know what they're doing."

"No problem, I spent one summer at Malibu—sailing Hobbies, surfing, and screwing anything that got up—and in my way!" "Sounds like my kind of gal! And you, pretty Maya Lady, you know how to sail?" "Never been on one—never even seen one—until just now!" "No problem, I'll take care of her!" Alex laughed as she grabbed Tiger's arm and pulled. "I don't doubt that!" 'Captain' chuckled.

"You gals got dudes? Husbands? With you?" he had already decided the 'little-one' could handle the boat situation. It was time for 'serious advances'. "Nope, just us two ", Tiger replied. "Let's cut this short, Captain— they hadn't heard any other name, Alex had decided 'Cap', or 'Captain' was suitable— "I'm in a hurry for some serious rest! I've been driving since five this morning. You want to hear a few 'old sea tales', come on over to number nine! I'll tell you some. We'll order some grub, on me," she pulled on her shirt, added, "And we'll get out of these clothes, shower, drink, eat and—what ever else the three of us come up with—as long as it is relaxing!" He didn't hesitate, "You're on Little One! I'll be up as soon as I close up here!" A quick round of nods, the two jogged away, he hastily began to gather up the loose items outside.

Headed on toward Villa number nine, Alex asked," You ever done 'three-ways" before? Girl/Boy/Girl? "Tiger wavered, then, "Maybe, I'm not sure—when we, me and the other little girl from Mazatlan, lived with the French-Canadian man, we took turns—but never she and I 'with' each other at the same time. One or the other of us would just back off and wait our 'turn'. Do you understand?" "Sure, but this will be different, It'll be the three of us together, at the same time—anything goes!" Tiger grabbed Alex around her shoulders, smiled into her eyes, said, "Oh! That sounds like fun!" As Alex wrapped her arm around Tiger's waist, she felt an inner pride to think she could teach—in part at least—the young Maya beauty something new!

When Alex turned on the shower to check for hot water, she called to Tiger, "When 'Cap' gets here, ask him what he wants to eat—for his belly! I'll have lobster—or something just as good—and a couple of bottles of white wine—California wine! One can really get 'clipped" in a place like this ordering Champagne! And, please call our order in to the 'room service'." Feeling the water—it was already hot—she stripped and threw her clothes toward the 'bedroom' area.

Still dripping water, but continuing to dry with a large towel, Alex came out of the bath and walked toward the porch. The glass doors were slid open, Tiger and 'Cap' were seated outside and chatting. She listened long enough to understand he was telling some funny tale about sailing. Wrapping the towel around her torso, Alex stepped down to the wooden porch floor. Passing by them, she pulled around a chair and waited for a break in the story. Alex slid down, leaned her head back and stared up at the night sky, and she shut her eyes.

"Alex—Alex—Alex. the male voice lightly spoke. Without opening her eyes, she replied, "Yes?" "The food is here—on the table inside—I wasn't sure where—," Cap said. "Ok, where's Tiger?" "She is still **in** the shower, but should be about finished. You care for a glass of wine?" "Please "as she shifted slightly—her butt was still uncomfortable. He lightly touched her arm, "Here's your drink." She opened her heavy eyelids, "Thanks." She slowly, but continuously sipped the entire contents. And closed her eyes. "Maybe you're too tired for company, maybe I should bow-out?" Still not opening her eyes, and with the glass hanging almost to the floor, she almost whispered, "Don't be silly, I'll bounce back as soon as we eat. Besides—", she hesitated, then, "Tiger would be pissed off." Again she went silent with her eyes still closed.

Alex heard sounds inside that sounded like grab-ass, Tiger had squealed. Shaking her head and setting upright, she twisted enough to see inside. Tiger had on her old sleeping tee shirt, and the bathroom door was shut. Forcing her body to move, Alex got up and went inside. Tiger, like a small girl, pointed to the bath door, whispered, "He's taking a shower—and it's this big!" She held her hands apart a 'good' distance. "Sounds like I need to eat! Get my strength back!" Alex responded as she smiled. Tiger poured three drinks, then she and Alex clicked glasses, Alex softly asked, "Tig? You know where the condoms are?" Tiger quickly stepped to one of the smaller Mitla bags, pulled out two and held these up—and she snickered. Alex thought, 'She's never had done 'this' before!'

'Cap'—the name seemed to work, they didn't ask, he didn't say differently—came out with a damp towel wrapped around his torso. Alex looked, he did 'wear' a sizable bulge. With what each wanted to eat on individual plates, they moved to the porch for the meal.

HOTEL OLTAS ALTAS, MAZATLAN, ROOM 303

It was after the last flight had left Mazatlan's airport for today and tonight. The two Agents had quickly installed a tee in the Hotel's phone line and installed an additional phone—it was cordless. The Hotel's 'hardwired' phone had been replaced with another cordless unit. Now, they paced as they talked, simultaneously with their 'Boss' in Mexico City.

The two—Kyle Larios (Agent #1), and Rudi Laporte(Agent #2)— had just finished explaining the situation. Bottom line, Alex and Tiger had given them the slip! Their Boss asked, "Well—What are you two going to do next? Besides screw-up!"

Kyle replied, "Sir, Rudi and I have discussed putting out an APB, to get in touch with the two gals again." "An All Points Bulletin? On two legally backed Representatives of the US Government? For what? For out-smarting you two dumb bastards? The US would come down on us—me! Like vultures! And get my ass in a sling with Colonel Gomez? That bitch has been after me since that fiasco three years ago!"

"I'll tell you what you're going to do!"—Boss continued—"Call Tony in Central Data, tell him you want a direct, fast-line—directly to you—day and night! Reporting Alex's credit card activities! And I do mean fast-line! When her card passes through an input device, you two better know it in minutes! Minutes, damnit! Not hours, not days—Minutes! You got that?" "Yes, sir!" they both snapped then waited.

Their boss lowered his voice, he seemed to calm down, "You guys lost them, you find them. And get answers, the heads of our departments have contacted the US departments, and got replies that backed-up the gals' documents—they are as clean as new snow. No help at disproving them and legally picking them up." "We under stand—whatever, has to be 'off-the-record', right?" "Right! And if you need help, in the field, you handle that too 'off-the-record!"

Rudi asked, "Sir, I'm not questioning the decision to go after these two, but is it really that important? So far, they're just screwing around." Silence, then, "Guys, let me fill you in on something you didn't hear from me!" He hesitated, then started, "Gomez recalled some info on the Alex gal three years ago, we had an Agent in the Mid-West of the States, he was on a case there. And he was Colonel Gomez's cousin!" "Was?" "Yes, WAS! This is the Alex part—he, the cousin, was banging Alex, and where and when 'Cuz' got it, Alex was present! Do you two see any connection?" Both replied, to the effect, 'There's more to Alex than they had suspected!'

"That's not all—working through the FBI, your innocent little girl, Alex, was responsible for the capture and 'putting-away' of the two high-level bastards that were bleeding the only three major food distribution companies in the USA." "The FBI? Sir?" Rudi asked. "Right! THE FBI! I'm telling you two, she is in and out, when she wants to, more things than you can shake a stick at!" Rudi remarked, "I know about her and sticks." "What?" "Sorry Sir, nothing, just nothing at all." "I'm telling you, Alex is not to be taken lightly. And she damn sure is not here—well where ever the hell she is—on a frigging vacation!"

PUERTO VALLARTA
VILLA NUMBER NINE

Alex paced back and forth in the open area between the bed and the coffee table at the sofa. Taking a few steps, then she shook one leg then the other—and her arms and she twisted her head, If she had wanted exercise earlier this evening to get her circulation going, she was now trying to prevent cramps. And hard exercise? She just had that! **The three of them had humped, pushed, pulled, twisted, kissed, and poked in just about all the positions—and combinations—possible!**

She drained the last bottle of wine, had another bite of what was left—she finished that off—then she called room service and ordered three more bottles of California white wine and three raw oyster cocktails. Turning to the two on the beds she said, "Hey! I'm going to shower, cool off! If there's a knock on the door, don't panic"—as if they would! "It's just room service with more survival supplies! **Cap, didn't miss a stroke!"**

Sometime before midnight, Alex lay flat on her back in the center of the huge bed, with her arms spread straight out, her feet far apart—she didn't bother to look around the room. Nothing else to eat, the bottles half empty—she had opened all three at once, no need to waste time pouring it into glasses—all the towels, wet and scattered about on the floor, and dishes, glasses, and service trays, Villa Number Nine was ready for the street cleaners! As 'Cap' and Tiger headed for the porch—still naked, but with the porches lights turned off—Alex said **"'If either of you want any more of me, you'll have to get it yourself!** My little white ass is fixing to crash-out!" She fell asleep. If they did, she didn't know it!

"Prepare to come about! ", Alex shouted at Tiger. "That's right! Pull that rope!" Alex pulled in the mainsail sheet, "Ready?" "Ready!" "Jib ho!" Alex slapped the tiller over as far as possible, the Hobbie quickly swung in the opposite direction, and the boom popped across. "Let go that line you've got! And pull the one on the other side!" Tiger, still lying flat on the wet canvas, did. She had learned quickly to give great respect to the mainsail boom when it snapped across! They had been out for about two hours.

At first, in the much lighter early morning breeze—it was directly 'on shore', out of the South-West—Alex had made runs up and down along the shore line, offshore only a few hundred feet. Then, she had explained the basics of sailing to Tiger. Now that the mid morning wind had piped-up, the real fun had started. The slapping, the wind thru the rigging, the sound of the higher surf, required louder communications. And the swells had increased to about three feet—just right for crashing through, or jumping! Doing this, they would yell and scream!

Headed back toward the resort—they had worked almost out of sight of it, not offshore—but along the jungle encroached coastline—Alex saw 'something' or someone as the two made quick time and got closer. Alex angled in toward the shore, as close as possible but not be in the breaking surf. "It's someone waving a white towel!" Tiger, lying flat on her stomach in the center, called out. Closer, Alex shouted, "I bet it's the guy with the car keys! I forgot! I insisted that he give the keys directly to me!" They laughed as Alex adjusted the sheets for more speed.

Slicing along, the windward hull a couple of feet above the water, when the'Cat' was even with the young man, she pulled the tiller hard toward herself. And she released both sheets simultaneously. Riding a swell, the Hobbie surfed in, slid completely out of the water and up onto the dry sandy beach. They didn't have to hop overboard and pull it out of the water.

The young man was dressed in a white uniform and white dress shoes, he stood where the white rocked path ended at the sand of the beach. Alex ran to him, extended her right hand—her tee shirt, which was stuffed in her tight jogging shorts, her shorts and tennis shoes were all wet. She said, "I'm so sorry! How long have you been here?" "Not too long, here are the keys, the car is at number nine." "Thanks, did things go ok?" "No problem! Is there anything else I can do for you? Or your friend—the Maya lady?" Alex had the feeling that maybe word had either gotten out or had been circulated about their 'activities' last night, but she didn't imply anything that pertained to that—she knew they were leaving soon, "Nope! Thanks again!" He reached into his pocket, started to say, "Here's—" She interrupted, "Keep it! Keep what is left!" "But, it is quiet a lot—" "Don't worry! There's a lot more where that came from!" He smiled and left.

They had beached at the opposite end of the beach from the dock, and 'Cap's' place. Tiger joined Alex at the end of the path. The two grabbed each other and jumped around as Tiger celebrated her first sailing venture. She also wore a tee shirt, jogging shorts and low tennis shoes—these were all wet—her tee shirt was very impressive! Alex had warned as they got dressed this morning, "Bathing suits, and especially tongs are ok for showing off, or sunning, but not for sailing! Too much jumping around, too much hard rubbing—all over your body! And your buns will be rubbed raw! Besides, tongs ain't got no pockets!'

The two looked at the 'Cat', the sails and the ropes were flapping about, and the boat was well above the surf line. "Let's drop the sails, coil the ropes"—she glanced at her sports watch, then toward the dock far down the beach, added, "and leave it here, We'll walk back and settle with 'Cap'. He probably can rent it again today—right where it is!" They started South, Tiger said, "Let's swing by that crowd up there—the ones at the pool. I feel like 'knocking em' dead!"

"Ok! But"—Alex stopped Tiger, stepped in front of her—face to face—"First, let's get our 'puppy-noses' up, at attention!" Alex smoothed down Tiger's wet, thin, white tee shirt over her large breasts, then grabbed Tiger's nipples with her thumbs and index fingers, pinched, pulled, twisted and then snapped her nipples very hard. "Oh! Oh! Alex!" but Tiger smiled as she watched her nipples double in size and become very erect. Alex did her own, then said, "Now! Let's knock em' dead!" Still dripping water and Tiger's long hair spread over her shoulders and back, she was very impressive. At the pool area—mainly the bar—they quickly drew a crowd—most appeared to be older wealthy men, then the two headed back to the beach. The men's mouths were still dropped open.

Back on the road again, Alex turned right at Route 200 and headed for Manazanillo. "This should be a breeze! It is only about one hundred and forty miles!" Tiger remarked as she looked at the map.

And Alex had settled their bill at the resort with her credit card.

CENTRAL DATA: MEXICO CITY

Within seconds after hanging up his telephone, Tony used his computer and shifted Hawkins, Alexandra and Morley, Margarita Calienta from the 'Suspects Level' to the 'Emergency Level'. The system instantly created other files and these were transferred to the computers in the 'Special Division'. Here, these files were monitored every second of the day and night. With sufficient personnel, the screens were watched all the time. Interfacing with GPS, any credit card device could be located, within a three foot radius, as soon as a card was slipped through it.

HOTEL OLTAS ALTAS, ROOM 303

The two Agents had their laptop plugged into the AC outlet and keyed to Central Data's Special Division, and pulled up to the file of Hawkins, Alexandra. The two took turns watching the small screen. It was just before noon—the screen changed, as an activity came through, it showed the resort's name, the location and the coordinates for the input device. "We've got them! They're headed south! They're near Puerto Vallarta!" Rudi yelled as he jumped up with his hands above his head.

They had already packed and settled their bill. Quickly getting together the few items—mainly the phones—they rushed out. Going down, Kyle asked, "Are we going to drive both our cars?" "Drive! Hell no! We are going to the airport, rent a light plane and fly down! Rent a car—or two if necessary—at Puerto Vallarta! We can have these two bitches before night fall!"

As the two Agents rushed down the stairs, Rudi remarked, "Kyle, I know this guy at the airport who operates a flying service—he'll fly any where, for the right price! Follow me, we'll drive our cars in the service gate—that's to the right of the main terminal—leave the cars there at his place. We'll not have to pay parking fees that way!" "And the cars will be ok until we can double back and pick them up?" "Sure! Old Sam is a good guy, he wouldn't mind at all." "And—this Sam—he knows his business when it comes to flying?"

"No problem, he's ex-USA Air Force—flew everything in 'Nam'—a little on the wild side, but really can fly anything, in and out of anywhere!"

As the three loaded the Agents' gear in the plane, Kyle asked, "What is this ugly thing?" He pointed at the plane. Sam laughed, replied, "Yeal, she's ugly alright! But the best damn plane ever built! It's a Swiss designed Pilatis PC6 slash B Turo-Porter. They've been built in several countries—this one was actually made in Argentina. I picked it up after 'Nam' for a song!" "And the large sliding door? I guess that's for ease of loading things!" "Yeal, like crates of pigs! Or heavy weapons—or for unloading troops in a hurry! I once carried a squad—ten fully armed crazy bastards—Delta Force I think—said they were in a hurry—going to get someone—that can mean to kill the SOB, or to rescue him! Any way, I put the wheels to the top of the rice, slowed down—she'll fly at fifty—the squad, the crazy bastards, jumped out! No chutes! Just jumped out in the damn rice paddy! Not a broke bone among them!" "Yes, that sounds crazy alright!" Kyle added as the three climbed in the Pilatis.

"Rudi, you remember how to fly one of these things?" Sam shouted above the high pitched whine of the turbine as Rudi buckled into the co-pilot's seat. "Probably so—flying is like riding a bike, you don't actually forget, may get rusty, but it'll come back to you." "I didn't know you could fly!" Kyle shouted from the bench seat along the left side of the huge rear compartment. "Was a hobby at first, then I worked at it for a while—bush flying mostly, short hops here and there! Before the boys came along, then my wife convinced me to get into a decent line of work! This government crap!"

After receiving clearance from the control tower and taxiing into take-off position, Sam shouted, "Rudi! Let's show Kyle how she'll takeoff!" With a few 'special' adjustments and manuvers, the plane jumped off the runway in only one hundred or so feet! "Whoa! That's really something!" Kyle yelled as they continued to climb at a very steep angle.

Sam didn't bother to gain much altitude—he swung the plane in line with the coast, headed toward Puerto Vallarta. "You guys want to go to the main airport? In Vallarta? Or some where close by? I can land in a pea patch if you want to!" Sam asked. Rudi reached into his inside coat pocket, pulled out a note, looked at it; replied, "We're really trying to catch up with a couple of people—the last know place they were is"—he looked again—"The Costa Azul Adventure Resort. I've got the GPS coordinates written here somewhere."

Sam laughed, said, ""You want to 'catch up' with the bastards! I know your kind of 'catching', more like 'arrest'! What did the bastards do—run off with their wives' jewelry?" "Not bastards, Sam, these two are bitches!" "Ok—so they ran off with their old man's money!" Sam laughed again. "Not exactly, as a matter of fact, they haven't broken the law, not yet!" Rudi responded. "Well—What's the problem?" Sam asked. "It's the—'not yet', we're concerned about!" Rudi laughed back. "Oook" Sam dropped that subject.

"The Costa Azul, you said! I know exactly where that is—it's North of Vallarta, we pass directly over it! But, believe me, there ain't no place to land there! That place is in the damn jungle! We'd have to have floats to land there! But—we can take a slow look at it! You want to do that? No problem, I'll just slow down, swing a couple of lazy circles over it. Ok?" "Sure, why not!"

As they approached the resort, Sam lowered the flaps and began to slow down, he asked, "You guys know what these two old bitches look like? Maybe they're out by the pool, sunning their fat asses!" "Not old, Sam, one's twenty-one, and the other—the leader—is thirty-two! And she is—" Rudi turned to Kyle, asked, "How did you call Alex?" Kyle replied, loud enough for Sam to hear, "Alex? She is as slick as a live snake dipped in mineral oil!" "Man! That is slick!" Sam laughed back. As he started a lazy clockwise circle, he called out, "You guys look down, out your side, I'll hold a couple of circles centered over the pool." They didn't recognize anyone.

Rudi motioned to Sam that they may as well go on then he remarked, "Nothing—as usual—we'll rent a car and drive back. Thanks anyway." Sam leveled off, cranked up the flaps and headed for the main airport.

After Kyle went and rented a car, he returned to the plane. While they unloaded their gear, Rudi asked Sam, "If we need you again, you got a card or something so we can contact you? This 'gig' isn't over yet." "Sure! I'd be happy to help out! Here's a business card with all the info. Nice to work with you again, Rudi, maybe we'll see each other again soon. Thanks for the business!" The two Agents watched as Sam took off, then they headed North toward the Costa Azul Resort.

ROUTE 200:

Heading on South, Alex suddenly became silent. It was still early afternoon. "What's wrong, Alex?" Tiger had 'sensed' a change. "I'm not sure—something from the past—I think." Nothing else for about twenty minutes, and even then, Alex started slowly, "Back when—before the collapse—I needed some information—these two men were up to something—I wasn't sure what—hacking away—first at most anything— any systems—" She again hesitated. Then, in a spark of realization, Alex snapped, "I found them by their credit cards' activities! Nailed those two bastards!" Alex stopped talking, glanced to Tiger. Tiger shouted, "Those Agentmen! They'll track your credit cards!" "Damn! We've been leaving a trail wide enough that a blind person could follow!" Alex quipped.

Another wait, then Alex asked, "Tig) where is the closest large city? A city with a large bank! A bank that I would feel sure they could deal directly in gold!" Not having to even think, Tiger blurted "Colima!

Go through Manianilla, continue South until you see the freeway! Take that! It goes into Colima! Look for the 'Central Zocalo' exit, get off there. The main bank is across the street from the Zocalo!" "We'll cut off that wide trail! No more credit card use, Mr. Secret Agent Men! "Alex shouted, then the two 'hi-fived'

In the bank's parking lot, as Alex got out one of the several small canvas bags—she had learned about plastic bags the expensive way—hidden under the rear seat, she whispered, "Kid, this is probably the first time gold has ever been smuggled into Mexico." "That's the truth I would bet." After deciding to go 'on vacation', she and Tiger had scrambled over the mountainside and gathered up all the gold coins they could—the coins Alex had dropped when she fell off the path along the mountain.

Walking out the bank's door with a large manila envelope, Tiger asked, "What's in that?", she nodded toward the envelope. Alex had done the deal in a closed office. "Five smaller envelopes, each containing one thousand US dollars worth of Mexican pasos."

Back on the freeway, headed back to the coast, Tiger asked, "What now? Where are you going?" "I'll just drive to Route 200, turn left and head on South until I get tired—or it gets close to dark. Then we'll do it your way, CHEAP! Find a cheap room! Cheap from here on, Kid!" They laughed together.

NORTH OF PUERTO VALLARTA:
COSTA AZUL RESORT

"May I help you gentlemen?" It was the same clerk that had checked Alex and Tiger in the day before, the one that had caused hard feelings with Tiger. Kyle glanced about—no one in hearing distance—he flipped his jacket lapel open and displayed his Internal Security badge—and his gun, said, "We are looking"—he unfolded a copy of the computer generated facial photo of Alex—"for this lady, Alexandra Hawkins", he slipped the picture to the clerk, added, "She is a Special Agent for the US Government." And he unfolded Tiger's and slide it to the clerk, added, "And this lady, Senorita Margarita Calienta Morley. She is a Special Archaeologist for the US Government."

The clerk wasn't sure if he was going to faint or have a heart attack! "You—mean—these—two—I—I—I" "You ok? You aren't going to die on us, are you?" The clerk got out, "They— just—left—before noon—." "Where did they go?" The clerk just shook his head. "Let's go in your office, this is serious official business!" In the office, Rudi closed the door as Kyle continued, "We want to talk to anyone—maid, waiters, bellhops—anyone that had any thing to do with them, even anyone that had seen them! And we want it now! Pronto!"

With the printouts spread on the desk, the clerk began, as discreetly as possible, to call different people into the office. The people were questioned, asked about any 'unusual' things, talk, visitors, or whatever. And one person's comments brought forth another person. But 'seen' the two? Hell, almost everyone there had seen them! The two gals were very difficult to miss! Like one 'witness' said, "Man! You would have to be blind to miss a set of tits like the Maya one has!" Even when things led to 'Cap', it still didn't produce any important information. "Hey guys! They were just two sex crazy gals! And money didn't seem to be a problem with the little one! I had no idea they were 'Secret Agent' chicks!" and Cap went on and on!

Back outside at the car, the two Agents hesitated, "Now what? So damn close!" "Head on south, their direction is definitely south!" "Guess so—Alex is sure to use her credit card again, probably tonight!" They drove from the dense jungle that surrounded the resort, turned right on Route 200, headed South.

ROUTE 200:

Alex decided to throw in the towel. Approaching La Mira, she saw a small sign that indicated a right turn, then only seven kilometers to a beach town, Playa Azul. And soon they were stretched out on two single beds in a very cheap motel in a quaint village at a beach. Later, they walked about—even along the beautiful 'unspoiled' beach, ate tacos from a push-buggy vendor—he was about ten—got cold beers at an outdoor joint and watched the sunset-into the Pacific.

The two took another stroll along the water's edge as they enjoyed the cool gently lapping sea on their bare feet and the light breeze that thrashed through the many palms that lined the beach. "Tig—This is a beautiful place—Why isn't it developed? There's not a hand full of businesses—or—people here." Tiger gingerly took Alex's hand, they slowly continued in the dim light, she sighed, replied, "Alex—You have not seen yet—but there are thousands of places—just like this—scattered along both of the coasts of Mexico. They can't all be—so called, developed! Or—is that ruined? Too many people, too much money, too—" she let it drop.

On a ways, they turned back toward the few lights. "How about if just I—and a few friends like you—had a small home in a place like this? No mega-buck set-up, just nice and comfortable. It is so nice—", she too let it drop. Silent, they strolled, still holding hands. "Alex, you really did need a vacation!" Tiger jerked her hand and she chuckled. "What?" "Now, right now, you're thinking about quiet relaxation—but—in a month—No! Less than a month! You would be 'bananas, bonkered out of your skull! In a place like this—This kind of a scene!" Alex jerked back, remarked, "You're probably right!"

Back at the motel, if Alex could just figure out what to do about all the loud music! It didn't take long—she and Tiger went to the place where the music was coming from and ordered 'slammers'!

The din throbbed away somewhere outside, far in the background as Alex and Tiger lay on the stiff, hard single beds and stared at the dark room. Only a shadow of light came through the two small windows that faced the beach. There were no curtains—that probably would have been too much trouble. Besides, curtains would have hampered any Peeping-Tom's efforts!

"Tig? You still awake?" "Yes, Alex." "This Agent business—I can't quiet figure it out—Why are they so interested—so persistent?" Tiger didn't reply immediately, then "Do you think they know about us going to look for the codex?" Silence then Alex, "I don't see how—we haven't really discussed our plans with anyone outside of HVG—How would they know?" "Maybe we made too much trouble—too much attention there in Mazatlan." "I don't think that's it—what harm was done? A little extra work for the local cops—a little bad publicity for Mazatlan—Playa Northa— so what?"

Silence again, then Tiger remarked, "Maybe it is something from our past—a long time ago—" "Maybe—", then Alex thought, and added, "Maybe, from that time when Tom, Arnie and I were out West—before the collapse. Tiger, did you hear, or do you remember hearing—that I had a 'quicky' affair with a Mexican Agent back then? And he was murdered?" "I don't recall hearing that." "Maybe someone down here thinks I had something to do with his death."

Another silent period, then Tiger remarked, "Maybe it is not your past they are interested in." "If it isn't mine, then that leaves yours." Alex waited. "Maybe", then she waited. "Maybe? Why would the Feds be interested in your past?" Tiger had never mentioned to Alex—Alex didn't know about Mike hearing it or not—Tiger softly replied, "I witnessed the slaughter at Amatenango—I saw Jackie, Niki and their Mother shot in cold blood! By the Federal troops—that is the reason I ran away—they wanted to—they tried to capture me—I ran!"

Alex had never heard this—but she didn't want Tiger to dwell on her horrible past, she decided to make as little of this idea as possible, "Tiger, that was a long time ago—what? Six? Seven years ago? Besides, you were only a child—I don't think they would care after such a long time." Tiger didn't verbally respond, she softly began to sob.

Alex got up and slipped in bed with her, and hugged her, and cooed, "Oh, Tiger—please don't—try to put all that behind you—I'm so sorry

I brought it up. Hell, The Feds—the Agents at Mazatlan, didn't have anything else to do—decided to come have a look-see. We probably will not see them any more."

Alex pulled her face to face, wiped her tears, then began heavy kissing. Soon, they were deep into sex, deep into the throbs of ecstasy. Later, exhausted, they both fell asleep tightly wrapped in each others' arms.

ROUTE 200:

"What happens if we pass them?" Kyle asked as he drove south. "That could be a waste of time. We may as well stop, settle down and watch the computer! Riding around looking for them is like looking for a needle in a hay stack!" The two Agents stopped and spent the night in Tecoman.

They took turns monitoring the computer. But there was not any new activity concerning Alex's credit card.

ACAPULCO
Monday
February 25th

Threading 'Betsy' through the slow and tight traffic in 'Old' downtown Acapulco—they had passed the huge Hyatt Regency with 645 rooms, all with a view of the famous bay—Tiger pointed out an older five story hotel. "If we can get a room on the front—those have balconies—the view is even better than at the Hyatt and the cost is only a fraction!" "Ok "as Alex judged if 'Betsy' could fit between the two cars ahead or not. "And, see the large boat, the one with two decks above the hull? That's the Midnight Cruise Beach Party Boat! We just have to go! It is fantastic! Dancing, music, and—and—free drinks! All you can drink!" "When?" "Tonight! Silly! Turn here! There's a parking lot under the hotel!"

Parked, and taking—this was a do-it-your-self-deal—only what was necessary, and they were able to get a room on the fifth floor—on the front. The old place at least had an elevator, and the view was great—and the room was ok.

"Don't wear hose, or panty-hose. And our skirts have to be loose enough to pull above our knees! And our shoes easy to get off, and on!" Tiger began to explain as they got ready to dress for the boat cruise. The cruise started at MIDNIGHT! It ended just before sunrise! Still drying, Alex asked, "Why? It this a boat cruise or a 'dress' foot race?"

"We have to climb off the big boat, get into a smaller one, and then maybe wade through the water." "What's this 'maybe' crap?" "Maybe it can get close enough, maybe not! Maybe the water has waves, maybe not!" "Ok! Ok! I've got the maybe part! Why don't we just wear shorts, or rolled up jeans?" "Oh no! This is a dress-up affair! Lots and lots of fancy ladies and men, and dancing!" "You've done this before!" "Yes, many times! I spent some time here—before I—", Tiger's expression suddenly turned serious. Alex stopped in mid motion, stared at her, decided any farther explanation would be about Tiger's unpleasant past, she didn't question. Alex jerked up tight a pair of tongs, quipped, more to change the subject than being serious, "Ok! I'm ready for the cruise!" Stunned, Tiger slowly smiled and forgot what she had been remembering.

After several trials—Alex jerked her shoes off and snatched her hem up to her crotch several times—the two finally got their clothes right. "Get all your valuables locked in the hotel safe—carry only the boat tickets—don't wear any jewelry—none! And don't carry a purse! Or any money! Only the tickets!" Tiger impressed upon Alex.

Earlier, they had bought tickets from the desk clerk—no buying of tickets at boarding time—and as they boarded, Alex decided that 'rule' was so buying tickets at the vessel wouldn't interfere with the 'cattle-herd' boarding tactics! On board, the party started instantly!

Looking at the bar—one had to go get the free drinks—Alex studied the bartenders' (about six) technique. One would pick up a bottle of Vodka, throw the cap in one trash container. One lined up paper cups—edge to edge. The bottle was turned up side down as the 'pourer' moved along the line of cups, then tossed the empty bottle into another trash container. Immediately following him was another guy, same action but with ginger ale—he threw his 'empty' into a different trash container. Another guy set the drinks on the top counter. The 'cup-liner-upper' started the cycle over. 'Round-and-round' they went!

The men guests even had a 'round-and-round' routine. To the bar, grab a drink, guzzle, toss the empty cup in a different container, round by a lady—it didn't seem to matter who she was—dance, round and round, and it was time to start another round again!

If a guy had a 'date' or mate, and if he decided to get 'her' a drink, then he grabbed two cups, drank one, threw away that empty, got another one and carried one to his 'partner'! If a gal was not escorted—like Alex and Tiger—she joined in the 'round-and-round' routine! She had to fend for herself!

Overall, it was a beautiful, wild scene! On all three decks! Each with its own band! And three different pieces of music at the same time! If one band took a break—no problem! Keep dancing to the one you could hear the loudest!

Tiger and Alex had no problems being asked to dance. When—not if—a guy reached for them, get ready! Because he would sling them to the floor and dance! Never a wasted step-or a word! No need for talk, one could not hear words!

Alex was thrown at her chair, she grabbed the bottom edge of the table to keep from being snatched up and thrown to the dance floor—again. She yelled into Tiger's ear—only about one inch away—"Do these guys ever give up?" "Oh, Yes! Soon!" Tiger was right, suddenly, all at once, it became deathly silent.

It shocked Alex, she jerked toward the crowd. No one was dancing, pouring, drinking or playing music! Everyone was taking off their shoes, or rolling up their pants legs, or pulling the rear of their skirt forward between their legs and stuffing the hem into the front waistband. The younger, 'modern' ladies simply stepped out of their skirts, rolled these tightly, pulled it around the back of their necks and stuffed the ends into the front top of their blouses. Alex thought as she watched this technique—'Strange order of dress, from top to bottom, skirt, blouse, then panties last!'

The transfer into the 'smaller boat'—Tiger's words, Alex hadn't seen or heard any other description—was only done from the hull's deck—thank goodness! A rigid boarding ladder? A transom water level platform? Stairs? Naw! Boarding NETS! Over the side! In the dark! Everyone looked like Marines jumping off for a battle at a Pacific island! As Alex looked in horror—Tiger had already 'left' her—a guy snatched her up and climbed over the rail! Alex screamed and head-locked around his neck with both her arms! And screamed again! He smiled! Over the rail, the hull below was blocked from any source of light—it was pitch black! Alex screamed, "This SOB is going to jump in the damn ocean with me!" He smiled, no one else paid her any attention!

But instead he lowered her to a guy below and forced her arms from around his neck. She guessed it was a 'he', because 'he' caught her by one cheek of her ass and her crotch! This one was standing down in the darkness! To add to the wildness, the craziness, the confusion, there were mothers, grandmothers, children, even suckling aged babies! All climbing over, carried over, or pushed over into the darkness that surrounded 'some' kind of craft! Somewhere below! Maybe!

Tiger's 'smaller boat'? It was an old World War II landing craft, and as the old vessel throbbed to the shore, there were lights on the hill. To Alex, these appeared to be maybe three, two 'D' celled hand flashlights! With batteries at least two years old! But she couldn't get lost! She had a handful of the person in front of her, and the person behind her had a handful of what was left of her skirt! But soon the stumbling stopped, everyone bunched together—like sheep that had been herded to the dip trough and no one had opened the lift-gate!

Bang! Lights! Show! Free drinks! 'Hawaii dancers'—with a definite Mexican flare! And loud music! All in an instant! No introduction! No build-up! No waiting! For about thirty minutes! Only! Then, pitch darkness again! It was back to the landing craft, and the procedure was in reverse—the same except for one major difference, a ground swell had developed. Alex estimated it to be two or three feet in height—she couldn't see, but she could feel it as the water surged from her knees to her breasts and she could feel the stern of the old craft as it rushed back and forth. She wasn't making any headway at boarding until someone behind her caught her by her thigh and crotch and pitched her up and forward. Caught by her arms and 'whatever', she was snatched on up and thrown to the others already aboard.

Getting back up to the main vessel's deck was worse! Much worse! But wild! Thrilling and very exciting! As Alex clawed her way over the ship's rail—completely soaked—she rolled to her hands and knees, and crawled to the center of the dance floor area. She looked, and felt, like an old alley cat that some mean ass little boy had just dipped in a bucket of cold, dirty water! Still on her knees and palms, behind her, Tiger shouted, "Wasn't that just fantastic!" Alex slowly lowered her forehead to the deck and shut her eyes.

CHAPTER 13

While Alex got the room key—she had decided to leave her other things in the hotel safe until they checked out—she noticed a young lady at one of the old sofas. She looked to be mid twenty, a few inches taller than herself, slim, trim and healthy. But most of all, she looked rested and refreshed. Her backpack was on the floor close-by and she was looking at a map. With the key, Alex looked at Tiger and nodded toward the young woman, said, "Let's check her out, maybe she could help with the driving—if she is headed South." Tiger just shrugged and followed Alex.

Wiping her still wet hair, Alex flipped her right hand as she tried to dry it. "Hi", as she extended her right hand, "I'm Alex", nodding to Tiger, "This is Tiger. Could I talk to you for a few minutes?" The stranger stuck her hand up, took Alex's and as they shook, she replied, "You two have been on the 'Midnight Cruise, haven't you?" "It's that obvious?" She smiled, nodded then remarked, "I'm in no hurry, what you got on your mind?"

The woman's name was Karen, Canadian, came South for the winters—this was her third season South of the border—single, could drive—she showed Alex her license—and, yes she was heading South and would love to help with the driving duties.

About a hour and a half later—Karen driving, Tiger over in the front corner asleep, and Alex stretched out on the rear bench seat asleep—Ole Betsy' rolled South, again on Route 200. Karen headed for a small town that Tiger insisted they visit—Puerto Angel. But Tiger would not explain why Puerto Angel was worth a visit! Alex guessed she wanted it to be another surprise.

TECOMAN

The two Agents hated to admit it, but they were stumped! Or either there was a problem with the system. It was mid morning of the twenty-sixth, and they had hot seen any activity in over forty-eight hours on any of Alex's credit cards. Nothing. Rudi called Tony in Central Data, inquired about the system—no problems—then he explained their situation. "I agree—It is as if they have vanished!" Tony casually remarked. "Yes", Rudi responded, "like the Maya gal, Margarita, can disappear." "What?" Tony snapped in return. "Yes, we saw her do it in Mazatlan! Strangest!

Thing you'll ever see. Here—face to face—then gone! Just gone! She and Alex did a demonstration gig in front of fifty or sixty people. Standing near Alex then Margarita just vanished!" "Are you serious?" Tony questioned. "Yes, dead serious! Why?"

"When I was at the University of Mexico City, I had an old history Professor—I can't seem to recall his name—but he described exactly what you just did! But he elaborated a lots more—said he stumbled across a village—only one village—where all the women and even the little girls could disappear—when ever they wanted to! Found this when he was a young man doing 'field work'. And he said the little girls thought their 'trick' was fun to scare strangers with! We, us students, thought the old guy had been smoking some 'bad stuff'." "Well, I'll be damn! Can you find any more about where this village may be?"

"Not sure—it has been years, the old guy may be dead—I do know for sure that he no longer teaches. It'll take a while, let me do some checking around, I've got a friend—ex-class mate—I think he may remember the old Professor's name. That will be a beginning." Rudi changed the subject.

"Tony, what can we do, now?" "It's obvious that the gals are headed South—drive on South, and I'll get in touch if—and as soon as—I find out more about this disappearing thing." "Hey, Tony, we owe you one!"

ROUTE 200:

Having rounded the 'bottom' of Mexico, their direction of travel was now more East than South. It was mid afternoon, Karen still drove. Twisting about several times, Alex finally gave up on trying to sleep any more, she sat up, said, "Good morning—or—whatever" as she glanced at her watch. "You want a relief from driving? I think I've recovered from last night!" "No, not yet anyway,I'm doing Ok." Tiger was still asleep, lying against the side window up front. "Sorry we didn't get to talk before I crashed-out! Karen, where are you from?" "Jasper, Alberta, at the Rockies." This was the opener for the 'standard four'. Where you from? How long you been down? How long you staying? What do you do for a living?

With Karen, the rest was; "Came down just after Christmas. Probably stay until the end of March. I work in a gift shop in Jasper National Park."

For Alex's answers to these, she slightly revised her story; "I'm-we—are from a small farming community in North-East Georgia. Drove down just after Mardi Gras. I guess we'll stay as long as Tiger wants to visit her folks—that's why we came, so Tiger could talk to her grandmother before—well, you know." And for a living, Alex only briefly remarked, "We're in the farming business."

Their conversation roused Tiger, looking around, twisting about, she asked, "Where are we?" "Not exactly sure, have not gone through Puerto Escondido yet." "Good! We need to do some shopping at 'Condido'" "Shopping?" Alex questioned. "Yes—Angel—well—like I said, it is very small." Mostly muttering, she added,"can't hardly buy alcoholic drinks there." "What? Can't hear you, Tig!" "Ok! It is very difficult to buy beer or wine—they have very odd rules as to when—and where—one can buy these! And your favorite,Champagne? They probably have never even heard of that!" Alex nor Karen responded, Tiger added, "And buy suntan lotion— straw hats, wide ones—and a few bed sheets, single bed size ones." Alex didn't bother—whatever Tiger was up to, Alex would just wait and see.

At Puerto Escondido, they shopped. Alex loaded the floor in front of the rear seat with bottles of California white wine and beer. The other two picked out fruit, crackers and tough bread. And the three had fun picking out three wide brimmed cheap straw hats. Tiger had suggested they not use their expensive 'Baja" hats—she didn't explain to Alex, but she thought these should be saved for more 'dressed-up occasions' Karen and Alex let Tiger decide on the best suntan lotion. Looking for sheets, Karen asked Tiger, "Why sheets?" "We may need, or we may not need—" was Tiger's only reply.

They left just before sunset with Alex driving. Not far out of 'Condido', she realized it was time to watch the sunset.

Pulling over, Alex stopped at a wide paved shoulder. There was a small footpath down to the beautiful and totally unpopulated beach.

"Come on, gals, let's wet our feet, have a beer and watch!" Alex exclaimed. Standing ankle deep in the cool ocean, in the last rays of light, Alex slid one arm around Tiger's waist and slowly squeezed them together. Tiger twisted face to face and gently put both arms around Alex's neck. As the sun disappeared, they held a long and hard lips to lips kiss. Parting lips, Alex sighed, placed her cheek to Tiger's, and slipped one hand down to Tiger's firm bottom and pulled tight—tight enough until she could feel Tiger's firm mound against her own. Tiger twisted her mouth to Alex's neck and with her tongue began a slow lick up, under Alex's short hair and continued a lazy circle around her ear. The two totally ignored Karen who was standing close by.

Back on the move again, Karen was in the rear, she leaned forward and asked, "I guess—just to better understand—what are your relationships? Between the two of you?" "Do you mean—are we kin? Sisters or something like that?" Alex asked. "No, I mean are you two serious lovers?" They didn't respond right off. Then Tiger began, "We have—both of us—serious lovers—men—back home. We've been together—as couples for several years now, but—but—" she dropped it, not sure of Alex's opinion. Alex picked it up, "We, Tiger and I, love each other. Love in all its meaning—we're very close—and—occasionally, we enjoy sexually love—deep, passionate sex." Tiger slipped close to Alex, kissed her cheek, and softly said,"Thanks, I needed that."

Tiger slipped away as Karen said "Then you two are 'bi'? Swing either way—male or female?" The two in the front chuckled, Alex replied, "Guess so. And while you're understanding, Karen, I'm an ex-nympho! I, in the past, 'did' anybody, anywhere, anytime, anyway! But, sweet Tiger here, Pulling over, Alex stopped at a wide paved shoulder. There was a small footpath down to the beautiful and totally unpopulated beach.

"Come on, gals, let's wet our feet, have a beer and watch!" Alex exclaimed. Standing ankle deep in the cool ocean, in the last rays of light, Alex slid one arm around Tiger's waist and slowly squeezed them together. Tiger twisted face to face and gently put both arms around Alex's neck. As the sun disappeared, they held a long and hard lips to lips kiss. Parting lips, Alex sighed, placed her cheek to Tiger's, and slipped one hand down to Tiger's firm bottom and pulled tight—tight enough until she could feel Tiger's firm mound against her own. Tiger twisted her mouth to Alex's neck and with her tongue began a slow lick up, under Alex's short hair and continued a lazy circle around her ear. The two totally ignored Karen who was standing close by.

Back on the move again, Karen was in the rear, she leaned forward and asked, "I guess—just to better understand—what are your relationships? Between the two of you?" "Do you mean—are we kin? Sisters or something like that?" Alex asked. "No, I mean are you two serious lovers?" They didn't respond right off. Then Tiger began, "We have—both of us—serious lovers—men—back home. We've been together—as couples for several years now, but—but—" she dropped it, not sure of Alex's opinion. Alex picked it up, "We, Tiger and I, love each other. Love in all its meaning—we're very close—and—occasionally, we enjoy sexually love—deep, passionate sex." Tiger slipped close to Alex, kissed her cheek, and softly said,"Thanks, I needed that."

Tiger slipped away as Karen said "Then you two are 'bi'? Swing either way—male or female?" The two in the front chuckled, Alex replied, as helped me overcome that problem!" And they all laughed.

Tiger turned toward Karen and asked "How about you? Where do you stand?" With no hesitation, Karen replied, "I'm a 'hard-core' lesbian—something must have happened—way back—I just can't handle a relationship with men. Sorry." "Don't be sorry!" Alex snapped, "It's your life! Enjoy what YOU want!" The three chuckled.

"Slow down! That was the sign for the junction with Route 175! That's where we want to turn!" "There's not a thing here!" "See, the small sign? Puerto Angel? Turn right!" Tiger exclaimed. They were both correct; there wasn't anything—nothing—except two very small signs. One pointed left to Pochutla and one pointed right to Puerto Angel. Alex turned right on a very narrow paved road.

Karen asked, "You two are saying 'An-hill', but the sign spelled it A N G E L, is not that Angel—like the 'spirit'? "Down here, it is pronounced 'An-hill!' Like the insects—ants' home!" Tiger explained. The sign had shown 8 K's to An-hill.

While traveling on the narrow, straight, and very dark road, Tiger began to explain their options for a place to spend the night. "There are four choices for spending the night. Well, five if you count sleeping in the wagon. Or six if you include sleeping on the ground." "Forget five and six, I'm not ready for those yet!" Alex remarked. Tiger hesitated, not sure if she should start at the bottom, or start at the top.

"Tiger! We're almost there!" Alex snapped. Tiger started at the bottom of her opinions. "There's a place, it was a jail in the Colonial days, no windows, still has iron bars in the peep-hole in the doors, the locks are still only on the outside—" "Move on!", Alex didn't need to hear any more. "There's a place, up on the shoulder, it is in a dense grove of low tree-8, but you can drive to it, but it is as if it was positioned wrong. The front—the only windows—face inland! Away from the view of the bay! The ocean! The building, their stuff is ok, but—" "That's two down! Keep on!" Alex remarked as she slowed for the sudden steep descent—and the fact that the road was dead-ended ahead. "The third is 'different! It's similar to that house we stayed in at New Orleans—one large room, bunks, very close together. And Army style bath. That's bath—singular. And—", she stopped. "And, what?" Karen snapped. "Gals and guys all bunk in the same room—and use the same bath—at the same time!" "Really? Now that's a different twist!" Alex remarked as she turned right—that was her only remark on this matter!

"And, so, what's the fourth?" Karen asked. "Slow down, Alex" And Alex thought, 'If I get much slower, I'll be stopped!' "The fourth is the first one we will come to—it's the next right turn just ahead. The place sets up there", she stuck her right arm almost straight up! Alex slammed on the brakes, she would just wait in the middle of the street until Tiger finished her tale! It wasn't as if she was blocking traffic, she hadn't seen another vehicle since turning off Route 200! Alex twisted toward Tiger, leaned her head back on the side window, and calmly asked, "Well, what's it like?"

"It's modern—I don't mean just'new', I mean almost far-out modern'— large rooms, well equipped, very clean, huge continuous balcony, and the view over the bay—the entire scene below—is absolutely gorgeous! But—but—it is very expensive!" Then Tiger wavered. "Expensive, as outrageously expensive—two, three hundred US dollars? Or moderately expensive—less than one hundred?" "Maybe thirty to fifty dollars." "For the three of us? Or each?" "Oh, for the room—they don't care how many!" "Ok! We'll go for that!" Alex quipped.

Alex turned back into her driving position, but Tiger caught her shoulder and gripped it firmly, said, "See that corner there?", as she point- ed to an opening in the curb only a couple of car lengths ahead. Alex nodded, started to ease forward. "No! Hit it! Get low gear and hit it as fast as possible! I mean to the floor! Swing that right turn at the corner as fast as possible! It goes UP—STEEPLY! Keep it to the floor, and in only a few more lengths of the car, you have to swing right again! It's UP—UP even more steeply! You got to hit that as fast as possible! Starting from here! Or you will not make it UP to the hotel parking lot!"

Alex had waited as Tiger spouted all this, she asked, "You're kidding? Right?" "No! No.! Not at all!" Karen opened the rear door on the right side, stepped out, craned her head back as far as possible and looked up, then said "I think she is not kidding! I think I am looking at the BOTTOM of the hotel! It is above us! It's damn near directly above us! UP THERE!" "Hop in, Karen! Let's see if we can make it to the top! ", Alex snapped. As soon as the door slammed, Tiger shouted, "Hit it, Alex!" The three laughed as Alex spun the tires and jerked it into the right turn.

Following Tiger's shouted repeat of her directions—she waved and waved, one hand for up and the other for the right—and her instructions—she even threw in several "Go Betsy! Go Betsy!"—they made it! Karen had been modest, she only screamed twice!

The fancy place was even more beautiful than Tiger had described. The view from the balcony or even from the bed—the entire wall which faced the bay was glass panels or sliding glass doors, and the head of the bed against the far wall was centered to this glass wall, the view. The entire arrangement and the view were fantastic! The moon was up, the dock and the few streetlights reflected on the bay among the boats at anchor. And with the two rocky out-cropping along each side with the palm trees, everything was just fabulous!

The only room available with "The View' had only one bed, but it was huge! It was about 10 P.M. as the three leaned on the continuous concrete parapet and stared at the scene, Alex asked, "Tig, is this the surprise? The one you've been holding back since you first mentioned Angel?" "Oh, no!" Tiger pointed a finger to their right, "That is beyond that rocky hill! We are not THERE yet!" "And what, may I ask, is over there?" Karen asked. "THE beach! We came to go to THAT beach!" Alex and Karen shrugged at each other then Alex asked, "How do we get there?" "There are two ways by land—a foot path over and between the huge boulders—and a small, rough road, an extension of the street we came in on." "Does this beach have a name?" "Sure! It is Zipolite!" Tiger beamed as she replied!

"Wake up! Wake up! You two sleepy heads!" It was Tiger as she tugged on their big toes. As the two slowly crawled from the huge bed, she added, "Dress for the beach—and we should carry every thing with us, go ahead and check out—we may decide to spend tonight at the beach!"

As the two got 'dressed', they didn't pay particular attention to what Tiger wore—the only obvious items were a long tailed older tee shirt, her everyday flat sandals and her sunglasses. The hats had been left in the car.

THE LOST CODEX OF PALENQUE

Alex jerked on her tong bathing suit and slipped an everyday tee shirt over it. Then got her flat sandals—and sunglasses. Quickly packing the rest, she did put her new 'Baja' fancy over-blouse and the new wedge strap sandals in the beach bag. Just in case there was enough people that she may want to impress. But she really couldn't envision that: she thought more of a small 'hidden cove' type beach (because of the huge rocky outcroppings) with maybe only a handful of 'locals'—mostly kids.

Dressed in Spandex jogging shorts—mid thigh length—-a soft knit sports top, her old low tennis shoes and her sunglasses, Karen was ready.

Down the many outside steep steps-without curbing or handrails—

Alex checked out—paid with cash—while the other two got the gear arranged in 'Betsy'.

Slowly driving over the many humps, following the crooked narrow dirt roadway, Alex spotted several young ladies walking ahead and in the road. The four wore tee shirts, wide straw hats and sandals. Each carried a straw beach bag. And they all wore sunglasses.

"You gals want a ride?" Alex asked as she stopped. "Sure! Thanks!" They piled in—some sat in others' laps. Tiger immediately told them, "Please! Please! Don't say ANYTHING about the beach! I want my two friends here to be surprised!" The four 'strangers' and Tiger laughed; Karen and Alex just looked at each other, they didn't recognize anything funny.

Starting down the last knoll, it gradually dropped to a huge level area that was semi-circular in shape. Alex estimated it to be almost a quarter mile wide at the widest point. It was surrounded by rocky outcroppings that had trees. The flat area didn't have any, only widely scattered saw grass and clumps of small low bushes. To their left, the beautiful beach was clearly visible. It looked to be about a mile in length—the surrounding 'wall' of huge boulders shut off the far end. The beach was white, wide and flat.

There were two small concrete buildings, one near each end of the beach. Spread along the length of the beach were several straw roofed palapas. And at each was an outdoor cooking station. And a lot of hammocks were strung under the palapas. People barely visible from the knoll were seen along the beach and shelters.

"Park here—don't drive on the flat part—it's too soft!" Tiger told Alex. The four 'hitchers' piled out, but they didn't rush for the beach, they waited on Alex and Karen. After securing the wagon, the seven walked on toward the beach—the shoreline. Tiger hung back with the four, and they whispered back and forth. As the group got closer to the people already on the beach, Alex and Karen slowed down their pace—and gradually came to a halt, the others waited behind these two.

Alex dropped her bag, ran over and grabbed Tiger by her shoulders, snapped, "You Joker! This is a nude beach! That's what your surprise is!" "Yes! Yes!" as Tiger and the 'four' jerked off their tee shirts! They didn't have on anything underneath! Everyone, including Karen and Alex broke out in laughter! "Ok! Ok! We got the joke!" Then Alex and Karen began to undress. The 'four' ran on to the water.

"The two concrete buildings are restrooms. The shower heads are mounted on the outside of the walls, over the concrete slabs. No need for showerstalls or walls here!" Tiger began to fill them in, she added, "Build by the Government! This beach is maintained, and watched over by them—nudity is Ok, but no 'hanky-panky' or rough stuff! And two soldiers HAVE to walk guard duty each day!" "Tough assignment!" Karen added.

"What's with the palapas? The hammocks? And the old steel lockers?" Alex asked. "Each place is a private business—you rent space for hanging your hammock, a locker for your 'stuff' and you can eat, buy beer, soft drinks at which ever palapa you want to." "Sounds neat! I see now why you wanted us to go ahead and check-out!" "Yes, we could spend the night here—if we had the gear! Hammocks!" "I bet we could borrow some!" "Sure! We'll see, about sunset!" "And the single bed sheets, those were in case we wound up in a hammock!" "Right! It can get cool at night! With the cool night breeze blowing through the hammock on your bare sunburned ass!" Tiger teased Alex!

After spreading the mats, piling their bags together, they applied a liberal coat of suntan lotion all over each other's bodies. Rubbing lotion on Alex, Karen softly remarked, "Alex, your shave—or hot-wax-is the smoothest, the neatest I have ever seen." Not wanting to bother to explain, Alex let it go at, "Thank you, Karen!"

Leaving their gear, they began a slow stroll. They kept their hats and sunglasses on, and their feet usually in the edge of the cool water. Strolling on, they saw a broad range of many things: age, nationalities, physical appearances—including sizes—and tan 'marks'. The different tans were interesting to Alex: from 'one-piece 'beauty contest suits' to tongs—bottom only. Probably European or from living near a secluded beach. To no suit marks at all. Fenced private pool she guessed, or like in her own case in the past at Lake Lanier, a fenced back yard. Karen had 'standard' jogging shorts and sports top marks. Tiger showed very little because of her natural brown skin, but she did slightly show a 'scooped neck, short sleeve and standard shorts marks. And herself? Tong bottom only—the others at Hidden Valley had quickly gotten used to her being outside, even working in the fields, with only a tong bottom.

The three strolled on, they approached a tall slim man—he looked mid forty, they appeared to stare forward—not at 'him'. Passing by, then Tiger cast a quick glance back—he wasn't looking their way. In a swift motion, Tiger grabbed Alex around her back and pulled her tight—hip to hip, said, "Alex? Did you see the 'wang' on that dude?" "Couldn't miss it! Being an ex-nympho at this place is like a little boy being shut in the candy store while he's bound and gagged!" Karen stepped closer to Alex's other side and Alex slipped her arm around Karen's back, just above her butt.

Approaching in the distance, Karen noticed two very attractive young women coming their way. The shorter one had an arm around the back of the taller one-—her hand looked low. The taller one had one arm across the other's shoulders, her limp fingers dangled to the girl's nipple. "Do you two mind?" Karen asked as she stepped between them and put an arm on the top of the two's shoulders—and let her fingers gently hang down and touch their nipples. Alex and Tiger quickly got the idea—they both had seen this situation during Mardi Gras—they each slipped a hand behind Karen and placed their hands on Karen's firm buns. They lightly patted as Alex replied, "No, not at all." Passing the couple, Karen nodded to the taller one, Alex and Tiger nodded to the shorter one.

On away, Alex twisted her face to Karen's shoulder, lightly kissed it, said, "Karen, you're a show-off! Those two must think you've got a tongue like a—a—", she stuck her head in front of Karen, almost to her breast, looked to Tiger and asked, "Tig, what was that you told me to say about your tongue?" "A tongue like an Iguana!" Karen squeezed their breasts, asked "Really? Alex? You think Tiger has a tongue like an iguana? That—is—very interesting!" "I guess, I'm not exactly an expert on iguanas! But if Tiger say they have huge tongues, I believe her! And she has a very large tongue!"

Karen gave their breasts a harder squeeze, and Alex softly said, "Karen, a couple more squeezes—and—I may do something naughty! My crotch is already having spasms! See?" She stopped, the other two stopped and looked down at her crotch—there was a rhythmical twitch in her mound and to each side. "I've seen a lot of crotches, but never one that had spasms!" Karen chuckled.

Jerking loose and throwing her hat and glasses on the beach, Alex laughed and said, "I've got to cool off!" Then she ran and dove into the surf. Pulling Tiger closer, Karen asked, "Was that for real? Her twitch?" "It's for real! I've thought at times, the little thing was chewing bubble gum!" "Tiger, let's cool off! Before I—", Karen didn't finish her comment, they both threw their hats and glasses up on the beach then joined Alex in the surf. The three swam, dove, frolicked—and played some grab-ass in the clear Pacific surf.

Back to the mats, they lay down to dry off. Then the vendors came: short brown men, all fully dressed in the same fashion—white dress shirts, black long pants, and black dress shoes and socks. Their hats depended on if they were selling hats or not. If they were selling hats, then they wore about twenty hats of a great variety. If hats were not their merchandise, they wore a 'standard'—all these about the same—white, narrow brim, dress woven hat. These guys were impeccably dressed and very business orientated. (Some how, this is true all over Mexico)

Their merchandise had a broad range: Jewelry cases—black velvet ones for a range of jewelry. Hats, mats, sunglasses, suntan lotions, watches, sandals, scarves, even different articles of clothing, and hammocks! And more! The only snack vendors they saw was a troupe of little girls with, of all things, 'cotton candy! The lively girls appeared to be trying a new business venture! The absence of roving food and drink vendors—so common at other beach—was probably the results of an'agreement' with the palapa businesses.

When Alex showed interest in the hammocks, Tiger checked the prices. Checking meant 'final argument' with one vendor. Waving him away, she told Alex the prices was outrageous! Compared to prices at a local market, besides, when they got to her village, the 'families' there had plenty—for free!

They had been on the mats for a while when suddenly Alex jerked her hat from over her face, popped her torso upright, jammed the hat on the top of her head. Looking around—and sniffing—she spotted the source of the mouth-watering odor—it was from a grill close-by. After digging out her wallet, she stood, kicked Tiger and Karen on their feet, and said, "Ok! Kids! It's time to eat!" Like scared jackrabbits, they jumped up.

Under the palapa near the grill were many small card tables and folding chairs. Enjoying the coolness of the shade, they ate piece-meal fashion: one of these, eat; one of those, eat; and had cold beers with the delicious tacos, enchiladas, quesodillas, grilled fish and shrimp, on and on. A lot of the other 'beach-combers' were also out of the noonday sun, eating, drinking, playing chess, reading, or just lying in their hammocks under the shade. During this time, the three had numerous conversations—they were able to get promises about using three hammocks to spend the night in. Many of the 'backpacker' set had hammocks and sleeping bags.

Three of the guys offered to sleep on the ground—in their bags—and loan their hammocks. All set to spend the night, Alex and 'her kids' moved in. Alex rented a single locker for their stuff—they could have used 'Betsy', but 'she' was too far away.

Another strolling period, and Tiger explained the boats that brought and picked up people at the beach as they watched this procedure. "These are the local fishermen, along here, they only fish at night. So—during the day—for a fee, of course—they haul people from Angel and carry them back. If the surf is 'up', it can be very exciting—even very dangerous!"

Late evening, most of the 'residents' and many of those who were going to return to Angel, made a trip to the restroom buildings and took showers. After a day in the sand, salt, and the lotion sticking it all together, the showers were very welcomed! As the three joined the others at the showers, it did seem a little strange to be showing with men! Particularly strangers! And out in the open! But Alex never noticed anything 'unusual'. For the three of them, after several hours of complete nudity, it just seemed natural. To everyone!

Back at the palapa, Alex quickly got together a group of serious 'sunset watchers', then at the proper time, they stood side by side and, in silence, watched the magnificent event. Later, someway, from somewhere, enough wood 'came' and a bondfire was started between the two adjacent palapas. People moved chairs close, and more or less had B.S. sessions—mainly about their travels. Alex, Tiger and Karen made a leisurely trip to the wagon, and brought back some of Alex's wine and beer. And Tiger's sheets! As the fire died down, others left and then returned wearing tee shirts or other loose shirts—it *was* getting cooler. The guys had shifted hammocks about until Alex, Tiger and Karen's hammocks were side by side.

Tiger had shown the other two how to spread the sheets in the hammocks, lay on the sheet, and then fold it over their bodies. It was the draft below one had to be mainly concerned about in hammocks. In the dim light from what remained of the fire, as the three lay in the hammocks, Tiger asked, "Alex? Are you Ok—with—the nude business? With strangers?" "It isn't at all what I and probably millions of others would have expected. No grab ass, no drunks, no gawking, no rude remarks. Just everyone accepting each other for what they really are—like the old saying; 'Richman, poorman, beggerman, thief, all the same when nude.'

It's been so serene, so pleasant, so natural feeling, so free of unnecessary wrappings—Yes, Tiger, I can't remember feeling so—relaxed. I really appreciate you letting me in on this occasion. Yes, thanks a lot!"

"Karen? And you?" Tiger asked. "I think Alex just said it all, thanks, Tiger! And have you two noticed? No one seems to care if it is male-female, together, or male-male, female-female or just loners. Just people, just couples—thanks, Honey, I've really enjoyed it."

Silence, then Alex lowly remarked, "But it does make me feel at times as if I am like Tiger—just invisible." Karen calmly asked,"Alex, what are you talking about?" Alex realized the subject had not been opened. she didn't answer Karen, instead she asked, in a somewhat coded fashion, "Tiger? You feel like it?" "I guess so—it's soft sand, you know, I'll have to—", she let it hang as she swung out of the hammock. Alex got out, and pulled on Karen's hands, motioned with her head for Karen to get up.

As she led Karen toward the light of the fire, she softly said, "Karen, don't touch Tiger, please." There were still six or seven people sitting around close to the fire. Knowing that Tiger had rather surprise 'strangers' than have any announcement, Alex didn't say a word to them.

The three stood side by side as they faced the fire. Karen stared at Tiger. Then she was gone! Vanished! Disappeared!

Most of the others had seen, and they made the 'usual' remarks as they jumped up from their chairs; 'Damn! She's gone!' 'What the hell was that!' 'I can't believe it!' 'She has vanished!' The few that had not been closely watching; 'What are you talking about?', 'She—what?' Karen grabbed Alex in a tight hug, snapped. "Alex! Where did she go? Pushing slightly apart, Alex shrugged, calmly replied, "I haven't a clue." Then in a louder voice, Alex said, "Ok! Tiger! They have the idea! You can come back!" She did, she was again standing next to Alex—the two nodded at the others and then led Karen back to the hammocks.

About midnight, rolled tight in 'Tiger's' sheets, the three went to sleep. Their plans were to leave at sunrise—about seven—for the long, rough haul to Tuxtla Gutierrez—on the other side of the Continental Divide. Tiger had warned them; "—only 179 miles, but it is the steepest, roughest, most curved paved highway in all of Mexico! It is common to take twelve or more hours!" Alex and Karen paid close attention! Plans were to spend tomorrow night in Tuxtla. Because the next fifty miles were just as bad—the fifty miles on to San Cristobal de las Casas! The last city before Tiger's home village of Amatenango!

There, at 'Ama', they would be over 2200 miles from El Paso!

ZANATEPEC
ROUTE 200/190:

"Jezz! Would you look at that!" Karen exclaimed as she stared at the 'wall' of mountains. "I told you so!" Tiger calmly remarked as she peeled an orange. "Well! Karen! It's your's!" as Alex stepped about and shook her legs and arms. For hours, this gigantic continuous chain of mountains had gotten closer and closer to their left side—but now, it was completely across their path. Now it was just as visible on their right as it had been on the left for so long! It was February 28th, about noon.

The three were stopped at a Pemex station at Zanatepec. Tiger had warned them to top-up even though it was 'only' eighty-eight miles to Tuxtla. From here on, they were to follow Route 190.

"Tiger! Be careful!" Karen yelled at her as she eased to the freshly broken off edge of the highway. Stomping with one foot extended—she wanted to see if it would shake, vibrate, she was as posed as a cat, ready to spring back. "It'll be Ok! If—you stay as far to the right as possible!" For over the next three hours, it would be switchbacks, broken off edges—edges that had fallen hundreds of feet down into the canyons! At times, Tiger and Alex walked in front of 'Betsy' as they removed large rocks and even rolled boulders out of the way.

"We are over the top!" Tiger shouted as they passed through the small town of Rizo de Oro. "Big deal!" Karen snapped, added. "Look down there! Jezz! This is like jumping off a mountain!" "Yes! The term—'The jumping off point' must have been created for just this spot!" Alex exclaimed. And for about three more hours, it was more of the same—except 'Betsy's engine didn't have to strain. It was the brakes that had to be protected from over heating. "Remember to pump! Don't keep your foot on the brake pedal! Pump!" Alex instructed, "And the first time the brakes don't slow us down, aim for the high side—stick the nose in!" "Right! Down there—" Karen pointed at the open sky BELOW, "Is not the way to go!"

"It's down there! We must take the boat ride on the Grijalva River— through the Canon del Sumidero! Karen! Have you ever 'done' it?" Tiger shouted from the rear seat. "No! 1 Never been any farther South than Oaxaca!" Karen replied. The only thing Karen did see was the broad—four lanes—concrete bridge as they crossed 'IT'. At Tiger's instructions, Karen had taken the off-ramp indicated as 'Downtown Tuxtla Gutierrez', and swung left onto Route 14. "Karen, Alex, look for the closest place for a room"—it was after dark—"It'll be easier to run back for the river ride in the morning!" And, Alex remembered Tiger's last boat trip! 'Oh, No, not again!' But, enjoying Tiger's enthusiasm, Alex didn't object.

Tiger began to whisper to Alex as the three got out what they wanted for the night at the motel. Alex realized Tiger was getting serious—complicated. "Karen, please excuse us—we don't want to appear impolite— but-there is something we need to do—and we can't exactly explain. Ok?" Slightly puzzled, Karen replied, "Sure, whatever."

Inside the room, as Alex and Tiger went through their bags, Karen watched. Spreading out their 'uniform' outfits—the black plain skirts, jackets, and man style blouses—the two looked at each other and shook their heads. Tiger quickly gather up the clothes and went out. Alex began to search again. She had packed away her pistol and the spare clip when they left Mazatlan. Locating it—it was wrapped in a small, soft cloth—she removed it from the Mitla bag. Stepping to the dresser—Karen continued to watch, Alex continued to ignore her—Alex laid it down, and slowly unwrapped the gun and clip. Quickly, she snapped out the clip, checked to be sure it was full, pulled back the receiver half way and looked in the barrel—it was empty. After slapping the clip back in, Alex got her larger, plain, black purse. She stuffed the pistol and spare clip into the purse, and laid it on the dresser, then folded the cloth and returned it to the Mitla.

Karen eased the back of her legs to the edge of the bed, and slowly lay back. Staring up at the ceiling, she thought, 'There is a lot more to these two than just a friend taking a young Maya gal to see her poor dying Grandmother!' She also recalled Alex's recent words—'We can't exactly explain.' Karen didn't ask.

"Well?" Alex asked as soon as Tiger stepped in the room. "Two hours— they'll be cleaned and pressed!" Turning to Karen, Alex said, "Ok! Kids! It's time for some serious eating and drinking! Damn! I could sure use a drink! After that—that—whatever we just rode over!" Then she chuckled.

Walking away from the door, Alex forgot to whisper as she said to Tiger, "Kid, this could back-fire on us. What if there are newspeople there?" "We'll be long gone before any news can reach Mexico City", Tiger replied. Karen wondered even more—a lots more!

CENTRAL DATA CENTER-.MEXICO CITY

Early morning "Rudi? That you?"—"This is Tony, Central Data! I've got something for you two! It's not exactly all you need, but it's a beginning! I've located the old Professor. He recalled the actual incident, the little girls that could disappear in front of his eyes. Said he would never forget that! But he couldn't recall the exact village, just somewhere close to San Cristobal! Out in a large valley area!"—"Yes, I know that covers a large territory! Anyway, the old guy suggested that we, I, now you, contact the people at the Franz Blom museum in San Cris! Someone, or something there could distinguish the exact location, the village of the disappearing girls, women!"—"Ok! Where are you two now?"—"The Hyatt, in Acapulco! First class!"—"I'd suggest you two fly from there to Tuxtla. It's just too far, too slow to drive. Rent a car at Tuxtla and head as fast as possible on to San Cris! Contact the museum, and then, well, whatever you guys have in mind."—"It's been fun, at least a break from my boring routine! Contact us if you need anything. Bye."

ACAPULCO
HYATT HOTEL

As Rudi hung up the phone, he said, "He suggested we fly to Tuxtla, drive on to San Cris." "How? All the flights from here return to Mexico City! The only flights into Tuxtla come out of Mexico City! That'll take forever!" Kyle snapped. "I know! I know! I'll try to contact Sam—in Matzatlan—ask what his situation is!" Rudi replied.

By his phone being 'patched' into the radio, Rudi was able to talk directly with Sam as he flew Southeast in the Pilatis. "Sam, ole buddy! This is Rudi! What you up to? We need a lift from Acapulco to Tuxtla

Gutierrez! ASAP!" He knew how to get Sam's attention, he added, "And money is no problem!" "Rudi, ole guy, you say the nicest things! I'm headed for Morelia—about an hour out—I can pick you up at Acapulco airport in—say—two hours! Is that ASAP enough?" "Sure beats the commercial game! Any particular place at the airport?" "Yes, the west side of the main terminal building, you'll see a lot of private small planes—I'll pull in there! I need to top up before we head out into 'no-man's land'! Got that?" "Yes, we'll see you there, we'll be waiting, thanks! We need all the help we can get!" "Still have not caught the two gals you're looking for I presume!" Sam rubbed it in. "Right—see you at the airport! Bye!"

After reaching cruising speed and the altitude he decided to fly, Sam clicked a few entries into the GPS unit, got a direct heading for Salina Cruz. He swung to that then settled back. "Rudi, you're a well-rounded, knowledgeable old guy, let me throw something your way, see what you think about it." "Sure, what you got in mind?" "The way I see the major airlines, I think they'll stick to their present routings—everything coming and going through Mexico City. At one time, I thought they may change—but—now I don't see that happening. I see more and more people—tourist types and business people—that want to do the Pacific coast—and the coast only. Everyone knows that having to go to the Big M.C. is a pain in the butt! Look at you guys—and I see it all the time." Sam hesitated, scanned the sky. "So, you're thinking something that runs up and down the coast?" Rudi asked. "Yes, and my old PC6 isn't the thing to do it in—just the looks of the old gal scares off a lot of the upper-class people!"

"I've located a Convair that's for sale—the price looks Ok, considering it has recently had a 'major'." Sam looked about again then con—tinued. "Convairs just can't compete against the new AirBus series on the major runs—to and from M.C." "So the old Convairs are being offered at reasonable prices?" "Yes—What do you think about such an arrangement? Such a venture?" Sam asked.

"I guess a decision like that may depend on if one had to go in debt, or if one had enough of his own money. Then it's a choice of keeping the money, or taking a chance of losing it if the business was a bust. And if you could find the help to run a business of that magnitude. You know you can't do it by yourself—maintenance, scheduling, ticket sales, publicity, all that takes people'—good people! And then there's the question of additional insurance! What about that? And what would you do with the

PC6? How does that sound to you?" Rudi thought this was enough for now, he waited.

"Sounds like I need to do more research—", but he did answer part of it, "I think I could find a buyer for the old gal here—some wealthy dude that just wants another play-toy—PC6's are fun to fly! If you don't really screw up!" "How does one go about selling planes?" Rudi asked. "There are bulletins, papers, and magazines—even Agents." Sam replied.

In only a few minutes, Sam remarked, "Salina Cruz, dead ahead! I'll change heading there." He began to work at the GPS, got a new course, then swung to it. "You guys keep a look out below! As soon as we approach the mountain range, I want to get a visual on Route 190, follow that highway across the Divide, and on to Tuxtla. The highway as a last resort is not much, but it sure beats what's off to both sides!"

Entering the airspace of Tuxtla Airport, Sam made radio contact and asked for permission to land. No problem, they started an approach. "Now the fun begins!" Sam snapped as he twisted the plane into a steep, dropping turn. "Landing at Tuxtla is like screwing a hole in the sky—screwing down into that hole Tuxtla is in!"

CANON del SUMIDERO
March 1st

It was early the following morning, "Ola!" the boat operator yelled as he jerked the boat left, jumping the wake of the other boat they had just ripped past! Alex, Tiger, Karen and the other couple in the long, slim boat screamed as loud as possible as the boat flew through the air! Crashing back to the river, the operator snatched the tiller of the 150 horsepower Yamaha outboard, swung the vessel's bow just in time to avoid ramming the vertical stone side of the canyon! Canon del Sumidero! At the Grijalva River!

Speeding on—left, right, left, right—they followed the winding narrow river between the high—hundreds of feet high—nearly vertical walls of the canyon. Suddenly, he slowed to a crawl, careful eased the bow into a crack in the cliff, went in a distance. Without leaning, Alex was able to touch both of the sides of the opening. "Hello!" the operator shouted! The echoes were amazing! So close together, they sounded as one continuous word!

Back in the main stream of the river, as their first start had so surprised them, he yelled "Ola!" But this time they knew what to expect! And what to do! Hang on! The instant acceleration caused the entire boat to leap out of the water! And leap forward!

At top speed—fifty or so—the sensation of watching the sides of the canyon was strange. The walls rose and fell, opened and closed as if swallowing, and disgorging the passengers! The early morning sun couldn't reach down to the river yet!

Walking toward 'Betsy', the three were still stunned! "What the hell was that?" Alex shouted! The three laughed. Jumping around Karen, Alex rushed Tiger and threw a headlock around her neck and shouted, "Kid! The next time you mention BOAT RIDE or CRUISE, I'm going to make you write a ten page dissertation before my little white ass gets involved!"

As soon as they were in the station wagon, Tiger—again in the rear seat—leaned forward between Karen and Alex. Placing one hand on each of their shoulders, Tiger quipped, "Ok! It is time to brace-up! And make it to the top!" "What?" they snapped! They thought the rough part was over! "Now! It's up! From the hole of Tuxtla! To the mountain top of San Cris!" Karen and Alex looked at each other, rolled their heads back, and one of them said, "Oh! Crap!"

It took HOURS to climb the fifty or so miles! Switchback after switchback, drop-off cliffs, sheer walls, and open sky below! Reaching the top, the narrow highway followed the very narrow—no wider than the highway—ridge of the mountains. Only sky above and to both sides and at times, even only the tops of the clouds BELOW them! There was almost no conversation since they had turned upward!

TUXTLA AIRPORT:
About noon:

"You ever driven to San Cris?" Kyle asked Rudi. "No, never even been to San Cristobal before. Why?" "Oh, it's such a pleasant, fun trip! Here, you drive!" as he threw the rental car's keys to Rudi.

SAN CRISTOBAL Early night:

Following Tiger's directions, Karen turned off of Route 190 onto the smaller side road that went up to San Cris. The town sat on the very ridge! But after only a short distance, Tiger said, "There! Pull in at the bus station." Karen didn't question. Nor when, after parking, Alex and Tiger quickly got their recently laundered suits and one of the smaller Mitla bags and headed inside the building. Karen locked the wagon, and followed them toward the Ladies restroom.

At the door of the restroom, someone swung the door open. It was a blonde, mid twenty, looked USA, a 'back-packer'. Seeing the two with their arms full, she held the door open for them. Alex smiled at the young woman, said, "Thanks, Sweetheart!" The two went in, and the blonde stepped toward the lobby. "Hello", as Karen extended her right hand, added, "My name is Karen! May I have a word or two with you?" "Sure— I'm in no hurry! Let's sit down so I can drop my pack. My name is Sue!"

Between Karen and Sue, it was quickly determined they were both headed south, without definite plans or schedules—just 'knocking about' south of the border. And that Sue had been in San Cris for two days, and she didn't have a room for tonight—yet. She had walked down to the bus station to check on a bus for tomorrow—a bus on to the border—with the idea of bussing on into Guatemala. Sue was from California, between classes.

The two were still chatting when Alex and Tiger approached them. Surprised, Karen stood, and stared. They were dressed in their 'official's uniforms', light tan hose, and medium heels, the small string ties neatly bowed around the collars of their 'men's' style shirts. And their larger black purses were pulled up tightly to their armpits. But mainly what was shocking were their official name plates—their badges. And Alex's plain, black rimmed glasses! Karen was taken back as she stared. And read.

"My name is Alex, and please don't call me by my other name", as she extended her right hand to the blonde. Sue stood, they shook, as Alex waved toward Tiger, "This is my boss—and my dear friend, Senorita Calienta—don't use the 'Morley' part—please!" As Tiger and Sue shook, Alex continued, "And I believe you've met Karen—at times, Karen has problems speaking!" Brought back to reality, Karen shook her head, said, "Oh! Sorry, yes, this is Sue!"

"So! You don't have a room?" Alex reconfirmed as she got under the steering wheel with Tiger in the front, Sue and Karen in the rear. "Well, no. I thought I might just stick around the station, see if something came along!" Alex chuckled, added, "According to—her", she nodded toward Tiger "we are going to bunk at the best hotel in San Cris!" "The Hotel Real!" Sue quickly remarked, "I checked it out—too rich for my budget!" Alex reassured the blonde, "We're on expense accounts. You can sack out with Karen. Karen? That Ok?" "Sure—sounds great with me!" It started to snow lightly as Alex drove up the steep hill.

ROUTE 190

"You sneaky bastard! That was the worst road I have ever driven!" Rudi blurted. "Now you know about the road from Tuxtla to San Cris! Wait until you see the one from San Cris to Palenque! What we just traveled will remind you of a 'freeway'!" At Kyle's' instructions, Rudi turned right from 190, headed up toward San Cris. Passing the bus station, neither of them noticed the station wagon with the Georgia license plate.

SAN CRISTOBAL
HOTEL REAL

Inside at the registration counter of the Hotel Real, the clerk and Alex had already gotten through the 'no room at the Inn' part. Alex leaned closer—she was directly in front of the clerk's face—and she loudly exclaimed, "You do NOT want me to call our Officials in Mexico City and tell them that Professor Calienta and we are going to trudge around in the snow, in the dark, in this one-horse 'burg' while we hunt a flophouse! Now! Recheck your reservations! And cancel two room now!" He quickly—1 fumbled through the pages, "Yes—I—guess these two are a little late—but these two are not adjacent rooms! With a connecting door! Like you demand! That is impossible!" "So, move someone!" "No, that has never been done! No!"

Alex didn't respond right off, she removed her purse from her shoulder, extended it over the counter to him. Placing one hand under the purse, he almost dropped it when she relaxed her grip. She pulled it back, almost whispered, "You know why my bag is so heavy?" she didn't wait for a reply, "Because it has my big, official pistol is in it. I am the Professor's personal bodyguard, and these two", she shook her head toward Karen and Sue, "are Professor Calienta's able assistants. We do NOT split up—understand?"

Sue's eyes were very large as she glanced back and forth between Alex and the clerk. Karen glanced back and forth between Alex and the entrance door—she estimated how fast she could exit if Alex stuck her hand in that purse! Tiger maintained a demure smile as she looked about the dining area and at the guests coming and going.

After ringing for a bellhop, whispering, waiting for his return, more whispering, the clerk turned to Alex, said, "We have it all arranged, Miss—" Alex held her fingers to his lips, snapped, "It will take you a while, we'll be at the bar! Just send someone to get us when you are ready. Thanks for your cooperation!" She turned, waved the other three toward the interior—toward the bar.

As the two Agents waited to be seated—they were in a restaurant about two blocks from the Hotel Real—Rudi asked Kyle, "Well? What did you think of the Real? Is not it as nice as I said?" "Sure! And you were right about calling ahead early this morning for reservations—it looked full to me!" "This place here is more of a local Business men's hangout. We probably should stay here after eating, circulate and ask about our two gals. If anyone has seen them, they're sure to remember them!" "Good idea! Besides, the 'chicks' here are nice looking!"

"Honey", as Alex touched the bartender's hand, "Get us a bottle of your best California white wine and four glasses", she motioned toward the other three, then added as she motioned to Tiger, "Professor Calienta only allows her assistants to drink that!" With the drinks poured, Tiger did something totally unexpected by Alex. Tiger, with her glass, stood then slowly stepped to the fireplace.

There was a fire in it, and in front of it was a conversation area. There were two sofas—one in front of each end of the wide fireplace These sofas faced each other. Tiger went to one end of the mantel, raised her glass—as if she was toasting the room—and sipped. Alex watched, and saw as Tiger's eyes began to glisten. Turning to Karen, Alex softly said, "You two stay here—Tiger has a problem." Alex left, headed for the fireplace—and Tiger.

Karen thought,'Tiger has a problem? And you are a border-line power maniac?' Karen twisted to Sue, calmly remarked, "Sue, stay here— Tiger seems to have a—slight problem." Sue grabbed Karen's arm, snapped, but not loud, "A slight problem! Who the hell are those two? And this—bull about assistants? And Alex—or whoever she is—putting the heat on the old clerk about two rooms? And—and—who the hell is Tiger?" "Sue, it's a little complicated—I can't exactly explain", using Alex's words from last night, "Just go with the flow—we'll be out of here soon." "Soon? Damn straight! The first bus south leaves at 4:30 A.M.—and my ass intends to be on it! What ever they're up to, I don't want to be a part of it! Are you with me? Or not?" "I'm out of here, yes, Sue, count me in with you!" They clicked glasses and drank. "Oh—Tiger is Professor Calienta's other name", Karen calmly remarked. Sue's eyes got very big again!

There were no others close-by as Alex gave Tiger a small danty handkerchief and softly said, "Here, before you make a mess of your face." Then Alex stared into the fire, and waited. "Alex, this is the first time I have ever been inside the Real. As street urchins, we were not even allowed close to the front entrance, they would run us away. Now, because of you, and the other members of HVG, I can stand here, hold my head high, and say, 'Look at poor little Margarita! Margarita is somebody!'" Alex knew she had to do something, and do it fast!

"Come on, Kid, let's get our glasses refilled—and—and—tour this joint! Look! Look at the parrots! They would enjoy our company! Come on!

you came to see, let's look it over!" Alex jerked Tiger's hand and they headed for the bar. Tiger smiled, and wiped her tears away.

Over half of the tables were already occupied and other guests were coming in. Alex quickly caught the headwaiter's attention and asked that a table for four be reserved in the name of Margarita Calienta.

The dining area was open up to the roof line. The dining room was surrounded by a continuous balcony at the second floor level—the level of the rooms for rent. There was no wall between the conversation area at the fireplace, or at the bar—all one large room. The parrots'—two pair— area was across the room from the fireplace. The parrots' swings consisted of chains and several bicycle rims hung from the roof. Their feed and water bowels—which kept the four there—were under the swings. There were no guests at the two tables closest to the parrots.

"Sue, please get some nuts from the bartender—we'll feed the parrots!" Alex asked. When she returned, Tiger quickly began to warn the three about the 'dos and don'ts' of being around parrots. And the fact that parrots can bite a finger off! She had suddenly forgotten her 'other' feelings! Alex backed off and smiled.

Alex returned to the bedroom after she had directed the hauling up of the bags and having moved the wagon to a hotel parking lot in the rear. Stepping to the open adjoining doorway, "Girls, I've got a table reserved, Tiger and I are going to stay dressed as we are. Karen, Sue, do you two have something suitable for diner dresses?" They both nodded. "Ok, get dressed, I'm famished!"

In the process, Alex curled an index finger at Karen. Together, and away from Sue, Alex asked, "Did you get an understanding with Sue?

Where she stands? Sexual wise?" Karen smiled broadly, "You'd never believe it possible! She's 'hard-core', like me! And, she's a 'sweetie'!" They hi-fived, Alex pulled Karen close, cooed, "Tonight's the night—I'm horny—I'm as horny as the bull in a field full of new two year old heifers." Then she slapped Karen on her bare rump, added, "Get dressed! I'm also starved!"

Alex didn't realize it, but it was also a Friday night.

During diner—Tiger had helped the other three order—when about half finished, a young lady came to their table. Looking at Tiger, she said, "Please excuse me. I had noticed your reservation card earlier, are you THE Margarita Calienta? The famous one?" Tiger beamed, extended her right hand, replied, "Yes, as a matter of fact, I am—and I'm the only 'real-one!'" Tiger looked toward Alex and winked. Alex smiled. "And—then—", the lady turned to Alex, "You must be the famous Alex—the famous body-guard!" Alex chuckled as she took the gal's extended hand, and replied, "That's me—just a poor working gal—trying to keep my boss here"—Alex motioned to Tiger, "out of trouble!" "I'm so pleased to meet you both! Wait until I get back to college! None of my friends will ever believe I met you two!" Then she left, returned to her friends—they began to whisper back and forth. Sue and Karen raised eyebrows, looked at the other two with inquisitive expressions. "Just another fan", Tiger calmly remarked. "You aren't really a bodyguard, are you Alex?" Sue asked. "Yes, I am really a bodyguard!" Alex and Tiger returned to their eating. And Sue wondered, 'An Archaeologist with a personal bodyguard! Wait until I get back to college! My Archaeology Professor will never believe ME!'

Giving up on finding any leads on Alex and Tiger, Kyle and Rudi paired together with a couple of the 'ladies' who seemed to be friends or they were working as a team. One of the ladies finally brought things to a head, she asked, "My friend"—she nodded at the other one setting next to Kyle—"and I have separate rooms at the hotel across the street. If you guys are interested, we could go over and look at the paintings on the ceilings!" Rudi and Kyle looked to each other, shrugged, Kyle responded, "May as well, I haven't seen any nicely painted ceilings lately!"

HOTEL REAL

Having another round of wine about the fireplace area—the conversations with others had reached the point of: Where you from, blab, blab—Alex slipped to the entrance door. Peering through the glass, she said to herself, 'We left in snow, we're back in snow!' Returning to the sofa, she wiggled her small bottom between Tiger and Karen, and softly said, "I don't know about you girls, but I'm about bushed. I'm ready to turn in." Leaning close to Karen's ear—Sue twisted across Karen's lap trying to hear—Alex almost whispered, "Besides, between that fire and these damn pantyhose—" They didn't need any more encouragement, the four headed up stairs.

Karen asked, "You two doing Ok?" Alex was too busy to reply, she had Tiger's thighs shoved far up, her face buried dee-'in Tiger's crotch. "Oh! Oh! Oh, it's you—Karen! What?" "I was just asking", Karen stepped to the bed, rubbed Tiger's voluptuous breasts roughly, snapped her nipples several times, then she stepped to Alex's backside, slapped her bare bottom, quipped, "Alex! You better come up for air before you faint!" Alex jerked her head up, rolled to one side, replied, "You're right!"

As she hopped to her feet, Alex tugged on one of Tiger's big toes, said, "Get up, Kid! It's time for a drink! Hang loose, no need to explode yet!" Alex look4round, added, "Where is Sue?" "I'm right here,", Sue answered as she walked in. Alex stepped to her, put her arm around Sue's neck,and said, "Come on, Sweetie, you look as if you could use a little cooling-off too!" And so they swapped partners.

Almost another hour later, then, "Well, Karen, it looks"—Alex said as she looked at Tiger lay flat on her back, her body still in spatic quivers, and Karen stood at the foot of the bed as she wiped her face and her firm breasts—her tall slim body glistened with sweat and juices—"like you and I are the only two left standing! What are we going to do about that?" "You sit—slide way down—in that chair, and I'll show you!" "And after—whatever you got in mind—I'll show you a trick, it's an old one, but it still works good. It is called sixty-nine, around-the-world style!", Alex remarked. "Goodness, Alex, how sweet you talk!" And Alex got into position, Karen pointed a finger, said, "Just a sec—I'll be right back!"

With her long, slim legs and her tight buns, Karen twisted to the other room, then returned with a black dildo—it was about two feet long, one and one half inches in diameter, with an enlarged bulge at mid-length, and it was encircled with ripples—it had two obvious heads. It was flexible, but firm, enough to get into most any hole. Shaking it at Alex's face, Karen growled, "Get ready, you little bitch, I'm going to put a real fucking on you!" as she spread her feet and slowly inserted one half of 'it' up into herself.

Alex smiled, snapped her legs straight up, hooked her elbows inside her knees and pulled these tight to her shoulders, then with pursed lips, she cooed softly, "Oh, please, Master, don't, don't—stop now."

The action over, Alex snuggled with Tiger, and gently wiggled her face to Tiger's breasts, then realized she had made it through another Friday night without a visit from Miss Hawkins.

But what she didn't realize was that the two Agents had returned to their room—the room next to her room.

CHAPTER 14

SAN CRISTOBAL BUS STATION
SATURDAY, MARCH 2th
4:28 A.M.

The four friends had already said their good-bye; Sue and Karen had thrown their heavy packs into the belly of the greyhound style bus—the two leaving were in line to board last. Suddenly Karen turned back to Alex, caught one of her elbows—Sue also turned back. Karen asked, "Alex, please tell me what you two have come here to do? If you don't, I'll wonder about it the rest of my life!" Sue just nodded in agreement. Glancing from one to the other—including Tiger—Alex replied in an enigmatic fashion, "Ok. Tiger is going to transgress back in time—hundreds of years in time—and visit with the Tzental Priests-—they are going to tell, or show, where a great treasure is—returning to our time, we are going to get the treasure—and no one is going to stand in our way!" Sue and Karen stared. "Hell! I thought you two had come to assassinated the Pope!" Karen chuckled.

The bus's door began to close as the two jumped to it, forced their way inside the bus, and waved through the glass. Settled into the huge comfortable seats, Sue leaned her head to Karen's shoulder, softly asked, "Karen, do you think Alex was telling the truth? All that mumbo jumbo about traveling back in time?" "Miss Alexandra Hawkins, Special Agent, telling the truth? Not on your life!" They chuckled as the bus to the Guatemala border pulled out.

HOTEL REAL

It was after seven, Alex and Tiger were again dressed in their 'official's' uniforms'—Tiger had again insisted. Not only did she want to impress the people of San Cris, but she also wanted to impress the people of her village. And, Alex wore her larger purse—the purse with her pistol.

The two were at the fireplace as they finished the cups of coffee from the small 'complementary table' nearby. Setting the empty cup down, Alex remarked, "Ok, Kid, let's go see your folks!"

Alex had left 'Betsy' at the loading zone near the front entrance door after they came back from the bus station earlier this morning. The bellhop had already loaded their gear and she had settled the bill—with cash—with the same clerk from the night before. And she had turned in the room key, but she had not locked the room door on their way out.

As soon as they got in the vehicle, Alex started the engine, then, "My watch! I've left my watch on the dresser! Leave the motor running, while I run get it!" Tiger just nodded.

Back in the room, Alex began putting on her watch, as she stepped out the door. Finishing with the watch, she took a couple of steps as she looked at the buckle. Suddenly the next door swung open, and stopped in mid motion, in the open doorway, stood Kyle—Agent-man #1!

The two froze, face to face! It took both of them a fraction of a second to realize the significance of their positions! Kyle should have stepped back and pulled his pistol—but he didn't! Instead, he lunged at her, his arms wide apart, with the intent of pinning her arms down to her sides.

She side-stepped—he hit the balcony's rail hard with his waist—, about his hip line. He almost fell head first over the rail. Alex stiffened both her arms and jabbed him in the back as hard as she could. The blow completed his out of balance situation. Slowly, he fell over as he grappled with his hands behind his back trying to grab the rail. Alex caught his wrists, and pushed very hard—forward.

As Kyle did a perfect flip, she watched. He landed—dead center—on a dining table below. The dishes, the food, the four people at the table, scattered as water from a dropped glass! The table collapsed with a loud bang! With her hands on the rail, Alex leaned over and looked—Kyle was gasping for breath, as a fish in a bowl of dirty water! Seeing no blood, she laughed!

Alex did not see Rudi—he was seated at a table across the room with his back toward the balcony and the stairs. And Rudi had not seen Alex. At the crash, Rudi jumped up, rushed to Kyle. Still not being able to speak, Kyle pointed up—up to Alex. Seeing her, leaned over and laughing, Rudi jerked out his pistol, held it pointed up, and ran for the stairs. Grabbing the bottom post of the ornamental iron hand railing, he swung around and up to the second step. And froze! He was staring in the muzzle of Alex's 40 caliber pistol. "Hold it, Cowboy! Slowly lay that 'shooter' down on the step—and back away!", she commanded.

As soon as Alex saw his hand get far enough away from his pistol, and as he began to straighten up, she slapped her left palm against the wall, propped her right forearm on the rail, and hopping both feet high, she kicked him—very hard—in his chest with both feet! The force knocked him off the step, he flew, stumbled back, hit the corner of the sofa and fell sideways. Hard. The side of his headed landed on the fireplace hearth, his face turned toward the fire. Scrambling, twisting, and trying to not faint, he struggled to keep his face away from the fire!

Alex grabbed up his pistol, stuck it into her waistband under her jacket. In one leap, she jumped to the floor, ran around the other end of the sofa, and out the front door. Quickly, she stuffed her pistol back into her handbag. Alex jumped in the wagon, and rapidly sped away. Tiger asked, "What was that loud noise inside?" "I think someone dropped something!" and Alex laughed.

Back in the dining room, the two Agents had managed to get up and come together, still rubbing their bones, trying to determine if any were broken. The clerk ran to them, yelled, "I know who did this! It was that little bitch bodyguard of Professor Calienta!" Kyle flipped back his lapel, showed his badge and his gun, snapped, "Shut up, stupid! We know who she is! That's why we're trying to catch her!"

Slowly, still flexing their limbs the two went outside, and crossed the street to the Central Park, the Zacolo of San Cris. It had stopped snowing, the early morning weather was bright and sunny. Glancing at his watch, Rudi said, "We still have no idea which way to go—to look for them. We'll wait until after nine, go to the Franz Blom Museum, see what they can dig up. There probably is a highly trained staff there—we'll leave it up to them!" "Yes—guess that's about it."

Speeding down the hill toward the bus station, Alex snapped, "Which way?" "Right! Back on 190! Go through the town of Teopisca—about twenty miles! After that, it's only a short distance to Ama! And it's on the right! I'll tell you when we get there—it's almost impossible to see from this highway!" "It is that small?" "No, it—the village—sets up on a bank—the shoulder of this road! Just can't see the top from this road!"

On the way, Alex explained what happened in the hotel, she closed with, "We've got to be more careful! Somehow, they have picked up our trail again!"

Slowly passing through Teopisca, Alex asked, "I don't see any people, no one! Is this normal?" "Not exactly—most everybody has probably already left—gone to Chamula!" "Chamula? For what?" "For the 'March the Fifth Celebrations! It is a very big deal! You'll enjoy it!"

'Betsy' coasted up over the edge of the steep bank and Alex eased on and parked by the lone, huge spreading tree. (She was to learn later this was a Ceiba tree—and as in so many cases of Maya villages, the very reason why a village was developed in a particular location.) If continued on, the road crossed through the village and disappeared down the other side of the ridge. To Alex's left, the main street went between the church and the concrete basketball court on the left, and a single row of small stone houses on the right. On the other side, her right, was a low spread out 'modern' building—Alex guessed it to be 'government', probably a school combined with offices. And Alex noticed—in the outer walls of the houses, thousands of small scars. These were about shoulder and waist high. Bullet scars, she imagined.

Over closer to the church were two heavy trucks with high stake bodies. A crowd of people—about thirty or so—all ages—were busy loading just about anything one could image! And walking toward the trucks, from beyond the trucks, were women with huge loads of clay pottery vessels. Some under their arms, and a stack balanced on the top of their heads. And men with huge sacks thrown up behind their backs (Alex learned these were sacks of charcoal that was produced here) Pottery and charcoal were two of the three main commodities—the third being vegetables raised in the gigantic field across the highway, but this was 'in trouble'!

Tiger got out, and ignoring Alex, she slowly walked toward the crowd. As she got closer, the people—everyone—slowed down their movements and gradually came to a halt. One teen-aged girl suddenly raced toward Tiger as she screamed, "Margarita! Margarita! It is Margarita Calienta!" Then, Tiger, at first a fast walk, then a slow trot, and then running at full speed, she shouted, "Susha! Susha!" All the others sat down their loads and rushed forward. Alex got out—and from habit, she slipped on her purse—and stepped to be under the shade of the large tree. She watched.

Alex watched the little kids jumping, dancing around, the teens and younger women as they slowly circled Tiger and studied her suit, her 'official badge', and her physical appearance. And the older people as they moved forward, calmly, one at the time, and either shook hands, or hugged and kissed Tiger. And Alex saw the lone, much older—with long flowing snow-white hair—frail woman as she was being assisted by one girl at each elbow. They came out of the church, and by the woman's manner, Alex deducted she was blind.

Spotting the old woman with the two girls, Tiger waved off the others, dashed toward the Lady. She screamed, "Grand MaMa"! Quickly kissing the woman's hands and cheeks, then Tiger bent to one of the girls. Tiger took the Ladie's elbow as the girl ran toward Alex, Stepping forward, Alex joined the girl, who yelled. "Come! Come! Senorita Alex!" Then she jerked Alex's hand and pulled her to a trot.

The people went back to what they were doing.

Joining Tiger and her 'Grand', Alex realized they were talking in some language other than Spanish or English. She recalled Tiger's statement back at Hidden Valley—it seemed ages ago now, but was really only weeks ago—'Grand MaMa' speaks only Tzental!" And Alex remembered her own response,'Well! We'll just have to go and talk to 'Grand MaMa!' And that was the reason they were here!

After introductions, and Tiger's brief description of Alex's physical appearances—as the blind Lady softly touched Alex with her long, bony fingers—'Grand' asked, through Tiger, "Alex, why do you have a gun?" The two girls 'mouthed' 'she smelled it.' Alex, again through Tiger, explained about her being Margarita's bodyguard. "Why do you, Margarita, need a guard?" "I'll explain later, please." The Lady just nodded.

"I hate to interrupt, Tiger, but why are all the people loading so much? So many different items?" "They are going to Chamula—as soon as they get loaded!" "Now?" "Yes, now—today! Now!" "Ask your Grand if she will ride with us? We'll go wherever everyone else goes!" Tiger nodded and said 'something'. Grand nodded and replied 'something'. Alex took all this as 'yes', she said, "I'll get 'Betsy', we can at least sit while you two talk about your adventures since you have been gone!"

Pulling up to the four, Alex hopped out and helped Tiger get her Grand into the rear seat. Tiger thanked the two little girls, they scampered off. Tiger slipped into the rear and the two began in earnest—in Tzental.

With her door open, Alex sat with her legs outside. Soon a husky young man, or boy—She couldn't decide his age—strolled to her. "My name is Mickey! I'm Margarita's cousin!" And as if she knew, he added, "I was Jackie and Niki's brother." Alex was confused with the,'I was'. Tiger hopped out, hugged and kissed him, then she tried to clear up their relationship. "His sisters and I were the best of friends. His Mother was my Mother's sister!" Again, 'were and was'. But Alex didn't ask, not yet anyway. "Mickey, how old are you now?" Tiger asked. "I'm eleven—but, as you two can see, I'm big for my age!", he proudly exclaimed. "Yes, you are!" Alex added.

Tiger returned to her Grand, Alex continued, "Mickey, you speak English very well! How did", he broke in, "My sister, Jackie, taught me before—", he lowered his gaze, twisted about to one side, and stared off into the distance. "Get in, have a seat! No need to stand around in the sun!"

He stepped past the front of 'Betsy', and sat down in the front passenger's seat. Looking at the dash—the controls—he asked, "You drove down here in this—station wagon?" "Yes, we did. Can you drive?" "Sure! I learned years ago!' 'At such a young age?' Alex wondered, she asked, "That's pretty young! Any reason why?"

"I learned when we were—", he stared at Alex's badge, changed the subject, "You work for the Mexican Government?" "No, the USA Government. Why?" "You have no connections with the Mexican Federalities?" He was persistent about him doing the asking! "No! None at all! As a matter of fact, we—I in particular—are in trouble with the Mexican Government! Why are you asking these kind of questions?"

"We—all our families—worked with 'Condor', about six to eight years ago" he turned from Alex, and started to look—he swung his view back and forth at the row of houses. With a cracking voice, he added, "My Mother— Jackie—Niki were killed, shot down as they tried to run away—by the Mexican soldiers, at the orders of your CIA Agent—", he stopped switching his eyes about, stared at one wall in particularly, then he slowly pointed, and struggled to get out, "Right over there."

Alex felt like a heel, not knowing more than she did about this lonely village-—Amatenango. He cleared his throat, continued, "Margarita's Mother and Father"—he pointed to a different house, then in just above a whisper, he forced out, "—were killed inside their home—there— Margarita got away. The few 'Old Ones' that survived that day by being inside the church thought—none of us were sure for years—." Alex realized she had never heard this from Tiger, she softly responded, "I'm so sorry, I did not know."

He wiped his eyes on his shirtsleeves, turned and faced Alex, then pretended a smile and quickly started again, "Well! I learned to drive when my PaPa and I lived with Condor in the jungle. We stayed on the move a lot—drivers were needed." Not exactly sure what to say, she casually remarked, "That's fine." She meant this to apply to his 'learning to drive'!

Mickey took it a completely different way, "No! Not fine! The 'Feds', at the direction of your CIA, called in the jet planes—most of us men—males, including my Father—were killed!" "Sorry, Son! I don't have any use for 'OUR CIA either!" as she remembered their—the HVG members—encounters with the CIA out West.

Suddenly Tiger twisted forward, patted Mickey on his shoulder and spoke to him in Tzental, he nodded. Neither one smiled as they got out of the car. "Alex, Grand says she will wait here—You want to come with us?" "Sure—", Alex decided to not ask, she just followed the two as they slowly walked toward the church. Passing the church, they continued to talk in their language—Tzental. Behind the church, they approached the graveyard, and Mickey pointed out where Tiger's Mother and Father were buried. It was obvious to Alex that Tiger didn't know this until this moment.

Stepping to Tiger's side, Alex took one of her hands—Mickey held the other one. For a brief period, the three stared at the two small wooden markers as tears slowly trickled down their cheeks.

Behind them, back toward the courtyard where the trucks were, someone blew the horn. Mickey quickly showed the two where his Mother, Jackie and Niki were buried. Not hesitating very long, he pulled their hands, said, "We'd better get back—"

Alex raised her head, a sudden cold breeze sprung up, it whipped the dry, red, dust from the barren ground—the swirling cloud of dust blocked out the sun. Shivering, Alex softly agreed, "Yes, it's time to move on."

Looking at the people, the loading operation, Alex said, "Tiger, looks as if the trucks are ready! What do we do now?" Tiger turned to Mickey, asked, "Mickey! Go with us! You can direct Alex while Grand and I talk! Ok?" "Sure! You know I'm on my own! I'd love to go with you two!" as he 'sized-up' Alex—he was larger than she! Not much, but just slightly.

Mickey ran to the two truck drivers—they briefly spoke—he returned. Alex and Tiger were in the wagon by then, he jumped in, said to Alex,

"Fall in between the two trucks! If you are in trouble, the trucks will help hide your wagon!" "In general, where is this Chamula?" "Back through San Cris—then head right, leave San Cris—on down into a huge valley. The road ends at Chamula—can't drive any further!" "Is it far? A long drive?" "No, not at all", he leaned across Alex, asked her to switch on, he looked at the fuel gage, added, "You've got plenty of petrol" Twisting his head toward her, they were face to face, he looked deep into her big black eyes, softly asked, "What tribe did your eyes come from?" He held his close position—suddenly Alex felt 'something,'something' from deep inside, she quickly gave him a kiss on his lips, snapped, "Cherokee!" He moved back to the other side, said, "Pull out! Get in line!"

HOTEL REAL

The two Agents were still in their room, just waiting for nine—waiting to go to the Blom Museum. Kyle removed his shirt, asked, "Rudi, look at my back. See if you notice anything unusual—anything serious." As he closely looked, he replied, "No, it is—it is—just slightly blue—all over!" "Great!" Removing his shirt, Rudi looked at his chest in the mirror—a perfect print of Alex's footprints, especially the two heels. These were a deep purple. Shaking his head, he said, "I'm going to have a hell of-a-time explaining this to my wife!" The two chuckled.

THE FRANZ BLOM MUSEUM

After a rather long wait, the frail, tiny lady let them in. She was dressed in a neat wool business suit, but it was entirely too large, it hung on her small frame. She wore low wedge heels, and her short snow white hair was in a natural fluff. She was using a silver tipped walking cane, and she wore a lot of expensive looking jewelry. As soon as Kyle and Rudi got inside, she said very loudly, as she peered over her half-glasses, "You'll have to speak up! I'm hard of hearing!" Rudi started, "Senora Bl—." She snapped, "It's Frau! Frau Blom! Frau Rachel Blom!" He started again, and after a lengthy shouting match, she motioned for them to follow her.

Inside 'Franz's office'—the walls were completely lined with shelves full of books, folders, envelopes, and stacks of tied together papers—she yelled, "It's here—somewhere!" as she swung the tip of her cane in a complete circle. Rudi and Kyle looked at each other—then at what they were faced with! "I know it is here! Because I remember that Franz spent about two years studying those girls! And he never—never did anything that he didn't write about! And write, and write!" The Agents just glanced about, no idea where to start! Suddenly, Frau Blom pointed with the tip of her cane, shouted, "There! Right there!" She indicated a thick brown folder with a string tied around it. She cleared a spot on the desk—it was piled high with papers and books—she just made the stacks higher!

Opening the folder, the Agents saw that all the scribbled handwriting was in German! "Excuse us, Frau Blom, but we can't read German! "Stupid! The damn name of the village will be the same! Regardless if the text is in German, English, or Spanish! Look for only the village name! You two would not understand the text regardless of what language it was written in!" She twisted, hobbled toward the door, shouted over her shoulder, "You do know the names of the villages in Chiapas, don't you?" She didn't wait for a reply, but asked, "Coffee?" she didn't wait.

She had a point! Separating the loose papers into two sections, they began to scan for a name—almost any name that they reconized. Suddenly, Kyle stopped, snapped, "Amatenango! And here it is again!" He sat back and stared into empty space, added, "Why the hell did it have to be Amatenango?" "Kyle? What difference does it make which village it **is?**" "I'll tell you later—Let's get out of here!" Rudi placed the papers back in order and returned the folder to the shelf. They thanked Frau Blom and went outside.

Kyle drove—he was doing all the driving since he was familiar with the area. Through town, he started to relate his past connections with the village. Before they approached the bus station, the two trucks—with the dull black station wagon in between—passed along headed in the opposite direction.

"It was because of 'Ama'—Amatenango—that I got out of the Army!"

Kyle started, "You do remember that I was an officer in the Army? Anyway, I applied to the 'Agency', got in! If it had not been for 'Ama', I could probably be a colonel by now!" "What happened at 'Ama'?" Rudi asked.

'We were chasing Condor! All over the region! The indications were that he was using the people of 'Ama' as contacts for information concerning our movements! He was always one jump ahead of us! We—the Mexican Forces—had a CIA prick assigned to us, was suppose to know everything about 'putting-down' subversives. Anyway—we couldn't actually discover the source of 'who-evers' info. This CIA guy demanded a simple solution! Right or wrong never entered this bastard's mind! If he had one!

Eliminate the villagers of Amatenango! That was his solution!

And before we—I and the other Lieutenant assigned to the troops—could stop him, that's what happened. Slaughtered—women, kids, what few men were still there—all except a handful that escaped and some old women that hid in the church. Horrible! This SOB—the CIA prick—he had his 'own'—USA—chopper—carried the two Nuns up—straight up in the chopper and pushed them out over the basketball court! I was there! Right there! They splattered all over the concrete slab! That was when I decided a career change was a necessity—for me!"

Suddenly Kyle snapped, "Calienta! I knew I had heard that name before! Just couldn't put it together! The Calienta families lived at Ama! The Margarita Calienta gal is going home! She must be one of the few people that escaped! That CIA bastard tried to round them up—but—we never did find—and 'eliminate' all the witnesses—some got away!" "Kyle! So what? That was a long time ago!" Rudi retorted. "You're right—six, seven, eight years ago? Screw it! I'd rather forget the whole damn affair!" The two didn't talk for a while.

"It still doesn't make sense? If the two, Alex and Tiger, were just going to Calienta's home, why all the mystery? Why all the trouble? Drive down? This damn far? They could have flown to Tuxtla, rented a car there! Why all the trouble? Why the tale about coming to get 'something' very old—lost for a very long time?" Kyle didn't respond, the two left it hanging.

Kyle drove at top speed as they rushed toward 'Ama', he didn't even slow down passing through Teopisca! Wheeling up the bank into 'Ama', he slammed on the brakes. They hopped out. And an hour later, the two Agents conceded there were no people—none—at Amatenango. They had methodically-with drawn pistols (Rudi had a spare)—slowly moved from house to house. No one.

Abruptly, Kyle jammed his pistol in his shoulder holster, turned around and headed back down the street—the one between the church and the row of houses. Rudi followed him, but he was confused. Stopping at a small unmarked building, Kyle suddenly kicked the door open. "What are you doing?" "This is the only liquor and beer store in 'Ama'"And he tossed the car keys to Rudi, added, "I'm going to get drunk! You drive!" Getting several bottles of Aguadiente, he stuffed these in his pockets, then opened one and took a large slug. He then threw a handful of Peso bills on the counter, muttered, "That's more than enough—even to repair the door."

Slowly walking back toward the car, Rudi thought 'My partner goes on a drunk binge, Alex and Tiger have given us the slip again, and we can't even find a village full of people! And—and—a 110 pound little gal kicks both our asses! All in the same morning!'

As Alex continued to follow the truck on toward San Juan Chamula, Mickey said, "Did Margarita ever mention"—Alex had quickly explained that the two of them had lived in the same 'village' for the last few years—"my sisters? Jackie and Niki?" "Don't seem to remember those exact names—but—we've talked about so much—" "Jackie, the older one, she was thirteen when—." He hesitated, then started again, "She was the best at what the girls of 'Ama' do—" "You mean—the disappearing 'trick'?" "Well, yes, but it is not entirely a 'trick'." "Mickey, I'm terribly interested in what they do—disappearing—but", she had almost said,'Tiger', "Margarita has not fully explained—yet."

Tiger and her grandmother continued to mutter, seriously, in Tzental at the rear. Mickey added, "The elder women never explained to me—but Jackie tried to." "Really? Would you please explain to me what you know." He continued, "There are two ways—two kinds of disappearing—if there are only a few others,'strangers', two, three, maybe four, they simply 'see' what the others are going to do—and jump to where the others are not going to look. Or, the girl, concentrates on only one of the 'strangers', see what he or she thinks—where he or she is going to look, then jumps to where he or she is NOT going to look!" Alex was amazed at his words; 'see' what the others <u>are going to do?</u> "See what they are going to do?", Alex questioned.

"Yes, it's as if they can SEE what someone thinks— BEFORE that person even realizes it!" "That IS a good feat in itself!" Alex commented then asked, "What's the other way they can disappear?" Alex had not heard—from Tiger—about there being two ways! Two methods!

"If there is a crowd—a lot of 'others'—the girls go to the Upper-world, and return when they want to—or when someone 'calls' them down." "The Upperworld? What's that?" "The sky, the air, 'above the earth', maybe even as clouds." "How can they?" "I'm not sure how—but—there is an old tale—the ancient Tzental Priests made a deal with the gods of the Upperworld—and ever since, the female Tzentals have been able to do it. Of course, it takes practice—they start very early—two or three years old." Strange, Alex thought! "Once, when I was two—three, Jackie", it was as if he was talking to himself, "she did it while she held me tight—we changed to air—floated about—then we came back."

SAN JUAN CHAMULA

"Jezz! "I had no idea this was such a big deal!" Alex exclaimed as the bottom of the valley became visible and she slowed down. The entire town—downtown where the taller buildings were—was surrounded by people, vehicles, tents, lean-tos! And scattered among this were many small cooking fires with whisper of smoke that drifted slowly upward. "Well over one hundred thousand! People from all over the world! Orientals, Europeans, and—" "Gringos?" "Yes! Gringos!"

Following the lead truck, they headed around the right side of the valley. The truck stopped, the driver motioned that she pull up along beside of him. And the truck behind, pulled up along side 'Betsy'. Immediately, the 'pottery women' began to unload their ware and head off into the thick crowd. Then the 'charcoal men' did the same.

The three were onside the wagon—'Grand was still waiting to get out, she seemed to sense that they were not 'ready' yet—when, suddenly, Alex and Tiger were besieged by the 'teen' girls of 'Ama'. Mickey backed off and waited. The girls chattered away with Tiger! "They say, you and I, have to change clothes! We must wear 'Ama' skirts and blouses, and sandals!" The girls had already selected what the two would wear—full 'wrap-around' dark red skirts and white pull-over blouses—the same as theirs! And they began to 'help'—they quickly undressed Alex!

Down to her pantyhose, one girl rattled off! "What?" Alex snapped to Tiger as she began to shiver. "She said you can't wear those! Your hose!" Tiger answered and pointed at Alex's hose! "My little white ass will freeze without hose!" The girl rattled again, and ran to one of the trucks.

Alex jerked on the blouse, and waited. Running back, the girl held up a pair of 'standard-cut' white cotton panties, said 'something'! "She said, put these on—they belong to her baby sister—but it's Ok!" Tiger laughed—

hard. "I haven't wore those"—Alex pointed at the panties, "since I was ten years old! And, my ass will still freeze!" Somehow, the girl understood, she began to twist about, wiggle her thights, her legs, as she said 'something'. "She said, warm up your bottom like she is doing!"

Tiger was almost bent double with glee!

Alex remembered the old saying; 'When in Rome, do as the Romans!

She did, and it worked! Even if she was only wearing 'baby sister's panties'! The 'teens' backed up, looked over the two, approved, and announced 'It was time to go! To head out! Into the crowd! Join into the fray! The mob! Alex quickly hid her purse insides the wagon, grabbed her wallet, and, by holding hands, they made a line, played 'follow-the-leader'! And, their 'Leader' was very fast and good at this! Mickey stayed with 'Grand' at the station wagon, he was still smiling as recalled watching the 'dressing' of Alex, and he thought, 'La Poco Chihuahua!'

It didn't take long as the girls dodged, pushed, shoved and twisted their way to 'it'—The Races! This pageant involved over two thousand official participants in the dances and rituals that took place in the center. These were just the 'official ones', because everyone in Chamula who could walk or ride participated—and a huge number of visitors came to witness this five day extravaganza! To eat and drink hearty, and to remember the true human nature of things. The deafing roar of hand-held bombas and skyrockets, the out of tune cacophony of handmade guitars and harps, the sound of old brass trumpets blaring before the racing standards

with their fancy flags. And the whistles, cheers, jeers, and laughter that encouraged the men as they charged through clouds of incense while they raced around the central plaza. All this was their music—the music of The Chamulas! Like their ancestors did thousands of years before, they remade the Maya world and renewed time itself through the drama of dance and pageant!

Alex jerked Tiger's ear close to her mouth, shouted, "Is everyone here crazy?" "Yes! Isn't it great fun!" Another rocket exploded skyward only a few feet from Alex. "Yes! If I don't get blown smithereens!" Then, their 'Leader' decided it was time to eat! And drink! She screamed—nothing that Alex understood—they were off again! Toward the food vendors!

Stuffed, and some what 'tipsy', Alex had no idea what she drank, she yelled to Tiger, "Do you have any idea where our vehicles are?" "Sure!" as she waved one arm toward an area that covered at least a thousand acres, "Over there!" Alex was beginning—just barely beginning—to understand how things worked—very vaguely! She grabbed Tiger's wrist, jerked and started 'over there'! Tiger didn't question. The two left the 'teens'—as if they cared, as if anyone, anywhere cared!

Back at 'Betsy'—Mickey and Grand were gone—Alex dug around inside the wagon and located a couple of bottles of white wine she had 'missed' while at Zipolite. She opened one, and sat on the end of the rear seat. Taking a swallow, she felt Tiger set down at the other end. "Alex, before it gets too dark, we need to locate some heavy, warm clothes!" Tiger calmly remarked. Lowering the bottle, Alex thought 'Oh,oh,something is up!' But she only said "Why?" "Because, tonight, we go to the Calvaries—and spend the night." Alex raised the bottle again, drank, and thought,

'Ok, what ever a 'calvaries' is!' she didn't bother to ask!

As they continued to lie on the rear seat, their heads on each others shoulders, their legs outside, Alex asked, "Have you spoken to your grand-mother about the Codex yet?" "Yes, she remembers about the tale, but not any specific details. She has agreed to help us—that's the main thing." "Help? How?" Alex asked barely above a whisper. "She's going to contact the head Shaman here—that may be where she and Mickey have gone now—at other times, he could be next to impossible to find. That's the reason I thought it was so important we get here—now." "And then what?" "Not sure—maybe get him to conduct a ritual—whatever—for more details of the old story—or stories—whatever. We'll just have to go along—for a while at least. Do you understand?" "Yes", Alex agreed.

Raising upright, Alex said, "Ok! Let's do the clothes bit, then make one more pass at the races!" They did, and returned just before dark—Alex thought finding the vehicles after dark would be impossible!

The other Tzentals drifted back, and they began their routine; someone build 'their fire' close by, the people had even brought their own three rocks and enough three legged stools. The women cooked a large pot of thick, rich stew for tacos. It appeared that a large supply of tortillas had been prepared at home. Smoothly, with no confusions, and in the Maya tradition, the men ate first, then the kids and 'teens' (under thirteen, being as this is the age of woman and manhood) next—the women ate last. After the meal, most of the thirteen and over crowd returned to the 'night' races! Tiger suggested to Alex that they skip that—and rest for the 'night' trip to the Calvaries. Alex agreed.

The two spent some more time straightening things in the rear of the station wagon. Alex sat aside the two beach mats, and she dug out Arnie's old 'winter emergency blanket'.(In the mountains at home, most everyone kept a blanket in their vehicles during the winter months in case they were stranded on the road) Laying aside what they thought would be needed to wear tonight, the two were finished there. Carrying the two mats and the blanket to the 'camp-fire' area—Alex saw that this affair was going to be like camping out—they spread these out.

Lying down, Alex thought,'Ah! At last! Rest!' With most of the Tzentals gone, it was nice and relaxing. Neither Alex nor Tiger noticed that the 'girls'—under thirteen and above about three or four—were also 'gone. With the stars out—the moon wasn't up yet—and the flickering light of the fire, Alex just enjoyed the different setting.

Suddenly, eight of the girls—the younger set—ran up! They were all holding hands, and the older ones helped the little ones along. Dancing about the area, the girls screamed, shouted and laughed as they demonstrated and explained 'something' to the few left here! Alex, startled, snapped upright, and watched! The girls hopped about in strange patterns, bowed, twisted, jumped, waved their arms and loudly exclaimed 'whatever', and they laughed a lot! All the words were in their language—Tzental!

Tiger jumped up, and joined the 'wild-ones'! And Alex had no idea—none—what was going on! She stepped to Tiger, caught her arm, shouted, "What is all this about?" In frantic Tzental, Tiger began to explain—with a lot of hand and arm motions! "Tiger! You are speaking Tzental!" Without hesitation, Tiger instantly switched to 'rapid-fire' Spanish! "No, No Tiger! English! Speak English!" The two laughed—and the girls

still carried on with their merriment! Suddenly, Tiger grabbed Alex in a tight bearhug—around Alex's arms. Jerking Alex off her feet up and down several times—Tiger began, this time in English!

"Oh, Alex! These are the memories I was forgetting! This—what the girls just done—is what I had forgotten! This fun! The girls' experiences! My memories of my times! Here! My first time! Oh, Alex! I'm so happy! I'm so happy you brought me! I love you so much!" And Tiger kissed her all over her face, head and neck as she continued to hug and bounce Alex up and down! And the eight little girls gathered around Tiger! And they were still in a dither, all excited about 'something'!

Knowing that Tiger was very strong and had extreme stamina when she was excited—or pissed—Alex had an idea this wasn't going to stop! She wiggled one arm loose, wrapped it around Tiger's neck and squeezed very hard, and yelled into Tiger's ear, "Tiger! What is going on? Why are you and the girls so excited?" and, "Tiger, please let me go!" Tiger dropped

Alex, released her hug, but caught both sides of Alex's face, pulled close, face to face, Tiger said, "It is the little ones—the younger ones—first time!" "Tiger! First time—WHAT?"

Tiger backed off, but she still held both of Alex's hands, still face to face, she started. "Each year, when we came here—the first time is always the most exciting! Like sex, you always remember that'first time! Oh, how we had fun! Like these little girls, now!" Alex was still missing something, she snapped, "What is IT! IT! What is so much fun? Exciting?"

"We—they—go and visit with girls our—their—own age of the other 'tribes'—the different tribes. And demonstrate—perform—for the first time—for the youngest Tzentals—their ability to disappear! To the little girls, or, whoever, who can't disappear! WE Tzentals are the only ones! Part of the excitement is finding—locating—kids who have never seen this done before! Then, we—they—disappear! Oh, Alex, I now remember—I can feel it again! All those happy times—the excitement of being able to fool the 'unknowing-ones'! It is so exciting to startle a 'stranger' for his first time! And to know they can't do it! They can't vanish! Like us!"

"Alex, can you imagine?" "Not for sure, but it sounds like real fun! And I can realize it must be exciting to be really unique!" Then Alex hugged and kissed Tiger, all over her face! Alex knew she couldn't actually feel Tiger's thrill, the same excitement, but at least she could now understand the WHY for such inner emotions. And Alex suddenly had the urge to make love—serious love—to the happy Tiger—but she knew it was not the proper time—Tiger was caught up in the girls' experiences!

Catching hold of two of the smaller girls, Tiger began to speak to them in Tzental. The two smiled, and hopped up and down in place. The others backed away slightly—they had heard and understood Tiger's plans. Turning to Alex, in almost a whisper, in English, Tiger said "Please, act surprised." Alex nodded.

Tiger backed off, the two tiny girls stared into Alex's eyes—Alex stared back—and the two disappeared! Vanished! And Alex was truly surprised— she had never seen anyone except Tiger do this amazing feat! And to be done by such small, so young little girls, it was really a surprise! Alex threw up her hands and arms, shouted, "Where did they go! Oh, goodness! They are gone! Vanished into thin air!" And she frantically looked around, even behind the others. And everyone—except Alex—laughed and shouted cheers! And the two reappeared! Instantly! Before Alex's very eyes! Alex hugged the two and exclaimed about the girls unusual 'trick'.

This started 'show-time', with Tiger as director, the others—the 'first-timers'—as the 'stars' and Alex as the audience of one! They all had fun—especially Tiger, and even Alex!

Show over, the girls bunched together around Tiger. Alex figured it out—they were cooking up another 'field-trip', another search for new ones who had never seen them perform. And—it wasn't difficult to see—they were talking Tiger into going with them. Tiger turned to Alex, they s-tared, Alex understood, but declined to go, instead she said, "Tig, you go ahead with them! I'll just stay here and try to rest. Go! Go! Have fun!" The group, with Tiger as Leader, held hands and headed off into the darkness.

Pulling the two mats closer to the fire—she kept these side by side—Alex then pulled the blanket up against her back, over her shoulders and around her neck. She folded it around to her front then sat down on one of the mats. Staring at the flickering flames and the glowing coals, she realized that this entire trip—the expense, the effort, the time, and yes, even the trouble, all these—was worth that one brief moment. The moment when Tiger remembered her happy days as a little girl—having so much fun!

Remembering her happy times before the losing her parents, before running away, before her horrible time in Mazatlan, Tiger was once again—even if only for this brief time—a happy little girl again!

Alex batted her eyes as tears fought their way out. But she smiled, and gently wiped these on her sleeves. She gave a deep sigh of relief to know that Tiger—they—had found what she was really searching for—her childhood memories! And Alex remembered that snowy mid-afternoon of February the fifth back at Hidden Valley when Tiger had tried to explain her sadness. Now, right now, Alex understood the feelings in a little Maya girl's heart.

It was slow, peaceful around the fire, The Tzental speech was harmonious, a pleasure for Alex to hear even if she didn't understand. One of the men—about middle age—tapped Alex's foot as she lay beside the fire. He extended a bottle of clear liquid toward her. Rising, she took it, said, "Gracias", and motioned for him to have a seat. The two sat, crossed legs, stared at the fire and passed the bottle back and forth. No words, but a very comfortable feeling for her. Whatever was in the bottle was pretty 'stout', Alex shifted, placed her head on the man's thigh. He leaned back on his hands. As they stared up at the stars, he slowly began to explain the patterns. Only understanding some of the 'modern' names—at times, he used the 'modern' names in conjunction with the 'originals', the Maya names—she occasionally replied, "Si. Si."

The blackness surrounding the bright stars seemed to grow larger—it seemed to engulf her. As she floated in the blackness, among the sparkling stars, Alex dozed off into complete bliss, no painful pressures, no thoughts, and—no dreams.

"What!" Alex jerked upright as Mickey and Tiger shook her feet, "It is time to leave", Tiger responded. "Leave?" Alex realized she was still on the ground—the man with the bottle was gone. "Yes, you can drive us over there." Alex took Mickey's hand and he pulled her to her feet. Shivering, and rubbing one hip, Alex started, "Drive? I don't think—"

"I can drive! Alex, please?" he interrupted. "Sure thing, Kid, because—", she shivered and wobbled, she let it drop.

"Tiger, show Mickey how to switch on the interior lights!" Alex was on the rear seat "So I can see how to change clothes! White cotton panties or not, my little white ass is freezing!" As Mickey backed the wagon out, he calmly asked Tiger, "Does she always talk like that?" "No, sometimes much worse!"

They were soon at the nearby hills that had great thirty-foot high crosses on the summits. "These are called, Calvaries" Tiger said, then added, "I thought it would be better if we followed the musicians, the independent 'monkey-men' and the fireworks guys." It was a steep hill, the three stopped a few times to catch their breath. Soon the Pasiones— the political representatives and their entourages ran the banners to the top of San Pedro's Calvario. They watched as the men with the banners circled the drummers, walked among the people, and observed the 'monkeys' feeding the huge crosses. Rockets traced large arches high into the night sky, the booms reverberated off the surrounding mountains punctuating the din of the crowd and the moaning sounds of the Bolen-Chop song. Seeing the fireworks men and the musicians gather their gear up, the three joined the exodus to the next Calvario—The Calvario of San Sebastian, another ridge top. Again, rockets left sparking trails through the dark sky.

Musicians announced the arrival of the banners with long doleful cries of conch-shell trumpets. And the drummers came with their net-bound water drums. Soon the banner runners continued the endless, circling route thru the Dance of the Warriors.

The Trio watched for hours, at last, about five A.M., Alex gave up to total exhaustion and lay down. "There is something else—", as Tiger pulled

Alex to her feet,"—Romeria. While we're out, we should go there." Alex didn't argue, "Sure, might at well—while we're out."

It was just after sunrise as Mickey drove along a rutted dirt road that passed around the outskirts of Chamula. The three were belted by a cold uncomfortable wind as soon as they stepped from the station wagon. And they slowly walked through the strangest, most haunting place Alex had ever seen. Thirty feet high crosses lined across the ridge like lost sentinels.

They gingerly made their way among the graves with their small, knee-high crosses as Tiger described the Day of the Dead. The Day when thous sands of Chamulas came to Romeria to have a picnic and share their food with their dead. Tiger almost whispered—any louder felt out of place—"These are doors," she added, "The Chamulas believe these open on that day to let the dead ancestors come back to share food and drink with their descendants."

Back in the wagon, as Mickey headed for 'camp'—the other Tzentals—Alex climbed over into the rear—behind the rear seat—kicking off her shoes, and wiggling a nest among the soft Mitla bags, she curled into a fetal position. Abruptly, she raised up and pointed a stiff index finger toward Tiger, snapped, "Tiger! Don't wake me even if the friging sky is falling!" She lay down and fell asleep. Tiger said to Mickey, "See? I told you!"

After a period of silence, Mickey softly asked, "Tiger? She called you Tiger? what is that about?" She explained how she got the unusual nickname—the time when Mike caught her in the woods at Hidden Valley—the time when Mike's brothers teased him about 'catching a tiger'—the time when she and Mike fell in love. She closed with, "Mickey, you would really like Mike! He's just a big, Ole Boy! Always jolly! Takes most anything in an easy-going manner—even if it is 'kicking-ass'! And he's very good at that! He and Tom—Alex's Man—served together in the military! Between those two, they know so much!"

"Mike sounds like fun!" He paused, then, "You sound as if you're really hooked on Mike! Are you?" It was a direct question, one she had not expected. Cutting her eyes from Mickey, she twisted and stared out the side window—but she didn't see. For the first time in a while, she seriously thought about Mike—She and Mike—how much he loved her—how badly he wanted them to get married—how badly he wanted them to have kids—And how Alex had suggested a 'solution' to her 'excuses'—how Alex had directly asked 'Why not get married? Why not have kids?' And her love for Alex drifted into her mind—now she was confused.

"Tiger? Are you Ok?" Mickey broke her deep thoughts. "Yes, of course!" she snapped as she wiped tears from her eyes. Turning back to Mickey as she took a hold of his shoulder, she replied, "Yes, Mickey, I love Mike very, very much!"

"Why don't you have any kids? Yet?" She didn't reply. Casting a quick glance to her eyes he saw the answer in her eyes. She had that weird Maya 'flash'—when their normally 'puffy, sleepy' eye lids stretched tight, and the vertical Mongolian folds at the inside corners appeared to fold cross-ways, the wrong way, accenting their eyes into narrow, dark, shinning slits. One had to be not looking, or blind, to not see when a Maya was not pleased! To see when they were pissed! He didn't ask, he realized he had made a definite mistake! And he didn't look at her eyes again until much, much later—until their situation changed—changed a lot!

'Tap. Tap. Tap.' Alex slowly rolled toward the sound, and opened her eyes. It was Mickey tapping on the window of the station wagon. Waving a 'get-in', she said, "Buenos dias, Mi Amigo!" Setting down on the end of the rear seat, he said, "I'm sorry to wake you—" "No problem! I'm as fresh as a new born colt on a warm spring morning! What's up?" "Grand, the two helper girls and—Tiger—" "So! You've heard, have you?" "Yes, she told me the story about 'Tiger'" he smiled, continued, "They have gone to meet with the Shaman—the one that Grand wanted."

"That's great!" Alex exclaimed as she climbed over the rear of the seat, added. "Let's go meet the Man!" "Well—there's something else—", he hesitated. "Ok! What?" "He expects to be paid." "No problem, I've got money. Pasos Ok?" He didn't seem to respond favorable, he added "It is not money so much—it needs to mean something!" "Gold? I've got gold coins!" Mickey slipped a slight smile. She had another idea, snapped, "Maybe he had rather have real gold nuggets! Given to me by my Father! They mean a lot to me!" Mickey broke into a large grin, "Yes! I'm sure that would be very fine!" Alex nodded, then climbed back into the rear, located her small Mitla and got out her jewelry bag. Holding up one of the gold nugget bracelets she shook it as he watched, she remarked, "See? Real—right out of the river—gold nuggets!" Then she got out the other bracelet, shook it, added, "These should be enough!" As she stuffed one in one pocket, the other in another pocket, Mickey gave an inquiring glance. "Never start with everything you've got, Kid, he might go for just one!"

He nodded in understanding. With one arm around Mickey's back, she followed him through the thick crowd.

Walking on, Alex became interested in something she noticed, she asked, "Mickey? I keep seeing kids, even small ones, run around without adult supervision. And it doesn't seem to bother anyone. Is there a problem of the kids getting lost? There is a lot of people here—and it's such a huge affair!" Calmly, as he led her on, "Can't get lost—for long at least." "How's that possible? A lot of the 'little ones' act as if this is their first time here!"

"Look at their clothes—their colors." "So? They could still not know where they are—where their parents—or whoever—are!" "You do *see* that the really small ones are nearly always with—holding hands with—usually an older sister." "Yes—but—" she wasn't exactly convinced. Mickey realized this, added, "If they—the little ones, or their guides—can't find their way back, their clothes will!" "What? I don't understand!" He chuckled, continued, "Look at their clothes! Each tribe wears different clothes, and especially different colors! Even thou most of the tribes can't understand each others' language, we all know each others' clothes! Their colors! If the kids act—or just indicate they want to find THEIR people, the ones around them look at the kids' clothes, recognize their tribe, then the 'strangers' direct the kids—usually just point in a general direction—and the kids head that way! Talking is not really necessary! And, here, each tribe always set-up camp in about the same area—year after year. Someone is bound to know where a certain tribe is."

"So! That's the reason everyone from a certain village—a certain tribe—wear the same outfits—at least the same colors!" "Yes!" He pulled her on, "Kind of like color-coded!" Alex elaborated, "Like electrical resistors—regardless of the configuration or the physical size—the different colored bands always show the exact resistance of a certain one!" "Yes, I guess—don't know what you're talking about exactly—but—our colors show we are Tzentals!" "And that's why the girls insisted I wear their skirt and blouse! If I got lost, the 'strangers' could point me back to the other Tzentals!" "Right! Now you got it!"

They went on, and Alex continued—she was amazed with such a simple solution. "Like in some of our larger cities, the kids of different schools wear different jackets, or sweaters. One can see where they are from!" "Wouldn't know about that—never been to your cities—large or small!"

Working on through the crowd, Alex also 'saw' something explained that she had wondered about ever since first seeing Tiger's style of blouses—the loose tailed, pullovers. Here, she saw, for the first time, how the mothers gently, and naturally, lifted the loose tails of their blouses above their breasts as they let their baby suckle. In a lot of cases, the mothers casually dropped the loose tail down over the baby and continued with 'what-ever' she may be doing at the time. The process looked so comfortable—and natural—Alex wondered why all mothers didn't wear these style blouses!

HOTEL REAL

"Kyle! Kyle! Get up! It is mid morning!" Rudi shouted as he rocked the bed with one foot. Raising up, twisting around, Kyle placed his bare feet on the floor. "Oh! Oh" as he grabbed the sides of his head. "I've been thinking", Rudi started, "What exactly is out assignments? The Boss didn't say 'capture' them. Or arrest them—and he made it damn clear to NOT put out an APB!" Kyle slightly nodded. "We are to find out WHAT, that's the key word—WHAT—are they up to! That's it! What are they doing—or going to do. So we'll concentrate on that!" "We've got to find the bitches first" Kyle moaned.

"Kyle, I've been out walking this morning. And there is hardly anyone here! It looks as if only the people with jobs—ones that have to be here, are here. Doesn't that seem strange?" "What? Of course!" "So, I asked about, and the common reply was—Chamula!" Kyle jumped up, pointed a finger at Rudi, snapped, "Of course! It's early March! The Grand Festival, the Running Thing! In Chamula!"

As the two Agents quickly got their gear together, Rudi remarked, "Game Plan! We find the old station wagon, 'bug' it with a GPS tracking transmitter, and we follow it! We'll not even have to get close to them!" "Them? You mean Alex! That little gal must have been a 'butch-bitch' D.I. in the damn Marines!" "Maybe—there sure is more to her than what meets the eye!"

After checking out, getting their bags in the car, and as Kyle pulled out of the hotel parking lot, he casually mentioned, "Sorry about the binge" then he hesitated, and as to himself, "I should have blown that CIA bastard's brains out the first time he mentioned his plans."

SAN JUAN CHAMULA

It didn't take the two Agents nearly as long as they had anticipated. "It's attached to the underside of the rear floor—just behind the gas tank. Drive off a distance, I'll check our reception" Rudi remarked as he got back in the car. They moved to another small group camped several hundred yards or so away from the station wagon—it was still in sight. "Ok! It's working just fine. This is going to make things much easier. Regardless where the wagon goes, by checking our own location with a GPS, we'll know which way to go to find the wagon." "Alex! We've got your little ass now!" Kyle exclaimed. Being able to see the wagon, they watched for any unusual swaps of packages or 'things' that might be, as Alex had said, 'very old and lost for a very long time.'

While at the de-staging area for the Runners, among the yelling, screaming, jumping, slapping each other, Alex, Tiger, Mickey and Dom Louise—the Shaman—they all played 'Make-a-Deal'. GrandMaMa and her two helpers had already headed back to camp. Dom Louise undressed from one odd, colorful costume and began to put another odd, colorful outfit on. He even swapped 'hats'—really unusual, comical caps. When down to his loose, baggy, diapers, Alex noticed that he appeared as hard—and as knotty—as an old hickory tree. She could only guess his age as very old'! But that didn't seem to matter—he wasn't even breathing hard!

Louise finally seemed to have a clear understanding of what would be necessary, the 'dealing' came down to just he and Alex. He settled—and appeared pleased—for one of her bracelets. With his large bag of 'whatever', he indicated for them to go to Alex's vehicle—he had decided they would drive over to the back side of San Pedro's Calvario. There, was a 'pil-na' that could be used for the ritual. As they made their way through the crowd, Alex asked Tiger, "What's a 'pil-na' anyway!" "A 'pil-na'?", then she hesitated. Alex wondered, and was on the verge of changing her statement to—'You don't have a clue, do you?' when Tiger began. "A 'pilna' is a portal, basically. But the word, the name, is more commonly used by 'your' people to represent the little sanctuary buildings, then 'pil-na' means 'underground house'—or—in some cases, these are called 'kunil'—'bewitching place'."

Alex was almost sorry she asked! "Whoa! Back-up! You said 'portal'—like a door? Or doorway? To the inside of a building?" Tiger explained more, "No Silly! An opening into the Maya Worlds! The Upperworld, the Otherworld—and the Underworld, which you don't even want to

HEAR about!" "Why?" Alex asked anyway! "The Underworld? That's where the Bad Demons live!" "There are Good Demons?" "Of course! They're our friends! They guide us when we ask!" "Ok! Back to the three Maya Worlds—" Tiger picked it up, continued, "Well—it is something similar to your—Heaven, Earth—and Hell. Except! We can go and come back!"

"That is what the—my—ritual will be all about! I'll travel to the Otherworld, see what happened—or—even what was said, or even thought! Back to a long, long time ago!""And if things go right, you will find out where the Codex is—now—Right?" Alex asked. "Yes", Tiger didn't smile—she wasn't joking. Alex studied Tiger's serious—almost sad—expression. But Alex didn't ask, 'What if things do NOT go right?' And she surely couldn't ask the Shaman—he only spoke Tzental!

As Rudi watched the station wagon with a pair of light-gathering field glasses, he said, "They're back—no unusual items—I wonder who the skinny old man is?" "Probably a Witch-doctor!" Kyle replied, added, "He may be asking Alex for some new tricks!" They chuckled, Rudi added, "Or the Maya gal how she flies away!"

When Mickey drove toward the three hills, Kyle followed, but at a discrete distance. Seeing the station wagon come to a halt, he turned in a different direction, then swung back and parked. The two Agents, with the binoculars could see what was going on.

The four walked the fifty or so feet to the small stone building—the 'pil-na'. It was a raised floor about eight feet square. The building had a rear wall and two end walls. These were only about five feet tall. The flat roof—like all the other parts—was stone—it was flush with the three walls, but extended forward enough to cover the entire floor.

Around the edges of the roof were badly eroded carvings. Inside the walls, was a raised—about only one foot high—stone slab. It was about three feet wide. The complete scene reminded Alex too much of a burial vault. Alex glanced just in time to see the sun drop below the surrounding mountains.

Dom Louise—with a small bowl from his bag—started a tiny fire—with tiny sticks, also from his bag—in the bowl. Alex and Mickey sat down on two small boulders close-by and remained silent as they watched. At the edge of the slab, Tiger turned, and sat down on it. Louise quickly removed her sandals and placed these to one side. He then poured some liquid in a ceramic cup and heated it over the flames from the bowl. Tiger lay down, flat on her back.

At first, when sipping from the cup, Tiger raised up, put her hand on Louise's hand—he held the cup, but, soon, he had to lift her head and more or less pour the liquid into her mouth. Like a cat after a bird, Alex slipped from her perch, crawled slowly on hands and knees to where she could see Tiger in the dim light.

In the beginning, Tiger appeared to be in a relaxed sleep, but with her eyes open. Suddenly, her eyes snapped shut, and her entire body became rigid—only her heels and the back of her head touched the slab! Then relaxed again. Another rigid spell! Then, for a while, she appeared to sleep peacefully. Slowly at first, her body began to have spasms. These became faster and faster, more and more violent! In one explosive moment, she showed all the physical signs of a scream of extreme terror! Great terror! Mouth wide open! Eyes snapped wide open! Fists in tight balls! Arms frayed wildly! Legs and feet rigid! Except she made no sound!

Tiger, with her eyes closed again, fell into a relaxed slow wiggle—her entire body, in a sensual wiggling motion. She even smiled! With a few short jerks of her head—from side to side, Alex thought she had multi-orgasms! Even Alex smiled as she also felt a tinge of excitement inside! Then Tiger appeared to be asleep—relaxed, with not a smile, but an expression of satisfaction—and comfort. And she remained this way for over a hour.

From the time Tiger sat down, and there after, the Shaman prayed in the low, murmurous Tzental language. After the drink, he sat crossed-legged, his eyes tightly shut, and maintained a slow, even rocking motion with his entire torso, his hands clasped tightly together.

Alex slowly rolled to one side, doubled into a fetal position but she never stopped staring at Tiger. Or stopped praying for her friend, her lover, her 'Baby Sister'.

Silently, the two Agents passed the light-gathering binoculars back and forth. No smart remarks, no teases, no jokes as they watched the ritual at the bottom of the Calvario. Occasional, Rudi wiped his eyes.

At first, it seemed to be a simple cough, and a single gasp, but it got much worst! Very rapidly! Tiger was gasping for breath—any breath! For her life! She was still in the state of being unconscious—unable to rise up even. But the muscles in her face and neck contracted, the arteries at her throat, the veins in her face extended, and still only a hollow gasp. The Shaman jumped up, pointed to Alex and shouted a few words! Swiftly Mickey dashed to between Alex and Dom Louise, dropped to his knees, cried out to her, "He asked if you love her!" "Yes! Of course!" The Shaman fired more words, Mickey translated "He said to go to her—talk her back! She is stuck in the White Light! Beg her to return to her world! Don't stay in the White Light! It is not her time to stay!" Mickey jerked Alex to her feet, and shoved her to Tiger!

She rubbed Tiger's face, sweetly spoke the words in her ears and kissed her about the face, but Tiger continued to gasp for air. Feeling Tiger's pulse—it was faint and getting weaker—Alex knew she had to hurry! Opening Tiger's mouth, feeling her tongue to be sure it wasn't folded back, Alex began mouth to mouth resuscitation. Alex would blow, but Tiger continued to only gasp. Taking as deep breaths as possible, Alex blew as hard as she could. Alex felt her skin—she was cold. "Mickey! Come rub her feet, her legs, her belly! Her blood is not circulating!"

The two worked frantically! The Shaman was standing, pacing back and forth across the small floor, his arms—hands clasped together—extended upward. He prayed to the Darkness above in a moaning, soulful voice!

Alex had no idea what the Shaman was saying or what he was asking for, but unconsciously she prayed—in all the old forms she had been forced to learn—and she asked The Lord for all the help possible! Most of this was not done verbally—she apologized—but her mouth was just a little too busy! But, as she gasped herself, she did manage one, she screamed, "Light! If we just had light! Please God? Light?"

Rudi, with the field glasses at his eyes, jerked more upright, closer to the windshield, "There is something wrong! Over there—something has happened!" Kyle jerked the glasses, looked, shouted "Let's go! Maybe we can help!" Rudi roughly grabbed Kyle's arm, snapped, "No! We—our sudden approach—would probably scare them! Do more harm than good! Besides, it looks as if the three are doing all that is possible!" Kyle snatched his arm loose, replied, "You're more than likely right—and you may be wrong!" He started the engine, switched on the headlights, and drove to the 'pil-na'. He aimed for a spot about fifty feet in front of the open side of the small building. There, he swung right and aimed the bright headlights directly on Alex and Tiger. Then he followed Rudi's advice—leaving the lights on, he remained in the car with Rudi. They waited.

Without hesitation, Alex hopped up and straddled Tiger's hips and gave mighty shoves to below her ribcage—pushed as hard as possible to where she hoped the diaphragm was. Then she rocked back on her toes and pushed upward under Tiger's armpits as hard as possible. And Alex repeated this, over and over—she had no idea for how long.

Suddenly, Tiger didn't gasp! She inhaled deeply, paused and then exhaled! Alex twisted off Tiger, and held off with the resuscitation effort. Soon Tiger was breathing in a slow—almost normal—fashion.

Slowly opening her eyes, Tiger looked into Alex's, slightly smiled, asked, "Alex? Is that you?" Alex kissed her all about her face and head, cried, with many tears, "Yes—It is!"

"Why did you make me come back? It was so peaceful—I wanted to stay so badly!" "Kid! I'm selfish! I want you for myself!" Alex cried a chuckle, added, "Besides! You are the only one that knows where the damn Codex is!" They hugged and kissed. Mickey stopped rubbing her legs. The Shaman stopped praying. And the two Agents sighed, wiped their brows and eyes as Kyle backed the car away, swung a half circle and slowly drove away.

As the scene returned to darkness, Alex never knew who was in the car—the car with the bright lights.

CHAPTER 15

It was almost midnight as Mickey pulled between the trucks and parked. They offered Dom Louise 'something' to eat—whatever was still available—and asked if he would spend the rest of the night with them. These are two of the many requirements of being Maya. He declined, said he still had other things to do. He walked off into the darkness.

As the three got a bite to eat, and Alex bought a six-pack of bottled beer from a 'roving vendor', the two Agents watched from their car. "Rudi, this isn't making much sense! Us setting here in the dark, watching a monitor! Let's head for our nice room at the Real, move our receiver in, and take shifts watching it for any movement. And get some grub, something to drink and lie on our comfortable beds!" "That sounds perfectly alright with me! Head out, Amigo!" Kyle drove away.

It had been decided that Tiger needed all the rest she could get. Setting in the wagon—Mickey up front, Alex and Tiger in the rear seat—Tiger was ready to give her account of her trip to the Otherworld. And what she understood about the Codex's history—and locations at different times. "Alex, you should take notes—in case something happens to me before—", she let it trail off. Alex dug around, located her 'little black-book', a pencil, and a flashlight which she laid in her lap. "Ok, I'm ready!" Tiger leaned over against the side window, propped her feet up on the rear of the front seat's back—and started.

"The drink was mostly Balche, with a few other herbs—I'm not sure what. At first, I felt as if I was just drunk. But, then, it was as if my brain suddenly opened—opened to everything! I was shocked when I saw the Vision Serpent! With his one, large, shining eye! I tried to get away even!

But I knew I had to confront him! And I was terrified when he opened his mouth! It was so large! And—and—I realized that the old tales were really true! He really was going to swallow me! I screamed and screamed!" She took a sip of beer, waited for a few moments.

She leaned to Mickey, pushed his face away from them said, "Mickey! You're too young for this! Close your ears!" Tiger laughingly commanded. He placed his hands over his ears—but not so as he couldn't still listen. Tiger slipped close to Alex, put one arm around her neck, placed her mouth close to Alex's ear, softly started, "Alex, you will not believe this—you can't believe it without having experienced it." In the dim glare from the flashlight, Alex could see Tiger's smile. "The Serpent stuck his tongue in my mouth. Not just in—but down through my mouth—down my throat—and completely filled my insides—all my insides! Full! And it— **his tongue—his** entire mouth was dripping, oozing with white, thick, semen!"

Alex quickly questioned, "Semen? Like—men's semen?" "Yes! All over! All inside me—not just my mouth like—well, you know. Then his mouth—dripping, flooding semen, opened! And opened! And he drew me into his mouth with his tongue! It swelled, pumped, drew, sucked, swelled so big! Oh! Oh!" She stopped, took another sip, calmly added, "I climaxed—over and over! Everything—me, it, inside me, all over my body." She made a lot of motions with both her hands then, "Me, inside him! All hot, slick, and slimy!" Tiger hugged Alex and wiggled her entire body tightly against Alex, cooed, "Oh, Honey, it was so thrilling, exciting, it makes me ache all inside, down there." The two held the embrace as they chuckled while Tiger went through a brief series of spastic quivers—then fell limp.

They chuckled again, Tiger straightened up, pulled Mickey's hand from his ear, said, "Ok, you can stop straining! You can hear the rest!" He just smiled at her and nodded. She started again, "When I thought I would just die from—my excitement, there was a sudden, explosive bright flash of red! Bright red! Blood red! Not a substance—just the COLOR of red! And, at once, I was among the clouds—No, I was a part of the clouds! White, swirling, misty, floating clouds. I didn't have a body—nothing! It was only my consciousness! I could think, I could receive 'messages'—not words, there wasn't any sound, only 'messages' back and forth—I could not speak, but I could convey 'messages ¹, and ask questions in a fashion. By thinking the 'message'!"

"I floated, then I realized I was at Palenque! The Priests, because they had heard about what the White Invaders were doing—burning all the Codexs— they, the Priests, had already decided to hide THE Codex when I was there!" She took a break from her account, said, "Alex, do you remember Nat saying that she wondered why 'The Lost Codex of Palenque' was always referred to as 'THE'—never 'A', or 'ONE'—always 'THE' Codex?" "I think so, it didn't seem very important when she mentioned it. Why?" "I now know why! The Priests were explaining it when I was there—well, as a cloud, air, or whatever!"

"Ok, why is it always specifically referred to as 'THE' Codex?" "Get this! It is what makes 'The' Codex so valuable! So important! Because it was—or still is—the only one that is about the real, true physical history of the Maya's journey into this—This! Part of the world! Not Maya's belief's— -tale's—Gods—or anything else! Just—only-their history of coming here! To Central America! And THE Codex was never exposed, discussed, or shown to the people! Their own people! It was, as we would say today, 'Top Secret'! Don't you see?" "Man! That's what every archaeologist has been wanting since—well—since John Lloyd Stephens wrote his books! His travels! And to think, we may actually get THE Codex!" The three clicked their beer bottles together and toasted their drinks!

They calmed down, Tiger returned to her tale. "As a part of the clouds, I floated forward in time. Between different time periods, I was always just a cloud. Next, The Codex was being buried at Toning—that's about forty or fifty K's south of Palenque. It stayed there for many years. I floated, then it was buried HERE! Right where we were tonight! Close to the 'pil-na'! It stayed there until two white men—not at the same time, but individually- —got too close to finding it. These men were S. G. Morley, my so-called Grandfather! And Franz Blom!"

"I floated again, then I was at a white, light blue, fast flowing river. Many low water falls, very beautiful, but strange scene. It was near Palenque! Almost back home! This river ended with the last, and very high, falls into an even larger river that ran crossways!" Anxious, Alex asked, "You know this river?" "Yes, it is the Agua Azul! It falls into the Tulija River!" Tiger continued, "Across the first river, the Agua Azul and around a knoll, or hill, or a cliff, there is a small cave. Very small, only large enough for an averaged sized man to crawl inside. Inside, there is an unusual rock—a cover—a door—I can't describe it, but I'll know it where I see—or—feel it. I have to be the one so I can recognize it! The Codex is behind 'that'- whatever 'it' is!"

Tiger waited, finished the beer,then in a very serious tone, said, "Things changed—more to like a dream—I was a person again, and you were there. I had it in my hand—I handed it to you—I slipped and fell—fell into the big river far below. I drown—I died in the river." She stopped. Alex thought, 'that was all the gasping for breath! Tiger fighting for her life!' "Then I was at the White Light, not wanting to return!" "No, Tiger, you didn't drown. You didn't die. You did come back!" They hugged as Tiger cried, "Oh, Alex, it was so beautiful—so peaceful, so pleasant. But the communications—not words, not voices—kept saying, 'Come back! Come back!' And from the opposite direction, 'it' communicated, 'Go back! Go back! It is not your time! You must return!" As the two hugged, kissed and cried together, Mickey quietly slipped out, walked into the darkness. The two cried themselves to sleep in each others' arms.

A while later Alex was routed when Mickey got back in the front and lay down. Gently, Alex got Tiger into a more comfortable position, then crawled over to the rear, got her lap-top computer and slipped outside. It was only a short time before sunrise as she E-mailed Nat at Hidden Valley. The message was brief: 'Background info completed. Acquisition should follow soon. Love BB&T'

HIDDEN VALLEY

It was early morning as Arnie and Jim sat at the breakfast table with their first cup of coffee. Tom and Mike were back on the road. Nat walked in with her coffee cup and a hard copy of Alex's E-mail received only a

few minutes before. She slowly placed the paper to the center of the small table then waited. They read it, jumped up, clicked cups as Arnie shouted, "I knew they could do it!" "I'll get in touch with the Big Guys, I know they will love this news!" Nat said as she headed back to her computer.

SAN JUAN CHAMULA

Back at Chamula, Kyle and Rudi were parked where they could observe—with field glasses—the activities around Alex's station wagon. Thinking their quary might move this morning, the two Agents had a early breakfast at the Hotel Real and drove over to Chamula. "I wonder what little Alex is up to—she has the boy and Tiger off from the others—looks as if she's explaining something to them", Rudi remarked to Kyle. Kyle had slipped down, and leaned against the driver's side window, "No telling—", he muttered. "There they go, Alex is leading her two prodigies into the crowd—headed for the plaza area." "How's she dressed?" Kyle asked without moving. "Warmer—jeans, heavy shirt and I saw her put on an insulated jacket", Rudi lowered the binoculars, added, "You know, with Alex's size and her short cut hair, dressed like she is today, she could easily pass for a small guy—maybe even a boy." Kyle chuckled then replied "Yes, with her pear sized breasts—those sure wouldn't give her away", he wavered, then continued, "Hell! Around here, all the crazy outfits, with one of those carved wooden mask, she could pass for a large monkey!"

About to nod-off—it had been over an hour of nothing—Rudi patted Kyle's knee, said, "Get up! Let's walk to the plaza and watch the races! I've never seen that! Besides, that wagon isn't going anywhere!"

Outside and stretched, they headed toward the huge crowd, then forced their way through it. They stopped where they could see the walled municipal building,and the path,the circuit of the Runners. This was sprinkled with pine brows and corn husks.

The huge thundering pack—it was about twenty men abreast—the banner carriers led the others round the corner. Rudi estimated the 'racing-group' was several hundred men—these followed the banner carriers, their Leaders. The banners had shafts of wood—round, and about fifteen feet long, and large flags—topped with a bundle of ribbons. The tips—spear points—were metal and appeared to be real silver. The leaders pumped the banners up and down, and occasionally touched tips with each other. At first, they ran clockwise, around and around the large plaza area. Suddenly, the leaders stopped, and reversed their direction—back through the group! The many followers flowed behind them. This direction only lasted for one lap! Then they reversed again, ran clockwise again.

"This obviously isn't a race of speed, is it?" Rudi asked, shouting to be heard over the thunderous roar of the crowd. "No! It's showmanship! To show their prowess in battle! War-like stuff! To win the passion—the approval—of the spectators!" "You mean past battles—past wars?" "Not necessarily! It is mainly a show of opposition against organized government! That's why they run around the Government Buildings here!" "And the reversal of direction?" "That was symbolic of a brief retreat! And, then another attack! Watch closely when they stop in front of the main entrance to the building! That will be a display of the final close-hand battle!"

The runners stopped, the leaders—the banner carriers—approached the wall and jabbed their 'spears' over it—many times—as they screamed in awesome sounds! "I see what you mean—the final thrusts!" Rudi waited, then asked, "But why against their own government?" "Ha! Not THEIR government! They've never been convinced that the Mexican Government ever exists! They believe they are Maya first, Chiapians next! Mexicans? Never!"

This race over—there would be many more—the runners filed from the open 'race-track', the crowd parted, they went on to a 'de-staging' area.

"And Condor? Was he a wise old Chiapian, strong in the old independent beliefs?" "No! Not at all! Condor was in his thirties when we—our troops—chased him. Oh, he was wise alright! College educated—Political Science, History, Law—the works! Independence? No, that wasn't his main point for his efforts! He knew that the Chiapians believed—still do—they were, and had always been, and would always be independent!" "Ok, but how did he win backing for an up-rising?"

"It was because of the land reform law that were written into the new Constitution after the country's revolution of—1924?—1927? I can't remember the exact year." "Land reform laws? I thought that went smoothly, it didn't turn out so good—but the transition was relatively bloodless." "Yes, for most of the country—where there were large tracts owned by few wealthy owners. And a lot of people—families—living at haciendas, farms, cattle ranches, giving the ownership to the residents, the people, taking it from the wealthy few, was relatively simple. The people could be easily identified!"

"But not here—Chiapas", Rudi interjected, "I can see, here, in Chiapas, the people 'appear' from the jungle, the 'cracks' in these mountains—they just show up along the roads!" "Right! And to split the large land holdings up and transfer the legal titles to 'them'—Who? It was impossible to say who got what! Only THEY knew where they actually lived. But—their great savior, 'Senor Condor', failed to explain that to his beloved followers! He kept pumping, we want our land! We want the titles to 'our' land! And that's how he got the people's support!" Kyle hesitated, then, "He had the right point—but it just couldn't be done!" "Legally, he was right—but it was impossible to identify the 'residents'", Rudi agreed with Kyle's remark.

Kyle commented as the next group of about two hundred men lined up for the next race, "Let's wander around, see if we can bump into Alex and her two 'partners-in-crime', and find a healthy slug of aguardiente." "Crime? That's the problem with Alex! So far, except for breaking every traffic law on the books, she hasn't committed a crime!" Rudi replied. "And spend money as if it came from a bottomless pit!" "It does." Rudi casually remarked. "It 'does' what?" "Oh, didn't I tell you? Tony—in Central Data punched around, found out our little Alex is a multimillionairess! Her own personal wealth—most all in gold holdings! And, besides that, she owns part of a fast rising food distribution company. With the potential of another pile of money!" Kyle waited then said, "Maybe we should stop being so rough on little Alex?" "Yea right!" as Rudi slapped Kyle's shoulder.

A few hours before sunset, as Kyle and Rudi sat in the car, they saw Alex, Tiger and Mickey when the three returned to the station wagon. Rudi remarked. "Well! Well! Looks like Alex went off and got tanked-up!" "What?" as Kyle took the field glasses, then he saw that Tiger—on one side—and Mickey—on the other side—were practically holding Alex up. Lowering the binoculars, Kyle asked, "Wonder what that's all about?" The two Agents had not a clue, and until well after dark, they didn't see any other action from the three in the wagon. Kyle started the engine, and headed for San Cris and the Hotel Real.

That night, in their room as they watched the un-changing signal on the receiver, they began to wonder if they were on a 'wild-goose' chase.

Darkness filled the valley, the temperature of the thin air plummeted rapidly and a light snow began to fall. The three sat in the station wagon, Mickey in the front—he leaned over toward the rear as he listened and watched. Alex had finished, she sobbed and sniffed as Tiger hugged her tightly around her shoulders and head. Lightly stroking Alex's hair and back, Tiger rocked and soothed Alex. Alex lapsed into a serious chill, with low moans and mumbles.

Mickey decided Tiger had been right yesterday—there were things he didn't need to hear. He started to get out, but Tiger snapped, "Not yet! I'll get Alex's purse, take out what money you think it will take to buy three blankets! Go find the Tzotzils and buy three, soft, fuzzy cotton ones—not wool! Alex doesn't like scratchy material! Their—the Tzotzil—red colors come the closest to matching 'our' reds. None of our people would understand if you showed up with Kakchi's bright blue blankets! Ok?"

"Sure, I think the Tzolzils are camped over there", he pointed. "And hurry, OK?" "Of course! She looks as if she needs it", as he looked at Alex, who was still shaking with the 'unusual' chill.

With a handful of bills, Mickey quietly slipped out into the darkness filled with small flickering campfires spread about the entire valley of Chamula. Under the low, overcast snow clouds, these lights reflected off the bottom and through the falling snow.

As soon as Mickey returned with the three blankets—he didn't have any trouble locating and buying from the Tzolzil tribe—Tiger leveled out the things in the rear. Helping Alex into the rear, she then crawled over and spread two of the blankets over themselves. Mickey curled up in the third one on the rear seat and immediately fell asleep.

After the two women snuggled tightly together, Alex's chill soon subsided and her sobs stopped. Tiger continued to soothe and rub Alex. They slowly, gently, began to kiss each other. In just above a whisper, "Tig—my jeans are too tight to be comfortable, please help me get them off." And Alex kicked off her shoes. They did, and while moving about under the blankets, Tiger removed her heavy full skirt and her delicate 'dress' blouse.

Alex cooed as she nuzzled into Tiger's large breasts while Tiger eased off Alex's jacket and shirt. With their naked bodies tightly pressed together and the blankets pulled snug around them, they were warm and comfortable—the two soon fell asleep.

Faintly hearing sounds outside the wagon, Alex twisted her left wrist close to her eyes. Depressing the light switch on her watch, she saw it was close to 4A.M. Uncovering and raising her head, she saw that several of the women had started cooking the early meal of the day. And she spotted a steaming pot of coffee at the edge of the small cook fire.

Feeling under the blankets, Alex located her tennis shoes, and slipped these on. Easing out the side of the blankets, she pulled the top one off and wrapped it tightly around her naked body, and up around the back of her neck and head. Tiger only slightly stirred as Alex pushed the other blanket tight against Tiger's body and head.

Opening the rear hatch, Alex climbed out and closed it back. Joining the women at the fire, they said their 'good-mornings', Alex in Spanish, the others in Tzental. One of the younger 'trainee' cooks gave Alex a cup of hot coffee. Fingering the edge of Alex's blanket, one of the older women said 'something' in Tzental that contained the word 'Tzotzil' in her statement. Smiling at Alex the younger one said, "She's saying, 'Your Tzotzil blanket is very pretty'." The younger one had related to Alex in English. "Thank you both!" Alex smiled back—in English. Watching the women go about their routines, Alex was amazed and she wondered—'Each with her own routine, going through her actions swiftly and smoothly. And no one getting in another's way. A few older women—a few much younger (she guessed to be only thirteen or older—the age of womanhood, or, whenever they started their 'period', which ever came first) women, watching and picking up on what needed to be done. And the most amazing thing, not a word spoken. When one of the 'trainees' finished filling several of the tortillas with the thick, rich, re-fried bean mix, she placed these on a piece of heavy, brown paper and handed it to Alex as she smiled. Alex nodded and smiled back. (It is permissible for women to eat while cooking, provided none of the men are up yet, or have left the area.

With the hot tacos and the cup of coffee, Alex went back to 'Betsy' and opened the tailgate. Placing the tacos to one side, she gently shook Tiger's foot, and said, "Tiger—Tiger—Wake up, we need to talk!" Uncovering her head, Tiger raised, and rubbed her eyes as she looked to Alex. "Are you feeling better?" she asked after their greetings. "Yes, I feel great as a matter of fact!" As Alex ate one of the hearty tacos she added, "Get some coffee, whatever— we need to talk about what and when—we're going to do next." Tiger pulled on the blanket, slid out then returning soon to the open tailgate, she sat down next to Alex. She had tacos and a cup of hot coffee also. The two looked like what they were—two Indian squaws!

"Do you think we have all the information concerning the Codex that is possible? Here? From your people?" Alex calmly asked as Tiger ate and sipped. "Yes", she managed between bites. "Do you want to stay and visit with your people longer? I guess there's no real hurry—we could—" Alex let it drop. Tiger thought, then replied, "No—I saw what I really came to see—that my parents were properly buried, in a proper place—, and to see if Mickey was still alive, and back at 'Ama'. And to see how the rest, the ones still alive were doing. They have a long, slow road to recover the lost of their male population—if that is even possible. Did you notice the large field across the highway from the village?" "Not much, why?" "That entire area should be alive with men and boys, cultivating, planting, and working the water system for the plants—but there wasn't a thing going on over there—nothing—just not enough men, boys—I can't think of a thing we, you and I, can do about that. Well, not now anyway. I guess we may as well leave—whenever you want to." Alex leaned close, wiped the tears from Tiger's cheeks, and gently said, "Tiger, I'm so sorry, but you're probably right. It is time to leave."

Hearing the two talk, Mickey roused up, removed the blanket and stepped out into the cool morning air. He joined the two, took Tiger's cup, had a sip then asked, "What's this talk about leaving? I thought you two came for a visit—or to stay." Alex decided it was time to fill Mickey in on why they were really here. And to ask if he wanted to join-up with them!

This took a while, and it ended with him saying, "Sure! Sounds exciting! Besides, there's not much to do around 'Ama' without enough men to work the fields—", he let it drop as he shook hands with Alex, then Tiger. "Ok! The quicker the better!" Alex quipped as she began find her clothes scattered among the blankets. And she handed Tiger her skirt and blouse. But she threw these to one side and quickly located her traveling jeans, her loose shirt and her tennis shoes—it was 'back-on-the-road' for the two!

Locating her little black book, and a pen, Alex stuck these in her jacket—she wanted to write some notes before it was 'too late'. Quick good-bys, the three left Chamula about an hour before sunrise. Alex began to jot down her notes about yesterday as Mickey headed for the highway. Tiger sat up-front, Alex half sat, half lay in the rear seat—with a blanket pulled over her legs.

Returning to San Cris, Mickey picked up route 190 southeast for a short distance, then turned off onto route 199 and headed northeast toward Ocosingo. And Palenque.

SAN CRIS HOTEL REAL

After a slow, but early—about an hour before sunrise—breakfast, the two Agents returned to their room. Inside, Rudi went directly to the receiver and looked. The numbers—the coordinates being received from the transmitter hidden under Alex's wagon were rapidly changing! Almost too fast to read! He snapped, "They're on the move!" "Well! I'll be damn! Finally!" Kyle exclaimed. "You think we should carry all our gear? Check out?" "Yes! I've got a hunch they are changing locations!"

As Kyle got their stuff, Rudi jotted down one set of numbers. Waiting a few nimutes, he captured another set. "They're heading northeast." Kyle stopped his actions, thought, then said, "There's only one road—highway—that heads in that direction from San Cris." And he knew they had returned to route 190 to take it. "That's route 199 to Ocosingo. From there, it swings more northward, and goes on to Palenque!"

At hearing the name Palenque, Rudi quickly stood, stepped to face Kyle. He started, "Kyle, old buddy, I haven't mentioned this earlier—I wanted to see more positive indications first. I asked Tony—with his mighty machines—to check for anything, any story, any info, about anything, 'old, and lost for a very long time' that could be related to Chiapas. Remember Alex's words, 'old and lost for a long time?'" "Yes, well?" "Tony's computer searches led to only one item!" "Ok, what!" "The Lost Codex of Palenque!"

The two sat down, almost in shock. Rudi spoke first, "And, now, they are headed toward Palenque." "Rudi, I'll bet you one month's pay—Alex is intending to retrieve that book!" "You'll not get a bet from me! She's after 'The Lost Codex of Palenque'!" Now, they rushed!

As 'Betsy' dropped from the high plateau, the curves became tighter, the descent steeper. They were running for the tops of the clouds, and Mickey worked harder and harder. He slowed because a section of the roadway— maybe two hundred feet long—had dropped about two feet below its original level. Rocks the size of basketballs had rolled down on the road. On a ways, he slowed, eased forward—half of the road had fallen into the canyon hundreds of feet down!

The mountains began a slow change, from the large rounded, to craggy with more sharp peaks and more cliffs. The surrounding canyons became narrower, steeper and much more rugged. They climbed steeply back into the 'old' rounded mountains again. Above the clouds again, Alex could only vaguely see the small villages below in the shadows of the clouds. The 'highway' changed to hard packed limestone as they began another descent. The vegetation got thicker and more lush, a striking dark green.

They passed over a ridge and headed down to Ocosingo. Approaching the side road—it turned right—into Ocosingo, Alex suggested that they stop there—at the bus station—use their restrooms, get a snack and drinks. They did, and while finishing the drinks—one can't carry off the bottles, and most all drinks are in glass bottles—Alex asked Tiger, "I thought you said the road from the Pacific to Tuxtla was the WORST!" "No, I said it was the WORST highway! This is an unpaved road!" The three laughed as Alex conceded, "Ok! You win on a technicality'"

It was a lot warmer at 'Oco' and as Alex slowly walked toward the wagon, she removed her jacket. Thinking the hardest part was over, she asked, "Mickey, you want me to drive for a spell?" He jumped at the offer, "Gladly! My arms have about had it!" Alex walked slower and slower as she approached the car. She was looking around at the scene—it was beautiful to her. Instead of getting in, she turned her back to the front fender, and hopped her bottom up and sat there. And she tossed her jacket on top of the hood.

At first, Tiger looked at Alex. Then she began to follow Alex's sweeping view of the valley. "Alex, you are not thinking what I think you are?" "Tiger! Look! This entire valley is just gorgeous! Beautiful! Look at that lush grass! One could put ten cows per acre, and they wouldn't run out of food! And—and—that lake! Unlimited water! It is splendid! And not even a single building close to it! And feel", she waved her arms around, "It is so warm here! And completely surrounded by high mountains, beautiful, rugged mountains! With timber at the lower levels! And this valley, none of the problems of being in the mountains! It is ideal!" Alex made a sweep with one arm, added, "Say—That thousand acres over there", she pointed a stiff finger, slowly moved it toward one side, continued, "down to the lake—out into the lake—An airstrip over there! A large home there! And a 'Recluse Lodge' there! ETC! ETC!" as she raised both hands and arms above her head. "Let's go, we still have a rough trip ahead," Tiger said, then, "Before you cook up another business deal!"

Alex hopped down, grabbed up her jacket and as she headed for the driver's door, she pointed a stiff index finger at Tiger, snapped, "Remember our talk about you and Mike? Living down here? Just keep this place in mind! Ok?" "Ok! I'll think about it!" then she threw Alex a kiss.

Leaving Ocosingo, they dropped to a river surrounded by thick jungle. There was an attractive natural water-slide in the river. "Well! We finally made it to the 'jungles of Chiapas!" Alex exclaimed. The other two didn't comment—they knew what was ahead! After only a few miles of the road following the river, it suddenly turned up! Ocosingo was again in view, but it rapidly dropped farther and farther down! Alex, with 'Betsy' straining at each switchback, they punched through the cloud layer, and on to above the clouds! Again pure white topped clouds that reflected the bright sunshine! In places, the higher mountaintops and ridges protruded above the clouds!

Alex didn't expect what she would see in the next four or five hours of majestic, awesome, and at times, frightening mountains—craggy peaks, vertical cliffs above and below, deep canyons with steep bare rocky sides! And tumbling rivers, dense jungles, all types of citrus trees, blooming yellow jungle trees fifty to a hundred feet tall, orchids, knee-deep pastures with inch wide blades of grass! And the road! Hung on the sides of cliffs, Alex eased along so close she could reach out the window and touch the rocky side! When she looked back—or upward—she saw that the road had hollow sections UNDER the roadbed large enough to be called caverns! And huge rocks continued to litter the road!

The angle of decline gradually decreased, sharp switch-backs became sweeping curves, the road was paved for some stretches and the jungle growth became thicker as they dropped toward the vast plain below. It was now visible—for as far as they could see.

Alex got her first glimpse of the Agua Azul river—way down and off in the distance. Seeing the back side of a huge billboard, and a smaller 'white' road that led off to one side, she pulled over in front of the sign. The sign showed: 'Cascadas Agua Azul—and it explained that the river was on private property—visitors were welcome—a small fee was required per vehicle to help defray the cost of maintenance. Women and men were expected to wear at least 'bottoms'. Littering, abusive language and fighting would not be tolerated—offenders would be ejected. And in much larger letters: The falls are extremely dangerous! The property Owner is NOT responsible for any injuries! Or deaths! There have been numerous deaths in the past!

Still parked in the side road, Alex turned to Tiger, said, "I want to visit Palenque! I've heard so much about it from you, Nat and Jim—We're so close! If we do this first", she pointed a finger in the direction that the side road went—"Then we'll have to hide 'it' for more time, more movements, more places"—she hesitated, then added, "Or we'll haul ass as fast as possible to get out of Mexico!" Mickey leaned forward, looked to Tiger. "No problem, Alex, we'll go on to Palenque-'do it'—and return to here. The road between the two is not nearly as bad as it has been", Tiger responded. Alex smiled, nodded, and pulled back on the main highway and headed for Palenque, They now traveled almost due North.

The two Agents following them were still over two hours behind.

In the small town of Palenque, Alex followed the signs, turned on a smaller but nicely paved road. The ruins were only a few kilometers out of town. Soon Tiger remarked, "It's only about two hours until dark. There is a motel—the last and only one on this road—The 'Hotel' Las Ruinas—you may should stop there, get a room. It's only about a half mile on to the site." Alex quickly did this while they waited in the vehicle.

The paved road turned up, got steeper and steeper. The air's temperature seemed terribly hot after being in San Cris, and the humidity was very high—Alex felt as if she could grab a hand full of water from the air! She immediately broke-out in a pouring sweat. Glancing at the other two, they didn't seem effected. Another trait of being May.

Parked at the smooth, paved, well laid out parking lot just outside the entrance, Alex quickly changed from her warm 'driving outfit' to cotton short-shorts and a loose cotton 'crop-top'. With Tiger acting as a private tour guide, the three walked pass the vendor's stands and the nice cool, large, palapa style restaurant on the right.

Standing in front of The Temple of Inscriptions, Alex was awed, not by the ruins so much, but by their backdrop! It was a black-green wall of impenetrable jungle, hundreds of feet higher than the ruins! The entire site, except for the north side, was as if surrounded by a dark green velvet curtain! As if she could walk up to it, push and her hand would not penetrate it! White veils of flowing mist drifted in and out the folds, up and down the entire face of this spectacular 'wall'!

The exposed ruins—there are still many that are buried—are set on a man-made plateau, hundreds of feet above the flat plain to the north. This plateau was carved into the sides of the Tumbala Mountains. The drama Alex saw was immensely increased by the contrast between looking north—across the miles and miles of the flat plain below—then looking South into the dark, hovering, mist-shrouded mountains. As she turned back and forth, she loudly exclaimed, "Awesome! Just fantastic!"

They wandered on, and Tiger explained, "Some of these monuments date back to 300 B.C. The cleared area is perhaps a halfmile in diameter, but with explorations covering an area of maybe fifteen square miles. Of the estimated five hundred individual monuments scattered around here, only thirty-four have the jungle cleared away." As Alex stood near the gap between The Temple of Inscriptions and The Palace, she counted thirteen separate structures in a panoramic view.

With her head tilted as far back as possible, with her mouth agape, Alex looked up at the square observation tower (all others found, are round) Tiger said, "Before it gets too dark, you just have to see the views from the top floor!" She started climbing the broken, ragged wall next to the tower. Alex then Mickey followed her. They could only get up there by walking the top edge of the remains of this wall. It was fourteen to sixteen inches wide, very irregular and as it neared the tower, it ascended steeply. With sheer drops of fourteen to fifteen feet on both sides, it was definitely no place for the staggers or to stump your toes!

After reaching the second floor of the tower, they hopped across the gap to the inside of the tower. But not too far inside! The opening down was very close inside—they had to land flat-footed and be sure not to take a step forward! After one of them hopped across, they had to move aside, or on up the steps to make room for the next person! Tiger had already headed up the narrow—almost vertical—stone steps when Alex hopped over. Following in order to make room for Mickey, Alex looked up. And realized why skirts are NOT recommended for 'Ruins Ramblings'! If Tiger had been wearing her traditional Tzental skirt, it would have totally exposed her bottom to Alex's face!

They wandered on, and Tiger explained, "Some of these monuments date back to 300 B.C. The cleared area is perhaps a halfmile in diameter, but with explorations covering an area of maybe fifteen square miles. Of the estimated five hundred individual monuments scattered around here, only thirty-four have the jungle cleared away." As Alex stood near the gap between The Temple of Inscriptions and The Palace, she counted thirteen separate structures in a panoramic view.

With her head tilted as far back as possible, with her mouth agape, Alex looked up at the square observation tower (all others found, are round) Tiger said, "Before it gets too dark, you just have to see the views from the top floor!" She started climbing the broken, ragged wall next to the tower. Alex then Mickey followed her. They could only get up there by walking the top edge of the remains of this wall. It was fourteen to sixteen inches wide, very irregular and as it neared the tower, it ascended steeply. With sheer drops of fourteen to fifteen feet on both sides, it was definitely no place for the staggers or to stump your toes!

After reaching the second floor of the tower, they hopped across the gap to the inside of the tower. But not too far inside! The opening down was very close inside—they had to land flat-footed and be sure not to take a step forward! After one of them hopped across, they had to move aside, or on up the steps to make room for the next person! Tiger had already headed up the narrow—almost vertical—stone steps when Alex hopped over. Following in order to make room for Mickey, Alex looked up. And realized why skirts are NOT recommended for 'Ruins Ramblings'! If Tiger had been wearing her traditional Tzental skirt, it would have totally exposed her bottom to Alex's face!

Each flight of steps exited at the center of a floor, and was only about sixteen inches from four door-size openings—one in each wall.

These openings came all the way to the floor—no low walls or parapets! This layout was repeated at each floor. There were two levels above the one that they had jumped to. The four openings faced North, South, East and West. Perfect for photos if one didn't move one's feet carelessly! Alex realized—there were five ways to fall! The four side openings, and into the stairwell! The floors being only about six feet square, this was a true example of where a few people made a 'crowd'!

More climbing, looking, going through the narrow tunnels, and a quick visit to the small museum and when at the small 'sunken' courtyard, Mickey stared at one of the many full sized stone carvings of a chieftain during a 'blood-letting' ceremony. "Ouch! That looks—", he cut it short when he noticed that Alex was paying attention to him. "Are you muttering about the old Chief with the sting-ray spine stuck through his—dong—or—the young maiden with the big tits on her knees in front of his—thing?" He just chuckled, and turned away. It would be dark soon, the three headed out.

Approaching the station wagon, they saw that 'something' was different'. Parked crosswise, close to the rear of 'Betsy' was a light colored car. The front of the vehicle faced their approach. And on each of the front fenders sat a man. They were dressed in sports—city style—clothes, with light jackets hung open. The bulges under their left arms were obvious. A few feet away, Alex stopped, raised a hand in front of Tiger and Mickey, said, "Well! Well! Tiger, look who's here! Our old Buddies from Mazatlan!

Let's see—", as Alex added she pointed a stiff finger first to one, then to the other, "It is tweety-dee-and—tweety-dumb!" She reversed her pointing, said, "Or is it tweety-dumb—and—tweety-dee?"

Tiger caught the joke, and pointed as Alex had, said, "No, it's Agentman number one—and—Agentman number two!" She too reversed her pointing, "Or is it—Agentman number two?—and—Agentman number one?" The two women chuckled. Kyle pointed his thumb to his own chest, said,

"I'm Kyle!" then he thumbed toward Rudi, added, "He's Rudi" Rudi followed, he thumbed himself, said, "I'm Rudi", thumbed to Kyle, said, "He's Kyle!!' They all laughed, including Mickey!

Alex stepped forward, slapped their knees, snapped, "What are you boys up to? I thought you guys got enough of us in Mazatlan!" On purpose, Alex had skipped their 'encounter' at the Hotel Real in San Cris. She wanted them to wonder—'Was that just a bad dream?' Rudi opened, "Alex, we know what you're up to!" She took one step back, placed her hands on her hips, raised her eyebrows and replied "Oh? Really? And what may that be?" "You have come to steal 'The Lost Codex of Palenque'!" She, Tiger and Mickey were surprised—shocked—but none of them showed the slightest sign.

Slowly, Alex pulled her shoulders as far back as possible, and raised both arms straight up—the short bottom of her crop-top snapped above her breasts, her prominent nipples sprung outward to attention! Holding her position, she calmly said, "So—search me." Tiger and Mickey both took the same positions. It was obvious the three didn't have anything as large—'about the size of a large briefcase' Tony had advised— as the Codex on their person.

Rudi hopped down, said, "Ok! Ok! Drop em. But we'll have to search your vehicle!" "Not here! Rudi, we've got a room at the Las Ruinas and my little ass is tired, and dripping sweat! Follow—or better yet, lead us there and you can search everything we've got while I shower and get a cold beer—or two—or three! Please?"

The Las Ruinas was a low, one story arrangement that enclosed a large area out back. For 'overnighters', the vehicles were driven through a breezeway into this secured area. There was parking, a swimming pool, and many lush flowers and flowering trees. Out front was parking for the restaurant and short-term visitors. At the breezeway were the desk clerk's station and a small outdoor eating and drinking area of the restaurant. Alex's and 'company' room was in sight of these.

Pulling in, through, and parking close to the room, Alex hopped out as the Agents pulled in next to 'Betsy'. The two Agents got out, Alex called out, "Hey! Rudi, I'd suggest you get a room." She stepped to him, slapped his back. "Tell the clerk that Alex said to give you"—she glanced toward the door next to their room—"room 103, that's next to ours! I just hate long walks late at night!" She laughed. He just waved her 'off' as he headed for the reservation desk.

Kyle stepped closer as Alex opened the rear of the wagon. She stuck one of the small Mitlas bags to him, snapped, "Feel! Is there a large book in it?" He did, shook his head. She passed it to the bellhop. And she repeated this for the other Mitlas. Heading for the room with the bellhop, she said, "Ok! Sport! It's all yours! Search a way!" Mickey and Tiger were already in the room. Not seeing any need to rush, Kyle ignored her, and joined Rudi at the desk.

Coming out, Alex saw that Rudi had showered also—his hair was still wet—he sat in a chair between their doors, his feet propped up on the rail. She was wearing tight, white jeans and a loose, thin, cotton blouse. She was bare-footed. She pulled up a chair, sat close to him and propped her feet on the rail as she continued to dry her hair. Kyle was busy at the rear of the wagon as he went through the piles—shifting 'stuff' from one side to the other. Seeing the bellhop/waiter, she waved him over, said, "Sweetie, bring me a cold Clara Gold"—she pointed at Rudi, he nodded, "Him one"—she called out—"Kyle! A beer?" He straightened up, replied, "Sure!" "Him one—and, Sweetie, please check with the two inside—what ever they want!" The waiter twisted toward the room door, Alex added, "It's unlocked—go on in! And if the one with hair down to her ass is naked—don't let her big 'hooters' make you tongue-tied!" Alex laughed. When the waiter came out with a very wide grin, Alex added, "Bring me a menu, please, I'm just famished!"

As they sipped, passed the menu around, and relaxed—and Kyle searched—Alex suddenly asked Rudi, "You a happily married man? With children?" "Sure—got two sons, one in the University of Mexico City, one only one year away from going there. Why?" "That's a shame. I don't—do—happily married men with kids. But, I'm attracted to— well—older men—but—", she let it drop. After a brief silence, she asked, "Kyle? What about Kyle?" "Single, never been married." "Why?" "Kyle has a mean streak—probably can't find anyone to put up with him!" Rudi chuckled. "Mean? Like bad, or just mean—selfish?" "Both, I guess." "I can understand that somewhat—my live-in mate has that problem, but, we've worked it out over the years."

"You live with someone? Full time? A guy? I would have never guessed you were a 'home-body! Got any kids?" "No kids—Tom, my man—is a lot older—really old enough to be my father—he's just not sure—his temper—about kids. So, I don't push it." Rudi continued, "You say he's mean—sorry mean or—" "Oh, no, not lazy, sorry trash mean—he's trained mean. Big, tough, bad! An ex-professional—Captain—a Delta Force guy." "And, Alex, that is where you learned—so much?" "I guess—and from Tiger's live-in, Mike." "Tiger lives with a man full time also?" "Sure! What did you think we were, just a couple of loose gals on the 'make'?" "Sorry, no offence, it is that I didn't expect you two as being regular house-wives—that's all." "It's Ok, I know we don't appear to be what we really are. Hey, I hope you two get to meet my sweet Tom someday!"

Alex waved her empty bottle at the waiter. When he brought her another cold beer, she said, "Ask the others—and take their orders for diner. I'll have the polio con mole, por vavor. And, Sweetie, put every-thing—including the beers—on my tab! Tonight, little Alex pays!"

Kyle was searching inside, at the rear seat area. Alex paid closer attention. Straightening up, he turned toward her, held up the large brown envelope, shook it slightly, asked, "Alex, what's this?" "Pasos! Four thousand dollars—US—Is that illegal? To carry a little traveling money?" He didn't reply, he turned back inside, then showed her the heavy canvas bag, "And this? More traveling money?" "You got it, Sport! Just some loose change we picked up around the house before we started this trip!" Giving up, he ignored the coil of rope—tow rope he thought. He returned the items to below the seat cushion, replaced it, shut all the doors and the tailgate.

Joining Rudi and Alex, Kyle said, as he tossed the keys to her, "Not a damn thing—not even a 'joint' or two—nothing illegal—considering the fact that she has a legal permit for her pistol!" "So? You thought I was a crook? A drug 'freak'?" Alex quipped. "Sorry, just doing my job." But he thought, 'Somewhere, sometime, some how, this is going to bust wide open!'

The waiter came to Alex, told her their diner was ready and asked where she wanted it served. "Outside—there at the tables", she nodded, added, "I'll get us together, we'll be on shortly." Reaching over, she patted Rudi's thigh, said, "Ok, Agentman, let's eat!" She stood, stepped to behind Kyle, patted his shoulder, said, "I hope you ordered oysters—you may need all the help you can get tonight!" She went inside and got Tiger and Mickey.

The pleasant meal over, some small talk, and while having coffee, Rudi asked, "Alex? What's next? The truth, please?" "The truth? Next? Tonight? I thought I'd screw out what little brains Kyle has!", she winked at Kyle, he glared back. "Ok, next? We're going to rest tonight, drive back to the Agua

Azul, go swimming, enjoy the sights—then—I'm not really sure—just go with the flow—we don't have a fixed schedule— any deadlines. And that's the truth." "The Agua Azul? Blue water? What's that?" Rudi questioned. This opened a round of lively conversation—very enthused from those that knew—to the two, Alex and Rudi, that had never been there. Tiger closed the boisterous, vivid descriptions with, "Oh! It is just fantastic!"

Standing, stretching, Alex asked the two Agents, "You guys bring swim suits? You'll probably need them!" The two looked to each other,

"No, not really—would tight, panty-cut undershorts work?" Kyle asked. "Sure! Done all the time!" Tiger replied. "We leave early!" Alex said to all. Then she headed for the room.

Later, rested physically, but not at all sleepy, Alex returned outside. Tiger and Mickey had quickly spread out on separated beds and 'crashed out'—sound asleep. There were still a few people in the restaurant, but she wasn't interested in that scene. She took a stroll around the pool, got a bottle of white wine and sat down at the rail again. In a short time, Rudi joined her, he mentioned that Kyle had 'left' with some 'lady' he met in the restaurant—he wouldn't be back for several hours. Alex didn't particularly pay attention—she was again thinking about the possibilities of 'something' in Ocosingo.

The two drifted into a casual conversation about her business interests as they passed the wine bottle back and forth. "Did you notice what really transpired between Marie and me—there in Mazatlan?" She asked. "Somewhat, of course not any real details—looked as if you formed some sort of partnership." "Yes, I rather like setting up things—businesses-but not getting tied down—that's boring. A partnership in Ocosingo-maybe." And she explained, roughly, what she was thinking about in 'Oco'. And she asked his opinions, the two kicked it around—and Alex 'stored-away' his comments.

"Rudi? What's your oldest son's—the one at UMC—major?" It almost sounded as if she changed subjects—but to her, she didn't, she had reasons. "Political Law—his Grandfather, my dad—was a Lawyer that specialized in political law. Why?" "Nothing really, just interested. When will he take his Bar Exam?" "Next spring—if things go right." He didn't push the 'why' point. She thought, 'His son may be just who I need to pursue the land acquisition!'

She returned to the original thought: Ocosingo. "I realize the major problem will be getting in and out of there—that drive is NOT easy, from either direction! My Tom can fly anything. I'm thinking a light plane—some kind that can drop in and out of that valley, close to the lake—", she let it drop, not knowing exactly many details. "Alex, you ever heard of a Pilatis PC6?" "Vaguely, Tom once mentioned—but only a little—about using PC6's in Nam. Why?"

"I've got a friend, has an old PC6, he's talking about 'moving-up'-to multi-engines—starting a service along the Pacific coast, regular schedules—now, he just runs rental-hops. He mentioned he would probably sell the PC6—wouldn't need it any more." "Really? That sounds interesting! A PC6? Turbo? Or piston engine?" She knew enough that there were two versions. "Turbo—that's needed for real short field work." And he explained the PC6's specifications. "That sounds like what I need! This friend, how would I get in touch with him?" "No problem—hang on, I'll dig out his card." He went inside for a brief time, she got her little black book and pen.

As she copied the numbers, she asked, "And this—Sam—he knows how to get in touch with you—your son?" "Yes", he didn't ask more about that, instead, "You're serious about this, aren't you?" She chuckled, "Oh, I'm not sure yet—just an idea—", she hesitated, looked off to the distance, added, "I've got another project I'm committed to—has to be completed about September, October", she returned to writing. "Another project? This coming fall?" "Yes", she only replied, and continued to copy the card's info. "Is—this project—is it big? Or—what?" he picked. **Rudi** was good at picking details, he didn't believe in pushing too hard.

Finished, she turned to him, took the bottle, had a sip and responded. "Big? Not necessarily—just got to buy some property—some houses—move my staff from D.C. to North Georgia—not over one million I guess." "One million? As dollars? US?" He was mildly impressed. "Yes—", she waited, thought, then, "And I need to unload some assets that aren't making me a dime!" She was thinking about her property and her sailboat at Lake Lanier.

"And, what about this project? The Codex project?" Rudi slyly slipped in. "Codex? What? I'm on a figging vacation! And looking for investment opportunities! And you think I'm hunting a damn old 'funny-book'! Go screw yourself!" She stomped off toward the cafe with the empty bottle. He waited, thought, 'And Alex has a very short fuse!'

Soon she returned with another bottle of wine, sat back down as if nothing had happened. She leaned forward, stared up at the star lit sky, and between sips, she casually named off several of the constellations—with their Maya, and their 'Modern' names. Again, Rudi was impressed.

Rudi thought, then asked, "Speaking of majors, what did you major in?" "Formally? Computers—everything from hardware design to systems designs", a pause, then, "And—financial Management—but—I got that the hard way—being on my own since I was fifteen!" She took a heavy slug, looked off into the darkness. Rudi didn't ask, he would wait. She didn't pass the bottle over. Instead she finished it, stood, threw the empty bottle overhand toward the lawn, and abruptly said, "Goodnight, thanks for the tips!" She went in her room, he thought, 'Yes, there's a lot more to little Alex than one would think!'

The following morning, Alex made sure they had everything from the room. She settled the bill, asked Tiger and Mickey to wait in the wagon. Leaving the engine at idle, Alex stepped to the trees close by. She had noticed that these had been recently trimmed. Looking about on the ground, she found what she wanted. It was a narrowly forked branch. The main part was about an inch in diameter—the two forked branches were smaller. It was about four feet long overall. Returning to the Agent's door, she forced the vee of the fork behind the doorknob—with the ends over the doorway trim. The door opened inward.

Stepping to the window, she banged on the glass very hard. Kyle pulled the curtain back, looked at her face. Then he cranked the window open. "The last one in the water is a dummy!" She shouted, then ran and jumped in 'Betsy' and raced off, headed for Agua Azul! The three laughed as they thought about the Agents trying to get out the door!

By driving very fast—and hoping the door trick would gain them more time—they intended to retrieve the Codex before Kyle and Rudi arrived at the river.

The side road down to the river was not paved, but it was as good as the unpaved sections of the main highway. It twisted and wound its way along the four kilometers to Agu Azul that was several hundred feet below the main highway.

This side road ended at a grassed open area adjacent to, and level with the river. The area was remarkable for its undeveloped condition; only a few open-air restaurants—palapa style—one 'modern' home that was built in a most spectacular setting at the very edge of the river, and several typical 'native' homes up-stream from the parking area. The entire open area was relatively small—maybe a quarter of a mile square.

There was not much talking, or at least they couldn't hear it above the rumbling and the roar of the huge river cascading about the area as it came down from above. It was as if the river didn't have a main channel, but flowed through the widely spaced trees in many different directions, came together at places, then re-divided and tumbled down again. The multitudes of drops were from one to twenty-five feet high. One part flowing out through the trees with numerous low drops while another part—at the same location—took the shorter route by dropping over a single waterfall fifteen to twenty feet, and then the two parts rejoined! At places, the river was exceptionally wide, at others, not wide at all.

But the main attraction was the color! For fresh water, it was unbelievable! It ranged from crystal clear to deep blue, with all shades of green and blue-greens mixed in. Each hue had its own location in this magnificent living scene! Rocks, concrete, tree roots, logs, everything solid in the water was encrusted with a marble-like substance instead of being eroded away! But the movement of the water was much too swift for any suspended material to precipitate from the water! Strange indeed!

Around the area were people prepared to stay a while—hikers down stream—tents and hammocks set up, and several 'camping vans' at the water's edge. There was no bank—no drop-off along the edge—the beautiful grass lawn was flat and only a few inches above the water. And there were no signs of the river recently being over the grass.

There was one large palapa with restrooms closeby that offered hammock spaces for rent. This was also at the very edge of the river. Alex parked there, hoping to gain some cover for their 'operation'.

The three were already dressed for their mission; all three wore longer legged Spandex jogging shorts—Alex and Tiger with fuller coverage jogging tops. And all three wore tightly laced low top tennis shoes. Showing the other two, Alex 'hid' the keys on top of the driver's side front tire. At the river's edge, Tiger studied the scene along the far side. Then, "There! That's the knoll! Around the face—the face above the larger river below—the river that runs crossways, below the last waterfall of this river!"

They briskly walked upstream to the closest falls—the river was wider there but the water wasn't running as fast downstream at the base of the falls—this was about fifteen feet high. They dove in and quickly swam to the other side. Then hiked downstream along the edge of the knoll. The flat walking space was six to eight feet wide here. But, at the corner, their foothold became much narrower. They hesitated before going on. Tiger got first in line, knowing it was she who would have to crawl in the small cave, Alex followed her, Mickey brought up the rear.

In line, they inched their way around the corner. The 'path'—but it was not a well beaten one—was now over the Tulija River. It was about a fifty foot drop—straight down to the water below! The path was very narrow, the margin for error was very slim! But the path became a little wider as it hooked slightly into the face of the cliff. Tiger raised a 'halt' signal, and carefully lowered to her knees, she crawled forward onto the wider area. She came face to face with the small cave.

It looked barely large enough to get her shoulders in—and not her hips at all! She realized this was all going to be done by feel—her body would close off any light from the outside.

She lay down on her stomach and with her arms extended in front of her head, she began a sliding, wiggling motion. Slowly, she entered the small opening. With her hands—her fingers—she felt along the right side. She just couldn't exactly remember what it was she was feeling for—couldn't remember what she had seen during the ritual. But she felt confident she would know when she felt it. Her hips were close to being inside.

Stopping her body's motions, she ran her fingers over, and around and around. Yes! It was a bias-relief of a face! An ancient Maya face! The downward arched nose, the thick lips, and the rearward slopped forehead— that was it! The stone cover for the reliquary!

Quickly she traced for the edges of the cover stone. Finding the four edges, she dug with her fingernails. Soon she was able to get finger-holds on the two opposite edges. At first, it didn't want to move—but by pulling, then pushing, it began to wiggle loose. With one hardy pull, it came out. She shoved it deeper into the cave, pushed it out of the way.

Reaching into the storage hole—the reliquary—she felt the edges of a package—it felt like it was cloth, or paper, coated with wax. Crooking her left arm, opening her fingers wide, she got a hold and pulled. Slowly, it slid out. It felt about the size of a large briefcase—or a large dictionary—and it was about as heavy.

Pulling the package with her left hand, and pushing against the cave with her right hand, and wiggling her hips and pawing with her toes, she slowly began to back out. With her head out, she hesitated, took several deep breaths—the musky odor in the cave had filled her lungs—and she batted her eyes to adjust to the bright sunlight. Gradually she arched her hips up, got her knees securely situated. As she pulled the package on out, she raised her shoulders and then leaned her forehead against the cliff above the small cave. Bracing with her head, she lifted the package with both hands. And slowly, carefully, raised to one foot, then the other.

Hugging the load in her arms, she turned back toward Alex, who had stayed as close to Tiger's feet as possible. Passing it to Alex, Tiger softly said, "We've got it, Alex, we did it." "Yes, Kid, you got it!" With much care, Alex slowly twisted around, leaning against the rock wall as she did. She moved a few careful steps toward Mickey. He was ready for the transfer. As Alex passed it to his arms, suddenly, behind her, was a scrapping, a scrambling and the sound of loose rocks moving—dropping over the edge!

Feeling Mickey take the package securely, Alex turned back, Tiger was clawing at the wall as her feet—and the pathway below her feet—slowly gave way! Her fall was imminent! "Get rope! Under the rear seat! Get help!" Alex screamed as loud as possible! As Tiger's hip hit where the edge had been, Alex knew she was going to fall! Tiger, with her arms still up, still clawed at the bare, hard rock face, looked pleadingly at Alex. In one swift motion, Alex bent to within range and grabbed Tiger's left wrist, as hard and as tight as possible. "No!" Tiger yelled. "Hang on, Kid, we're in for one hell-of-a-fall!" As Tiger's full weight fell, it jerked Alex head first from the ledge. "Ball up! Before the water! Ball up! Tight!" Alex shouted as they fell. Folding her legs up, tightly together, Alex kicked the cliff with both feet—very hard, this propelled her farther from the cliff—and she snatched Tiger with her.

It seemed like hours, but was only a second or two. Alex prayed very rapidly that the water would be deep enough! At the last instant before they hit the water, Alex felt Tiger fold up, Alex coiled as tight as possible, but she kept her hold—with one hand—on Tiger's wrist. The force from slamming into the water was like being struck by a moving car. Or kicked by a bunch of mules—all over their bodies, all at once! The time it took to reach the surface seemed like ages. Their heads popped up, Tiger was strangled, she gasped for breath! Alex took a deep breath, forced her way down, stuck one hand between Tiger's crotch, forcing her arm through, up to the crook of her elbow. With strong, sweeping strokes of her legs, she lifted Tiger until she knew her head was completely out of the water. Alex knew this was a 'regular' trick of coordinated swimming teams. With her head against Tiger's stomach, she heard Tiger gasp several times, then begin a near normal breathing cycle. Knowing from skin diving experience, that she could hold her breath for three minutes, Alex stayed, lifted, still kicked. Soon, she felt Tiger pat the top of her head. Calmly, Alex surfaced, looked at Tiger, "You got any broken bones? Any bleeding?" "No, don't feel any! You?" "No! I think we're in great shape!" The two smiled and hugged as they steadily, in long, strong strokes and slow long kicks, floated with the current.

Their choice was clear—the low land on the opposite side of the river. On the side where they fell, it was vertical, solid, smooth rock. Not knowing what was downstream—a waterfall perhaps?—the two rolled to their backs and began a steady back stroke toward the, lowland side. Soon, they crawled up on the shore—it was a beautiful white sand beach, about fifty feet wide—lay on their backs and rested. Minutes later, Alex raised, propped back on her hands, surveyed the situation. They were about a hundred yards downstream from where they had fallen. The Tulija's current was steady, about two miles per hour. The water-fall from the Agua Azul up above was tremendous—in volume, and force—and with swirling currents—turbulence—where it fell into the bigger river. "Want to stay clear of that!" She said to no one.

Looking along the upper edge of the cliff, downstream, the knoll flatted, and there appeared to be a lower level—maybe even a path? To the edge? Then another heavily wooded knoll. "Stay here, rest, I'm going to hike downstream—be sure there's not a waterfall too close. If you see anyone over there—", she pointed in the direction of the cave, "Wave at them—whoever—give them the old Army Ok sign! Ok?" Tiger just nodded as she continued to stare toward where they had fallen. To Tiger, it seemed impossible that either of them were still alive!

Alex walked about a hundred and fifty yards beyond the low spot—she didn't see, or hear any waterfalls in the Tulija. Returning toward Tiger, she stopped at the low area, estimated, 'if they started about where they fell—the cave—and swam across, they would be angled by the current to about the low spot. And if they missed—whatever—they would have enough clear distance down stream to return to the low shoreline—the beach. Walk back, and try again!

Back with Tiger, She sat down and waited, waited for someone, something to appear somewhere on the top of the cliff. They were setting directly across from the low spot—a path 'up-there' they hoped.

Alex decided she should as well take advantage of the wait, the sun, the beautiful soft, white sandy beach. She stripped off her top and bottom, spread out to sunbath in the buff. Tiger stood, slowly began to stroll along a line formed by the white sand and the low scrubby brush. She continuously looked down. "What are you doing? Why don't you come sunbath? It is so comfortable in the buff!" Alex called out to Tiger as she got farther off. Tiger turned, came back to Alex, and muttered 'something'. "What? I didn't hear you!" "Not much, just—we don't want to be here after dark!" "Dark! What?" "Night cats—tracks all along." Alex jumped to her feet, shouted, "Night Cats! Here?" "Alex—you finally made it to the real jungle of Chiapas! Yes! Night cats! Even a few Jaguar tracks!" "Damn!" Now Alex became anxious! She jerked her bottom and top back on, and began to pace as she watched the top of the cliff 'over-there', and the bush-line 'over-here'!

Mickey had quickly hidden the package behind a large boulder close to the corner of the knoll and covered it with some brush. He ran along the edge of the Azul, back toward the waterfall—to get upstream.

Kyle and Rudi's car was parked near the station wagon. The two were casually strolling about, looking at the beautiful scene. Especially the numerous skimpily clad ladies—many tongs and a lot of 'topless' beauties. "Isn't that Mickey? Swimming from the other side?" Rudi remarked. "Yes, those two gals are probably over there somewhere!" Mickey, without speaking, not even noticing them, ran to the wagon, got the keys and ran to the tailgate. He unlocked it, and with frantic motions, began to look for the rope! "Something is not right!" Kyle shouted as he started to trot toward the wagon. Rudi followed.

"What's wrong, Kid? What are you looking for?" Kyle snapped. "Rope! I can't find the rope!" "It is under the rear seat's bottom! What do you need rope for?" Mickey, leaving the tailgate open, unlocked the door, and jerked up the seat bottom, and shouted, "They fell in the big river! Below the big falls!" Without asking, the two Agents stripped their clothes off, except their briefs, and threw their shoes, clothes—even their pistols—in the rear of the station wagon. Mickey, with the coil of rope, ran toward the low falls—upstream—Kyle ran after him. Rudi, noticing that Mickey had left the keys in the door, took the keys, replaced these on top of the front tire, and locked up the wagon. Then he ran to the river, went to join the other two.

Mickey held one end of the rope as he inched close to the edge of the cliff. They were along side the knoll, Kyle held the rest of the coiled rope. After some waving and jumping about, Mickey turned to the other two, shouted—the thunder of the falls at their feet was tremendously loud— "They are Ok! They both are on the other side of the big river! They kept waving that way", he pointed toward the knoll, and down stream of the main falls. Kyle eased closer, looked around the corner. "Can't go that way! That's how they fell off! Trying to go that way!" Mickey yelled.

Rudi motioned that they follow him. When clear of the edge, he said, "There may be a path farther back, maybe it goes around behind this knoll—comes out at a better spot along the cliff! Alex and Tiger can see the top of the cliff better from where they are! Let's work our way back, look for a path!" Knowing that the two gals were ok, they slowed their pace and soon spotted a path around the knoll—and the trees were not nearly as thick in this area.

Following the path, it led to a natural saddle—the higher knoll back toward the Azul, and a lower hill to the left. The area opened out, there was little underbrush, and there were signs of several old fire sites—probably from campers. As Mickey headed for the edge of the cliff, Kyle stopped him. "Don't rush, we'll tie the rope off to a tree, use it as a safety line, then check out the girls!" They did, and while holding the rope—with a twist around their wrists, the two went directly to the edge and waved at Alex and Tiger. Rudi kept a respectful distance back.

Kyle quickly recognized that Alex was using 'standard' military hand signs. He and Alex got the gameplan conveyed. "They are going to walk about a hundred yards upstream, swim across—the current will angle them downstream to about here. We are to lower the rope with something heavy tied to it—a rock or whatever—to help stabilize the rope. Then we pull them up—the two of them at the same time", he relayed to Rudi and Mickey. Quickly getting a rock about the size of a football, Mickey then helped Kyle as he tied a double-basket loop around it. "Mick, how much do you think Tiger weights?" "About one-twenty, or maybe twenty-five." "Plus Alex's one-ten, that's quiet a bit—" "Senor Kyle! I can get more help! Ok?" "Sure, Kid! No need of taking a chance! Go ahead!"

As Kyle and Rudi finished rigging, and lowering, and communicating with the two below, Mickey ran back to the Azul. At the edge of the river, he thought about getting the package—now—and carrying it on to the wagon. But—that wasn't the problem—It was when everyone returned, the package may be too difficult to hide in the station wagon. And—with the others there, around the wagon—he gave up on the idea. Running up to a falls where several young men were, he asked for help. Returning to the cliff with four 'healthy' young men, they were ready.

On their first attempt, Alex missed catching the rope—or—the rock. They returned to the beach, changed their approach slightly. "Tiger, as we get close to the rope, you grab me around my thighs, when I yell 'UP', you lift me! Hold your breath, it'll probably push you under! And this time, we go all the way to the cliff BEFORE we get close to the rope! We'll hold hands, and both of us can claw the wall—that should slow us down some! Ok?" "Got it!" And this attempt worked.

Alex quickly took a turn of rope under her arms, and helped Tiger climb up on her shoulders and straddle her neck with her legs. "Hook your legs under my arms! Lock your feet together behind my back! And hold on to the rope! I'll use my feet to fend us off the wall! I'll walk up!"

Leaning out as far as possible while holding the rope, Kyle looked over the edge, but he couldn't see the two below. Returning to the 'pulling end', he waited for two minutes then decide it was time to try hoisting, "On three, we pull our arms in, hold, and move our hands forward, one at the time, and again on three, we all pull together. And no way do we turn loose until they're both over the edge—until they turn loose the rope! Got it? Any questions?"

None, Kyle began, "One, two, three!" They pulled. On the second pull, it was clear the two were on the other end by the strain on the rope. In about twenty minutes, Tiger appeared over the edge. She unlocked from Alex, crawled forward, still holding the rope. As Alex came up, still 'walking', she simply pulled on the rope, walked over the edge. Taking a few more steps, she then turned loose, and gave a 'patty-pat' hand clap to the guys! Then she helped Tiger to her feet—they hugged, and kissed—mouth to mouth very passionately! The guys applauded!

There was a lot of hand shaking, pats on the backs, and hugs.

Alex and Tiger made sure they kissed each one of the guys—mouth to mouth! This brought a lot of whistles! And 'cat-calls'!

CHAPTER-16

Before heading back to the Azul, Rudi caught one of Alex's elbows, asked, "Young Lady, just what were you two doing to fall in the damn river?" "My mistake—I wanted to look down at the big river—below the falls. The path gave way, we fell." She let it go at that.

While walking the path toward the Azul, Tiger whispered to Mickey, "Where is it?" He glanced around, Alex had the two Agents by their elbows, bending their ears about something, he replied, "Behind the largest boulder close to the corner of the knoll, covered by bush." She nodded in understanding. After a leisurely swim across the river, Alex and Tiger stepped to the wagon. Alex got the keys, unlocked the vehicle, and Tiger whispered to her, "Keep those two busy—for fifteen minutes, and we'll be ready to go." "How?" Alex questioned. "I'll disappear—get it-reappear—and I will not even get my feet wet." "Ok, I'll take care of Agentmen."

Tiger got out a change of clothes, said loudly, to everyone, "I've got to change—I think I need to!" Alex got out her pocketbook, headed to Kyle and Rudi. They stared at the purse—it was the larger dress purse. She noticed their reaction, said, "Relax! I've also got my spending money in here! Come on, you two, little Alex is buying the drinks!" She took their elbows and slowly, very slowly directed them toward the farthest palapa that had drinks—mainly beer—for sell. They still had on their briefs, only their briefs, but no one seemed to notice—or care. She glanced over her shoulder—Tiger was not in sight! She had already disappeared! And Mickey was sitting in the passenger's front seat. As they sat down, and ordered beers, Alex made sure their backs were toward 'Betsy'.

"WOW!" Alex exclaimed when she saw the light plane as its wheels barely cleared the roof of the 'sleeping' palapa. Kyle and Rudi looked to their left, Kyle chuckled, replied, "That's the 'hop' out of Palenque Town—there's a strip over there—for the 'bucks', you can fly up here!" She stood, looked at the plane as it taxied around and eased back to the parking area. "I'm amazed! Rudi! Could a PC6 do that?" "Of course, even better! A PC could carry more people!" "Even from Ocosingo?" She asked in excitement. "Sure! It would be a snap!" "What's this about a PC6?" Kyle asked the two. "She's got the 'hots' for Sam's old PC6!" Rudi joked. "Oh—Rudi—It's just an idea." she tried to appear modest.

After a couple of rounds—Alex kept watch over their shoulders—she saw Tiger reappear at the wagon, open the rear door, put something inside, then she got in the rear seat and closed the door. "Guys, order us another round"—she stood, bent close to their faces, added, "Please excuse me, but, little Alex has got to go pee, be back in a sec." With her purse still on her shoulder—and she hadn't paid for the drinks—she walked toward the restrooms—and the station wagon.

She looked close to be sure the tailgate was shut, it was. Opening the driver's door, she asked Mickey, "Their stuff still in the rear?"

He grinned, "Sure is!" "Tiger, you ready?" "Sure am!" Quickly, Alex hopped in, started the engine, glanced in the rearview mirror—the two were still seated under the palapa—she drove away from the beautiful Agua Azul! The three broke-up in laughter! "Between explaining about not being able to pay for the beers, breaking in the car, hot-wiring it"—Alex laughed— "It'll take them hours to catch up with us!" Then Tiger climbed over into the rear and rolled down the tailgate window.

As dark approached, Mickey leaned over to Alex's knees, reached down toward her feet. "What ARE you doing?" she snapped. "Unplugging the brake light switch—just in case." "Oh, Ok, I thought you were getting kinky on me!" "That comes later!" Tiger reached over from the rear, slapped his shoulder, exclaimed, "You shouldn't talk to your elders like that!" "Tiger! Tiger! Let Jesse rob this train his way!" The three laughed.

But the three didn't know about the GPS transmitter hidden under the rear floor.

Later, as Alex drove on, as fast as safely possible, Tiger got close to the rear of the front seat, said, "There's something wrong." Alex immediately let off the gas. "No, nothing like that! I meant, how did they find us at

Palenque?" The three went silent, Alex got back up to speed. A while later, Mickey said, "I've got friends at Zapata—'Condor' buddies—if you're willing—we could probably swap vehicles there—" Alex didn't answer right off.

The two Agents had not lost as much time as Alex had hoped for. They quickly convinced the restaurant owner to go with them to the car. Forcing open one rear window, they unlocked the doors, and pulling the trunk latch, they got to their cases. They had spares for just about everything—including the extra car keys. And, most importantly, the GPS monitor was still in good receiving condition. "They are headed slightly east of due north." Rudi quickly checked the position of the station wagon.

When Kyle roared out of the 'lawn' area onto the road, he suddenly skidded to a stop. "What are you doing?" Rudi asked. "Our shirts! They are in the road!" He hopped out, ran back and got these. On about fifty or so feet, he stopped again. Rudi didn't have to ask, he had also seen their shoes scattered along the road! Next, it was their pants—with their things still in those. Farther on, it was their holsters, and last—as Kyle now drove more slowly—it was their two pistols. "I guess it was worth it—but we've lost more time!" Kyle snapped.

Driving as fast as conditions allowed, Kyle said, "I'm telling you! The next time we catch up with that little bitch—her ass is mine! I don't give a damn what kind of official crap she has!" Rudi ignored his partner's anger as he leaned against the side window and tried to doze off. It had all the indications of being a long, long night!

After a couple of near-accidents, Rudi sat up, said, "Kyle! Back off the gas! We've got them on the monitor! If we have a wreck, we sure as hell will NOT catch them!" Kyle seemed to relax, replied, "Yeah, you're right, she just pissed me off." Rudi twisted back over, but he didn't try to go to sleep. Instead, he thought—'Why would Alex and Tiger even remotely get in a situation where they might fall off the cliff? And why would they run now? Not before now?' A while later, without rising up, he calmly said, "They've got the Codex. They got it at the river." "What?" Kyle snapped. Rudi explained his logic. Kyle agreed. "And, now, they are running for an airport!" Rudi remarked. "And, with the Book, if they fly away, our ass is grass!" Kyle added.

"This friend? The swapping vehicles thing—is it close by?" Alex asked Mickey. "Very close! Only a few K's before we would have to turn off this highway!" "Ok! Let's do it!" In just a few minutes, he said, "Slow down, the turn—to our right—is just ahead. Should see a sign for Zapata!"

Driving into the small town, she slowed, then noticed a Pemex station, Alex stopped there. As the attendant topped up the tank, Mickey talked to him. Pulling out, he said, "There's a small bar—about center of town—pull into the dark side street—you two wait in the car—I'll check around inside. The gas-man said my friend was probably there."

It didn't take long, Mickey and a young man jogged to Alex's open window. "Meet Jose, Alex, we've got a deal for you!" The two quickly explained; Swap the station wagon for his VW van. And he would drive about for the next few hours in the wagon. If it is 'bugged', the Agents will more than likely catch up with him. You write Jose a bill-of-sale, he doesn't want to be charged with stealing it. He gives you one for the same reason! And Jose would appreciate 'some' money for this deal.

"How about one thousand dollars—US—in Mexican Pasos?" Alex asked. Jose thrust his right hand to her replied, "Deal!" "Deal", she responded. The four quickly transferred all their gear—Alex made sure to get the sack of gold coins. When she got out the large brown envelope, she removed one of the smaller envelopes, handed it to Jose and said, "One thousand, US, in Pasos!" He didn't bother to open it. He slipped it deep inside the front of his pants. Working fast, it only took about ten minutes until Jose drove off in 'Arnie's Betsy'. He headed on through Zapata, continued on south-east.

As Mickey turned the van around, Alex lay down on top of the gear in the floor in front of the rear bench seat. Tiger lay on the rear seat, they both covered up with blankets. Mickey pulled an old hat far down on his head and put on a pair of sunglasses. When he approached the Pemex station again, he checked the gas gage, said, "We're in luck—the van's tank is full! It's over one hundred miles to the next station! At Francisco Escarcega!" Just beyond the station, he said, "There they go! They've taken the bait!" as the Agent's rental car sped in the opposite direction, the 'wrong' direction! Turning right, back onto route 186, Mickey guided the van toward the Gulf of Mexico.

By driving fast—he wanted to check out his 'new' wagon, and he didn't like the idea of being stopped by two Federal Agents out in 'no-where'-he crossed the bridge high above the Rio Usumacinta River and arrived at the small 'jungle' town of Tenosique before the Agents caught up with him. There appeared to be a sizable crowd at the only bar in the small town, and he knew this bar was a 'regular' for many of his old 'Condor' friends—friends that really hated Federal Men of any sort! Parking in the light in front of the bar, he casually strolled in, waved at friends, got a beer, and waited.

Kyle roughly swung open the swinging doors, smartly stepped inside the bar. Rudi was slightly behind and to one side. As Kyle glared, Rudi sized-up the situation: about twenty, very mean looking bastards, men with ugly scars, men wearing big knives, men drinking from glass beer bottles. And a very, very big man behind the bar—he was the ugliest, and meanest looking of all. Definitely not a good scene—not at all!

Kyle stepped forward, crudely pushed a chair out of his way and shouted, "Where are the two women and one guy from the dull black station wagon out front!" No one moved, no one replied.

Seated at a table in the middle of the others, Jose finally said, "Try a different questioia, Mr. Federal Agent Man!" Six or eight big men stood, drained their bottles, and took the bottles by the necks. The two Agents didn't say anything. But Kyle stepped forward, toward Jose then stopped—Rudi had caught his elbow. "Try—who owns the station wagon out front! Mr Agent Man!" Jose loudly remarked—he wanted the 'regulars' to understand the situation.

"Ok—Who owns the wagon?" Rudi asked. "I do—got a bill-of-sale right here in my shirt pocket!" Jose pulled it out and waved the hand-written document around. "Yeah? Since when?" Kyle snapped. Jose had been waiting for this—"Since Alex—the famous personal bodyguard of Senorita Tiger Calienta—sold it to me!" In the brief time while they transferred the stuff, Tiger couldn't resist filling Jose in with 'who' they were! The 'regulars' Oh'ed and Ah'ed at hearing the women's names! A brief silence from the Agents as the two contemplated their situation. Then Kyle said, "We are going to search the wagon!" "Search away! Just don't steal anything!" Jose replied as a few of the 'jungle-men' chuckled.

"Not a damn thing!" Kyle said as he slammed the tailgate. "Yeah, it's like they and all their gear have vanished! Disappeared in thin air!" Rudi added. Kyle reached under the rear and removed the GPS transmitter, showed it to Jose, who only shrugged, he didn't indicate any interest. "Let's get the hell out of here!" Rudi said. Jose and many of his friends had stood outside the bar and watched the search. As the two Agents headed for their car, Jose called out, "You guys want to buy a used station wagon? With Georgia plates?" The two didn't respond, Kyle turned the car around, and headed back toward route 186.

On reaching the junction with 186, Kyle hesitated, blurted, "Damnit! We've lost them again! Now what?" "They were headed North, we go North, start checking the airports. Campeche, follow up with Merida, then Cancun." "Rudi? What happens if we do find out that they have flown away? Out of Mexico?" "We find a dark, ugly bar, you pick a fight and we get slightly beat-up, we call the Boss, say several CIA pricks jumped us! And the gals got away!" "Rudi, that's the best plan I've heard yet!"

"Alex! Alex!" Mickey called as he shook her shoulder. She raised up, opened her eyes, said, "It's daylight—where are we?" "Just coming into Campeche—The City" The vehicle wasn't moving, she looked out and saw they were stopped at a Pemex station. "Well, I guess it's my turn to drive", as she got out of the van. Reaching back in, she shook Tiger's foot, yelled, "The house is on fire! The house is on fire!" The station attendant, as he filled the tank, looked at Alex, nodded, said, "I've got one like that too!" When Alex and Tiger returned from the restroom— Mickey had waited at the van—he said, "You need to pay for the gas. This city looks large, even from here—I've never driven in a city this big before!" "Once you get used to it, they're all the same—the traffic is just faster!"

They were still outside, shaking the kinks out and rubbing the numb spots, Tiger asked, as she looked toward the city, "Alex, isn't there an airport here? One large enough for 'whatever'—a flight to the USA?" Alex didn't reply. "Could we hole-up here? Do what's next? Here?" Taking Tiger's hand, Alex responded, "I'd rather go on to Merida—can't exactly understand why, but—", she dropped the subject. Tiger didn't question, she hugged Alex, then got in the front passenger's seat—it was Mickey's time to sleep on the rear bench seat. Beyond Lerma and approaching the outer-limits of the city, they stopped at road-side vendors and bought fruit and other snacks and drinks for the trip on north.

After Alex worked their way through Campeche—she had decided to go straight through instead of taking the 'new' half circle 'By-pass' around the Southeastern part of the city—she said, "We should get to Merida about mid afternoon. Plenty of time to find a room—even look around some before dark."

Entering the edge of Merida, Alex began to describe different things. Realizing Alex seemed familiar with the city, Tiger asked "You have been here before, you told me", Tiger recalled that Alex had mention Merida some time in the past.

"Yes, I came down for one summer—when I was sixteen, I think. My Dad was staying here at the time—tracking down and making gold deals.

He and I didn't have much—spend much—time together. I was at that independent stage—he was dealing—and—staying drunk a lot. Anyway! I found my own way around. Merida is just great to get about in! Regular buses to everywhere! A very nicely layed-out city. Especially considering it's a city of over a half-million. And its location is central to so many of the ancient ruins—monuments—scattered around here. But, I wasn't seriously interested in ruins then—it was boys—well, men!"

She hesitated, as if she had 'lost' the subject then slightly shook her head, started again, "Well—The transportation, out and back to Marida is dependable! I would day-trip out, and return to the hotel where I was staying." She stopped again. "I? Alex, you used the word I a lot, didn't your Dad—" "No, he didn't", Alex interrupted.

"Sorry. You stayed in the same hotel the entire time?" "Yes, the El Presidente." "Sounds expensive!" "It was! But—" "I thought you said your Dad was a—" "A bum? Yes, and he was! But, he wasn't a 'Cheap-Bum'! When it came to me anyway—What I wanted, what I wanted to do. He just never took time—didn't want to—I guess—to spend time with me—he just never—."

Tiger quickly changed the subject, "You know where you're going? This is a very wide avenue!" "It is the 'Itza'—the main 'drag' coming in from the South! Yes, if I can remember, turn right—the next street after the zoo—go to the center." It was as if Alex was talking to herself, trying to recall the area. "The Central Zocalo will be on the left—turn left on 16th—that's the East side of the park—the Zocalo." Alex hesitated. Tiger asked, "You're going to the Hotel El Presidente, aren't you?" "Not only can you disappear—you can read minds too!" Alex said then smiled at Tiger. "Joke! Joke! You know by now, that is part of the vanishing 'trick'!" Even though Tiger never appreciated others calling 'it' a trick, it was Ok if she or Alex called 'it' a trick.

Entering 'downtown', Alex described different places and things—"On the left—see the small sign—El Grotto, that's where Dad hung out the most—drunk or sober—making deals." "Grotto? That's the name for—cave? Why is it named Grotto?" "Silly, because it is a cave!" "In the center of 'downtown'?" "Yes! Merida is full—that's a bad choice of words—undermined with caves! Even some of the hotels use 'their' cave! The Hotel Colon uses theirs for a sauna—hot springs and all!" "What about private homes? Those have caves also?" "Yes, especially in the Colonial District—

North of center—a lot of owners have decorated—'whatever'—theirs for bars, party rooms, wine cellars, 'get-aways', whatever!"

The traffic was at a crawl, Alex asked, "Have you noticed that there are not many overhead wires here?" Tiger stuck her head out the window and looked about, replied, "I see what you mean! How's that possible?" "Caves, connecting natural tunnels. All the major wiring and water system are run through the tunnels and the caves!" "That's great! Who would have thought of that!" "Thomas Edison did!" "THE Thomas Edison?" "Yes, THE Thomas Edison! He laid out Merida's first electrical system, and, like he did in New York City, he decided that underground was the way to go. He hated to see overhead wires!"

"And speaking of New York, did you know that the New York Post—the newspaper—has been available in Merida since—" Tiger interrupted, "Since before 1839! Ha! Ha! I read John L. Stephen's 'Incidents' when you did! Remember?" They laughed together.

Turning north on 16th, slowly pass the Zocalo, then in the next block, Alex exclaimed, "There! On the left! The Cafe Express! THE BEST place to eat in all of Merida! My very favorite!" "We'll have to get there!"

Again, Alex spoke as to herself, "four, five—next street one-way West—yes—here", she turned left, and went only one block. Stopped by the stop sign, she pointed, "El Presidente! I knew I could recall where it is! How to get from the Itza!" The tall—taller than the other buildings around it at least—hotel was across 18th and on their right.

As Alex pulled the VW van under the entrance canopy, she said, "Now, if they just have a room!" The Doorman didn't step forward, or offer to help the 'ladies' out! He just glared at the dirty van.

Seeing the Doorman's non-action, Alex said, "Come on—leave Mickey asleep! Watch this!" The two, rather grubby looking by now—Alex's jeans and loose shirt, Tiger's full skirt and her blouse, all wrinkled—Alex hopped out with her large purse and the keys. Tiger got out—she had her purse also. Alex briskly stepped directly to the Doorman, she held out the keys, snapped "Bellhop! Please get our things out—and bring my little baby inside! We'll be at Reservations!" The Doorman glanced at Mickey asleep on the rear seat and the Doorman appeared as if he would faint! Alex jerked the keys back, said "Oh? You're too busy? I'll do it myself! And ask the Management about the 'crappy' service out front!" The two got back in the van, and Alex drove into the hotel's parking lot.

They doubled over with laughter as they woke Mickey, and rolled the Codex inside the old blanket that came with the van. Alex got out another small envelope, hid the remaining ones and the canvas bag of coins under the rear seat's bottom cushion again. With the four Mitlas shouldered, a paper sack of fruit, food items and the beach bag full of beer and wine bottles—some empty, some still full—and Mickey with the heavy bundle (the Codex) in his arms, they walked back to the main front entrance. As they approached, Alex said toward the Doorman, "I forgot! He can walk!" as she nodded to Mickey.

Stepping to directly in front of the reservations clerk, Alex saw that he continuously turned his head from side to side as he avoided her. Mickey and Tiger, with their arms full also, stood to each side, slightly behind Alex. The man kept turning his head. Alex snapped, "Hey! Are you looking for—'A', the hotel 'Dick'? 'B', a city cop? Or, 'C', the mule we rode in?" He stopped his turning, and with a sneering expression, leaned forward, and in almost a whisper, said, "The service entrance is that way.", he motioned toward the rear of the lobby with his bald head. Alex enjoyed moments like this—when men really screwed up! In a loud voice, she said, "Service? Service is when you get your thumb out of your ass and look through the reservations book and get us a room on the top floor! That IS the fifth floor, is it not? Or do you know? A room or suite with a balcony! And at least two beds!" She nodded toward Mickey, added, "We don't sleep with HIM! He still wets the bed!" It was all the three could do not to laugh!

The clerk flipped through the book, then said, "The only thing available—on the top floor—is the Presidential suite. It is rather expensive!" Alex hated 'rather expensive' almost as much as she disliked 'no'. To her 'rather expensive' implied they didn't know the damn price! She slipped the strap of the larger Mitla off her shoulder and she let it fall. She removed the smaller one, unzipped it, then jerked out the still sealed envelopes—the one with one thousand dollars—US—, in pasos.

Sticking the envelope in the clerk's face, she quipped, "If that's not enough to get us started, there's more where that came from! Just apply that to my account. When we use it up, just you let me know! Ok? Now, give me the key, and ding your bell for a Bellhop! My kids are about tired of your lazy attitude!" The clerk ripped open the envelope, counted, then gave a slight gasp. "What? That's not enough?" "No, no, this is plenty—Senorita—" He hesitated as he turned the book toward her so she could sign it. "Senorita? It IS Senora! You think my kids are 'bastards'? Senora

Alex—and Alex is all you need to know! Got that?" From this incidence on, things went very well, very smoothly with the employees at the El Presidente!

As they and the bellhop—with their bags and the sack of food—got on the elevator, Alex whispered to Mickey, "Sorry about the bedwetting joke—I just couldn't help it." "That's Ok, it was the coolest! I'll have to remember it!" Mickey was still carrying the 'bundle'.

The bellhop left after Alex tipped him handsomely, then the three quickly reached an agreement. At least one of them, armed, would be with the Codex until 'help' arrived or until they flew out of Mexico.

Alex got on the phone to Room Service—the other two looked over the suite. It was about eighteen feet wide—with a balcony the full width—the sleeping area, though not walled off, was nicely arranged along one side. The other side was settees and stuffed chairs that faced the all-glass wall at the balcony. Toward the kitchenette—even with a full size refrigerator—was a fourplace dinette set. At the far end of the suite, was a handy dressing area—closets, counter, lavatory—the walls and all the doors—there were doors between the main room, the bath, and to the closets—were covered with mirrors, a lot of mirrors!

The bath was the nicest part of the entire apartment. The same width as the main room, and about eight feet in the other direction, it was huge! The entire inside of the bath—including the ceiling—was ceramic tile. And like the rest of the place, the colors were pastel shades of light yellow, with some trim in cream, some in bright gold. At the door to the bath, the one between the bath and the dressing room, was a low step-over threshold. Inside the bath, there were floor drains and ceiling mounted sprayheads. Across one end was a large tub with side spray nozzles and two hand-held units.

Talking on the phone, Alex watched the two as they looked in wonder at the interior and the excellent view from the balcony, where there were four chairs and two small tables. Hanging up, she joined them on the balcony, casually remarked "You two should see my suite in D.C., Tiger, maybe you and I can run up sometime soon." (Just before the last time she had left D.C., she had made a deal with the Hotel Empire. She leased the suite, 518, the one she liked so much, for one year. With the agreement that the hotel could rent it out when she didn't need it. But, it was to be 'hers' as soon as she got to D.C. If occupied, it was to be vacated—no questions asked.)

They enjoyed the view, then, "I guess I had better put what fruit was left, in the 'frig'—and look for me a drink!", Alex said as she headed in. They followed. As soon as the three saw 'it'—the blanket wrapped bundle—they stopped. Mickey had placed 'it' on the floor at to the wall between the two king-sized beds. They stared at the Codex, then, Alex waved her fingers at it, snapped, "No! We're not going to open it until Dr.K gets here! She'll know the proper procedure. We may do harm by not opening it in the correct fashion!" They stepped on to the kitchenette.

Sipping on a warm beer, Alex ran her fingers up and down Tiger's long hair, "I'm going to call up a beautician—after we shower, she can brush out your hair, trim the ends." Stepping to a mirror, she felt her own hair, added, "And do SOMETHING with mine!" On the phone, she ended with, "Yes! Someone that knows about wigs!" She hung up, turned to Tiger, and said "Ok, Kid, it's 'scrub-a-dub' time!" Mickey 'retired' to the balcony as the two women started to remove their shoes.

Stepping back to Tiger, Alex untied the waistband to her full, heavy skirt, let it drop to the floor, and said, "Let me show you a trick—leave your panties and blouse on—I'll leave my jeans, shirt on. We'll do 'laundry' while we shower!"

"Tap-Tap', on the door, Mickey went, peeked through the view-port-the young man in the hall appeared to be a waiter as he held up a menu close to the hole. After Mickey let him in, he refastened the 'night-chain', said, "Follow me!" Mickey knocked on the bath door, then eased it about half open, shouted—the shower heads were on full blast—"Alex! What do you want to eat!" He motioned for the waiter to write it down—and—to lean closer, close enough to see. Alex stopped what had looked like an Indian War Dance as she stomped her clothes, she called back, "Butter broasted chicken—pollo! "And she recalled her favorite in Merida, "And, a club sandwich on the side! An order of toastatos—con strawberry jam! And, a bottle of California white wine!" "Tiger? You?" he asked. "I'll have the same! I don't think I've ever had a side order of a club sandwich!" The girls laughed, hugged, and Alex waved them away! They had been staring at the two wet, naked women.

"And you, Senor?" the waiter asked. "Do you guys make a 'killer' burger?" Mickey asked. The waiter smiled, "The best in all of Yucatan!" "Great! I'll have that, fries, and a large Coke!" "Sorry, no Cokes in Yucatan—only Crystal soft drinks." "Ok, a large jugo de fruta—fresh!" "We only serve the very freshest fruit juices!" "Ok! Hey, on that white wine?

You can save yourself some trouble—bring two more bottles, we'll stick it in the 'frig'!" "Is there anything else, Sir?" Mickey almost whispered, "You don't happen to know where there is a teenaged chick— a chick—that can—you know—be 'had'—for a price even?"

The waiter at first hesitated as he thought, then, "Yes, I do, as a matter of fact", he leaned closer, added softly "She works—only on call, special occasions, not regular—with a couple of our regular 'Ladies'." He pulled out a card—a 'business' card—it showed two names, room 405, 'Special Services'. "This will get you 'in', just ask for 'arrangements' to get 'Suzie' to come over." "Hey, man! Thanks a heap! I'll see that 'Mom' treats you right!" He added, "What's a fair price? Straight, no 'special features'?" "One hundred—US." "Ok! No problem! Thanks again!" Mickey knew he had 'collected' more than that by just picking up Alex's change—she nearly always left the change on the tables or counters.

Coming out of the bath, still drying, Mickey went in. Tiger asked, "Don't you think you should contact HVG?" "Not yet, it's not even dark, no telling where they are. I want to directly communicate with Dr.K—via our computers—I'll do it about ten tonight."

Seeing Tiger get her hairbrush, Alex said, "You may as well wait for the beautician—I think your ends need trimming." Looking in the mirror, Tiger nodded in agreement. They were still nude when there was a 'tap-tap' on the door. Alex checked, it was the beautician. After introductions, and relocking the door, Alex and Tiger told the attractive young Maya woman what they wanted done to Tiger's hair. Trim the ends, brush it out and braid two small side strands—to hang beside her cheeks.

As the beautician worked—she had spread out a small sheet on the carpet—on Tiger's hair, Alex paced, and repeatedly glanced at her own hair in a mirror.

Stopping in front of a mirror, Alex asked, "What do you two think about a blonde? A curly, bushy-headed blonde?" "How?" Tiger only replied. "A wig! The only way I see." Alex responded. The Hairdresser stopped, stepped very close to Alex's bare back then stroked her fingers through Alex's hair. As she breathed on Alex's neck, she said, "Your hair is too short to wrap into a bun", she felt some more, added, "And too course to fold up". She twisted Alex to face to face and remarked sweetly, "What do you think about a boy-cut? You would make a—darling", she smiled, and slowly dragged her fingers down Alex's neck, her shoulders, on down to the top of her breasts, "a cute—little boy." Slowly, and maintaining their eye to eye contact, Alex raised her fingers to her own nipples, and, using her thumbs and index fingers, gave these a slow, twisting pinch. "And these?" she asked as she continued to twist her already prominent, hard nipples. "And—those, are the cutest of all." The beautician's lips were wet as she slowly lowered her gaze to Alex's erect nipples. And she was very impressed with Alex's glabrous condition.

"Hey! You two! We going to do hair? Or what? Please? Before you two get all slobbery and choke on your tongues!" Tiger's pun broke their trance. The beautician returned to Tiger's hair, remarked, "Just an idea—the boy-cut. Then a wig would cover your sides and back—if cut high enough. Think about it!" Alex continued to look in the mirror, she asked, "Tig—what do you think Tom would think?" "It will grow out, besides, a change might shock Ole Tom into—well—whatever!" Alex stepped smartly to the two, quipped, "Ok! Let's do it!" Then she asked,

"There are blond wigs available? Here? I will not have to go out, will I?" "No problem! I've got exactly what you need! A silvery blond Marilyn Monroe!" "You don't by chance happen to have MM's tits, do you?" "No way!" And the three laughed.

The door between the living/sleeping area and the dressing room was open. So far, they hadn't seen any reason to close it. Still drying, Mickey came out of the bath, but on seeing 'a stranger', he quickly wrapped the towel around his hips. She had finished with Tiger—powdered and brushed off any loose hair. "Mickey, this is Laura—the beautician! Laura, this is Mickey—my son!" Alex introduced them. Tilting close to Alex's ear, she whispered, "Is he really your son? You don't have any stretch marks—scars—" "You noticed, did you? It was a miracle!"

Alex noticed as she looked in the mirror that Tiger and Mickey seemed to be having problems finding something to put on. She said, "Why don't you two go buy some new 'rags'! And especially, Mickey new dress slacks! Guys do not wear jeans in Merida! It is—only—what Laura? Six or eight blocks to the shopping district?" "Ten or twelve" Laura corrected. Then Alex gave directions, "Go out the front entrance, keep in that direction, cut across the Zocalo, to 16th, head right—South—on 16th. You will soon see anything you can imagine to buy! Right, Laura?" "Yes, and the shops—a shop for each different article—will be open until about ten tonight."

"What colors do blondes wear?" Alex quickly asked Laura. "Pale yellows, creams, off-whites, or shinny white—nothing bold or dark.

They're suppose to be delicate you know." The two threw on 'whatever' as Alex said, "Tiger, get me a new slip-dress, soft yellow or cream.

And, you Mickey, get what ever money you two may need from my purse—just be sure to replace it back in the drawer." He smiled as he thought why her purse was in a drawer—because her pistol was still in her purse. And 'his' pistol—the one Alex had gotten from Rudi—was in another small top drawer in the same dresser.

Laura was almost finished with Alex's haircut when the two left. As soon as they closed the door, Alex said, "Excuse me", she stepped and locked the door and secured the 'night chain', turned and looked into Laura's eyes, asked, "How about a drink—of whatever is in the 'frig'?" "Sure, I need a break anyway." There was a bottle of wine—it had cooled off by now. As Laura poured drinks, Alex called Room Service, "There's been a glitch here. Please hold that order until I call you back." Stepping to Laura and taking the glass, she asked, "You ever been with a little boy before?" Laura slowly reached her hand around to Alex's bare small bottom, pressed it, replied, "Not one like you—not one as cute as you." "Let's shower—get this hair off me", Alex cooed as she directed the young beautiful beautician toward the dressing room. Getting undressed for Laura wasn't a problem—she wore a snap-down the front white uniform. With one jerk, she dropped it to the floor—she was naked underneath. Kicking off her low top slip-on shoes, she was ready.

Outside, the streetlights began to come on as darkness approached.

As Rudi swung right onto route 180 leaving Campeche, he said to Kyle, "That was about four hours pissed away!" "Tell me about it!" "And we will not get to Merida in time to check any flights there. You know a good place we can spend the night in Merida?" "Yes, right downtown, on avenue eighteen, about six blocks North of the Zocalo—'The Hotel El Presidente." "That sounds expensive." "It is, but what the hell, this may well be our last time on THIS expense account!"

Alex paced, twisted more, and looked at herself in the large mirrors even more. Striking a pose, she studied what she had on, what she looked like. She had on the white spike heels from the Playa Northa gig, a pair of light tan pantyhose, and the new MM silvery blond wig. She bent closer to the mirror and twisting her head back and forth, she examined her 'new' blond eye brows and lashes, the pale blue eye shadows and light blue lipstick. Laura had painted these for her, and had insured her that it all was removable—with face cream, oil, or, as Alex had suggested, suntan lotion—because Alex had so much left over from the 'beach-business'!

Changing poses, she settled on; stiff left leg, her weight on this. Her right foot turned outward, her right knee slightly bent, her right heel slightly lifted. Her left fingertips to her left hip, her right finger tips to the rear of the wig.

But her eyes were not right! Who had ever seen a blonde with black eyes! She quickly looked through her bags and located the 'fancy' sunglasses she had worn at Mazatlan. Yes! These hid her eyes, and went with the wig! She was ready! If she just had a dress to match the rest of her glamorous appearance!

At the 'tap-tap', she rushed to the door, looked through the 'peekhole'—she saw Tiger and Mickey. Silently she removed the chain and unlocked the door. Stepping back, she got her pose 'just-right', and said,

"Come in! The door's unlocked!" They rushed in—Tiger first, her arms full of packages—Mickey next, his arms full of packages—and then the young waiter from earlier this evening! He quickly put his fingers—but not very tightly together—over his eyes. "Lock the door!" Mickey snapped as he looked at the waiter, then the door. He did, turned back to stare at Alex—posed—through his fingers. Tiger and Mickey were full of giddiness! The shopping! The shops! How the shops specialized! The low prices! And everything was there in that one district! The two rattled on and on! In mixed English, Spanish, and Tzental! Tiger even threw in a little French!

Suddenly realizing that Alex was still posed, the two stopped in mid motion, in mid sentence, and stared at Alex. Tiger said, "You look wonderful!" And she started again about how marvelous the shopping was! Mickey only said, "Great! Just great!" And he too began again about the shopping trip! Seeing that Tiger was frantically looking in the new bags for 'something', and Mickey was showing off his new clothes. Alex turned more toward the waiter, asked, "Well? What do YOU think?" He tried, "I— I—I—" "That's close enough! I'm glad someone finally noticed me!" Alex snapped then added, "Please! Go get the food! I'm starved!"

When the waiter went out into the hall, Mickey rushed to him, slipped him a five dollar bill, asked, "Hey, Buddy, would you please stop by 405 and ask the 'Ladies' to have Suzie 'available' at ten? Time looks tight here— the eating and all—" "Sure! No problem!" The waiter replied then asked, "Is she really your Mom?" Mickey just nodded. "Man! She is—is—", the waiter stalled. Mickey finished it, "She is something else!" "Yes, that's it! Something else!" Then the waiter, as he shook his head, went on to the elevators.

Back in the room, Mickey saw that Tiger had located the dress she had picked out for Alex. It was a simple slip-dress, with tiny spaghetti straps—very similar to Alex's favorite—but a different color and a different material. The color was a pale yellow, mottled with a creamy—even lighter shade of yellow. The material was very stretchy—almost Spandex, but much lighter weight. The two finally got it up over Alex's hips, then her bust and the straps over her shoulders. Looking in a full height mirror, Alex saw how marvelously it stretched over her erect nipples, and tucked under—even into—her small tight butt. She exclaimed, "Oh! Tiger! It is just ME! It is beautiful! Oh, thanks, Tiger! You knew exactly what I wanted!"

Noticing Mickey stare at her bottom—how the thin material covered it like a coat of paint, she turned to Tiger, placed her fists on her hips, said, "That poor boy has got to get 'laid'—soon!" Mickey just grinned, and went out on the balcony, and thought, 'Right! And tonight's the night!'

The waiter soon returned with the food and drinks. He sat a very attractive meal, and stood to one side, helped, and poured drinks as these were needed. All very professional, he didn't mention—or show—any signs about the 'posing-session' earlier. But he did wink at Mickey and gave him a 'thumbs-up' sign. While the waiter cleared the dishes away, the three had coffee on the balcony.

Noticing the waiter start toward the door with the cart, Alex said to Mickey, "Please go sign the bill—and be sure to add a tip." He jumped at the opportunity. Inside, just the two of them, Mickey added a 'very handsome' tip. "Man, that's a lot—is it going to be Ok with—", the waiter nodded toward Alex. "With Mom? Sure, her money comes from a bottomless gold mine!" The waiter shook his head in amazement and left.

Only shortly after the waiter left, Alex said, "You two going to be Ok—here by yourselves?" She waited. "Alex, I've got—a date—at ten. Is it Ok if I leave before then?" To Tiger, Alex remarked, "He's been in Merida not over eight hours—and he has a date! And I was concerned about his sex life?" She turned and hugged Mickey, softly said, "Of course." He went inside and started getting ready. "Tiger—why don't you offer him—a—well, you know what."

Stepping inside to the Mitlas—she knew exactly where—she took out two condoms, tossed these to Mickey, and as she pointed a stiff index finger at him, snapped, "Be sure and use those—I'm not ready to be an aunt yet!" He nodded—and smiled back.

Returning to the balcony, Alex caught her arm, said, "I want to make a sweep through the downstairs—try out this new disguise—just look around. See if those two Agents show up? We're so close—Are you sure you'll be Ok?" "I'll be OK! Remember? Mike taught me to shoot as good as most anyone!" Then Tiger went inside.

Alex turned and looked out over the lighted city—and wondered. She thought, 'Brace-up, little Alex, it's going to be long, rough night!' She went in, got her purse—the one with the pistol—from the drawer, slipped the strap over her left shoulder, got the sunglasses—she would wait to put these on—and left. Stepping out of the elevator at the lobby level, she began a systematic search. And mentally 'mapped' the different areas. At the main dining room, she chit-chatted with the waiter as she looked among the guests—no sign of the Agents. Again at the two smaller cafes—one was open-air into the lobby—nothing. And at the two bars, and even the pool area, still nothing.

Leaving the hotel by the front main entrance, she headed south—to the area of the Zocalo. A quick pass through the tourist and the spectators at the nightly exhibition dances, the traditional dance teams sponsored by the city of Merida. No one in sight that even vaguely resembled the Agents. A quick pass through the park—only young families with their kids enjoying the cool of the evening and the band's nightly music around the central flagpole—no Agents. She then made quick swings through the six or seven more popular cafes along Avenues 16, 17, and 18. While on 16th, she had a quick drink in the Express and watched the foot-traffic on the sidewalks and the small park across the street. On purpose, she avoided the south-west of the Zocalo—where 18 and 19 intersected.

She hesitated, glanced at her watch, it showed 1:0:15. Rushing—she wanted to contact Nat soon—she returned to the hotel. And as she approached the 'open-air' cafe in the lobby, she saw the two Agents! Kyle and Rudi! It appeared as if they were having a late-night snack and coffee. She slowed her pace, entered the cafe where she would not be noticed by the two. To be sure, she ordered coffee—and watched the two. No mistake, it was them! But, how was this possible? She knew for sure, the van was not 'bugged'! They didn't even know about it! And they surely had not had the opportunity! She out-waited them, they soon left and went directly to the elevator. She shifted about, watched the elevator's indicator—it stopped at the third floor! It was obvious to Alex that they were at least spending this night here! At The hotel El Presidente! Not taking the chance of a face to face consultation at—or in—the elevator, she took the stairs.

Reaching the third floor, she removed her 'spikes'—too difficult to run in—or maneuver in! And it made climbing the stairs easier. At the fourth floor, she suddenly stopped when she saw Mickey come out of a room! She ran toward him, he was startled at seeing he. Not asking any details, she roughly grabbed his arm, and headed back for the stairs. Running up the stairs, he asked, "What's going on?" "Not now, wait until we're in the room!"she snapped.

Out of breath, Alex could hardly explain after Tiger let the two of them in. As she chained and locked the door, Alex tried. "They—here—Kyle—Rudi—on the third—floor—a—room-I guess—I saw them—in the cafe—, downstairs!" Mickey quickly got her a drink of water as she sat down on the edge of the bed, "But how could they find us?" Tiger asked as to herself. "I don't think—", Alex got her wind, continued—"If they knew that we were here, they would have already come to us! They didn't seem in a hurry." "Just dumb luck? You guess?" Mickey asked. "Yes, just dumb luck!" The other two sat down as they contemplated their situation. But Alex knew what had to be next—now!

"Mickey, get the lap-top! I—we—had better send a message—now!" With the computer, and a drink for Alex, the three moved to the balcony. Satellite communications can be better without steel overhead—the reinforcing in the concrete roof above. After link-up, Alex entered the following message to Nat—Dr.K.

From: A&T, TIHOO(JLS-Y,VOL1,PG41)

Acquisition complete. Expect trouble from fierce competition. Urgently need assistance. Contact 'STILL", promised! Will remain on for your response. W? W? W? A&T,PAKAL'S CASA,-0.

HIDDEN VALLEY

Tom just happened to be at home. He, Arnie and Jim stood around Nat's computer when they heard that the 'in-coming' was from Alex. As soon as the message appeared on the screen, Nat snapped, "Arnie, get my copy of Stephens, volume one—see what's on page forty-one! Then she commanded, "Jim, get on your cellphone! Contact Bill Stillwell, now! Regardless of where he is, or what he is doing! I'll hold this connection as long as possible! What Alex wants to know, is some answers to— What? When? Where?" Then Nat wondered, 'Pakal's Casa'? The Ruler of Palenque? The king? The president? She stepped to Jim, whispered, "Wasn't there an El Presidente hotel in Merida?" He nodded, yes.

It didn't take Arnie long, he said to all, as he quoted Stephens, "The Indian town of Tihoo, the very loyal and noble City of Merida."

They are in Merida, Yucatan!" "Ok!" Nat snapped, "Merida, El Presidente hotel, room 502!" The—0. in Maya is 502.

But getting Secretary Stillwell on the phone was taking longer. And Mike was tied-up in Central Florida.

MERIDA-HOTEL EL PRESIDENTE

Alex passed the laptop to Tiger, snapped, "Watch for an answer, I've got something else to do tonight!" She rushed inside and frantically began to remake her disguise. She carefully removed the wig and placed it on the foam 'head-stand'—this came with the purchase of the wig. After a lot of pulling and wiggling, she was out of the dress—she kept the pantyhose on. At the lavatory in the dressing room, she removed the blond eye make-up with suntan lotion. Then with pan-cake foundation, she applied a liberal coating to her face—she was trying to get her skin darker. Looking the mirror, she decided it was as good as it was going to get. She grabbed the jeans and her loose 'driving' shirt, these were still slightly damp, but would have to do.

Back at the beds, she slipped on the jeans but not the shirt—yet. Grabbing up her purse, Alex dumped the contents on the bed. Picking out the loose paso bills, and the coins, she put these in her right front pocket. Then she stuffed her wallet in her left front pocket. Taking the empty purse, she adjusted the strap for a snug fit over her left shoulder. With it unzipped, she checked the pistol—she tried inserting and drawing it from the purse. Satisfied, she left it in, and left the purse unzipped. After pulling on the loose shirt, she stepped to a mirror and looked. Not right, Alex dug through her clothes and located an old windbreaker jacket. With this over her shirt—over the 'hidden' purse—she was now pleased with her image in the mirror. She quickly put on her low quarter tennis shoes and tied these very tight.

With a black eyebrow marker, she leaned close to the mirror and began to apply a thin line—a mustache—above her upper lip. Mickey, inside, had been watching her very closely, he asked, "What are you up to?" "Personal) I've got to settle a very old debt!" As she continued with her mustache, she looked at Mickey's reflection in the mirror and questioned, "What were you doing in a room on the forth floor?" "Personal, something I've wanted to do for quiet a while." "Touche'!" Alex replied. "To-what?" "Touche', that's French for,'you get back what you give!" and she smiled at him.

"We have a reply!" Tiger called from the balcony. The two rushed out, Tiger quipped, "Goodness! Who do we have here?" as she looked at the 'new' Alex. "Don't ask", Mickey responded. She didn't. The three looked at the small screen as it showed:

W? RWB GULFSTREAM
W? 03/08 ASAP
W? SU CASA

Alex quickly interpreted, "Red, white, blue Gulfstream. Bill Stillwell's government jet is white, trimmed with red and blue stripes. 03/08, that's tomorrow, and as soon as possible." "Su casa— your home", Tiger interjected, "Your home—Dr,K must mean here, at our hotel!" At Alex's directions, Tiger entered: CAP.T-T-T? The three waited. A reply appeared, 'Squad Leader' "Great!" Alex exclaimed as she realized Tom was leading the 'rescue mission'! "Tiger, send 'Thanks, love, blab, blab, and OUT. Then shut down."

Back inside, as Alex paced, she told the other two, "I'm going out for a while—not sure when I'll be back. Hold the fort here—take turns sleeping—and stay armed. Mickey, have you checked that pistol? The one I got from Rudi?" "Sure, it's ready." Strangely, she kissed each of them on their cheeks. Then she left.

It was almost midnight as Alex rushed down the stairs. At the lobby level, instead of heading straight out through the lobby, she turned right. Entering and going through the kitchen, she saw that everyone was busy— no one paid any attention to her. Leaving the hotel by the rear service entrance, she turned right and quickly crossed to the sidewalk opposite the hotel and she headed south—toward the Zocalo.

Past the park, at Ave. 19, she turned right. She knew that where she was headed was near the middle of the block, on her right.

At the small sign overhead—'El Grotto'—she went through the wide double doors, and slowly eased down the wide steps. Looking about she saw there were tables, chairs, booths, and still a large crowd of men, no women, and the heavy layer of smoke came down about half way to the floor.

There was one big, ugly, scar-faced bartender at the end closest to the entrance—another bartender at the far end of the long bar. He appeared younger—and not as ugly. The one closer, stared, and started toward the end of the bar. Alex quickly decided to take the 'direct' approach—she briskly stepped toward the bartender. She knew without their cooperation, she would most likely get thrown out on her ear!

As the bartender watched—he didn't speak—she removed a handful of bills, and separated what she guessed to be about twenty dollars—US. Handing these to him, she whispered something to him. He took the money and stuffed it into his pants pocket. Then he got her a bottle of Superior Beer. Slowly, she started, and for the next hour or so, she searched among the customers. Without attracting too much attention, she carefully looked at their faces—in particular their eyes. But, every man had dark skin—and black eyes. Having covered everyone, she took a seat close to the wide entrance, waited, and watched for any newcomers.

Another hour passed, the crowd began to thin out. Giving up—for tonight anyway—she emptied her bottle, carried it to the bartender—the same one she had talked to earlier. She leaned close, whispered to him. He nodded, she took out what she estimated to be about fifty dollars and slid the bills to him. Again, he put these into his pants pocket—not his apron. And again, he nodded to Alex. Leaving the El Grotto, she hesitated when she reached the fresh, cool morning air.

The typical early—it was still before sunrise—morning mist began to drift in. She headed east, turned left with the intention to go directly back to the hotel. Alex wasn't a 'happy-camper', she was tired—she was tired of sneaking around. She stopped, the sound of the footsteps behind her stopped. She crossed the street, stepped under the large spreading trees in the park. The two men followed—she recognized them from seeing them in the bar—she snapped around, jerked out her pistol—they froze in place—she said "You best go in a different direction, unless you two want to start breathing through your bellies!" They turned around and headed back toward the all-night bar. She replaced the pistol in her purse and went north toward the hotel.

Approaching the front main entrance, the Doorman slid from his stool and held up a hand in front of her. Her appearances didn't exactly indicate she was a guest. Jamming her hand in her right pocket, she jerked out some bills and slapped these in the man's extended hand. As he stuck these in his pocket, he opened the door. Briskly, Alex walked straight through the long lobby and took the elevator to the fifth floor. If she had met the two Agents, it would have not gone well for them—little Alex was pissed.

CHAPTER 17

It was just after noon as the three—Nat, Jim and Tom—waited at the Blairsville airport. Restless, Tom paced, then suddenly stopped, pulled open his jacket and removed his Army 45 pistol from the shoulder holster. While he checked the clip, Jim watched. And he watched Nat—she was squatted down, checking her 'standard' travel bag. The one she had grabbed up at the last minute before they left Hidden Valley.

She assured the presence of the main items: her 35MM camera, her small camera(about the size of a pack of cigarettes—it took micro-film size photos) and her chemical analysis kit. And removing her four different passports, she waved these toward Jim, asked, "Do you think I'll need these?" "Only the one that shows you to be an American citizen!" Removing that one, she pushed it in the left large pocket of her 'safari jacket'. Coming across her all-fiberglass boot-knife, she took that out and slipped it into the top of her right boot—between her tight 'safari pants and the boot, it wasn't noticeable.

As she removed and checked the clip of her 9MM Russian made semi-automatic pistol—it was small, but very deadly. Jim said, as he looked at Nat, then Tom, "I wouldn't want to meet you two in a dark alley!" Nat stopped—still holding her pistol—she smiled up at Jim, said, "How about on the roof of the Castillo—at Chicken Itza—on a cloudless night?" He grinned at her remembrance of their first 'serious' encounter, he replied, "Now! That's Ok!"

Nat continued with her equipment, she slipped the pistol in her right jacket pocket. She had her full length Russian mink coat pulled open—away from her jacket. After checking her emergency medical kit and her bag of gold Krugerrand coins—her 'traveling money'—she straightened up. And listened, she could hear the jet as it approached. "I'll not need my furs"—she also had on the Cossack's fur cap—"in Merida!" She stepped to Tom's van, removed the furs, threw these inside.

As Tom came to the van to lock it, she asked, "You brought your 'legal' Mexican permit for your pistol, didn't you?" "Sure! Right here in my wallet!" She had 'fixed' these—her's and Tom's—last night.

The Gulfstream screamed to a crawl—full brakes and the thrust reversers activated. As soon as it taxied back, and turned around at the parking apron, the forward side door popped open and the stairs were lowered. The three were amazed at the sight of the first man to exit and come down—It was Bill Stillwell! They had not expected The Secretary of Agriculture to be on the plane—on this trip! "Bill", or "Still", the three shouted as they rushed to greet him. "We didn't ex—" Jim started, but Stillwell interrupted, "Hell! I wouldn't miss this for the world! I knew Alex was up to something! All the weird questions we got out of Mexico! My staff—and I—had to try hard to fend off those questions! Come aboard!"

The jet took off, reached cruising altitude, and turned off the seat belt lights. Stillwell shifted, faced the three—and—said—"Ok, gang, you've got two choices—either tell me exactly what Alex is up to— or—jump out!" They laughed, Nat went to the bar, fixed drinks, passed these around then sat down. And she began, at the beginning, with the 'old tale' about 'The Lost Codex of Palenque'. Over an hour later—and a lot of questions by Bill—she ended by quoting Alex's last message.

Stillwell went to the bar, fixed another Jack Daniels on the rocks, turned toward the others, said, "Fierce competition—the Mexican Feds." "Yes, we guess. If they know what she has, they'll do most anything to stop her", Nat responded. "Let me ask", Bill continued. "What do you—your group—intend to do with this—as you've said—'priceless artifact'? Is our little Alex going to turn 'it' into another million dollar deal? Or what?"

They knew his implication, but Nat quickly answered, "No, Sir, she has agreed that we'll turn it over to the museum authorities—in Mexico—after we, Jim and I, have photo-copied it. And we have ascertained the Codex is an original. That it is really THE Codex—thousands—thousands of years old." "No money required?" Bill asked again to be sure he had the point clear. "No money from anyone—for the Codex, Sir" Nat replied.

He shook hands with the three then sat down and added, "Seeing that! Is worth the trouble! Alex doing anything without making money? That, I've got to see!" The four laughed.

MERIDA, HOTEL EL PRESIDENTE

It was mid afternoon as Alex came out of the bath room—she was still drying. Stepping into the large room, she saw Mickey—he was propped up in one bed, watching TV. Finished drying, she wrapped the wet towel around her torso, stepped out on the balcony next to Tiger. Putting one arm around Tiger's waist, Alex said, "I'm going to get dressed—as the blonde again, make a searching sweep through the hotel—maybe go 'outside' for a bit—this waiting is getting next to me! You two going to be OK?

Here?" "Sure", Tiger replied as she turned and kissed Alex's cheek, "If anyone shows up, we'll handle it—take off."

Alex returned to the dressing room and began to 'do' her eyebrows and lashes to the blond color—then she got dressed, and added the wig. Ready to leave, she checked her appearance in the mirror—same outfit, same white spikes, and her purse—with her gun—she twisted about, thought, 'Not bad! Maybe I like being a blonde—for a change at least!'

For one last opinion, Alex twisted to the balcony where Tiger was. "What do you think? How do I look?" as she turned about, she thought she had new glamour! She was full of giddness! But, unexpected, Tiger only nodded and cast an attempted smile. Her eyes were slightly wet, on the verge of real tears. Alex knew there was a problem, she stepped face to face, placed both hands on Tiger's hips and looked into her big, black eyes. She didn't have to ask, she waited. "Oh, Alex, I'm so sorry—but-what happens to us—you and me-after we leave here?"

Alex felt the young Maya Beauty's pain, she placed her cheek to Tiger's, and softly replied, "I know—I'm the one that is suppose to have all the answers—but—that's the one question—I—Oh, Tiger, I love you so much—and I don't have the answer. There's so much involved—you and Mike—Tom and I—and—you and I. Can you live with—we, you and I-just wait and see?"

Tiger put her hands on Alex's hips, held this, then slipped her hands up, and took Alex under her arms, slightly pushed her away until they were face to face. As the two stared into each other's eyes, Tiger slowly smiled—a real smile—and replied, "Yes—we'll just see where it goes—

I can live with that." Then the two embraced in a hard, long passionate kiss.

Downstairs, Alex went through the same routine as last evening. No sign of the Agents. Unknown to Alex, the two Agents were still at the airport checking all out-going flights, even the ones to Cuba and the smaller rental businesses. And their plans were—if no news here—to move to Cancun the next day before the first early morning flight out of there. She strutted through the lobby, nodded at the same clerk that had checked them in. He didn't recognize her, but he did concentrate on her tight, twisting strut! Face to face with the Doorman—the same one—she asked that he get her a cab. He also didn't show any signs of recognition!

"The shopping district—close to the Market", she told the taxi driver, "I want to shop—pick up a few things! Just follow along, please, and maybe help with my packages?" "Si! Si, Senorita!" he happily commented.

Alex sat back for the short ride South as she thought, 'If anxious, shop! Besides, I may not make it back here soon, or, ever!' What she loved about this district was the many small shops that specialized: hose in one, panties in one, skirts in one and on and on. And this same approach included most everything: pots in one, frying pans in one, brooms in one, etc, etc! Not one huge mega-store with all items scattered about, where finding what you wanted was the major problem!

After clothes—she bought a rather large amount—she decided to look at hammocks. She hopped in the cab and told the driver her intentions, he drove about two blocks and stopped at the ten or so hammock stores. Knowing the best approach—she had learned this during her summer at Merida—she decided before going in the first shop. Her choice was:

three double hammocks, and one single—all in Dacron thread, and all in bright fancy colors! Not deciding before 'shopping' was asking for trouble! Total confusion! Because there were so many choices! It still took her over an hour!

It was nearly dark as the driver headed back toward the hotel. As the Doorman briskly stepped to the taxi, he saw the huge pile of packages. He immediately rang for a bellhop. Then he started to help Alex out—as he stared at her crotch—it showed with her short dress hiked well above her knees. She smiled at him, spread her knees farther apart as she reached for his hand, asked, "Remember me? Yesterday? The VW van? My 'baby' asleep?" He gasped, batted his eyes, replied, "I guess so—that was you?" "Yes! I'm Alex, My baby's name is Mickey, his sister's is Tiger—she eats men that piss her off!" Alex rose, and laughed as the bellhop got all the packages loaded on a cart. Handsomely tipping the driver, she threw him a kiss, snapped, "Muchas Gracias Senor!" The Doorman held the door open this time! Inside, Alex said to the bellhop, "Sweetie, take that stuff up to 502, here's a tip!" she passed him a bill. She headed for the closest bar.

While she had one quick 'slammer', then a glass of wine to slowly sip as she looked about—still no sign of the two Agents. But, just in case, she put her sunglasses on. Returning to the lobby, she swung by the desk clerk's counter. As she stepped close—it was the same clerk as yesterday—he quickly asked, "May I be of assistance, Senorita?"

In just above a whisper, Alex said, "I told you once, it is Senora—I don't have bastard kids." He gave a start, dropped his lower jaw, stared. "Yes, it's me, Alex, remember? The thousand dollar deposit?" "Of course!

Please excuse me! I just—I—" "Didn't recognize me, did you?" "No, not at all! You're—you're—" "Beautiful is the word you're searching for! Isn't it?" "Oh, yes! Of course! Beautiful!"

She gave a slight laugh, asked "I just wanted to check—see if there was any of my money left—more or less get an idea where we—you and I—stand. Money wise, that is." He quickly pulled the account card for 502—there had been so much activity to it, he didn't need to be told the room number. "Senora Alex—just guessing today's—tonight's charges, you will still have several—over three at least—hundred dollars left. Are you planning to check out?" "Maybe, maybe not."

She turned to leave, but the clerk said, "Oh, excuse me—" Alex twisted back. "You have guests! Came in about thirty minutes ago." "How many? What did they look like?" she snapped.

"No problem—they were—well—very noticeable. Two large men— one dressed in—well—work clothes. One in a three piece light blue suit, he wore a silk tie. One slim tall gentleman—a so,so suit, And one—one—" Alex helped, "One beautiful Lady!" "Yes! With an odd accent." "Russian, she's Russian—and she is my Mother!" He almost fainted, "Your Mother? But she looked only a few years—", he realized he had made a mistake! "It runs in the family—young motherhood!"

Turning to leave, she wondered, 'A three piece suit? And a silk tie? No one at Hidden Valley even owned a silk tie! Thrilled, she almost broke into a trot, but her heels, and the skin tight dress were not suited for that! She walked very briskly, with an accented extra twist to her buns—a tighter snap.

Rushing through the long, narrow lobby, she failed to see the two Agents that sat in the open-air cafe! Kyle said, "Man! Look at the twist on that little blonde chick's ass!" Rudi responded, "Yeah! Small tight buns!" And, at the same moment they both realized they had recognized Alex! By her walk! By her bottom! Rudi slapped a bill on the table and they hurried toward the elevator!

Alex pushed the 'Up' button, the doors opened immediately. Stepping inside, she twisted to the control panel, depressed the 'Five' button.

The doors began to close. These were almost shut when four sets of fingers stopped the door's motion. The hands pulled the doors open—and Kyle and Rudi swung inside. The doors closed, the elevator started up.

Mustering her control, Alex didn't turn, didn't react to them at all. She glanced up at the ceiling and watched the floor indicator. Slightly shifting her feet, she got ready to run. The only thing she could think of was getting out of arm's reach! Gaining enough distance and time to get her gun out of her purse. And, damnit, she had zipped up her purse! She knew what to not move—her hands toward her purse! Passing the third floor, Kyle said, "So! Alex! We meet again!" She did nothing. "Alex, I would know your tight little ass in the dark—with both hands tied behind my back!" Kyle quipped.

Still looking at the indicator, she calmly said, "Jerk, you've got the wrong babe! If you want my ass, it'll cost you two hundred—US, for fifteen minutes. If you last longer, then it's a 'free-bee'—and Carol Sue, that's me, ain't never had to give a 'free-bee'." The elevator passed the fourth floor, shifting her weight to her left foot she got ready to jump with her right!

The doors began to open, Alex bolted forward—and ran directly into Tom's big chest! She screamed, "Tom! Look out!" The man behind her lunged, forward, his arms spread as if to catch her by the waist or hips. Roughly pushing Alex to his left, Tom hit the Agent dead-center of his face— solid, directly in the nose—it splattered blood. The blow knocked the man back in the elevator—the top of his head bent the rear wall of the elevator! That was Kyle!

Rudi jumped out, turned, faced Tom in a half crouch, planted his feet apart, and reached for his pistol under his coat. Alex kicked him forcible—

very forcible—in his crotch with the hard, pointed toe of her shoe. He doubled forward, his knees struck the floor as he grabbed his crotch. The pistol fell, Alex kicked it across the hall. With her fingers straight and stiff, her palms flat, she popped both sides of his head—directly over his ears—the slaps were awful sounding. Tom, in one swift motion, grabbed the back of the man's coat collar and his belt. Lifting, and in a swinging movement, Tom threw him into the elevator—head first. The top of his head bent the rear wall of the elevator.

Alex swung one arm and her head inside the elevator, punched 'L' for lobby. "Going Down!" she yelled, added, "This is my Sweetie—Tom—I'm so glad you two got to meet him!" The doors closed, it started down. Turning to Tom, she grabbed him around his neck, threw her legs up around his waist, shouted, "Tom! I'm so glad to see you!"

"The others are in your room! Let's go!" he responded as he walked and carried Alex toward 502. With her legs still locked around him, she leaned back, asked, "With my wig, my get-up, how did you know it was me?" "Didn't. I just didn't like the bastard's aggression toward a sweet, innocent looking little blonde!" Tom laughingly replied. "Oh, Tom! You're so sweet!" and she kissed him all about his face and neck.

"Where did you learn that 'number' you did on that other guy?" Tom asked. "I don't know for sure! Seems like I saw some 'big lug' do it to a cowboy out West! A long, long time ago!" They both laughed at her remembering 'the incident out West' before the collapse, years ago.

The doors of the elevator opened when it reached the lobby. The two Agents—as others in the area watched—crawled out, twisted about and leaned their backs against the wall. Kyle said to Rudi. "Remember your idea about me picking a fight? Us getting slightly beat-up?" Rudi just grunted. "Well, forget it! I think we just had it!" Then Kyle pressed his handkerchief tighter against his nose and muffled by his compress, he added, "What's next?" "I suggest", as Rudi still clutched his crotch, "We crawl back on the elevator, go up to our room—order two ice-packs-one for your nose—one for my balls!"

Bill Stillwell had heard the commotion at the elevator, he stepped to the door, released the thru-bolt, and pulled the door open to the extend of the night-chain. Looking through the narrow gap, he saw as Tom tossed 'someone' into the elevator, and Alex when she jumped up on Tom. Watching Tom carry Alex and approach the door, he unhooked the safety chain. At the first 'tap', Bill jerked the door wide open. Standing in the middle of the doorway, with one hand on his hip, he pointed a stiff index finger at Alex, snapped "Tom! Who's the dizzy blonde? I thought you were going to look for Alex? And you come back with a blonde 'fluzzy'!"

Alex unlocked her legs, wiggled loose, jumped to Stillwell, put both her fists on her hips, shouted, "Bill! You know it's me! Alex!" She poked him in his large waist, snapped, "You big Politicrat! Give me a kiss!" She caught his silk tie, pulled it as he bent down, and he kissed Alex on her lips. Leaning away, she added, "Silk tie! I should have guessed it was you!"

Turning toward the others, Alex saw that the dining table had been cleared off and moved to the center of the room. And The Codex was finally unwrapped, on the table, as Jim and Nat examined it. Nat was doing some sort of chemical test at an insignificant—but colored—spot on one of the 'pages'.

Alex stepped to Nat's hip—she was bent over with a very small eye-dropper—Alex didn't interrupt, but she extended her right hand over Nat's back. Jim smiled as he took Alex's hand. Holding the shake—after greetings—she asked, "How's it looking?" "So far—good, only a few more tests." Releasing the shake, Alex moved her face close to Nat's ear and whispered, "Glad you could make it." Nat only slightly nodded as she very carefully located the tip of the dropper exactly where she wanted it.

Moving away from the table, Alex saw that Tiger and Mickey were almost finished with packing their 'older' things. Stepping to the two, she hugged them, said, "Thanks, Kids, now—if we only had room"—she saw the Mitlas were bulging—"for all the 'new' stuff!" "No problem!" Tiger snapped, then flipped down the bed's covers, took a pillow, and jerked off the pillowcase. Mickey knew this 'game-plan', he quickly removed the other three pillowcases and began to pack the 'new' articles.

Noticing her jeans, the loose shirt and her tennis shoes—even the old windbreaker laid out on the bed, Alex said, "Tiger, you know what I need better than I do. Thanks."

Tom and Bill had slipped to the 'frig' in the kitchenette. Holding the 'frig' door open, Bill called out, "Damn! Alex! I expected better hospitality! There isn't anything to drink here but 'Girlie' stuff! How do guys like Jim and I get Jack Daniels here?" While Alex grabbed up her jeans and the loose shirt, she snapped back, "Try calling Louise and ask her to order some!" Bill nodded to Tom, calmly remarked, "Room Service', where's the phone?" as he left the kitchen area and headed for the dresser.

With her things, Alex stepped to the dresser, jerked her pistol from her purse and laid it on the dresser close to the phone. Dumping the rest of the items from her purse onto the dresser, she headed for the dressing room—with her empty purse, clothes and tennis shoes. Bill hesitated on the call to Room Service as he studied Alex's pistol. Picking up the phone, he called toward Mickey, "Hey! Kid! What's Room Service's number?" Bill knew that the first thing young people learned when 'hotel-living' was Room Service's number! Mickey told him, he dialed.

"Yes, this is room—' Kid! What's this room number?" "502" Mickey replied without stopping what he was doing. Bill continued to Room Service "Please send up a large bottle—the largest you've got— of Jack Daniels", he estimated, added, "And two, no, make that three—bottles of white wine—California white wine! And"—"Kid?" "A pitcher of fresh fruit juice!" "And a pitcher of fresh fruit juice—and something to snack on!'—"I don't know!" he hesitated. Mickey finally quit, stepped to Bill, took the phone, snapped, "Six club sandwiches, one 'killer' burger—and three large plates of sliced fresh fruit! And please rush it up! We're kind of in a hurry here!" Mickey hung up, looked at Alex's pistol. He removed 'his' pistol from the top drawer and placed it next to Alex's. Then he returned to Tiger and began to help her finish the packing.

Bill had watched Mickey with the pistol. As Tom walked close, headed for the balcony, Bill caught his arm and said, "And you were worried about these two gals?" as he pointed to the guns. Tom just shrugged, went on out on the balcony. Bill joined him as they watched the street lights come on.

Meanwhile, back in the dressing room—with the door to the big room closed for the first time—Alex removed the wig then stripped. She quickly applied suntan lotion to her face—particularly to her eyebrows and lashes. Letting this soak, she wiped her armpits and crotch with a warm, wet wash-cloth. Then sprayed these areas with body perfume. Roughly wiping her face, she checked her brows and lashes in the mirror—'yes', good enough. After pulling on the jeans and putting on her tennis shoes—she tied these very tight—she adjusted the shoulder strap of her purse. With a tight fit, she was ready to try the pistol in the purse. Realizing she was bare-breasted, she slipped on the loose shirt—but didn't bother to button it. Another look in the mirror, she slightly ruffled her 'little-boy' cut. And with a sly smile, she knew this was going to surprise the 'guests'—Tom in particular!

Returning to the larger room—she carried her new dress, pantyhose, spikes, and the wig—she saw that Jim and Nat were still busy with The Codex, Mickey was propped up on one of the beds—he watched her—and

Tiger had joined Tom and Bill on the balcony. "Pack it!" as she tossed the things to Mickey.

He didn't get up, he slipped the wig on his head, rolled the dress into a small ball, stuffed it into one of the 'packed' pillowcases close by. He spread out the hose on the bed next to himself, carefully rolled these up—looking to see that no one was watching him, he sneaked a quick 'sniff', then shoved these in the 'case'—and he forgot about the wig.

The three on the balcony turned and watched Alex. The two men, in mild shock at seeing Alex's new 'cut' for the first time—just waited and watched. Standing in front of the mirror at the dresser, with her shirt flipped open, she picked up her pistol and inserted it into the purse-holster. The grip stuck out toward her left breast. Lowering her hands, then quickly drawing the gun, she tried the fit of the purse. 'Ok', she buttoned her shirt—but not any higher than the bottom of her breasts. She tried the draw again—still Ok.

Tom started to step toward the inside, but Tiger stopped him with her hand on his arm, as she said, "It's a personal matter—some old debt to settle—" Tiger let it drop off. Bill took Tom's other arm, squeezed it, said softly, "Tom, I thought this affair was a simple robbery—ride into town—steal a priceless artifact—get the hell out of Dodge. But—it looks as if Alex is getting ready for—a—personal vendetta—or— an assassination. I fail to get the gist of—", he too let it drop.

Satisfied with her gun and shirt situation, Alex looked through the other items from her purse—these were scattered on the dresser top.

With the eyebrow pencil, she bent close to the mirror and began to 'draw' 'her' mustache. She wanted to look exactly as she had last night.

Tom had waited long enough, he pulled his arms from the two, went to Alex. Standing behind her as she continued to apply the marks above her upper lip, he looked in the mirror. They made eye contact, Alex hesitated. "Alex, whatever it is—I'm behind you all the way." "Thanks—are you sure you want to get involved?" "I am already involved—you know that." She started with the pencil again. Finished, she turned, they were face to face. "Ok. Just do exactly as I say—when I say. Ok?" "No problem, Senor Chico!" he pulled her hips forward, added, "I guess I can't kiss you?" "Right!" and she gave him a slim smile.

The two were still facing each other when the 'tap-tap came at the door. Not moving, Alex said, "Mickey, please get that—and be sure who it is!" "Ok!" as he jumped from the bed. Seeing Mickey with the blond wig on, Bill said to Tiger, "That's all we need! A blond-headed Maya!"

The two hugged and laughed. "It's the food!" Mickey called as he looked through the peek-hole. "Is it our 'regular' waiter?" Alex asked as she pulled Tom's hips tighter to her. "Yes!" "Ok, let him in—he has been so sweet!" Mickey jerked the door open, said, "Come on in! I'll help you. As you can see—things are—well—in a mess here!"

It wasn't the mess that the waiter saw first—it was Tom and Alex pressed tightly together. Alex looked at the young man and said "Hi. I'm glad to see you—I'm famished!" His mouth fell open as he looked at the 'new' Alex, but he managed, "Alex? Is that you?" "Senor Chico for tonight!" She pushed Tom back, called out, "Ok! Folks! It's chow time!"

Mickey helped the waiter get the cart into the kitchenette, they unloaded the food and drinks onto the counters buffet style. As Mickey helped maneuver the cart out the front door, the waiter asked "Was that really your Mom?" "Yes, she is really—" The waiter finished it, "Something else!" They laughed. "Hey, I like the wig!" the waiter added, just shook his head as he went toward the elevator.

Noticing that everyone had finished eating, and had gotten their glasses refilled, Nat and Jim went to Alex, and turned her to face the others as they stood at her sides. Nat opened, "Comrades! It"—she pointed at The Codex still on the table—"is real! A genuine, authentic, thousands of years old—Maya Codex!" "And from what little we have 'read' so far"—Jim added, then continued, "It will be the most profound, true history of the Maya known to date!"

Alex placed her fingers over her lips as her eyes glistened. She pulled Jim and Nat tight to herself. Stillwell stepped forward, said, "Folks, this calls for a toast!" Everyone raised glasses—even Mickey with his fruit juice—"To Alex! For her unfailing determination!" They clicked their glasses and sipped. Alex stepped forward, turned to Tiger, then Mickey, "To Tiger and Mickey! Without them, it would not have been possible!" Again, they touched the rims, and sipped. Alex had another toast—"To my sweet Tom for being so understanding!" Tom added another, "To Jim and Natashia for knowing the difference between real—and fake!" After clicking and sipping, Jim said, "To Bill Stillwell—for having the plane that's going to get our asses out of here!" Cheers, and another round of drinks!

"That brings us to a point! Let's get the hell out of here!" Bill stated loudly! Jim and Nat quickly, but carefully, wrapped The Codex in the old blanket. The others gathered up the rest. And Alex slipped on her windbreaker. Someone asked Alex, "What about the two Agents?" "Screw them!

What can they do? Go to the City Police? Tell the cops some 110 pound little gal kicked their asses? Besides, The Chief and I go way back! We're old friends!" She didn't bother to explain that when she was here before—when she was sixteen—she had 'picked-up' the 'wrong' man one Friday night. The bastard got rough—really rough. A City Detective came to her rescue. He later became The Chief! And over the years, they had stayed in contact with each other.

As the group packed into the elevator, Jim asked, "What happens if we run into those Agent-guys? In the lobby, say?" Mickey—with the largest load—snapped, "I'll ask them to help carry part of my load!" The others laughed.

Coming out of the elevator and falling into a single line, the entourage did make an unusual sight—especially for the lobby of El Presidents. Alex led the way: her tight jeans, loose shirt with the tail our, the old windbreaker with faded elbows and frazzled collar and slightly dirty 'white' tennis shoes without socks or hose. Her short hair ruffled. And her mustache was slightly cocked.

Following her was Bill Stillwell: at over a foot taller, well over twice as wide, and almost three times as heavy, his shirt collar unfastened, the silk tie loosened and flopped to one side of his huge belly, he was definitely a contrast to Alex. His suit coat hung open, and was weighted down by the quart of Jack Daniels in one pocket, and the bottle of wine in the other. His long hair that normally covered the bald spot on top had fallen away and now hung over his ears.

Behind him, was Nat: her 'chick' tightly fitted safari outfit, tall zip-up high heel boots, and her immaculate face and hair, she was another contrast. But she carried—baby fashion—the 'bundle' of the old Indian blanket. Her suave leather bag was strapped under one of her jacket's epaulets.

Jim followed: his typical college Professor's suit—over-sized, baggy and wrinkled. His hair—never in place—was true to form, scattered and disturbed. And, as all Professors, his shirt collar was loose, his tie hung untied. His shoes had never even seen any polish!

Next in line, Tiger's outfit was impeccable! For traditional Indian dress! It was just never seen in the lobby of El Presidente! Her full wrap-around skirt—dark red with the 'Ama' darker, almost black, band near the hem. And her white, ruffled short sleeves, and the deeply scooped neckline, the blouse barely covered her enormous bosom. Her braided 'tails' hung directly over her nipples. The flat, leather strap sandals went with the rest, perfectly—but not in the lobby of this hotel!

Mickey wore his new 'Merida' apparel: loose, almost peg legs, pleated slacks—a pale blue—of soft cotton cloth. The shirt was of a silky type material, large collar, no pockets, long full sleeves, and was open almost to the waist—it was made that way. His smooth, hairless, brown chest contrasted wonderfully with the light blue of the shirt. And his 'ribbed Merida' loafers fit the outfit. But, it was the blond M.M. wig that really set it off! Especially with his straight jet-black hair showing out from under the wig!

Bringing up the rear was Tom in his 'normal' Western Wear: high heel, pointed toe boots, tight jeans, a light blue denim shirt with pearl capped snaps. A Levy jacket—fitted, but now, it hung open—that barely hid his Army 45 under his left arm. And not a hair out of place.

They all carried a lot, with Mickey the most—including the four 'borrowed' hotel pillowcases. On seeing Alex's group, all the others within sight, stopped and stared. Approaching the reception clerk's window, Alex held up a 'halt' sign. The others stopped, but slowly gathered around her—they didn't want to miss a word! Or sight!

The clerk—the same one—was on a stool at a side desk, he was tallying up the day's tickets and transposing the various charges to the individual rooms' expense cards. Out of the corner of his eye, he caught sight of a movement. He glanced over his half-spectacles and not recognizing Alex, he turned back to his accounting duty. As she tapped the glass with the room key, he looked again. But, he didn't say anything. "Hey! It's me! Alex!""He looked at her face—then at the others who had pressed close—their faces over the top. He realized who they were—but not Alex. He stared ihto her eyes. "Yes, it is ME! Again! Alex!"

With a gasp, he almost fell off backwards. He—in jerked motions— looked to each side, even toward the outer wall! "You looking for, A, a door to run out? Or, B, a hole to crawl in?" she calmly stated. He buried his face in his cupped hands, moaned, "Oh, no, not again."

Alex dropped the key to his side of the glass partition, said, "We're out of here! If there is any money left—after you add up my expenses—please see that the young waiter—his name is on my tickets—gets what is left! Ok?" Without standing or looking at the 'stranger', he just nodded. As she stepped away, she called back, "And if I own you anything—just send me a bill!"

The seven, with their loads, filed out the front main entrance, and ganged up around the Doorman's area. "Drop everything—except the 'you-know-what" As she tossed the keys to Mickey, she winked at the Doorman, said, "Baby-boy, please get the limo!" He ran around the front, headed for the parking lot. Standing among the piles, Alex suddenly became serious. She explained exactly where and how she wanted each person to set in the van. They began to understand that whatever Alex was up to, it was going to be soon. She closed with—"Mickey will be driving. Tom, you and I will go in—down. Bill, you'll be 'back-up', stand at the top of the steps. You others stay in your place—no swapping seats. Understood?" The Doorman had gotten interested—he even nodded in agreement. He didn't know, but it had sounded like instructions for a robbery of some sort! And coming from the 'little weird one', he didn't doubt anything!

Mickey drove south on 18th, Alex said "At the corner, at the end of the park, turn right! Go until you see a small sign—it'll show 'El Grotto'. Park directly in front of the two double doors under the sign." She sat in the front passenger's seat. As soon as he turned the corner, he said, "It's no parking here!" "So? Pull the right side tires up on the sidewalk! It'll be OK! And don't leave for any reason! None what so ever! Even if you"—she nodded toward Nat on the rear seat "and Nat, have to point your guns!" Alex pulled out her gun, jerked back the breach—this loaded a round into the chamber—Tom did the same. They then put the pistols back 'in'.

The van had barely stopped rolling, Alex jumped out, opened the sliding side door—Tom and Stillwell were seated closest to the door. Standing in their way, Alex snapped, "We're going to get someone!" "As in, kidnap?" She didn't reply to Bill, she headed for the door of the El Grotto. The two huge men followed her. Just inside, Alex told Stillwell, "Stay here, keep your coat open, act as if you are armed. Watch the room, watch for any 'incoming'" "I am armed—with all the crazy political situations now-day, most of us are armed. And did you forget—I'm also ex-military." She patted his arm, said, "That's great, just do what you feel necessary." Turning around, she started down the wide concrete steps—Tom followed. She glanced back up at Bill, he had moved to the left side of the steps—better shadow coverage and a better view of the room—the marjority was to the right of the steps.

Alex went directly to the big, ugly bartender—the one she had made the deal with last night and she started to whisper to him. Tom hung back a few steps and swept the room with his sight: about twenty customers, mainly at small tables—in groups of two to four. Most big and ugly. One other bartender, younger, not as big and slightly better looking. A couple of 'Ladies of the evening' working among the men. And two waitresses—hauling beer. The room was large and dark—and smoky. A few drunks with their faces down on their arms.

Finished at the bar, Alex just nodded for Tom to follower her. They worked their way toward the far end. Hardly anyone noticed them, Alex's disguise was working—almost too well. The two men she had run off from the park last night saw her. Tom noticed the two as one pointed toward Alex while leaned close to his partner's ear and whispering. Tom kept watching the two and saw when they stood up, still staring at Alex. Taking 'several quick steps to them, Tom pulled open the left side of his jacket—he let them see the big 45. Calmly, Tom motioned for them to set back down. They did, and remained motionless.

Slowly she worked her way among the men in a particular area. She was concentrating most on their eyes. She came to one with his head on his arms. Gently, she raised the drunk's head, and opened one eyelid. Tom was where he could watch her, and he saw, contrary to the others so far, this man's eye was crystal blue. Blood shot, but definitely blue. And his facial skin—if washed—would probably be white.

Alex pulled up a chair and sat down next to the man. Tom shifted his position to have a better view of the larger part of the room. Twisting the man's face toward herself, she studied his features. Gently shaking him, she got no response. The man was very drunk. She whispered into his ear-and finally got a grunt, then, "No, go away." Alex's actions were beginning to draw attention—from the wrong men. The few standing close-by began to move away. A few men seated close-by began to stare and talk to each other as they looked at Alex.

Standing, Alex stepped behind the man and tried to straighten him up, but he was too heavy for her. Tom came to behind, and by grabbing the man's collar, he pulled the drunk upright. Unexpected, Alex jerked the man's shirt open at his chest—the buttons popped off. Two big men at a table close-by started to stand—Tom decided it was 'Power-play' time. He drew his 45, pointed it at the ceiling then motioned the two to set back down. They did. The talking dropped off, but the staring in-creased—almost everyone in the room was watching.

Outside at the van, Tiger was still in the rear—behind the rear bench seat. Mickey maintained his seat under the steering wheel—with his pistol laid on his lap. Nat had slipped to the end of the rear bench seat—the end close to the side sliding door. Her gaze at the doors of the bar was steady. Jim was at the other end of the bench seat, leaned against the window, he was asleep.

Nat was suddenly disturbed by the sight of two men staggering toward the van. The three began to watch the two men as they approached the van. Seeing the two women, one called out as he patted the side window of the sliding door and shouted "Ola! Mujeres! Puska para dineros?"

As Mickey grabbed his pistol and reached for the door handle, Nat caught his shoulder, snapped, "You two hold your positions! I'll take care of this!"

Briskly Nat slid the side door open, and smiling, she hopped out—she also slipped her hand in her right pocket and gripped her pistol. "Ola Hombres! Bueno!" The closest man reached forward as to grab her. A quick glance—she saw they both were wearing open strap sandals—she stomped the bare arch of his foot with her high, small diameter heel—and twisted, then dragged it sideways—she saw the skin rip open and the blood begin to flow. He cried, "Ah! Ah! Bitch!" as he doubled forward, and reached for his wounded foot.

The other man leaped forward—but—the sound was unmistakable— 'ClickClick!' as Nat breeched the gun—loading a round into the barrel. The 9MM pistol was pointed at the man's chest—he stopped, threw both hands high overhead. "Vamos! Hombre! Pronto!" she quipped. With no hesitation, he backed up a few steps, twisted around and ran as fast as possible!

The one on his knee close to her again reached as if to catch her ankle—or leg. She hopped one step back and with the inside flat of her boot, side kicked him in the face. The force drove him upward, then back. But toward the doors of the bar! Not wanting him to be in the way as he got to his knees, she kicked him again—hard in his ass with her pointed, stiff boot's toe. He lunged forward, to the bottom of the building's wall next to the doors—now—he would not be in the way! Then he lay there, only slightly twisting about and moaning in sever pain—in several places!

Inside, on the steps, watching the crowd inside, Bill heard 'something' through the double doors. He carefully backed up, pushed one door partially open—he saw Nat as she was getting back in the van. "Dr.K? You guys Ok?" "Sure, just a couple of drunks moving past." and she chuckled as she motioned for him to 'go-away'. He eased down about halfway of the steps and resumed his watch.

Back on the rear seat, Dr.K looked to Mickey as he softly commented, "Lady, you're 'bad' with your feet—your boots." She nodded and smiled in return, replied, "A little something I picked up in years of ballet!" Then he nodded toward Jim—he was still asleep—asked, "How does he sleep like that? That hard?" "Practice! A lot of practice!"

Tom quickly glanced at Alex, she had her face close to the man's left nipple—and she 'traced' something with one fingertip. She jerked up, pulled his head to her hip, "Ok! It's him! Let's get him out of here!" She stuck her left arm under the man's right arm, lifted—but that was not enough! Tom shifted hands with his pistol—he could shoot with either hand—and jerked the man to his feet by hooking his elbow under the man's other armpit. With one foot, Tom roughly shoved the table and chairs out of their way. They headed toward the steps. The crowd, as soon as they saw Tom's big automatic, parted and moved away.

Two men off to Alex's side jumped up as if to interfere. In a smooth flash, she whipped out her pistol, pointed it directly at the bigger one, shouted "No! No! Hombres!" They stopped in mid motion, raised both hands above their heads. Alex glanced at the two bartenders—they were not moving and they had all four hands in plain view on the top of the counter. 'Good boys', she thought.

When they got the man to the steps, Bill relieved Alex, she turned her back to the steps, gripped her gun with both hands, then backed up the steps. And she kept sweeping the room with her sight—and the barrel of the pistol. No one moved.

They didn't hesitate to see what the situation was outside—they rushed to the open side door, pushed the man into the van, down on the floor between the rear bench seat and the front seats. Bill, then Tom jumped to the bench seat, and propped their feet on the drunk's back. Alex hopped in the front seat, shouted, "Hit it!" as she closed the door.

Back in the Bar—El Grotto—on seeing the four leave, the younger bartender ran to the older one, asked quickly, "Who the hell was that?" Without changing his 'poker-face' expression, the big older one only replied, "C.I.A." "C.I.A.! No stuff! That old man was always bragging that he was 'somebody important'! Guess he really was! To get picked-up by the C.I.A.!" The Big One quickly cast a glance in both directions, gave one nod to his partner, then softly said, "The Little One—that was Alex- The Bodyguard." "No stuff! Man! The famous Bodyguard to the famous Senorita Margarita 'Tiger' Calienta! And they really are C.I.A.?" The old barkeep just gave one small nod. "Wait till I tell my wife! She'll flip!" the younger one said.

Then they both went back to drawing beers for the customers.

Mickey followed Alex's instructions as he headed for the airport. Tom kept a watch out the rear—he didn't see that anyone followed them. On away, Alex handed Nat a flashlight, and said, "Tom, Bill, roll him up on his right side! Nat, look around his left nipple! Be sure! There is a—or is suppose to be—a small tattoo—a little eagle over his nipple—and—a name under it" And Alex added, "I sure as hell don't want to haul the wrong man to Georgia!"

Shifting and twisting, looking, then Nat said, "One eagle—and-W. Hawkins!" No one spoke as Alex bent forward, put her face in her hands and began sobbed.

She cried as a wave of relief swept through her mind—not a relief that tonight's situation had gone so well, but for other deeper reasons. As in so many of her seemingly impulsive undertakings, she had never had any doubts that she could pull it off—one way or the other. But relieved that she had made a definite decision to take positive action. Right, or wrong—at least she had decided.

Still not sure when she had first comprehended that she was strong enough, in a situation of power—and, yes, even wealth—and determined enough, she wondered, 'Did the idea start when she was in the nightmarish hell trapped in the burning wheat—a few years ago, in North Dakota? Or had it started when she realized she was alone—hopelessly alone—when she found her Mother dead? When she was only fifteen? And as usual, HE was gone—and she wanted, needed, him so badly—but—he was gone. And she had to handle everything—alone.

She did know that the idea to take action had fought its way forward through her mind on this trip, when she decided to not stop at Campeche, but to continue North to Merida. An uncanny feeling—a sense—had pressured her from within her mind—'He is in Merida! He is in Merida! Now is the time! Now! Now!' For so many years—yes! Probably even since the moment of finding her Mother dead, she had been able to force the thought back—back deeply into her subconscious mind. Except when she was not in control—when she tried to overcome restless sleep. But with hard, relentless work, actions—even drinking a lot—she had fought her way through the years. And her lack of self confidence, her vacillations, had nagged at her during all these years.

Not knowing if she was headed in the right direction or not, if she was condemning or forcing a vindication, at least this was maybe—just maybe—a solution better than what had plagued her for almost seventeen years! If it didn't work, she had at least tried!

By the time they reached the airport, Alex had regained her composure, and she had wiped her mustache off with her tears and shirttail. Driving to the plane was no problem—Stillwell just flashed a bunch of fancy documents and a badge to the military guards at the service entrance gate—and Mickey drove through. "Swing around the right wing tip", Bill said to Mickey, added, "The ramp—the steps—are in front of that wing."

Feeling secure, they took their time transferring the 'goods'—Bill and Tom put W. Hawkins in the rear seat and strapped him in, he was still 'out'. And Nat—the former Dr.Natashia Karsky, the world famous Russian expert on Maya hieroglyphs—-was the one to carry 'The Lost Codex of Palenque' up into the U.S.Secretary of Agriculture's government jet.

Adding his last load of bundles to the growing pile behind the rear seat, Mickey took a keen interest at the interior of the Gulfstream.

Back at the front door while he waited for others to settledown, he tilted his head into the cockpit. The pilot, Co-pilot and Bill Stillwell were discussing flight plans. Finished with that, Bill asked Mickey, "Kid, your first time inside a Gulfstream?" "First time inside any airplane!" "Let me give you the standard tour then!" Bill quickly spieled off the techni- cal specifications, comments concerning the planes capacity and capabilities, etc., etc.—a edition he had often made to strangers of the Gulfstream.

"Kid, you seem very sharp! Why don't you come with us? I know I can find you a position in my department—and that 'gang of outlaws', the HVG, down south—would love to have you there! What'd you say?" "Sorry, Sir—I feel I'm needed back at 'Ama'." "Family?" "Not exactly, like you mean family, but, yes, family—our group. You see, we operate very similar to Alex's HVG—we all work, raise, sell, and stock for everyone in the village. No 'mine', 'yours', 'his'—it's all 'ours!" And Mickey grinned, added, "Besides, I'm only—seventeen" —like Alex, he had added a couple of years—"Your law does not exactly encourage youths like me!" "Mick— you every heard the true story of Audy Murphy?" Mickey shook his head no. As Bill put his big arm over Mickey's shoulders, he started, "Well! Let me briefly tell you the story of MY HERO—"

Meantime Alex had dropped into one of the seats and wrote another bill-of-sale, transferring ownership of the VW van from her to Mickey.

But she suddenly realized that she didn't even known his last name—his family name! Tiger was within talking distance, Alex asked, "Tig, what's Mickey's family name?" She smiled, called back, "Same as mine! Calienta!" Alex finished the document, got Nat to stamp it with her 'personal' notary seal and sign it as witness. Bill just shook his head as he watched this, the two just shrugged and smiled back at him.

With the bill-of-sale, Alex dug through the pile, got the two unopened envelopes of pasos and 'her' laptop computer. Squeezing by in the narrow aisle, she joined Bill and Mickey at the bar area. "Here, Mic, I wish it could be more—but—" she thought, but didn't say, 'I don't want to spoil you too soon, too quickly!' She dropped the subject as she gave the items to him. Then she hugged and kissed him, trying to not get all in tears. She quipped, "Ok! Now, swap me that gun!" Mickey looked surprised, he thought of the Agent's pistol as his own! Realizing his reaction, she softly added, "Sorry, Kid, but no guns—not yet—Ok? Besides, we can add it to Tom's collection. He collects guns—especially the ones WE TAKE from Assholes!" Then Mickey smiled, removed the pistol from the rear of his beltline. She quickly popped out the clip, pulled the receiver back—ejecting the round from the barrel. He picked it up and handed it to her. She pushed it back into the clip, slammed the clip back in. As she placed the pistol into a drawer at the bar, she said to Stillwell, "Don't let me forget that. Ok?" He just nodded in return.

Back to Mickey, Alex seriously said, "Promise you'll get someone—maybe there in San Cris—to teach you about the computer! I want us—you and I, and others—to be able to communicate with the computers! E-mail, all that stuff. Promise?" "Promise!" Nat had overheard, she interjected, "Mic, get in touch with Frau Rachel Blom, at the Blom Museum in San Cris. Tell her Dr.K said for her—her people—to teach you about computers! We go way back! Just mention your connection with me! She'll do it! Ok?" "Sure thing, Dr.K! Thanks for the tip!" Nat then rejoined the others. He leaned close to Alex's ear, whispered, "What does the 'K' stand for?" She smiled, whispered back, "Killerlady' it's a KGB code."

"Alex?" Bill interrupted as he looked at the laptop—Mickey had slipped it out of the case—"Alex? Isn't that the same brand, same model as Jerry White's Operators—and our Field Agents—use?" As she shook Mickey's hand, she just smiled to Bill and shrugged. "Alex!" Bill snapped as she turned and headed for the rear. But she suddenly realized she had forgotten something! She rushed back to Mickey as he started down the exit steps, jerked the blond wig off his head! She quipped, "That's mine! I want to see if blondes really have more fun!" Everyone that saw her laughed out loud! Mickey stepped on down, and waved over his shoulder. He didn't want the others—his new friends—to see his tears.

As Mickey reversed the van away from the plane, he recalled Alex's words, 'Room 502 is paid for until check-out tomorrow—but that can be pushed until two PM.' Headed for the exit gate, he thought, 'Time for serious decisions—like Alex would say—A: Head for home to 'Ama'? B: Go back to 502 and party down? C: Go by 405, get Suzie, head for Cancun, then party down? No problem! He quickly decided on C!

The plane taxied toward the take-off position, Alex suddenly pounded one knee with a fist, snapped, "Damn! I forgot something!" Tom stopped her hand, "What? Alex—Forget! No!" "Yes! I intended to slip a note to the two Agents!" She held her hands up in front of her face, and spread her hands far apart, "See this! Big print! We've got it! And you'll get it! I really wanted that!" Nat—as she passed her cellphone around the edge of her seat, said, "Call the hotel! Have them deliver it! Personally! From Alex's Gang!" "Great idea!" And Alex quickly worked it out as all the others laughed.

When the seat belt light went off, Nat stood, stepped to the bar, and asked, "Anyone for a nite cap?" All the others held up a hand, and from the rear, Mr. Hawkins mumbled, "La Camarera—La Camarera—" Alex started to rise, but Nat held up a halting signal to her, then headed back. Standing beside Hawkins's seat, she leaned her face close, asked, "Si? Senor Hawkins?" "Hey, you're new here! And a real Looker! Bring me double, up, provor!"

Returning to the bar, she poured a shot of ginger ale. Taking out a small prescription bottle, Nat dropped two tiny white tables in the drink. As she passed Alex, she winked, said, "He'll sleep like a baby." Alex nodded and smiled back. Then Nat poured and served the others drinks. At Jim, as she handed him the glass, she smiled, softly said, "Coffee? Tea? Or, me?" "Decisions—decisions—I'll have—", he hesitated. Nat twisted her backside close to his face, contracted her buns a few times in her skintight stretch pants, quipped, "Maybe this will help you decide!" He lightly popped her bottom, "No doubt!' I'll have that!"

While having drinks and moving around some, Alex—with Tom and Bill Stillwell at the bar—she slowly began a discussion. The opening was "What about a HVG/CHIAPAS group? Using our systems—our expertise, in the food distribution—and, no offense Tiger—", as Tiger began to pay attention, "But what I've seen so far—from one end of Mexico to the other, things are similar to our—the U.S.—days in the very early nineteen hundreds. And transportation! Man! A few fast moving, closely controlled trucking companies could work wonders! They just need to know exactly what, when, where—and where to!"

Bill became involved, "For instance, a central info system—info distribution—education of the system—", and he added, "Their Secretary— Minister—of Agriculture, Senor Diaz, and I have become familiar with each other—contacts over the—Alex, the Special Agent 'problem'." Bill clicked his glass to Alex's glass, then sternly said directly to her, "Little Lady, the next time—give me some warning! Up front! Ok?" She batted her big black eyes, sheepishly smiled, humbling replied "Yes Sir." As Alex turned away, she thought, 'Yes—with the publicity—even the troubles—that she and Tiger had gotten, it wouldn't be very difficult to start a food distribution company in—and around—Chiapas! And use Ocosingo Valley as the operation's center, the headquarters.'

While still up, and seeing the others settled in, Alex decided it was time. She stepped to where Tiger was seated, took her hand, raised it— Tiger stood—"Do you folks want to hear the details about the Famous Margarita Calienta's adventures in Mazatlan?" Alex announced. That was all it took! Tiger began! And continued for the next hour—or so!

When it was obvious to Alex that Tiger would not have any problems carrying on, Alex went to Tom, slipped past his knees and sat down next to the window. Later, as Tiger concluded her rendition—she ended with her being recognized in the Hotel Real in San Cris—Tom leaned across Alex. Gazing into her eyes, he quietly asked, "Alex, it is Friday night, are you, your usual horny self?" She turned her eyes away, stared at the darkness, darkness only interrupted by the red reflections of the lights on the white wing.

In silence, Alex wavered as her memory recalled when she, Tom and Arnie were thrown together by the unusual circumstances which preceded the beginning of their last season as Major Buyers—the season of the collapse of the food system. It had only taken two—maybe three Friday nights for Tom and Arnie to realize Alex had an 'unusual' habit—freelancing for sex in a determined fashion. And, at times, the two men teased Alex about this. Later, only when she and Tom had became seriously 'involved'-sex-wise—had Alex vaguely explained Miss Hawkins.

After deciding to try life as a couple, Tom had become accustomed to Miss Hawkins' Friday night appearances. Alex slowly realized that he was enjoying Miss Hawkins—perhaps even more than Alex. In the beginning with Tom—as she had for so many years—Alex willingly allowed Miss Hawkins to take over her mind, her body, her self. But living together with Tom almost constantly for the three or so years, Alex gradually began a denial toward Miss Hawkins—maybe Alex even became jealous of Miss Hawkins's intrusions, her interruptions.

Miss Hawkins wasn't a very agreeable social person—she seemed to have only one thing on her mind, sex, hard and heavy—but the other members of HVG had learned to accept her on Friday nights. And Miss Hawkins had also adjusted—she routinely swept Tom away from the others. And this too bothered Alex more and more as she lost 'her' time with 'her' friends. And Alex blamed Miss Hawkins for this.

Over the past four weeks, Alex's own character, her self, had made adjustments—maybe even permanent changes. Alex couldn't, at least yet, determine if these were caused by her brief—but intense—love affair with Tiger. Or Alex's open admission—mainly to herself—to enjoying the girl-girl scene again. Maybe it reminded her of the earlier years—the years before Miss Hawkins and her obsession with men. Either way, whatever the reason, Miss Hawkins had felt left out, rejected, or even repulsed. Slowly, quietly, Miss Hawkins had slipped away.

Unexpected, Alex suddenly felt free of her, Miss Hawkins, her bothersome character. And Alex admitted to her self—to Alex—that she truly, deeply, loved Tiger—with much more than 'sisterly' feelings. But, as she had told Tiger on the balcony of the El Presidente, at this very moment, she still didn't know the answer as to where their relationship was going.

"Alex? Are you Ok?' Tom's soft question brought her back to reality. "Tom—I may as well tell you now—Miss Hawkins is gone. I no longer care if it is Friday night or not." She hesitated, turned back to him, stared into his eyes, added, "Anytime is perfectly Ok with little Alex." Then she kissed him hard on his lips.

"There is still snow on the ground—at Hidden Valley", Tom quietly commented. She leaned her small head against his large shoulder, closed her eyes and dozed off into peaceful sleep.

It had been four weeks and one day since Alex and Tiger had left the valley.

The end.

EPILOGUE

With the greetings and congratulations over, Alex led Arnie out on his porch. "Arnie, I'm really sorry about not being able to return with your 'Betsy'. Anything you want—a new station wagon, a new car or pickup, whatever, I'll gladly pay for it!" "Well, I've kind of gotten accustomed to your sports coupe, the seat is very comfortable. It is a little difficult to get in and out—it's so low. If you'll just let me borrow it, just for 'quickie' runs, no hauling I promise! Maybe I can do without a car."

Alex hugged him, said, "Oh, Arnie! How sweet!" While holding her close, he started, "What we really need around here is a tractor. The Bill Brown estate has one, only a few years old. His daughter, his only survivor, she came when you two were gone—she wants me to handle the liquidation of everything, including the property—about twenty acres, probably fifteen of open bottom land. The tractor is a Ford diesel—not too large. And of course, there will be the implements: a set of discs, a couple of turn plows, a snow blade, and the bush-hog—and we'll need a new fuel storage tank—", he turned her to his side and pointed with a stiff finger beyond Mike and Tiger's place, added, "Over there." She looked, he continued, "And over there", he pointed at a different location, "We need to build a storage shed for the tractor and tools—I think we'd be even!"

Alex dropped her chin to her chest, covered her face with one hand, mumbled, "I knew this wasn't going to be simple."

The two were outside in the open, just strolling about. Alex took one of Tom's hands, stopped and stepped around until they were face to face. "Tom, when we were at Chamula—I had this 'thing'—with a Shaman—" She hesitated, looked directly into his eyes. Slightly narrowing her eyes, she concentrated, continued, "I saw something—I learned something." She gently turned loose his hand and took one step back. "Alex, you don't hav—", she was gone! She had disappeared! Tom jerked around, she was not to be seen! She had vanished! "Mike! Help! Mike!" He knew Mike had experience with Tiger's 'disappearing feat'!

It was one Saturday, mid morning, when the 'Big Guys'—Tom and Mike—were home. Alex got them and Tiger together for a stroll. Alex started, "Someday, I want to show you two the most beautiful valley I have ever seen, it is in Chiapas. I want us—the four of us—to give some serious considerations of a—say a vacation home—a retirement place—an operation center for HVG / CHIAPAS—maybe a lodge, rooms, suites for rent, B&B style—and? Or? A place-for Mike and Tiger to raise a home full of kids!"

Tiger smiled and tugged on Mike's arm—she knew Alex was talking about the beautiful valley of Ocosingo!

"It's amazing how Arnie and your Dad have hit it off!" Tom exclaimed as they looked down at the two older men below. "Yes, it is—but I'm still not sure how things will work out—in the long run—", Alex let it drop off. "You mean, how your 'Old Man' is—was—hooked on wandering about searching for gold—and staying drunk?" She didn't respond. "Maybe he's tired of it—like I was and didn't know it. The 'war-thing'—caught up in one world—until you came along."

They watched as Arnie appeared to explain different points involved in the gardening activities. "Maybe—I guess, I'll just wait and see." Alex commented. "Yes, wait and see—at least Old Hawkins is off the 'sauce'—", Tom let it go. She turned and hugged him, softly replied, "Yes—wait and see."

Lightly kissing her forehead, Tom added, "He is genuinely impressed with your achievements, Alex, you can't deny that." "Yes—finally." She pressed her face tight to his chest.

He kissed the top of her head, then gently turned her around to face the scene below. The two older men had moved to the stream and squatted down. "What are they doing?" "That, my dear little Alex, is two old 'farts' panning for gold!"

One day, Jim and Nat got Alex off to one side. Nat started, "Alex, word has leaked out about The Codex. Several publishers are screaming for publication rights to our manuscript concerning The Codex. We, Jim and I, think you should be listed as the leader of the expedition that recovered The Codex. And, you should be one-third owner. Are you willing to go with that?" "Are we talking big money here?" "Yes, a lots of money. I feel we can get at least one million for exclusive publication rights. This is going to be the hottest news ever! About the true history of the Maya!"

But Alex didn't seem to respond, Jim asked, "Alex, what are you thinking?" "It sounds nice—but—the way I see it. True, I financed and pushed the recovery—but without Tiger—hey! She actually got it—and damn near paid with her life—and Mickey, no one would have The Codex—not yet, at least." Then she hesitated. Nat asked, "Ok, what do you propose?" Nat could feel that Alex had something in mind—already.

"True, without you two, we wouldn't know what it 'says'—how about 50% to you and Jim, and, 50% to the three of us—Tiger, Mickey and myself? And the three of us be listed as 'The Expedition', and not with a specific 'Leader'. Really, I just tagged along—Tiger got all the answers! And-and—Tiger be listed as an Assistant Archaeologist?" Again, Alex waited. Then she added suddenly, "And, in the credits, you give thanks to the Department of Internal Security, of Mexico, for their cooperation and help", she chuckled, added, "Hey! We may want to go back sometime!"

Nat extended her hand, said, "Deal!" "Deal!" Alex replied as the three shook hands. As they walked away Alex thought, 'Boy! Oh boy! Is Tiger and Mickey going to be surprised! About $160,000 each!'

Jim stepped to Nat, and said, "UPS said they would be here in about two hours. Is it ready?" She had just finished gluing the label to the heavy plywood crate. She looked at the label, it showed:

Frau Rachel Blom c/o Franz Blom Museum
San Cristobal de las Casas
Chiapas
Mexico, S.A.

As she thought, 'The Lost Codex of Palenque' is going home! She smiled and answered, "Yes! It is ready!"

It was pitch black, they had been in bed for a while. "Tom? You still awake?" "Yes, Alex." "Tom, I've had my eye on a Pilatis PC-6, a turbo model. If I buy it, will you teach me how to fly it?" "Yes, Alex." "I want to fly it down to Chiapas—Ocosingo, Chiapas. Will you go with me? Off season, of course." "Yes, Alex." "Tom—go to sleep." "Yes, Alex."

She thought, 'Yes! Little Alex is off to her next adventure!'